FOR STARTERS

A PLACE FOR NEW BEGINNINGS

ANNA-MARIA ATHANASIOU

CONTENTS

LA CASA
D'ITALIA

FOR STARTERS

"*Everything is determined, the beginning as well as the end, by forces over which we have no control.*

... we all dance to a mysterious tune, intoned in the distance by an invisible piper."

Albert Einstein

This is for you, Mum and Dad -

You always, always believed in me and said I could achieve anything.

I didn't manage to have the dream restaurant I always wanted but at least I succeeded in creating one all the same.

TEN STEPS BACK

Tugging on her black, six-inch-high ankle boot, Dani looked over her shoulder at Jez. "Feeling any better?" she asked.

"A bit. My head's still pounding though." He stretched, then pulled himself up and rested leisurely on the headboard, pulling at the sex-mussed-up sheets. His dark green eyes scanned her appreciatively. Dani shuddered inwardly; his look alone could do that.

"I'll bring you some more paracetamol and I'll make you a hot drink before I leave. Coffee okay?" Jez nodded. She looked at her watch; it was five thirty. Then she reached over for her other boot and slipped her foot in. They really needed a polish, she'd had them a while now and they were looking a little worn out. She made a mental note to do it tomorrow.

Whilst zipping up her boot, she stood and smoothed down her skin-tight black trousers. Dani moved over to the dressing table and leaned in closer. *Crap, her roots needed doing.* Another mental note she needed to add to her list; arrange a hair appointment. She picked up her hairbrush and brushed back her long blonde hair. *Long, artificial blonde hair was a pain in the ass to keep*, she thought as she passed it through her hair tie. Her eyes caught Jez looking at her through the mirror and she smiled shyly at him.

"Don't put it in a ponytail. Leave it loose," he muttered.

Dani nodded, pulled her hair tie out and shook her head, allowing her hair to cascade down her back. She put her hair tie around her wrist. She'd put it up once she was out of the house. As Dani walked over to the wardrobe, she could still feel Jez's eyes on her. She took her red top off its hanger and slipped it on.

"You should wear the black halter top."

Dani sighed. Just once, she'd like to wear something without having to change it for him. She turned and smiled tightly at him.

"I thought I'd wear this, break up the black a bit," she explained as she fingered the buttons.

"The black works better." He continued ruffling his dark blonde hair. Dani sighed again.

"Okay, I'll change." She begrudgingly shrugged off her top, put it back on the hanger and reached into the wardrobe for her black halter top. Jez nodded his approval as she zipped it up.

"That's better. It shouldn't be too busy tonight and I'll be back at work tomorrow."

"We'll manage. It's midweek. Julie's the only one that's off tonight. I'll be back by midnight – one, tops. Let me just get you your drink and I'd better get off."

"Thanks, I'm parched." He turned to the TV and flicked through the channels. Dani left the bedroom and ran down the stairs to the kitchen. Jez looked edgy, he was a terrible patient, she thought. Luckily he didn't have a temperature. Dani flicked on the coffee machine and reached for the coffee pod, slotting it into place. She then leaned against the counter and waited.

Within a few minutes, the kitchen smelled of rich filtered coffee. Dani poured it into a larger cup and splashed in the milk, feeling decidedly glad that she'd recently invested in their coffee machine. There was nothing better than freshly made coffee. Then taking a bottle of water, she ran back up to Jez. She was surprised to find him in the shower.

"You haven't changed your mind, have you? We'll manage; if you're feeling shitty you should stay home."

"I thought a shower would make me feel better," he said.

"Oh. Maybe. I've left your coffee on the dressing table and I brought up some water. Don't forget to take some paracetamol too."

"Okay. I will. Thanks. I'll call you later, see how you're doing," he called as he rubbed his shaggy hair. Dani watched him and her pulse raced. Even ill, he looked sexy as hell. His body toned and lean – he wasn't a huge fan of exercise – his physique was purely genetic. It made Dani a little sick. She worked out five times a week to keep in shape. Even after five years she still got a kick out of looking at him. He opened one eye to look at her as the shampoo washed over him. "You'll be late if you don't get going," he frowned. Dani shook her head, ridding her thoughts and she grinned.

"Okay, I'll go." She reluctantly left the bathroom and ran down the stairs picking up the car keys as she headed to the door.

There was a cold blast of air as she opened the front door and she tightened her coat around her. Jeez, it was freezing. Dani hated this time of year – it was so dark already. Dani shuddered as she walked down the path to her parked car. She quickly sunk into the low car and turned on the engine. It roared and Dani cranked up the heating.

She loved the Porsche but she would have much preferred a more practical car for in-town driving, especially when it came to parking. A Smart maybe, she mused. Jez wouldn't hear of it though. Like everything, it had to be his way. He'd insisted she get a Porsche. It was all about image. He couldn't have his girlfriend driving a Smart. It wouldn't reflect well on the bar. *Everything* was about image. It drove Dani insane.

Jez owned a bar in Kingston, which he'd had for over five years now. Dani had gone to work there while her mother was ill. It was supposed to be temporary but she ended up staying. Originally Dani had wanted to continue her studies but never seemed to get around to it. A lot of that was to do with Jez. She'd started a hotel catering course but dropped out when her mother was diagnosed with cancer, just two years after her father had died. Chloe, Dani's older sister, had moved up to Leeds with her husband Adam, who had been offered a job in a very prestigious law firm. By then, Chloe was six months pregnant with her second child, so Dani offered to stop her studies to nurse and look after their mother. The distance and Chloe's pregnancy made it hard for her to help out with the day-to-day care of their then-terminally ill mother.

Once she'd started seeing Jez, it became harder to focus on anything other than him and his business. They'd been together for nearly five years and Dani was hoping he'd take the plunge and marry her. The only commitment they had to each other was their house.

Dani had been left a substantial amount of money after her parents both died. They'd had a bed and breakfast in Brighton and once it was sold, the inheritance was split between Dani and Chloe. Dani had used some of it to buy the house with Jez three years ago. The rest she'd allowed Adam to invest for her. The only other item she'd bought was her car.

Dani pulled into her designated parking spot and stepped out of her car. She quickly locked it up and walked towards the bar. The road in front of the entrance was being resurfaced, so Dani had to carefully walk around the coned-off area over an uneven surface. The wind was freezing and Dani shuddered. Her halter top was not going to keep her warm in the bar tonight, she thought. As Dani stepped past the last cone, she lost her footing and her knees buckled. She heard a snap as she grabbed onto the wall for balance. Shit! She looked down at her boots to see the left heel snapped in two. Wonderful! Now she'd have to go back home and change. She hobbled through the door and dumped her bag on the bar.

"What happened to you?" Earl, their head barman, furrowed his brow as Dani sat on a bar stool.

"I just snapped my heel on the bloody pavement outside." She looked around the bar as she cringed in annoyance. It wasn't too busy. There were mainly workers popping in for a drink before they went home. "I'll have to go back home and change."

"Sure, we can manage. How's Jez?" He leaned on the bar as he spoke, his mischievous dark eyes widening.

"Grumpy. He's not a good patient."

Earl laughed, showcasing his perfect white teeth in stark contrast to his dark skin, "No, he's not. I'll hold the fort 'til you get back."

Dani looked at her watch. It was six thirty. In the evening traffic, it would be an hour round trip. She sighed. *Mental note to self: keep a spare pair of heels at work.*

"It'll take me an hour there and back in the traffic. Sorry to dump on you, Earl."

Earl smiled at her and then patted her hand, "Don't worry, Dani. You get off, we'll be fine."

"I'll help you bottle up and get everything set up first and I'll go once the evening rush hour passes."

"Sure. The rest of the staff will be in by then. Are you sure you can manage, hobbling around like that?"

"Yes, I'll be fine."

Dani proceeded to oversee the restocking of the bar and she reset the tills for the evening shift. She sat at the bar and ate a sandwich, then picked up her phone to call Jez. The time had flown by and it was almost nine. His phone was switched off and Dani was about to call the house but thought better of it. He'd probably dropped off to sleep again.

"I'll go, Earl. I won't be able to hobble around when it gets busier."

"Sure, Dani, we'll manage." He smiled widely and shooed her off.

"Thanks." Dani collected her bag and headed back outside to her car, lighting up her fourth cigarette of the day.

The drive home was worse than she'd expected and it was nine thirty as she pulled up outside their house. Dani let herself in, then pulled off her boots as she sat on the stairs. They were definitely beyond repair and she sighed. She really loved those boots. Scooping them up, she started climbing the stairs towards their bedroom. The sound of soft music, coming from their room, filtered down the stairs. Coldplay. *That was odd*, she thought, while hearing Jez talking. Dani stopped momentarily on the step and strained to hear. He wasn't talking – it was moaning.

Crap, he must be in pain, thought Dani and just before she called out to him, a woman's jacket draped on the banister caught her eye. It wasn't one of hers. Her footing faltered, trying to process what she was seeing. There was something wrong with this picture. There was a distinct smell of Jez's Davidoff Coolwater aftershave mixed with scented candles. His moaning continued and Dani realised it wasn't because he was in pain. She'd heard that moan before. In fact, she'd heard that exact same moan not just five hours ago. Her stomach clenched while her feet stayed rooted to the floor as she took a few seconds to pull herself together. Dani took a tentative step closer and slowly pushed the door ajar.

"That's it, ride it... ah yes... ah."

The room was lit solely by candles and through the dim light Dani could see a woman with long blonde hair cascading down her bare back as she straddled over Jez, in the full throes of passion. Dani watched, frozen in horror, as she saw Jez grasping the woman's hands as she continued to ride him and he moaned, both totally oblivious to their audience of one.

"Oh, Jez... ah."

"That's it, faster... oh God, that's it!"

Dani clenched her teeth and threw her damaged boots in the direction of them. They hit the wall directly above the bed head with a loud thud, shocking the occupants out of their sex-filled oblivion. The woman screamed out and Jez bucked upwards, shocked.

"Fuck! Shit, Dani!"

Dani flicked on the main light switch, flooding the room with bright light as she stared at them both, her hands fisting by her side. As the blonde turned to look at who had rudely interrupted their moment of passion, Dani realised it was Julie, the new bar woman. Julie closed her eyes and her hand shot to her mouth. At least she had the decency to look ashamed, thought Dani fleetingly. Julie quickly released herself from Jez and tried to cover her nakedness up with the quilt. Jez stared, stunned and wide-eyed, at Dani.

"You fucking prick!" Dani's teeth still clenched as she spoke.

"Dani..."

"Don't even speak to me!" she seethed. Dani then focused on Julie.

"You. Get the fuck out of my house!" Julie quickly grappled around on the floor, gathering her strewn clothes. She pulled on her panties and then slithered past Dani and exited the bedroom, her face red as she tried to cover herself up.

"Dani..."

"Shut up! Shut up! You asshole. I wasted five years on you!" Her brain worked overtime, trying to remember any other times that he'd made excuses not to be at work. "Is she the only one, or have there been others?" Dani demanded.

Jez pulled himself up and reached for his boxers, avoiding eye contact. His silence confirmed what Dani had dreaded to hear.

"You're pathetic! I don't want to waste another second in your presence."

Jez's gaze shot up to her. "You're leaving?" he whispered.

Dani's mouth opened in disbelief. He was expecting her to stay; was he that delusional?

"What, you thought we could work this out? Are you insane? I never want to set eyes on you again. You've made me look like a fool." In the distance Dani heard the front door open, then shut.

"Dani, they meant nothing..." He edged forward

"Fuck you!" Dani reached for the coffee cup she'd previously made for him and hurled it at him. Jez ducked and it smashed against the wall, the remains of the coffee splashing against the pale blue paint.

"Jesus, Dani!" His head whipped up to look at her.

"At least have the decency not to lie anymore! *I* meant nothing to you, not them! I need to get out of here. I can't stand to look at you." She turned and headed downstairs. Her body shook as she held on to her temper and the tears that burned her eyes. She rummaged about in her bag and pulled out her cigarettes. With a shaky hand, she lit one and dragged hard on it as she moved to the kitchen. She felt humiliated and broken and the image of Julie on top of Jez seared into her brain as she closed her eyes. She dragged again on her cigarette and opened the fridge, pulled out a bottle of tequila, then splashed a generous measure into a glass. She could hear Jez coming down the stairs and she drained her glass.

"Dani? I'm sorry. Please don't go."

She ignored him. If she spoke, she knew she'd break down and she didn't want him to see how utterly devastated she was. She stubbed out her cigarette in the sink and pulled open the drawer that housed the bin liners. She retrieved the roll and pushed past him and headed back upstairs.

"What are you doing? Dani, talk to me." Jez sprinted up the stairs behind her as she continued to ignore him. Dani ripped off a bin liner and shook it violently open, then she opened her drawers and started emptying their contents into it.

"Dani? Stop it!" Jez looked on horrified as he watched Dani systematically empty her clothes into another bin liner. She looked detached and her eyes were hard.

"Dani! Please just stop it!" His voice was louder, betraying his alarm. He moved closer to her and hesitantly reached over to her.

"*Don't touch me!*" she fumed as she spun around to face him. "Don't *ever* touch me again."

Her mind had gone into automatic pilot. She needed to focus on getting out of there; if he touched her, she'd cave. Her heart pounded against her chest as she stared at him, his face confused and frightened. She needed to pack up her stuff and leave.

"Dani please don't leave. I love you. I was just being –"

"Stop talking. Every word you say is a lie. We are a lie. My whole life with you has been one big fucking *lie*. You don't love me. You never did. How can you treat someone you love like this? Answer me? I'm just glad I found out before it was too late. And to think I wanted you to marry me," she snorted. "Jesus. At least it's only me I need to think about now and not anyone else." She turned around and continued her methodical packing.

"I do want to marry you – I love you, Dani." He slumped in the chair and put his head in his hands.

Dani huffed as she walked into their bathroom and started scooping her belongings into the next bin liner. She looked down at her contraceptive pills and shook her head. Thank God she'd kept taking them. The thought of being pregnant to Jez now turned her stomach. Then she looked at the antibiotics she'd been taking for an infection she'd had, and a few more pieces to the puzzle fell into place. She'd had so many infections over their five years together. *Jesus Christ!* Jez never wore a condom. He hated them. She could have contracted all sorts of diseases. Dani clenched her eyes shut and put her face in her hands. She felt like a prize idiot.

She straightened up abruptly. She had to get out, as far away as possible. She'd go to Chloe and stay with her. Two hundred miles was as far away as she could get and he wouldn't be able to come and bother her. Dani lifted the bag she'd filled and dropped it next to the other two. She pulled off another bin liner and started clearing out the wardrobe. Jez looked up, stunned that she was still packing.

"Where will you go?" His voice was quiet.

Dani ignored him as she threw her dresses, jackets, trousers and skirts into the bag. Jez continued to stare blankly at her. Dani pulled another bag out and filled it with her shoes and handbags, not caring if they got tangled.

"Dani, talk to me. Please, just stop it." He sat watching her move around their bedroom detached and distant, and the realization hit him. She was really leaving; this wasn't an act. She was actually leaving.

Dani lifted a couple of the bags she'd filled and headed downstairs, leaving them at the bottom. She then walked through to the lounge and scanned the room. She'd spent the three years decorating and furnishing the whole house and now looking at it, all she wanted was to get away from it. She walked over to the small bookshelves and pulled out her old photo albums and her files containing all her personal documents. She unplugged her laptop and packed it away in its case. Then Dani walked through to the kitchen and scanned it to see if there was anything she needed. Her eyes fell on the coffee machine. She quickly unplugged it and emptied the contents into the bin, then wrapped it in kitchen paper and placed it in another bin liner.

Jez had followed her down the stairs and watched her. He'd put on a T-shirt and jogging pants, his face ashen. His hair was dishevelled but he still looked stunning.

"Please don't leave me, Dani. I promise, I'll never cheat on you again. We'll start over. Just please don't leave me."

"I can't stay, Jez. You've destroyed everything. I'll never trust you, *ever*. I can't be with someone I can't trust, however much it hurts," she spat out.

"We've got so much together, been through so much together…"

"It means nothing to me, Jez, nothing if I can't trust you. I gave you everything and you've betrayed me. Everything we had has crumbled away. I can't get over this. I don't want to. I'm a jealous person as it is – you know that. You know how I am. You managed to make me believe that I could trust you. How will I ever believe what you say to me ever again? I have to go, get away…"

Dani pushed past him and ran up the stairs, collecting the remaining packed bin liners, and left them at the bottom of the stairs. She pulled on her biker boots and opened the front door. The blast of cold air hit Dani and she shivered. She quickly packed her belongings into her car, squashing them into the small boot and piling the rest on the passenger seat.

Dani ran back into the house and up the stairs as Jez stood immobile in the hallway. She took one last look around the bedroom. The Coldplay CD was still playing as she left the room and came down the stairs. Jez stood in the hallway, rubbing his face as he watched her move through the lounge and then the kitchen. Dani looked on the windowsill and spotted her green orchid that Chloe had sent her for her last birthday. It was budding again. She lifted it off the windowsill and carried it through to the hallway where Jez was sitting on the stairs.

"Where will you go?" he asked softly as he stood up.

"I'm not sure."

"Then stay tonight. Let's talk it out, Dani. Please don't go like this. It's late..." he pleaded as he moved swiftly over to her, his hand reaching out to touch her stony face.

Dani jerked back and Jez's hand dropped. "Good bye, Jez."

"Jesus, Dani, don't leave like this. After five years, we can't just be over!"

Dani clenched her eyes shut, not wanting to see the devastation in his handsome face. "I can't stay... I just can't."

"Dani, I love you. Please don't leave me." His fingers touched her arm and Dani felt her tears prick the back of her eyes again. She had to leave and leave now.

"You didn't love me enough. I needed that. Someone who only needs and wants me."

She turned away and walked towards her car, clutching her orchid. She slipped into the car and started the engine. Dani pulled out onto the road and drove away without looking back, her tears falling freely down her cheeks.

Dani drove towards Twickenham and the M3 so that she could join the M25. Dani wasn't very good at getting around London, so she pulled into a service station and programmed her GPS. Thank God her car was fitted with one. She filled up with petrol and bought some cigarettes. It would take her at least four hours to get up to Leeds. She looked at her clock. It was nearly eleven. If she called Chloe now, they'd have to stay up until she arrived at three or four in the morning. Dani didn't want to put her out. She knew Chloe slept early because of the children. Rosie wasn't two yet and still woke up in the night. Dani decided she'd set off, then stop half-way up. Nap in the car and get up to Leeds around seven. At least they'd be up by then.

Dani pulled out of the service station and headed towards the M25. Her tears pooled in her eyes as she tried desperately to calm down. Her hands were shaking and the shock of what had happened began to dawn on her.

She'd left him. She'd left Jez. In her eagerness to get away, she hadn't really appreciated what that meant. She was hurt and angry, which had resulted in her impulsive decision to leave. It meant she was leaving everything behind: her home, her job, her life.

Tears fell, blurring her vision, and she knew she really shouldn't be driving. She blinked hard encouraging them to fall. At the age of twenty-five, she'd have to start over again, when she'd hoped that she would now be looking forward to the next chapter in her life. Dani pulled over on the hard shoulder and rummaged around for a tissue. She roughly dried her eyes. Her phone buzzed and she knew Jez was trying to call her. She reached into her bag and looked at the screen. His photo flashed across it – a picture she'd taken of him resting his chin on his hands, propped up on the bar. He was smiling his sexy smile and Dani's heart broke at the image of him. Fresh tears rolled down her face. If she answered, he'd convince her to go back. She just couldn't. Cheating was a deal breaker. She shut off her phone and dropped it back in her bag.

Dani shifted her car into gear and continued to head towards the M25, deciding to stop at the first service station and pull over for a nap. She suddenly felt bone weary. Her head was pounding from the crying. She checked her GPS. The next service station was on the M1. With any luck, she'd be there in an hour.

It was still dark as Dani drove into Leeds City Centre. It was six thirty. The early morning traffic was still light. Dani turned onto the inner ring road and followed the signs towards Harrogate, glad she had her GPS. She'd only been up to Leeds by train since Chloe had moved up, so the roads were unfamiliar. Dani yawned as she stopped at traffic lights, her head pounding from lack of sleep, crying, chain smoking and numerous cups of coffee she'd drunk on the way up.

She'd been driving for almost three hours after she'd taken a restless nap in the service station. Her neck was stiff and she was feeling light headed. She looked over to her phone and reluctantly switched it on. She knew there'd be numerous messages from Jez. The traffic lights changed to green and Dani pulled off and drove towards Harrogate Road. It was still too early to call Chloe. As her phone connected to her network, ten messages beeped through and Dani's eyes filled with tears again. It had taken her the first couple of hours of the journey to calm down, but now she just felt an overwhelming sense of loss. She glanced at the passenger seat crammed with her belongings. After five years with Jez, all she had was her car and the black bin bags full of her clothes and possessions.

Dani roughly dried her eyes with a tissue she'd been holding the whole journey. She stopped at another set of traffic lights and looked around. There were a few shops along the street, and further down, she could see a small grocery shop that seemed to be open. Once the lights changed, Dani pulled into the small parking area in front of the open shop. To her delight she saw that it was a small Jewish bakery too.

Dani checked her reflection in her visor mirror. Her eyes were blood-shot and puffy from the crying and she looked drawn. *What the hell, no one knew her here anyway*; she thought as she flipped back the sun visor and stepped out of her car. The smell of freshly baked bagels wafted through the street. Dani took in the smell and pulled her biker jacket tighter around her. The air was icy cold. She was still wearing her halter top and skin tight trousers. Dani shuddered as she headed for the door.

Within fifteen minutes, she was back in the car driving up towards Harewood, past all the huge houses with their perfectly tended gardens. It was really quite beautiful, even in the dark and only lit by the street lights. All the houses were floodlit, showing off their different facades. Dani munched down on her bagel as she headed past the entrance to Harewood house. Nothing like a hefty dose of cream cheese-covered bagel to lift your mood, she thought. Dani looked at the time; it was seven fifteen. She pressed her speed dial for Chloe's mobile and waited for it to connect.

"Hello, Dani?" Chloe answered, her tone clearly baffled as to why her sister was calling her so early in the morning.

"Hi, Chloe." Dani's voice was shaking as she spoke.

"Dani, are you alright?"

"No, I'm not. I'm about five minutes away."

"What? What do you mean?"

"I drove up through the night. Jez and I broke up."

"Oh crap! Dani!"

"I'm sorry to spring this on you but I just..." Dani's voice broke. Saying it out loud made what had happened real.

"Don't be silly. Just get here. You know the way?"

"GPS." Dani let out a stifled sob.

"Okay, good. See you in a bit."

Dani closed off her phone and carried on driving down the country road. Dawn was breaking and the sky was fiery red. There were frost-covered fields on either side of the road and the trees were bare and white. Dani checked the temperature. It was two degrees. The thought sent a shiver down her spine. She turned into Chloe's road and followed it about a mile down, before she spotted their house set back to the right. Dani's heart swelled. Thank God she had Chloe, her one true constant. She swerved into the wide driveway and brought her car to a halt.

Adam and Chloe had bought their house six years ago. It was a large, sprawling, stone-built residence set in an acre of land. They'd refurbished it over the last year and Dani had yet to see it finished. Dani quickly pulled out her packet of cigarettes and took one out. She lit it with shaking hands. The thought of reliving what had just happened over nine hours ago was not something she was looking forward to. It still felt like a dream. A nightmare. She opened her car door as she dragged on her cigarette. She didn't want to smoke in front of the children. At least she'd get to see them and actually spend some time with them. She smiled to herself; well there was the silver lining she was looking for – out of all this mess she'd at least spend time with her nephew and nieces.

It had been six months since she'd last visited. She'd been up for Rosie's first birthday. Sophie, who was five, had started school this September and Oliver was now in year five. Dani took a final drag on her cigarette and stubbed it out in the ashtray, then she looked at the packet of Davidoffs. She had two left. Maybe it was time to quit this bad habit too. Dani opened up the glove compartment and put the packet inside. She looked at the front door and sighed. There were three carved pump-kins of varying sizes on the doorstep. Dani had forgotten it was Halloween; her mind flitted back to the bar. They were having their fancy dress party tonight and she wondered how they'd manage without her. Dani rubbed her face and climbed out of the car, then headed down the path, her hands shaking as she shoved them into her pockets.

Within an hour, Dani was settled into the spare room. Chloe had arranged the bed for her while Adam brought up her eight bin liners full of her belongings. He sloped off, knowing the sisters wanted some privacy, but not before hugging Dani.

"I'll put some coffee on and toast up the bagels you brought." His kind face smiled gently, his blue eyes magnified by his glasses as he blinked down at Dani.

"Thanks, Adam."

Chloe scrunched up her nose as she grinned at him and he left, taking Rosie and Sophie with him.

"You're so lucky Chloe," sighed Dani, watching them leave.

Chloe pursed her lips and slumped on the bed. "I know. He's a saint." Feeling her sister's pain, she asked, "Want to tell me what happened?" She cocked her head to one side as Dani fished out her shoes, which were tangled around various bag handles.

"He cheated on me. It's as simple as that." Dani looked up at Chloe as she spoke. Chloe took a sharp intake of breath, "I walked in on him."

"Oh Dani, I'm so sorry."

Dani shrugged, trying hard not to start crying again. "She was one of our staff and she wasn't the first, Chloe." Her voice cracking as she spoke.

"Oh God." Chloe put her hand to her mouth.

"I suppose it's better I found out now, rather than later." Dani opened the wardrobe and placed her shoes in the bottom. "I just feel like an idiot and that I wasted all that time waiting around for him to commit."

"Oh Dani. *He* was the idiot."

Dani snorted. "I feel like I've moved ten steps back. I'm starting again, from the beginning." Dani opened up the next bin liner and started hanging up her crumpled clothes. "It's not just him I left – it's my job, my home, everything."

"What are you going to do about the house?"

"I didn't think that far ahead, to be honest. I just needed to get out of there, away. If I'd stayed, I'd have forgiven him."

Chloe smiled at her sister. Dani portrayed herself as being tough and confident, but Chloe knew she was soft. She'd always tried to see the best in everyone.

"Don't worry about the house. Adam can sort it. He'll know what to do."

"I'm sorry for dumping on you. But it's just until I get a job and get back on track."

"Dani, will you stop it? I'm thrilled you're here, we all are. Not so much about the reason why you're here, granted, but I'm so glad you are.

I've missed you." She got up and hugged her. Dani clung to Chloe as she tightened her grip.

"I'm so glad I have you, Chloe. I don't think I could cope if you weren't in my life." Tears sprung into her eyes again as they held onto each other, both reluctant to let go.

Chloe sniffed as she tried to hold back her tears. "I'm glad I have you too, Dani. I've missed you so much."

2

NASTY HABITS

Stretching out her legs, Dani felt something against her calf. She sleepily opened her eyes to see what was obstructing her much-needed stretch. Sat cross-legged, perched on the edge of her bed, was Sophie. Sophie was staring at her with large blue eyes.

"Hi, angel," yawned Dani. She'd decided to have a nap after unpacking. Her head still fuzzy after her deep sleep, Dani tried to focus on Sophie. In the dim afternoon light, she noticed Sophie was holding something. Dani propped herself up on her elbows to get a better look.

"I brought you my lamp. You don't have one." Sophie looked down at the lamp she was holding. Dani sat up as her head started to clear.

"Thank you, Sophie. Are you sure I can borrow it?"

Sophie nodded and scrambled closer. "It's a Snow White lamp," Sophie explained proudly.

Dani knew this was a real honour; Snow White was Sophie's favourite heroine. "I know. Isn't it your favourite?"

Sophie nodded, "You can borrow it until you get one. Mummy said you're sad so this will cheer you up."

Dani's heart burst at the sight of her beautiful angelic face and her blonde curly hair. "Shall I plug it in? It is getting dark in here."

Sophie nodded and got down from the bed and placed the lamp on the bedside table. Dani rubbed her face, reached over for the plug and pushed it into the socket. Sophie then switched it on and the small lamp gave a warm hue to the darkening room. Dani looked at her watch; it was nearly four.

"Thank you, Sophie, that's much better. Here, get under the covers. It's chilly." Sophie scrambled up onto the bed and Dani enveloped her in the quilt as they snuggled face to face. "You know, in Greenland, where the Eskimos live, where it's freezing, they give Eskimo kisses."

"What are Eskimo kisses?" asked Sophie.

"They rub their noses together." Sophie giggled. "Like this." Dani pulled Sophie closer and rubbed her nose. Sophie giggled again and Dani hugged her tightly. *Sophie was just so perfect*, she thought. "Are you going to dress up for Halloween?"

"Yes, we're going to a party. I'm going to be a witch and Ollie's going to be a vampire."

"Ooh, scary!" Dani mock-shivered, to Sophie's delight. They were distracted by the door opening and they both pushed themselves up to see who had entered the room. Ollie peeped his head around the door and smiled shyly.

"Hi, there. Are you back from school?"

"Yes." He edged in, hovering nervously at the door. He was the image of Adam, big for his age and his face kind and gentle, the only difference was that he had Chloe's colouring, brown hair and hazel eyes, which sparkled behind his glasses.

"Come here, darling, and get in the covers."

He beamed and ran up to the bed and scooted inside. His eyes rested on the lamp and he frowned.

"Dani just gave me an Eskimo kiss."

Ollie gave a puzzled look at Dani, and she explained to him what that meant. Then she bent down to him and rubbed her nose against his and he blushed.

"Come on, we'd better get you ready for your party. Where's Mummy?"

"She's in the kitchen finishing off the fairy cakes we're taking."

"Let me wash my face and we can go down."

By the time Dani entered the kitchen, Chloe was packing the fairy cakes into a plastic container.

"Sleep well?" she asked.

"Amazingly, yes. What time are you going to the party?"

"In an hour."

"Where's Rosie?"

"She's having her nap, otherwise she'll be grizzly at the party. I need to go and wake her up, actually. And I have to dress her up."

"What's she going as?" smirked Dani.

"A pumpkin."

"Oh no, how cute! She'll look adorable. What do you need me to do?"

"Um, can you sort out these two with their dinner? I'd rather they ate properly before we go."

"Sure."

At five fifteen, Ollie, Sophie and Rosie were ready, all dressed up and each holding their trick or treat bags. Chloe bundled them in the car, also dressed as a witch. Dani waved them off and went back into the empty house, closing the door behind her. She still felt groggy from her lack of sleep. She needed coffee. Dani ran up to her room to bring down her coffee machine. As she entered, she noticed on the far bedside table a lamp in the shape of Dr Who's Tardis. Ollie must have put it there. Dani's eyes filled with tears. After all the pain and upset she'd suffered over the last twenty hours, these two amazing children had managed to make her feel loved. Her heart ached at the thought of them.

Dani poured her coffee and sat down at the kitchen table, looking at her phone. She hadn't switched it on since she'd arrived at Chloe's. Reluctantly, she pressed in her PIN and waited for it to connect to the network. One by one, the messages beeped through. Twenty-three. Jez was being relentless. Dani stared at the phone, wrestling with herself as to whether she should read them. She knew he'd try anything to get her to go back to him. What she wasn't sure about was his motive. Was it her he wanted back, or his manager?

The bar ran like clockwork while she was managing it. Jez was much more into the public relations side of the business, the image and playing his role. He was brilliant at it, but the day-to-day running of the bar he found tedious. Dani had always been the organised one, from ordering and negotiating supplies, to staff rotas, and to private parties and events. Dani huffed. She wondered now about his 'public relations' with other women. *Well tough shit!* Trust was the most important thing for Dani. She could never be with someone that she couldn't trust, regardless of how much she loved him.

Dani looked back at the phone and deleted all the messages. Whatever he had to say was too little, too late. Dani's stomach rumbled. She hadn't eaten since morning. She stood up and made her way over to the stove, where Chloe had left spaghetti and bolognaise sauce out for her and Adam, for when they got home. She was craving nicotine and her thoughts flitted to her discarded cigarette packet in the glove compartment. Dani took a deep breath and decided to substitute her craving for the next best thing – something sweet.

Dani paced over to the fridge and opened it. Scanning down the shelves, her eyes fell on a foil-covered pie dish. She pulled it out, then opened up the foil. To her delight, it was half an apple pie. She placed it on the counter and served herself a large portion, then popped it into the microwave just to take the chill off. Dani much preferred to eat desserts rather than savoury food. She loved other food too, but desserts were her weakness. She opened up the freezer and pulled out a tub of Ben & Jerry's Karamel Sutra ice cream, and scooped a generous dollop on the warmed pie. *Heaven in a bowl*, she thought. She took a big spoonful and savoured the taste. Scrumptious. Chloe knew how to bake a mean apple pie.

Dani was jolted out of her dessert-induced trance by the front door opening. Adam was home from work. She heard him drop his keys on the console table in the hallway and hang up his coat in the closet. He paced through to the kitchen and grinned as he saw Dani licking her spoon.

"I hope you left some for me," he joked.

"Good job you came now, otherwise I might have finished it all." Adam sat next to her. "Shall I get you something to eat? Chloe's taken the kids to a Halloween party."

Adam twisted his mouth, then rubbed his eyes, "I need a drink first. Do you want one?"

"Do I ever!"

Adam snorted, "What do you want?"

"Tequila, if you have it. Otherwise brandy."

"I think we still have a bottle in the bar from when you were last here." Adam got up and headed into the lounge. He came back grinning, with a half-full bottle of Jose Cuervo and two heavy crystal tumblers. He poured the amber liquid into the glasses and slid back into his chair.

"Cheers." Adam lifted his glass and eyed Dani.

"Cheers." They both took a sip and Dani relished the warmth in her throat.

"So, are you gonna tell me what that asshole did?"

Dani almost choked at his unexpected question. Adam raised an eyebrow as Dani recomposed herself. "He cheated on me."

Adam's eyes turned icy. "And you just walked out on him?"

Dani nodded as she pursed her lips.

"Good. You're way too good for him."

Dani stared wide-eyed at him.

"What? Chloe thinks the same too. He was a prize douche bag. I tolerated him because of you."

"Douche bag?"

"Wanker, then!" he sneered.

Dani laughed at her brother-in-law's accurate description, then sighed.

"Yeah, maybe. But it still hurts. I feel like an idiot. It means I have to start again, all over, from scratch." Dani took a deep drink from her glass.

"What about the house?" Adam watched as Dani frowned.

"I don't know. I haven't thought that far ahead."

"I'll take care of it. I'll get it valued and ask him to cough up half, or we can sell it and split the profits." He paused a moment, gauging her reaction, his blue eyes magnified by his glasses as his gaze swept over her face. Dani looked into her glass, unable to look up at him. She knew he was right but she wasn't ready to deal with the logistics of separating herself from Jez. This time yesterday, she had been in bed with him and now she was over two hundred miles away, sitting and talking about how to extract herself from him, mentally, emotionally and physically. It felt far too soon and way too real.

"I'm sorry, Dani. I was going all lawyer on you. You can decide what you want to do when you're ready." He took a sip from his drink and mentally kicked himself. He'd never liked Jez from the moment he'd met him. He was everything Adam despised in a man. Jez was driven by what people thought of him, selfish, pretentious and self-absorbed. He used people to get whatever he needed and it was obvious he'd never had Dani's best interests at heart. He'd stopped her continuing her studies and totally controlled her life. In the five years they'd been together, Dani had become consumed with everything to do with Jez and she'd lost sight of who she was.

Adam looked at her drawn, sad face and knew that if Jez had been anywhere near, he'd have beaten the living shit out of him. Lucky for Jez, he was down in London.

Dani looked up at Adam's kind face and forced a smile. "It's okay, you're right I need to get on with it. I'd appreciate you handling it; I really haven't got the strength to deal with that. I need to get myself a job. That's my priority. I need to be busy."

"Any ideas?"

"I really don't know; a bar or restaurant, something with a lot of hours. And then I need my own place. I can't stay here indefinitely." Dani rubbed her tired face and took another drink.

"You can stay as long as you like. We love having you here. All of us. The kids are so excited you're here and Chloe, she misses you a lot. Me too."

Dani screwed up her nose and smiled, "I love being here too. I've missed you all so much."

"Good. About the job, I can ask around. There are loads of places, I'm sure a few are looking for staff, especially with Christmas around the corner. I'll get the paper tomorrow and you can have a look. Are you okay for money?"

Dani's eyes shot up to Adam and she grinned at him. He really was the best, "I'm fine, Adam, thanks for asking."

"You need anything, anything at all, and it's done."

Dani scraped back her chair and flung her arms around him, catching him off guard. "You're the best, Adam."

Adam awkwardly put his arms around her, feeling embarrassed by her sudden outburst as she squeezed him. She pulled back and his rugged face flushed. "Well... er... thanks."

Dani sat down and smirked at him. For all his confidence and strength, he still wasn't comfortable with displays of affection. Dani found it amusing to see a six foot four, burly man recoil when affection was openly bestowed upon on him.

Dani placed the dirty dishes into the dishwasher and began wiping down the kitchen counter, when she heard the familiar sound of Chloe's car pull up. She opened up the kitchen door that led into the garage. Chloe was juggling her bag and a fast-asleep Rosie. Dani quickly took her bag and mouthed that she'd get Sophie and Ollie.

"Hey guys, how was the party?" That was all Dani needed to say, and Ollie and Sophie immediately gave her a blow-by-blow account of every detail, as Dani helped them into the house, both of them carrying bulging bags of sweets and a balloon each.

Within an hour, all three children were tucked up in bed and Dani sat with Chloe in the kitchen. Adam worked in the office, tactfully leaving the sisters alone.

Dani twiddled her hair nervously; her nicotine craving had kicked in hard. She looked at the clock. It was nine fifteen and normally she'd have been at the bar and would be on her fourth cigarette. Chloe was rambling away about Adam's company Christmas charity dinner, as she looked through her kitchen cupboards, jotting down what she needed to get from the supermarket.

"So it'll be the first time since Rosie was born that I'll get to go out to the swanky do. Last year she was just too small. And I know Adam's dad could've babysat, but I would have been worried all night and..." Chloe opened the fridge and peered in, then looked over to Dani who was staring at the clock, oblivious. She closed the fridge and sat down at the table. "Hey, stop that."

Dani looked up and sighed.

"Has he called you?"

"Yes."

"And?"

"I didn't pick up. I'm not ready to talk yet. I could kill for a cigarette."

Chloe pursed her lips together. "I've some sugar free pastels if you want, or a lollipop."

Dani shook her head. "I quit one nasty habit, I don't want to substitute."

"Which nasty habit is that, the cigarettes or Jez?" smirked Chloe.

"Both."

Chloe laughed. "What do you want to do tomorrow? We could go to Betty's in Harrogate, if you like. You'll love the cakes there."

"Sounds good, but I need to search for a job and I really need to get my hair done too."

"I'll book you an appointment at where I have mine done. I doubt you'll get in until Monday, though."

Dani shrugged, indicating that was okay, "I think I should sell my car too. It's not economical and to be honest, it's really not me."

Chloe sat next to her and hugged her shoulders. "If that's what you want to do. We can put it in the paper."

"I just want everything that reminds me of him out of my life. I feel... I feel... argh! I don't know. Angry? Foolish? Pathetic. Probably all three. I'm so pissed off at him and at myself for being so blind. Adam told me you both didn't like him." Dani looked up at Chloe, whose face dropped.

"Well, we just thought you deserved better. He seemed to take over everything." Chloe smiled nervously as she watched her sister's brow furrow. "It doesn't matter what we thought, anyway. We only ever wanted you to be happy. It's down to you, Dani. Were you happy with him?" Chloe got back up again and started to empty the dishwasher.

Dani leaned back in the chair and took a deep breath. Had she been happy with Jez? She really couldn't answer. She'd met him when she was going through a rough time. Her mother was terminally ill and she'd gone to work for him at his bar. Jez had only had the bar a few months and was finding it hard work. When Dani started working for him, he

21

soon realised she was more than just a bartender. Within a few weeks, Dani was helping him with the day-to-day running. Jez didn't waste any time, and within those same few weeks, they were seeing each other. After Dani's mother died, they moved in together. Their relationship moved at a fast pace, all initiated by Jez, and Dani had been sure that they would eventually get married.

As time had passed though, he never seemed to make that final commitment. Looking back, Dani tried to see if he'd ever shown her any signs that marriage was on his mind. She knew she was blindsided by his good looks and charm, and he seemed to be able to say the right things to her, whenever she felt that maybe he wasn't marriage material. Was she happy with him though? She sighed deeply as she looked at Chloe's expectant face. If she had to think about it, she thought to herself, maybe she hadn't been that happy after all.

She'd fallen into the relationship feet first. A combination of her mother's condition and Dani's need for companionship had pushed her towards Jez. Chloe had moved two hundred miles away, leaving Dani lonely. They had always been close and Dani had practically done everything with Chloe and Adam prior to their move.

Jez was devastatingly handsome, in a rock star kind of way, with his shaggy dirty blond hair and effortless, edgy sense of style. He could charm anyone with his seductive manner, women and men alike. Jez was always the centre of attention and one of the reasons his bar was so successful was purely down to his personality. Dani loved watching him in action, and he played his role perfectly. Everyone was made to feel special as he lavished them with attention and stroked his clientele's egos with just enough vehemence to ensure they'd want to come back for more.

He was also calculating and shrewd, and every action he undertook was ultimately to benefit him. Dani's heart sunk. Even down to her. He'd needed her, she'd known that, but she really had hoped their relationship was more than his need for a reliable and loyal bar manager. Now that she'd extracted herself from him, from his overpowering influence, she could see that she was obviously nothing more than a very good member of staff with fringe benefits.

"I was happy sometimes, when we worked together. He was great when we worked together," mumbled Dani.

"What about when it was just the two of you?" Chloe's eyebrows rose.

Dani rubbed her face. They hardly spent time alone together, only in bed. They were always surrounded by people, staff or customers. They were always at some event; they rarely had time for just the two of them. Dani hadn't really noticed that until now.

"We didn't spend that much time alone. I suppose that's not a good sign either." Dani huffed air up her face as her eyes pooled with tears. How had she been so blind? She'd been swept away by him, totally. The signs were there but she hadn't seen them. She put her head in her hands. Why hadn't she seen them? She'd loved him. She'd overlooked everything and believed in the lie he'd convinced her she was living.

"Oh Dani, don't get upset. He's not worth it." Chloe crouched next to her, pulling her hands away from her face.

"I can't get that damn image out of my head, Chloe," Dani sniffed. Chloe got up and pulled off some kitchen roll. "God knows how many more he's been with. I need to go to a doctor too."

Chloe's eyes widened.

"He never wore a condom, Chloe."

"Shit! Dani!" Chloe's face showing her horror at what that implied.

"I know. I can't believe how stupid I am."

"I'll get you into Adam's dad's surgery tomorrow."

"I don't want him to examine me!" Dani said, horrified that Chloe's father-in-law would know all her sordid details.

"No, silly. There are other doctors there. It's a large surgery. I go to Doctor Evans. She's a woman. She's really nice. Try not to worry."

Dani screwed her eyes up and shook her head. She felt so unbelievably stupid and let down, used in the worst possible way. She vowed to herself that she'd never let anyone make her feel so low about herself again.

3

HAVING YOUR CAKE AND EATING IT

D ani looked at her weary face in the mirror, her hair loosely falling down her back as she sipped her espresso. The colour specialist rolled his stool up closer, holding a book of hair swatches. He smiled at her reflection, his shock of black hair in stark contrast to his pale skin.

"So, Dani, have a look at these. See which you feel is the closest to your present shade." He fingered the ends of Dani's hair as he spoke. Dani looked down at the book and sighed.

"I think I'm tired of being blonde. Maybe I should go back to my original colour."

"Oh, okay." He rolled his stool up closer, then sat down and pointed to the section with the chestnut samples of hair. "Something like this, then? Maybe with a few low lights for texture?"

Dani nodded. "I want it shorter too. More layers. Up to here." She showed him, indicating with her fingers to just over her breasts. "It'll be easier to look after."

The colourist nodded, his light blue eyes sparkling. "Going for a big change, then?"

"Yeah, something like that," Dani huffed.

After two and half hours, Dani emerged from the salon looking like a completely different woman to the one who had walked in. Chloe was waiting in her car. Her jaw dropped as Dani slipped into the passenger seat. "Wow, Dani, you look amazing."

"You like it?"

"I love it. You look sophisticated and chic. The colour is fabulous on you and I love the fringe."

Dani beamed. *Nothing like a new look to change your mood*, she thought. "Let's go to Betty's for brunch."

"Unch," repeated Rosie from her car seat.

"Brunch. B-b-b-brunch," corrected Chloe. "I hope she grows out of this." Chloe rolled her eyes. "The only thing she says correctly is Mummy and Daddy."

Rosie had difficulty pronouncing the first letter of most words. She'd learned to talk early, but for some reason she omitted the first letter, making her both difficult to understand and comical.

"She will. Don't you remember Ollie couldn't say his Rs and Sophie used to change the word completely! It's just until it clicks. She'll find the first letters!"

Chloe nodded and sighed.

"It's so cute." Dani turned to look at Rosie. "Do you know you're cute?"

Rosie beamed at her and kicked her legs, her big brown eyes wide. "I could eat you, you're so cute!" Rosie squirmed and giggled as Dani reached and tickled her tummy.

They managed to get a table in the celebrated tearoom. It was Dani's first time in Betty's. As she walked through the entrance, Dani immediately fell in love with its old world charm. Her eyes scanned the shop, taking in all the different tea canisters at the rear end, set high on wooden shelves. Then her gaze fell on the sumptuous pastries, biscuits and enormous variety of bread displayed in glass cases. The smells were so enticing; Dani breathed in deeply, ensuring her senses were flooded with them. The hostess guided them to a table by the window and Dani looked around the airy, bright room.

"Oh Chloe, I've died and gone to heaven. This place is amazing. Why have we never been here before?"

Chloe smirked at Dani and shook her head. "I knew you'd like it. Well you always came up for a flying visit and we never seemed to have the time. I love it here." She placed Rosie in a high chair and took her seat.

"Well, it's my treat. It's the least I can do, after everything you've done for me." Dani took the menu from the waitress and opened it up.

They decided to go all out and ordered a couple of glasses of pink champagne. They both opted for the breakfast rosti and for Rosie, they ordered a scrambled egg muffin. Rosie played with a cloth book as they waited for their food to come.

"Are you going to get in touch with Jez?" Chloe inquired. Dani's face hardened. "You're going to have to talk to him sooner or later."

Dani sipped her champagne and sighed. The truth was she was

scared to talk to him. If he tried to talk her around, she knew she'd cave. He made her weak and these past few days without him had made her realise how much he'd influenced her over the last five years. She was consumed with him and he'd taken full advantage of that. She was still unbelievably hurt, but that wasn't the reason she couldn't bring herself to answer his persistent calls, or call him herself. She knew he would only need to say the right thing and she'd go running back to him. That very fact made Dani feel powerless and pathetic. She really needed to toughen up.

"Yes. I just can't seem to muster up enough courage."

Chloe frowned.

"If I talk to him, he's going to try and get me to go back. I'm not sure I'll be able to say no." Chloe's mouth opened to say something, but she closed it as Dani continued.

"I know what you're thinking, but the bottom line is, I did love him. I know he couldn't have felt the same way about me, but that just makes it worse." Dani took a deep breath and shook her head as if she needed to clear it. "Anyway, I need to concentrate on positive thoughts. I need to get moving on. Like for my interview tomorrow." She forced a smile and Chloe nodded.

They'd spent the weekend searching for suitable jobs. Adam had managed to secure Dani an interview at a very popular Italian restaurant that he frequented. It was always busy and was a family run business. The turnaround of staff was minimal, indicating it must be a pleasant working environment. The vacancy had arisen due to a member of staff leaving the area. Luckily, Adam had been in the restaurant on Friday and had overheard they were looking for a replacement.

Dani's phone rang and she closed her eyes. Surely Jez couldn't be ringing so early; he never got up before one. She looked down at the number and saw it was a local. Apprehensively, she answered it. "Hello?"

"Hello, Miss Knox?" said a female voice that Dani didn't recognise. Chloe looked at her as she took another mouthful of rosti.

"Yes?"

"This is Dr. Evans. I have your blood and urine test results from Friday."

"Oh. Right. Thank you. Do I need to come back in?"

"No. That won't be necessary. They are all clear. But I suggest you schedule an appointment in a month for when you need a repeat prescription for your contraceptive pill."

"All clear. That's great news. Thank you for calling." Dani's relief evident and Chloe smiled, realising who the call was from. "Okay. I'll call in a couple of weeks for an appointment, then."

"Good. Well good bye, Miss Knox."

"Good bye and thank you." Dani pressed the end call on her phone and popped it back in her bag. "Thank God for that. I think I need a dessert to celebrate."

"Just one?" Chloe smirked and Dani giggled. Her heartbeat sped up as the enormity of what she'd been told sunk in. She'd been given the all clear. The wave of relief flowed over her. It could have been... no, she wasn't going to think about it anymore. Her insides churned. She was never going to be that foolish again. Note to self; buy your own condoms.

Dani broke into her citron torte and placed it in her mouth. It was a perfect combination of sweet and zesty lemon zing. Dani moaned. It was divine. Chloe had chosen the fresh raspberry macaroon and they'd also ordered a Montagne de Chocolate, which they shared with Rosie, and a mille feuille.

"If I die now, I'll be happy. These are just delicious. We need to take some home for the kids and Adam. I feel guilty," said Dani as Chloe licked her spoon, then spooned up some of the chocolate to feed to Rosie. Rosie's mouth was wide and ready in anticipation.

"Well, she definitely takes after me in that department. She hasn't stopped eating!" Said Chloe. Dani grinned. "Now your hair is back to your natural colour she looks more like you."

Dani screwed up her nose. "You think? I don't see it." She looked back at Rosie, who was chewing contentedly on her chocolate cake, her full lips covered in chocolate. "Do you look like your aunty Dani?" she asked a wide-eyed Rosie, who immediately rewarded her with a grin.

"Ani!"

"D-D-D-Dani!" corrected Chloe and she shook her head.

***

"We're off!!" called Chloe up the stairs. Dani leaned over the railings and looked down to where her sister was standing in the hallway.

"Have a good time."

"You sure you don't want to come? It'll take your mind off everything." They were leaving for a bonfire party held at a neighbour's house.

"I'm sure. You go on. I'll be fine."

Chloe nodded and went out of the front door, closing it behind her. Dani paced back to her room and sat back down onto her bed. She opened up her laptop and started up her email. She knew this was a chicken's way out, writing rather than talking, but she knew she'd be able to get everything down exactly as she wanted to say it. Dani always seemed to get flustered when she had to say what she felt. She smiled at her screen saver. It was a collage of pictures; all of them were of her parents. She missed them terribly. Dani smiled, thinking about how her mother used to moan about how no one seemed to talk anymore.

"People are either texting, emailing, tweeting. Tweeting? What the hell is that all about? Why don't people just talk anymore? Pick up the phone and chat. You have something to say, just say it!" she'd tut.

Dani could visualize her shaking her head and busying herself in the kitchen. She was always baking. There were always homemade cakes or biscuits in the house. Then later, when Dani's parents owned the bed and breakfast, her mother always made sure there were homemade goodies in each of the rooms. Dani was sure this was why she loved desserts so much. Lucky her mother had taught both Chloe and herself to bake.

It was easy for their mother; she'd always been a straight talker. Dani was much more like her father. He hated hurting anyone's feelings; he was a soft, gentle man who'd adored his wife. Dani often thought that Chloe and Adam had a similar dynamic to their parents. Chloe was the feisty one and seemed in control of pretty much everything. The house ran like clockwork. Chloe had also finished her law degree but when she'd fallen pregnant, she'd opted to stay home. They'd been lucky that Adam's career had allowed them that luxury. Nevertheless, Chloe had thrown herself into motherhood and being a corporate wife with as much drive and enthusiasm as she had for her legal career.

Chloe pretty much excelled at everything. She'd taught herself how to sew and she now made the children's fancy dress costumes and volunteered her services to the school whenever they put on a production. Her garden was immaculate, all due to Chloe's handiwork. The remodel of their home was all Chloe – her ideas and her vision. Dani was in awe of her. When she put her mind to it, Chloe just seemed to achieve whatever she wanted. Her ambition had also pushed Adam. Even though a lot of his success was down to his extreme diligence and proficiency, it was Chloe that nudged him that bit further.

Dani looked at the blank screen, then sighed hard as she started to type.

Jez,

I'd like to say I'm sorry for not answering or replying to you but to be perfectly honest, I'm not. These past few days I have had time to stand back and reflect on our relationship. All I seem to come up with is that I gave you every part of me, so much so that I lost myself. You had me totally and completely, but I was never enough. These past few days I seemed to have found myself again. I realised you never loved me, not in the way you should have. If you love someone, you don't hurt them but you did, deeply. I can't be with someone I don't trust. It's as simple as that. I would never be able to trust you, ever.

I don't want to get into the amount of pain you've caused me because I know you don't really care. Your actions proved that. Your words mean nothing to me unless you can back them up with true feelings and actions.

Please stop pestering me. Whatever you have to say won't make any difference. We are finished. And after five years, that hurts to say, but it's the truth.

I've asked Adam to deal with the house. You'll hear from him shortly. I also took half of the money we had in our joint bank account. I'll send back the cheque book and card.

Please don't call me anymore. I'm not ready to speak to you. I'm not sure if I ever will be.

Dani

Dani wiped the tears from her eyes with the back of her hand. Her finger hovered over the 'Send' option. She knew the email was cold and harsh, but it was how she felt. Her heart felt like it had encased itself in ice. Trust was paramount to her, and Jez had shattered her with his betrayal. She felt herself harden every time the image of Julie straddled over Jez came searing back into her mind. She hit the 'Send' key, then shut down her computer. She knew she'd be hearing from him soon – his ego couldn't take the rejection.

Dani's attention was directed to the fireworks exploding in the sky. She watched as they lit up the dark with a myriad of different coloured stars. She hoped she'd get a job soon. She wasn't used to sitting around – it gave her too much time to think and she really didn't want to do that. She needed to lose herself in work – distract herself from the constant pain she was feeling.

Dani was emptying the dishwasher when Chloe, Adam and the children returned.

"Did you have a good time?"

Ollie grinned broadly, "It was brilliant! We got to toast marshmallows on the fire and I helped Dad with the hotdogs. Did you see the rockets?"

"Yes I did! They were awesome."

Chloe ushered them upstairs to get bathed and changed, and Adam leaned on the door, eyeing Dani. "You okay?" he asked.

Dani shrugged.

"Nervous about tomorrow?" Adam walked through the threshold.

Dani half-shrugged. "I sent an email to Jez."

Adam's eyebrows shot up. "Oh, I see. What did he say?"

"I turned off my computer after I sent it."

"Well at least you got whatever you wanted to say off your chest, eh?"

"I suppose." Dani slumped onto one of the chairs around the kitchen table.

"I think we need a drink." Adam turned around and headed for the lounge. He came back with a couple of glasses and a bottle of brandy.

Dani grinned at him. "What about some cakes?"

Adam's blue eyes sparkled. "Cakes?"

"Oh yes. And not just any cakes, Betty's cakes. We went there today and brought some back."

"Excellent." He rubbed his hands together.

Chloe came down into the kitchen to find Adam and Chloe working their way through the box of cakes. "There better be some for me." She retrieved a spoon from the drawer and sat down with them.

"I tell you what, that Betty knows how to make cakes." Dani licked her spoon.

"The recipes were made by a man, Dani," corrected Chloe.

"A man?"

"Yep. A Swiss man."

"Who's Betty, then?"

Chloe shrugged, "I think she was some random young girl. The story goes that she interrupted a meeting when they were deciding on a name. Not sure, though."

"Well I'd marry any man who could make me cakes like this."

Adam laughed loudly. "That's why I married Chloe, for her cakes!"

Chloe's mouth dropped open and she mock snarled at him.

"That and her ass," he corrected.

Chloe's face broke into giggles. "Too right and my ass!" she got up and wiggled it in his direction and Adam playfully slapped it. Dani laughed for the first time in five days as she watched the two of them fool around.

4

THE INTERVIEW

Dani brushed her hair for the umpteenth time as she checked herself in the hallway mirror. Her brown hair was going to take some getting used to, after being blonde for nearly five years. She loved the new length though. It was great having layers. It gave her hair body. She shook her head from side to side, watching it move.

Sophie watched her from the stairs where she was sitting in the hallway. "You're funny," she giggled.

"Am I?" Dani winked at her. Sophie nodded. Dani turned to face her. "So, do I look okay for my interview?"

"You look pretty," Sophie grinned. Dani beamed at her. Why was a compliment from a five year old such a thrill?

"Do I?" Sophie nodded and Dani walked up to her and squeezed her. "I'm so glad I'm here," she sighed.

"Me too."

Dani lifted her up and rested her on her hip, then walked through to the kitchen where the rest of the family were eating breakfast.

"Ani!" shouted Rosie and Sophie giggled.

"It's Dani, D, D, D, Dani!" corrected Chloe. "Morning! You look lovely, Dani." Chloe smiled up at her. "Are you nervous?" she asked as she placed some buttered toast, cut into strips, on a plate for Rosie.

Dani twisted her mouth, "A bit. I really need the job. The skirt isn't too short, is it? I don't want to look slutty." Dani motioned to her black pleated skirt that came a few inches over her knee. She'd paired it with a cream turtle-necked sweater, thick black tights, knee-high black boots and her black leather biker jacket.

"No, you look smart and edgy," Chloe answered, pleased with her description.

Adam looked up at her. "They'd be mad not to take you. You're way overqualified and experienced."

Dani shrugged. She just wanted to get a job and start afresh. She could do the job standing on her head, but maybe they wouldn't want someone overqualified.

"Did you give Dani her present?" Chloe asked Sophie.

"No. I'll go and get it." Sophie wriggled from Dani's arms and Dani lowered her to the ground. Sophie ran to the kitchen counter and picked something out of the drawer, then she ran back over to Dani.

"Here, this is for good luck." Sophie held out a bracelet made from dry macaroni threaded on a string of elastic. "I made it," she said gleefully.

"You made this for me?" Dani crouched down so she was eye level with Sophie, clearly moved. Sophie smiled bashfully. "It's lovely. Thank you. Put it on for me." Dani put out her hand and Sophie carefully slipped it on her right wrist. Then Dani jiggled her wrist and it rattled. Sophie smiled widely. "It fits perfectly." Sophie looked across at her mother and Chloe winked at her.

"She made it out of macaroni because you're going to an Italian restaurant," explained Chloe.

"Oh, I see. Good job I'm not going to a German restaurant – you'd have made it out of frankfurters!" laughed Dani, and Sophie giggled. "Eskimo kiss?" Sophie nodded and stepped closer, tilting her face up as Dani lowered her nose to Sophie's. They rubbed noses and then Dani hugged her. "Thank you for my bracelet. I love it."

"Come on, Dani. If we don't leave soon, the traffic will be a bitch." Adam put down his coffee cup.

"Itch," repeated Rosie.

"B-B-B-Bitch," corrected Adam, to Chloe and Dani's horror. He bent down to kiss Rosie, Ollie and Chloe.

"Adam!" chastised Chloe.

"I was just correcting her." He put on a look that said, 'what's the problem?'

"One day she's going to repeat something and you'll regret it." Adam shrugged and chuckled.

Sophie held Dani's hand and fiddled with the bracelet she'd made her.

"Will you see us to the door?" Adam asked Sophie, and she nodded.

"Good luck, Dani. Call as soon as you're done," Chloe said.

"Thanks. I will."

They made their way to the door and Adam kissed Sophie and went out to start the car. Dani put on her cream, woolly peaked hat, tilting it a little as she looked at herself in the hallway mirror. "Bye, Sophie. I'll see you in a bit." Dani stepped out of the door into the cold, crisp morning and turned to Sophie. "Wish me luck, angel."

"Good luck," Sophie called out to her as she closed the door behind them and went back into the kitchen.

Adam pulled up outside La Casa d'Italia. It was ten to nine. She was forty minutes early but she didn't care. Dani hated being late. The building was set on the river and was a converted old stone mill. It had been beautifully restored and from the outside it looked like it had three floors. The entrance way had a glass extension to it and the original windows had been replaced with long larger ones, presumably to let in as much natural light as possible. There were ten large sandstone planters along the front with sculptured bay trees in each one. At the side was a large car park and further around was a deck overlooking the river. Dani presumed this was for the warm summer months. Definitely not for now – it was freezing today. She looked up at the building from the car window. The top floor had window boxes at each of the windows. It looked like a residence. There were already a couple of cars in the car park.

The whole area had been re-landscaped with sandstone-paved footpaths. Trees lined the road along with periodically positioned benches. *It must be well used in the warmer months*, thought Dani. *The offices and businesses must use the area for lunch breaks.*

Dani looked over at Adam and he gave her a reassuring smile. "I'll wait with you until it's time, if you like."

"No, it's okay. I don't want you to be late."

"I'm a partner, Dani, I can do what I damn well please. If you sit here until it's time to go in, you'll freeze." He handed her a coffee which they'd picked up on the way, and she took a welcome sip. She'd have preferred an espresso, to give her a buzz, but the cappuccino would have to do. She could have also done with a cigarette. Her cravings weren't really subsiding, but she was pleased she'd stuck it out going cold turkey for five days. She'd promised herself if she made it a whole week without a cigarette and also got a job, she'd buy herself some new boots. Footwear was always the best therapy.

"If they don't take you on here, there's a new hotel that's opening. I know the owner. He's bound to be looking for staff. I know you prefer restaurants and bars, but it's an option too."

Dani looked over to him and smiled. "Thanks."

She was lucky she had Adam and Chloe. Her heart cracked a little at the thought. She'd hoped by now she'd have her own family instead of intruding on theirs. She knew they loved her being with them, but it just made the fact that she didn't have her own even more apparent. Her life had taken several steps backwards in the last couple of days. She was back to being single, out of work and crashing in their spare room, instead of building her own future. She'd lost everything: her home, her job and her man.

"Hey, stop that. It'll work out Dani." Adam squeezed her hand.

"Thanks for this, Adam," she mumbled.

"They were looking for someone anyway, Dani." He knew she was feeling indebted to him for getting her the interview. "They won't take you on because of me. I just heard they were looking, that's all. With any luck, I might get a discount if you get the job," he joked, trying to ease her tension with humour. "Our company spends enough bloody money in there," he snorted.

Dani grinned. She looked over to the building and felt something. She wasn't sure what, but it felt warm and homely. Even though the outside was urbane and polished, it still felt welcoming. Her attention was distracted by a tall man jogging towards the building. He was wearing long, grey shorts with a matching hooded top, covering his head. His breath formed clouds in the cold air as he steadily moved closer. Dani unbuckled her belt and reached for her bag.

"You get off. I'll go in and wait. Thanks for the lift. I'll call you when I'm done."

"Only if you're sure."

Dani nodded and Adam slipped his arm around her, giving her a hug. "Good luck. Not that you need it," he grinned.

Dani opened the door and stepped out. She swung her small bag over her shoulder, smoothed down her skirt, then reached into the car to retrieve her CV and coffee. Closing the door, she waved bye and blew Adam a kiss, causing him to grin and blush.

Dani watched him pull away up the street. There were a few cars driving into neighbouring buildings further up. Dani checked the time. It was just past nine. Thirty minutes to go. She looked back at the building and noticed the jogger had stopped and was leaning against the small wall that enclosed the car park. He was lighting up a cigarette and his brilliant blue eyes looked up as he felt her watching him. Dani smiled tightly, embarrassed that she'd been caught out staring. Dani took a sip of her coffee, then sat down on one of the benches that ran across the paved area opposite the restaurant. She tried to refrain from looking back up again and fiddled with her cup, but she felt his eyes on her still, and was desperate to get a second look. That quick glimpse of him was enough for her to want to take in the rest of him.

It was his eyes that had drawn her attention. They were so intense and steely blue. He was tall and obviously fit, and his exposed calves were toned and tanned. Dani shifted in her seat, looking anywhere but at the jogger. Then, in a feeble attempt to look casual, she let her eyes drift over to the restaurant and across towards where the car park was, hoping her peripheral vision would be able to focus on him. To her horror, he was still staring at her and she felt herself blush. *Crap! How embarrassing!* He was blowing out the smoke in a steady stream and his mouth twitched. Dani hastily picked up the brown envelope with her CV in and stood up. *Shit, she'd have to go in, even if she was fifteen minutes early.* She dropped her half-full coffee cup in the dustbin next to the railings and walked towards the restaurant entrance.

She couldn't get the image of his beautiful sculptured mouth out of her head as she walked steadily across the road. *That's all she needed.* She had already been nervous and now she was flustered. What was even more disturbing was that she knew he was still watching her. She just hoped she wouldn't trip up.

As Dani reached the door, her heart thumped against her chest. Calm down; she willed herself. She took a deep breath and pushed open the heavy glass door and stepped inside, pleased she was out of the jogger's view. She smirked to herself and shook her head, then pushed open the second glass door and walked into the entrance area of La Casa d'Italia.

The interior was a complete contrast to the grey stone exterior. The walls were light and the floor was a beautiful cream granite. There were light-coloured, leather high-backed chairs around a selection of round, square and rectangular beech wood tables. In the entrance area were a marble desk and a cloakroom. The restaurant opened up and the bar area was to the left, lit by a mixed selection of large, funky-shaped bulbs, all hanging at different heights.

The main body of the restaurant had the tables arranged so that each had enough distance to ensure privacy. There were booths along the right side and further in. At the rear, raised up by three steps, was what looked like a private dining area with a black delicate curtain made entirely of fine strands of cord. In the centre was a large, planted lemon tree, which made an unusual focal point. The kitchen was to the right and semi-exposed so that customers could see inside. The whole feel of the restaurant was chic and intimate without being claustrophobic. It was airy and the ceilings were high, paired with concealed lighting and beautiful modern chandeliers.

Dani loved it immediately. She'd expected the generic style of the Italian restaurants she'd previously been used to. Green, red and white everywhere and Italian statues, even paintings of the Coliseum or the Leaning Tower of Pisa; but there was nothing of that here, except for the unmistakable sound of Puccini floating from the kitchen. Dani could hear a deep baritone voice singing along and she grinned to herself. The restaurant was thick with the aroma of a sweet vanilla smell, making Dani's mouth water.

Dani stood awkwardly, unsure what she should do. She squinted to see if she could see who was singing in the kitchen and then, deciding she really couldn't loiter in the entrance for another fifteen minutes, she paced towards the kitchen. Standing by the kitchen door, she took a deep breath and tentatively pushed it open and peeped inside. She was greeted by the sight of the back of a man. He was of medium height, dressed in full chef attire with a red bandana around his head, waving a slotted spoon in the air in time to Tosca as he belted out the familiar piece. The smell of whatever pastries he was frying was deliciously overpowering. Dani waited until he finished his duet with the iPod docking station and then quietly, so as not to startle him, she coughed. "Excuse me."

The man shot around, clearly surprised. His eyes were wide with shock.

"I'm so sorry. I'm here for an interview."

The man quickly recovered and his face changed from shock to a wide smile. "Interview?" he repeated. Dani nodded. He quickly fished out the pastries he was frying, then put down his spoon and turned off the burner that housed a large deep frying pan. Then, taking the remote control out of his pocket, he turned down the music. Further into the kitchen, Dani could see a young woman and another man. Both were dressed in whites with white bandanas. They seemed to be preparing vegetables. They both glanced in her direction momentarily.

"Sorry, my name's Daniella Knox." She held out her hand and he took it, lifting it to his lips and planting a kiss on it. Dani grinned, embarrassed at his gesture.

"Matteo. Pleased to meet you, Daniella." He had a thick Italian accent, which made him endearing. He openly appraised her, making Dani shift nervously.

"I'm supposed to see a Peter Becker." Her voice made Matteo's eyes dart back to her face.

"I see. I'll get him for you." He walked over to an intercom placed on the wall. "You like Puccini?"

Dani furrowed her brow, a little puzzled at the question. "Yes."

"Verdi?" he demanded.

"Yes." She felt like it was a test.

He nodded and smiled, then pressed the intercom. A calm voice answered. "Yes?"

"Chef, there's a Miss Daniella Knox to see you."

"Oh, she's early. Okay, I'll be down in five minutes," the calm voice answered.

"I'll make her a coffee."

"Okay."

Matteo turned to her and smiled. "Coffee?"

"Um, yes, thank you."

He nodded. "You like cannoli?"

Dani bit her lip nervously. "I don't know, I've never had one. Is that what you're making?" she asked bravely.

"*Si*. I get you one to try." He moved over to the other side of the kitchen and walked into what Dani presumed was a walk-in fridge. Matteo emerged with a tray of around twenty long pastries, which had a creamy mixture piped in them, each end rimmed with chocolate and chopped pistachios. He lifted one off with some tongs and placed it on a plate, then returned the tray to the fridge. He motioned to Dani to leave the kitchen and he followed her out and led her to the bar.

"Sit down, Daniella. What coffee would you like?" he placed the plate in front of her and pulled out a thick paper napkin and fork and set them on the bar. He was stout and middle aged – early fifties, Dani guessed – but he moved with grace and every gesture was done with a flourish. His face was kind and he had a mischievous glint in his eye. It made Dani smile. She sat up on a bar stool and placed her CV on the bar.

"Espresso, please." Matteo beamed and set to work on the large, impressive coffee machine.

"Try the cannoli." He eyed her as she picked up the fork. "It's better if you eat it with your hands," he suggested.

Oh! Dani set down the fork and picked up the pastry and took a bite.

Oh my! she thought as she chewed. It was delicious. The flavour of the shell was crossed between vanilla, pancakes and a crispy ice cream cone. The creamy centre had a hint of orange. It was a perfect combination of slightly bitter dark chocolate and sweet cream. Dani moaned as she savoured it, closing her eyes in appreciation. Matteo's eyes widened as he placed her coffee down and then picked up his own.

"That's absolutely delicious. You made this?"

Matteo nodded. "I'm the head chef. Usually my pastry chef prepares my recipes, but she's off today."

"This is your own recipe?"

Matteo nodded, clearly pleased with her reaction. "I make them smaller than usual, so they stay crispy," he explained.

"No wonder my brother-in-law loves this place," she muttered as she picked up the cannoli and took another bite.

"You like Italian cuisine?" he asked.

Dani grinned at his continuing inquisition. "I love it, Matteo!"

Matteo beamed, obviously delighted with her response. Dani put down her delicate pastry and sipped her coffee. It was seriously strong and exactly how she liked it. If she got this job, she'd need to enrol in a gym fast, purely so that she could keep sampling everything.

Her attention was distracted by some footsteps coming from the rear of the restaurant. She turned to see who it was and was faced with a slim, well-groomed man in his late forties. His hair was greying and cut short. He wore an immaculate charcoal grey suit with a crisp white shirt and pale blue tie, matching his eyes. His face lit up as he focused on Dani.

"Morning, Capo," he said to Matteo.

Dani looked puzzled. *Capo?*

"Morning, Chef," Matteo replied to the grey-haired man.

That's funny. Thought Dani. *I thought Matteo was the chef.*

"This is Daniella Knox."

Dani slid off her seat and extended her hand. The grey haired man took it and shook it firmly. His eyes twinkled as he smiled. "Peter Becker. Pleased to meet you. I hope Matteo has been looking after you."

"Yes, thank you. I've sampled his divine cannoli."

"Divine?" Peter's eyebrows shot up at the description.

"Mmm, definitely."

"Well, please finish it. Capo, do you think I could have an espresso?"

"Sure, Chef."

Dani frowned again, then took her final bite of the cannoli. Closing her eyes as she chewed, she then licked some of the creamy filling she had on her index finger. Both men looked on, transfixed. Dani wiped her hands on the napkin and looked expectantly up at Peter.

Recovering quickly, Peter straightened. "Shall we sit over here? It's a little more comfortable." He motioned to a table. Dani picked up her CV and paced over to the table. "Shall I take your jacket?" He gently helped Dani out of her jacket and placed it over a chair as Dani took off her hat, ran her fingers through her hair and sat down.

"This is my CV." She handed it to Peter.

He opened up the envelope and pulled the three-page document out as he sat down opposite her. Matteo watched on as he sipped his coffee. Peter's eyes darted up to Dani as he read it. "You managed a restaurant and bar in Kingston?" He looked impressed.

"Yes, until last week," Dani answered nervously.

"Why did you leave?"

Dani inhaled sharply. "Er, personal reasons. I loved my job but my personal circumstances... er... changed. So I decided to move up here to Leeds, where my sister is. I wanted a fresh start."

"I see." He smiled tightly, then looked back down at the CV. "You studied hotel management, but dropped out after the second year?" His eyes narrowed as he spoke.

"Yes. My mother became very ill, so I gave up my studies to look after her."

"Oh. You didn't want to carry them on?" He smiled at her as he spoke.

"No. She passed away and I wasn't really focused on restarting, so I decided to work instead."

"I'm sorry." Peter's face softened, noting that she had shifted uncomfortably in her seat. Dani shook her head, indicating it didn't matter.

"Well, from your CV, you're more than qualified to work as a waitress. Maybe I should tell you a little bit about La Casa."

"Yes please, I'd like that." Dani relaxed, glad the focus was off her painful past. It was something she didn't want to dwell on.

"Well, it's a family run restaurant. Mrs Ferretti is the owner. I am the restaurant manager. Matteo is the head chef; he's Mrs Ferretti's cousin." Peter looked over at Matteo and he nodded. "Mr Ferretti is the general manager, though he's spending more time at the other family businesses at the moment." Dani noticed that Mr Becker's face hardened a little, then he smiled tightly. "Shifts start at ten thirty through to three and five through to closing. We are open every day apart from Monday."

"So the restaurant closes for a couple of hours in the afternoon?" Dani asked.

"No, we are open straight through. A couple of the staff stay on over the afternoon. It works on a rota and voluntary basis. The staff are paid on the twenty-seventh of each month. We work bank holidays, so you can choose to be paid double or have a day off later on. You are also entitled to two half-days off, which also work on a rota basis, unless it's for something specific."

"That's what I've been used to. Is there a uniform?"

"Yes, you'll be supplied with four sets. Mrs Ferretti insists that all the staff are immaculate." Dani nodded. "Tips are kept by each waiter or waitress."

"Oh, they're not shared out?"

"No. Whatever you make, you keep. Mrs Ferretti believes that this way the staff will not slack off. I have to say I agree." He smiled as he shuffled forward. "The restaurant gets very busy, Daniella. Most days we get a minimum of three covers per shift, so the waiting-on staff need to be professional and focused."

"That's good to hear." Dani thrived off pressure. She hated being idle.

"I'll get you all the pay details and hours, rules and regulations and you'll need to fill out an application form. When would you be able to start?" Peter rose from the table.

"Whenever you want."

Peter's eyebrows shot up. "Good. I'll just go and get you all the details for you to mull over."

Dani watched as Peter turned and headed back the way he'd come in. A family business run by a married couple was exactly what Dani wanted. She'd always envisaged herself working as a husband and wife team in an establishment like this. The thought made her mind drift back to Jez and her heart sunk, as she sighed to herself.

"Would you like another espresso, Daniella?" asked Matteo, jolting her out of her thoughts.

"Er... yes, thank you. Call me Dani." She stood up and walked over to the bar. "How many people work here?"

Matteo nodded and began to make her espresso. "In my kitchen we are eight, out here there are fifteen." Matteo placed her coffee on the bar. "It gets pretty crazy here over the weekend and holidays. Weekdays are busy too, but steady."

Their attention was drawn to the back of the restaurant, where Peter was coming towards them holding a thick document.

"If you'd like to fill in the application form, and then this is for you to read through." Peter pulled out a silver pen from his inside pocket and handed it to Dani.

"Thanks." She took it and perched herself back onto the bar stool.

"I'll get back to my kitchen. It was a pleasure to meet you, Dani. I hope to be seeing you very soon." Matteo came around the bar and extended his hand to her. Dani took it and he lifted it up to his lips and kissed it again. Peter snorted at him.

"Thank you very much for my first cannoli, Matteo," blushed Dani.

"The pleasure was all mine, Dani. Call me Capo."

"Capo?"

"It means boss in Italian."

Oh!

Matteo smirked and winked at her as he headed towards the kitchen.

Dani looked down at the application form and began to fill it in. Peter studied her as she concentrated. He moved back, giving her some space as she scribbled away. "I can give you a tour once you're done."

"I'd like that."

Dani handed him the form and pen as she slipped off the bar stool.

"Well you've seen the main restaurant. Come this way and I'll show you the private area." Dani walked beside him as they approached the three steps. "We reserve this area for any small private parties, or for customers who want a quieter dining experience. It gets pretty loud down there."

Dani scanned the room. It had six large tables that had white table-cloths and were set up for six, though they could easily sit eight. There were small booths with padded seating, which seated up to four along the rear. The lighting was more subdued and the atmosphere was definitely more intimate. Peter took Dani through to the back, where there was a door which led out to a fire exit and a small foyer area with a lift and stairwell. He guided her up the stairs.

"Upstairs are the offices and a private room for functions." Peter opened up a large double door, which led into a spacious function room. The tables were set out but not laid. There was enough room to accommodate a hundred people and at the rear, there was a small bar area. The decor was very similar to downstairs except it had a hardwood floor, making it cosier.

"It's a lovely room."

"It is. We use it for birthday parties, small weddings, that kind of thing. Come this way and I'll show you the offices and then the staff area."

They walked back out of the function room and moved to a door that had 'Private' on it. The door opened onto a wide, well-lit corridor with five doors, two on either side and one at the end.

Peter opened the first door, which had 'Manager' on it.

"This is my office." Dani peeked inside. It was surprisingly roomy and functional. The decor was minimalist, clean and sharp. Dani noticed a bank of monitors showing different parts of the restaurant.

"Opposite is the store room." He motioned to the door facing them. "Next to that is Capo's, er... Matteo's office." They walked further down the corridor and he motioned to the door on their left. "That's Mrs Ferretti's office. She's not down yet, though. And this office here is Mr Ferretti's." He frowned as he spoke, seeing the door slightly ajar. He tentatively pushed it open and put his head round the door.

"Oh, you're here," he said warmly to whoever was in the office. Dani could see a large window overlooking the river, making the office bright. "I was just showing Daniella around. She came for an interview."

"Oh, I see. Well show her in," the raspy voice of the occupant replied.

Peter turned to Dani. "Come in, Daniella."

Dani walked through the door and turned to where the voice was coming from. Her eyes locked on the magnificent blue eyes she'd only seen less than forty minutes ago. There, sitting behind a large dark wooden desk, leaning back in a black leather chair, was the jogger. His elbows rested on the armrests as he stared directly at Dani. She came to an abrupt halt and her breath hitched. *Holy shit!*

Mr Ferretti gracefully rose and walked around from the desk, his eyes focused on Dani the whole time. His beautiful sculptured lips twitched into a smile. He strode the few steps from his desk with purpose as he put out his hand for Dani to shake. It took Dani a moment to shake herself out of her shock-induced trance.

"This is Mr Ferretti. Jerome, this is Daniella Knox." Peter's voice jolted Dani and she lifted her hand to shake the hand of the gorgeous man standing two feet in front of her. He licked his lips, and Dani felt her heart skip as she watched his tongue run over his bottom lip.

His eyes were fixed on hers. "Pleased to meet you, Daniella." His voice was smooth. He gripped her hand as he shook it.

"Pleased to meet you, Mr Ferretti," breathed Dani as she held his hand, enjoying the feel of his long lean fingers encasing her. As they shook, Dani's macaroni bracelet fell down from under her sweater cuff and Jerome's eyes darted to it. Arching his eyebrow, he reached with his left hand to finger it. His fingertips were warm and Dani noticed the silver coloured wedding band on his ring finger. He returned his gaze back to Dani for an explanation.

"Um... my niece made it for me. For good luck," Dani explained. Jerome nodded and smiled softly. Dani blushed, aware he was still holding her hand.

He turned the wrist of the hand that held Dani's to reveal two thin black leather plated bracelets. "My daughter made them." And his face lit up with a broader smile. He released her hand and stepped back. "So you're here for the waitressing job?" he asked as he perched himself on the end of his desk, his stance seemingly casual.

"Yes," Dani answered, trying hard not to run her eyes over him. He really was incredibly good looking. He'd taken down his hood to reveal his hair. It was dark and cut short on the sides, but longer on top and a little unruly. His jaw line was strong and he had cheekbones any woman would die for. Dani noticed he had a slight scar under his right eye. He oozed masculinity with a confidence that bordered on arrogance. He was beyond handsome, but it was his poise and assurance that made him utterly irresistible.

"Daniella used to manage a bar in Kingston. She recently moved up to Leeds," Peter explained. Jerome raised his eyebrows, suitably impressed. "Is Gia in?" Peter asked.

"No, she has a hair appointment at Level One. She should be back in an hour." Jerome let his eyes travel over Dani.

"Oh okay. Well I need to show Daniella the basement."

"Sure." Jerome stood back up again. "It was nice meeting you, Daniella." He reached over to shake her hand again.

"It's Dani. It was nice meeting you, Mr Ferretti." Dani took his hand and shook it.

"Please call me Jerome."

Dani nodded, then shuffled out of the door, avoiding any more eye contact.

By the time Peter had shown Dani the basement, where the staff area was, as well as the extensive wine cellar, some of the staff had already come in. Dani looked at her watch. It was twenty to eleven.

Peter saw her out to the entrance way as Dani slipped on her jacket and tugged on her hat. "Well, I'll be making my decision in a couple of days. I'll be in touch with you if you've got the job."

"Thanks very much, Mr Becker."

"Is there anything you'd like to know?"

"No, I think you covered everything. Thanks again." After shaking

Peter's hand, Dani left through the heavy glass door and stepped out into the cold crisp air.

Peter walked back into the restaurant and headed up to his office deep in thought. He'd seen roughly twenty applicants for the job and Dani was his last. She was the most qualified and her appearance did fit the restaurant perfectly. As he opened the door to his office Jerome stepped out of his.

"Still here?" he called over to him.

"Yeah, just going over to the gym to get changed. All my stuff's there. I think I need to start bringing my change of clothes here. It's easier." He indicated to his clothes. "Was Dani the last applicant?"

"Yes," Peter answered slowly. "She's the best for the job. Too good, actually."

Jerome cocked his head. "What do you mean, too good?"

"Well, she won't want to stay if she gets offered a better job. It's a step down for her."

"She came for the interview. She must need the job. You said she'd just moved up, right?" Peter nodded. "Why did she leave her old job?"

"She said personal reasons. I didn't press, but it looked like it was man trouble by the way she shuffled uncomfortably."

Jerome nodded. "Well, we need someone. The Christmas bookings are full."

"Capo liked her," Peter chuckled.

"I bet he did!" Jerome laughed. "He's a sucker for a pretty face."

"Oh, I think Dani's a bit more than that!"

Jerome smiled awkwardly and shrugged. "See you later, then."

"Sure."

Jerome ran down the stairs and out of the back entrance that led out onto the car park. He paced over to his car and opened it, but was distracted by a voice. He looked around and his eyes fell on Dani. She was talking on the phone and he strained to hear what she was saying.

"... from the bus station. Okay... number thirty-six. Sure." She twiddled her hair as she spoke, totally oblivious of Jerome. "I'll call you and you can pick me up. Yes, it's a lovely place. I really like it. He said he'd let me know. Okay, thanks, bye." Dani turned to put her phone into her bag and looked over to where Jerome was standing by his car. She felt herself blush and she smiled tightly.

He narrowed his eyes at her and strode over to where she was standing. "Do you know where you're going?" he asked.

"Er... yes, the bus station," Dani answered.

"And you know where that is?"

"Not exactly. I presume it's towards the centre."

Jerome's face softened into a smile, "I'll drop you off. It's on my way."

"Oh, no it's okay... I don't want to trouble you." Dani felt herself heat up instantly. *Crap!* She couldn't be in a car with him. She was flustered when he was six feet away from her – God help her in the confines of a car.

"It's no trouble. Like I said, it's on my way." He motioned to his car with his hand. "I don't bite, Dani – well not hard, anyway." He arched one eyebrow at her and smirked.

Dani stifled a grin at his comment. Shit! If she didn't want to blow her chances at getting the job, she'd better get in the car. It would only be for a few minutes anyway. She nodded nervously and eyed the black, sleek sports car behind him. The curves of it were smooth, stylish and graceful, *much like the owner,* Dani mused.

"Okay. Thanks." She walked over towards the car and Jerome opened up the passenger side for her. He smirked at her and she positioned herself onto the low seat. He closed the door and moved around, slipping smoothly into the driver's side. Dani fixed her eyes on the dashboard, trying hard not to look at his toned thighs exposed by him sitting down.

Jerome shifted the car into reverse and turned so he could look out of the rear window. His left arm moved to rest across the top of Dani's seat so he could see better, his gaze pausing on Dani momentarily. *She really was very attractive*, he thought.

"So you've recently moved to Leeds?" he asked as he turned out onto the street.

Dani swallowed hard before answering. "Yes, I came up last week."

"Do you know the city at all?"

"No, not at all. I just drove up using my GPS."

"You drove up?" Jerome sounded surprised.

"Yes."

"Where are you staying?"

Dani shifted in her seat nervously. "Near Harewood."

Jerome raised his eyebrows and nodded. "It's very nice there. My old family home was in Harewood."

"Oh really? Yes, it is really nice."

Jerome continued to drive into the city. The roads were busy and the traffic was slow moving but Jerome didn't seem to mind.

"The bus station's not far, but the one-way system takes you around the houses," he snorted. He pressed something on the wheel and the sound system started up. Dani relaxed a little. At least the awkward silences were filled with music.

"Do you have family here?"

Oh hell... was he going to carry on with these questions the whole journey? "My sister and her family."

"You're staying with them?"

"Yes."

"And the man who dropped you off?"

Dani's eyes darted to Jerome and he turned to look at her. She flushed, remembering how he'd caught her looking at him. "He's my brother-in-law."

Jerome took a deep breath and smiled, pleased with her response. "I see."

He looked relieved and Dani felt that maybe she should elaborate. "He told me you were looking for staff," Dani added. "He arranged the interview with Mr Becker."

"Oh, does he know Peter?" They'd stopped at the traffic lights and he turned to look at her. His eyes softly blinked as she looked at him. She noticed how beautifully they were framed by dark, lush eyelashes that naturally curled up, giving his otherwise masculine face a softness.

"Well, his company comes to your restaurant quite a lot." Dani's eyes blinked at him and he cocked his head to the side.

"Which company is that?"

"Cope, Baxter and Holmes; the solicitors."

Jerome nodded, seemingly satisfied with her answer. The lights changed and Jerome dragged his eyes from her and pulled into the traffic. Dani shifted her eyes back to the dashboard and then looked out of the window. The road looked familiar, but she wasn't sure. She was convinced they'd just passed by this same spot. She frowned. *Strange.* Maybe she recognised it from when Adam dropped her off.

Jerome smiled to himself as he hummed along to the song that was playing. Dani had never heard the music before but she liked it. Feeling like she needed to make conversation, she asked. "Who's the artist?"

"Eros Ramazzoti. Do you know him?"

Dani shook her head.

"Do you like it?"

"Yes, it's very soothing. Italian?" *Contradicting herself*, Dani thought – even the singer's dulcet tones were not calming or soothing her racing pulse.

"Of course," he smirked, arching his eyebrow at her again, Dani flushed and looked out of her window. Jerome switched on his indicator and turned to park up against the pavement, smoothly slowing down to a stop. "Well, here you are, Dani." He swivelled his body to face her as she fumbled with the seat belt.

Releasing the belt, she gathered up her bag and the documentation Peter had given her. "Thanks for the lift."

She looked up into his dreamy eyes and he smiled. "It was my pleasure." He licked his lips and Dani made herself drag her gaze away. He was really way too handsome.

"Bye then, and thanks a lot." She pulled the handle of the door and clambered out of the low car.

"Bye, Dani," he answered gently. "Hope to see you soon," he added.

Dani leaned down to look back inside the car. Feeling a little braver now she was out of its confines and knowing that this could be her final chance to ensure she secured herself the job, she replied, "Well, I think that depends on Mr Becker doesn't it?" She smirked wryly. "Thanks again for the lift." And before Jerome could answer, she closed the car door, but not before seeing his eyes widen in surprise. She walked quickly towards the bus station, knowing full well Jerome was still looking at her, grinning to herself.

Jerome took a few seconds to recover. Then he cracked a smile and shook his head. *So she had a feisty side to her too?* he thought to himself. He pulled out onto the road and headed to the gym, which was on the completely opposite side of town. He sighed as he looked at the clock. It was already half past eleven. By the time he'd get showered and changed, it'd be lunch time. He really wanted to go back to the restaurant, but he needed to work at the gym today.

Liz had let things go. She'd lost interest in it, like he knew she would. He'd have to spend more time there or get a manager, now that Jonathan had been sacked. His heart sunk at the thought of Liz, knowing he couldn't put off the inevitable and long overdue confrontation with her. Jerome turned up the music and with a heavy heart, drove towards the gym.

5

LA CASA

Peter Becker sat in his office, looking through each one of his shortlisted applicants. He knew there was no contest as to who was the best for the job. He pulled out Dani's file again and checked it over. He'd liked her from the very first instant. The fact she'd arrived early to the interview had scored major points for Peter. Punctuality was important for him. After years working in Switzerland, where everything ran to a precise and accurate timing, he found tardiness almost intolerable. She'd been extremely pleasant and her CV showed she was more than qualified for the job and he knew instinctively she'd fit in with the rest of his team.

He heard the familiar footsteps of Jerome echoing down the corridor and into his office. He glanced at his clock. Nine thirty. Peter took a deep breath. Things must be bad at home for Jerome to have already gone to the gym and run down to the restaurant so early. He felt for his friend and boss. Liz was making him miserable. Peter reset all the monitors and started up today's surveillance. Then he pulled back his chair and made his way to Jerome's office.

Peter walked in and scanned the large office. It was empty. Then he heard the shower running from the en suite Jerome had.

"Jerome?"

"Hey, Peter. I won't be long," Jerome called out. Peter sat down on the leather couch and looked out of the window. The rain was thrashing down. *Jeez, had he run in this?* He was dedicated. Peter wished he had half his drive. Ever since he'd known Jerome, he was always so focused. He pushed himself to excel. He had to be the best he could be, and in his professional life he'd succeeded. Sadly that couldn't be said for his private life.

The restaurant had been his starting block. He'd worked hard and studied harder to make the business thrive. He'd expanded into the night-club and bar business by acquiring Sky, a rooftop nightclub. And then, to satisfy his wife Liz, he'd opened up an in-town gym, Level One, and a beauty salon for her to run. Peter knew Jerome's first love was the restaurant but over the past few years, Sky had taken up more of his time and now, more recently, so had the gym. He knew the latter was purely because Liz had lost interest.

Jerome's businesses thrived, but as he continued to conquer the business world, his private life seemed to be crumbling around him.

The Ferrettis were all about family. They were second generation Italians and were very close knit. Jerome was the only one of the three brothers who had married. Cosimo, the eldest, had followed in his father's footsteps and become an accountant, carrying on in the family business. Arsenio was the youngest brother, who was a partner in a law firm. Both brothers had the same drive as Jerome but neither had married, both for entirely different reasons.

From a young age it had become perfectly clear to Cosimo and his family that his interest in the opposite sex was non-existent. His father, Alessandro, had found the news hard to take but had accepted it never-theless. Arsenio, on the other hand, had made it his mission to make up for his eldest brother's lack of interest in the fairer sex and had, as a result, become renowned for his playboy status. Jerome fell smack in the middle of this wide and extreme spectrum. The only problem was that both Jerome's brothers were happy in their lifestyle choices, whereas Jerome sadly, was not.

Jerome had had every intention of following in his elder brother's footsteps by carrying on in the family business, but it became apparent at an early age that Jerome struggled academically. He became disruptive in school and an unruly teenager. Fortunately, at the age of ten, one of his teachers recognised that Jerome didn't lack intelligence but that he was dyslexic. After being diagnosed, Jerome threw himself into sports, at which he excelled, and with the help of his teacher he managed to pass his GCSEs. Jerome's second passion was cooking. He'd always helped his mother when he was young and as he'd grown, so had his interest. He enrolled in a local college and completed a two-year catering course with a distinction. At the age of eighteen, he managed to secure a place at the prestigious Lausanne Hotel School in Switzerland, where he completed his Diploma in Hotel and Restaurant Management.

Peter scanned the office, his eyes flitting over the many framed certificates Jerome had acquired over the last seventeen years. Jerome had come a long way since Peter had known him and his family. Jerome had been a moody, angry teenager the first time they'd met on one of their holidays to the family home in Italy. It was just after his father had died and he'd taken it very badly. Peter smiled at the memory.

His thoughts were interrupted by Jerome coming out of the bathroom. "Morning. You're here early."

Jerome shrugged and nodded as he knotted his tie.

"You ran in this?" Peter motioned to the window with his head.

"Yes. I got soaked. Certainly got my blood pumping through my veins. Just need my caffeine and nicotine fix and I'm set up for the day," Jerome joked, but the smile didn't quite reach his eyes. "Decided on our new staff member yet?"

"Yeah. I'll be calling her soon."

"Her?"

"Dani. You met her yesterday."

Jerome nodded and stifled a smile.

"How's the gym doing? You seem to be spending a lot of time there lately. Customers are asking about you."

Jerome raised his eyebrows at the comment. He knew this was Peter's way of finding out what was going on between him and Liz. Jerome sat behind his desk and rubbed his eyes with his thumb and forefinger. "The business is doing well. I just need to find a good manager." He shifted in his seat, avoiding eye contact with Peter.

"I thought that was Liz's role." Peter brushed his grey trousers nervously.

Jerome sighed, then rubbed his forehead. "She's finding it too much, I think."

"Too much?" pushed Peter.

Jerome looked up at him and sucked on his top teeth, his eyes narrowing as he toyed with the idea of confessing what was really going on. He knew he could trust Peter, but he wasn't sure he wanted to admit to his friend what he obviously already knew. Peter waited patiently for his response.

"It's not working out. I think she liked the idea of having a gym and salon but it's a lot of work."

"Well, maybe she could go part time and you employ an assistant for her." Peter disliked Liz. She was spoilt and self-centred. Jerome was permanently trying to cover up her faults and in the process ran himself ragged just trying to keep her happy, which she never was.

Jerome nodded slightly. "It's a bit more complicated than that."

Peter left his gaze fixed on to Jerome and waited for him to elaborate.

"The assistant she had unfortunately left a week ago. Liz hasn't been in since, so I've had to cover them until I find suitable replacements."

"He left? He was very good. Did he find a better position?"

Jerome huffed and closed his eyes, rubbing his face. "Yes, you could say that. The position he found" – he paused a moment, then looked up at Peter – "was on top of my wife," he mumbled.

Peter shot up from his seat. "What! He and Liz were having an affair?" Jerome closed his eyes and clenched his teeth. Peter looked down at his friend and regretted his unguarded outburst. This was obviously painful for him. It did, however explain why over the last few weeks Jerome had been spending more time at the gym and at home. He'd obviously been trying to either find out for sure or trying to work things out with Liz.

"I'm not sure if it's in the past tense yet," Jerome ground out.

"Forgive my frankness, Jerome, but are you telling me that you think the affair is still going on?"

"Yes," Jerome said quietly.

Peter's jaw dropped as he stared at a grey-faced Jerome. A thousand thoughts ran through Peter's head, ranging from wanting to kill Liz for doing this to his friend and to slapping Jerome into some sort of action. Why was he so calm? Why hadn't he thrown her out? He was a successful, wealthy, good-looking guy and he was allowing some trumped-up nobody to make a fool of him. Then his eyes dropped to the silver framed picture on Jerome's desk of Alessandro and Kara – of course, his children.

Peter paced over to Jerome's desk. "What are you doing about it? Do you need me for anything?"

"To be honest, I really don't know what to do. It's no secret Liz and I have had problems from the start. The children made it harder too, for her." He rose from his seat and began to pace around the office. "I want to make it work, but the last six months have been difficult. Nothing makes her happy. She spends all day out of the house and as little time as she can with the children. I'm lucky we have such a great nanny. She blames my working hours. That I'm always either here or at Sky." He rubbed his forehead again. "But I need to be here and there. It's my job. It's what gives us our lifestyle, that she takes full advantage of and enjoys," he huffed.

He walked over to the window and looked out over the river as the rain continued to pour down. "She wants my full and undivided attention and doesn't give me any leverage on that at all. I can't split myself into pieces."

"And the guy? The affair? How do you feel about that?"

"She said it was a one off. To get my attention. But..."

"You don't believe her."

Jerome shook his head.

"What are you going to do, Jerome? You can't just leave things as they are. You'll go crazy. I know I'm no relationship expert, but I know you. This situation is going to break you. You're already a wreck splitting yourself up."

"I know." He turned around to look at Peter. "I need to get Level One back on track. Here's covered with you. If you need more staff, we'll get it. And then I can concentrate on my marriage. I don't want my kids to suffer. I grew up with both parents and when Papa died, it destroyed me. I know it's not the same as a divorce" – Peter's eyes shot up to Jerome's weary face – "but if your parents aren't together... I don't want that for them."

"Jerome. If you're miserable in a marriage, your children will suffer too. Look, now they're being brought up by the nanny. Liz was never the maternal type." Peter restrained a sneer.

"I know, but I have to make this work, Peter, for them." Jerome's eyes gazed at the picture on his desk and his face softened.

"Does anyone else know? I mean about the affair?"

"Just Cosimo. He saw her with this assistant. He went to the gym on his lunch break and used the back entrance. I gave him a key. They were in her office. They didn't see him."

"When was this?"

"Three weeks ago."

"Jesus, Jerome. I'm so sorry." Jerome turned back to look out of the window. Peter noticed his veins pumping in his neck and he realised that Jerome was holding back.

"Look, Jerome. I know I really can't give advice – well, not with my track record. Two failed marriages and a string of bad relationships, and now only six months into a new marriage. But the one thing I know is that if your marriage is shaky, you need to protect yourself."

"You sound like Cosimo." Jerome's voice was low as he leaned his hands on the windowsill. At first Peter thought it was for support, but then he noticed his friend's hands were gripping the ledge so hard, it revealed the whites of his knuckles.

"Well he's right. I don't want to pry but... well, if you end up divorced, you don't want her walking off with half your businesses."

Jerome released his grip and Peter braced himself, wondering whether he'd overstepped his mark. They were close, but that didn't mean Jerome would be happy with Peter's straight talking. It was his marriage and wife Peter was talking about, after all.

"I'm hoping it doesn't come to that, Peter. But thanks for the advice." He turned back to him and Peter visibly relaxed. "I'd rather no one knows about this. Firstly, I need to see how best to deal with the situation and secondly, I don't want Mama getting upset."

"Of course, Jerome." Peter smiled at him. "Come on, I need a coffee."

Jerome smiled weakly and nodded.

"Don't worry about La Casa. We'll manage without you until you get Level One organised." Peter patted his back as they headed towards the door.

"I'm not worried about here, Peter. I know you've got it covered. I just... well... I just like being here." He stifled a sigh. This felt like home. He was always at his happiest in La Casa.

Ollie snuggled up to Dani as he continued to read his book out aloud to her. Sophie listened as she stuck pictures she'd cut from a magazine into her book. It was raining heavily outside and was already dark. Dani was glad for the fire, she hated November – it was so depressing. Dark by four o'clock and the sun rose so late. They could hear Rosie babbling away in the kitchen with Chloe as she prepared their dinner. Chloe was singing "You Are My Sunshine" to Rosie as she sat in her high chair. Sophie kept giggling when she heard Rosie repeat the last words, again omitting the first letter.

Dani's phone vibrated on the side table and she disentangled herself from Ollie to reach for it. She hoped it wasn't Jez again. His phone calls had dropped to one a day now. She looked at the time. Ten past five. The number didn't look familiar but it was local.

"Hello?"

"Hello, Dani?"

Dani's heart stopped for a second. She recognised Mr Becker's calm voice. "Er, yes."

"It's Peter Becker from La Casa d'Italia."

"Hello, Mr Becker, it's nice to hear from you. Well, I hope it is, anyway," she joked.

He let out a laugh. "I like someone with a sense of humour. Well, I'm ringing to offer you the job. That is if you're still interested."

"Yes I am, very much so. Thank you. Thanks a lot." She couldn't contain her enthusiasm. *Finally, something to take her mind off –*

"Did you manage to read through the material I gave you?" Mr Becker interrupted her thoughts.

"Yes. Everything's fine. When would you like me to start?"

"Could you come in tomorrow morning around nine so we can run through everything? Then we'd like you to start on Friday."

"Yeah, sure. That's great."

"Good. And you'll be able to pick up your uniform and meet Mrs Ferretti too. Get acquainted with the place and staff."

"Sounds great."

"Okay, then I'll see you at nine then."

"Yes, and thanks again, Mr Becker."

"Good bye, Dani."

"Bye."

Dani turned off her phone and shrieked. "Yeah!" she jumped up from the sofa and jumped on the spot, to the delight of Ollie and Sophie. She grabbed their hands and they immediately stood up.

"I just got a jo-o-b. I just got a jo-o-b!" she sang as they formed a circle and danced around with her. Chloe came in from the kitchen with Rosie on her hip to see what all the noise was all about.

"Mummy, Dani's got a jo-o-b!" mimicked Ollie and then carried on dancing round in a circle with Sophie chanting.

"Oh that's great news, Dani." Rosie wriggled on her hip itching to get down and join in. Chloe lowered her down and Dani took her hand. "Are you going to sing too? Dani's got a jo-o-b!"

"Job!" repeated Rosie. Sophie and Ollie stopped instantly and gaped at Rosie.

Chloe's face lit up and Dani scooped Rosie up. "Yes, Rosie. Job."

"Job," Rosie repeated as she beamed at Dani.

"That's it, Rosie. See, I told you it would click." Dani looked at Chloe as she grinned.

"Double celebration, then. I think this calls for chocolate cake." Chloe cheered.

"Yeah, chocolate cake! I'll make us one of Dani's special chocolate cakes! I need helpers," Dani cried. Sophie and Ollie jumped up and down and they all scrambled into the kitchen.

By seven o'clock, Dani had bathed the children and was getting them into bed, while Adam and Chloe had dinner together. She was pleased she was here. At least she could help them out, give them some time alone together. They never went out alone. Chloe never felt she could leave the children with a babysitter she could trust. If they were really stuck, Adam's father always volunteered and he was great with the children, but Chloe still found it hard to leave them. As Dani brushed Sophie's hair, she made a mental note. Her first evening off, she would babysit for them so they could go out.

Dani found Adam and Chloe in the sitting room drinking coffee and eating the chocolate cake she'd made earlier.

"Congrats on the job, Dani." Adam grinned at her. "I knew they'd take you on."

"Thanks, Adam. I have to say I'm excited."

"I put your car in the paper. It goes in next Thursday. I put my number for a contact."

"Good. I really wouldn't know how to deal with all that."

Adam smirked. "What time do you need to be in tomorrow?"

"Nine." Dani curled up in the armchair.

"I'll drop you off. We need to set off by eight."

"Oh great. And I know which bus to get home. Though I'm not sure how I'll get home once I start working. I'll probably finish around midnight. Not sure I'd like to travel at night on the bus. I'll need to get a car organised."

"Use your car until it's sold."

Dani nodded. She just wanted to get rid of it. It was another reminder of Jez. Then, as if he was reading her mind, he added.

"I've got the letter I drafted for Jez regarding the house for you to look at. When you've read it, let me know if you need to change anything and I'll get the ball rolling on that too." He popped a forkful of cake in his mouth and chewed as he eyed Dani. Her face dropped and he felt bad for causing her mood to change from excited to melancholy. Chloe straightened up on the sofa and caught Adam's eye. He cringed as she glared at him.

Adam pulled up outside La Casa d'Italia at eight forty-five. The heavy rain from yesterday had been replaced by a light drizzle. Dani hugged Adam, then quickly jumped out of the car and ran in through the heavy glass door. She carried a small holdall with her shoes in. She was wearing her silver Hunter wellingtons to protect her feet and a waterproof mac.

Once inside, she took off her hood, opened up her mac, smoothed down her black skirt and adjusted her white blouse. A sweet smell wafted from the kitchen and Dani took a deep breath, relishing every molecule.

Wow, what a fabulous way to start your day. She could hear the familiar Italian opera coming from the direction of the kitchen and Capo's distinct baritone voice.

Dani looked around the restaurant and felt excited and a little nervous. It had been a while since she'd worked under someone else's supervision, and the thought was a little daunting. Dani stepped through into the restaurant and walked over to the kitchen. She paused at the door, then pushed it open. There were already a number of people in the kitchen. She recognised the two from when she was there for her interview. Capo was vigorously mixing a cream mixture in a bowl and a petite blonde woman was rolling out pastry on a floured surface.

"Dani. *Buongiorno!*" Capo smiled widely, genuinely pleased to see her. "Welcome to our family!" he gushed. Dani grinned, overwhelmed by his greeting.

"Thank you, Capo."

"I tell Chef you're here. This is Carmen, my patisserie chef."

Carmen dropped her rolling pin and quickly wiped her hands, then extended one to Dani. "Pleased to meet you, Dani." Her smile was warm.

"Likewise. What are you making?" Dani eyed the pastry.

"Almond crust for the cheesecake."

Dani bit her lip. "Oh, I'm going to love working here." She shook her head and Carmen laughed.

"It'll be ready in an hour or so, you can try some."

"Really?"

Carmen nodded.

Capo quickly introduced Dani to the rest of the kitchen staff, then took her out to the restaurant. She sat by the bar and changed out of her wellingtons, replacing them with her shoes.

"Espresso?" he asked.

"Sure, but do you want me to make it? I need to get to know everything."

"*Si*. Have you worked one of these before?"

Dani looked at the huge coffee machine. She had her own and they'd had one in the bar, but both were tiny in comparison.

"A smaller one, yes."

Capo waved her around the bar and he showed her the controls and how to work the various valves. The glorious aroma of freshly ground coffee filled the room. Capo placed the coffee on the bar and then let her make one. He beamed as she handed it to him to taste.

Peter Becker came down to the restaurant and walked up to them as they sipped their coffee.

"Morning, Dani. Welcome." He held out his hand for her to shake.

"Morning, and thank you, Mr Becker."

"Call me Chef from now on."

"Chef?"

Peter nodded. "It's what they all call me. It's a habit I continued from the time I worked in Switzerland. Confusing, I know." He shrugged. "Can I have one of those?" he looked at Capo, who motioned to Dani to do it, to Peter's surprise.

Once they'd had their coffee, Peter took Dani through the daily schedule. He showed her the rear entrance which she would now use, and he assigned her a locker in the changing rooms. Dani was pleased to see there were showers too. They made their way back into the restaurant and Peter explained how the touch screens for the orders worked and how they split up the restaurant.

Dani started to feel more relaxed as Peter went through the menu with her and suggested she take one with her to study.

"The first week or so I'll have Rosa and Pino with you. They're our oldest members of staff."

The restaurant had started to smell of all the different aromas and Dani felt her stomach cramp with hunger. It was almost ten thirty and the staff were already coming in. Peter introduced Dani to a few of them, then left her to get acquainted with them.

"Hi, I'm Rosa." Rosa was in her late thirties with dark brown thick wavy hair that she pulled back into a ponytail. She extended her hand and smiled sweetly at Dani.

"Dani." Dani shook her hand.

"Have you worked in restaurants before?"

"Bars and clubs mainly, we served food too though."

Rosa nodded. "Chef asked me to help you out, just until you know what's what."

"Great. Thanks for that."

"Let me get your uniform and then I'll introduce you to everyone."

"Sure."

Dani followed Rosa up one flight of stairs to the store room, where the offices were. The store room was surprisingly large. On the right hand side, stacked on shelves, were cellophane packs with what Dani presumed were the uniforms. The rest of the store room had everything in it. From stationary to boxes of glasses, cups and plates, all housed on shelves that reached the ceiling. Rosa pulled out a number of blouses and skirts and Dani checked them for the size. Rosa gave her four sets and two sashes that they wore in a lime green. The blouses and skirts were both black and very stylish with an asymmetrical neckline.

"It's a lovely uniform." Dani lifted it up to check it against herself, and Rosa nodded.

"Mrs Ferretti designed them."

"Wow, really? She has great taste."

"Yes, she does. Come on, we'll go across to the dining room for our lunch and our meeting."

"Lunch?"

"Yes, every day all the staff have an early lunch at ten thirty. Chef goes through a few things with us, bookings and any specials. Well, we can't work in a restaurant on an empty stomach!" Rosa laughed at Dani's surprise.

"No, I suppose not."

Rosa guided Dani through to the private dining room where most of the staff were already busying themselves with setting the tables up for their meal. Dani smiled to herself. They really were like a big family. Everyone was helping, even Chef. He opened up the dumbwaiter and was pulling out one of four large steaming serving platters. Dani looked around, slightly bewildered.

"Come on, Dani, come and meet everyone."

Rosa made her sit down as Capo and Chef placed what looked like cannelloni and salad on the table. The smell was amazing.

To her left sat a tall, attractive man. He looked of an Asian origin. He turned to her as she sat awkwardly, and his eyes twinkled as he introduced himself. "Hi, I'm Benjamin Kuchiki. But call me Kuch." He held out his hand for her to shake.

"Dani. Pleased to meet you."

"You look a little overwhelmed."

Dani uttered, "Just a bit. I wasn't sure what to expect but this... well, this is unbelievable."

"The Ferrettis are great. You'll love it here." He grinned a cheeky grin, showcasing his perfect white teeth, and Dani immediately liked him.

Dani took a good look around the table and knew instantly she would indeed love it here. She learned that Kuch was the head barman. He was half-Italian, half-Japanese. Most of the staff had some connection to either Italy or the Ferrettis. Dani was introduced to all the staff throughout the lunch and was shocked to see Chef and Capo join them too. The cannelloni was, of course, delicious, stuffed with spinach and ricotta, then smothered in a tomato sauce, topped with cheese and baked. They had left one space between them, and another space to the right of Chef was free. Everyone was eating and catching up, when the double doors opened and everyone's attention was drawn to whoever was walking towards the table. Immediately, all the staff put down their cutlery and began to stand. Dani, having her back to the door, wasn't exactly sure what was going on and hastily followed her fellow colleagues.

"Sit, sit. Please sit. I'm so sorry we're late." The voice of a woman purred in a thick Italian accent. Everyone retook their seats and Dani twisted around to see who the sultry voice belonged to.

Dani looked on wide eyed at the stunning woman who glided towards her, flanked by an equally breath-taking Jerome. Dani caught her breath at the sight of him dressed in an impeccable dark blue, three piece suit, a dark coloured shirt and matching tie. He looked even more handsome than she remembered, dressed for work. She dragged her gaze away from him and focused on the woman. It was as if Isabella Rosellini's serenity, Sophia Loren's beauty and Gina Lollobrigida's voluptuous raw sex appeal had been blended and poured into this one woman. She was dressed in a navy blue dress with a deep V-neck. The dress clung to her curvy body as she sashayed in her kitten heels towards the tables.

She smiled widely at Dani, her dark eyes sparkling, and Dani reeled at the unbelievable resemblance to Jerome, who was walking just a step behind her. Then suddenly it hit her. Mrs Ferretti wasn't Jerome's wife, she was his mother, and an overwhelming feeling of relief flowed through her. The feeling caught Dani a little off-guard and she quickly shook it off. Looking closer at her, Dani realised she must have been in her late fifties, though she looked at least ten years younger.

"This must be Daniella." Mrs Ferretti eyes widened as Dani scrambled to her feet. Mrs Ferretti extended her beautifully manicured hand for Dani to shake. "Welcome to La Casa d'Italia."

"Thank you," breathed Dani as her eye caught an exquisite white gold and diamond bracelet on Mrs Ferretti's wrist, which shimmered under the lights.

"This is my mother, Gia Ferretti, Dani." Dani's eyes focused on Jerome as he spoke, then she turned back to Gia. "I'm very pleased to meet you, Mrs Ferretti." Dani felt herself heat up under Jerome's intense gaze. The rest of the staff carried on with their meal, seemingly oblivious, as Gia appraised her. "You have a lovely restaurant."

Gia smiled widely. "Thank you, Daniella, I hope you'll be happy here. Please continue with your lunch."

"Thank you."

Gia stepped back and headed to where Chef and Capo were sitting and Chef stood to pull out her chair for her to sit between them.

"Nice to see you again, Dani." Jerome stepped forward and extended his hand for Dani to take.

Dani instantly heated up as she shook his hand, relishing his firm grip as his long fingers tightened. "Thank you. It's nice to be back," she replied and he arched his eyebrow.

"Have you learned your way around yet?" he asked with a mischievous smirk.

"I'm getting there. I'm a fast learner," she replied, feeling a little braver.

"I'm sure you are. Well, I'd better let you finish your lunch." He nodded as he retreated and walked over to sit next to Chef, directly opposite her.

Dani slumped back into her chair feeling flushed, her heart racing and her palms sweating. *Crap, that's all she needed, a crush on her boss.*

Once lunch was over, the staff went into overdrive clearing up and getting ready for twelve o'clock service.

"Dani, come and sit here by the bar and observe. You'll get a better idea how La Casa operates." Peter pulled out a stool for her and Dani jumped up onto it.

Mrs Ferretti came over and sat down next to her. "So, Daniella, tell me a little about yourself." Dani felt herself heat up under her intense gaze. She contemplated correcting her about her name preference but then thought better of it. She actually rather liked the way her name rolled off Mrs Ferretti's tongue in her thick Italian accent. Mrs Ferretti smiled warmly at her making her feel more at ease.

"Well, er... I used to live in London and managed a bar down there. I moved up here last week. My sister and her family live in Harewood." Kuch slipped an espresso in front of Mrs Ferretti and she nodded her thanks. "I see. Would you like an espresso?"

"Yes please."

Kuch busied himself with her coffee as Dani waited for the next question from Mrs Ferretti.

"So you haven't any other family, then? Mother? Father?"

"No. They both passed away. My father when I was eighteen, and my mother four years ago."

"I'm sorry. My boys lost their father when they were young too. He died twenty years ago." Mrs Ferretti smiled tightly.

Kuch placed Dani's coffee in front of her. "Thanks." He winked at her and smiled, then busied himself with what seemed like stock checking. A pretty blonde girl called Nicole that Dani had seen up at lunch was helping him. Dani presumed she was bar staff too. They interacted well together, seemingly familiar and comfortable. Watching them made Dani think of Jez and how they'd worked together.

Her errant thoughts were disrupted by Mrs Ferretti. "So you don't have a boyfriend?"

Dani clenched her teeth and shook her head.

Mrs Ferretti nodded, understanding Dani wasn't altogether happy about talking about her private life. "Well, La Casa has been around for fifteen years now."

"It's a lovely restaurant, Mrs Ferretti."

"Thank you, Daniella."

"I'm crazy about food, especially Italian, so it's going to be great working here."

Chef came over to where they were sitting and stood by Mrs Ferretti. "Do you want me to bring you over the bookings for lunch, Gia?"

"No, Peter, I'll come over to the desk. I just wanted to meet Daniella, get to know her a bit." Mrs Ferretti looked at him warmly.

Dani could see they were close by the proximity of Chef's stance. He rested his hand protectively on the small of her back as she slipped off the stool. "She prefers Dani, Gia," he corrected, and Mrs Ferretti's eyebrows shot up.

"That's okay, Mrs Ferretti, I actually like the way you say my name," Dani blurted out, then kicked herself, worried she might have offended her.

Mrs Ferretti laughed slightly, throwing her head back, and Dani blushed. Peter shook his head and grinned. "The accent, eh?"

"Well, yes it makes everything sound... well... better."

"I like you, Daniella. You've got spunk. Please call me Gia from now on though."

"Oh, okay."

"I'll be back in a bit to go over how we work. Okay, Dani?" added Chef with a stifled smirk.

Dani nodded as Gia and Chef walked over to the desk. Dani sipped her espresso and watched the restaurant staff as they prepared their stations. Chef went up to each section giving them their reservations.

"She likes you." Dani turned to look at Kuch, who was leaning up against the bar. "It normally takes her a few weeks before she lets you use her first name."

"Oh. I thought I might have offended her."

"No, she definitely likes you. So, you're here alone, then? No boyfriend? Fiancé?" He grinned cheekily at her.

Dani looked down at her coffee and shook her head. "No. Bad breakup."

Kuch nodded as he pursed his lips together, realising it was still painful for her. "So, was he a psycho or a cheater?"

Dani's eyes shot up at his comment and stared at him for a second. He grinned at her and she shook her head in disbelief at his perception. "A bit of one, and a lot of the other," she replied, and Kuch bobbed his head knowingly.

"Yeah, there are some assholes out there. He was an idiot, if you ask me. You're better off without him."

"Thanks, Kuch. I had to get away." Dani's voice was quiet as she shifted on her stool.

"Two hundred miles will do it, then."

"I hope so."

By one o'clock, the restaurant was practically full. Dani watched on in awe at how smoothly the service went. Gia was an outstanding hostess. Everyone got special attention, new and regular customers. It was soon clear that the reason people came to La Casa d'Italia was not only because the food was out of this world, it was because of Gia. She gave the restaurant glamour in an unthreatening way. Men and women alike loved her.

Dani scanned the restaurant. Chef was checking the tables discreetly as the waiters and waitresses busied themselves, showing no signs of stress at all. Dani let her eyes roam over to the kitchen and all seemed to be running like clockwork. She looked around, feeling like she could really feel at home here. If it was this busy on Thursday lunchtime, Dani could only imagine what a Saturday night would be like.

"So how was your first glimpse of La Casa?" Dani's heart raced as the now-familiar raspy voice of Jerome jolted her out of her thoughts. She slowly spun around in her seat to find Jerome resting himself against the bar. She took a sharp intake of breath just at the sight of him. She'd presumed he'd left, seeing as he hadn't been around since they'd finished lunch. His eyes bored into hers and she tried hard not to think about what was under that immaculate suit he was wearing.

Using all her effort to get her brain out of the bedroom and into gear, she answered. "It's an amazing place, and so busy."

He sniffed and smiled at her comment. "This isn't busy." His eyes quickly darted to something or someone behind her and he smiled widely and nodded. Dani turned to see who it was. A party of six businessmen had walked in and were obviously pleased to see him. "Excuse me, Dani. I really have to say hello to these customers." His tone was genuinely apologetic as he shrugged at her.

"Of course. Don't worry about me." He gave her a curt nod, narrowing his eyes and hesitating as though he was about to say something, then he thought better of it. Dani's eyes followed him, watching him stride gracefully over to the businessmen. They seemed thrilled to see him and to Dani's surprise, they all hugged him affectionately. He then directed them towards the raised dining area separated by the thin curtain where Pino, one of the waiters was waiting. Then something extraordinary happened.

As Jerome worked his way through the now-full main body of the restaurant, he was stopped by a number of customers. He took time to talk to every one of them, oozing charm as he gave them his undivided attention. He laughed at the comments they made and seemed to be familiar with most of them. Dani stared on, totally mesmerised as she saw the complete and utter transformation from the intense, brooding businessman to the charming, social host. It seemed that Jerome not only had his mother's extraordinary good looks but also her most outstanding feature, her charm.

Dani couldn't take her eyes off him. She'd seen Jez in action when he turned on the charm at the bar, but this – this was in a whole other league. Then it struck Dani. Jerome was being genuine. This was who he was. He clearly loved being here and talking to all the familiar faces. His restaurant wasn't just his business, it *was* him, a true embodiment of who he was: warm, welcoming, stylish with a unique flair and totally intoxicating, and his whole being changing into this alluring lethal weapon. Jez had only played his part to get what he could from people. It was purely business for him.

It took Jerome fifteen minutes to get back up to the table of businessmen. He talked to them while they drank their drinks and left them a menu. Then he walked over to the kitchen and went inside.

Dani turned back around and was faced with Chef observing her. "So, think you'll be able to handle it tomorrow?"

"I'll do my best. I can't believe the buzz. It's very..." she searched for the right word.

"Lively? Loud? Busy?" suggested Chef as he cocked his head at her, amused at her enthusiasm.

"Intoxicating, I was going to say."

"Really? Intoxicating." He mulled over the word. "I suppose you're right, you do get a buzz from being here. It helps that Jerome's here today." He eyed Dani as he spoke and she looked around nervously. "He's not been here much these past few weeks and the customers have missed him. La Casa *is* Gia and Jerome. They're a formidable team," he continued.

Dani's eyes flew up to Chef's face. "They are. I can see that just from the couple of hours I've been here."

"Well, you can leave if you want. I think you have a feel for what you're letting yourself in for tomorrow," Chef joked. Dani smiled.

"I'll go and get my things from the locker and head off, then."

"Ten thirty tomorrow," Chef reminded her and Dani nodded. Chef shook her hand and walked off towards a table that was about to leave.

"Here you are, Dani." Kuch put a polystyrene container on the bar.

"What's that?"

"Carmen sent it out for you, mascarpone cheesecake with an almond crust. She said she promised to give you a piece to try."

Dani looked down at the box stunned. "Really? For me? I won't get her in trouble will I?"

Kuch laughed and shook his head, "Carmen's Jerome's cousin, Dani. She won't get into trouble."

Jeez, was everyone related to the Ferrettis? "Tell her thank you. I don't want to go in there when they're in the middle of service. Are you related to the Ferrettis too?"

"Ha! They wish I was," joked Kuch.

Nicole chuckled at his comment and shook her head. "I'll tell her for you."

"Thanks. See you tomorrow." Dani picked up her box with her cheesecake in, and walked to the back of the restaurant and down to the changing rooms.

She quickly changed into her wellingtons, put on her mac and picked up the holdall and new uniform. She then made her way up to the back entrance which led to a small area set aside for, she presumed, the staff to smoke. It was sectioned off from the car park, making it private so customers couldn't see them. Dani looked at the ashtray, which was full of water from the drizzle, and felt her nicotine craving come back. Thankfully, the drizzle had now stopped, though the air was heavy with damp.

Dani looked down at the polystyrene box and she opened it. *Nothing beats a nicotine craving like a serious sugar rush.* The first thing that hit Dani was the exquisite smell of toasted almonds. Dani contemplated saving it until she got home. Not a chance – who was she kidding? Without any cutlery, she'd have to just use her hands. She rummaged in her bag for a tissue and was pleased to find some antibacterial wipes. *Great,* she thought, *at least she wouldn't have sticky fingers.* She carefully picked up the delicate slice and took a bite. She moaned as she savoured the amazing combination of creamy, crunchy, sweet and an ever-so-slightly tart combination of the vanilla cream. Pure heaven. She took a second bite from the decadent slice and the light crust crumbled, dropping the other half into the box.

"You look like you're enjoying that."

Fuck! Dani gulped and clenched her eyes tight, cringing. Slowly, she turned as she quickly licked her lips from crumbs and turned to be faced with the glorious vision that was Jerome Ferretti. He was smirking at her as he stood by the door with a lit cigarette in his hand as his eyes twinkled with amusement.

"Sorry. I'm afraid I'm having a sugar craving since I quit smoking." She licked her fingers free of the creamy remnants and Jerome's eyes intensified slightly.

"How long is it since you quit?"

"A week and..." Dani looked at her watch. It was two fifteen. "...six hours and fifteen minutes."

Jerome threw his head back and laughed out loudly.

H-o-l-y cow! God, he looked even more breath-taking when he let his guard down, thought Dani.

His whole face lit up and his face creased around his sculptured mouth. "How's that working out for you?" he asked as he took a deep drag on his cigarette, then let out the smoke in a steady stream, his eyes steady on hers.

Dani lifted up the box and shrugged as a form of explanation. Jerome laughed again and Dani's heart skipped a beat as his eyes glittered.

"Well, I'd better be off." Dani closed up the box and put it into her hold all, then quickly wiped her hands with a wipe.

"Do you know where you're going?"

"Er... Yes, thanks. See you tomorrow."

Jerome narrowed his eyes and nodded. "See you tomorrow." His mouth twitched into a smile.

Dani quickly walked through the car park and on to the street. She reached into her bag for her smartphone and pressed the map app. She waited for it to load then checked out her direction.

Okay, left then straight. She walked towards the direction of the city centre in the cool afternoon air, glad to be away from Jerome. She really was going to have to get over this crush. They'd be working together, for goodness sake.

She'd walked about a hundred metres when she heard the familiar roar of a car engine. Her heart stopped. *Surely not.*

The black car slowed down by Dani and Jerome let the passenger window slide down. "Get in, Dani. By the time you find the station, the rain will have started again." He motioned to some ominous black clouds.

"You really didn't need to..."

"Just get in Dani," he interrupted.

Crap. Dani opened up the car door and slid into the ridiculously low car. The same music was playing in the car as last time and Dani racked her brain to remember the singer. She smiled tightly at him as he watched her put on her seat belt, before he pulled out onto the road. Dani's heart raced. She couldn't believe he'd left the restaurant to drive her to the station. She felt a shiver go up her spine, thrilled that he had. She focused on the shops they passed and then her eyes moved to his left hand that rested on the wheel. His wedding ring glinted. Dani smiled, remembering that before she'd met Gia she'd thought the Mrs Ferretti that Chef referred to was his wife, not his mother. She also remembered her relief that she wasn't. Well he must be married. She looked again at his ring.

"How are you getting to work?" His voice jolted Dani out of her unsettling thoughts.

"I'll drive. I have a car."

"Ah yes, I remember. GPS." Dani smiled, pleased that he had.

"If you don't want to drive, we do provide a taxi service to take you home."

"Oh, I might consider that when I sell my car."

Jerome stopped at the lights and turned to look at her. "You're selling your car?" he sounded surprised.

"Er... yes. It's not very practical."

He furrowed his brow at her comment. "Practical?"

"Or rather, it's not really me."

Jerome looked confused and Dani smiled at his expression.

"What car is it?"

"Porsche."

"Porsche?"

"Yes. Not me at all."

"No, it doesn't suit you," he agreed, looking puzzled.

Dani shrugged, "I know, I'm more of a Smart girl."

Jerome laughed, "Yes, you really are a smart girl!"

"No, I didn't mean it that way." She shook her head as she chuckled at his comment.

Jerome set off as the lights changed. "Oh, I know you didn't. I'm just messing with you."

Dani grinned as she looked at him. She took in his immaculate profile and let her eyes drop to his throat where she watched his Adam's apple work on a swallow. Jeez, he was so damn good looking, all designer stubble and chiselled jaw.

"Here we are." He pulled into the parking bay and stopped. He turned to look at her and she flushed as he caught her staring at him. Dani fumbled with the seat belt and opened the door.

"Thanks for the lift. *Again*," she joked, trying to defuse her nervousness with humour.

"No problem."

Dani pulled herself out of the car and then bent down to look at Jerome. "What's this car?" she asked.

Jerome raised his eyebrows at the question. "My car?"

Dani nodded.

"It's a Maserati."

"Italian?" smirked Dani.

Jerome laughed, "Yes, it's Italian."

"Of course it is. Well it *really* suits you. Thanks for the ride and *ciao*."

Jerome's jaw dropped a little as she closed the door before he could reply.

FIRST DAY

Adam pulled up outside La Casa d'Italia and killed the engine. "You look nervous, Dani."

"I am, a bit." She unbuckled her belt.

"You're very early." It was ten to nine. "What will you do until ten thirty?"

"I really want to get acquainted with everyone and the place."

Adam nodded.

"Is anyone in?" he peered over to the car park of the restaurant. There were four cars parked in it. Dani looked to where he was looking and she felt a little thrill when she recognised Jerome's Maserati. She was sure Chef said he hardly spent time here. Maybe he just checked in. She nervously adjusted her ponytail and fingered through her fringe.

"Nice car," whistled Adam as he spotted the Maserati.

"Yes, it's Jerome's, the owner." Dani tried hard to keep a 'matter of fact' tone in her voice.

"Oh. The others?"

Dani shrugged. Adam narrowed his eyes at her, and Dani felt nervous as he watched her fumble for the handle. She realised he was trying to work out why she knew Jerome's car and not the owners of the other three.

"I think they're Chef's, Capo's and Mrs Ferretti's. What type of cars are they?"

Adam looked over and squinted through his glasses. "Alfa Romeos and a Fiat," he replied.

"Yeah then, they're their cars. They seem to have a preference to all things Italian." Dani shrugged and pulled herself out of the car.

"You're sure about getting the bus home?"

"Yeah, I'll drive down for the evening shift. I think I'm getting to know the way now."

Dani threw him a smile as he pulled away from the curb. She walked towards the back entrance, away from the car park, rounded the wall that shielded the back door and the smoking table, and pushed open the door. She was immediately greeted by a wonderful sugary lemon aroma. She headed straight to the kitchen and walked in through the door.

Capo was busy talking to a supplier but his face lit up when he saw Dani. "*Buongiorno,* Dani! First day, eh?"

"*Buongiorno,* Capo. Yes, it is. It smells delicious." Dani's eyes rested on Carmen, who was busy whipping up a creamy mixture. "Morning, Carmen. Thanks for my cheesecake – it was to die for," she groaned. Dani had managed to save a small piece for Chloe, who was seriously unsatisfied with the small morsel she got to try. "What are you making?"

"Limoncello and lemon cream tart."

Dani's mouth pooled with saliva as she thought of it. "Sounds like heaven. I love lemon," she huffed and backed away as if it was too tempting and Carmen laughed.

"I'll give you some to try later."

"Oh no, Carmen, I can't..."

"Nonsense. You need to try everything so you can recommend it to the customers. The first batch is ready."

"I'm going to have to work out every day if you're going to make me try everything, Carmen. Espresso anyone?"

"*Si,* Dani." Capo winked at her as she left the kitchen.

Dani placed her holdall on the floor by the bar, which contained her work shoes, a towel and a few cosmetics. She needed to invest in a few backup items to keep at work, maybe some spare shoes. Her heart sunk as she thought about her last night working at the bar. If she'd had a spare pair there, she'd have never caught Jez out. What troubled her was that she wasn't sure if she was sad or pleased about that.

The restaurant was lit only by the lights over the bar and the light coming from the kitchen. The dull day outside did little to brighten up the restaurant through the large windows. Well at least it wasn't raining today. As Dani started to use the coffee machine, she glanced up at all the bottles housed on the shelves. She should really be taking note of them all. Grappa, calvados, Armagnac, Cognac, Campari, amaretto, Martini and limoncello were on the first shelf. Dani wasn't accustomed to seeing such a diverse selection. The bar in Kingston focused on the more popular drinks. Here, there was a huge array of liqueurs. Her eyes drifted over to the counter, where she picked up the drinks menu and leafed through it. She absent-mindedly placed the cups onto the coffee machine and pressed the button. *Even the coffee menu was extensive*, she thought. She'd really need to study this. She'd pored over the menu last night, trying hard to commit every dish to memory, but she knew it would take her a few days yet. There were so many dishes and Italian words she wasn't familiar with. Maybe she should start Italian lessons.

"Is that for Capo?" His now familiar raspy voice made Dani start. She swung round and caught her breath at the sight of Jerome casually sat on a bar stool, staring straight at her in a way that made her feel uneasy and thrilled at the same time. His stunning blue eyes swept over her. He'd obviously been to the gym as he was dressed in a grey hoodie with a towel tucked around his neck and matching jogging pants. Sweat glistened on his brow.

"Yes," she forced out. *Oh my... how long had he been watching her?*

"I'll take it to him." He slipped off the stool and waited for Dani to pass it to him. "Could you make me one?"

"Sure." Dani blinked.

"A double, please." His sculptured lips twitched.

Dani nodded and turned away to face the coffee machine as he continued to study her, her face flaming, then he rushed into the kitchen with Capo's coffee. Dani could hear them talking in Italian with a few English words peppering their conversation. Dani squirmed inwardly as she listened. Jerome sounded so damn sexy when he spoke Italian. He could have been talking about the price of fish for all she knew, but it still sounded so seductive.

Dani busied herself, placing the coffee cup on a saucer as she heard him come back through. She'd go down to the staff changing room and get settled in. She sipped her espresso nervously. Why did she feel so self-conscious and flurried around him? She'd really needed to get a grip. She reminded herself again that they were going to be working together and he was more or less her boss. Although... Chef did say Jerome spent less time here.

"Carmen sent you this to try." He placed a dessert plate with a slice of the lemon tart on it. She'd even presented it with lemon swirls, mint leaves and seared the top in a criss-cross pattern. Dani flushed. Jerome sat on the stool and smirked. "You're here early." He cocked his head to look at her as Dani placed his coffee on the bar. "Thanks."

"I wanted to get acquainted with everything."

Jerome nodded and pushed the plate towards her. "Well you seem to be getting very acquainted with the desserts."

Dani's face dropped. Oh no, she was getting Carmen in trouble. He chuckled. "Capo's recipe is the best limoncello and lemon cream tart. You need to try all the menu," he reassured her, realising she'd misunderstood his previous remark. "There are some spoons under the counter." He pointed and Dani relaxed a little.

"One of your favourites is it?" Dani asked. He watched as she grabbed two spoons.

He furrowed his brow as she pushed a spoon over to him. "Yes, I love lemon."

"Me too... but I can't eat it all. So we can share." She gestured towards the dessert with a smirk.

Jerome pursed his lips and twisted his mouth. "After what I witnessed yesterday, I think you could easily eat it all."

Dani grinned up at him as his eyes lit up, "Yes, you're right. I could, but I shouldn't."

Jerome nodded slowly and smiled a sexy smile that had Dani captivated for a few seconds. "Are you always so... self-controlled, Dani?" His voice dropped a little as he spoke.

Dani swallowed hard as her mouth dried. *Ha! Self-controlled? Her?* "When I need to be," she answered. His eyes were still on hers and she had to look away. Dani cut into the tart and popped it into her mouth, needing to occupy herself with something delicious, other than Jerome. It was, of course, mouth-wateringly divine and she couldn't suppress a small moan. "That's absolutely... wow!"

Jerome clenched his teeth and his eyes widened as he watched her.

"I think I may have changed my mind," Dani joked, hoping to lighten what seemed to be a rather intense atmosphere. It worked. Jerome let out a loud laugh, which lit up his whole brooding face. Dani's heart stopped for a split second. She didn't think he could look any better, at least not until she saw him in these rare unguarded moments.

He picked up his spoon and cut a piece. "You look quite determined. I have to say I'm a little scared."

"You should be. Desserts are my weakness and now I've stopped smoking, they are my one and only vice. I can be quite ruthless, violent even." *Shit! Stop the flirting! He's your boss!* She watched him chew slowly and swallow.

"I'll bear that in mind. Never come between you and a dessert," he chuckled, taking a smaller piece, then holding it in the air as he continued to watch her.

Quick, change the subject... "I'm going to have to start a strict exercise regime if I'm going to sample the menu."

"Why do you think I work out every day?" He raised his eyebrows and popped the tart in his mouth. Dani focused on his chiselled face as his tongue slowly stroked over his lips, relishing the flavour.

Dani shrugged and grinned, trying hard not to imagine what his body must look like under his sweatshirt. Then, as if he'd read her mind, Jerome loosened the towel from around his neck and unzipped his top, revealing a grey T-shirt, which clung to his sweat-drenched torso. *Holy fuck!* He rubbed the towel over his face, then set it on his knee.

Dani quickly placed a piece of tart in her mouth, then set down the spoon. "I'd better go get settled in."

Her heart raced as Jerome took another spoonful. His brow arched. "You're leaving the rest for me?"

"Well, yes. You worked out this morning, so you can afford to eat it," she replied, grinning, then moved around from the bar, her pulse racing as she reached down for her bag.

"Did you find the way alright this morning?"

"Adam drove me down. I'll drive down for the afternoon shift. I think I've got the hang of the one-way system now." Jerome swivelled around to face her and he nodded.

"See you." Dani walked away towards the back of the restaurant and down the stairs forcing herself not to look back at him. She felt his eyes on her all the way to the exit, which made her shiver.

Peter was sitting in his office checking over the monitors from the night before. Nothing unusual. He flicked through to the morning, seeing Jerome's arrival at six twenty. Jesus, he started early. Things must be really bad at home, he thought sadly. He pressed fast-forward and saw Dani arrive. He checked the time. Eight fifty five. She was an hour and half early. He reset the monitors and stood up to go downstairs. He was met by Jerome making his way to his office. "Morning."

"Morning, Chef."

"Been to the gym?"

Jerome nodded his reply.

"You're changing here, then?"

"Yes. I jog there, work out, then jog back. I prefer to now. It gives me at least an hour and a half."

Chef shook his head. "You're a machine."

Jerome shrugged. He contemplated explaining his enthusiasm for exercise was purely to relieve stress and a way to forget, but thought better of it. He didn't want to dump on Peter again.

"Shall I bring you up a coffee?"

"Er, no thanks. I've had one and I'm getting straight off this morning. I've got interviews at Level One."

"Oh, good. Let's hope that gets sorted out. So you won't be around today?"

Jerome's brow creased as he thought about not being around. "Not sure. Maybe later."

"Okay, see you later, then."

By nine thirty, Dani had changed into her uniform and placed her few items into her locker. Carmen took great delight in introducing her to the team. Dani then spent the next hour getting to know the kitchen staff. There was Jamie the sous chef, two brothers named Enzo and Franco, Rico the pot-man and Vanessa. Silvanna would also usually work, but today was her day off. Capo had left them to it for his regular morning meeting with Chef.

Dani watched on as Franco and Enzo put the finishing touches to the staff lunch, linguini with a seafood sauce. It smelled mouth-watering and Dani couldn't believe how hungry she felt, even after sampling her lemon tart.

The private dining room was a hive of activity as Dani entered it. The restaurant staff from yesterday had set up for the staff lunch. Dani spotted Rosa and Kuch. They were already sitting down and had left the seat between them free.

"Hi, Dani, come and sit here." Dani noticed that everyone seemed to sit in the same place as yesterday. That thought made her smile. It really was like a big family. Growing up, Dani's family had always sat in the same places at meal times, a tradition Chloe also followed. Dani scanned the table and realised that the place opposite to her was the one Jerome had occupied yesterday. She felt a little thrill, then shook her head. She really shouldn't be thinking like that.

"Are you ready for today?" Kuch cocked his head at her.

"I'll tell you at three o'clock, shall I?" Dani rolled her eyes. It was true she was a little nervous. She really didn't want to let them down.

"Well, Fridays are always a little crazy. Businessmen usually, and lots of them," Rosa explained.

"Great, now I'm even more nervous." Dani slumped in her chair as Rosa smirked.

The lunch progressed quickly. Gia joined them, floating in, looking stunning in a black pencil skirt and cream deep scoop top clinched at the waist with a red belt. She was so striking, Dani found it hard to believe she had a son in his thirties. Capo and Chef sat on either side of her. Jerome's seat remained empty and Dani found herself focussing on it, almost willing him to appear, but he didn't. Chef briefed the staff with their stations and bookings and then everyone got up to start their preparations.

"Dani, you can help out Rosa today. Just until you're familiar with everything." Chef had pulled her to one side as the rest of the staff cleared away the table, "I see you came in early today."

"Yes, I wanted to get to know my way around, meet the staff. I also got a lift in with my brother-in-law. Is that alright?"

Chef nodded, "Yes, of course it is. I need to see which days you can work through. We do it on a rota system."

"Um, well to be honest, any day suits at the moment. I don't have any plans as such, so whenever is okay with me."

"That makes my job easier," he grinned. "Well, good luck today." He gently patted her arm and then led her towards the door. Dani fleetingly looked at his profile as they walked out. For all his efficiency, he still had a warmness about him. She knew she was going to love working here.

Dani had always enjoyed the thrill of pressure. When she'd worked alongside Jez, the bar would be literally bursting at the seams. She'd had to deal with drunks, witnessed fights, put up with overly friendly customers, but she had been more than able to live up to the challenge and still maintain her professionalism.

La Casa d'Italia was a whole other league. The bar had been more concerned with everyone getting served as quickly as possible. At La Casa, the aim was to also serve quickly, but without the sense of urgency. The whole concept was to be efficient without making the customer feel any of the pressure the staff were under, ensuring their dining experience was as relaxed and enjoyable as possible.

Gia was instrumental to this. She had a grace about her that put everyone at ease. Dani watched her talk to customers, giving them her undivided attention, yet she was fully aware of everything else going on around her. Glasses that needed filling, dessert orders to be taken, bills to be prepared, tables to be cleared; her eyes never missed a trick. Between Peter and Gia, they managed to ensure that the restaurant ran as smoothly as possible, and from what Dani could see, it did.

Rosa walked Dani through every step with meticulous detail and before long, the restaurant was already on its second cover. Rosa had been right: it had up to now been predominantly businessmen and the second wave was starting to come in.

"You up for taking an order?" Rosa asked as they cleared a table. "Table twelve are ready for their desserts. Take them the menu and then take the order."

Dani's eyes widened. "Are you sure? I don't want to mess it up."

"I'll be close by. You'll be fine. Go on," she encouraged as Dani took over the menus.

Table twelve was occupied by four women. They'd been clearly enjoying themselves throughout their lunch. Dani handed them the menus and moved back towards the bar out of the way, giving them a chance to look over them.

Kuch leaned over to speak to her. "So how's it going?"

"Okay. My first order." Dani motioned to table twelve.

"The women? Dessert? Women always seem to be watching their weight. Why they ask for the dessert menu, I'll never know. They just read it and then order coffee." Kuch rolled his eyes and Dani grinned. Chef came over to check she was alright and then Dani walked back to the table.

"Are you ready to order dessert?" Dani smiled at them as the four women looked up at her.

A striking blonde answered first, "God, I want them all but I've eaten so much already." The other three agreed with disgruntled moans.

"Oh that's a shame, our chef's desserts are pretty special."

"Yes I can see. Which one would you recommend?" the petite brunette asked.

"Well, the mascarpone cheesecake is just heavenly with a rich, creamy and almondy texture" – she paused as all four women focused on her – "the limoncello and lemon tart is also very scrummy, it's light with just enough tang... it's hard to choose between the two." Dani's eyes widened to emphasise the point. Her audience were riveted as she continued. "But I love the cannoli too, a divine combination of sweet, orange cream, crispy shell and chocolate." Dani added a sigh and licked her lips.

The occupants of the table stared at Dani as she described each of the desserts and Dani watched them all visibly swallow.

"Crap, you make them sound better than sex," the petite brunette moaned and the table erupted into giggles. "Maybe we should order a couple and share."

"Bang goes the diet," the taller brunette to the left of the blonde huffed. "Order all three and we'll share."

"Sure. Thank you." Dani beamed at them and walked over to her service station as she tapped in the order.

Rosa was over to her grinning. "You did great."

Dani grinned as she pulled out the cutlery she needed.

Peter watched her from the bar and Kuch leaned over to him. "She's good. Didn't think for a minute they'd order desserts." Peter raised his eyebrows and nodded, clearly impressed. "She did make them sound better than sex," Kuch muttered so only Peter could hear and they both stifled a laugh.

By quarter to three, the restaurant was starting to empty. The tables remaining were either on dessert or coffee. Rosa was working the afternoon shift today with Augustino, another waiter. He was of medium height, slim with dark short hair and seemed to have a great sense of humour. He'd been joking about with Kuch as he waited for his coffee order.

"How do you feel after your first shift, Daniella?" Gia had walked over to where Rosa and Dani were clearing a table that had finished.

"Okay. It was very busy, but once I'm familiar with the menu, I think I should be fine."

"I think you'll be more than fine," replied Gia. "So you need to be down for five thirty."

"I was going to stay, if that's alright? I'm curious to see how busy the afternoons are."

"If you're sure, I don't see why not."

Dani smiled, "I just need to tell my sister I'll be staying on, otherwise she'll worry."

"Of course. Take time out to call her."

Dani quickly made her way down to the staff room and opened up her locker to grab her phone and call Chloe.

"Hi, Chloe."

"Hi, how did it go?"

"Great, it's so busy, but everyone's helpful. Look I'm staying on, so I won't be back this afternoon."

"Oh, okay. What about getting home tonight though? Do you want me to get Adam to pick you up?"

"No, they have a taxi service which can drop me off. Don't worry."

"Really? That's great. Okay, then. I'll probably see you in the morning."

"Yeah, sure. See you later. Bye."

Dani looked down at her phone and saw two missed calls from Jez and her heart sank. She wondered whether it was because of the letter Adam had drafted about the house. Surely he couldn't have got it so soon; she'd only approved it last night. Crap. She knew she'd have to call him eventually. Maybe she should before he got the letter. Dani switched her phone to silent and placed it back in her locker.

The changing room was filling up with all the staff as she locked up. Each one of them acknowledged her with a smile, nod or a kind word as they got ready to leave, thankfully making her forget about Jez.

By the time Dani went back up to the restaurant, there were only a handful of tables still full. Rosa and Augustino were resetting the tables while Chef was at the main till going over the bookings for tonight. Dani looked around as she entered through the door and her attention was alerted to a new table in the raised section. Gia was sitting at the table with two men. One had blackish, slightly long wavy hair, with dark eyes and fair skin. He was dressed in a pin striped navy blue three-piece suit with a white shirt and white tie. He was immaculate. The second man looked ten years younger than the first, probably in his early thirties. He was also in a suit but his was far less conservative. It was light grey with a soft sheen and paired with a white shirt and matching grey tie. The younger man had chestnut hair with a slight wave, which was sharply cut and gelled. They were talking with Gia and their conversation stopped momentarily as Dani walked past their table.

Dani headed straight to where Rosa was. "What do you need me to do?"

"Just help set up the tables. I need to go and see what they need." Rosa motioned to Gia's table.

"Sure."

Dani busied herself as Rosa went up to the table. Glancing up, she could see that the men were familiar with Rosa and they engaged in friendly banter. Gia beamed across at the men as they spoke. The younger man's gaze flitted over to where Dani was setting up and Dani smiled nervously and then looked away as Rosa walked over to the bar.

"Do you want me to get the drinks for you?" At least this was an area Dani felt confident in.

"Would you? That'll be great. I need a double espresso, two San Pellegrinos, a Campari with ice and a slice of orange and a glass of Pinot grigio."

Dani slipped around the bar and started on the order. She was just putting the espresso on the tray when Jerome strode in from the back entrance, his eyes lighting up as he saw the occupants of Gia's table. All three men greeted each other warmly with hugs and kisses, which Dani found unusual but extremely endearing. Jerome dragged back the chair to join them. His eyes scanned the restaurant and he narrowed his eyes as he saw Dani behind the bar. Dani gave him a small smile and carried on with the last of the order. Upon seeing Jerome focus temporarily on Dani, the younger man bent closer to ask him something and Jerome's expression hardened. Gia quickly said something and the younger man smirked as his eyes flitted back over to Dani.

"Looks like you made a hit with Seni." Dani hadn't noticed Augustino had come over to the bar.

"Sorry?"

He motioned to the table. "The guy in the grey suit is Arsenio, Seni for short, Gia's youngest son."

"Oh, I didn't know she had another son."

"She has three. The other guy is the eldest, Cosimo."

"Really? She doesn't look old enough." Dani quickly looked over again at the table and saw the slight resemblance between the three men. Jerome was very much like his mother, dark and sultry. Cosimo, on the other hand, had her dark hair, but his features were less striking and his eyes were dark. Arsenio was fairer than both his brothers, but had the same sculptured lips as both Gia and Jerome.

"Yeah, I know. They come here every Friday for lunch together. Family get-together."

Dani pursed her lips together and nodded.

Rosa placed their drinks on the table and looked expectantly at Jerome.

"I'll have a San Pellegrino, Rosa, thanks." She nodded and headed back to the bar.

"So, it's her first day, then?" Arsenio sipped his water as he eyed Jerome.

"Yes." Jerome shifted in his seat.

"Well it's nice to see Peter finally hired a pretty girl for a change instead of just men."

"Arsenio, you know you're not allowed to date the staff," Gia chastised as Jerome visibly stiffened.

"I'm just saying, Mama," huffed Arsenio as he continued to stare at Dani.

"So, Jerome, how are Liz and the children? We haven't seen them in ages," Cosimo asked in his smooth calm voice. Jerome turned to him.

"They're fine, Cos. I should bring them down this weekend so you can see them."

"I'd love that." He smiled kindly and Jerome softened. Cosimo had a unique gift that made you feel relaxed. His voice was soothing and he was gentle in his tone. He was also very shrewd and even though he knew the details of Jerome's private life, he would never make an awkward situation worse. Quite the contrary, in fact. He always endeavoured to make everyone feel at ease. He was less fiery than both Jerome and Arsenio, a quality he'd inherited from his late father.

Dani watched on as the Ferrettis enjoyed their lunch together. Gia sipped her espresso as the three men caught up with each other's news.

Another few customers came in for late lunches, which kept Rosa and Augustino busy. Capo had left and Jamie the sous chef was preparing the orders with Carmen. Dani helped out with the drinks, then went into the kitchen to thank Carmen for her limoncello tart. She found her putting the finishing touches on a salad. "Hi, Carmen."

"Hi," Carmen smiled back.

"Thanks for the tart. It was heavenly."

Carmen raised her eyebrows at the description. "Thanks. Have you come to try something else?" she teased.

"Oh no, no." Dani shook her head as she smirked, then added. "Why? What do you have in mind?"

Carmen laughed softly, "Let me bring you some panettone bread and butter pudding."

"Oh hell! I swear you're trying to kill me with these desserts. I'm like a junkie, here for my next fix!" Jamie chuckled at her comment from where he was preparing a sauce for pasta. "Remind me when it's your birthday, so I can return the favour," called Dani as Carmen disappeared into the walk in fridge.

"It's her thirtieth birthday on Sunday," whispered Jamie.

"Seriously?"

Jamie nodded as his soft face and green eyes lit up mischievously.

"In that case, I'll bake her a cake. But don't tell her."

Jamie grinned and nodded as Carmen re-emerged from the fridge carrying a large tray. She cut out a portion and positioned it on a plate, then warmed it through. She then served it with a zabaglione cream.

Dani's mouth watered at the sight of it. She could almost feel her behind expanding from the delicious aroma alone. Dani shook her head slightly. *Note to self: dig out the fitness DVD tonight and start it.* Since moving up to Leeds her exercise routine had flown out the window.

Peter pulled back a chair and joined the Ferrettis as they had their coffee. "How did the interviews go?" He directed his question to Jerome.

"Good, actually. They're a couple who are suitable. I'm thinking of taking them both on. It would mean I wouldn't need to be there so much."

Peter nodded slowly as Jerome answered nervously, his eyes purposely focused on Peter. Gia narrowed her eyes and was about to say something when Peter turned to her and added, "How come Dani's still here?"

Jerome visibly relaxed as he realised Peter had purposely deflected a possible barrage of questions. He knew it was temporary but he was grateful all the same. "She wanted to see how busy it gets in the afternoon. She's very willing."

"Glad to see you employed a pretty girl, Peter," Arsenio smirked as he glanced back at Dani.

"I didn't employ her for your benefit, Seni. She was the best for the job." Peter shook his head and stifled a smile. "Off limits." He mock-scolded him, arching his brow.

" Jeez, I'm only saying." Arsenio rolled his eyes. "Anyone would think I _"

"Save it, Seni. You can't keep your hands off any good-looking girl, so don't play the innocent," interrupted Cosimo. "Hell, sometimes I think all they need is a pulse!"

Arsenio opened his mouth to defend himself, then stopped, knowing full well he could never win this argument. He was a good lawyer, but he had to admit he'd never convince his family otherwise – there was too much damning evidence. He decided to use humour instead.

"A pulse definitely helps." He stifled a smirk.

"Arsenio!" Gia gaped, horrified as the four men chuckled.

Jerome looked at his watch. It was four thirty. "I better get off. The kids will be home from school." He pushed back his chair and stood up in one fluid movement. "I'll call you when I bring them down." He rested his hand on Cosimo's shoulder as he spoke.

"Great. Looking forward to it. I've got those papers you asked for. I'll put them in your office."

Jerome froze for a second and then nodded. He said his goodbyes to the rest of the table, then headed for the exit, but not before scanning the restaurant to steal a glimpse of Dani as Augustino teased her while she made some coffees. He strode out into the cool November air and lowered himself into his car. He checked around the car park and realised that Dani hadn't brought down her car. There were only his mother's, Chef's and Arsenio's rather flashy gun metal Lamborghini. Jerome started up his car and headed out of town towards his home. His stomach started to tighten at the thought of having to be in the same vicinity as Liz. He rubbed his forehead then cranked up the volume of the stereo in an attempt to change his mood.

HOME SWEET HOME?

Jerome swung his car in through the electric gates. It had taken him roughly twenty minutes to get home, and by the time he'd got there, he was feeling nervous. Nina's car was parked in the garage as he pulled up next to it, achingly aware that Liz's car was missing. Jerome tried to suppress the tirade of thoughts and questions that forced their way into his head as he approached the door adjoining the garage to the house. Why wasn't Liz home? She hadn't been at Level One today. So where was she? She should be home, now that the kids were in from school. He found himself in turmoil over how to deal with the situation. He didn't want a fight but he needed her to know that if they were going to make it work, she'd have to change. Even if she did change, could they ever go back to normal? He was worryingly unsure if he could handle it or if he could even forgive her at all. Who was she with? His stomach clenched as he rubbed his forehead. He had to make this work; he had to at least try. He couldn't just give up, not when the stakes were so high... this was his family. His heart thumped against his chest as he wrestled with himself and twisted the handle of the door.

Jerome could hear Alessandro's voice and his heart instantly began to slow down. The kids would have been home almost an hour. He thanked his lucky stars he'd found Nina. At least his kids were looked after by a nanny that truly cared for them. The sound of their voices and the smiles on their faces were always enough to make Jerome almost forget about Liz. He found them sitting at the kitchen table, assembling some magnets and metal balls.

"Hi, Jerome." Nina grinned up at him as he dropped his keys on the kitchen counter, her mop of ginger curly hair in a bundle on top of her head.

"Hi, Nina." Jerome smiled down at her.

"Daddy!" Both Kara and Alessandro jumped out of their seats and threw themselves at him. He crouched down, scooped them up and straightened with ease as they clung to him.

"Hey guys. What's that you're making?"

"We're just seeing how high we can make it go, Daddy," replied Alessandro. He walked over to the table, putting both of them down after he squeezed them tightly and kissed them. They proceeded to explain what they were doing and Nina discreetly rose from the table and let Jerome have some private time with his children.

Nina had worked for the family nearly eight years. She'd started when Alessandro was nine months old. Liz was finding childcare very demanding. That, along with her wanting to continue her modelling career, meant Jerome needed to find a full time nanny. At first, Nina had come in at eight and left by four. But as time went by, she ended up staying longer. Jerome was at the restaurant and Liz wanted to be able to come and go as she pleased. She hated the fact her baby restricted her. The family moved from the flat above the restaurant into their present home. A large six bedroom house set in an acre of land in the suburb of Bramhope. Jerome hoped that having their own home, away from the restaurant, would make Liz happier. Nina was asked to move in with them and Jerome converted an outhouse into a one bedroom residence for her to live in.

At first, Liz seemed content. She enjoyed the idea of having her own home and spent a lot of her free time redecorating it. She began to work again – small contracts, mainly catalogue modelling and some promotional work. She aspired to be a successful catwalk model, but at the age of twenty-six, she had never yet achieved that level of success. When she fell pregnant with Kara, the real cracks in their marriage began to show. Liz realised her chances of ever making it big were now even less. She spent little time at home and Nina took on the care of the children. By this time, Jerome had opened Sky and it meant he worked long, unsociable hours. Liz enjoyed the fact her husband owned a popular nightclub and she spent a considerable amount of time there with him. However, like many things with Liz, after a while the novelty and glamour wore off, and she lost interest. Especially as Jerome was constantly playing his role as host and giving Liz less of his undivided attention.

The agency Liz worked with found her a few jobs but not the high profile ones she sought after. So in an attempt to please her, Jerome suggested they open a gym and beauty salon for Liz to manage. She spent every day at either one or the other, so it seemed the ideal business for her to be involved in. It had been two years since they opened Level One.

Jerome sat on Kara's bed as she snuggled into his side. He'd changed out of his suit and put on some lose black lounge pants and a thin apple green sweater. Alessandro was curled up on the bed, with his head resting on Jerome's stomach. He giggled every time he heard it gurgle. "It's funny, Daddy."

"The film?"

"No! Your tummy."

"My tummy's funny?" Jerome furrowed his brow.

"It's gurgling." Alessandro gazed up at Jerome, his eyes almost an exact replica.

"That's because it's working hard to digest my dinner."

"Well it's working super-hard then," he snorted and then rested his head back on Jerome's stomach.

They'd settled down to watch *Shrek* before they went to bed. Jerome had prepared dinner for them. He loved to cook and whenever he had the chance to, he took full advantage. Today was one of those times. He'd purposely come home early so that he could prepare dinner for his children.

Both Alessandro and Kara loved it, especially as Jerome let them help. He prepared one of their favourite dishes: Piccata Milanese. Kara mixed the rich tomato sauce as Jerome pan fried the veal coated in breadcrumbs and Parmesan. Alessandro kept checking the spaghetti, pulling out a strand every so often to see if it was ready. Once they'd eaten, Jerome bathed them both, then sat to watch their favourite film. His agitation grew as the evening progressed when there was still no sign of Liz. He contemplated ringing her but he didn't. Whatever he had to say to her he wanted to say it face to face.

Nina had helped tidy up, then left Jerome to enjoy his children, retreating to her place. She genuinely liked Jerome – they'd fallen into a familiar relationship but still managed to keep a respectful distance, and it was because of him and the children that she'd put up with Liz for the last eight years. That and the fact that Liz spent less and less time at home. Nina took her instructions from Jerome. It was only as a courtesy that she followed Liz's rare instructions, and her respect for Jerome was why she put up with Liz's rudeness and belittling comments. Nina gave Liz a wide berth and avoided her as much as she could.

By eight o'clock, both children were asleep. Jerome made his way back down to the kitchen and found Liz sat at the kitchen table on her phone. She looked up at him as he walked in and her face stiffened.

"Look, I've got to go. I'll call you later... Sure, bye." She switched off her phone. Jerome crossed his arms and leaned against the door frame, his eyes focused on her nervous face. "What?"

Jerome arched his eyebrow at her comment, making it perfectly clear he was waiting for some sort of explanation.

She just stared at him, her pale blue eyes cold.

"Where have you been?" His voice was low but steady.

"I had an appointment with an ad agency. It went on longer than I expected." Her tone was bordering on arrogant. She pushed back her chair and stood up, then paced over to the fridge.

"Why didn't you call?"

Liz opened the fridge and pulled out a bottle of open wine. "I didn't think you were home. You're not usually." The last three words were laced with sarcasm and Jerome inhaled deeply trying to keep calm. She poured herself a glass of wine, then turned to face him.

"You also have two children. Didn't you think about them?"

"I *know* I have two children, Jerome, I don't need *you* to remind me. I spoke to them when they got home from school. Jesus," she sneered.

"So the rest of the day, where were you?"

"Is this how it's going to be, Jerome? Twenty questions about where I go and what I do? For the last six years you never bothered and *now* you interrogate me?" she spat out.

Jerome straightened. "I didn't think I had a cause to wonder what you were doing before." He clenched his teeth as he spoke.

Liz huffed, "Oh, just go back to your beloved Casa. You'd much prefer to be there than here with me."

"Don't turn this on to me, Liz. It's my work. It's what provides *you* with this." He lifted his hand in the air, gesturing to their surroundings. "Provides you and the kids with everything you need and want." His voice was a little louder, betraying his feelings.

"And you never let me forget it, do you? Well I was at work too. I'm trying to get my career going again, but what do you care, eh? You're so wrapped up in Casa and Sky or Level One, that what I want doesn't count." Liz took a drink of her wine and put down her glass.

"I don't care!" He stepped closer to her, his fists clenching. "Who the fuck do I work so hard for? All I do is try and make you happy. But you never are. I don't know what you want anymore. Jesus, I don't think I ever have." He rubbed his forehead in exasperation. "I set up Level One for *you*. Something you could get involved with and you just abandoned it, leaving me to pick up the mess you left it in and –"

"I don't want something *you* set up for me. I want my *own* career, something I've done on my own," she interrupted. "I'm thirty two. If I don't do this now, I'll never do it!"

Jerome closed his eyes and took a deep breath. He looked at her as she fiddled with her long blonde hair with her perfectly French mani-cured nails. She looked immaculate as always, dressed in a black short woollen dress showing off her long slim legs, her four inch heeled ankle boots making her as tall as Jerome. They stood staring at each other in silence, then Jerome tried a different tactic.

"Liz, we're a family, a team. I'll support you in whatever you want, but you need to support me too. If you didn't want Level One, you should have just told me." His voice was softer, hoping he could thaw her out.

"I want my modelling career back, Jerome. That's what I want," she replied coolly. It was a statement with no room for negotiation.

He rubbed his face with both his hands. She still hadn't explained where she'd been all day and he knew he had to ask. If they were going to work things out, he had to know everything.

"Where were you today, Liz?" Her eyes darted away from him and he knew. "Were you with *him*?"

Silence.

"You said it was over. It was a one off. Was that a lie?" Jerome's voice was barely audible.

"We just met up to talk. He's pretty upset."

"*He's* upset! Are you kidding me?" Jerome shouted, then muttered something in Italian under his breath. "Did you sleep with him?"

"I'm trying to let him down gently, Jerome…"

"Answer me!" Her reply had tipped his temper over the edge.

"Stop shouting, you'll wake the kids," she hissed.

"Oh *now* you remember you have children, now it suits you! You lied to me. You said it was once and it was a mistake. This was not a one off. This has been going on for a while. Why would you need to let him down gently? It's either finished or it's not Liz, so which is it?"

"I'll finish it." She glared at him as she answered.

"Do you want to be with him?" he asked angrily.

"I said, I'll finish it," she spat out, then pushed past him and headed upstairs.

"*We* haven't finished yet."

She turned to look at him over her shoulder, her cool eyes filled with loathing. "Well I have. Just leave me alone, Jerome." Her eyes darted to the clock. "Go back to work, Jerome, go to your Casa." Her tone was heavy with bitterness, then she headed up the stairs.

He slumped into a kitchen chair and held his head in his hands and leaned on the table. His pulse was racing. It was eight thirty and he knew he'd have to go down to Sky. It was Friday night and the club would be heaving. Maybe he should just stay and thrash it out with Liz. He glanced towards the hallway. He really didn't feel like arguing anymore. He was feeling too angry and hurt and he knew himself too well. He'd end up saying things that he'd regret, when all he wanted to do was to try and work things out. He heard Liz close her door and he quickly picked up his phone and rang Nina.

"Hi, Jerome."

"Hi. Look, I'm off out in half an hour. Liz is home but I'm not sure if she's staying in. Can you keep an eye out? I'm sure she'll let you know if she's going out but she might –"

"Don't worry, Jerome." She interrupted him, knowing what he was trying to say. Her heart went out to him. He had so much to deal with and no support at home. At least she could hopefully help in that part of his life. "I'll make sure the kids are okay."

"Thanks."

As Jerome walked into his busy restaurant, his mood immediately changed. Peter caught his eye and he nodded his hello. He reciprocated, then scanned the room, noting where each staff member was stationed and which customers were in. Gia was talking to a large table when she noticed him. She momentarily furrowed her brow as she saw his pensive expression, then she smiled at him. Something was wrong, she could see it in his face. He immediately smiled at her and moved down to the bar, where he saw some regulars waiting for their table. Kuch winked his hello as he poured his drinks order, then automatically prepared an espresso for Jerome and pushed it over to him.

Jerome mouthed his thanks, wishing he could drink something stronger. He had a long night ahead and an even longer day tomorrow. He needed to keep his head straight. Peter came over and gave him a quick rundown of the evening, joking with him about some of the customers. After knowing Jerome for over fifteen years, he'd learned how to bring him out of a bad mood. Talking work always distracted Jerome from any problem he was battling with. It took Peter roughly ten minutes to soften Jerome's hard expression. Jerome's eyes rescanned the restaurant and found Dani coming out of the kitchen with an order. His gaze followed her as she placed the plates down at a table with a young couple. His brow creased as he saw the man openly appraising her, but was pleased to see that Dani didn't seem to notice.

"How's she doing?" He motioned to where Dani was with his chin.

"Good. Very good actually. I gave her four tables at the back and she's doing great."

Jerome nodded. He finished his espresso and put it down. "I'll go and do the rounds before I head up to Sky."

"Good. There are a lot of people in today that have been asking about you."

Jerome smiled and huffed, then headed to a table of four who were desperately trying to grab his attention. It took Jerome roughly forty minutes to go around the main restaurant. He headed back to the bar and contemplated going out for a cigarette. As he moved towards the back of the restaurant, he noticed Dani talking to the table of two again.

"Who's that on table twelve?" he asked Peter.

"It's a Joseph Mann? He was asking about you."

"Joseph Mann from college? You're kidding me. I haven't seen him in ages – at least five years, maybe more. I didn't even recognise him." Jerome looked back over to the table in shock. "I should go and say hello."

Joseph Mann was an old college friend of Jerome's. They'd been at the local college together. He'd been on the chubby side and walked very much in the shadow of Jerome. Jerome liked him immensely. Joseph had helped him when Jerome struggled in college and they had hung out a lot together. He'd always been a shy boy until he'd met Jerome. When Jerome went to Switzerland, Joseph had landed a job for a large chain of hotels and slowly worked his way up. He'd moved to America over five years ago and they'd lost touch.

"Joseph?"

"Hey man, how are you?" Joseph got up instantly and they hugged each other affectionately.

"Where've you been? Last I heard you were in Baltimore?"

"Come and sit down, join us." Joseph beamed, genuinely pleased to see his old college buddy.

Dani quickly pulled over a chair. Jerome took it from her and sat down. "Thanks, Dani." He smiled at her, his gaze lingering, and she nodded.

"This is Jenny. Jenny, Jerome's the restaurant owner." Joseph motioned to the petite blonde sitting opposite him.

"Pleased to finally meet you Jerome." Jenny's accent was clearly American and she extended her hand.

"Likewise."

"Jenny's over from California, visiting. I'm trying to recruit her."

"Recruit her?" Jerome asked.

"Yes, I've bought a property in Skipton which I've had converted into a spa and boutique hotel. Jenny will hopefully be in charge of the spa. That's if I can convince her," he chuckled.

"Wow, that's great, Joseph. When did you get back?"

"A few months ago."

"And you waited this long to come and find me?" Jerome shook his head at his friend. "You didn't want to stay out there?"

"I loved it out there. But my parents are getting on now and I'm an only child. I couldn't convince them to come out, so this was the next best option for me. Anyway, how about you? This place is still incredible. He was always a fantastic chef, Jenny, and a charmer."

Jerome snorted at the compliment. "Yeah, but the written stuff was your forte. I couldn't do that for shit. God, it's great to see you. America obviously agreed with you – you look fantastic."

"Yeah well, out there they're obsessed with keeping fit and slim. You either go the obese way or the fit way. I lost four stone and run every day now." Joseph chuntered, "Bloody hate it, but it took me two years to get in shape and I'm not gonna go back to how I was."

Jerome sat with them and they caught up with what was going on in his life, his businesses and his family, genuinely pleased to have reconnected with his old friend. Dani cleared the plates from one of her tables and then headed to the bar to collect a drinks order she'd placed. Kuch slid over the tray to her.

"How's it going? You seem to have got the hang of it."

"Yeah, I have to say I am enjoying the rush."

He winked at her as she lifted off the tray and headed back to her tables. She served the drinks, then headed towards Joseph's table with a dessert menu.

Jerome excused himself and headed to the back to have a cigarette. He stood there for a moment, enjoying the solitude. Once alone, his thoughts drifted back to Liz. He dragged hard on his cigarette as he tried to process what had happened tonight. He realised her affair with Jonathan, her assistant, was obviously more than she'd admitted to, and he was having a hard time processing that. What frightened him the most was that he didn't feel the extreme hurt and pain he should be feeling. Of course, the news had affected him, but not in the manner he'd expected. Over the years, their relationship had lost that passion, that intense feeling of not being able to be without that one person. Most relationships moved from that phase, to a deeper level of love; the physical animal attraction becoming a more spiritual and deeper connection. But Liz's constant unhappiness with pretty much everything had chipped away at their marriage. In the ten years of being together, Jerome had done everything in his power to try and make her happy. It was his love for his children that was instrumental to this. They were what fuelled his perseverance. Deep down, he knew if he didn't have Alessandro and Kara, Liz and he would have never lasted this long. He stubbed out his cigarette and headed back inside. If his feelings for Liz had been deeper, he knew he wouldn't be as calm as he was.

Peter tactfully hovered at the back of the restaurant, keeping an eye on Dani as Jerome strode in through the door. Jerome went immediately to Peter's side, watching Dani approach Joseph's table to take their dessert order.

"I think I'll just have an espresso. They all sound delicious, but I'm pretty full." Jenny put down the menu and looked at Joseph.

"I know..." agreed Dani.

Jerome narrowed his eyes as he listened to their conversation and Peter leaned closer to him and whispered, "Just watch."

"Don't you wish you could eat dessert first?" continued Dani. "Luckily I've tasted all of them. Our chef's recipes are pretty special."

"Which one would you recommend?" asked Joseph as he leaned closer.

"Tough choice. If you're a chocoholic, the chocolate and hazelnut ravioli with vanilla cream is heaven on a plate." Dani widened her eyes to emphasize her comment. "The espresso pana cotta is so light it melts in your mouth, as is the panettone bread and butter pudding." Dani gave a slight shudder, half-closing her eyes. "Delicious."

Jenny stared, mesmerized, as Dani described the different dishes. "Oh hell." She reopened the menu. "I'll have the ravioli, I love chocolate."

Joseph licked his lips and swallowed. "Screw it, I'll have the bread and butter pudding and run a couple of extra miles tomorrow."

Dani grinned and took their menus. "You won't regret it."

Joseph huffed and rolled his eyes.

Jerome leaned back against the service station and shook his head slightly.

"Every one of her tables has ordered dessert tonight," Peter said.

Jerome's eyebrow arched as he turned to Peter.

"Well, wouldn't you?" snorted Peter.

Jerome exhaled as he nodded his assent.

By ten thirty, the restaurant had started to slow down. Dani's tables were all on coffee.

Rosa came over to her as she was preparing a bill. "You did great today, Dani. Friday's pretty busy and you handled it well." Rosa rubbed her arm affectionately.

"I only had four tables, Rosa, but thanks."

Joseph and Jenny were getting ready to leave and Joseph signalled to Dani for the bill. Jerome had joined them while they enjoyed their dessert, which they both finished, despite their initial comments on how full they were. Jerome's eye caught Peter's. and Peter walked over to Dani. "Table twenty's meal is on the house. Once Jerome gets up, just go over and tell them that it was with our compliments, okay?"

"Of course. First, I'll just go and take them their coffee."

Peter nodded. "Once you've done that you can go. You've been here all day." He looked at his watch. It was ten forty-five. She'd been here for over thirteen hours.

"It's okay. I'm alright staying until the end."

"I'll organise a taxi for you, then."

"That's okay. Kuch offered to give me a lift home. He lives about a couple of miles from me. I'll be driving in tomorrow."

"Oh. Well, that'll be easier for you. Tomorrow will be hectic. We're fully booked from six thirty." He flashed a grin and walked back over to the till where Gia was.

Dani took over the coffee Joseph and Jenny had ordered, along with a fresh espresso for Jerome. *He drank more coffee than her*, she thought fleetingly as she placed it in front of him and cleared the dessert plates. His eyes wandered over to her as she worked quickly around them.

"She's very good," Joseph commented, catching Jerome unaware.

"Yes, she's new, but she's doing well."

Dani brought over two shot glasses of grappa that Peter had sent over and placed them on the table, along with some cream Jenny had asked for. "They're to go with the coffee," she added.

"Thank you." Jenny eyed the drinks.

"It's grappa. It's quite strong but it's lovely. It complements the coffee," explained Dani, and Jerome stifled a smile at her comment.

"You drink a lot of coffee then, Dani?" asked Joseph, effectively stopping her from leaving his side. He sat back in his chair so that he could see her better.

Dani knew he was trying to open up a conversation with her. He was being subtle, but Dani had had her fair share of men flirting with her. Her reply needed to be polite without giving him the complete brush off. "Yes, something like that," replied Dani, as a smile curled on her lips and her eyes involuntarily darted for a split second to Jerome. She stepped back and nodded, then walked to her station.

"She's *really* good Jerome." Joseph stared after her.

Jerome smiled stiffly at Joseph and nodded. He drained his espresso, then got up and excused himself. Once he'd vacated his seat, Dani went over to inform them that their meal was on the house. Of course, Joseph protested. Joseph searched for Jerome who was by the bar and he made his way over to him in order to thank him. They spoke a little more and then Joseph and Jenny left.

Dani began to clear the last of her tables when she felt Jerome come up behind her.

"He left this for you." Jerome held out a fifty pound note. "He asked me to give it to you."

"Really? Thanks. I never got to thank him." Dani took the note from Jerome, clearly shocked.

"Don't be so surprised. You did really well today. I have a feeling he'll be back again, you can thank him then."

Jerome gazed down at her intensely as he spoke and Dani felt herself heat up. "Er, thanks," she muttered, then turned back to her table as she put the note into her pocket, not wanting to make a complete fool of herself.

Jerome walked into the kitchen and Dani relaxed. She didn't see him again that night. It worried her how much she was bothered by his absence.

By eleven thirty, Kuch was ready to go. He was also dropping off Nicole. After bidding everyone goodnight, they headed to the back of the restaurant and out to the car park. As Dani lowered herself into the car, Carmen caught up with them.

"Hey, this is for you." Dani looked at the polystyrene container she was holding.

"For me?" Dani squeaked and instantly her mouth flooded with saliva. She knew whatever was in the box would be delicious. Carmen nodded as she grinned at her. "Thanks, Carmen."

It was midnight by the time she got home. Everyone was fast asleep.

Dani took off her shoes and crept into the kitchen and flicked on the lights. She placed the box on the table and contemplated whether she should save it for the morning. *Ha! Who was she kidding? Not a chance!* She pulled a fork and spoon from the cutlery drawer and sat down at the table, then flicked open the container. She gasped. There it sat, a slice of the scrumptious limoncello and lemon cream tart. But that wasn't what had taken her breath away. On the inside of the lid there were nine words handwritten in black marker pen.

Enjoy it all this time, you deserve it. J

Dani's hand flew to her mouth as an overwhelming giddy feeling spread through her whole body.

Holy shit!

FAMILY MATTERS

Dani drew her car into the car park and stopped next to Gia's Fiat. Jerome's sleek car was parked on the other side and Dani felt a little thrill. Quickly checking the time, she got out of her car. It was nine fifteen. She'd made it down in forty-five minutes. Feeling pleased with herself for not getting lost, she stepped around the wall that hid the staff smoking table and bumped into Franco and Enzo, who were having a quick cigarette.

"Morning."

"Morning, you're early," Franco commented as he stubbed out his cigarette.

Dani shrugged and then stepped through the back door and headed into the kitchen. The sweet smell of vanilla wafted through the air. "Morning, Carmen."

"Morning." Carmen grinned at Dani. "Strawberry, fig and goats cheese tart." Carmen gestured to the work surface, which had a number of ingredients on it and was covered in flour.

"Oh crap!" moaned Dani and backed away.

Carmen laughed loudly. "Go get yourself a coffee."

"I will, where's Capo?"

"He's coming in late today. He always does on a Saturday and Sunday, because he works through," explained Carmen.

Dani slipped out the back to ask if Franco or Enzo wanted a coffee.

"You drive a Porsche?" Enzo asked, wide eyed, clearly shocked that a waitress could afford to buy and run a Porsche.

Dani scrunched up her face, embarrassed. "Um, yeah, but I'm selling it."

Franco peered round the wall, looking at the number plate, and shook his head in shock. "It's only a couple of years old."

"I need something more practical," she explained, feeling her face redden, and she hurriedly headed for the back door, wishing she'd taken the bus instead.

She set to work on the coffee machine and started taking note of all the liqueurs as she waited for the coffee to filter through. The dulcet tones of Frank Sinatra could be heard from the kitchen and Dani hummed along to a familiar song. She put the coffees down and took them on a tray into the kitchen.

"Frank?" asked Dani, surprised that the usual Italian opera wasn't on while they all worked in the kitchen.

"Yeah, we thought we'd go more contemporary," sniggered Rico, his round face creased as he grinned. "Don't you like Frank?"

"Love him, Tony Bennet and Dean Martin. My parents always listened to the fifties music," replied Dani. She left the kitchen and headed back to the bar area, slid onto a stool and lifted up a wine list. She opened it up and continued to familiarise herself with the extensive wines and drinks La Casa d'Italia had to offer. The sound of footsteps alerted her to the back of the restaurant and she held her breath in anticipation of seeing Jerome.

Peter strode through the door and Dani smiled tightly at him, trying hard not to reveal her disappointment. She shook her head slightly. This really had to stop, she thought to herself.

"Morning, Dani, you're in early." Peter was next to her by now and she noted he had a hard black book in his hand.

"Morning, Chef. Yes, I wanted to get to know the route down so..." she shrugged. "Shall I make you a coffee?"

"Sure, I'd love one. I'm trying to see how we can fit in all the bookings tonight. It's going to be a manic evening." He perched himself on a stool and opened up the book as Dani set to work on his espresso. "Thankfully, everyone's in tonight," he mumbled, almost to himself.

"I can help if you like." Dani placed Peter's coffee down and then came to have a look at the bookings. He moved the book towards her and let her look down the list.

Jerome quickly dried himself with a towel, then dressed in the suit that hung on the back of the door. He slipped on his boots and walked down to Peter's office to let him know that Liz and the kids would be down around two thirty. He pushed open the door, only to find the office empty. He lowered his brow and just as he was about to leave, his eye caught the image of Dani sitting at the bar on one of the monitors. She was talking with Peter. He edged closer and leaned onto the desk, to get a better look. They seemed to be discussing the bookings for tonight. Jerome watched on as Dani pointed to parts of the restaurant and gestured enthusiastically, making Peter grin then laugh at some comment she made. He checked the time. Ten to ten. She was early again.

As he continued to observe their interaction, he noted that she'd put her hair into a plait. He smiled to himself. All the other female staff just put their hair into a ponytail, but in each of the three days Dani had been coming, she'd had a different look. The thought pleased him. Attention to detail, he thought wistfully. Jerome stood and watched, secure in the knowledge no one was aware. Between them, they managed to accommodate the bookings. Peter beamed at her and then patted her arm. Jerome looked at the clock again. It was five past ten. His attention was directed to the monitor showing the car park. Capo was pulling up. Next to his mother's car he noticed a silver Porsche. He leaned closer. *So Dani had driven in today* – he smiled at the thought. In the far corner of his mind, it pleased him that she wouldn't be getting a ride home from Kuch. He frowned to himself. That really wasn't any of his business. Jerome straightened and headed back to his office.

Sitting down at his desk, he picked up the sealed envelope that he'd been avoiding since yesterday. He picked up his letter opener and sliced through the seal, then pulled out the weighty document and started to read it.

Dani sat in her usual place between Rosa and Kuch for lunch. The seat opposite her was vacant and she felt disappointed for the second time that morning. Her eyes drifted over to Gia, who was elegantly cutting through her ravioli. She really was an extraordinary good-looking woman, thought Dani. Gia was listening intently to Peter as he spoke and she was nodding as he continued. Her eyes lifted to Dani and she smiled at her. Dani reciprocated nervously, embarrassed she'd been caught out staring.

"I hear you drove down." Kuch's comment jolted her.

"Yes."

"Porsche? Are you some rich kid who's just working for fun, then?"

Dani laughed. "Hardly. I'm selling it. It's great but... well, it wasn't my choice."

"The ex?"

Dani nodded tightly. Kuch narrowed his eyes at her.

"You know, it gets better – with time, I mean. He must have been bad news if you moved two hundred miles away."

Dani nodded again and looked down at her half-eaten ravioli.

"Apart from Capo, Chef and Jerome, we're all single here, so you're not alone. Either we are divorced or still looking. It's the nature of the business. Unsociable crappy hours don't help. Not many people put up with that or even understand the buzz."

Dani looked back up at him. "When I was in college, the very first lecture we had, the lecturer's opening speech pretty much said that. That this business had the highest divorce rate and if you didn't love it, the unsociable hours and long shifts would eventually get to you. I love the rush, though."

"Me too. People go to restaurants for happy occasions, birthdays, to meet up with friends, on dates. That rubs off on you. So if you're having a shitty time but you're surrounded by people who are out to have a good time, it lifts you up."

"You're right," agreed Dani as she picked up her fork and knife again.

"You went to college, then? Smart *and* pretty." Kuch raised his eyebrows and Rosa huffed at him. Nicole, who was sitting opposite him, arched an eyebrow and he winked back at her.

Shrugging, Dani grinned at the compliment. "I never finished my course."

"Oh." Kuch's brow creased.

"I never seemed to be able to get round to it," she offered as an explanation.

"The ex?" Rosa asked softly and Dani nodded.

"Screw the ex. Stick with us and you'll wonder what you ever saw in him." Kuch grinned at her and gently squeezed her shoulders.

"So, you're single too, then?" Dani asked.

Kuch twisted his mouth and rocked his head from side to side, indicating that he wasn't. "Well, not exactly. Let's just say it's complicated."

Dani snorted, "Isn't it always? She's not married is she?"

"No, but she may as well be," he sighed. "Like I said, complicated," he added cryptically.

Rosa laughed. "Tell me about it. I've been divorced for eight years and it's still complicated." She shook her head.

By eleven thirty, all the staff were getting the restaurant ready. Gia came up to Dani as she was folding the napkins. "Daniella." Her thick accent extenuated every letter, making Dani smile.

"Yes, Gia?"

"Peter tells me you helped him out this morning with the reservations and that you were here early."

"Um, yes. I came in early because I was unsure of the route. I didn't want to be late. The traffic from Harewood can be very busy," Dani explained, unsure of where the conversation was going.

"Ah yes, you come in from Harewood? That *is* far." Gia's huge eyes widened in surprise, then a thought seemed to pass through her mind but she dismissed it. "We used to live not far from there, before we bought this place. It's a lovely area."

"It is," agreed Dani.

"Well, Peter was very grateful for your input today. Are you staying on this afternoon?"

"I'm not sure. Chef hasn't told me but I can do if needed. I was going to buy myself some new boots in the couple of hours off, but it's nothing important."

"I'll ask him. I think we might need more staff today."

"Sure. It's no problem. To be honest, I'd prefer to work. It keeps me occupied."

"Boots? You should go to Harvey Nichols."

"Oh, I will. Thanks, I really don't know the shops in Leeds."

Gia smirked and nodded, then gracefully walked towards the front desk where Peter was resetting the till.

Jerome put down the document and rubbed his eyes with his thumb and forefinger. He had to hand it to Cosimo. He hadn't left anything out and he had been meticulous in handling all his assets. Jerome knew he was lucky to have such a diligent accountant and a mother who was stubborn. He picked up his phone and dialled Cosimo's number.

"Jerome. How are you?" Cosimo's voice was soothing as he spoke.

"Hey, Cos, I'm fine. I managed to read through everything."

"I see. You're pretty well covered. She can't get her hands on anything except the house. All three businesses are not in your name." He paused, waiting for some comment but it never came. "Thankfully, Mama kept La Casa in her name, while Sky and Level One are part of the Ferretti Leisure Group too, of which Mama is the CEO. The only thing she can claim from you is a percentage of your earnings. That, I'm afraid, we can't do anything about. We could reduce them but if she decides to get her lawyers to dig, we'll have to let them know when the decrease was implemented. It'll look bad, so I wouldn't advise it." He paused again, hoping Jerome would speak. Cosimo knew this was hard for Jerome. After a few seconds, he continued.

"You'll need to get Seni to draft up a settlement. That's if you decide to go forward."

"I'm not sure what I want to do yet, Cos," sighed Jerome. "I'm not ready for Seni to know anything either. With all due respect, Cos, it's bad enough you know."

"I'm sorry Jerome, I truly am. But you have to be smart. You're lucky Mama insisted that everything stayed in her name."

Jerome's mind drifted to the conversation they'd had with their mother ten years ago. He had to hand it to Gia – she knew a thing or two.

"I've had our lawyers redraft my will." Gia was standing in her sumptuous living room by her Italian marble fireplace. Cosimo, Jerome and Arsenio were slumped on the sofas, but this conversation caused all three brothers to immediately sit forward.

"Er, why? Is everything alright?" Cosimo was first to speak.

"Everything's fine, but it's time to put things in order."

All three men physically relaxed.

"I need to protect you all in case of... well, many things, to be perfectly honest." Her eyes darted to Jerome and he tensed.

Gia took a deep breath. "The A and C Ferretti Chartered Accountant Company will go to Cosimo. As you both know, he has taken Papa's modest company and built it up to be one of the largest in northern England." Both Jerome and Arsenio smiled at Cosimo as he shifted awkwardly in his seat. "I have asked our lawyers to transfer the company from me to Cosimo from now."

"Why?" interrupted Cosimo.

"It's your company. I kept it on my name to protect you."

"Protect me?"

"Well, I wasn't sure about your personal life. I didn't know if... well, you won't be getting married, will you? So..." Cosimo smirked as Gia struggled to be tactful.

Jerome's eyes narrowed as it began to dawn on him why this meeting had been called.

"No, Mama, marriage isn't in my future," Cosimo replied softly and Arsenio sniggered, causing Gia to frown at him.

"Arsenio's share of his inheritance is still in a trust fund until he's ready to branch out on his own. This will remain in my name until you decide what to do with it. It is willed to you in the event of my death, should that happen before."

Arsenio stared at Gia wide eyed. "I have my own trust fund?" he'd been twelve years old when his father died and Gia had never revealed to him the extent of his inheritance. It had grown considerably over the last ten years.

"Yes, you have. When Papa died, he left everything to me. I then took fifty percent of it and split it into three for each of you. Cosimo used his share to expand the accountancy business. I used Jerome's to set up La Casa, and yours was put in a trust fund for when you decided which direction you wanted to go in."

Arsenio slumped back, stunned, and Cosimo smiled wryly at him.

"As for La Casa, we bought the building using the money from selling our home and then to set up the restaurant and apartments, Jerome's inheritance was used. As you all know, the restaurant has become very profitable and has paid back its original set up costs plus, a few times over." Gia smiled tightly at Jerome as he regarded her, his posture tense.

"I have managed to recover the money I used from the sale of the house, so effectively, La Casa is solely Jerome's." Jerome relaxed slightly. "However, it will remain in my name and it will be willed to you when I die." Jerome opened his mouth to speak, but Gia interrupted him before he could: "In the light of your recent... relationship."

"Liz is going to be my wife, Mama." Jerome clenched his teeth as he spoke.

"Yes, well, because of that, I would prefer, for the moment, to keep everything in my name. You will have full control, as you do now. There's no question that La Casa is a success because of you, there is no doubt about that at all. I just... well, what you've built, what you've achieved, *you* did that through hard work. I never want that to be taken away from you." Her eyes darted to Cosimo, then back to Jerome.

Jerome rested slowly back into the sofa, understanding perfectly where this was coming from. His relationship with Liz and her sudden pregnancy had caused a rift between him and his mother. Gia hadn't liked Liz from the start, but once his girlfriend had fallen pregnant, Gia had resigned herself to the fact that she was going to be in their lives, one way or another. Liz may have tricked her way into their family, but she wasn't going to lay claim to whatever her son had built up until now.

"It's for your own protection, Jerome." She repeated the words, knowing he would undoubtedly want to reopen this discussion at a later date.

This conversation wasn't over, thought Jerome as he took a deep breath and slumped back deeper into the sofa.

Both Level One and Sky became part of the Ferretti Leisure Group, which Gia remained CEO of. Jerome had been given the title of General Manager, purely as a formality, though he was, in fact, the acting CEO.

Over the ten years, he'd had various arguments with Gia about taking control officially of the company but she'd never budged. She gave him full power of attorney to do whatever he saw fit and never questioned his decisions, but she was never going to give him the company – not while he was still married to Liz.

In the last year and especially the last few weeks, Jerome had realised Gia's original perception of his marriage to Liz had been correct. She had known they'd have problems. If he went ahead with a divorce, he knew Liz would be ruthless, even if she was the one at fault. The idea of splitting up his family home weighed heavy on his tense shoulders. His eyes focused on the photos of Alessandro and Kara. He'd needed legal advice, as well as financial and he knew that Arsenio was the only one who could help him. He didn't want to lose his children, but he was finding it increasingly difficult to go home to a wife that had obviously used him for his assets and whom he couldn't trust anymore. His home wasn't the sanctuary it was supposed to be. In fact, it was proving to be the opposite. He felt tortured and miserable there.

"Thanks for putting this together, Cos. I need to do some thinking before... well, I need to see where Liz is in this. If she wants us to be over, then so be it. If the decision is down to me..." He stopped and rubbed his face. "I'll let you know, okay? But this is between me and you for now."

"Of course. I would never say anything," Cosimo replied softly.

"I know." Jerome slipped the document into the envelope and put it into his desk drawer, eager to change the subject. "The kids will be down around two thirty today, if you want to come down."

"I'd love to see them. Like I said, I've missed them." Cosimo lavished all his natural paternal affection onto Alessandro and Kara. Jerome knew that his life had come with a great personal sacrifice – missing out on being a parent was one part of that.

Cosimo very much kept his personal life exactly that: personal. He had a number of friends but he'd never brought any of his partners to meet his family. Jerome wondered whether he might be celibate and had asked him a few years ago.

"No, Jerome, I'm not. I just don't want to make anyone uncomfortable. I'm not sure how well Mama and Seni would be able to handle seeing me with anyone and to be honest, I'd prefer to have that part of my life separate to the rest."

"Don't your partners mind?"

Cosimo shrugged. "It's the only way for me, so if they don't like it..."

Jerome nodded. Cosimo had always been a private man. There was a six-year age gap between the two brothers, and that and Cosimo's homosexuality evoked a distance in their filiation. It was the death of their father that caused the dynamics of their relationship change. Cosimo had taken his role as the oldest brother seriously after Alessandro senior died. He was in his early twenties and Gia found it gravely difficult to overcome the shock of losing her husband so suddenly. She suffered from depression, and Cosimo was left to guide and comfort his two younger teenage brothers. As a result, both Jerome and Arsenio became very close to Cosimo, their grief bonding them.

Their father's death led Cosimo to recognise that regardless of how uncomfortable his family felt about his homosexuality, they needed and loved him. So rather than pull away from them, he became very present in their lives and over time, they accepted his identity.

Saturday lunch was always busy at La Casa d'Italia. The difference to the week days was the change in clientele. They were mainly shoppers and families, which made a welcome change. The noise level was notably louder and the atmosphere more relaxed.

Dani had been given a larger section today and had volunteered to stay on for the afternoon. Most of her section was on dessert, so she started to reset the tables. Gia had gone into the kitchen and Peter was talking to a large party at the back of the restaurant. As Dani replenished her cutlery, her attention was directed to the front door. A statuesque blonde had walked in with two children, a boy around eight years old and a younger girl. They were all immaculately dressed. Behind them stood another woman with curly red hair, which was piled on top of her head. Dani looked around for Peter, who had his back to the entrance and hadn't seen them enter. The rest of the staff were busy. Dani dropped what she was doing and walked over to the front desk.

"Good afternoon. May I help you?" asked Dani smiling at the striking woman. She was pale and had ice blue eyes that stared at Dani. Her expression was that of distaste and Dani tried hard not to shrivel under her gaze.

"You're new." The icy blonde's eyes moved away from Dani as she looked into the restaurant, effectively dismissing Dani.

"Yes. I'm sorry, would you like a table?" Dani answered politely. The blonde momentarily smirked at her and then, ignoring her completely, walked towards the rear of the restaurant. The children followed her and the redhead smiled apologetically. Dani stared after them wide eyed and was about to say something, when Gia came out from the kitchen and upon seeing the children, her face instantly lit up.

"Nonna!" the two children cried and ran past their mother and towards Gia, who flung her arms around the children, showering them with kisses.

Dani swallowed hard as it began to dawn on her that the rude blonde was Jerome's wife. She took a deep breath, relieved she hadn't made a total fool of herself. She studied the blonde as she slowly approached Gia. She was tall and in addition to her height, she wore four inch high black ankle boots, making her tower over Gia. She'd slipped off her coat to reveal a smock-styled grey dress that only a slim tall woman could pull off and manage not to look pregnant. Her hair was straight and long, falling loosely down her back. Dani's heart sunk. She was stunning and the fact that all the male customers had stopped to stare at her confirmed that.

Gia straightened after hugging and kissing her grandchildren, still holding them close to her as she greeted Liz cordially. Gia momentarily released the children to shake her hand and give her a rather lukewarm peck on the cheek. Liz stiffly shook her hand and reciprocated the kiss but it was obvious that there was no warmth between the two women.

Dani moved back to her station and cleared a table that had left, and headed over to the kitchen. The redhead was sitting at the bar chatting with Kuch and he pulled a face at her as she caught his eye. Dani smiled back at him and took the plates into the kitchen. Peter approached her as she came back out.

"Dani, run up to Jerome's office and tell him Liz is here, will you?" he asked tightly. Dani nodded and her eyes flitted to where Gia was settling them onto a table in her section. *Oh! So he was here, then?* she thought, realising he hadn't come down at all. At that moment, Dani could not think of anything worse than serving their table.

Dani moved quickly to the back entrance and ran up the flight of stairs two by two, leading to the offices. She flung open the door, only to be faced with Jerome walking from his office down towards her. Dani stopped in her tracks as her heart skipped a beat at the sight of him, flawless in his black three piece suit. His face was set hard but his expression changed when he saw Dani.

"Er, your wife is here... well I mean your family. They just arrived," Dani blurted out.

"Yes. I know. Thank you."

Oh!

He stifled a smirk and Dani turned back around and headed back down the stairs, feeling flustered. She really wished she hadn't volunteered to stay on this afternoon. The morning had gone so well. Now she'd have to serve Jerome and his frosty wife. She could hear Jerome walking behind her and she skipped quickly down the stairs.

"How was lunch today?" his voice was soft as he caught up with her.

"Um, busy."

"Are you staying on this afternoon?" he turned to look at her as he spoke.

Dani smiled tightly and nodded, "Yes."

"Good."

Good? Why good? "Thank you for my tart." Her voice was low as they approached the door.

Jerome put his hand on the door handle and turned to look at her. "It didn't seem fair that I ate the most of it last time. I hope you enjoyed it." His eyes burned into hers and Dani swallowed nervously, transfixed. *Christ he was just so...*

"Yummy," muttered Dani. *Crap! She'd said that out loud. Jesus, get a grip.* "Um, it was really yummy. Er, thanks."

Jerome frowned a little before he opened the door to the restaurant and motioned for her to go through.

"Thanks," mumbled Dani as she entered the restaurant and headed straight to her station, her eyes focusing on anything other than the Ferretti family. Jerome walked steadily over to the table and both children ran excitedly over towards him. Dani turned and her heart melted at the exchange between the three of them. His whole demeanour softened as they clung to him. He'd lifted up his daughter and was holding his son's hand as he took them back to the table. Liz was texting on her phone at the table, indifferent to anyone and anything.

Dani noticed that Peter had gone over to speak to her and she momentarily stopped what she was doing to begrudgingly accept his hand. Gia was fussing over her grandchildren, clearly enjoying every moment, when the front door opened. Cosimo and Arsenio entered the restaurant, and the over-excited children ran towards them both, nearly knocking the packages their uncles were carrying out of their grasp.

The whole scene was a joy to watch. Jerome's stature had relaxed and his normally broody face had softened as he watched the interaction between his brothers and children. Gia glowed more than normal, taking a break to enjoy some quality time with her family. Only Liz sat quietly as the Ferrettis chatted animatedly. All of them watched the children open up the presents their uncles had bought them.

It took fifteen minutes for them all to calm down. Peter placed their drink orders and Kuch set them on a tray ready for Dani to take over.

"Let me introduce you to Nina. She's the Ferretti's nanny."

"Hi, pleased to meet you. Kuch tells me you just started this week." Nina extended her hand for Dani to shake as she smiled warmly.

"Hi, yes."

"Oh, you'll love it here. The Ferrettis are great people."

"Yeah, they are. How long have you worked for them?" agreed Dani.

"Eight years."

Dani's eyes widened. "Wow."

"Yes, Jerome's great and the kids are angels," Nina said with a wide smile.

Dani waited for a comment about Liz but it never came, so she took the drinks to the table. Gia, thankfully, helped her. She felt decidedly flustered as the Ferretti family members that she hadn't met stared up at her. She wanted to make a good impression.

"Let me introduce you to Liz, Dani. She's Jerome's wife." Gia smiled at Dani.

Dani extended her hand to Liz. "Pleased to meet you Mrs Ferretti. Sorry about earlier." Liz extended her pale hand to Dani and weakly smiled at her whilst giving a slight nod. Then releasing her hand quickly, she diverted her attention back to her phone. Dani flushed a little at the obvious brush off. *Great, she'd obviously offended her,* thought Dani, but before she could say any more, her thoughts were interrupted by Cosimo, who had risen from his seat.

"Hello, Dani. I'm Cosimo. I hear you are newest member here." He had his hand extended and Dani shook it, pleased to be distracted. He smiled kindly at her and Dani began to feel less awkward.

"Pleased to meet you. Yes, I've been here just a couple of days."

"Hello. I'm Arsenio, the younger good-looking brother."

Cosimo smirked and shook his head, mildly exasperated. Dani turned to where the voice came from. Arsenio was standing behind her, his eyes twinkling mischievously. He extended his hand and Dani reached for it. "Hello, pleased to meet you."

Arsenio lifted her hand to his mouth and kiss it, causing Dani to redden, and she heard a huff from Cosimo.

"Don't scare off the new staff, Seni," Cosimo chastised in good humour.

Arsenio released her hand and winked at her. "I don't think she scares that easily, do you?"

Dani stifled a grin. "No, I don't." Then she backed away from the table and went to her station.

Jerome was sitting next to Liz in an attempt to show his family that they were fine, but it was obvious from their body language that they were anything but. Liz was facing away from him and Jerome was sitting with his arms crossed with a tight smile on his face.

Gia ordered food for everyone and before long they were all eating. Nina sat at the bar and ate while she chatted comfortably with Kuch. He'd stayed on this afternoon too, along with Pino and Richard. The restaurant remained busy and thankfully Dani wasn't only focused on the Ferretti table.

"Aren't you hungry?" asked Gia as she looked at Liz's untouched food.

"It's a little too rich for me," Liz replied coolly.

"Shall I ask Capo to make you something else?" Gia pressed.

"No really, I'm fine." Liz picked up her mineral water and sipped it. Her phone vibrated and she looked at who was calling, "Excuse me, I need to take this." She rose from the table and to Dani's surprise, Jerome, Cosimo and Arsenio also rose from their seats as she got up. Liz smiled tightly at them and headed to the back of the restaurant to take her call.

"Is she ill?" asked Gia.

Jerome shook his head. "No, she's just watching her weight. She's talking to her agent about a job and..."

Gia took a deep breath and interrupted, her agitation obvious. "She's far too thin and surely she's too old to start modelling again."

"Mama please," Jerome mumbled. "She really wants this, so don't make it harder for me." He clenched his teeth as he spoke and Gia sat back in her chair. Jerome's eyes kept focusing on Liz as she talked. She laughed softly to whoever was on the other end of the phone.

Jerome was trying hard not to show his increasing agitation. This was supposed to be their family time together and she had spent the best part of it either texting or talking on the phone. His mood had not gone undetected by Cosimo and he did his best to keep the conversation flowing at the table so that neither Gia nor Arsenio would notice.

Dani cleared their table and Gia asked her to get some chocolate and amaretto cake for the children, and espressos for the rest of them. Liz paced up and down and then finished her phone call. She walked back to the table and sat down. Jerome turned to look at her as she settled in her seat, indicating he wanted to know who the phone call was from.

"It was Graham, my agent. He's trying to get me to do a show in Manchester," she explained, she looked smugly at Jerome and he took in a deep breath.

"Well that's great news," he answered softly and Liz smiled at him. He leaned in and kissed her quickly on the cheek and her eyes darted to him. "When will you know?"

"By next week. The show will be just after New year." Liz sat back in her chair and for the first time since she'd arrived, she genuinely smiled.

9

NEW BOOTS

"That smells wonderful," Chloe yawned as she slumped into the chair by the kitchen table. She'd found Dani in the kitchen, whipping up some chocolate frosting for one large and one small chocolate cake that were on the cooling rack.

"Sorry, did I wake you?"

Chloe shook her head.

"There's coffee ready."

"Oh thanks, I need it. Who's the cake for?" Chloe moved over to the coffee machine and poured a cup.

"Carmen. She's been giving me desserts every day and it's her birthday today. I thought I'd bake her a birthday cake, as a thank you."

"Oh, that's nice of you. What time did you get up?" yawned Chloe.

"Six."

"Jesus, you'll wear yourself out."

"I love it there. Everyone's really nice."

Chloe smiled and took a sip from her coffee, "I'm glad. Need a hand with the frosting?"

"I'm fine. I made a small cake for you, too. I thought the kids might want some."

Chloe grinned, dipped her finger in the frosting and then licked it off. "Delicious."

Dani pulled into the car park at nine forty-five. The Sunday morning traffic had been very light and she'd made it down in less than thirty minutes. Her heart sank a little when she realised Jerome's car wasn't there. Carefully, she lifted out the cake and made her way into the restaurant.

Jamie was busy working over some huge pans when she walked in.

"Wow! You made that?" Jamie whispered, impressed.

Dani nodded. "Is she here?"

"She just popped into the store room. Let me put it in the fridge at the back and we can bring it out at lunch. She'll be thrilled," he grinned. Franco and Enzo came over to inspect.

"You realise you'll have to make one for everyone's birthday now," Rico chipped in as he leaned closer for a look. Dani had decorated it with chocolate fudge frosting and piped 'Happy Birthday Carmen' on it.

Dani shrugged, indicating she was happy to make cakes for all the staff, as Jamie took it quickly away.

"I'm off to get changed and grab a coffee before lunch."

By ten thirty, all the staff were in the dining room. Lunch was veal, with a rather rich mushroom sauce. Dani sliced into it and relished the flavour as it melted in her mouth.

"This is wonderful," she muttered to herself. Rosa giggled.

"How you aren't fat, I don't know. I've never seen anyone eat so much and stay so slim."

"I'm starting my fitness video tomorrow. Carmen has totally ruined me these past few days."

Dani glanced over at the empty chair opposite her. *Stop it!* She scolded herself. But she just wanted a glimpse of him. Tomorrow she'd be off and it would be Tuesday before she saw him again.

Dani was dragged out of her daydream by the doors opening and the sound of children running. Everyone turned to see who had come in the door. Gia stood up instantly as her grandchildren ran to her. Dani took a deep breath and turned to see Jerome sauntering into the dining room, his handsome broody face making Dani catch her breath.

Within seconds, the staff made room for his unexpected visit and both Alessandro and Kara settled with their father to enjoy lunch. Dani smirked to herself, wondering whether her constant wishing had made him appear. She shook her head and inwardly laughed at her ridiculous thought. She was just glad he'd come, and the fact Liz wasn't with him was a bonus.

Jerome sat with Kara on his knee as Capo and Chef cleared away their plates and put down fresh ones for the unexpected guests. Dani found it hard to keep from looking at Jerome as he spoke quietly to Chef. The staff finished off, then Jamie went over to the dumbwaiter. He fumbled with a lighter, then pulled out the cake Dani had made and walked over to where Carmen was sitting. As soon as the rest of the staff saw the cake with its candles lit, they all began to sing a rendition of Happy Birthday. Carmen stared dumbfounded as Jamie placed the large cake in front of her and she blushed at all the attention, then he whispered something in her ear.

Blowing out the candles, she looked around the table and her eyes locked on Dani and she mouthed "Thank you." Dani shook her head, indicating it was nothing. Gia caught Dani's eye and cocked her head to one side, then gestured to the cake, asking if she was responsible for it. Dani nodded shyly and Gia's eyebrows shot up, clearly impressed. Silvanna did the honours of cutting up and serving the cake.

Matteo took a mouthful and savoured it. "Jamie, this cake is –" Before he could finish, Gia stopped him and whispered in his ear. Matteo looked shocked at what she'd said and turned to look at Dani. "Dani, you made this?"

"Er yes." Dani blushed as the whole table turned to look at her. "As a thank you for all the desserts Carmen's been letting me sample." Dani tried to keep her eyes focused on Matteo as she spoke.

"Well it's... how did you put it?" he waved his fork in the air as he tried to recall Dani's words she'd used to describe his cannoli. "Divine? That's right, isn't it?" he beamed. There was a rumble of everyone's agreement around the table, and Dani felt herself heat up even more.

"Thanks, Capo," she muttered.

Kuch turned to her as he chewed, then swallowed. "Wow, smart, pretty and can bake. Your ex was a fucking idiot!"

Dani grinned at him as he chuckled and bumped her shoulder. All the while, Dani avoided looking across the table as she felt Jerome's steely blue eyes staring into her.

"Well she's set a precedent now, she'll have to make everyone a cake for their birthday." Rosa popped the last piece in her mouth and stood up to start clearing the plates. Everyone was getting up to wish Carmen a happy birthday as they loaded the dumbwaiter with the dirty plates.

"I don't have a problem. I love baking. I'll need to know when everyone's birthdays are."

"Mine falls on a Monday. Does that mean I won't get one?" pouted Rosa.

"Don't worry. I'll make it for you on the Sunday," Dani reassured her.

Carmen came over to Dani and hugged her. "Thanks for that, Dani. A great surprise. It was really sweet of you."

"My pleasure."

As Dani turned to leave, she almost fell into Jerome who'd been standing behind her, waiting to wish his a cousin happy birthday. Dani flushed again as he steadied her, putting his hands on her arms. "Sorry," she muttered as he let her go.

"No problem." He stepped to the side, hugged Carmen and kissed her affectionately, his big body dwarfing her tiny frame, "*Buon compleanno.*"

"*Grazie.*"

Dani watched them for a moment. Carmen caught her gaze and smiled. "So you need to make a cake for Jerome next. It's his birthday on the fourteenth." Dani's eyes broadened as she swallowed. *Oh crap...*

Jerome turned to look at her, his mouth twitched seeing her reaction.

"He turns thirty-four."

"Oh, sure. Friday then, right?" Dani tried to recover her composure, but it was hard when Jerome just stood staring at her as he cocked his head to the side.

"I'm looking forward to it," he drawled with a grin.

Determined not to make herself look totally thunderstruck, Dani straightened herself and stared back at him. "A chocolate cake, or would you prefer something else?"

The question knocked him off guard for a split second. He furrowed his brow, then half-squinted as he thought about the question. Then, in a low voice, he answered, "Surprise me." His eyes stared at her in that intense way that made her heart race.

Dani took a deep breath, "I will." Then she turned to leave, but not before she saw his eyes lose their composure.

Sunday lunch was extremely busy and before Dani realised, it was three o'clock. She'd decided to take her couple of hours off and venture into town, finally getting to treat herself to some new boots. She'd earned it, after a week of going cold turkey without a cigarette. She was pleased her cravings were starting to subside. A lot of that was to do with the change of environment and her constant supply of desserts.

Rosa drew her a map to guide her to the town centre and pinpointed the major department stores. It took Dani less than ten minutes to walk into town. It was cold, and thankfully, she'd changed into her black leggings, biker jacket and boots. Her jacket blocked the wind but her ears were still vulnerable and ached from the frosty air. *She should have worn her hat*, she thought to herself. It didn't help that her hair was pulled into a messy off-side bun.

She entered the shoe department of Harvey Nichols and sighed at the huge array of footwear. Footwear was too tame a word to describe the selection her eyes gazed over. They were like works of art. Dani moved around the displays, eyeing the beautiful designs. She sauntered over to where she spied some black, high ankle boots. There were a number to choose from, each more fabulous than the others. Her eyes fell on a pair that looked familiar and she picked them up. She chuntered to herself when she saw the price. They were the same ankle boots Liz had been wearing. *A little out of my price range*, thought Dani, as she returned them to the display. Dani moved along and picked up a black ankle boot with a gold buckle. They were five inches high with a small platform.

"Can I help you?" The voice of the assistant jolted Dani.

"Um, yes. I need a size four."

The assistant looked at the boot, "I think that is a size four. It's the last one." The assistant took the boot from Dani's hand to check, then she nodded. "Yes, and I think it's reduced. Shall I bring you the other one to try them?"

"Please."

Dani settled on a seat and removed her boots, then slipped on the new boot. The assistant came over with the box that housed its pair and for the first time Dani noticed the motif. The black box had a large Q with Mc inside. Dani's heart sunk. She couldn't afford Alexander McQueen! The assistant handed her the second boot to try and Dani reluctantly put it on. She stood up and looked down at her feet.

"They're a fabulous design. You can wear them with everything." The assistant stood back to admire them.

"Yes, they are. How much are they?" Dani cringed.

"They were eight hundred and forty-five but they've been reduced to four hundred and twenty. They're the last pair."

"Still out of my price range, but they are so lovely," Dani sighed, then thought to herself, *screw it* – if she sold her car next week, she'd be flush. "I'll take them. Like you said, I can wear them with everything. They even make my leggings look good!" chuckled Dani and the assistant grinned in agreement.

Jerome sat in his office, staring out of the window. Alessandro and Kara had gone into his mother's flat above the restaurant and were no doubt being spoilt rotten. At least one good thing had come out of his and Liz's argument this morning: Gia got to spend full and undivided attention on her grandchildren. He looked at the time. It was just past three and the restaurant would be slowing down. He really needed a cigarette. Shrugging on his jacket, he made his way down the stairs and out to the back, then lit up his cigarette. He heard footsteps coming down the corridor and the door flung open.

"Oh there you are!" Peter grinned. "Is Gia in the flat?"

Jerome nodded.

"Nice surprise you coming down on a Sunday."

Jerome huffed as he blew out smoke. Peter was fishing – Jerome usually stayed at home on Sundays so that they could spend time together as a family. Today though, it had started with Liz leaving early to see her agent about the possibility of her new modelling job. Jerome had questioned the need for her to go out on a Sunday, which had consequently escalated into a full-blown argument. Jerome couldn't be sure whether it was a genuine appointment or whether she was using it as an excuse to see Jonathan. It was beginning to eat away at him, all the constant doubt. So rather than staying at home to fester, he came down to La Casa. At least he'd be distracted and in the back of his mind he knew it would annoy Liz too. He knew he was being petty, but she didn't seem to be showing any indication she was trying, or that she even wanted to try and make things work, full stop.

Jerome knew it was going to need a lot of hard work and patience to get through this rather large hiccup in their marriage, but he was getting the feeling it was all one sided. The truth was, he wasn't sure if he wanted it badly enough. He'd wrestled with himself from the moment he'd found out about the affair and he still couldn't grasp how he felt. He was torn between his loyalty to keeping his family together and his true feelings.

Their relationship had never been perfect. They'd had problems from the start, but Jerome had fallen for Liz and was determined to make their relationship work. They'd met on a photo shoot for an advertisement Liz was featured in. Jerome had also been asked to be in it. His friend had suggested he earn a bit of money being an extra in commercials. His good looks earned him an extra part in a coffee shop scene, in which Liz was one of the main characters for a local bank's advertising campaign. While they waited around in makeup and for the scene to be set up, they began to chat to each other. Liz had pretty much spotted Jerome within the group of extras right from the beginning and was trying any way possible to lure him away from the numerous women who were vying for his attention.

She approached him on the pretence that he should consider taking up modelling professionally. Liz managed to get his number so that she could give him some details on a photographer for some headshots.

From that phone call, they had met up and began dating. Liz was totally smitten with Jerome and he equally with her. She lacked confidence then, and gave off a vulnerability that he found endearing. From the start though, Liz found it troublesome that women were constantly throwing themselves at Jerome when he was working. His long hours were hard for her but she didn't want to lose him and after only a few months together, she fell pregnant.

The Ferrettis were sceptical of how long the relationship would last, but begrudgingly accepted Liz. Within the first few months of their hasty marriage, it was obvious that the chances of them lasting were slim. Even moving out of the second flat above the restaurant to a rather grand large residence on the outskirts of Leeds did not help. The arrival of Kara, three years later, revealed the already gaping cracks in their marriage.

Jerome turned to Peter as he stubbed out his cigarette. "Mama was complaining she never sees the kids alone, so I thought I'd surprise her." He couldn't face an inquisition from Peter. His nerves were already raw from the morning's slanging match with Liz. And to be honest, he just didn't want to face it all just yet.

"Well, she's certainly loving it," Peter continued, hoping Jerome would open up. Jerome gave him a weary smile and headed back inside.

By five thirty, Jerome was heading back home. Nina would be back within a couple of hours so he'd be able to leave for Sky around nine o'clock. As he swung his car into the driveway, he noted that Liz's car was there, and his body went through a number of reactions ranging from relief to anxiety. *At least she was home*, he thought. What mood she'd be in and how he was going to respond to her was making him feel anxious. He brought his car to a stop, and the kids got out of the car and headed in through the kitchen.

Liz was pouring herself a glass of wine and she beamed at her children as they came in. "Hey, did you have a nice day?" she directed the question to the children as they hugged her. They quickly told her about going to La Casa and that it was Carmen's birthday. Liz tensed slightly but carried on listening, her cool blue eyes focused on their faces the whole time. They continued to tell her about their time with Gia and Liz maintained her smiley façade. They ran up to their rooms, leaving a taut Jerome leaning against the kitchen counter.

"How did your meeting go?" He tried hard to keep his tone calm.

"Very well, actually. They want me in the fashion show. There's going to be loads of coverage too." Her cool eyes lit up as she found it hard to hide how excited she was.

"That's great news." Jerome straightened and paced slowly up to her. "And it's just after New Year?"

"Yes, they're trying to secure the right venue. One of the hotels is going to host it, I think. And it's not going to be in Manchester now; it'll be here in Leeds. I'm really excited. It'll mean I need to keep in shape over Christmas, though." Jerome knew this was a dig at the over the top festive celebrations the Ferrettis always had. Jerome nodded and smiled at her, genuinely pleased that for once she seemed happy. Their morning spat was seemingly forgotten.

"I need to go and ring Mum and a few of my friends too." She collected up her wine glass, grabbed her handbag and headed upstairs, leaving Jerome staring after her. He looked at the clock. It was almost six thirty. He decided to bath the kids and get them ready for bed before he left. He knew there wasn't a chance Liz would do it once she got on the phone. He shrugged out of his jacket and hung it on the chair, then climbed the stairs. He could hear Liz's excited voice as he passed her room and headed to where his children were.

Liz had placed her glass on the bedside table and pulled out her phone. She redialled the number she'd rung on her way back from her meeting. This time, the phone was switched on and it rang three times before Jonathan answered.

"Babe."

"Hey, great news, I got the job."

"I knew you would. They'd be mad not to take you."

"Finally, I get to do a runway."

"All that training we did in the gym – and out – paid off, then," he sniggered and Liz giggled. "When am I going to see you?"

"I can pass by yours tomorrow."

"Make it in the morning."

"Sure, as soon as I drop the kids off."

"Can't wait. We'll have all day."

Liz squirmed on her bed. "Mmm, sounds perfect. Bye."

Dani placed her new boots in her locker and changed back into her uniform. Rosa and Nicole had made it back.

"What did you buy?" asked Rosa.

"Some ridiculously expensive boots I really can't afford. But the upside is, apparently they go with everything!" Dani chuckled and Rosa laughed.

Nicole grinned at Dani as she brushed through her blonde hair and pulled it through a hair tie. Dani heard her phone beep through an email as she bundled her bag into the locker. Curious to see who would be emailing her on a Sunday afternoon, she fished out her smartphone and opened her email option. She instantly wished she hadn't. The email was titled "Sorry".

Her face drained of colour as she slumped into one of the chairs. Nicole eyed her reflection in the mirror. "Dani? Are you okay?"

Rosa closed her locker door so she could see Dani. "Dani?" Rosa stepped closer as she saw tears spring into Dani's eyes and run down her face. "What is it?"

Clenching her eyes shut, Dani shook her head.

"Hey, come on now." Rosa sat beside her and glanced at her phone. "Is it him? The ex?" Dani nodded. Nicole came over and crouched down as Rosa slipped her arm around Dani's shoulder.

"I'm sorry, I just wasn't expecting it," Dani sniffed. "I've avoided his calls and text messages because I know they'll upset me. But..." she wiped her eyes roughly and Nicole ran to the toilet to get some toilet paper. "He emailed me and it caught me off guard." She took the paper and blew her nose. "Thanks," she muttered.

"What's he say?"

"I only read the first line. But I need to read it. I can't put it off any more."

"Well if you're sure? We'll leave you to it. But if you're not up in ten minutes, I'm coming down."

Dani nodded at Rosa and forced a smile. Then both Nicole and Rosa left the changing rooms, leaving Dani staring down at her phone screen, and she started to read.

Dani

I cannot believe you need to communicate with me via a lawyer. I received the letter outlining your demands with regard to our home. True to Adam's over-zealous efficiency, I presume that the three independent valuations he has attached are accurate. I would never have contested even one!

All I want is to talk to you. I want to explain, but you won't take my calls or answer my texts. I'll do whatever you want, but please pick up your phone and talk to me. I realise you are up in Leeds. If it means I come up in person for you to talk to me, I will, and if you won't, then I'll just come up anyway. I can't accept that after five years together you can write me off so completely.

I'm sorry, so deeply sorry that I hurt you. If I could change that, I would, in a heartbeat, but I can't. I behaved badly but I don't want to lose you. You mean the world to me. We don't need lawyers, we just need to talk. Me and you. Please forgive me and call me.

I love you and I'm miserable without you.

Jez x

Dani sobbed quietly in the still of the changing rooms. She almost felt guilty for putting him through this. He made her feel that way, even via an email, he still managed to control her. The truth was, she missed him too. Her new job had distracted her and a lot of the reason she'd wanted to work as many hours as possible was that it kept her mind occupied. At Chloe's, she had time to think and she just didn't want to. She needed to distance herself from him. It was the only way she'd gain perspective. When she was with Jez, he consumed her totally. She lost sense of who she was and now, being away from him, she realised to what extent he'd managed that.

She knew she'd have to call him, or at least send him a reply. Dani looked again at the email. He'd threatened to come up if she didn't. *Crap!* She'd never be able to handle that. She was in pieces over an email. To see him face to face, that would be almost unbearable. She needed to keep him away from her, as much as possible, until she felt strong enough to face him. Whatever happened, she had to reply, but she couldn't right now. She looked at the time. It was ten to five. She put her phone away and headed to the mirror. Shit! Her eyes were red and her face blotchy. She retrieved her cosmetic bag from her locker and removed her morning's make up and re-applied it.

She checked herself in the mirror as Rosa walked back into the changing room. "You okay?" Rosa asked softly.

Dani nodded. "Do I look like I've been crying?"

"No, not at all," Rosa lied. "Come on, nothing like work to take your mind off everything." Rosa rubbed her arm. "Or food! Capo made us pizza tonight."

Dani grinned. "Pizza will definitely help."

Dani worked around the restaurant quietly and efficiently, keeping herself busy. She was pleasant and professional throughout the evening, but Peter noticed that she was not her usual bubbly self. As Rosa came to the bar, Peter came up to her. "Is Dani alright? She seems a little off."

Rosa's eyes darted to Kuch, then over to Peter. "She just got an email from her ex and it upset her, that's all."

Peter glanced over to where Dani was taking an order and nodded. "Is she coming out with you tonight?"

Rosa's face dropped and she cringed. "I forgot to tell her about our night out."

Kuch pulled a face. "Rosa," he chastised. "We can tell her anyway. She can borrow something of yours or Nicole's to wear."

"You're kidding, right? She's half my size and at least six inches taller!"

Nicole snorted behind Kuch and he smirked, "It doesn't matter, she can wear whatever she has. I think she needs a change of mood."

"You coming too, Chef?" asked Kuch.

Chef twisted his mouth. "Just for a bit." Kuch smiled and nodded.

By eleven o'clock, La Casa had emptied. The kitchen staff were already down in the changing rooms and the restaurant staff were finishing off.

"Come on, come out with us. It'll do you good." Rosa was almost whining.

"I haven't anything to wear and I'm really not good company tonight." Dani scrunched up her nose. Rosa felt bad for her, especially as it was her fault Dani hadn't known.

"You can wear your new boots. You said they go with anything," she coaxed. Dani lips curled a little. "Come on. It'll be fun. Drinking, dancing, flirting…" insisted Rosa.

Dani sighed, "So I'm going out in leggings and a sweatshirt?"

"And fabulous boots, don't forget the boots." They'd made their way into the changing rooms. Carmen was just grabbing her jacket. Dani stared at her in total surprise. Gone were her chef's whites and bandana. Her tiny frame was squeezed into a black halter top and skinny jeans, and she wore sky-high black ankle boots. She'd styled her short blonde hair into dishevelled spikes and her makeup accentuated her blue eyes.

"Wow, Carmen, you look amazing!"

"Thanks." Carmen blushed at the compliment. "You're coming, right?"

Before Dani could answer, Rosa grabbed her elbow. "Yes, we'll see you there." Rosa opened up Dani's locker and looked inside. "Okay, let's see what you've got."

Kuch slouched against the wall by the smoking table as he waited for the girls to get ready. He heard Jerome's car pull up. Within a moment, Jerome was walking around the wall. "Hey Kuch. What are you doing out here?"

"Waiting for the girls to get ready."

"I came to get change from the safe," Jerome explained. "I'll see you there, then."

"Sure," Kuch nodded and Jerome strode in through the back door, almost bumping into Nicole coming out.

"Ready?" Kuch straightened up expectantly.

"Not quite. Have you got another shirt, apart from the one you're wearing?"

Kuch creased his brow and looked down at his apple green shirt. "Um, no. I've a couple of tops though. Don't you like it?"

"I love it, just Dani's nothing to wear and I've nothing spare and Rosa's things don't fit her – Dani's too tall. I thought she could wear your shirt over her leggings."

"Oh. Um, okay." Kuch stubbed out his cigarette and Nicole grabbed his face and kissed him hard on the lips. Kuch wrapped his arms around her and kissed her back, and for a moment, they forgot where they were. The sound of Jerome's footsteps alerted them and Nicole pulled away, stifling a grin. Within a few seconds Jerome came out carrying a large bag.

"Still waiting?" Jerome asked.

"Yeah, women, eh?"

Jerome grinned and shook his head as he disappeared around the wall.

"That was close," muttered Kuch.

"We're gonna have to tell everyone sooner or later." Nicole picked up his hand and toyed with it.

"Yeah, but I don't fancy your cousins' inquisition. They're gonna freak and I really just want to enjoy what we have without the drama."

Nicole kissed him quickly on the lips. "I know, you're right. Come on, go change and give me your shirt."

"There, you see? It looks perfect," Rosa beamed.

"The boots are fabulous," added Nicole.

"Yeah. One of the best feelings in the world is wearing new shoes. That and slipping into clean sheets," sighed Dani.

"I can think of a few more," sniggered Rosa. Dani and Nicole laughed.

Dani looked at herself in the mirror. Kuch's shirt was secured with a gold chain belt Nicole had and was open to the waist. Dani wore a black vest she'd worn under her sweatshirt, that matched the black embroidery down the front of the shirt. Her leggings and, of course, her new boots, completed her look.

"Come on. It's almost midnight."

Dani grinned. She had to admit she didn't look bad. The smoky eye makeup helped. Dani hugged Rosa and then Nicole to express her thanks, glad they'd cajoled her into going out. After the day's events, it was exactly what she needed. A chance to forget – even if it was just for a little while.

10

SKY HIGH

The elevator doors opened out onto the fourteenth floor and they were immediately greeted by two men, both immaculately dressed in black suits, standing in the reception area. Two women dressed in smart black trousers and backless halter neck tops stood behind an Italian marble front desk, which matched the rest of the foyer.

"Hey, Kuch, how you doing?" one of the men moved forward and shook Kuch's hand.

"Great, man. glad it's Sunday." Kuch shook the other man's hand. The women acknowledged Rosa and Nicole warmly.

"They're all in there waiting – your usual table."

"Thanks guys, see you later."

The suited man who'd spoken to them opened up the heavy double door and Dani followed Kuch, Nicole and Rosa in.

Dani stood for a second, taking in her surroundings, her senses spiked. The sound of the music pounded out its intoxicating beat and the lights were an array of ultra violet blues. Dani could feel the music vibrating through her whole body, but that wasn't what had her almost dumbstruck. The club was huge, filling the top two floors of a fourteen story office block in the town centre. It was set out on many levels and was predominantly white, which showcased the lighting perfectly. The walls and the ceiling, predominantly made of glass, unveiled a picturesque panorama of the city. Dani stared up – the sky was in full view, giving the illusion it was open air. Definitely living up to the name, she thought.

Kuch made his way through the mass of people, to where the rest of his colleagues were already seated on sumptuous white leather couches. Most of them had made it. As Dani took in her surroundings, Kuch caught her expression and grinned. He leaned in to speak to her.

"Stick with us and you'll wonder what you ever saw in that asshole. We're gonna change your life." He planted a smacking kiss on her cheek and Dani screwed her face up, embarrassed. "Come on, what you drinking?"

"What are you having?"

"I don't drink. Well, rarely."

"You're kidding? A barman who doesn't drink?" Dani couldn't keep the surprise out of her voice.

"Yeah I know. Hey, I just don't need it. I'm high on life – can't you tell?" he joked, gesturing to himself with a sweep of his hand.

Dani smiled widely. He was really trying to distract her from any troubled thoughts. She realised he was obviously in on the 'getting Dani to forget the ex' scheme. "I'll have a tequila, straight – gold if they have it."

Kuch nodded and placed the order with the waitress who was standing near him, then Dani had a thought and she clasped Kuch's arm. "Shit, I'm driving. I'd better not."

"I'll take you home. Leave your car at La Casa and pick it up tomorrow."

Dani twisted her mouth as she contemplated the idea.

"Lighten up. Let your hair down. Come on," he coaxed and Dani smirked as he winked at her, then she nodded.

Jerome stood looking down from one of the private bars. He had a bird's-eye view of the club and was scanning the area when he spotted Kuch, Nicole, Rosa and Dani approach the staff table. He leaned forward, resting his forearms on the glass and chrome railing, narrowing his eyes as he tried to focus. The hairs on the back of his neck prickled. Dani's shirt looked familiar – he was positive that Kuch had been wearing it earlier. He felt himself stiffen. He knew Kuch was a terrible flirt. In fact, that was one of the reasons he'd been taken on at La Casa – that, his mad skills as a barman, his genuine friendliness and his disarming good looks. But the idea of him making moves on Dani made Jerome disturbingly uncomfortable.

As Jerome straightened up, he watched Kuch give Dani a hard kiss on her cheek, then after a moment he spoke to the waitress. Jerome clenched his teeth. *Shit!* He really had no right to get riled. He tried to think logically. Of course Dani was going to get hit on. But he knew it was bothering him a lot more than it had reason to. He paced towards the stairs that led to the lower level where the staff table was, and walked towards them.

"This place is unbelievable." Dani spoke into Nicole's ear. "Do you come here a lot, then?"

Nicole nodded. "Nearly every Sunday night."

"Really? That explains the great service, then."

Nicole smiled wryly and twisted her mouth. "Yeah, that and the fact my cousin's the owner."

"Wow! Yeah, that'd do it," chuckled Dani.

"Talk of the devil and he shall appear." Nicole motioned to whoever was walking up behind Dani.

Dani pivoted around to see who Nicole was beaming at. Her heart stopped as her eyes narrowed in on Jerome as he strode steadily through the crowd. *Holy shit!* The lights flashed across him and Dani couldn't quite see if he was looking at them or not, but regardless, for a couple of seconds, she stood stock-still and openly gaped at him as he moved fluidly towards them. Dragging her gaze away, she turned to Nicole. "This is Jerome's club?"

Nicole nodded, grinning at Dani's obvious surprise.

"And he's your cousin too?" even with the loud music, Nicole could hear the shock in her voice.

"Yes." Nicole looked past Dani and grinned wider. "Hey."

Dani shut her eyes for a moment in an attempt to calm herself. Then with consummate practice, she turned around, replacing her stunned expression with a gentle smile.

Jerome's eyes darted to Dani, then refocused on Nicole. "Hi, you made it. Didn't keep Kuch waiting too long, then?" he joked as he kissed Nicole's cheek.

"Yeah. It's busy." Nicole looked around the club.

"Not as busy as last night." Jerome then looked at Dani, his eyes raking over her as she stood awkwardly. "Hello."

"Hi, it's an amazing club." Dani blinked up at him.

"Thanks." Jerome's eyes locked on Dani's as she spoke.

"I didn't realise Nicole was your cousin too."

Jerome's mouth softened into a small smile. "Yeah, on my dad's side."

"Carmen is Jerome's cousin from his dad's brother. I'm from his dad's sister," explained Nicole.

"Oh. Big family, then?" Dani dragged her eyes away from Jerome's to look at Nicole.

She huffed, "Yeah, you could say that."

The waitress came over and handed Nicole and Dani their drinks. Dani grasped hers, desperate to knock it back. Jerome's close proximity was making her giddy; she could feel her heart thumping in her chest. "Cheers." Dani turned to Nicole.

Nicole lifted her glass in reciprocation and clinked Dani's glass. Dani took a large gulp of her drink, relishing the warmth in her throat. Nicole started to talk to Jerome about some family member and Dani glanced around the club, watching the hundreds of clubbers dancing, and felt herself involuntarily move to the beat. The rest of the table were talking animatedly behind them. Dani could hear their laughter and turned slightly to see. Her eye caught sight of Rosa, who mouthed "are you okay?" and Dani nodded. Jerome noted the exchange and narrowed his eyes as he refocused back on to Dani, wondering why Rosa was so concerned for her.

"Hey."

Jerome turned to his right to see who had interrupted his thoughts. Peter stood next to him and Jerome flashed a smile. "You made it?" he looked genuinely pleased.

"Yeah. Well it's Carmen's birthday after all, and I managed to get Angie to come too." He motioned to the attractive woman stood next to him. She must have been in her early forties, roughly the same height as Peter, with dark brown shoulder length hair. She had petite features, making her look younger.

She smiled up at Jerome as he leaned down to kiss her cheek. "Nice surprise, Angie."

"Yeah, well I haven't seen everyone for a while." She waved at the table and everyone acknowledged her. "I'll just go say hi." She started to walk over to the table, when Jerome said.

"Let me introduce you to our new member. Dani, this is Chef's wife, Angie. Angie, this is Dani."

"Oh, pleased to meet you. Peter told me about you. How are you settling in?" Angie shook Dani's hand.

"Very well, thank you. Everyone's been great."

"Yeah, they are. Are you Italian too?"

"Er, no." Dani's brow creased as she replied.

"Oh, it's just with your colouring... I just assumed." Angie shook her head.

"Are you?" asked Dani.

"Yeah. I work with Cosimo, Jerome's brother, the accountant."

"Oh. You're related, then?"

Angie laughed. "No, but I feel like I am."

Dani grinned at Angie as she rolled her eyes.

"It was nice meeting you, Dani."

"Likewise."

Angie moved over to the table and started talking to everyone. It was obvious she was well liked and it struck Dani that her reception was in complete contrast to Liz's at La Casa. The staff had been polite to her but then had pretty much ignored her. Angie, on the other hand, was sitting with all the staff, comfortably socialising with them.

As they were all talking, the music stopped momentarily and the lights dimmed. Then the first words of a song rung out which made the hair on Dani's body stand on end. The clubbers hushed to hear the lyrics, waiting for the final line of the refrain. When the singer sang "I can change your life", the lights brightened and began to move in time to the beat, as the dancing clubbers threw their hands in the air, shouting and singing along. Dani stood for a moment, swept away by the energy pulsing through the whole club, and felt overwhelmed by the significance of the lyrics.

"Come on." Kuch grabbed her elbow. She turned to look at him. "This song is for you. Change your mood." Nicole beamed at him and he winked at her.

Rosa came up behind her with Pino. "Come on, Dani, let's dance," she coaxed.

"Far East Movement, girl. Gotta love them," added Kuch.

Pino made some smutty remark about Kuch showing everyone *his* Far East movement, which was rewarded with a playful punch to his stomach. Kuch then took Dani's drink and put it on the table, then guided her to the dance floor, followed by Rosa, Carmen, Pino and most of the table. Jerome clenched his teeth as he watched Kuch dance closely to Dani. She was clearly enjoying herself, laughing at something Kuch whispered.

Nicole put down her drink and was heading to join them, when Jerome caught her by the elbow. "Is Dani alright? She looked a little off." He explained he'd seen the exchange between Rosa and Dani.

Nicole's eyes flitted to Dani, then back to Jerome. "Her ex got in touch with her today and she got upset. We're trying to snap her out of it."

Jerome furrowed his brow and nodded, then looked back over to where she was dancing. "You think Kuch has the hots for her?"

Nicole grinned wryly. "Um, I think he likes her, Jerome. We all do." Nicole eyed him. *Crap, if he was this protective over Dani, he'd never be comfortable with her and Kuch*, she thought to herself. How they'd managed to keep it from everyone for a year was a miracle. They'd need to start being more careful. "He's just being a friend, Jerome. Lighten up." She shook her head and went over to join them.

It didn't take long for Dani to loosen up. She ended up dancing with all the staff and being introduced to Kuch's brother, who was the resident deejay. Rosa, Nicole and Kuch kept Dani close by and Jerome remained a moderate distance from the party, occasionally going over. He stood mainly by one of the private bars, talking with customers or staff, but his eyes were constantly flitting over to Dani.

"Man, I'm boiling. I need some water." Dani fanned herself with her hand, leaning towards Nicole, speaking close to her ear.

"Go get some from the bar and tell them to put it on our tab."

Dani nodded and headed to the private bar on the same level as their table, her heart still pounding wildly. Her body was covered in a slight sheen of sweat from the dancing and she contemplated shedding Kuch's shirt, but thought better of it. *Well, at least all that dancing would have helped burn off some of those extra calories she'd consumed over the last few days*, she thought to herself, squeezing between two rather large men and waiting until the barman finished opening a couple of bottles of beer. She leaned over the bar, hoping to catch his attention, when her eyes fell on Jerome.

Her heart raced faster. *Holy shit, he looked good enough to eat.* He was slouched against the bar arrogantly – he had a way of oozing confidence without it being annoying. He'd taken his black suit jacket off to reveal a deep V-necked, charcoal grey T-shirt, which accentuated his perfectly toned pecs and strained over his tanned arms. He was talking to a party of four men that he seemed to know well. He laughed at something they said, and his normally brooding face lit up as he threw his head back laughing, causing his face to crease. He looked insanely handsome and Dani had to catch her breath. *Crap, she had it bad.* Why did she always fall for the most inappropriate men? Jerome turned, catching Dani's gaze. She instantly flushed. *Thank God for subdued lighting.*

He smiled at her, his eyes intense as always, and Dani gave a weak smile back. He excused himself from the group and leisurely paced over to where she was standing, slipping in a tight space next to her. Panic washed over Dani as the proximity between them vanished.

"Hi, need a drink?" he asked casually. Before she could answer, the barman was over within a second. Jerome looked down at Dani, waiting for her to answer. He arched his brow and cocked his head waiting for her response.

"Er... tequila. Straight. Gold. Oh, and some water, please. Thanks."

Jerome shifted his gaze to the barman and he immediately poured Dani her drink. He placed it on the bar, along with a bottle of water, and then looked at Jerome. "I'll have the same."

Dani shifted on her feet nervously and focused on the bartender pouring another, then he placed it next to Dani's. Jerome picked up his glass and waited for Dani to do the same. Her hands were clammy and the glass felt satisfyingly cool against her palm. She lifted up the glass and muttered, "Cheers."

Jerome clinked her glass, holding her gaze. "*Salute.*"

"Um, *salute*," Dani repeated, blinking up at him as he took a small sip from his glass. Dani took a gulp. She wished he'd stop looking at her so intensely. Even in the dim light of the club, his eyes shone like laser beams, causing her pulse to race. The drink was making her feel a little reckless, and she really was in danger of embarrassing herself.

"Having fun?" he asked as he leaned closer so she could hear, and Dani took a deep breath, relishing his unique scent. *God, he smelled delicious.*

"Um, yes. I am. Everyone's been great."

Jerome nodded, then his eyes travelled over her. "Nice shirt." He arched his eyebrow and took another sip, eyeing her over the glass rim.

Dani looked down at the shirt. "It's Kuch's. He let me borrow it for tonight. I didn't bring any going out clothes with me."

Jerome nodded, seemingly satisfied with the explanation. Dani picked up her water bottle and frowned, then looked over to the barman. "Something wrong?" asked Jerome.

"Er, I'd like a glass. I can't drink out of bottles. I'll spill it." She shrugged apologetically.

Jerome's eyebrows shot up in surprise. Then reached over the bar and grabbed a tall glass. He gently took the bottle from her hands, opened it and poured the contents into the glass, then handed it to her.

"Thanks." Dani took it and proceeded to drain it.

"More?" Jerome looked at the empty glass and Dani shook her head.

Nervous and unsure of what to say, Dani picked up her glass. "Thanks for this. I'd better get back." She gestured to the table where everyone was.

Jerome nodded. "Are you driving?" his brow furrowed as he spoke.

"Um, no. Kuch said he'd drive me home. I'll pick up my car tomorrow."

Jerome tensed a little but he gave a slow nod again.

"Thanks again." Dani lifted her drink and quickly made her way back to the table, glad for the increasing space between them so she could breathe again.

By two fifteen, Dani was feeling tired and a little light headed. For the first time since she'd left London, she felt more optimistic. She was glad Rosa and Nicole had insisted she came out.

Kuch, Nicole, Rosa and Dani rode the elevator down to the underground parking and settled into the seats of Kuch's car. As Kuch pulled up the ramp, he turned right onto the quiet street in front of the building. Dani strained to see if she could see Sky from her window but the elevation was too steep from this angle. Her eyes dropped down and she noted the name of the building. Ferretti House.

"Do the Ferrettis own this building?" She turned to Nicole who was sitting next to her in the back seat.

Nicole scrunched her nose up and nodded. "Cosimo's accountancy business takes up five floors. Arsenio's lawyer firm another five, and the remaining two are taken up by Level One."

"Level One?"

"It's a gym and beauty spa. Liz runs it. Well sort of, anyway." Nicole shrugged.

"Oh." Dani couldn't hide her surprise.

Dani found Chloe in the kitchen when she finally surfaced. It was almost eleven by the time she'd showered and dragged herself downstairs.

"Morning."

"Morning."

"What time did you get in last night?"

Dani moaned, "About a quarter to three." She rubbed her face. "We went to a nightclub after work. From what I gather, it's a Sunday night ritual. Apparently it's owned by Jerome."

"Apparently?" Chloe stopped what she was doing and came to sit down with Dani.

"Well it is. And in fact the whole building belongs to the Ferrettis."

"Really?" Chloe's eyes widened, clearly fascinated.

"I know, right? It's a huge high rise in the city. Very swanky. The top two floors are the nightclub and the other floors have the family accountancy and law firms. They've got a gym and beauty spa too."

"Wow. Well I'm out of touch with what's going on, so I wouldn't have known. Adam probably does. He deals with the law firm sometimes, and of course eats in the restaurant. So the Ferrettis have quite an empire, then?"

"So it would seem. And a lot of their family work for them. You know, cousins. Not really sure how many, but they seem close knit." Dani got up and started to make the coffee.

"What was the club like?"

"Off the charts. It had a glass roof and walls. It felt like you were in the open air."

Chloe looked impressed.

"Yeah. I've got to go pick up my car. I didn't drive. Oh and Jez sent me an email. He got Adam's letter."

Chloe cringed. "How was that?"

Dani shrugged and pursed her lips, "I'm going to have to speak to him. Its ten days now. I'll get in touch this afternoon, once I'm back from getting my car."

"You need a lift down?" Chloe glanced at the clock.

"No. I'll get the bus. I know you've got a lot on. I'll just have my coffee and head off." Dani looked out of the window. The sky was clear and the sun was out. "At least it's a nice day."

―――――

Dani walked down the river bank towards La Casa d'Italia and turned into the car park. There was only her car parked up and Dani huffed. *What did she expect?* It was Monday and the restaurant was closed but she still couldn't shake off her feeling of disappointment.

As she unlocked the door, she saw Gia's green fiat turn in through the car park gates. Dani waved at her and Gia gave her a megawatt smile. She opened the car door and stepped out. "Dani, you know we're closed today right?"

"Yes, Gia. I came to get my car. I left it here last night."

Gia opened up her small boot and pulled out a couple of orchids. "Oh. I see."

"Do you need a hand?" Dani peered into her boot.

"Do you mind? I went to IKEA and bought all these orchids. I'll need two trips."

"Of course. Here let me help."

They gathered up the eight orchids and headed for the back entrance. Gia pumped in a security code and the door opened, then they both headed for the elevator. Gia chatted away, making small talk until they got to the second floor. She placed the flowers on the floor so she could unlock and open the polished dark wooden door. They stepped in through the threshold and Dani faltered, taking in the elegant apartment.

The hallway was finished with a light marble surface, which opened out to a sumptuous living area with dark, hardwood flooring. Covering the floor was an enormous silk woven rug in cream and gold hues that matched the classic styled sofas. There was a large glass coffee table in the centre, topped with perfectly stacked books, candles and decorative bowls. The centre had a vase containing white old-fashioned roses.

In front of the sofas was a large marble fireplace, with an array of framed photos and small ornaments. The decor was stylish, rich and warm, but above all it was a perfect reflection of Gia. It almost seemed out of place with the urban view of the city of Leeds from the large balcony windows. The apartment suited a view looking out onto the streets of Rome or Milan.

"It's a beautiful apartment, Gia."

"Thank you, Daniella. Since the boys moved out, I've been able to make it a little more feminine," she grinned. "Would you like a coffee?" Dani followed Gia into the kitchen, which was state of the art. Gia placed the orchids into the sink and started on an impressive coffee machine.

"Yes, please." Dani scanned the kitchen as she stood and watched Gia gracefully move around the kitchen.

"Please sit down."

Dani sat on a kitchen stool while Gia ground some coffee beans. "How long have you lived here?"

"About fifteen years. We bought the building and converted the top floor into two apartments before we opened La Casa."

"Oh, there are two apartments?"

"Yes. The other one is only two bedrooms. When we moved in here, Cosimo lived in the other apartment while Jerome and Arsenio lived with me. Then Cosimo moved out and Jerome moved in there with Arsenio. Well, they needed their privacy." She shrugged. "When Jerome met Liz, Arsenio moved out and they lived there for a short while."

Gia placed the cups under the coffee machine and waited for the coffee to filter through. Her face tensed as she spoke. "Well, the flat was too small for them once Alessandro was born, and they moved out. Arsenio moved back in for a year or so, then moved out again. I think he didn't like the idea of living too close to me," she chuckled. "I saw all his – um, how shall I say? Comings and goings?" She arched her eyebrow and Dani instantly understood what she was implying and laughed.

"Then Peter moved in until nine months ago. He got married recently." Gia placed the coffees on the breakfast bar and then brought over some biscotti.

"Wow, you've had quite a lot of neighbours, then."

Gia hopped onto the bar stool next her. "Yes." Gia rolled her eyes. "So, have you settled in? Peter has only good things to say about you."

Dani smiled shyly at her comment. "Yes, I really like it here."

"Good, well it's going to start getting busier. Christmas is always a little crazy."

"I don't mind. I like being busy. I haven't any commitments, so I'm glad to be working." Dani's eyes dropped to look at her cup and Gia sipped her coffee, giving a small nod.

"If I remember correctly, you live with your sister?"

"Yes."

"You're close?"

"Very. We only have each other."

"It's important. Family. Our family is – well, it's big. My boys never really needed friends. They had each other and cousins."

"Yes, I didn't realise how many of your relatives worked for you." Dani picked up her coffee and took a sip.

Gia laughed, "We're a big family. Both sides." She picked up a biscotti and waved it in the air as she started to explain. "Matteo is my cousin. Franco and Enzo are his nephews from his wife's side, so they are somewhat related to us. Carmen is my late husband's brother's daughter. Nicole is his sister's daughter. Rosa is Matteo's cousin on his mother's side and so is Pino..." Gia stopped for a moment as Dani stared blankly at her. "Maybe I should stop," Gia laughed.

"You lost me at, 'we're a big family'," Dani chuckled. "I think it's safe to say pretty much everyone is related to you, one way or another, here at La Casa."

Gia gave a throaty laugh as she let her head fall back. "*Si*, we are a big family almost living under one roof. Eh, that's why we called it La Casa d'Italia. It means the house or home of Italy."

"Um, that's a very appropriate name," mused Dani.

"Have you ever been to *Italia*?"

Dani grinned at how Gia peppered her conversation with Italian words. It was endearing and sexy at the same time. "No, unfortunately not. I went on a school trip to France once, and for the last three years, my boyfriend took me to Ibiza. My parents owned a bed and breakfast in Brighton, so every summer we helped them out. Then my mum got sick and I just never had the time to travel. But I'd love to go some day. I'd love to go to Venice – it seems so romantic," Dani said quietly and Gia smiled softly at her.

"I come from a small town on Lake Garda, in the Lombardy region in the north of Italy. We have a house there and every summer we used to go. The rest of our family would either be there or come over, so my boys were always surrounded by family."

"And your late husband, was he from there too?" asked Dani, glad that the subject had changed focus.

"Yes. He was friends with my cousin. School friends."

"Matteo?"

"No, his older brother." Gia grinned as Dani shook her head. "I know, complicated."

"I feel like I should be taking notes, just to keep up!" Dani giggled.

"Yeah, and I'll test you on it later," joked Gia. "We met at a christening. Alessandro, my husband, was over from his studies here in England and over the summer we got to know each other. I was only seventeen when we met, still in school. We carried on our relationship in secret, because he was five years older than me. Only Matteo and Gianni, Matteo's brother knew."

"Sounds romantic."

Gia smiled wistfully, obviously recollecting some memory. "It was. We didn't have emails and Skype then, so we used to write to each other through Gianni. I kept every letter he ever wrote to me," Gia sighed. Dani watched her as she looked vacantly into the kitchen, miles away. Sighing hard, Gia brought herself back to the present. "We kept in touch over the year and then the following summer, he asked me to marry him. I was eighteen then. He took me out on the lake and proposed under the stars.

"Of course, my parents were shocked. But thanks to Gianni and Matteo, they managed to talk my father round."

"You were so young."

"Yes. We got married within a month."

Dani's jaw dropped. "Really?"

Gia chuckled. "Yes. Alessandro wanted me to go with him to England and there was no way I could go without being married, so we got married as soon as we could. I fell pregnant almost immediately with Cosimo."

"Wow. That must have been hard."

"I was madly in love with the man of my dreams who worshipped me.

There was nothing hard about it. He worked hard and I made sure his home was his sanctuary. I was the luckiest person in the world."

Dani pursed her lips and nodded, knowing that was exactly what she wanted. It was what her parents had and what Chloe and Adam had. She knew she'd never had that with Jez and for the first time since she'd walked out on him, over ten days ago, she felt at peace with her decision. She knew she could face the phone call she'd been putting off. Dani looked back over at Gia and smiled at her.

"You were and are lucky," agreed Dani.

"This man you left, did you feel like that? About him, I mean."

Dani screwed her face and then answered, "It doesn't matter. He didn't feel like that about me. It took me leaving him to realise that."

Gia nodded knowingly. "*L'amore e cieco*. Love is blind. Hold out for someone who feels like that about you. You're worth it. Aim for that, Dani, demand it," she added, and patted her arm. "Always aim for the best, the top. Aim high."

Dani nodded, mesmerised by Gia's passion. "Come on, help me put my orchids in the pots – that's if you have time."

"Sure, I've got time." Dani hopped off the stool and followed Gia to the sink.

"You like orchids, Daniella?"

"I love them, Gia."

11

FROM THE BEGINNING TO THE END

"Do you still go out to your family home?" asked Dani. They'd placed the orchids in two pots, grouping them into fours. Gia was carefully arranging some moss on the top.

"Yes, every year I go just after New Year here. The restaurant slows down then, so I can spend a month or so with my family there. I try to go over in the summer too. It's beautiful at that time of year." She positioned one of the arrangements on the dining room table and stood back to admire it. "That's better," she murmured to herself.

"They look lovely," agreed Dani. She glanced over to the balcony and noted that it was full of plants and flowers. "You like plants, I see."

"Yes, I miss a garden. I love my apartment – apart from anything, it's easy to keep. But I miss having a garden to walk around. In Desenzano Del Garda, our home there has a very large garden and it overlooks the lake."

Dani noted, "Well, I suppose this is a miniature version – a balcony overlooking a river."

Gia laughed at her comment. "*Si*, I suppose it is."

"Did you never want to live back in Italy again?"

"Sometimes. But my boys are here. They're all I've got and I've been here for so long now. I did think about packing up and going back when Alessandro died. I found it very hard being here without him. I'd never been alone before. I moved from my father's house to my husband's. But Cosimo was studying and the two younger boys were in school." Gia picked up the next pot she'd been arranging and walked over to a large console table, placing it at one end. She stood back again to admire it.

"Jerome was a handful. He took his father's death very badly – well we all did. Him more than the other two, though. But thanks to Matteo, he began to cope better."

"Matteo?" Dani asked happy to hear any information about Jerome.

Gia smiled. "Yes. If it wasn't for Matteo, Jerome would have never wanted a restaurant and we would never have La Casa."

"Oh." Dani stared with curious eyes at Gia.

"Let's have another coffee."

"Um, okay, as long as I'm not stopping you from anything?"

Gia huffed. "No. It's nice to have a little female company. I'll tell you how we started up, if you're interested."

Interested? Dani huffed to herself. She couldn't think of anything she wanted to hear more.

After Alessandro died, Gia suffered a deep depression. His death was sudden. She was left alone with one son at university, completing his accountancy degree, and two unruly teenagers. That summer, she took them all to the family house in northern Italy. They had always spent their summers there, usually just a couple of weeks, but this time they went for the whole summer. Gia needed her family's support.

Alessandro Ferretti had provided well for his family. He had a thriving accountancy business that he had primed for his three sons to expand. Cosimo was already on track, two years into his degree. Once Alessandro died, the company was headed by his loyal employees, his managing director taking control until Cosimo had finished his studies. His life insurance ensured the house was fully paid off and that Gia and his family were left with a substantial inheritance.

It was on this holiday in Desenzano Del Garda that the family first met Peter. He was managing the restaurant that Gia's cousin Matteo was a chef in. They frequented it throughout their holiday. Peter had just divorced his first wife and moved to Italy from Switzerland. Over the holiday, Peter got to know them well. He'd explained that he was just working there until summer was over and then he hoped to go back to England. He'd worked around Europe and felt it was time to go back home.

Gia was cooking dinner one evening with Matteo. His family lived close by and he'd come over on his night off to see them all.

"I really need to do something, Matteo. Alessandro provided for us but I'll go crazy if I don't have something else to do. And the money won't

last forever." She took a teaspoon and collected some sauce she was stir-
ring, and motioned for Matteo to taste it.

He took the spoon and put it in his mouth. "It's perfect, Gia." He
nodded as he licked his lips. He watched her as she started to fry the
chicken piccata, smiling to himself. It was Jerome's favourite dish. "How
are the boys? They seem okay, except for Jerome. He's very quiet."

"Yes. It's hit him hard and he's struggling at school. Thank goodness
for Cosimo. He spends every moment he can with Jerome. He just
seems lost."

"He needs something to interest him, take his mind off what's
happened."

They all sat down to eat – Matteo, his wife Marcella and their two
daughters. Jerome came into the large kitchen and checked the pots on
the stove as everyone settled into their seats.

"Thanks Mama." He hugged Gia in appreciation for cooking his
favourite meal. "I would've helped you if you'd asked."

"You like to cook, Jerome?" asked Matteo as he served himself.

"Yes, I like helping Mama," Jerome replied awkwardly.

"He's very good. He often cooks for us – desserts too."

Matteo grinned. "You should come down to the restaurant and watch
if you like." Matteo eyed Jerome as he spoke. "Maybe even get to work a
little."

Jerome's blue eyes sparkled a little and he looked over to his mother
for approval.

"Would you like that? I know you love the food there, you'll get to see
how it's made. Maybe steal a couple of recipes," joked Gia, hoping Jerome
would relax, he always looked so tense.

"Yes, I'd like to," muttered Jerome and Gia sighed inwardly.

"Great. I'm at the restaurant by seven. Come around the back anytime
after that, but before eleven thirty, because it'll be too busy then." Matteo
smirked at him as he sat down, pleased to see a small smile crack Jerome's
worrying face.

Gia took a deep breath and mouthed '*grazie*' to Matteo, who reciprocated with a wink.

The next day, Jerome was waiting at the back door of the restaurant at
six forty-five. He spent the rest of the summer working alongside Matteo.
They forged a close bond over their love of cooking. Gia was forever
grateful to her cousin and christened him *Capo*. Matteo was Jerome's
mentor, her son's leader, the boss.

A lot changed that summer on Lake Garda. Gia revelled in Jerome's transformation from a moody, awkward teenager to a thriving, enthusiastic young man. Watching him work alongside Matteo, she realised this was what he loved to do. Academically he struggled, unlike Cosimo. But in this working environment, he became a new person. The pressure fuelled him and the creativity of putting together a dish seemed to fulfil what he was obviously lacking. He became sociable, made friends and shook off that perpetual chip on his shoulder that was seemingly dragging him down. It had been hard to follow in his elder brother's footsteps, but now he had carved out his own path. A path that he felt he could excel in.

Gia watched Jerome working one afternoon and wondered whether she should suggest he stay with Matteo and work alongside him. The very thought of not having him close to her, especially now, was unbearable. Maybe she could convince Matteo to move out to England. After they'd finished their shifts, they all sat on the terrace overlooking the lake and drank their fresh lemonade.

"I think I know what I'd like to do." Gia directed the comment to Matteo. He widened his eyes expectantly. "I think I'd like to open a restaurant."

"Here?" asked Matteo.

Gia shook her head and her eyes flitted to Jerome. "No, in Leeds, back home."

Jerome shifted in his seat for a moment, then leant forward. "But you don't know anything about the business, Mama."

"No, but I know how to cook, and if you really like what you've been doing these past few weeks, maybe you should go and study it."

"You'd do that? Open a restaurant for me?" Jerome gasped, clearly shocked.

"Would you like that? Is it something you'd like to do – in the future, I mean?"

Jerome looked over to Matteo, who had a huge smile on his face, then back at his mother as he tried to process what her suggestion would mean.

"I'd love it, Mama. For the first time in my life, I feel that I'm good at something other than sport."

"You are." Matteo patted his arm warmly. "For all his fiery temper outside of the restaurant, in there" – he motioned to the restaurant with his head – "he's calm and focused. Nothing seems to pressure him, and it gets crazy in there I can tell you!"

"But I can't run a kitchen now, Mama." His expression tensed.

"I'm talking about in a few years from now – at least four. We need to find a premises, do some research. You can go to college and get the necessary qualifications and then, when you're ready, we can start."

"Why don't you come and work for us?" Jerome turned to Matteo, unable to hide his excitement. Gia stifled a smile.

Matteo stared at Jerome, overwhelmed at the suggestion. "Well, my home is here. And there's my family too."

"But it would be a family restaurant; you'd be working with us. And it would mean we could set it up quickly if we already had a chef. Then, when I finished, we could work together." Gia had never seen Jerome so enthusiastic about anything before, except for when AC Milan was playing football.

It was on that hot and sunny summer afternoon that Gia, Matteo and Jerome first hatched their plans for the opening of La Casa d'Italia.

"Once I got back home, I started looking for premises." Gia picked up her coffee and took a sip. "It took us roughly two years to find this place and set up La Casa." Gia lifted her hand and waved it in the air as she spoke. "Matteo came out alone at first, until his daughters finished their schooling. Then his family moved over. We'd kept in touch with Peter once he'd left Italy and asked him to come and work for us."

"That explains why you're all so close."

"We are like a big family, even those who aren't actually related," grinned Gia. "It is very much Jerome's place, though. I know I set it up but it's Jerome that worked hard for it to become the success it is now. When we started, the restaurant only took up half the ground floor. We never thought we could ever fill the whole of it. After five years, we expanded it and made the second floor into the function room and offices."

"And you have the nightclub too," Dani added.

Gia smiled. "I heard you went there last night."

"Yes. It's a great club." Dani felt herself flush a little and wondered whether she'd said too much. She didn't want Gia to think she was being nosey or that she'd outstayed her welcome. Dani looked at her watch. It was quarter to two. She really should be leaving.

"Well, I'd better go. I've taken up enough of your time. It was really lovely hearing about La Casa."

"It was my pleasure, Daniella and thanks for the help."

Dani shrugged, indicating it was nothing. They made their way to the front door and Gia opened it.

"Good bye, I'll see you tomorrow."

"*Ciao. Domani.*"

Dani headed for the stairs, skipping down them, regardless of the slight twinge she felt in her thigh muscles. *That'd be the dancing*, she mused. The last couple of hours had been quite an eye opener. At least it explained why everyone was so close. And it was Jerome who'd wanted the restaurant? Well, that didn't surprise her. Dani realised he was very much the drive behind its success, but she wondered why he didn't spend as much time there. She huffed to herself – *who was she kidding*? She just *wanted* him to spend more time there. He was probably too busy running his empire.

Dani stopped for a moment, just in front of the door leading out to the car park. She'd really enjoyed Gia's company and her words of wisdom about finding the right person came back to her, in a rush. She was right, of course she was right. Gia must still be in love with her husband not to have remarried. Or maybe no one could match up.

Her thoughts were disturbed by the bleeping sound made from the security pad outside the door. Dani waited a second and then the door unlocked. She stepped back to avoid being hit by the door as it was pushed open. The watery sunlight from outside filled the dimly lit entrance and Dani inhaled sharply at the unmistakable large silhouette of Jerome.

He let out a low gasp and muttered something in Italian under his breath. Then, recovering, he added, "Sorry, I wasn't expecting anyone on the other side." He locked his questioning eyes on her.

"I was just up at Gia's." Dani felt her face flame as Jerome's eyebrows shot up. "I came to get my car and helped her take some flowers up to her apartment," Dani explained quickly.

Jerome's face softened and he nodded. "Oh, I see." He stepped in and closed the door. Then he reached his right hand over Dani's shoulder and pressed the light switch, which lit up the corridor. "You just came now?"

"No, a couple of hours ago."

Jerome's eyes widened at her comment.

"We had coffee."

"Ah," he said mildly, blinking down at her. The intense stare of his magnificent blue eyes softened slightly.

Dani shifted on her feet nervously as he continued to stare at her. He was making her unbelievably uncomfortable but as ridiculous as it seemed, she didn't want it to stop. Her pulse was speeding up, and she knew she'd need to say something if she wanted to let this brief moment last. "Sky is quite a club."

"You liked it then?" His face lost some of its intensity and he leaned back against the wall.

Dani could smell his cologne in the small confines of the corridor and she took in a deep breath, filling her lungs with it before she answered. "Yes. It's very... unique."

"Unique?"

"Its location, the roof. And the glass – I mean the ceiling," Dani answered, mentally kicking herself for sounding so flustered.

Jerome nodded as he narrowed his eyes at her, and Dani wasn't sure if he was displeased with her answer.

"We had a great time. It was good to let off steam," continued Dani, rambling off anything just to fill the oppressive silence.

"Are we working you too hard?" He cocked his head to one side and stifled a smirk.

Dani relaxed a little, pleased he wasn't being so serious. "No, not at all. I really love it here."

Jerome licked his lips and smiled, his eyes sparkled, framed by those dark lush lashes.

"I'm very glad to hear it."

"Well, I better go." Her voice tightened with unease. She really didn't want to leave.

Jerome reached for the door handle and opened the door. "I'll see you tomorrow, then."

"*Domani*," replied Dani.

Jerome's face lit up into a huge smile. "Picking up on some Italian?"

"Trying. See you." And she hopped out the door into the car park, leaving Jerome staring after her, again.

Jerome slowly climbed up the stairs to the first floor and turned to go through the door that led him to his office. His mind cluttered with a number of unwelcome thoughts. He wasn't entirely sure what to make of his reaction to Dani. He knew he liked her, that was evident, but what troubled him was how much. It also disturbed him how much it irritated him that Kuch and Dani had forged some kind of close relationship. How far that had gone or was going to go he wasn't sure, but the thought of her with Kuch or any other man did not sit well with him. He paused a moment and headed up the next flight to his mother's apartment, still trying to rationalise his feelings. What Dani did in her own time shouldn't have really been any of his concern, but Jerome knew that it was.

Jerome had ended up staying later than usual at Sky last night. He normally left by one thirty on Sundays as his Mondays were a full working day, regardless that La Casa was closed. He knew the reason he'd stayed was because of Dani. Kuch had stayed close by her all night, along with Rosa and Nicole. He'd danced with her and occasionally put his arms around her, but nothing more than how he behaved with Nicole or Rosa – in fact, with all the women he interacted with.

Because of this, for the first time in a long while Jerome had skipped his workout and had gone to Level One at around nine, allowing himself a lie in and the chance to take his children to school. Liz had been edgy when she'd seen he was still home in the morning and her uneasiness had rubbed off on to Jerome. He'd obviously messed up some plans or her routine. She'd come downstairs exquisitely dressed, which seemed unnecessary for the school run. Flustered, she'd explained she was going into town to meet a friend for coffee and maybe some shopping. Jerome watched her as she became overly focused on packing the children's school bags, and he knew she was hiding something.

Jerome paused outside Gia's door before he knocked hard on it. Then he turned the knob and opened the door. Gia usually left the door unlocked when she was home. "Mama?" he called out.

"*Si*." Gia came out of her kitchen and smiled widely at Jerome. "This is a nice surprise."

Jerome walked over to her and they greeted each other by kissing both cheeks. "I was coming to get some paperwork from the office and I thought I'd pop in and see you."

Jerome shuffled out of his leather jacket and draped it on the back of a chair.

"Are you hungry? I was just making some risotto."

Jerome faltered a second and then smiled at his mother's expectant face. "Sure, I'd love some." He walked into the kitchen and went over to the stove. Gia had just started adding the stock and the rich aroma of seafood wafted out of the pan. "I'll do it if you like. You sort out the table." Gia grinned at him, handing him the wooden spoon. He started to stir, slowly pouring in the next ladle full of stock.

"I bumped into Dani as I came up." His comment was casual.

"Yes, she came to get her car and ended up staying for coffee. She helped me bring up my flowers. She's a lovely girl." The last sentence was almost said to herself as she paused, hovering over the table.

"Um, yes." Jerome continued to stir.

"She's going to settle in just fine here. I told her a little about La Casa, who everyone was." Gia snorted. "I think I confused her a bit."

"How so?"

"Well, trying to explain who everyone is and their relationship to us. She's only got her sister, poor girl, not like us and our huge family. I think she's still heartbroken over whomever she left in London."

"Oh, is that what she said?" Jerome sprinkled the Parmesan shavings into the risotto and stirred, trying to keep his tone level.

"No. But I can tell."

Jerome turned off the gas and served the risotto onto two plates, then took them over to the table where Gia had sat down.

"This is nice. Lunch. Just the two of us. I love our family and our business family, but sometimes it's nice just to have a one on one, don't you think?" Gia snapped open her napkin and placed it on her lap.

"Yes, it makes a change," grinned Jerome.

"So how's Level One doing?" Gia forked some risotto and placed it in her mouth.

Jerome poured Gia a glass of wine and then poured himself a small glass. "I've thankfully found two managers who'll be able to work in shifts. I'll also need to restructure and maybe promote a couple of staff to assistant managers, so that they can help out when the managers are sick or on holiday." Jerome took a sip of wine and then picked up his fork.

"So Liz won't be working there anymore?" Gia asked trying not to sound irritated but failing miserably.

Jerome tensed at his mother's tone but smiled tightly. "She can go in and overlook things. I'll leave that up to her. Now that she's focused on restarting her modelling career, she may not have as much free time."

"I see. Well she certainly looked happier on Saturday."

Jerome chewed on his food slowly, then swallowed. "Yes, she did."

Gia's eyes narrowed as she watched Jerome take another forkful and place it in his mouth. She was in two minds about whether she should voice her opinion regarding Liz's modelling career, and the lack of interest in a thriving business her husband had built up for her, when Jerome's phone vibrated in his pocket. He scowled and pulled it out.

Saved by the bell, he thought. He looked at the number, which he didn't recognise, and then answered it. "Hello?"

Gia continued to eat and Jerome's eyes flitted up to her. She pointed to her plate with her fork and indicated it was delicious. Jerome grinned at her. He always got a kick out of her compliments.

"Hi, Jerome? It's Joseph."

"Hi, Joseph, how are you?"

"I'm good, other than running around like an idiot, trying to get my hotel on track. I have had a bit of a run in with my accountant and I seem to remember your father had an accountancy firm."

"Yes, but Cosimo runs it now."

"Great. Do you think you could give me their number? I need a company that isn't living in the dark ages." He sounded exasperated.

Jerome chuckled, "Sure." He quickly gave him Cosimo's number, then told him he'd call Cosimo and let him know that he'd be getting in touch.

Gia watched Jerome joke with Joseph and then make arrangements to meet up this week to see the hotel, glad she hadn't mentioned her thoughts on Liz, and spoiled their rare time together. She'd never understand why he put up with Liz and her unreasonable demands. She knew her son deserved better, much better. But she was resigned to the fact that there was little she could do to change his situation. She just needed to accept it and make the part of his life she was involved in as fulfilling and as trouble-free as possible.

Dani sat cross-legged on her bed and stared at her phone. She couldn't pluck up the courage to call Jez. Now that it was time to do it, her previous good intentions had dissolved and she couldn't face it.

It was four o'clock and she knew he'd be starting to get ready to go to the bar in an hour. Maybe she should email him. At least he wouldn't interrupt her and she'd get to say what she needed to say. She sighed to herself. What did she want to say? That he'd hurt her? That she felt used and her time had been wasted on someone who had no intention of committing? She knew she deserved to be treated better and when he said he loved her, he was lying. She buried her face in her hands. Why did she feel guilty? She didn't need to explain her actions. *He'd* betrayed *her.* Why did she even want to explain herself to him? Screw it. She pulled over her laptop and started up her email, then started to compose a reply.

Jez

I asked Adam to deal with the house as I can't face it. I really don't feel

I can speak to you, I've said all I wanted to say. Nothing has changed. I want a fresh start and I'm beginning to get my life back in some sort of order. Please stop harassing me.

You say you love me. I know that's not true but if you really do, you'd leave me to get on with my life.

Please don't make this harder for me. Agree to either buying me out or selling the house. The choice is yours.

Dani

Dani's finger hovered over the 'Send' option and wondered whether the email was too cold. She knew this was the coward's way out, but she still wasn't ready to talk to him. She pressed 'Send', then shut down her laptop.

It was dark by the time Jerome pulled into his driveway. Liz's Mercedes was parked up and Jerome went through his usual feelings of relief that she was home and anxiety as to what mood she was in. Lately, he never knew what her mood would be and he didn't want an atmosphere while the children were there.

He stepped into the kitchen and strained to hear where everyone was. The TV was on and Jerome could hear Kara and Alessandro talking with Nina. It was six thirty, so the kids would have had dinner. Jerome scanned the kitchen to see what remnants were left, but it was spotless. *Nina was a real marvel*, he thought, opening up the fridge and checking what he might put together for himself later. Maybe he'd just get take out. He huffed to himself – Liz would flip out. There were a number of plastic bottles with wheatgrass in the door shelf and some pre-cut and prepared salad in bags filling the other shelves. Jerome shook his head, thinking it was ridiculous that a restaurant owner's wife lived off this food. He shut the fridge and headed towards the dining room and opened up the bar. He reached behind the bottles to the back, and pulled out a bottle of Tequila, then splashed a generous measure into a heavy crystal glass. He smirked to himself as he thought of Dani and how she'd reacquainted him with it. He took a swift sip and savoured the taste. *It tasted better cold*, he mused.

Jerome headed to the lounge where his kids were and peered

around the door at them. It took them all of a couple of seconds to notice that he was leisurely leaning against the door frame. They both jumped up and ran over to him. Hugging them both, he joined them on the sofa as they watched some children's program and Nina rose from her chair.

"Where's Liz?"

"She's in the studio."

Jerome nodded. He sighed inwardly, knowing this was how it would be, now. She'd be working out constantly and watching every single thing she ate.

"Are you hungry? Shall I make you something?" asked Nina. She knew on Mondays Jerome usually ate at home, as La Casa and Sky were closed.

Jerome shook his head. "I'll sort myself something later. I'll just go up and see Liz. See what she's up to." He drained his glass, then got up, leaving Nina with the kids.

Jerome climbed the stairs and walked past Liz's room. It had been their room but over the last six months, Jerome had slowly moved into the spare room. At first it had been because of his unsociable hours. He'd come in around two o'clock when he was at Sky and in the beginning, he'd come in as late as five. This had disturbed Liz's sleep. He also woke up early, which also bothered her. So to avoid any arguments, he'd started to sleep in the spare room. Now Jerome realised it was less to do with the hours he kept and more to do with the fact his marriage was falling apart.

Jerome headed to the end bedroom, which they had converted into an exercise studio. It was a fully fitted gym, spacious enough for floor exercises. Over the years, Liz had had various personal trainers who had come out to the house while the children were small. She still used the studio even though Jerome had set up Level One for her. He had hoped her obsession with her looks and fitness would have made her take an interest in the business, which would facilitate that. But it seemed that her interests had lain elsewhere.

Jerome pushed open the door of the studio. The Pilates instructor on the DVD Liz was watching gave out the next instruction and Liz was about to settle into the position, when her eye caught Jerome in the large mirror.

"Hi, you're home early." She sat up and hugged her knees.

Jerome paced into the room. "Yes. I felt a little worn out. I'll finish off the last of my paperwork at home." He didn't want to make it obvious he was keeping tabs on her, but Liz was no fool and she'd purposely made sure she'd been home early today. He only needed to ask Nina what time she'd come home. Liz scowled at the thought. She sometimes felt that Nina was his personal spy and not just their babysitter.

"How was your day?" Jerome asked, narrowing his eyes. Liz averted her gaze and rose from where she was sitting.

"It was fun. I did a little shopping, had lunch with some friends, then came home." She reached for the remote control and paused the DVD, still avoiding his eyes.

"Which friends?"

"Um Joanne. You don't know her." Liz fumbled with the towel she had next to her.

"You said friends. Who else?" His voice was deceptively soft.

"Did I? My mistake. No one else just Joanne."

Jerome scowled, then determined not to argue he added. "What do you want to eat tonight? Shall I cook?"

Liz shrugged her slim shoulders, "I was going to just have a salad." She seemed to compose herself and looked up at him. "But we can eat together, if you like."

Jerome nodded. "I'll poach some lemon sole for you, to go with your salad."

Liz forced a smile and nodded. "Sounds great. Get Nina to bath the kids until I'm done here. I'll be finished in about an hour."

"Okay." He smiled tightly and left the room, slowly closing the door behind him. He paused outside the door still feeling the tension. Something was amiss; he knew Liz too well.

Walking slowly towards the stairs, he hovered outside her room. The door was slightly ajar and he pushed it open and walked in. His eyes scanned the room that had once been familiar but now felt alien to him. It was tidy, as usual, nothing untoward. Jerome then walked over to her walk-in wardrobe and stepped inside. It looked pretty much as it always did, apart from that Liz had managed to take over the section that used to house his clothes. He shook his head and turned to walk out again, when he caught sight of a large bag with Harvey Nichols printed on the side. He narrowed his eyes and crouched down to pull it out from under Liz's collection of long coats. He peered inside. The bag contained a black, grained leather Paul Smith holdall. It had a brushed stainless steel J hanging from the handle. It was a fine piece of craftsmanship and Jerome ran his fingers over the handle, then fingered the J. He pushed it back under the coats and straightened. *Well, maybe she was trying after all*, he thought. She'd really gone all out for his birthday this time. He stepped back into the bedroom and made his way back downstairs, feeling a little uneasy at his original ungracious thoughts.

Jerome set to work on dinner, deciding he would eat the same as Liz to show that he was being supportive. He poured himself a second tequila and placed the bottle next to the wheatgrass in the fridge door. He smirked to himself, knowing full well it would annoy Liz but he had to say he did much prefer it chilled. He grinned to himself as the image of Dani smiling shyly at him came full force into his head, catching him unawares for a second.

He shook his head and scowled, then took a moment to process what he was feeling. He swallowed hard and closed his eyes. In the ten years he'd been with Liz, he had never ever looked at another woman, never thought about another woman or ever wanted to be with any other woman, until now. How much that was credited to the breakdown in his and Liz's marriage, he still couldn't assess. All he knew was that he seemed to be thinking far too much about Dani, when he really had no place to.

12

FAST CARS

Working at La Casa, Dani found that her days flew by and before she realised it, it was Thursday. She'd hardly seen Jerome the last two days. He'd been around though – his car was always present, a constant reminder. Dani was appalled at how much the sight of the sleek, black Maserati made her giddy every morning as she pulled up into the car park. She slid out of her seat and closed the car door behind her. It was nine thirty.

The familiar sound of Pavarotti accompanied by Capo could be heard as Dani opened up the back door leading into the restaurant.

"*Buongiorno.*"

"*Buongiorno,* Dani! *Come stai*?" Capo beamed. Dani had made it her mission to learn Italian, so every day, Capo would throw a few new phrases or words for her to pick up on and then he'd test her on them.

"*Bene, e si*?" she replied, grinning.

Franco winked at her and she blushed slightly. "*Eccellente*! You remembered?"

Dani wrinkled her nose shyly. He really was such a good man and after what Gia revealed to her about him being instrumental in helping teenage Jerome, Dani couldn't help but feel genuine affection for him. "Espresso?"

"*Si.*" He beamed. Dani's eyes swept around the kitchen, focusing on each member of staff, every one of them nodding their hellos and indicating they too wanted a coffee. It had become their new morning ritual. Dani would come in at around nine thirty and make each of them a coffee. Previous to this, they'd staggered their coffee fixes, but since Dani had arrived, they all enjoyed their ten minute break together.

Dani immediately set to work on the coffee machine, remembering each colleagues' preference. Double espresso for Franco, Americano for Silvanna, Jamie liked a cappuccino and the rest were espressos, except for Carmen, who liked a ristretto at this time.

As the machine bubbled away, Dani's phone rang and she searched for it in her bag. It was Adam. "Hi."

"Hi. I just got an inquiry about your car." Dani had forgotten that it was being advertised in the paper today.

"My car? Already?" Dani jammed her phone between her shoulder and ear as she moved the coffee cups around, then put the next ones under the spouts where the coffee started to filter through.

"Yeah, I know. He's a dealer and wants to get in before anyone else I think. He wants to see it today."

"Oh, well I'm working most of the time, so I won't be able to show him it."

"I know. I was going to tell him to come there around lunch time and I'll come down there to show him, if that's alright. See what he's going to offer."

Dani carried on arranging the now full cups on the tray as she spoke. "Sure. Just come in for the keys."

"Great, it'll be around one thirty."

"See you at one thirty, then. Bye."

Adam hung up and Dani took her phone away from her ear. She looked up and caught sight of Jerome's reflection in the mirror behind the bar, observing her. Dani instantly blushed. His mouth twitched into a smirk. "*Buongiorno.*"

Dani took a deep breath and turned around to face him. "*Buongiorno.*" Her voice betrayed her nervousness. *Why did he make her so nervous?* Jerome leaned forward on the stool he was sitting on.

"Are they keeping you busy?" he jerked his head in the direction of the kitchen.

"Er, no. I just offered... I mean... that's okay, isn't it?" *Crap, maybe she shouldn't be so presumptuous.* This was their morning ritual and usually only the kitchen staff were around. She'd gotten so comfortable with most of the staff now, but maybe she was overstepping the mark. Jerome cocked his head to one side, unsure of what she was implying.

"Of course it is, as long as you make me one too." He grinned, making his whole face light up. Dani's heart fluttered, visibly relaxing. She loved

149

it when he smiled, the wrinkles around his eyes softly meeting the laughter lines around his mouth. "I'll take those through for you while you make it."

"Oh, um, thanks. Do you want a double?" Dani remembered he only had a double in the morning.

Jerome hopped off the stool.

"Yes, that's right." He lifted the tray and walked towards the kitchen. Dani stood for a moment, drinking in his perfect physique as she absent-mindedly twiddled the end of her ponytail. He was wearing dark blue suit trousers and a matching waistcoat over a white shirt. Dani focused on his behind. She'd never noticed what an amazing ass he had. He tended to wear his suit jacket, so it was usually covered. *Holy mother of God, he was just so yummy.* He pushed open the kitchen doors and slipped into the kitchen. Dani blew air out of her mouth, shaking her head. *Shit, she had it really bad.*

Peter stared at the monitor while Dani began to make coffee for her and Jerome. He sighed inwardly. *Crap. That's all he needed.* He rubbed his hand over his face and tried to process what had unfolded before his eyes.

Peter had come in early today and found Jerome freshly showered and hovering outside his office. He'd noticed that Jerome had been spending more time at La Casa over the last few days, even if it was holed up on the first floor. He'd hoped it was because the staffing at Level One had finally been organised and that things were slowly working themselves out between Liz and him – until today.

When Peter had arrived, Jerome had been standing nervously at his door.

"*Buongiorno.* Were you looking for me?" Peter asked, as he stepped closer and they greeted each other warmly. Then he unlocked the door.

"I wasn't sure if you were in yet," replied Jerome.

They walked into the office and Peter quickly pulled out a large file. Jerome, in an unguarded moment, allowed his gaze to rest on the monitors. He watched Dani arrive and head to the kitchen. Peter reached into a drawer, oblivious of Jerome's focus.

"Can I give you this to take to Angie? It's all the invoices. I forgot to take them home last night. You're going to Level One, aren't you? I've told her you'll leave them in reception and she can come down and get them."

"Er, yes, in a while. Sure, I'll take them."

Peter handed him the file and shrugged out of his jacket so he could settle into his chair to review the monitors and place some orders. He looked up at Jerome and caught him staring at the monitor that showed the main restaurant. Dani was walking out of the kitchen. He was about to ask Jerome if he needed anything specific, remembering he'd been waiting, when he caught Jerome's gaze riveted to the monitor. It took Peter all of a millisecond to understand why Jerome was spending more time at La Casa. It was because of Dani. One look at Jerome's face and the way he was looking at the monitor was enough. Peter furrowed his brow. That was going to at the very least, make things awkward and at the worst, make things extremely difficult.

"So, did you want anything?" Peter asked, pulling Jerome out of his trance.

"Um. No. I'll just take these then." Jerome quickly turned and headed out of the office.

Peter leaned back in his chair and stared at the monitor, watching Dani start to make some coffee, then reach for her phone. Jerome entered the restaurant and he hesitated before walking over to the bar and lowered himself onto a bar stool. He put the file down as Dani carried on with her phone conversation and simultaneously made the coffees. All the while, Jerome observed her as she obliviously carried on.

Peter stared at the monitor, gauging Dani's reaction. *Double crap*, thought Peter. It was bad enough Jerome had the hots for Dani, but what made things more complicated was that Dani obviously felt the same way about him. Peter rubbed his eyes with his thumb and finger, then scanned the monitor recordings from the night before.

From behind the bar, Dani stared blankly at Jerome shifting back on the stool."

"So you found a buyer, then?" Jerome waited for her to respond but it was clear she was confused.

"For your car. The phone call," he explained.

"Oh. Yes." Dani gave a slight shake of her head. "It went in the paper this morning. Adam's coming down at one thirty to show him it."

"Your brother-in-law," he confirmed.

"Yes."

"And you'll be buying another? A Smart?" He stifled a smile and Dani grinned, remembering their previous conversation.

"Possibly. I do like them. I suppose you think I should buy an Italian car," Dani teased.

Jerome shrugged and his smile widened.

"I think they're a little out of my league." Dani lowered her voice.

"Oh I don't know. I think you could have whatever you wanted. That's if you really wanted it, Italian or otherwise." His blue eyes fixed on to Dani's face and his expression suddenly became intense. Dani stood still, unable to reply. She knew they were talking about her car, but the atmosphere had changed and she felt that his comment meant something entirely different. She swallowed hard. *Pull yourself together, girl.*

"Er, well. I need to look at all my options. I don't want to rush into anything and make a mistake, again." *Well two could play at this game,* she thought, feeling a little reckless.

Jerome rested his elbow on the bar and pulled his bottom lip between his thumb and forefinger, his eyes still boring into Dani's. Dani found it hard not to focus on his mouth, wondering how soft those sculptured lips were. His gaze alone was making her heat up.

"So this car, was it a mistake?" He dropped his eyes momentarily to his cup, then picked it up to take a sip.

Dani's chest heaved as she took in a deep breath. "Yes. It didn't, I mean, it doesn't suit me. Too fast, and... well, I just need something more suited to my needs." Dani looked away from him, unable to continue with what was fast moving into a conversation a lot more complicated than she had originally thought. She knew he wasn't talking about her car anymore and her heart pumped so hard, she was worried she'd make a fool out of herself if they continued this conversation laden with double entendre. *Why was he so God damned sexy? And was he deliberately flirting with her?*

"You don't like fast cars?" Jerome asked softly, placing his cup down before licking his delectable lips.

Shit, he was going to continue, thought Dani. Taking her cup, she looked him straight in the eye.

"I love fast cars. I just don't trust myself with them. I don't think I can handle them so well." Dani tried hard not to let her nerves show as she sipped her coffee. *Crap, maybe she'd overstepped the mark.*

Jerome's mouth twitched and he slightly cocked his head to one side. Edging further forward, he replied. "Really? You strike me as someone who'd have no trouble with speed. In fact I think you could handle pretty much..."

"*Buongiorno.* What are you two talking about?" Gia's familiar Italian accent broke through the highly charged atmosphere and both of them turned to look at her as she gracefully walked towards them.

"Cars," they both answered, then shooting a sideward glance at each other, they smirked. The previous intense conversation seemingly pushed to one side, the charged atmosphere instantly evaporated.

"Really? Well Jerome loves cars. Always has. You too, Dani?" She bent over to kiss Jerome's cheek and he reciprocated. Gia then turned to look at her. Dani noticed that though they both looked very similar, Jerome had blue eyes as opposed to Gia's dark brown ones.

"Yes, I like cars. But we were talking about my car specifically. I'm selling it."

"The Porsche?"

Dani nodded. Jerome rubbed his forehead nervously, then took a sip of his coffee.

"German cars are very... hard. I much prefer Italian: smoother, sleeker and a joy to ride."

Jerome spluttered into his coffee cup and Dani barely contained her laugh. Gia patted his back and looked puzzled at the two of them. "What? What did I say?"

"Nothing, Mama. You just pretty much said what I was saying to Dani, that's all." He licked his lips, catching Dani's gaze. Dani blinked hard at him, then she turned to Gia and asked brightly if she would like an espresso.

"*Si.*"

Dani turned back to the coffee machine, glad to focus on something other than Jerome, thankful for Gia's interruption. Dani dreaded to think how much further the conversation would have gone, her previous bravado fading fast. She smiled to herself as she pressed the button. He had been flirting with her and she couldn't contain how thrilled she was.

Jerome looked down into the car park where Adam was talking to the car dealer. He was in two minds about whether he should go down or not. He'd purposely hung around La Casa today. The past few days, he'd avoided being down in the restaurant but he'd observed Dani from the monitors. He was unsettled about his obvious feelings towards Dani, and the blatant flirting episode this morning had thrown him off balance. He knew better than that. It was totally unprofessional, but he'd be lying if he said that he hadn't enjoyed every second of it. He grinned to himself. *She gave as good as she got*, he thought. Jerome turned back to his desk and decided he'd better make his way to Level One and check up on his new manager. He'd been splitting himself in two over the past three days and he knew that had a lot to do with wanting to see Dani. He shook his head, appalled at his behaviour, and shrugged on his jacket, then headed downstairs.

Adam walked into the restaurant and headed over to the bar. Kuch was over in a flash, recognising Adam as a regular customer, though he didn't know his name.

"Hello. What can I get you, sir?"

"I'll just have an espresso. I'm waiting for Dani." He slipped onto the bar stool.

"Sure." Kuch's eyes narrowed at the comment, then he immediately started to make his coffee.

Dani's section was busy. She'd been totally preoccupied throughout her shift. This was her sixth day and she already felt like she'd worked there for six months. A lot of that was to do with the staff but it was also because Dani loved it, thrived off it. Dani moved to the bar to collect a coffee order and smiled widely at Adam. "So, what did they say?"

Kuch frowned, confused as to who the man was and what they were talking about.

"Kuch, this is my brother-in-law Adam. Adam, Kuch. I'm selling my car," she explained and Kuch's expression relaxed.

"Pleased to meet you Adam, officially anyway," grinned Kuch, holding out his hand for Adam to shake.

"Likewise."

"Well?" she asked Adam.

"You're busy. What time are you done?"

"In about forty minutes."

"Okay. I'll hang on and then we can go for a coffee and I'll fill you in."

"Okay." Dani took the tray of coffees Kuch had prepared and went back to her section.

Jerome entered the restaurant and walked towards the bar area. He stopped to speak to a table for a moment, then headed to where Adam was sitting. "Hello. Adam, isn't it?" Jerome held out his hand to shake.

"Yes. Hello, how are you?"

"Great, thanks. Are you waiting for a table?" Jerome settled onto the barstool next to him.

"No. I'm waiting for Dani to finish." Adam motioned with his head.

Jerome turned to look across to where Dani was. "Oh. I see."

"She asked me to sell her car for her. The dealer seemed keen."

"Ah yes, she mentioned she wanted to sell her car." Jerome smirked to himself, remembering their earlier flirtatious conversation.

"How's she settling in?" Adam asked.

"Brilliantly. It's like she's always worked here. She's fitted in incredibly well."

Adam's eyebrows rose at Jerome's enthusiastic response. "Yes, well she's very good at her job. And I know she loves it here. She's had a bit of a rough time of late, so it's definitely something she needed to take her mind off everything."

Jerome narrowed his eyes and before he could stop himself he asked, "Rough time?"

Adam smiled tightly, wondering whether he should elaborate on his sister-in-law's recent break up. Then he thought, *what the hell, Jez was history*. "Bad break up with a boyfriend." Then he twisted his mouth, indicating it was a difficult situation.

Jerome nodded sympathetically. "Oh. I see."

"Yeah. They have assets together. So I'm trying to get that sorted for her."

"Ah, that must be, er... difficult."

"Yeah. Putting mildly." Adam shrugged. "He's lucky he's two hundred miles away," Adam muttered under his breath. Jerome nodded at Adam.

Wanting to change the subject, Adam replaced his frown with a smile. "I'm coming in tomorrow with a couple of clients."

"Did you book? It's pretty busy on Fridays."

"Yeah, my secretary has."

Jerome looked at his watch. It was two thirty, and he really should be going. He slipped back off the stool. "Well, I better go. It was nice seeing you. See you tomorrow, then." Jerome extended his hand and shook Adam's, then turned to Kuch, signalling that the coffee was not to be paid for. Kuch nodded discreetly.

Once finished, Dani walked over to Adam, eager to hear about her potential buyer. "Thanks, Adam." Dani looked at the clock. It was four thirty. Her eyes scanned the car park and she felt a twinge of disappointment when she couldn't see Jerome's car.

"So. I'll sell it to the dealer. He said he'd give you a good deal on a car. You really want a Smart?" Adam asked.

"Yeah. I don't go far. They're economical. They're just me." Dani shrugged.

"Okay. I'll sort it out. You'll be able to get a really top of the range one and you'll have a decent amount of cash."

"I want a convertible."

Adam chuckled, "Okay. I'll see what I can organise."

Dani reached across and hugged him and he awkwardly reciprocated. "Thanks. Really, for everything."

"No problems, Dani. I'll be in tomorrow with some clients," he mumbled, embarrassed at Dani's outburst.

"Yeah? That's great."

"A convertible eh?" he sniggered. "I'll see what I can do."

By the time Dani got home, it was eleven thirty and everyone was asleep. She let herself into the house and quietly crept through to the kitchen. Still wound up from a very busy night at La Casa, she decided to bake Jerome's birthday cake tonight. She turned on the oven and then closed the kitchen door. Within a few minutes, she was mixing up the sponge batter and pouring it into the prepared tins. It was almost midnight as she shut the oven door and put the timer on for forty minutes, feeling thoroughly pleased with herself.

Dani quickly tidied up the kitchen and set about preparing the filling and frosting ready for her to assemble the cake in the morning. As she put everything into the fridge, she spotted the Tequila bottle in the door. She lifted it out and poured herself a generous measure, then sat and waited for the sponge to finish baking.

Her heart fluttered thinking about tomorrow. She wondered whether Jerome would remember she'd promised to make him a birthday cake. She took a large gulp of her drink just as the timer beeped. Dani got up and took out the perfectly baked sponges and placed them on the kitchen work surface. The whole kitchen smelled wonderful and Dani smiled to herself as she turned off all the lights and headed upstairs to bed.

13

TALKING ITALIAN

I t was still dark outside as Dani made her way into the kitchen. Chloe was feeding Rosie her cereal, while Sophie and Ollie ate theirs. "Morning."

Sophie, Oliver and Chloe instantly replied and Rosie, having a mouth full of cereal, spat out, "Ani!" causing mushed up Weetabix to spray everywhere, resulting in Sophie and Ollie dissolving into hysterical laughter.

"Dani, D-D-Dani," corrected Dani, stifling a laugh. Then she planted a kiss on Rosie's head. "I thought she'd gotten over it."

"Sometimes she gets it right," chuckled Chloe as she wiped herself clean of cereal. "You were very busy last night." She gestured to the sponges.

"Yes, it looks like since I made the last cake for Carmen, I'm now expected to make one for everyone's birthday."

"Oh, I see. Well, it's great to see how quickly you've settled in and you're obviously loving it."

"I do. They're all so nice."

"Adam told me about your car. That's good news too. Any more from Jez?" She hesitated over the last sentence.

"No, not since I sent him the email. I just hope he doesn't do anything stupid like... turn up," cringed Dani.

"Well, I know you don't want to, but you may need to speak to him."

"I know, you're right. I'm just... well, to be honest, I'm scared I'll cave."

"He's two hundred miles away. That helps," grinned Chloe. "Come on guys, let's get you all washed up to go." Sophie and Ollie got up as Chloe pulled Rosie out of her highchair. "Ring him. Sometimes you think things will be worse than they are."

Dani nodded and started to clear up the breakfast things.

"Who's the cake for, then?"

"Er, Jerome."

"The owner?" Chloe's eyes widened.

"Uh-huh." Dani shuffled over to the sponges, avoiding eye contact.

"Really?"

"Yeah." Dani looked up as Chloe hitched Rosie onto her hip. "Carmen, the girl I made the last one for, practically forced me into it. Looks like I've started a tradition." Dani shrugged, trying to make light of it and Chloe nodded slowly.

By nine forty, Dani was nearing La Casa d'Italia's car park. For the entire journey down, she'd had butterflies thinking about seeing Jerome. Her cake had turned out perfectly and she felt a real thrill that she'd made this for him, even though the feeling was totally inappropriate. She was behaving like a love-struck teenager and her reactions were totally ridiculous, bordering on ludicrous.

As soon as she drove through the entrance, her heart dropped. His Maserati wasn't there. Dani parked up and sat for a moment. She shook head and unbuckled her seat belt. This was stupid. How could she be feeling so devastated, all because he wasn't here? She had no right, no right whatsoever. She'd better get her head together before she did something she'd regret. This was a great job and a new beginning – she couldn't mess it up.

Dani pushed open the kitchen door and was hit with the delicious smell of rich tomato sauce. Jamie grinned at her. "You made him one, then?" He paced over to see the cake as Dani placed it on the work surface.

"Yes." Her attention was distracted by the fridge door opening, and Capo stepped out.

"*Buongiorno,* Dani." He beamed as he strode over to her. By this time Franco, Enzo, Carmen, Vanessa and Rico had come over to inspect. "You made Jerome a birthday cake?"

Dani nodded shyly, "I said I would."

Capo looked down at it and grinned. "You even wrote 'Happy Birthday' on it too. That's fantastic! *Fantastico!* Quick, put it in the fridge, Jamie, so we can surprise him later," he said, his excitement evident.

"Great job, Dani. He'll be thrilled," beamed Carmen, her blue eyes danced as Dani blushed. "I'll get you a cannoli." She hugged Dani and walked over to the fridge.

"Coffee?"

Everyone nodded and Dani almost skipped her way to the bar, with a new bounce in her step.

Jerome decided to skip the gym this morning. Instead, he made his children pancakes for breakfast, seeing as it was his birthday. He also felt he should make more of an effort with Liz. Maybe if he was around more she'd be less difficult. They were going to have to broach the subject of Jonathan sooner or later but he wasn't going to do that today.

Jerome placed the pile of pancakes in the oven to keep warm and prepared some fruit salad. He knew Liz wouldn't touch the pancakes. He could hear his children and Liz walking around upstairs getting ready for school, so he went out into the hallway and called up.

"Anyone for pancakes! Come and get them while they're hot!"

Kara squealed with joy. "Daddy, you're here!" Then she ran back to her room and Jerome heard her whispering loudly to Alessandro. He grinned to himself as he paced back to the kitchen and started to set the table.

There was a thunder of footsteps coming down the stairs, then Alessandro and Kara burst into the kitchen.

"Happy birthday, Daddy!" They both flung themselves at him and he hugged them tightly.

"Thank you. Come on, sit down."

They both quickly sat at the table, then Kara put a small parcel on the table and Alessandro a large card. They grinned at each other as Jerome reached into the oven and took out the warm pancakes and put them on the table.

"This is for you, Daddy." Alessandro pushed over the card and small parcel.

Jerome's eyes brightened. "For me?" He sat down and took the card.

"Alessandro made the card for you," Kara explained excitedly as Jerome opened the large envelope.

Jerome pulled out the card, which was cream in colour and framed in blue. Alessandro had stuck a picture of himself and Kara along with a picture of a Maserati, a chef's hat, a picture of AC Milan's badge and an Italian flag.

"They're all the things you love." Alessandro smiled shyly at his father as Jerome opened the card to find it covered in different sized Xs, and at the bottom they'd written "Happy Birthday" and signed their names.

"They're all our kisses," Kara explained.

Jerome's heart almost burst as he gazed at his children's expectant faces. "It's absolutely amazing. I'm going to put it in my office."

Alessandro grinned. Their attention was drawn to the door opening and Nina walked in.

"Happy birthday, Jerome. Morning munchkins." She winked at them, then she hugged Jerome from behind and handed him a beautifully wrapped box of chocolates, "I know they're your favourite." Jerome looked down at the large box which had "Hotel Chocolat" emblazoned on the top. "It's their Winter Pudding Selection. They are to die for!"

"Thanks, Nina. You didn't need to buy me anything." He gave her a peck on the cheek and she rolled her eyes. He said that to her every year.

"I know. I wanted to. Ooh, you've been busy." She spied the pancakes and immediately started to serve the children.

Putting the chocolate box to the side, Jerome then reached over to the small parcel. He picked it up and ripped open the paper. Two thinly plaited, black leather bracelets fell out. Jerome picked them up and noticed that within the first bracelet there was a silver letter A attached, and in the second bracelet there was a silver letter K.

"Kara made them," Alessandro said softly as he saw his father finger them.

"Nina helped me, *a lot*," added Kara.

Jerome looked over to Nina, then over to both of his children. His eyes welled with tears, clearly moved by the personal gifts. "They're beautiful. I can't believe you made me my card and my gift. You're both amazing. Thank you."

Nina stood up quickly, moved by how overwhelmed he was. "Here let me put them on. They've a special clasp so you can take them off easier."

Jerome held out his wrist and Nina took off his old ones and clipped on the new ones.

"They fit perfectly." Nina looked pleased with herself.

Kara jumped up and sat on Jerome's knee and Alessandro followed. Jerome squeezed them both and kissed them. "They're the best birthday presents ever. How lucky am I? Come on now, let's eat the pancakes. You'll be late for school. What do you say we have dinner down at the restaurant tonight?" His eyes caught Nina's and he mouthed "Thanks." She shrugged it off. She adored the children and she loved Jerome like her own family. He'd been so good to her over the time she worked for him, it was the least she could do.

Liz stepped into the kitchen while they were clearing up. "Morning." She looked over to Jerome. "You have been busy." There was a slight hint of sarcasm in her tone, but Jerome chose to ignore it. "Happy birthday." She walked over to him and gave him a peck on the cheek. The gesture was about as warm as the November morning frost.

"Thanks. I made some fruit salad for you." Nina quickly ushered the children to get their coats on and gather their school bags.

"Oh thank you. Didn't you go to the gym, then?"

"No. I thought the kids would like to have a birthday breakfast." He turned from the dishwasher and faced her. She was flawlessly dressed in black woollen slacks and an ice blue sweater that emphasised her cool blue eyes. Her blonde hair was swept into a ponytail. "I thought we could have an early dinner at La Casa with the children."

Liz was about to answer when Nina came through. "I'll take the kids this morning."

"Thanks Nina," replied Jerome and Liz nodded. Both Kara and Alessandro ran in to hug and kiss their parents. Kara held Jerome's wrist to quickly admire her work. She ran her fingers over the bracelets she'd made and beamed, then exited the kitchen as fast as she'd run in. Jerome stared after his children, glad he'd spent the morning with them. He frowned to himself. *He really should do it more often*, he thought. He caught Liz watching him and he smiled tightly.

"So? What do you say?" Jerome pulled out a chair for Liz to sit down. She stood for a moment, contemplating her next move. Over the past six months, they'd skirted around each other and become distant. Every action was tense and deliberate. Jerome's stomach knotted, feeling her hesitation. It was as though she didn't even want to be in the same room as him anymore. *How had they become this way? Why had they become this way?*

"Let me get your present." Liz's voice interrupted his thoughts and she turned around, leaving the kitchen to head for the stairs. Jerome flicked on the kettle to make her some tea and he placed the fruit salad on the table. *Jeez, he felt uncomfortable. How can you feel so uncomfortable with your own wife?* He shook his head, unsettled by his continuing disturbing thoughts.

Within a few minutes, Liz had returned holding a small bag with

"Harvey Nichols" on the side. "Here you are. I saw your old ones and thought you needed a new pair." She held out the bag and Jerome narrowed his eyes, taking the bag from her. He pulled out the parcel inside and unwrapped it. Inside was a slim box with "Paul Smith" on the front. He opened the box and ripped off the tissue paper to reveal a black pair of leather driving gloves.

"Thank you. They're" – *not what I expected* – "er, lovely." He fingered them, feeling the smooth soft leather. Pulling himself together, he quickly responded to her expectant look. "My old ones are looking a little weathered." He tried hard not to show his devastation as he instantly worked out that the holdall he'd discovered was obviously not for him. The silver "J" was clearly for Jonathan. He put down the gloves and busied himself with Liz's tea.

"So, about tonight?" he pressed, trying hard not to sound agitated. He really didn't know how much longer he could hold on to his temper. However, he didn't want a full blown row on his birthday. He'd just have to ride it out today and then he needed to speak to Arsenio and needed to fast.

"Sure. I'll bring down Nina and the kids around six. Is that alright?" She looked up at him and smiled. "They'll like that. And I'm sure your mother will be pleased too." Her tone was a little cooler at the mention of Gia.

"Great." Jerome sipped his espresso.

"Aren't you eating?" Liz asked as she spooned up some fruit salad.

"No. I just had one pancake to keep the kids happy. I'll get something at La Casa." Liz stiffened. Every time she heard him mention La Casa it annoyed her, it was as though he referred to that as his home, rather than here. He was so attached to the place she'd found it hard to stop her jealousy over the time he spent there. Now there was Sky and Level One too. She'd fallen very low on his pecking order.

Jerome looked at the clock. It was almost nine. "I'd better go. I need to check up on how the new manager is doing. What are you doing today?" He placed his cup and saucer in the sink as he spoke.

"I'm going down to the agency to see what else there might be for me. Better strike while the iron is hot," Liz grinned.

"Good. Well let me know, then. I'll just go and get changed." He picked up his gloves. "Thanks for these." His gaze rested on her face and she smiled.

"Glad you like them." She looked down to her fruit salad and continued to eat as Jerome walked out of the kitchen and up the stairs.

He reached Liz's room and paused a moment, then entered it, heading straight for her wardrobe. As soon as he stepped through the threshold, he bent to retrieve the bag he'd spotted a few days ago. He looked inside and the exquisite leather holdall was still there. He quickly pushed it back into place, then headed for his room to get ready. His gut instinct told him that the holdall was not for him but he'd wait – give her the benefit of the doubt.

He walked into his bathroom and turned on the shower, then glanced at the clock as he pulled out one of his dark blue three piece suits. He'd have to be quick if he was to make lunch with his staff. Jerome pulled out a white shirt and dark blue tie, then headed back to the bathroom. At least she'd agreed to come down this evening. Jerome stripped and stepped under the cascade of hot water, feeling utterly wretched. His marriage was over. He knew it, and deep down he knew that he couldn't forgive Liz. He just needed to be smart and not make hasty decisions.

"That smells delicious." Dani peered into the large pot Jamie was carrying from the dumbwaiter.

"It's the Milanese sauce to go with the spaghetti and piccata. They're Jerome's favourite. Capo always cooks them for Jerome on his birthday."

"Oh. So he will be coming?" Dani asked, unable to stop herself.

Jamie snorted, "Of course. Don't worry, your cake won't be wasted."

Dani grinned, glad he'd interpreted her comment as concern over the cake, rather than concern over the possibility of not seeing Jerome.

It was ten thirty and everyone was sitting down. Gia looked at her watch nervously. He was late. Jerome wasn't usually late. Everyone began to serve themselves and start to eat on Gia's instruction. By eleven, she'd become agitated, and reached into her bag to retrieve her phone. Just as she placed her glasses on her nose, the door opened and her eyes shot up. Dani felt herself hold her breath, knowing instinctively Jerome had entered the private dining room.

"I was just going to call you," she tutted in good nature. Everyone turned to look at Jerome and stood.

"I'm sorry. Please sit down. I got held up at Level One." He shook Capo's and Peter's hand, then hugged them affectionately as they wished him a happy birthday. He bent down and kissed his mother, who in turn squeezed him tightly and muttered something in Italian to him. He smiled down at her and whispered "Thank you," then pulled out his chair and sat down. Gia squeezed his hand, then started to serve him his lunch.

Dani tried hard not to focus her whole attention on him but it was difficult, seeing as he was sitting opposite her. His striking eyes flashed up at her and for a second, she felt like a rabbit stunned by headlights from the sheer intensity of his stare, until his face softened. He smiled at her, making his excruciatingly handsome face crease around the edges of his mouth, causing Dani's breath to hitch, then she forced herself to smile back. She couldn't believe how happy she felt that he was there, sat in front of her.

Jerome chatted warmly with Capo and Peter as everyone finished up lunch. Peter excused himself, then went over to the bar. Kuch got up with Nicole and they started to help Peter pour Prosecco into champagne flutes. Capo signalled to Jamie, who immediately stood up and made his way to the dumbwaiter.

Peter, Kuch and Nicole paced over to the table holding the glass-filled trays and started passing the glasses to everyone. Jerome grinned at Peter as he shook his head.

"Okay, everyone." Peter tapped his glass with a spoon as he stood next to Jerome and the tabled hushed, everyone diverting their attention to Peter.

"As you all know, today is Jerome's birthday and true to tradition, it is my job to make a small speech. Most of you know that I've known Jerome for many years. And every year that I've known him, I'm thankful that not only can I call him my boss and colleague, but also my very good friend." Peter turned slightly so he looked down at Jerome, who stared up at Peter, clearly moved. "La Casa has been my home since it opened and I'm honoured to be part of this large, extraordinary family. Jerome, happy birthday. I wish you health, fortune but above all, happiness. To Jerome." And with that, everyone stood up to toast to a rather dumbfounded Jerome.

Jamie then approached the table with Dani's cake. He'd placed candles on it which were lit and everyone started a rendition of Happy Birthday. Gia hugged him as he continually shook his head, blinking back tears that settled on the rims of his lids, making his eyes shine brighter. He stood up to blow out the candles as Kuch, Carmen, and Richard took photos of him with their phones and Nicole snapped away with a very professional-looking camera as he leaned forward and blew them all out in one go.

"I hope you made a wish," joked Capo.

Jerome smirked at him and his eyes darted for a second to Dani.

"Of course." He looked down at the cake and shook his head again.

"Dani made it," Capo explained and Jerome's brow creased, looking back at the cake. His eyes shot back up to Dani and for a split second, they locked on hers. Before he could say anything, Gia handed him a cake knife. He firmly cut the cake and then Gia took the knife and started to cut it up and serve it.

Dani sat in her chair, avoiding looking up at Jerome, as Rosa chatted to her about how lovely the cake was. One by one, the staff dug into their cake and went over to Jerome to wish him happy birthday personally. He was desperate to talk to Dani, to thank her, but his attention was constantly under demand. Capo made his way over to Dani to congratulate her on a delicious and light cake.

"It's really *divine*." He winked. This was obviously going to be their continuing joke. Dani screwed up her face, embarrassed at the attention.

She got up from the table, uncomfortable with the continuous praise, and helped clear the plates, while Jerome continued to talk to Gia and Peter. She walked over to the dumbwaiter and started to load it as the staff finished off their cake and wine, suddenly feeling very uneasy. The truth was she had wanted to make this cake for Jerome – in fact, she'd revelled in the idea of it – but now that she was receiving all this attention, she thought that maybe she'd behaved inappropriately and crossed the line. She'd only been there a week; maybe she was pushing her luck.

"Thank you." His raspy voice sent shivers down her spine and she slowly pivoted around, her eyes falling on Jerome's steely blue gaze. He stood close enough for her to catch the smell of his chosen cologne and she breathed in deeply, taking it in, smiling tightly at him, her focus trained on his eyes.

"Well, I said I'd make you one." She tried to sound casual but she could hear the tightness in her voice as she spoke. She swallowed hard. *Holy mother of God, he was just so gorgeous.*

"Yes, you did, and as I asked, you totally surprised me. *Buon compleanno*? You even wrote Happy Birthday in Italian." He grinned and his whole face lit up.

"I'm trying to learn. Capo keeps teaching me words and phrases." Dani shrugged, feeling slightly less uncomfortable and glad she could now string a sentence together.

"Oh, I see. And you made me a lemon mousse sponge cake?" He cocked his head to one side and narrowed his eyes at her.

"Er, well, I know you like lemon, so –"

"I love it," he interrupted, his voice a gentle whisper. "Thank you. It was... well, as Capo says, it was divine. *Torta al limone,* one of my favourites."

Dani couldn't help but grin widely. "*Torta al limone,*" she repeated and nodded, committing it to memory.

Jerome laughed softly, his eyes sparkling. "We'll have you talking Italian in no time."

Dani chuckled, thinking that was a long way off yet, when Jerome leaned forward and gave her a kiss on her cheek. It was just an innocent gesture of thanks, but the charge of electricity that surged through her body had her reeling, knocking her off balance. She swore she felt a flash of something. Jerome pulled back sharply and his face tightened. His hand lingered on her arm a moment longer than necessary, to steady her sway as she let out a soft gasp. The whole episode far too intimate for such a public setting.

Oh my God, what was that?

"Thank you again," he muttered, clearly unsettled.

"Um, it was my pleasure," Dani breathed, blinking up at him, meaning every single word.

BIRTHDAY BLUES

Gia sat on a bar stool sipping her espresso, talking with Nicole as the lunch time rush was easing up a little. She was feeling a little tired today. Her eyes scanned the restaurant and they gravitated to the rear where Dani was serving. She was talking warmly to a table of four men. She recognised one of them as Adam Holmes, a regular.

It was approaching three and Dani would be coming off her shift. The restaurant was still busy and Gia realised that they would be short-staffed. The rear was still busy with four of the tables only just seated. She spotted Peter also clock watching, then he paced over to her.

"Still busy. We're not going to manage with just three staff." Peter's eyes ran around the restaurant. "I'll ask Dani if she can stay on."

Gia nodded. "Yes. You're right. Jerome will be back within the hour too, so we should be fine, if she stays on. The children are coming down later and so are Arsenio and Cosimo for Jerome's birthday." The Ferretti weekly get together had been moved to the early evening because of Jerome's birthday. Gia sighed, pleased she'd have all her family together.

"You go off, then. We'll manage." Peter patted her arm and she slipped off the stool.

"We're full again tonight. I left the bookings at the desk."

"Leave it to me, you just go and relax," he added warmly.

Gia nodded and headed up to her apartment. She took the elevator up to the first floor to collect her bag from her office. As she walked down to her door, she heard Jerome talking. She paused a moment. She was sure he'd left to go to Level One. She entered her office and gathered up her bag, then decided to pop her head round the door. But as she approached Jerome's office, she heard him raise his voice in frustration and she stopped just outside, the door slightly ajar.

"Seni, don't start with me... of course, but I need to be one hundred percent certain... Exactly, that's why I'm talking to you. I need to get as much information as possible, so when I'm ready, everything will be in place. I can't fuck this up. There's too much at stake, personally and financially. I need your word that whatever goes on is between you, me and Cosimo... I know, but you're gonna have to control yourself... I appreciate that... Yes, get on to it ASAP... I don't care about the cost, it's my sanity that's suffering. Yes, I'll see you later on... about six... Yes, sure, see you then."

Gia stepped away from the door, feeling decidedly uncomfortable about her eavesdropping. She quietly walked back down the corridor and headed for the elevator. She mulled over what she'd heard, and deep down she knew it was to do with Jerome's personal life. Gia clenched her jaw. If Liz was causing him problems again, she didn't know if she could carry on her pretence. Gia stepped into the elevator and pressed for the second floor. Her dislike for Liz had just increased.

Jerome put down his phone, then immediately called Cosimo. He knew Arsenio would be ringing him so he felt he needed to warn him.

"Happy birthday." Cosimo's calm voice made Jerome relax a little.

"Thanks, Cos. How are you doing?"

"Just winding down for the weekend. Thank God it's Friday."

"Good for you. Look, I spoke to Seni. I told him about Liz."

"Everything?" Jerome heard Cosimo's voice shift from relaxed to focused.

"Pretty much. I've asked him to get a private investigator, so I can have concrete proof. I want to be able to get out of this marriage without her being able to make it hard. I want primary custody of the children and I'll only get that if she willingly gives it. So I have to be able to pay her off and have some serious leverage to be able to secure that."

"So Seni's looking into every legal loophole?"

"More that he's going to see how far he can bargain with her legally."

"I'm not sure I follow."

"If she's continuing the affair..."

"You think she is?" Cosimo interrupted.

Jerome paused a moment. "Yes," he sighed deeply, confirming his thoughts out loud. After ten years of struggling to keep Liz happy, he couldn't believe he was having this conversation. He didn't know how much of the blame was his. He knew his work had taken over a large portion of his life. *Had his marriage broken down because his work had taken over, or had his work filled in what was seriously lacking from his marriage?* He couldn't be sure. What he did know was that Liz had never made it easy for him and in the last five years especially, he was perpetually trying to find the balance. He'd obviously failed.

"I want to make sure, though. That's why I need a private investigator. The most important thing for Liz is that she maintains her lifestyle. That's where I can bargain."

"She can't claim on any of the businesses, Jerome. You've Mama to thank for that."

"I know, and once she realises that, that's when we'll be able to negotiate. If she can't get a payoff legally, I can offer her one privately. That's when I'll be able to push for custody."

"You're telling me she'd sell out her own children?" Cosimo's voice became higher, betraying his disbelief.

Jerome rubbed his face as he processed what Cosimo had asked. *Would she? Could she? Or were his feelings of hurt and anger clouding his judgement?* "I'd like to say no but to be honest, I'm really not sure."

"Jesus, Jerome, how have you been putting up with this for so long? Why the hell have you never spoken to me about it before? Look, I know Liz is difficult and self-absorbed, but what you're saying is that she's willing to trade off her own children. What kind of a person is she? And why have you endured it?"

Jerome sat back in his chair as the overwhelming feeling of devastation washed over him. He was talking about his wife and the mother of his children. Someone he had loved once. Sadly he knew he didn't feel the same way now.

"Sorry, Jerome. I don't mean to judge, it's just you must have been – or rather, you must be living through hell."

"To be honest, I didn't even realise it. I buried my head in the sand, or work in my case," Jerome scoffed. "I don't like thinking of her in that way, but I've got to be realistic. My children are worth more to me than any of my businesses and I'll take a serious hit to secure them. You asked me why I put with it? I put up with it for them."

"I thought you were off this afternoon." Adam looked up from his empty dessert plate.

"I was asked to stay on. It's pretty crazy here today." Dani quickly cleared the table and moved to the next one to take a dessert order.

Jerome entered the restaurant and walked over to the bar. Kuch had stayed on too. "Want an espresso?" he asked as Jerome leaned up against the bar.

Jerome shook his head. "I'll have a whisky." His face was set hard as he spoke. "Actually, I'll have a Jose Cuervo instead."

"Sure." Kuch's eyebrow arched as he replied, sensing his boss's anxiety. He quickly poured a generous measure and placed it by Jerome. "It hasn't eased up today and we're full tonight too." Kuch started to put a drinks order together that came through while he continued to speak to Jerome.

"Um." Jerome ran his fingertips around the rim of his glass, staring blankly at it.

Kuch eyed him and scrunched up his brow. He didn't like seeing Jerome so pensive. Over the couple of years he'd worked for him, he'd gotten to know Jerome well and if something was eating at him, work was the only way to drag him out of a black mood. "Your friend Joseph's in. He's at the back in Dani's section."

Jerome's eyes jerked up to Kuch, then he turned around to look over to where Dani was now placing Joseph's order in front of him. Joseph commented on something that made Dani laugh softly. Jenny was also there, and the three of them spoke for a moment. He remembered he was supposed to pass by and see Joseph's hotel. With everything going on at home and trying to get Level One in some sort of order, it had totally slipped his mind.

"I'd better say hello." Jerome picked up his glass and took a deep drink, leaving less than half of the measure. He turned to head up to where Joseph was, when he was greeted by Adam coming towards him.

"Hello, Jerome, nice to see you again." He held out his hand to shake.

Jerome smiled warmly at him. "Adam, good to see you too. Was everything okay?" The rest of Adam's party was heading for the door.

"Perfect. And the service was excellent." He grinned and his eyes sparkled mischievously behind his glasses. Jerome's smile broadened. He liked Adam. He'd only met him within the restaurant, but he was always friendly and genuine.

"Well of course it was." Jerome chuckled at Adam's comment and what it implied. He looked up to where Dani was. "Did you sort out her car, then?"

"Yes. The dealer's going to part exchange it and she'll get another car."

"A Smart?"

Adam's eyebrows rose. "Yes, she told you?" He shook his head, indicating that a Smart wouldn't be his first choice.

"Yes, we kind of discussed it." Jerome's mouth twitched, remembering their rather highly charged conversation.

"Well, it's what she wants and she can be quite headstrong when she wants something. I hear it's your birthday today. Many happy returns."

"Yes it is. Thanks. Her cake made my day." He motioned with his head to the direction of Dani.

"Dani made you a cake?" Adam turned to look at Dani and she smiled nervously.

"Yes. She seems to have been cornered into making the staff's birthday cakes, from now on."

Adam turned back to Jerome. "Well she certainly knows how to bake. One of her many talents."

"Yes, it was…" Jerome paused, trying to find the appropriate superlative. Adam narrowed his eyes at him, waiting. Then Jerome decided to change tactic. "Well, it was very sweet of her. I appreciated the gesture."

Adam's expression relaxed a little. "It was nice seeing you." Adam put out his hand and they shook.

"Likewise."

Adam caught up with his party as they left the restaurant. He turned to wave to Dani when he reached the door, but her attention was directed to one of her tables. His eyes fell on Jerome who was still standing by the bar, his gaze riveted on Dani as she spoke warmly to a couple. He frowned, then walked out of the door.

Jerome headed up to where Joseph was sitting and greeted him warmly. Joseph insisted he sit with them. He explained that Jenny had agreed to manage the spa so they were hoping to open before Christmas. Jerome visibly started to relax, his previous bad mood forgotten thanks to Joseph distracting him with news of the hotel's progress and the varying problems he'd encountered. "Cosimo has been a godsend. He's taken over all my accounts now, so thanks for that."

"Glad I could help. Are you fully staffed up?"

"Mostly, yes. I'll need a couple of managerial staff after the New Year, but until then Jenny and I will manage."

"When exactly are you thinking of opening?"

"Ideally, I'd like to open now, but it looks like I'll need another month."

"Can I get you anything?" asked Dani softly.

"An espresso please." Jerome looked up at Dani and she smiled.

"Of course. Have you decided on dessert?"

"I really shouldn't," moaned Jenny. "But they're so good here."

"The cannoli is light and the combination of creamy ricotta and crisp shell isn't too sweet."

"Damn, you're good!" Joseph shook his head, chuckling. He dropped the menu onto the table. "How can anyone say no to you? I swear if you read out the whole dessert menu, everyone would order the whole lot!"

Jerome grinned up at Dani, causing her to blush. "So is that a yes to the cannoli, then?" Dani asked sweetly and Joseph laughed.

"Definitely. I shall hold you personally responsible for every pound I gain."

Dani laughed softly at his remark and went to the bar to order their coffee.

"Where did you find her? I could do with someone like her." He leaned forward, directing his question to Jerome.

"We got lucky."

"I'd say. I've been watching her. That table over there have been constantly bringing her back and forth for no reason and she hasn't batted an eyelid. They've been rude and difficult and she's handled everything they've thrown at her."

Jerome swivelled round discreetly to see which table Joseph was talking about. He immediately recognised the party of three. They were regular customers. David was a large plumbing merchant with a number of branches throughout the region. He was in the restaurant a minimum of twice a week. He was flashy and rude and Jerome didn't like him at all, but he spent an awful amount of money in both La Casa and Sky, and had also enrolled himself and his executive staff at Level One. "Yes, he's a regular."

Dani brought over their coffees, then paced over to the kitchen to get the desserts. David summoned her over and said something to her which made Dani tense a little. She nodded and went into the kitchen. "Table eighteen would like some more tomato sauce, Capo."

"More?"

"Yeah, he's just showing off to his guests. There was more than enough."

Capo shrugged and ladled some into a white porcelain gravy boat, "*Detto, fatto!*"

Dani looked at him, puzzled.

"It means, no sooner said than done." He beamed.

"Oh I like that. *Detto, fatto.*" She committed it to memory.

Carmen put out the cannolis on the counter. "We use it a lot."

Dani snorted. *I bet they do*, she thought. She picked up the gravy boat and took it to David's table and was surprised to see Jerome stood by him.

"Ah, thank you, Dani. You're a sweetheart." David grinned at her, then patted her arm and she nodded curtly. Jerome flinched at the overly familiar gesture but was pleased to see Dani was unfazed by it. She went back to retrieve the cannoli and took them over to Joseph.

Jerome left David's table and walked over to where Dani was just entering another order. "Is David giving you a hard time?"

"No, it's okay. He's just showing off to his friends." She shrugged it off. The truth was she really didn't like David in the slightest. His comments were always lewd and he pushed the boundaries of familiarity, making Dani edgy. But she knew it was part and parcel of the job.

"He's harmless, but he is an ass," muttered Jerome.

Dani stifled a chuckle at the very apt description. "Yeah, he is. Don't sweat it, I can handle him." She shrugged, looking up at him.

A grin spread across his face. "I'm sure you can."

The staff had all returned for the evening shift by five o'clock. Kuch was restocking the bar while the rest of the restaurant staff who'd stayed on busied themselves getting the restaurant back into some sort of order. Luckily, there'd been a lull around five. Peter was checking over the reservations for the evening at the bar.

"What's it like tonight?" asked Dani.

"We're rammed packed, and I'm worried we've overbooked." He rubbed his forehead.

Dani leaned over to see.

"We've this large party in, so they'll take up four tables. That might leave us short if the first lot of customers linger over coffee."

Dani's brow creased as she scanned over the restaurant. "Why don't you put the party over in that part there?" she pointed to where she meant. "If the tables are connected that'll open up space here. Bring down a table from the private room, just for tonight, so you can accommodate at least one of the parties if the earlier customers take their time."

Peter narrowed his eyes and pursed his lips together. "Yeah, that'd help."

"And it won't infringe on other tables. They'll still be enough space between them."

"You're right. It'll alleviate the stress. Thanks. I'll get Richard and Pino to bring a table down. Once the rest of the staff gets down, go and get something to eat."

"Sure, no problem."

Dani sat in the private room with Pino, Richard, Kuch and Augustino. Capo had sent up their dinner of mushroom risotto and salad. It was delicious. They ate quickly, knowing the restaurant would start filling up.

"Man, it's been crazy today." Pino stretched. "I hardly had time for a smoke. You seem to have got the hang of everything." He gave Dani a wink.

"Thanks."

"We'll be going out on Sunday again. Are you up for it?" Kuch stood up and collected their plates.

"Um, sure."

"Good, don't forget to bring some clothes," he chuckled, "and leave your car."

Dani grinned, "Okay. Do you think you could send me the photos you took today? I never got to take any." Dani flushed a little as she asked. She had desperately wanted to take photos but thought it might be inappropriate.

"Sure. Message me your email and once I get home, I'll download them and send them to you. Nicole will probably put them together in an album. She's photo mad. You want just the cake or all of them?"

"Er... just send all of them. Thanks, Kuch." Dani's stomach fluttered a little at the thought of having a photo of Jerome. She shook head slightly. She really was behaving ridiculously but it still made her smile.

Kuch nodded and headed for the male changing room as Dani made her way to the female changing room to freshen up and re-apply her makeup. She looked at herself in the mirror and frowned. Her hair needed redoing. She pulled out her hair tie and brushed it, then decided to put it up into a loose French plait, allowing a few tendrils to come out. She checked herself over. Yes, definitely more of an evening look. She was going to have to bring a few extra accessories down if she was going to work more afternoon shifts.

Luckily, the restaurant was still quiet when she returned to the floor. There were a few people sitting at the bar and around five tables were already seated. Dani scanned her area and was pleased to see it was still empty, giving her time to get herself organised. Her eye caught sight of a table in the main restaurant. The Ferrettis were all seated together in Rosa's section. She recognised Jerome's older brother, Cosimo. She liked him, he seemed like such a gentleman. There was also Arsenio, who had Jerome's daughter sat on his knee. He was teasing her and she squirmed on his lap as he blew raspberries into her neck. Gia was sitting next to Jerome's son, and Liz and Jerome were sitting next to each other. Dani narrowed her eyes to focus on Liz. She really was very pretty, even though she always looked so moody.

Dani moved to her section and started to get her tables ready. She was working with Richard and Pino again. They were already setting up. Dani spotted Rosa at the bar talking to Nina. She waved, seeing as they hadn't spoken today. Rosa had taken the morning off.

Dani made her way down to the bar and after greeting both Nina and Rosa, Dani asked, "How was your morning off?"

"I stayed home and did housework – joy!" huffed Rosa. "I heard about your cake. Capo saved me some."

Dani scrunched up her nose and Nina looked puzzled.

"Dani made Jerome a birthday cake. Apparently he was blown away," Rosa explained.

Nina's eyes widened as she looked at a blushing Dani. "How nice of you."

"She's going to make one for everyone's birthday," added Rosa.

"That's a lot of cakes," Nina mused.

"Yeah, it's Silvanna's birthday next Thursday."

"Oh, well, I better ask her what cake she likes, then," Dani giggled. "Nice to see you again, Nina. I'll see you later." Dani quickly went back to her work station and made a mental note to ask Silvanna what she'd like.

"So Liz, what's new?" Arsenio's eyes twinkled at her and Jerome tensed.

"What do you mean?" she looked up from her salad.

"Well, you've got yourself a... what's the word... um, a new... gig." Jerome's eyes bored into Arsenio's as he continued to talk. A smile twitched around his mouth. "A fashion show, right?"

Liz nodded coolly.

"Anything else brewing, something else other than that, maybe?"

"Well, I was with my agent today, and he's put me forward for an advertising campaign."

"Really?"

"Yes, it's for a holiday brochure." She felt Jerome shift in his seat and she turned to look at him.

Jerome tried hard not to look agitated that Liz had forgotten to tell him and he was only now hearing about it. There was a time he'd been the first to know of any good news. He sighed inwardly, realising if Arsenio hadn't asked, he would have probably found out at an even later date. The thought saddened him but he wasn't about to let it show. "That's great news," Jerome said softly, "I'm pleased for you."

"If I get it, it'll mean I need to fly out on location. Spain, I think."

"Sounds very glamorous," Cosimo chipped in.

"Talking of glamorous, that Dani's looking better every time I see her." Arsenio licked his lips, shifting his focus to her.

"Arsenio!" Gia scolded and she signalled that he should keep his mouth shut in front of the children, who were in fact oblivious. "Don't talk like that about the staff," she hissed.

"I'm just saying. I can look at the menu, but it doesn't mean I'm going to order, Mama." He stifled a smirk and she pursed her lips at him.

"So how's your birthday been?" asked Cosimo, trying to change the subject.

There was so much tension at the table between everyone and Arsenio was just making it worse. Jerome's face was stony and tense, Gia was flustered and Liz was cool and indifferent. He sometimes wondered why they had these family gatherings. *Weren't families supposed to enjoy each other's company?* Everyone was just so uncomfortable, it made Jerome sad just thinking about it. Thank goodness the children were there to lighten the atmosphere. "It's been good," he lied, and Arsenio sniffed.

"Dani made him a birthday cake. It was a lovely surprise," Gia gushed.

"Really?" Arsenio cocked his head to one side and lifted his eyebrow.

"Yes, she made one for Carmen on her birthday too. Capo saved some for us. I'll go and get it." Gia moved back her chair and headed for the kitchen, taking Kara and Alessandro with her. Liz, glad of an excuse to also get up, excused herself and went to the bathroom.

"So she knows how to cook too. She's really making this very hard," joked Arsenio as his gaze found Dani again.

"Seni, watch it," warned Jerome, his jaw flinched as he spoke. "And what's with the twenty questions? I asked you not to rock the boat." He sat forward so no one could hear.

"I was being polite. I didn't ask anything unusual. Christ, Jerome lighten up. What is this? The birthday blues? Since when have you been so uptight?"

"Give me a break Seni." Jerome rubbed his face roughly. "This isn't easy for me and you're not helping."

Jerome leaned back in his chair and Arsenio instantly felt bad. He knew this must be hard for Jerome, but he'd never really liked Liz, and now that he had good reason not to, he was pleased he could be less guarded around her. Cosimo frowned at Arsenio. "Okay, okay, I'm sorry. I'll ease up. I was just joking around."

Jerome sighed deeply and nodded at Arsenio.

Gia came back with cake for everyone. Arsenio took a forkful and popped it in his mouth.

"Jeez, that's delicious."

Cosimo nodded in agreement.

"And to think that it was delectable Dani's hands that made it. Somehow it makes it *so* much more delicious."

"Arsenio!" scolded Gia again.

Arsenio chuckled as he lewdly raised his eyebrows in quick succession and licked the spoon, causing Cosimo to stifle a grin and shake his head. Jerome's face softened and he smiled at his brother who winked at him, then took another deliberate spoonful.

15

APOLOGIES

Dani walked through the front door and carefully closed it behind her. It was just before midnight and she was trying hard not to wake anyone. She slipped off her shoes and hung up her coat and headed for the kitchen. She needed a drink. She'd have to find her own place soon. The thirty-minute drive every night was beginning to get to her. She'd need to start flat hunting. *Maybe on Monday,* she mused. Yet another thing to add to her to do list. She snorted to herself as she flicked on the kitchen light. That to do list was getting longer and longer by the day.

"Hey."

Dani jumped out of her skin and she let out a muffled cry as her hand flew to her mouth. "Jesus, Adam, you scared the living daylights out of me. Did I wake you?"

He smirked at her, leaning against the kitchen counter in his T-shirt and drawstring trousers.

"No. I was waiting up for you." He pulled out a chair and sat down as Dani opened the fridge and pulled out the tequila bottle. She motioned to it and Adam nodded.

"Waiting for me? Why?" Dani reached up to the cupboard and pulled out two glasses and place them on the table and poured two large measures.

"Sit down, Dani."

Feeling pretty wired after her encounter with Jerome today and the busy evening that had followed, she was hoping the drink would relax her. She carefully pulled out a chair and sat down, puzzled as to why Adam would be waiting up for her.

Adam lifted up his glass and Dani clinked it with hers. "*Salute.*"

Adam raised his eyebrow, "Yeah, cheers." Then took a large gulp.

"So?" Dani took a large gulp and rested back in the chair.

"Jez sent me an email," Adam explained.

Dani's stomach clenched. The way Adam was looking at her only meant one thing. "Oh. Bad news?"

Adam twisted his mouth, indicating he wasn't sure. "After a paragraph of him tearing into me about my – how did he put it – *overzealous attitude*, he's decided to buy you out."

Dani let out a breath she'd been holding. "Oh, I see. That's good news, then, isn't it?" Dani looked at him expectantly, but from the look on his face, she could see there was something else, something maybe not so good after all. "What is it, Adam?"

"He's decided to buy you out at the asking price I stipulated. The price was an average of the three valuations and he was happy not to dispute that –"

"Adam, just get to the point. What's the condition?" Dani interrupted. After five years working alongside and living with Jez, she knew there must be a condition and after more than ten years of knowing Adam, it was increasingly obvious he was trying to soften the blow.

Adam snorted. "His condition is that he meets up with you before he hands over the money. Actually, he wants to hand over the cheque in person. He wants to see you, so you can talk."

Dani leaned forward and rubbed her face as Adam looked on. Adam clenched his jaw and gripped his glass. He knew Jez's game – Jez was trying to get her back and knew that he only needed to be with her for a few hours and she'd start to feel sorry for him and he'd guilt her into getting back with him.

"Look, you don't need to answer him yet. I can send him an email to say you're considering the offer. I can stall him." Adam was hoping that if Dani had more time away from him she'd feel stronger.

"How long before I have to answer him?" Dani interrupted.

"A week or so, and then it'll take a few weeks for the paperwork to be drafted. I'm sure he'll need a month to get the money together, unless he has it in cash somewhere?"

Dani shook her head. "I don't think so. He'll be borrowing it." She took a deep breath. "I want to get this done as fast as possible Adam. I need to. I'm trying to get my life back on track and this is hanging over me."

"I'm not altogether happy about his motive, Dani. You know he'll try and –"

"I know, Adam. I know what he'll try to do. But if you're there, he won't be able to try anything..."

"He stipulates that he wants to see you *alone*, Dani. No one else, just the two of you." Adam's voice hardened. He took another drink from his glass as Dani sat back in her chair.

"I need to talk to him."

"Are you sure? You don't have to. I'll deal with this."

"No, Adam. I'm fed up of feeling intimidated by him. I'll call him and try and talk him around. There's no way I'm going to go down to London to see him. It's just too soon."

"I'll do whatever you want. But I won't stand for him making you feel guilty. He was the asshole."

Dani nodded and drained her glass. "Thanks, Adam, for everything. I mean it."

Adam smiled a small grin at her and patted her hand. Wanting to change the subject, he grinned more broadly. "So, I heard you made your boss a cake today."

Dani's eyes jerked up to Adam's face. "Er, yes."

"He was very" – Adam paused as he tried to find the appropriate word – "well, he seemed very pleased that you made him one."

Dani blushed slightly and grabbed the bottle. "He told you that?" She poured them both another drink, purposely avoiding Adam's gaze. She felt an overwhelming thrill at the thought of having pleased Jerome, in any way.

"Yes, he did."

"Well, I seem to be the birthday cake baker. I'm making one for Silvanna next week for her birthday too."

"I see. Well, that's nice. You seem to have really settled in there." Adam took a sip from his glass and got up from the table. "Well, I'd better let you get to bed. It's late."

"Sure. Goodnight."

"Goodnight."

Dani sat for a moment, staring into her glass. Her emotions were all over the place. Jez had finally come to terms with her leaving, though she knew he was still going to try and win her back. Even if it was just to satisfy his ego. She wasn't sure how she felt about that. On the one hand, she was pleased he was still fighting for her, but on the other, she knew she'd moved on. Moving two hundred miles away from him had helped, a lot. She knew the only way to get over him was to go cold turkey. Cut him off dead, which was exactly what she'd done.

Dani took a sip from her glass and checked the time. It was half past midnight. He'd be busy now. The bar would be full on a Friday night. Maybe this was the best time to call him – at work. He wouldn't be able to talk much.

She drained her glass and got up from the table and headed up to her room. No time like the present. After closing her bedroom door, she sat cross legged on her bed. Taking a deep breath, she opened up her bag and took out her phone.

Jerome drove into the car park of the Ferretti House and pulled into his designated spot. He checked the time – it was eleven twenty. He was late and he felt mentally exhausted. Dinner had been tense and once it was over, he'd decided to go home rather than stay on at La Casa. He knew that he had left Peter shorthanded on a very busy Friday night, but he needed to spend time at home. In hindsight, he realised his decision to go home had only unsettled him. Instead of finding some clarity, he had in fact become even more confused.

Once they'd reached home, Jerome had taken the children up for their bath while Liz went straight upstairs to the gym to start her evening workout. Jerome had put the children to bed, then, ensuring they were asleep, he went to find Liz. He'd decided it was time to lay things down on the table, and delaying it was only eating away at him. Liz had been showering when he entered her bedroom.

"Oh, sorry, I didn't realise." Jerome stood just past the threshold of the doorway as Liz came out of the bathroom wrapped in a towel, her hair crudely tied up.

A smile curled over her lips and she fixed her cool blue eyes on him. "That's okay. I've just finished my workout."

"I'll come back later." Jerome suddenly felt uncomfortable. Something in the way she was looking at him made him stop from coming in further.

"No, don't go. Sit. Did you want something?" her voice had softened and she readjusted her towel that was secured around her chest.

Jerome hesitated, then stepped closer and stood by the bed. He wasn't sure where to start. He was still annoyed that he'd found out about her possible job in Spain at the same time as the rest of his family. But he didn't want to start by accusing her of keeping secrets. It would only escalate into a huge fight, which in turn would mean their already-strained relationship would become even more unbearable. Jerome decided on a much softer approach, in the hope he'd get a clearer picture of where his marriage was going.

"I wanted to talk to you. I think we need to clear the air. It's been... well, it's been very strained and I know we've argued about where we stand and over the last few weeks it's been difficult. But we need to see if this, us, is going to work."

"I see." Liz leaned back against the chest of drawers, her eyes never leaving Jerome's.

"Liz. I don't want to argue. Really, I'm done with the shouting and the screaming. We just need to see if we can make this work."

Moving away from the chest of drawers, Liz stepped closer to the bed, "Jerome, I only wanted your attention." Her voice was low.

"Well, you certainly got it," he muttered. Liz stiffened at his remark. Jerome took a deep breath as he prepared himself for his next question. "Are you still seeing him?"

Liz's eyes stayed focused on Jerome, and then she pulled out the tie that was holding up her hair, allowing her blonde locks to fall loosely over her shoulders. "No. I told you it was just the once. How many times do I need to keep telling you?" She tried hard to keep the agitation out of her voice.

"So when you went to see him –"

"I was just taking some of his things back. He didn't want to come down. He didn't want to bump into you. You can understand that, can't you? I've told you I'm sorry. Truly, I am, but over the past year we've become strangers." Liz kneeled up on the bed, trying to close the distance between them and Jerome rubbed his forehead. He continued to stare at her and her expression softened again. "Don't you miss me?" Her voice was barely audible and Jerome sucked on his teeth. Liz cocked her head to one side. "Don't you want me anymore?"

"Liz, please don't do this. We need to talk."

"We are talking, aren't we? I've told you it's over. He's not at Level One. I'm getting on with my career. Things are finally going my way. It's just down to you, now." She shuffled closer, so that she was now kneeling on the bed in front of him.

"Me?" He furrowed his brow and looked down at her.

"Yes, you. Do you forgive me? Will you ever forgive me?"

"I... I don't know."

Liz took hold of his hand and gently squeezed it. "Please try, Jerome. I know I'm the one who was wrong, but you pushed me away. You cut me out. I'm not blaming you, I'm just trying to make you understand."

Jerome took a moment as the arguments and screaming matches they'd had over the past few weeks, regarding Liz's apparent 'one time' slip up, returned forcefully into his head. He didn't want to start that up again. There wasn't any point to it. All it did was make him feel angry and out of control. He was determined that it wasn't going to happen to him again. Was he willing to forgive her? He knew right now he wasn't. Would he ever be able to? He just wasn't sure. He wanted to, so that his family life would resemble something more normal than it was now. His family was everything to him and if it meant he had to try and get past this for them, he had to at least try.

"Liz, please." Jerome closed his eyes as she pulled him closer to her, then she reached up to stroke his cheek. He knew what she was doing. He knew she was trying to distract him so that they wouldn't need to talk. So she wouldn't answer the many questions he wanted answering. Before he could protest, she sealed his mouth with a tender kiss. Her hands found their way into his hair, pulling him flush against her. Jerome resisted for a moment, but as Liz deepened the kiss, he surrendered, allowing his arms to encase her. Liz loosened her towel, allowing it to drop, and Jerome's hands roamed over her bare damp back. It felt good to have her naked and in his arms again, and for a moment, he was lost in her. She pulled him down onto the bed.

"I need you Jerome," she gasped, reaching down and taking hold of his trouser zip.

Jerome grabbed her hand to stop her and then pulled himself away from her. "Don't, Liz. I can't. I just... It's too soon." He clenched his eyes shut as the image of her and Jonathan seared into his head.

"Jerome, please. I only want you," she breathed, looking up doe-eyed into his tormented face. But she knew she'd lost this time. Pushing him would only make him close off more. "Please forgive me," she pleaded. His stormy eyes opened. "I need you to forgive me."

He breathed deeply, then gently prised himself away from her. "I know. And I'll try. But we need to take things slow, Liz. You hurt me, a lot. Just give me some time." Jerome shuffled off the bed and Liz covered her perfectly toned body with the towel. She squinted her eyes at him and nodded. Feeling rejected wasn't an emotion Liz was accustomed to, but she hid it well. She was very good at that, when she needed to be.

"I need to get ready. I'll be late."

Liz nodded softly watching him edge to the door.

"We need to talk more, Liz. I'm trying to get work more organised so I can spend more time with you, and I'll support you in any way you want in your career. But you need to understand that I cannot be split in two. You're going to have to also compromise."

Liz licked her lips nervously and nodded again. "I'll try harder."

"Okay. I'll go and get ready." He looked at his watch. It was almost ten. He was going to be late.

Dani pressed the speed dial and held her breath while her phone connected and started to ring. Her heart was thumping so hard and she wondered whether she should just hang up. Maybe this wasn't such a good idea after all. It rang for the fifth time, then someone answered.

"Dani?"

It was Earl, the head barman.

"Hi, Earl. How are you?"

"I'm well. It's nice to hear from you." His voice seemed a little guarded and Dani felt instantly guilty. Earl was a good guy and she'd worked with him for five years. When she'd left, she hadn't even said goodbye to him or even called, and Dani knew he deserved better than that.

"I'm fine, Earl... I'm sorry I never said bye. I just had to leave, but I should have rung you."

"That's okay, Dani. I understand. How are things?"

"I'm getting there."

Earl snorted, "Well, I wish you all the best. We all miss you here."

"Thanks, Earl. I miss you guys too."

There was a pause, and Dani wasn't sure what to say. Before she opened her mouth, Earl's quiet voice broke through the silence. "Jez has been in a mess since you left."

Dani sighed, knowing Earl was a loyal friend of Jez's. "Earl." Dani's voice took on the tone of a mild scold.

"I'm just saying. He sacked Julie."

"Oh." Dani wasn't sure how she felt about that piece of information.

"I know he feels bad about everything. Give him another chance, Dani. At least let him speak to you."

Crap. Now she had Earl making her feel guilty. "That's why I'm calling. So we can talk. Is he there?"

"Yeah. I'll call him over."

She heard Earl call Jez's name over the loud music. He must have motioned to him that it was her, because she didn't hear anyone speak.

Her heart banged against her chest. Was she really ready for this? At least she could hang up on him if it all got too much.

"He's coming, Dani." Earl's voice jolted her out of panic.

"Thanks Ear –"

Before she could finish, Jez had grabbed the phone. "Dani?" his voice sounded a mixture of stunned and surprised.

"Hi, Jez," Dani answered softly, trying hard not to let her voice betray how nervous she was. It disturbed her how much hearing his voice pleased her.

"Thank God. Jesus, Dani, I've missed you." His relief was evident. He sounded vulnerable, something Dani had never experienced before.

He must have walked out of the bar and into the office at the back because the pulsing music had faded. Dani's throat tightened and her stomach clenched. Now she had him on the phone, she really wasn't sure what to say. She could do pleasantries, but that seemed ridiculous. Maybe she should just stick to business. Taking a deep breath, she spoke. "I'm calling because we need to sort out the house," she blurted out in a rush.

"Er, okay. How've you been?" His tone became nervous.

Dani sighed. He wasn't going to let her guide the conversation. "I'm fine, Jez."

"Well I'm not. I'm far from fine."

"Jez –"

"No, I need to say this, Dani."

"You said it in your email."

"Dani, Jesus! I fucked up. Let me apologise. You're the best thing that's ever happened to me and I fucked it up. I'm miserable without you. Please come back. We can work it out. I sacked Julie – she was nothing to me."

"Jez, please stop. I didn't call for you to apologise. I called because we need to sort out the house. I'm getting myself together. I've got a job. I'm starting over."

"That's it? You're cutting me off dead? You can't forgive me after everything we've been through? Dani, I told you I'm sorry, that it was my fault. I behaved like an idiot, but you mean too much to me to lose you. I love you. Please don't just end it."

"I didn't end it. You did. I will never be able to trust you again and I can't live like that. You don't betray someone you love, Jez. I just won't get past it," Dani said, the waver in her voice betraying her. Her palms were sweating and she rubbed them on her skirt.

"So that's it?" His voice had lost its arrogant edge and Dani realised he had really been thinking that she would go back to him.

"Jez… yes, that's it. I'm sorry, but I can't be with someone I don't trust."

"Jesus. Five years and now we're done?" His voice was a whisper, betraying his disbelief.

Dani's heart broke hearing him so obviously devastated, and the image of his handsome face, ashen and pained, came into her head. She was infinitely grateful she wasn't face to face, because there would have been no way she would have been this strong.

"Jez –"

"Dani, I just can't believe it…" He paused a moment as he processed what was happening.

Dani's eyes filled with tears. He must have genuinely loved her. He seemed to desperately want her back. Dani blinked hard, releasing the barrier, and tears fell freely down her hot cheeks. Hearing him so vulnerable was breaking her and for a moment, she questioned her decision. Five years they'd been together and on the whole, they were happy. They'd been through so much.

"Are you seeing someone?"

His question jolted Dani out of her thoughts. *What?* It took Dani a couple of seconds to register what he'd asked. "Excuse me?" Her tone was puzzled.

"I said are you seeing someone?" His voice had hardened.

"I beg your pardon?" *How dare he ask her about her private life! Seriously, of all the…* and then it dawned on her. He thought that she could only refuse to go back to him if she had someone else. He couldn't, or rather wouldn't believe that she could reject him if she was single. Dani roughly wiped away her tears.

"Well?" Gone was vulnerable Jez, and arrogant Jez was back.

Well, two can play at that game. "That is none of your business." She tried hard not to let her voice falter.

Jez snorted. "I see. Well, you didn't waste time did you? Okay, you want to play it that way, fine. I'll have your half of the money by the second week of January. You want it, you'll have to come and get it. On. Your. Own. That's what I stipulated. I won't quibble on the value."

"Fine. I'll tell Adam. He'll be dealing with it." Dani tried to sound monotone, not wanting him to realise how angry she was. *The nerve! He really couldn't believe that she could be on her own and be strong enough not run back to him? Jeez, he really didn't think much of her after all.*

"Fine. Good bye, Dani."

And before she could answer, he'd hung up.

Jerome switched off the engine and headed for the elevator. At least work would take his mind off Liz. Maybe she really was ready to make a go of their marriage. Something had broken in him though, and he really wasn't sure if he could get past it. He wanted to, for the sake of his children, but was that the right reason to stay? He still wasn't sure.

The elevator opened into the foyer and Jerome was greeted by Paul, his head of security and good friend. "Good evening, Jerome."

"Good evening, Paul, everything under control?"

"As always *Boss,* and happy birthday." Paul nodded curtly and winked at him as the rest of the staff at the front desk also wished him a happy birthday.

Jerome thanked everyone and Paul opened the door leading into the club. "Thanks Paul."

Jerome weaved his way through the club, acknowledging his staff with a wave, a nod or a quick word until he reached his office, which was situated at the rear, concealed by mirrored panels. His phone vibrated in his pocket, signalling that he'd received an email. He furrowed his brow. *Who would be emailing him at this late hour?* He walked into his large office and sat on his chair, then pulled out his phone. The email was from Kuch and was titled "Birthday boy". Jerome chuckled, opening it up. There in front of him were a collection of photos from this lunchtime. Jerome quickly opened up his office computer and opened his email so he could get a better look. The phone screen wasn't big enough to see them properly.

Jerome smiled to himself as he looked at the photos. There was one of Peter doing his speech, with him looking awkward, and his mother smiling widely. There were various shots of him, a few as he blew out the candles and then a selection of him posing with the staff. There were two pictures however, that had him inspecting the monitor more closely.

One was of Dani sitting while resting her chin on her hand, looking wistful and totally oblivious that she was being photographed. Jerome stared at the photo, mesmerised by it. She really was quite beautiful. He shook his head slightly, then moved to the second photo that had really grabbed his attention. This was again a picture of Dani but this time, he was in the photo too. It was taken when Jerome had gone over to thank her for the cake and he had leaned down to give her a kiss on the cheek.

Jerome enlarged the photo so he could focus on their faces. He rubbed his forehead nervously, focusing on their expressions.

There it was in vibrant Technicolor. If ever a picture could say a thousand words, then this was the perfect example. Both of them were in what seemed like an innocent exchange, even though their body language was far too relaxed and familiar. But what struck Jerome most was that they both had their eyes closed. If all the background had been erased and the picture focused just on their faces, it looked like a couple intimately embracing.

Jerome sat staring at the photo for what seemed like an age. He really needed to tread extremely carefully. He was very vulnerable at the moment and he wasn't sure whether his feelings for Dani were a result of that, or maybe they were the cause. He took a deep breath, then closed the photo. His eye caught sight of all the staff email addresses Kuch had sent the photos to, including a new one: Dani's. Jerome saved it to his contacts file, then opened up the 'Reply all' option.

Thanks, you made my day.
Jerome x

He pressed the 'Send' option and twisted his mouth. He knew he'd only sent it so that Dani would get it, but by sending it to all his staff, his gesture seemed innocent.

Dani stared at her phone. The bastard had hung up on her! She clenched her teeth in anger. *Yes, angry was good*, she thought. And to think he almost had her caving. She actually started to doubt her actions. Thank goodness for two hundred miles.

As she glared at the phone, it signalled that an email had come through. *It better not be from Jez*, she thought, opening up her email option. It was from Kuch. Dani instantly relaxed. It must be the photos. She shuffled off the bed and switched on her laptop so she could see the photos. Within a few minutes, they had all downloaded and Dani looked through each one of them, focusing all her attention on Jerome. He was just so good looking, and wow, was he photogenic. His eyes glistened even in the photos. Dani ran her fingers over his lips on the screen. *Jeez, she needed to get a grip.*

Dani scanned through the next few and stopped at the one of her. She always looked better in photos when she didn't know they were being taken. She clicked onto the next one and let out a small gasp. Dani licked her lips and leaned closer to the screen, then enlarged the image. She clasped her mouth. *Holy mother of God!*

Her trance was interrupted by another email coming through. Dani quickly opened it and let out her second gasp within a minute. It was from Jerome. She read the six words three times as a huge smile crept onto her face. She knew he'd sent it out to everyone, but she didn't care. *He'd* sent it to *her.* And that alone gave her a thrill.

Dani saved his email address to her contacts and opened it up to send him a reply. Crap, should she really send him one? What would she say? Wouldn't it be rude not to acknowledge his email? His first email at that. Unsure, Dani quickly wrote:

My pleasure :)

That was pretty harmless wasn't it? She wasn't overstepping the mark? Dani looked at the screen, then pressed one more key.

She stared at the screen. *Was that too familiar?* He'd sent a kiss. She closed her eyes and the image of the photo came into her head. Sod it. It was just a freaking kiss. She hit the 'Send' option and screwed up her face in excitement. *God, she really had it bad.*

There was a sharp knock at Jerome's door and Paul walked in with the club manager Gino.

"Hey, boss. Just a quick drink to wish you happy birthday before it's all over." Gino grinned, putting down three glasses and a bottle of Blue Label. "You know it's our tradition, celebrating you getting one year older!"

"Yeah, and getting your scar," added Paul as they sat down. Jerome ran his middle finger over the half-inch scar he had under his right eye as he grinned.

Gino had been Jerome's manager since they opened the club four years ago. He'd previously worked in another club along with Paul, which Jerome had frequented in his early twenties. They forged a bond on Jerome's twenty-first birthday.

There had been some trouble at the bar the night they'd all met, and Gino was trying to calm a heated discussion between a couple of drunks and possibly drugged-up customers. At one point, one of the customers lashed out at Gino and before security could get in to disperse the fight, punches were flying. Jerome was standing a couple of feet away with a few friends celebrating his birthday. Seeing what had happened, he immediately shot up and went to Gino's aid; his renowned hot temper getting the better of him. Thankfully, Paul and his team were there within seconds, but not before Jerome caught a punch just under his right eye. The drunken assailant was wearing a ring that had cut him.

"Jeez, that's thirteen years ago."

Gino poured generous amounts into the three glasses, then handed them out. "*Salute.*"

They all clinked their glasses and took a sip.

"So how was your day?" asked Gino, eyeing his boss.

The computer indicated he had another email, and Jerome's attention was distracted by it before he could answer Gino. He opened up the email and smiled broadly at Dani's response. He quickly pressed 'Reply', typed, then pressed 'Send'.

;) x

He looked up from his computer at Gino and Paul who looked on, clearly amused at their boss's reaction.

"My day was good. In fact, it was better than good, actually." He grinned as he took a drink from his glass.

16

HEAD RUSH

Dani flopped down into her chair around the table as Pino and Richard carried their food over. She'd worked the afternoon shift with them and it had been continuously busy. Sundays were always hard. There was never a breather. Customers streamed in steadily at different times compared to the weekdays. She was looking forward to her Monday off tomorrow. Her to do list was getting longer and she didn't seem to be putting a dent into it.

"It's been crazy today." Dani helped herself to seafood risotto.

"I know, hardly had time for a smoke," Pino huffed.

"You should pack it in," grinned Dani.

"Yeah. How did you manage it?"

"I just decided to stop. I only smoked around ten a day, fifteen tops. But moving up here helped. You know, new beginning and a change of environment. Saved me some money too." Dani shrugged, deciding not to elaborate much more.

"Ah, there you are, Daniella." Gia's melodic voice interrupted them and Dani turned around to look at her walk gracefully towards them. Pino and Richard immediately stood up.

"No, no, sit. You don't mind if I join you?"

They all answered simultaneously that they didn't mind and Richard quickly fetched another plate and spooned on some risotto.

"Oh, *grazie, Ricardo.*"

Dani smiled. She loved the way Gia converted everyone's name to Italian. "Did you need me for anything, Gia?" Dani asked.

"I noticed you haven't had a shift off since you started and you've worked most afternoons. I was wondering if you were saving them up for some time off later?"

"No, not really." Dani shrugged. The truth was she just preferred to be working and her Monday off was more than enough for her.

"You've worked every shift this week, haven't you?" Richard asked as Dani took her first forkful.

She nodded, chewed and then swallowed quickly. "Yes. I prefer to be busy at the moment and to be honest, by the time I get home, I'm only there for an hour or so, then I need to head on back, so it's really not worth it."

"Yes, it is a long drive from Harewood," Gia mused.

Dani nodded.

"You're still living with your sister?"

"Yes, but I'm going to start looking for a place of my own. I love being with them but I think I need to be on my own now and it's also a bit far away too."

"Yes, everyone should spend some time on their own. I never did when I was younger. That's the time to do it. Unfortunately my time alone is now," she said wistfully. "Not that I regret getting married so quickly – no. But you need time to grow on your own. I was lucky Alessandro and I grew together." She smiled almost to herself, clearly remembering something from her time with her husband.

"You should get an agent to find you a flat to rent around here," suggested Pino. "Or are you going to buy somewhere?"

"I think I'll rent for a while. I'm expecting some money to come through after the New Year, so I may look to buy then. I'm not sure."

"Some big trust fund, eh, Dani?" laughed Richard.

Dani wrinkled her nose, feeling a little embarrassed at the attention. "Not quite," she answered softly.

"Well, it's been a great help for Chef that you've volunteered to work extra. It gets hard juggling the rota." Gia smiled softly at Dani.

"Actually, I might ask for next Thursday night off, if that's okay. It's my sister's birthday and I would like to babysit for her so she can go out. She doesn't get out much."

"I'm sure that would be no problem. Make sure you tell Chef today."

"I will."

"Are you alright in the back restaurant with Pino and Ricardo tonight? It's a full restaurant from seven thirty and will be full from early on too?"

"I'm fine wherever, Gia."

Gia smiled warmly at her and affectionately patted her arm. In the couple of weeks Dani had been working at La Casa d'Italia, Gia had grown fond of her. She was good natured, professional and all the staff and customers liked her.

"Good. Well I'll see you later. I'm going to go and have a rest until seven. I'm feeling a little tired today." Gia gracefully rose from the table and headed out of the door. Dani watched her leave and then she looked down at Gia's plate. She hadn't touched her food. Strange.

Gia had been right. From the second Dani entered the restaurant, it had been packed out. Dani wondered how much busier it was going to be over Christmas. Matteo and his team were in their element, churning out each and every order like a well-oiled machine.

Dani rushed into the kitchen. "Table twenty-four wants an extra portion of the aubergines." She cringed at Matteo. "I'm sorry, but they keep adding things."

Matteo's eyes rolled and Jamie went to the back to quickly put a portion in the oven.

"Five minutes." He pressed his fingers and thumb together, emphasizing his reply. Dani nodded, leaving the hot busy kitchen and entering the buzzing restaurant, making her way to the troublesome table twenty-four.

"Your extra portion of aubergines will be five minutes."

"Oh aren't you a sweetheart," replied David. He'd come in again and Dani had been lumbered with him. All the staff disliked David – he was crass and obnoxious. He'd been sending her up and down for extra food, then drinks that he ordered periodically. He seemed to be enjoying watching Dani pander to his every whim. Dani remained professional and carried out every request with a smile. But he was starting to become more familiar. Touching her arm or leaning closer to her as she poured his wine.

"I see David's giving you a hard time." Richard cringed.

"David?"

"Table twenty-four. He's a regular and a pain in the ass. Spends a load of money in here but he thinks the restaurant is at his beck and call. I really don't like him."

"Yes, he was in on Friday too."

"I have a feeling he likes you." Richard gave her a knowing look.

"He's with his family," Dani replied, appalled.

Richard shrugged. "Like he cares."

Dani rolled her eyes. "Well, I've handled worse."

By eleven thirty, the restaurant had emptied and all the staff had made their way down to the changing rooms to get ready for their weekly night out.

"So glad I've got tomorrow off," sighed Nicole as she applied mascara.

"Have any plans?" asked Dani, vigorously brushing out her ponytail and then pulling it into a loose low ponytail off to one side, styling into a fish tail that fell over her shoulder.

"Just chilling with a friend. I love the way you style your hair. You're always doing something different with it."

Dani scrunched her nose at the compliment. The truth was Jez had only liked her hair loose and she'd never had a chance to experiment. Now he wasn't around, she loved the fact she could wear it any way she pleased.

"Thanks. So, is it a boyfriend?" Dani slipped on her red halter top and tucked it into her skin tight black trousers, then leaned over to the mirror to apply her red lipstick.

"Um, well er, sort of." Nicole blushed as she answered in a hushed tone. "I don't really talk about him. It's a bit complicated, so no one knows."

Dani raised her brows up. "Oh, okay, well I won't breathe a word."

"Thanks," grinned Nicole.

Once Rosa was ready, they went upstairs to meet up with Kuch who was standing by his car waiting for them.

"Wow, you girls look fabulous. I'm a lucky so-and-so escorting you three." He smiled coyly at them.

"I like your shirt, Kuch... although I think it looked better on me," Dani teased.

"Ha, I think you're right. You can borrow it again anytime." He winked, opening up the back door for her to get in with Nicole, then Rosa slipped into the front.

Sky was packed out and they needed to squeeze through the clubbers to get to the staff table. Most of the kitchen staff had made it, along with the majority of the restaurant staff. Kuch immediately ordered their drinks, then went over to the deejay box to speak to his brother. Rosa was itching to dance, so she coaxed Dani to go with her and they joined Carmen, Jamie and Silvanna.

Jerome watched over the club from a balcony on a higher level, effectively giving him a bird's-eye view. He was able to observe the whole club without being detected. It also meant he could watch Dani. Her scarlet red top made it easier for him to spot her. He was pleased to see she wasn't so much the centre of Kuch's attention this week. Maybe she'd given him the brush off, he thought. Jerome carried on scanning the club, secure in the knowledge that he was hidden from the lower floor clubbers, but his eyes were constantly drawn back to wherever Dani was.

Dani dropped into one of the white leather sofas next to Carmen and fanned her face. "I need to cool down."

Carmen grinned and jerked her head towards one of the huge glass walls. "There's a large veranda out there for the smokers."

Dani twisted around to see where Carmen had signalled to. "I didn't notice that last week. That's so cool! I'm going out there for a bit. You coming?"

Carmen shook her head. "I'm not that hot and the height freaks me out."

Dani shrugged and got up and began to weave her way through the crowd, towards where Carmen had gestured. The flashing lights reflected off the glass walls, so unless you knew where the veranda was, it was hard to notice. Dani pushed through the heavy glass doors and was instantly hit by the cool dry air. She took in a deep breath and looked around. Once the door had closed, the music from inside became muted. Only the vibration through the decked floor gave away Dani's location.

It was a huge area scattered with white leather sofas and low glass tables set in intimate U-shapes, ensuring privacy. There were outside heaters periodically placed, which helped warm up the veranda. The edge was secured with high glass walls allowing the view to be unobstructed and the area was sheltered by a canopy. Dani looked closer at the canopy and realised it was probably retracted in the summer. There were roughly twenty people puffing hard on their cigarettes, though the area could comfortably accommodate five times that. Dani chuckled to herself as she watched a party of two couples stub out their cigarettes and re-join the clubbers inside, glad she'd managed to ditch *that* habit.

She'd cooled down considerably now, her halter top providing very little protection from the cold breeze that blew around the veranda. Her curiosity piqued, now that she was out there, she decided to walk towards the edge but then stopped a few feet away, not quite feeling brave enough to go right up to the balcony edge.

"It's a bit daunting at first." Jerome's raspy voice startled her, causing her to let out a small yelp. She spun to her left where he stood, his expression amused as he steadied her, placing his hand on her waist. "Sorry, I didn't mean to sneak up on you." He'd followed her out, pretending to himself that his real reason for being out on the veranda was for a cigarette.

Dani's cheeks flushed, embarrassed that she'd overreacted to his voice, but her ears were buzzing from the loud club music and out on the soundless veranda, unexpectedly hearing Jerome's alluring voice had startled her.

"That's okay, I just didn't hear you come out. Sorry, what did you say?" Dani had turned a little so she could look at his face, forcing Jerome to drop his hand from her waist. Dani drank him in, from his slightly unruly dark hair, down to his black boots he wore under a midnight blue slim fitting three piece suit. *Gorgeous...*

"I said that it's a little bit daunting at first." His eyes almost glittered in the subdued lighting. Dani frowned, not understanding what he meant. "The height." He looked over to the glass balcony in explanation.

"Oh, yes. Well, I was thinking about going and looking down but..." Dani screwed up her face and she saw Jerome frown for a second. He shrugged himself out of his jacket and gently placed it over her shoulders.

"You must be freezing."

Dani was about to protest because in his presence, she'd forgotten it was cold. Once the warmth of Jerome's jacket touched her frozen skin, engulfing her in his scent, she stopped.

"That's better. Can't have you getting ill now, can we? So are you going to go and look?" he cocked his head and flashed a crooked smile at her. "Isn't that why you came out here? Unless you've fallen off the wagon." His smile widened.

"Er... no. I just wanted to cool down a bit."

Jerome nodded and then stepped closer to Dani. Her eyes opened, wondering why he was suddenly invading her space and she held her breath as his hand reached out. *Oh my, what was he doing?* Jerome's hand then slipped into his jacket's pocket and retrieved his cigarettes and lighter. Dani felt herself blush again. *He was just getting his cigarettes – calm the hell down*, she chastised herself as she let out the breath she was holding and smiled tightly, embarrassed at her erratic thoughts.

"You don't mind, do you?" he held up the packet and twisted them a little. Dani recovered enough to shake her head slightly. He pulled out a cigarette and then shielded it from the slight wind so he could light it. Dani stared at him, mesmerized by the simple action, watching his chiselled cheek bones accentuate when he sucked. He dragged on the cigarette and then blew out a steady stream of smoke, his face betraying complete satisfaction.

"Come on. I'll stand next to you if you like. It really is something, being fourteen floors up."

Dani twisted her mouth, unsure if she really needed to go up to the edge. Jerome fixed her with his eyes, and Dani knew she'd have to suck it up. "Okay."

Jerome shot her a smile and gently guided her by placing his hand on the small of her back and they both stepped towards the glass. Dani stopped a foot away, nervousness gripping her. *Jeez, it was really high.* Jerome stepped right up to the glass and took another drag from his cigarette and regarded her. He then looked out over the city of Leeds and pointed. "La Casa is over there. If you go up to the apartments at the top of La Casa, you can actually see Sky." He turned a little to the left. "Over there is the way back to Harewood." He grinned and Dani shuffled a little closer to the edge. "On a clear day you can see for miles out past the city centre."

Dani was now up to the glass, taking in the view, but refusing to look down.

"In the summer it's really something up here." He smiled softly down at Dani as she looked up at him.

"I can imagine," Dani answered quietly. They stood for a moment, looking out over the glittering city in the eerie quiet, with the cold air breezing over them. It was surprisingly peaceful and Dani wanted this moment to last forever. Jerome stood only inches away from her but his presence had totally enveloped her. She started to feel a little giddy and her face was flushing from a sudden surge of acute emotions. She wasn't entirely sure if it was the height, Jerome's proximity, or the warmth from a nearby heater, but all of a sudden she felt increasingly warm.

Their quiet was interrupted by a voice. "Um, Boss?"

Both Jerome and Dani turned around sharply to find Paul, the head of security, standing a couple of feet away. The two men looked at each other and an unsaid communication passed between them.

"I'll be right in, Paul," answered Jerome, suddenly becoming tense. Paul nodded curtly and allowed his eyes to flit over Dani, then he abruptly turned and headed back in to Sky.

"Well, that's my cigarette break over with," sighed Jerome, returning his attention to Dani.

Dani chuckled. Jerome took a final drag from his cigarette, then reached over to stub it out into a nearby ashtray. "Thanks for the tour." She motioned to the view, then shrugged out of his jacket. "And thanks for the jacket. Here." She held it out for him to take.

"Keep it on if you're staying out."

"No. Thank you. I think I've had enough of a head rush for one evening. I'm going back in." Dani's warm skin instantly cooled once she'd removed the jacket.

Jerome lifted an eyebrow in amusement as Dani stepped away from the edge. "Head rush?"

Dani smirked. "Yeah, head rush. I'm not too good with heights." That wasn't entirely true – it was the hefty dose of Jerome's close proximity that had her head spinning, but she couldn't admit to that. *No wonder I'm giddy*, thought Dani.

"You'll get used to it. It can get quite addictive, the rush."

Dani narrowed her eyes at Jerome. "Maybe I'll need to ease myself into it."

Jerome laughed, taking back his jacket and Dani grinned, feeling decidedly reckless, encouraged by his subtle flirting. *God, he was just stunning when he laughed.* Dani's heart skipped a beat. She turned away from him and headed towards the door, scared he'd catch her openly admiring him while he slipped on his jacket. She was sure it was written all over her face. Jerome followed her, allowing his eyes to drift over her exposed shoulders and back, then down to her behind. He managed to reach out for the door before her and she glanced up at him, his hand taking hold of the handle.

"You look flushed." Jerome's comment made Dani redden more.

"Yes, well... um... it's probably the adrenaline, or the heater." *Or the fact you're so close to me and sexy as hell.*

Jerome blinked down at her, his dreamy eyes sparkled and a smile curved over his lips.

"Or maybe it was because of your jacket," Dani added bravely. She pulled the door open and stepped back in to the hot pulsating atmosphere of the club. Jerome faltered a second before following Dani, her comment jolting him. She moved quickly through the crowds and Jerome let his eyes follow her back to where the rest of the staff were gathered. He really couldn't make her out. She sometimes was shy, then out of the blue, she'd come out with some unexpected remark. He furrowed his brow and shook his head. He really needed to stop spending so much time thinking about her.

Jerome opened up his office door and was confronted by a grim-faced Paul.

"Who was it this time?" he asked, slipping into his chair.

"No one important. They've been taken by the police."

"It's getting harder to keep them out. We know the major dealers but they've so many runners. Did you catch them before they did any major dealing?"

"Hard to say, boss. They had a fair amount of cash on them."

Jerome rubbed his face. He was adamant that his club stayed clean. He had a zero tolerance of drugs but he also wasn't so naive as to think that the dealers would keep out of his prestigious club. It was inevitable, but he'd be damned if he'd let them get away with it.

"Where did you catch them?"

"They were loitering around the back bar. We moved them out to the back. Thankfully, they didn't cause a scene."

Jerome knew Paul wouldn't openly threaten anyone, but he had what could only be described as a very persuasive manner. "Follow it up with your leads. That's the third incident this month," Jerome added, clearly agitated.

Paul nodded.

"I really need to know we can control it, especially with Christmas coming."

"I'll get in touch with some of my old colleagues down town."

"Good. Everything else under control?"

"Of course," Paul smirked.

Jerome visibly relaxed. He had enough to deal with, and he didn't need to worry about security here as well. With his police training and contacts on both sides of the law, he knew Paul was the best. If there was anyone Jerome could trust it was Paul. Jerome sat down at his desk, allowing his eyes to drift to the photo he had of Alessandro and Kara. "Do you still have contact with that private investigator?"

"You mean Scott?"

Jerome nodded and Paul stepped closer to the desk.

"Yeah. You think we should be using him to find out who's behind the runners?" Paul tried hard not to sound affronted. The club security was his domain and he wasn't comfortable letting someone else take over. In the four years he'd been in charge at Sky he'd never needed anyone's input to keep the club clean.

"No. I know you have that covered."

Paul loosened up, but Jerome didn't even notice. His thoughts were focused on how he was going to get the number of the investigator without arousing suspicion. "Seni asked me if you knew of anyone. He's working on a case that needs some... well, subtle investigating."

Paul pulled out his phone and scrolled through his contacts, then reached for a pen and paper and scribbled down the number. "Here. Do you want me to call him first, tell him Seni will be calling?"

"Sure. Thanks. He's discreet, isn't he? From what little Seni told me, he needs total discretion."

Paul looked down at Jerome staring at the piece of paper he'd handed to him. He knew something was wrong. After closely working alongside Jerome for over four years, he'd become somewhat of an expert at reading Jerome's moods. "Yes, he's solid, you don't need to worry. Is there anything else? You seem preoccupied. Don't worry about here, we'll keep things clean."

Jerome sighed and nodded. "I know, Paul. I'm fine, just a lot on my mind. Thanks again for this." Jerome slipped the paper into his jacket pocket and stood back up again. He knew Paul would be the best person for the job. But he couldn't let him know about Liz – he was too close. If Jerome was being perfectly honest, he really didn't want his friend and colleague knowing his personal problems. It was bad enough Cosimo, Seni and Peter knew.

17

BLIND LOVE

Adam unbuckled his seat belt and turned around to face Dani. "Well? What do you think?"

"It's great, nippy, easy to park, fast enough and a lot roomier than I thought." Dani looked around the interior of the Smart car she'd just test driven.

"But?"

Dani smirked. Adam knew her too well. "I really wanted a convertible."

Adam nodded. "Well, you can wait until one becomes available."

"I need a car, Adam. I'll just have to take it," she sighed.

"Let's see what the chances are of getting a convertible first. You never know." He could see that she was disappointed and was hoping the dealer might ring around again and try and locate one.

Dani opened the door and followed Adam into the office of the dealership. She stood awkwardly while Adam explained that Dani had her heart set on a convertible.

"The only convertibles I have are a Peugeot and a Fiat. I can try and see if my contacts down south can get hold of one, but I can't guarantee anything. Give me a day or so and I'll try my best." He smiled hopefully at Dani.

"What Fiat is it?" Dani asked.

"A 500."

"I'm afraid that means nothing to me. What I mean is: is it a big car?"

Adam chuckled and shook his head. She really was quite clueless when it came to cars. "No, it's a small car, Dani," Adam explained.

"Can I see it?"

The dealer smiled widely and immediately grabbed a set of keys, then ushered them out onto the forecourt to show them the car.

Dani grinned as he approached the small pearly white car with a red soft top. It had a thin green, white and red strip along the side. "Can I test drive it?"

"Of course." The dealer handed her the keys and Dani jumped into the driver's seat. Adam opened up the passenger side and buckled up.

"It's like Gia's – Mrs Ferretti's. But hers is green and isn't a convertible" – she turned to look in the back – "and it's a four-seater."

Adam huffed, "For midgets, maybe. Come on, let's see what it drives like."

Within thirty minutes, Adam thrashed out a price with the dealer and arranged for the car to be road ready by Thursday.

Dani grinned to herself as they drove away from the car dealership, glad to see the back of her Porsche. Another reminder and tie to Jez eliminated. One by one, she was managing to tick off each task on her ever-increasing mental to do list.

"I think La Casa and the Ferrettis are having quite an influence on you," Adam joked. Dani smiled tightly.

Dani's grin dropped. *Oh crap*, she'd hoped he hadn't realised just how much they were unconsciously influencing her. She lifted up her hand and ticked off each of the criteria on her fingers. "It's a small, nippy, easy to park, convertible," Dani answered in justification. "Just what I wanted."

"Yeah, whatever." Adam shook his head, unconvinced.

By four fifteen, Jerome was sitting in the office at Level One feeling decidedly better. He'd managed to find two managers that would be able to start almost immediately. He was lucky it was the end of the year and the gym business was slowing down, so they'd be eased in gently before the influx of new memberships after the New Year. He'd be splitting himself in two again until they were settled but nevertheless, things were getting in order.

He pulled out the paper with the number of the investigator Paul had scribbled down for him and turned it in his hands, unsure of what he should do. He knew he couldn't be permanently second guessing Liz, and this would be the only way he'd be sure if she was still seeing Jonathan.

He scraped back his chair and put on his jacket, tucking the paper into his inside pocket, then headed out of his office.

The elevator opened up onto the seventh floor where Arsenio's office was situated. His office was a far-too-large corner suite, which suited him down to a tee. It was decorated in the style that only Arsenio seemed to be comfortable with. Ultra-modern, very masculine, sleek, black and white, and devoid of any warmth. In short it was the epitome of what a tough successful lawyer would select. The only item in the whole of his vast office that indicated Arsenio had a softer side was a black and white framed picture of Alessandro and Kara on his desk.

Arsenio's assistant was not at his usual station, so Jerome popped his head around the slightly opened office door. Arsenio was pacing around his desk talking on his phone just in his white shirt and black suit trousers. He'd taken off his tie, jacket and shoes and continued to move around. Jerome smirked as he watched his younger brother, who was clearly agitated, walk up and down the plush off-white woollen carpet in his socks. *It was a good job he'd taken off his shoes*, thought Jerome, *he'd wear a hole in the totally impractical carpet*. Arsenio waved him in and signalled he'd be one minute.

"Stop talking," Arsenio snapped at whoever was on the other end of the phone, "I expect a revised proposal within an hour... I don't care that it's nearly four thirty. My client has given you more than enough leeway and whatever happens, I want this deal signed, sealed and delivered by end of business tomorrow. Otherwise, I'll advise my client to go elsewhere."

Arsenio scowled at his phone as he pressed the off switch. Jerome stepped closer and lowered himself into the chair in front of the desk. "Problems?"

"No, not really. Just some hotshot lawyer thinking he can play hard-ball. Anyway, to what do I owe the pleasure of this visit?" he grinned, settling himself into his chair.

"I was at Level One and thought I'd come and see you," mumbled Jerome, suddenly feeling unsure if he was ready to broach the subject of a private investigator.

Arsenio raised a quizzical eyebrow. "Jerome, just spit it out, what do you need?"

Jerome took a deep breath and reached into the side pocket of his jacket, then handed the paper over. Arsenio read the name and number, then looked up at Jerome, waiting for an explanation.

"Paul gave me his number. He's a PI; someone trustworthy."

Arsenio leaned back on his chair and nodded, watching Jerome slouch down nervously.

"Paul said he'd ring him first to let him know you'd be in touch."

"Good. Does Paul know why?"

"No. I said it was for one of your clients."

"I see. Okay, I'll ring him in the morning and set up a meeting."

"Fine." Jerome sat staring blankly at a framed black and white photograph of a glass building's elevation that was positioned behind Arsenio. *God, even the art he displayed was cool and clinical*, thought Jerome.

"Look, Jerome, I know you're really not comfortable talking about this, but we need to work out some sort of strategy." Jerome's eyes darted back to Arsenio but he didn't speak. He just clenched his jaw repeatedly. So Arsenio continued, "If the investigator digs up that she's still... well with this asshole, you'll have your grounds for divorce."

Jerome stood up and walked towards the vast window and stared out of it blindly. Divorce. There was that word again. A word he'd never thought he'd use in relation to himself. The very thought depressed him.

Arsenio's heart sank as he watched his brother try hard to hold on to his emotions. Out of all the brothers, Jerome was the most sensitive. This was a lot harder for Jerome than he was showing, but Arsenio wanted to protect him in the only way he knew he could. Legally.

"But that won't secure you full custody, Jerome. I take it that is what you want? She's not the first wife to play away and the courts don't really care."

Jerome took a deep breath but still remained silent.

"If you want to get full custody, she has to be seen as a danger to the kids."

Jerome slowly turned around to face Arsenio, his brow furrowed.

"She's not a danger to the kids. She maybe neglectful, indifferent even, but she'd never hurt them, Seni." *Crap, he couldn't believe he was actually having this conversation about his wife, the mother of his children, the woman he once loved.*

"Look, Jerome, I know this is hard." Jerome huffed at this comment. "But I'm talking to you as your lawyer. The kids..." He stopped a moment, searching for the right words. "What's important is that the kids stay with you. No judge will ever grant the father full custody over the mother unless she's deemed unfit. She can be screwing around every night for all they care, she's still their mother. The best you can hope for is joint."

"What if she agrees to it herself?"

"You actually think she'll give up the kids?" Arsenio couldn't hide his disbelief.

"Maybe, if she's given the right incentive."

"What do you mean?"

"Well, Cosimo has checked over my financial status and, as you well know, I only have the house in my name. So she's only entitled to half of that and a percentage of my earnings. I'm sure she thinks she's entitled to more. If I can give her some deal, a package that will set her up, she may agree to giving up custody."

Arsenio leaned back on his chair. "You really think she'd do that? I know she's a selfish bitch, but give up her kids?"

Jerome flinched at his comment and broadened his eyes.

"Sorry. But you know I've never liked her."

Jerome clenched his jaw tighter and closed his eyes momentarily.

"Look, Jerome, I know you're not comfortable talking to me about your personal affairs and if you'd rather I get another lawyer, one that specialises in family law to deal with this... we've a whole floor dedicated to –"

"No. I don't want anyone else," Jerome interrupted. It was difficult discussing his private life with Arsenio, but he knew that his brother would do the utmost to protect him, even if his manner was a little too abrasive for Jerome at the moment.

"I won't sugar-coat anything, Jerome, just so we're clear," Arsenio warned.

"I wouldn't expect you to," snorted Jerome as he headed back to the chair and slumped back into it.

"I'll try and be more respectful, okay?"

Jerome nodded, then leaned forward. "So how does this work, then?"

"The investigator, you mean?"

Jerome nodded.

"Well, after we've had the meeting... do you want to be here when I see him?"

Jerome shook his head. The last thing he wanted was to hear the no-holds-barred conversation between Arsenio and a PI.

"Okay. Well I'll fill him in on the details. If he's been recommended by Paul, he'll have all the latest equipment so he'll track her car and phone. He could bug the house too if you want."

Jerome shook his head. "No, Nina's there most of the time."

"Sure. He'll take pictures and videos, then after a week, he'll give me a report and we'll go from there. I'll need her car registration. I have her phone number and the name of the asshole."

Jerome leaned over onto the desk, took a pen and pulled off a piece of paper from a block. He scribbled the information down and left them on the desk. "Thanks. Let me know how it goes." He pushed to his feet and paused a moment. "I really appreciate this, Seni. I'll be honest with you; I'm finding it extremely hard to get my head round it all. I never wanted this, or even thought... I'm still not sure what I want to do." He stopped himself from saying any more.

Arsenio got up from his seat, rounded the desk and pulled Jerome into a hug. "Whatever you need, Jerome. I'll do whatever. I'm here." He pulled away. "Just so you know, from experience, things get better. A year from now, you'll be past all of this." He gave Jerome a reassuring smile, hoping it would appease him. His brother had been looking very drawn these past few weeks and Arsenio hadn't noticed it until now. "I'd better let you get back. Call me."

"Of course."

Arsenio sat down in his chair as he watched Jerome leave. He could kill that bitch Liz for what she'd done to him. He just hoped the investigator would pull up enough dirt to make Jerome feel he really had no option but to kick her to the curb. The sooner the better. She'd single-handedly broken him down. He used to be the life and soul of the party – he'd walk into a room and everyone was drawn to him and not only because of his good looks. He had incredible charisma – even Arsenio could acknowledge that. Over their late teens and early twenties, Jerome had women throwing themselves at him and Arsenio had always felt a little envious of the attention Jerome had consistently received. But it became abundantly clear that Jerome was not the kind of man who thrived off the attention of women. He was polite and courteous, but to the best of Arsenio's knowledge, he'd only had a couple of girlfriends prior to Liz. Arsenio had always been around to pick up the slack though. He'd seen glimpses of the old Jerome when he was at La Casa, but over the years, Jerome had lost that individual magnetism that just drew you in.

Arsenio picked up his phone and punched in a number, then jammed his phone between his ear and shoulder so he could put on his shoes. "Hey Mary, is he busy? Great, tell him I'll be there in five."

Arsenio walked out onto the twelfth floor of Ferretti House and smiled at the pretty receptionist. "Go right through, Mr. Ferretti," she beamed.

Arsenio winked at her and made his way to Cosimo's end office. The door was slightly ajar and he could hear Cosimo talking to Mary, his secretary. He pushed it open and strolled in. "Hello."

"Good afternoon, Mr Ferretti," Mary replied as she picked up four large folders off the top of Cosimo's desk and tucked them under her arm, then pushed her designer spectacles back up her nose. Arsenio loved Mary – she was like the generic secretaries of the nineteen fifties; prim and proper and highly efficient. She was in her late fifties and would've no doubt been described as an attractive woman when she was younger. "Can I get you anything?"

"No thank you, Mary."

"Well, I'll leave you to it," she turned to Cosimo. "Mr. Banks called while you were on the phone earlier. He's running late. Your mobile was off so he asked me to tell you he'd be done by five thirty."

"Thanks, Mary. If he calls again, put him straight through and let Mr Mann know he won't be there before five thirty." Cosimo focused on Arsenio as Mary walked out of the office, closing the door behind her. Cosimo pulled out his phone and turned it on, leaving it on his desk. Arsenio lowered himself into the leather chair and leaned forward. "What's wrong?"

"Jerome came round to see me today."

"Oh?"

"He gave me one of Paul's contacts. A private investigator."

"I see."

They both sat for a minute in silence. Then Cosimo sighed.

"How was he?"

"Not good, Cos, not good at all. You know he doesn't open up but I get the feeling he's hoping it's a one off, I think. That if he makes an effort, they'll be able to get through this. The last thing he wants is a divorce."

Cosimo shook his head. "That's never going to happen. She's never been happy."

"She's a fucking bitch, that's what she is and he just can't see it. I can't believe he got sucked in by her!"

"*L'amore e cieco,*" murmured Cosimo

"Love is blind, my ass!" scoffed Arsenio. "I'm going to meet up with this investigator in the next day or two. Track her car and phone."

"He asked you to do that?"

"Yes, and then get a report back to him. We need some concrete evidence that she's still with this guy. Maybe hack her phone?"

"It's not legal, Seni."

Arsenio raised an eyebrow at Cosimo and he huffed. The irony of this statement made him smirk. "It's not for court, it's for leverage. She won't have a leg to stand on. And secondly, I want Jerome to hear, so that he'll stop doubting and get rid of her."

"He won't be pleased and he won't thank you for meddling," warned Cosimo.

"Maybe. But at least he'll know and in the end it'll be for his own good."

"Do you want me to be with you when you speak to the investigator? Don't take this the wrong way, but Jerome will feel better if we're both involved."

"Yeah, you may be right. Sure, I'll let you know when he's coming."

Their attention was drawn to Cosimo's desk phone ringing and he picked it up to answer it.

Mary's muffled voice announced it was Mr Banks on the line.

"Thank you, Mary... hey, sorry about earlier." He smiled widely at something the caller said and his eyes darted to Arsenio, who was watching him with amusement. "So, five thirty up at the Lodge. I've let Joseph know you're running late... um, sure." Cosimo shifted nervously in his seat. "Can we talk later? I've someone in my office at the moment... okay. See you then. Bye."

"So who was that, that got you all flustered over?" teased Arsenio.

"I wasn't flustered." Cosimo tutted. "He's just a client – Mr Banks. He's a landscaper that I've recommended to Joseph Mann, Jerome's college buddy," explained Cosimo, avoiding eye contact as he nervously rearranged his immaculate desk.

"I think he doth protest too much!" laughed Arsenio.

Cosimo glared at his younger brother. "I've work to do before I leave, so if you don't mind..."

"Okay, okay, I get the message." Arsenio pushed to his feet and smirked. "A landscaper eh? So you like the outdoorsy type?"

"Seni! Just leave, will you?" Cosimo growled, clearly embarrassed that his brother had picked up on the importance of Mr Banks.

"Okay, I'm leaving. Have fun." He winked at Cosimo and sauntered out of his office.

18

PLANS

After a few days of relatively mild weather, the temperature had dropped and the rain came down relentlessly. Dani looked out of Adam's windscreen, the wipers working double time as he pulled into La Casa d'Italia's car park and as close to the back door as possible. The doorway was obstructed by a rather flashy gun metal-coloured sports car. Dani's heart flipped, focusing on the only car that ever interested her, Jerome's Maserati, parked up next to Gia's.

Adam whistled through his teeth, "That's a *very* nice car. Whose car is that?"

"I haven't a clue. What is it?" Dani shrugged.

"Lamborghini. Are you working through again?"

"Probably. I'll get the work taxi home or Kuch will drop me off."

"Okay, see you in the morning, then. Remember, we're picking up your car tomorrow, so we need to set off earlier."

"I know. I can't wait." She was grinning she opened up the car door and shook her umbrella until it sprung open, then slid out under its shelter. Dani quickly tucked her newspaper inside her waterproof coat and bobbed down to say bye. "Thanks. See you in the morning."

Dani ran to the back door and pushed her way through, eyeing the mystery car. Shaking off all the remaining water from her umbrella, she closed it and walked downstairs to the changing rooms. After storing her belongings in her locker, Dani restyled her hair into a soft high bun, pulling a few tendrils out. She applied her lipstick and made her way to the kitchen. She checked the time. It was nine fifteen. Just in time to make the kitchen staff their first coffee.

Dani realised that Capo couldn't be in this morning the moment she heard the dulcet tones of Dean Martin floating out of the kitchen, rather than the standard opera Capo seemed to prefer. Dani pushed through double doors. "*Buongiorno tutti.*"

Carmen looked up from her work station and grinned. Everyone greeted Dani and she went through the morning ritual of seeing who was in so she could prepare the first coffee of their shift.

"Where's Capo?"

"He went to see a supplier down at the market. He should be back soon, though," answered Jamie.

The music shifted to one of Dani's favourites: "Sway". She smiled. "I love this song so much."

Enzo grinned and turned it up so she could hear it in the restaurant, then wedged the door open.

Dani called her thanks to him, then skipped her way through the restaurant, softly singing along to the tune, and got to work on everyone's coffees. Within a few minutes she had taken them through to the kitchen, and everyone came over for their much-needed coffee break.

"Will you put it on again?" Dani asked Enzo.

"Sway? Sure, you like Dean Martin, then?"

"Yes, but especially that song." She swayed a little as it started up again and Carmen grinned, joining her and singing along to the song. It was infectious and before long, Jamie was twirling Silvanna and Enzo held a wooden spoon like a microphone and accompanied Dean Martin. Carmen spun Dani around one way, then the other, then as she re-spun her, Dani lost her footing and staggered a couple of steps back, slap bang into Arsenio, who had just walked through into the kitchen, having heard the music through the opened door.

"Oops, sorry." Dani flushed instantly and the rest of the staff stopped.

He took her by the waist in a firm grip and grasped her hand, then swayed in time to the music. His hazel eyes fixed on her, smiling mischievously down at her. "Don't apologise. Believe me, you just brightened up my rather miserable morning. Don't stop on my account." He held her closer, moving in perfect time to the music, then spun her round as the song finished, leaving Dani a little dumbstruck and shaken. He winked at her, then bowed curtly and she shook her head and dipped a curtsy. "I wish my place of work was as much fun as here," he chuckled.

"Well, we all know lawyers are as dull as dishwater, Seni," Carmen teased.

Arsenio leaned against the doorframe, regarding Dani closely. Enzo had turned down the music to its previous level and the rest of the staff got back to their stations. Dani busied herself collecting the empty cups and putting them on the tray. "Ah, but we make up for it on our time off, cus!"

Carmen huffed at him and started beating some cream. Dani lifted the tray and took it over to the dishwashing area trying to distance herself from the disarming Arsenio.

"Do you think you could make me an espresso, Dani?"

"Sure." Dani shuffled past him and headed quickly to the bar. Arsenio followed her out and sat on one of the stools. She could feel him watching her.

"I see you've settled in here."

"Yes. I'm really enjoying it."

"I can see," Arsenio chuckled. The coffee filtered through and Dani heard the familiar footsteps of Peter walking into the restaurant.

"Morning. Jeez, it's awful out there today." He ran his hand through his damp hair as he spoke, then shook off the rain from his overcoat.

"Morning, Chef. Coffee?" Dani felt instantly better, now that Peter was there. She wasn't sure she could handle Arsenio's constant barrage of flirting, however flattering it was.

"Please. This is an unexpected surprise, Seni." Peter's eyes flitted to the back of Dani's head as she worked the machine.

"Don't worry, Peter, I came to see Jerome. But I have been entertained while he's getting ready."

Peter huffed at his comment. "He's back, then?"

"Yeah, he ran in this." Arsenio motioned to the window where the rain lashed against it and shook his head.

"He's nuts."

"Yep, that about sums him up."

Dani passed the two espressos over, then reached for her newspaper she'd left on the bar and headed to the far end of the restaurant, giving them some privacy. She sat down at one of the unset tables and opened it up at the "Flats for Rent" section, hoping she might find something suitable.

"Daniella, *buongiorno*." Gia's familiar smooth voice made Dani abandon what she was reading and look up.

"*Buongiorno*, Gia. Shall I make you a coffee?"

"*Si, grazie.*" She leaned to see what Dani was looking at. "Are you trying to find another car?"

"No I bought one already. I'm getting it tomorrow."

"Oh that's good news." Gia seemed genuinely pleased.

"I was just checking for apartments closer to town."

Gia nodded at her. "Any luck?"

"Not really. All the nice ones are too expensive and all the places in my price range are awful. I only need it for six months, maybe a year. I plan to buy my own place eventually."

Gia furrowed her brow and mulled over something, then focused on the bar where she heard Arsenio talking with Peter. Dani folded her paper and headed to the bar, following in Gia's footsteps.

"Arsenio. This is a nice surprise. What are you doing here?" they kissed and hugged each other warmly.

"I had something to discuss with Jerome, but he's just come back from Level One. I left him showering. I'll be going back up again in a few minutes. He should be done by now."

Dani quickly made Gia's espresso, then proceeded to make a double. She passed Gia hers, then pushed the double espresso in front of Arsenio. Puzzled, he looked up at Dani for an explanation.

"If you're going up to the office, Jerome will probably want his coffee," Dani mumbled, then felt herself blush.

"That's very thoughtful, Daniella. Yes, take it for him, Arsenio," Gia prompted. Peter smiled stiffly as Arsenio took the cup.

"Sure." He said his goodbyes and headed for the back of the restaurant.

Peter eyed Dani for a second while she cleared away the empty cups.

"Um, Chef, I was wondering if I could have next Thursday night off. It's my sister's birthday and I'd like to babysit for her so she can have a night out for a change. I was supposed to ask you over the weekend, but it completely slipped my mind. I hope I haven't left it too late."

"Next Thursday? Sure. I'll make a note. It's your first night off since you started, isn't it?" Dani nodded her response. "Well, I can hardly say no then, can I?" he chuckled.

"What a lovely idea, Dani. It must be hard for them to go out. They have small children, no?" asked Gia sipping her espresso.

"Yes. They have three. It's the least I can do. They've been so good to me."

"You're working the afternoon shift today, right?"

"If you need me to."

Peter nodded, scribbling something in his book. "I think so." He passed the booking book over to Gia for her to look at. "If you don't mind, Dani?"

"Not at all." She smiled at them both, before leaving them to look over the bookings.

By the time Arsenio made it up to Jerome's office, Jerome was already dressed in a dark blue suit and on the phone when he walked in. He quickly finished his phone call and turned his attention to Arsenio.

"Here I brought you your coffee."

Jerome couldn't hide his surprise. "Don't look so shocked, the delectable Dani told me to bring it up to you." He dropped himself into the leather couch at the side of the office. "She's definitely brightened up my morning," he mused.

Jerome cleared his throat ready to say something, but Arsenio stopped him. "I know, you don't have to go on about it. I was merely making an observation," he huffed. "Anyway I thought you'd like to know how the meeting went with Scott. I saw him yesterday."

"Oh, right. And?"

"Well I was right, he's got all the right equipment. He reckons he'll be up and running by the weekend and he'll submit a weekly report. He can do a lot more if we need him to." Arsenio stopped and waited for some reaction, but instead he was met by a steady stare from Jerome sipping his coffee. "Anyway, I paid him half his fee and he'll bill us for his expenses as they occur and then, when we're done, we'll pay the balance."

Jerome immediately opened up his drawer and pulled out his cheque book. Arsenio waved at him indicated he didn't want the money.

"He's billing me, so when it's all done we can settle then, so just put that away for now."

"What did you think of him?" Jerome's voice was hoarse and Arsenio knew from his expression he was feeling guilty for doing this.

"He was very efficient and matter of fact. He's done this a hundred times. He didn't seem fazed by the task and was confident that he'd have the information we needed. That is, if there is anything for us to find out." He added the last sentence purely as a courtesy to make Jerome feel better. But he knew he'd find out what they all already knew to be true, and probably then some. "It'll just be him doing the surveillance, unless we – I mean you – see fit to expand it."

Jerome leaned back in his chair and nodded. "So, next week, then?"

"Well yes, that's the plan. After the weekend, to be specific."

Jerome stared out of the window, mulling over what Arsenio had said. So this was it. He was investigating Liz, his own wife. He sighed inwardly. He really wasn't sure if he wanted to know the details. He wasn't sure if he could stomach them. He wasn't sure if he could carry on not knowing either. Jerome huffed to himself. He just wasn't sure of anything anymore. "Thanks for doing this, Seni."

Arsenio smiled stiffly at him. "Look, I won't read the report. It's really none of my business. I won't get involved, unless you want me to. You decide, one way or the other. You know I'll support you."

Jerome nodded, then got up. Arsenio realised it was his cue to leave, or at least change the subject.

"Well I'll leave." Arsenio stood up and looked out of the window. "The rain hasn't let up since last night and you ran in this?"

"Yes," Jerome smirked.

"You're insane."

"Yeah something like that," he chuntered.

Jonathan paced up and down, clearly agitated as Liz continued to explain. "I have to make an effort with him, Jonathan. Look at me." She was perched on the end of his bed. They'd spent the first two hours of her visit making love, but now it was time for Liz to make him understand that she had to lie low for a while. She didn't want to rock the boat at home – well, not until she had secured herself a good modelling contract. Secured her future. Her meeting with her agent had gone well this morning. There were still some areas to be ironed out for the fashion show, but the holiday brochure shoot in Spain was officially signed today. There was a possibility of another magazine fashion shoot and Graham had suggested she put herself forward for different projects that could prove to have more longevity, hence her unscheduled visit to see Jonathan and celebrate.

Jonathan stopped pacing and looked up at her. She'd slipped on one of his T-shirts that barely covered her. He was besotted with her. It killed him whenever she left him to go back to her other life. Their affair had been going on for almost seven months now. Jonathan remembered the first day he saw her, his first day at Level One, January the second.

Jonathan had applied for the position of manager at Level One. He'd been a personal trainer for over ten years, working in various health and sports clubs, but had been ready to take on more responsibility. Ultimately, he wanted his own gym but he knew that was out of his grasp. Financially, he wasn't able to fund such a business venture. He'd been interviewed by Jerome and liked him, knowing they could work well together. Jonathan furrowed his brow at that thought. He certainly didn't feel that way now. Now his feelings for Jerome bordered on envy and resentment. Envious that Jerome had Liz when he couldn't, and resentment for Jerome standing in his way of them being together.

Liz had sauntered into Level One at around ten. He remembered it as if it was yesterday. She was cool and distant and when Jerome introduced them, her handshake was weak. Apart from the fact she was stunning, tall, blonde, with ice blue eyes and delicate features, she had an aloofness about her that only made her more attractive to Jonathan. Untouchable. He instantly wanted to break through her cool exterior and unleash whatever she was trying hard to hide.

Jerome had left them alone to get acquainted, his other business needing his urgent attention. Jonathan couldn't understand how Jerome wouldn't want to work alongside Liz and find managers for his other businesses. If she were his wife, he'd never let her out of his sight.

It was on that morning Jonathan knew Liz was going to mean a lot more to him than just being his boss. They spent all day together as Liz went through the workings of Level One. He watched her begin to warm up to him. Her cool blue eyes sparkled when he made a joke, her stiffness and distance softened as they sat and drank their tea in her office. The time had literally flown by and when five o'clock came around, when it was time for her to leave, Jonathan couldn't wait for the following morning. In those few hours, they'd built a subtle rapport. A rapport that you would expect from a couple of colleagues who'd worked together closely for a lot longer than just seven hours. Jonathan realised on that same day he had to have Liz and no one was going to stand in his way.

"What do you mean, make an effort? I hope you're not thinking of sleeping with him again." He stepped closer to her, his hands fisted at his sides.

Liz lifted her hand up and gently touched his arm, warmed by his possessiveness. "No. I told you it's been over six months. Not since you and I..." Jonathan took a deep breath. The thought of another man touching her made him positively violent. "He thinks you and I are over. And I want him to think that. He has to think that, Jonathan. You understand that, don't you? I need to get everything in place. My career. So we can eventually be together. The fact that he found out has made this harder, so you're going to have to be a bit more patient. You know I only want to be with you, and going back to that house kills me too, but we have to be smart. No phone calls."

"What?"

"He may check my phone. He's not convinced we're over."

"Well, get another phone. Another number. I can't not speak to you!"

"Okay. I will. But I won't be able to come here. Not for a while."

Jonathan moved closer clenching his jaw. "No way. I have to see you, be with you. You have to find a way."

"It's just until he stops doubting me," Liz pleaded. Jonathan leant down and slipped his hand around the back of her neck, then firmly pushed her back against the mattress. His dark eyes bored into hers, his full lips crushed against hers and he laid his big, hard, dark body over her. He ravished her mouth, holding her head still. He couldn't get enough of her and these stolen hours were what he lived for. He'd go insane if she denied him of these, even for a short time.

Liz's hands instantly grasped at his bare back, feeling every taught muscle as it rippled under her soft hands. There wasn't an ounce of fat on him. His body was a well-oiled machine that never tired, and every slab of muscle Liz touched was rock hard, encased in his dark velvet skin.

"Fuck this, Liz. Just leave him. We don't need his money, we don't need anything of his. I can ask my cousin Gabe. He can finance us. We can borrow from him and set up a gym. He's got a bit of money. I can't bear not seeing you."

"I can't either, but it'll be worth it. I don't want to owe anyone, Jonathan. I want to do it on our own," groaned Liz, feeling his hands hastily leave her head and roam down her sides. She loved the way he never hid his raw desire for her. He wasn't controlled like Jerome; he took from her and was rough and Liz revelled in it. Craved it. She needed her man to be insane about her, to be jealous of her. She needed that full and undivided attention, and Jonathan gave her that, in heaps.

Jonathan shoved up the T-shirt she was wearing and lowered his lips to her nipple, tender from their previous celebratory sex, and sucked hard.

"Ah!"

"That's right, you scream for me," he mumbled against her delicate skin. His hands ran over her behind and he yanked her close to him. "Can you be without this?" He circled his hips and pushed his throbbing erection against her. "How long can you last?" He thrust against her. Liz whimpered as he continued to suckle her. She grappled with his briefs to release what she needed. "One day? Two? A week?" He punctuated with a thrust. "Tell me?" he demanded. "Can you do without this?" He plunged his now-released erection into her and she gasped.

"No. No, I can't. Fuck me, Jonathan. Fuck me hard."

Jonathan growled as he pulled her legs up and pushed them against her stomach so he could penetrate her deeply, knowing she thrived off being totally taken. He pummelled her fast and hard. It was animalistic. Liz clawed at the sheets to anchor herself as Jonathan continued to hammer into her. He felt her start to shake and he slowed down, wanting to savour her orgasm. "Give. It. To. Me." Liz moaned and pulled at the sheets even tighter. "That's it. Give. It. To. Me. Now!" She exploded around him and he gazed in awe at her arching up, almost screaming her release, his ice queen melting just for him and only him. As she continued to pulse around him with aftershocks, he plunged back into her faster and harder, chasing his own release.

"I could fuck you all day." His voice was gruff as he spoke through clenched teeth, never halting. "I want to fuck you all day, every day and I will, Liz. I will!" he threw his head back, emptying himself into her. With almost no time to recover, he withdrew from her, yanked away the T-shirt and flipped her onto her front. He covered her slim body with his, then grabbed her wrists and lifted them above her head and pinned them there with one hand.

"You'll find a way. I have to see you, Liz, otherwise I don't know what I'll do." He nibbled at her ear, his breath short and fast.

Liz moaned and wriggled beneath him, relishing his dominance. "I'll think of something," she breathed.

His hands skirted down her side and slipped underneath her as he kissed her shoulders. "I know you will. You won't last without this. Without me being inside you. You need it."

His fingers slid over the most sensitive spot and he began to massage her, toying with her. She was putty in his hands again. "Tell me that you need it. That you need me," he demanded softly.

"I do, Jonathan. I need you. I need this." She wriggled her behind into his now-rock-hard erection. He was always ready for her, always hot for her and she loved it. She loved that she did this to him.

"Yeah, you do, and I'm going to keep you satisfied. Whenever, wherever."

Liz groaned against the mattress. She knew she couldn't be without him. Even a day was too much. She was going to have to find somewhere. Somewhere neutral. A place they could escape to. "Oh God... I'm so close... "

He stopped for a moment, allowing her to calm, then he took her wrists and guided them around to the base of her back. "Kneel up for me, babe." Liz did as she was bid, desperate to be filled by him again. "Yes, that's it. I love your beautiful white ass." He stroked her cheeks with his free hand, then guided his extensive length slowly into her. "I'm starting slow. How's that? Um... you feel so good. Is that good, eh?"

"Oh Jonathan, push deeper, yes, yes." Liz pushed back against him.

"Is that deep enough?"

He pulled her wrists towards him in a quick jerk and she groaned. "God, yes."

He gripped her hip with his other hand, knowing there was no way he'd get his own way. She liked it hard and rough and he was going to give her whatever she wanted, because he knew that was the only way he could keep her. He may have played the alpha male in bed with her but he knew it was what she wanted, how she wanted him. She was in control, she'd set the rules and he was more than willing to oblige.

Jonathan thrust into her, marvelling at how such a delicate slim woman revelled in hard sex. The rougher the better. She didn't want a smooth, sophisticated Italian, she needed a rough diamond, a rough black diamond like him to keep her satisfied. And he was more than happy to. He yanked her hard against him and she let out a yelp. He felt her instantly start to tighten. "That's it, Liz, scream for me, let me hear you..." before she could reply, she climaxed loudly and he pounded her until he found his release, collapsing on top of her as he let out a guttural shudder.

"Christ, I can't go a day without this, Liz. Find a way."

Liz tried to slow her breathing but it was hard. After six glorious orgasms, she was exhausted. Jonathan rolled off her onto his back. His smooth toned chest glistened with sweat as it rose and fell from his deep breathing. She turned to her side and propped her head up on her elbow.

"I'll see if I can find somewhere. But we have to be patient, stick to the plan. If we want to start up on our own, we need money and the money I've been stashing over the last five months isn't enough."

"I know. I just wish we didn't need *him*."

"We don't. Once I file for divorce and I take what's due to me, he's history."

He turned to look at her. "Promise me you won't fuck him. I'll kill him if he touches you. I mean it, Liz."

Liz looked over his shoulder at the clock it was three forty-five. The kids would be home in forty five minutes. She needed a shower and to get out of there fast if she was to make it home before they arrived.

"I have to go." She hadn't promised him, because she couldn't. If she needed to sleep with Jerome to convince him she was being faithful, then she would, but she wasn't going to openly admit that to Jonathan.

She padded into the bathroom and turned on the shower, reluctantly washing off Jonathan's scent.

19

EVERYTHING'S NEW

Dani stifled a yawn as she boxed up Silvanna's chocolate cake. She huffed to herself. Why did everyone always choose chocolate cake? Dani could almost put one together with her eyes closed. At least she'd added the amaretto and almonds, just to make it a little different this time. It was so much more enjoyable making or creating new kinds of cakes. Staring out of the kitchen window into the darkness, her thoughts drifted to Jerome and his lemon mousse cake. Her mouth pooled with saliva and she shook her head, unsure if it was the thought of the cake or Jerome that had her salivating. Dani covered the smaller extra cake she'd made for the children with the glass dome, then headed off to bed. It was almost two and she had an early start tomorrow.

"So this is your insurance and the tax is paid up for a year already, see?" The dealer pointed to the documentation. "You've two sets of keys. The log book will be with you in a couple of days and the service log is in the glove compartment."

"Thank you." Dani pressed the fob to unlock the door.

"It's been fully valeted and thankfully the rain's stopped, so it hasn't been ruined," puffed the dealer.

Adam paced around the car, inspecting it. The dealer shifted nervously, then reached into his inside pocket and pulled out a cheque. "This is the balance we agreed on." He handed it over to Adam and Adam indicated it was Dani's. Dani tried hard not to smile, taking the check from the dealer's hand.

"Thanks." She read the amount and then immediately passed the cheque over to Adam. He slipped it into his inside pocket without a word.

"It was a pleasure doing business with you." Adam reached out his hand and shook the dealer's hand.

"Likewise." The dealer shook Dani's hand and walked back towards the showroom.

"What do you want to do with the money?"

"Just put it in my account. I may need if I find my own place."

"You're looking for a place?" Adam furrowed his brow. "You know you don't need to."

"I know. It doesn't look as if I will for a while. Well, not until I get the money from the house, anyway."

"We've only just got you back, I don't think Chloe would be happy if you left. Or me, for that matter."

Dani stepped closer to Adam and hugged him. He enveloped her small frame in his huge arms. "Thanks, Adam. Thanks for today, for everything."

He sniffed nervously. "Still think your car's a tin can on wheels."

Dani chuckled and shoved at his shoulder. "It's perfect. Now I'd better get off or I'll be late."

"Do you know your way?" Adam stifled a smirk.

"Sat nav." Dani winked.

"Of course." He chuckled, then opened up his car and pulled out the large cake box and placed it on the passenger seat as Dani held open the door.

Liz sat opposite Graham, watching him intently while he continued with his phone call. She tried hard not to look nervous, but she really needed this fashion show job. They'd had a few problems with the organisers but they'd assured her she was definitely booked. It was a high-profile job with large media coverage. Liz knew it would be in all the press and magazines. It was the exact exposure she needed. Graham pulled off his earpiece and dropped it on his desk, continuing to pace around the room.

"Well?" Liz asked impatiently.

"They're insisting it's still on. They're just in discussions with the venue owners, just ironing out details, they said." Graham shrugged.

"Other than that, nothing more. The designers are ready to organise fittings for the last week of December."

Liz nodded.

"The Spain dates have come through. You fly out on the fourteenth of December and you're back on the nineteenth. There won't be any problem, will there?"

Liz shook her head.

"Good. There's also that protein shake I told you about. They're looking for a new face to represent them. Would you be interested in that? It's not fashion but it's a huge contract. Worldwide."

Liz furrowed her brow. This wasn't an area she'd ever thought about before. "Worldwide?"

"Yes. It's an organic protein shake, and they're going to hopefully be sponsoring a fitness DVD that will be sold worldwide."

"Wouldn't they want an athlete rather than a model?"

Graham snorted. "Have you seen women athletes? I wouldn't call them glamorous. They need a pretty face and a good body to sell the product. You've been working out hard and it shows. I really think they'd go for you. It might mean you have to create a little more definition, but you own a gym, for Christ's sake, that shouldn't be hard for you."

"I'm not sure, Graham, I've always done fashion."

"I know, Liz, and that's what most young models want, to be the face of some big designer but this... well this campaign isn't short term. It's a whole branding. If it takes off, it'll be everywhere: supermarkets, gyms and health shops. Holland and Barrett are interested in stocking it. You remember when all the power drinks came on the market? How big they were? Well that's what this product wants to be. High protein, no carbs, no fat, great taste. They're already talking about power bars and snacks as well as ice cream. I really think it will be huge."

Graham walked over to his computer, which was set on his desk and clicked his mouse, then swivelled the screen so Liz could see. "These are the preliminary mock ups of the campaign. It's slick and cool; less of the big muscly beefcakes and more lean and glossy."

Liz leaned forward to look at the screen. He was right. The campaign almost rivalled a top-branded alcoholic beverage, like Martini or Absolut.

"And the best part is the money."

Liz's eyes flitted up to Graham. He smirked. "They're paying more than you've ever been paid before, a lot more."

"Seriously?"

Graham nodded slowly.

"Okay, then. Put me forward. Let's see what they're offering."

"I'll send them your portfolio today."

Liz got up to leave. Putting on her coat, she moved to the door. She really hoped the fashion show came together quickly. If this protein shake was as big as Graham thought, her appearance in the show could clinch it.

As soon as she was back on the street, she headed to her car. She needed to get a new phone. Jonathan was getting more and more possessive and needed reassuring. She smiled to herself as she slipped into her car. The thought of Jonathan had her insides quivering. Looking back up at the agency building, she noticed a "For Rent" sign. Liz quickly typed in the number of the letting agent and called them. Within a few moments, she found out that there were four small offices for rent on the third floor up, just above her agency. They could either be rented together or separately. Liz took all the details and made an appointment to see them in the afternoon.

Silvanna beamed at Dani as everyone sang Happy Birthday to her. She was a shy girl and the attention was a little overwhelming, her flushed appearance betraying her discomfort. "Thank you Dani," she said softly, hugging her. "The last cake I ever had on my birthday was when I was a child."

"Really? I'm so glad I made one for you, then. No one should have a birthday without a cake. Then it would be just like any other day." She winked at Silvanna.

The staff quickly finished up and started to prepare for the evening shift. Dani had worked through again and was disappointed that Jerome hadn't made an appearance all day. His car had not been parked up this morning when Dani had pulled into her usual parking space. She was waiting to see his reaction to her new car.

The evening shift was busy and it was eleven thirty before the last of the customers left. Peter sat by the bar chatting to Kuch and Nicole while they finished cleaning down the surfaces.

"You look tired, Chef." Kuch narrowed his eyes at Peter wiping his hands on a cloth.

"It's my throat. I think Angie passed on her sore throat to me. It's killing me," he cringed, trying to swallow.

"Honey, lemon and brandy," chipped in Nicole as she turned off the light over the bar. "Come on. You need to go home and get to bed."

Peter nodded and Nicole hurried up the staff so Peter could lock up. He was still holding the bookings book in his hand. "Dani, I'll leave this on the bar in case I come in later tomorrow."

"Sure, no problem. I'll tell Gia."

"Thanks. I don't want her looking for it."

Dani nodded, shrugging on her coat and following everyone out into the car park. She headed over to her new car and unlocked it.

"Is that your new car?" Kuch asked in surprise.

"Yes."

"Bit of a come-down, isn't it?" he joked.

"Well that depends how you look at it I suppose," Dani answered cryptically.

Kuch laughed, realising she was referring to her ex. "Very true. Well you know I love *all* things Italian, so it's definitely a step up." He winked at her.

Nicole stifled a smirk and Dani watched her blush. Kuch unlocked his car and then opened up the back door for Nicole. As she stepped into the car, Dani watched Kuch's hand slip over her behind and squeeze it. She didn't flinch at all and slipped into the back seat. Dani stood for a moment, thinking it was an inappropriate gesture for friends, and then the penny dropped. *Nicole and Kuch were seeing each other!* she huffed to herself. Of course, it made sense now: Nicole's secrecy about her boyfriend, Kuch being evasive about his relationship status. They were keeping it a secret. Rosa took the front seat as usual and waved to Dani who was still standing by her open door. Why were they being secretive? Was it the "no relationship with staff" policy? Dani smiled to herself, thinking back to her first day. She'd picked up on their obvious chemistry, but hadn't put two and two together. She watched Kuch pull away and Nicole waved at her through the glass. Dani reciprocated, still a little dumbfounded. Was Rosa their cover? Dani noted she always sat in the front seat when they went anywhere. She shook her head and started the engine, thinking that relationships were really complicated.

Dani adjusted the heater onto full blast before she drove off, thinking that at least she could sleep in tomorrow on her first morning off. Frowning to herself, she realised she wouldn't be there to tell Gia about the bookings Peter had left. Maybe she should call Gia first thing.

Liz dialled the familiar number and waited.

"Hello?" Jonathan's puzzled voice made Liz smile.

"Hi."

"Liz?"

"Yes, it's me, this is my new number. You can call me on this. I'll have it on silent but I'll see your missed call and ring you the second I can."

Jonathan sighed. "That's great, babe. How did today go? Jesus, I missed you." He sounded needy and Liz felt a rush at the thought of him.

"I've got the dates for Spain, so you need to book the same flight. We'll have four to five days together."

"Awesome. And the fashion show?"

"Still being hammered out, but I'm in. But there's more."

"More?"

"My agent's putting me forward for a big new contract."

"That's great news. What is it for?"

"I'll tell you when I see you."

"When will that be?" Jonathan sounded almost whiney.

"Well that's the third bit of good news. I've found a place for us."

"A place?"

"Yeah. It's a small space over my agent's office, with underground parking. I signed the lease today. We have our own new place now." He could hear her smile as she spoke.

"Oh my God, that's just the best news! No more looking over our shoulders." The relief in his voice sent a hum through Liz's body.

"I know. Who would suspect me of anything? It'll look like I'm at my agency. It's the perfect cover. So tomorrow, get there for nine o'clock and I'll meet you in the car park just after. I'll text you the address."

"You're amazing. I can't wait. I fucking love you, Liz."

"I love you too."

20

SEXPOT

Dani stretched her arms over her head. It was the first time she'd had a shift off since she'd started at La Casa. She wasn't entirely sure what to do with herself. If she'd been living alone, she'd have been doing her laundry or housework, but thankfully, Chloe had managed to take over all of that. She sighed to herself. Well she needed to arrange a doctor's appointment. She yawned, trying to recollect all the items on her mental to-do list. Maybe she should start on her fitness DVD. She reached over to her phone on the bedside table and looked at the time. Five past eight. The message icon showed she'd had a message come through at three forty-five this morning. *Strange*, she thought. Her heart plummeted, wondering whether it was Jez. Dani quickly opened it and was relieved to see it was from Peter, telling her he was pretty sick and wouldn't make it in today. He asked if there was any chance she could go in this morning as they'd be short staffed.

Dani pulled herself out of bed and headed for the bathroom, thankful for a reason to get up. Her fitness DVD could wait, but her doctor's appointment couldn't. She'd call the surgery later.

Dani pulled into La Casa's car park at nine forty, parking next to Jerome's Maserati. She headed for the back entrance and was greeted by Franco and Rico having a cigarette.

"I thought it was your morning off." Franco looked surprised.

"Chef asked me to come in. He's sick and we're always busy on Friday lunch." Dani shrugged.

"Can't keep away, eh?" winked Rico.

226

"Something like that." Dani winked back, then practically skipped through the doorway.

It wasn't long before Dani was serving up the morning coffees as usual. She stepped back into the restaurant and started on her own. The reservations book was on the bar where Peter had left it last night. Opening it up to today's date, she scanned the large list of bookings and mentally tried to accommodate them in the restaurant. She was so engrossed in what she was doing, she didn't sense Jerome walking into the restaurant. He stood observing her for a moment. Dani nervously twiddled with the end of her ponytail. *She often did that when she was concentrating*, he noted.

"So you're not a *Smart* girl after all?" His raspy voice made Dani jump and she swung round to face him. He gave her a crooked grin that made his whole face light up, then started pacing towards her. Dani stood transfixed for a moment, caught in his gaze. "Your car?" he added, mistaking her hesitation to respond for confusion. He'd reached her by now.

"Oh, I see. Hmm, it would appear not." Dani shrugged, pulling herself together. She couldn't believe how happy she was to see him. To anyone watching, the evidence was all over her face. Lucky for her, they were alone. He stepped a little closer and leaned against the bar in that casual manner he had. His exquisite burgundy three piece suit, crisp white shirt and black tie erased any casualness about him. He always looked so comfortable and confident in his own skin. Whatever he wore only extenuated his incredible good looks and perfect body. In Jerome's case, the man definitely wore the suit, not the other way around.

Dani put down the book and hopped onto a bar stool. "I went for the Italian option rather the Smart option." She grinned, and Jerome let out a soft laugh.

"Well I'm very glad to hear it. They're a little more stylish and definitely racier." He arched one of his eyebrows.

"Apparently." Dani paused, unsure of what to say next, her body suddenly feeling very aware of his close proximity. "Would you like an espresso?" Dani jumped back off the stool, needing the distance and something to occupy her fidgety hands.

Jerome fixed her with his brilliant eyes. He was doing that staring thing again, making her flustered. "I'd love one."

Dani rounded the bar and got to work on Jerome's coffee, glad she had something to occupy her attention. Desperate to fill the silence between them, Dani placed the cup and saucer on the bar and added, "Um, I just hope they're reliable too."

Jerome was sitting directly opposite her now and though the bar was between them, Dani felt a distinctive pull, which had her leaning up against the bar.

"Well, that all depends on how you handle them. They're surprisingly fast but very smooth, as long as they're serviced regularly, and cared for. And if you're not overly rough with them, they'll fulfil your every need," Jerome answered. His voice had become smoother, lower, more intimate. His eyes blinked slowly at her and his smile was softer, sweeter.

Dani swallowed, trying to calm herself. *Why was he so damn good looking and why did she always feel they were having an entirely different conversation?* "I'll try to remember that," she answered quietly.

Jerome rested his elbows on the bar and laced his fingers together, then rubbed his clenched knuckles across his lips. He continued to stare at Dani and for a few seconds, neither of them spoke. *He always touched his lips when he thought*, Dani noted. She just couldn't seem to drag her eyes away from his mouth.

"*Buongiorno.*" Gia's melodic voice jolted both of them. "What are you two talking about?"

Both Jerome and Dani turned towards Gia and said in unison. "Cars." They both looked at each other. Dani shook her head as she stifled a laugh and Jerome chuckled.

"Cars? What is it with you two and cars?" Gia was up by the bar and she leaned to kiss Jerome who'd already gotten off his stool.

"Dani's just bought a new one, Mama." Jerome picked up his coffee and took a sip, his eyes flitted over to Dani.

"Ah, *si*. You got one like mine. They're a dream to drive, and fast too!"

Dani stifled a grin and turned to the coffee machine.

Jerome masked his chuckle with a cough and answered with a straight face. "That's exactly what I said, Mama. She most definitely picked the best option." His eyes caught Dani's for a split second.

"Er, espresso, Gia?" asked Dani. The question was redundant, seeing as she had already turned to the machine and started preparing it.

"Please, Daniella. I thought it was your morning off."

"Chef asked me to come in as he's not well."

Gia perched herself on the stool next to Jerome. "Oh?"

"He messaged me last night. He didn't want to bother you with it." Jerome pushed the open book towards his mother. "Dani was just looking over the bookings for lunch and tonight."

Dani placed Gia's coffee on the bar and smiled gently at Gia.

"Well come over to this side of the bar and let's get it all sorted." She beckoned Dani with her hand and then patted the stool next to her.

Jerome got up from his stool, quickly knocked back the remains of his coffee and buttoned his suit jacket. "I'll leave you two to it. I'll be back by twelve to help out."

He bent down to kiss his mother goodbye and then turned to Dani. "Thanks for coming in today. We really appreciate it." His eyes danced as he looked down at her.

Dani felt her face redden slightly. "Um, that's okay. I'm happy to help."

"Well we'll have to compensate you." Gia patted her arm affectionately. "Won't we, Jerome?"

"I'm sure we can work something out," he replied to his mother, but his eyes stayed fixed on Dani. Dani sat mesmerized by the intensity of his stare. Her heart thumped hard against her ribcage, convinced that it was audible in the quiet of the empty restaurant. Then Jerome stepped back and was gone. *Holy shit, what was that all about?*

Between Gia and Dani, they managed to organise the lunchtime and the evening bookings. Dani suggested they implement a program on the computer for reservations and table planning. Gia grinned at her, explaining Peter had often suggested it but because she wasn't very computer savvy, they'd stuck to writing everything down in the book, for her sake.

"I could teach you if like?" Dani suggested.

"How to use the program?"

"Yes. I could show you on Monday, when the restaurant's closed."

"But I know very little about computers, Dani," cringed Gia.

"It's not so hard once you get used to it, Gia. I could show you a little bit every day and on the afternoons I'm not working."

"You'd do that?"

"Sure. I used this program all the time before. It just makes everything easier and you can store everything too. You'll be able to see how often customers come in, log in their details, and other stuff. It's really useful."

"Well, if you can spare the time, I'd really like that." Gia smiled back.

Jerome pulled up at Level One. Peter's illness had thrown his schedule out, and he'd have to quickly deal with anything pressing, then get back to La Casa. Thank goodness his new managers were settled in and proving to be more than capable. He pulled out his phone and hit Liz's number on speed dial. It rang a few times before she answered. "Liz?"

"Hi."

"Hi, um look Peter's sick, so I'm going to have to cover him today and probably tomorrow. I know I said I'd try and spend more time, but –"

"It's okay, Jerome. Really. I understand," interrupted Liz.

Jerome swallowed hard as she spoke. This was not the reaction he was expecting. He was convinced she'd be aloof at best, angry at worst.

"What's wrong with him? I hope it's not too serious," she continued.

"His throat," Jerome answered, still reeling over her response. "It might mean that I get home a bit later for the kids."

"That's okay. I'll be home for when they get in. Don't worry, really."

"And there's tomorrow, you know Saturday's hectic…"

"I can bring them down after lunch so your mum can see them, if you like. I've a few meetings at my agents over the weekend, so really don't worry about me."

Jerome's mind went into overdrive. This was a complete turnaround from the moody, frosty Liz of recent months. He was hoping it was the recent developments in her career but his gut feeling screamed out something entirely different.

"Okay, that's good. I mean, it's the possibility of work, right?"

"Fingers crossed." He could hear her grin down the phone and he instantly felt better. So maybe her good mood was connected to her work after all. "I'll know in a day or so. I won't tell you anymore. I don't want to jinx it. But I'll be spending a lot of time up at the agency. Graham's really pushing for me to get some high profile jobs."

"Well that's great news. I'm really pleased for you."

"Thanks," she replied softly.

"Okay, I'm off. Shall I let Nina know?"

"Sure, I'm just in with Graham now."

"Oh sorry, I didn't mean to interrupt. Send him my regards. I'll call her then, and Liz, thanks for being so understanding about work. I know I said I'd try and spend more time with you. It's just one of those things."

"It's fine. Really. I'll speak to you later."

"Bye, then."

"Bye."

Jerome hung up and looked at his phone for a moment unable to grasp what was going on. The change was too quick; a complete one-eighty. He hit the speed dial for Arsenio, feeling decidedly uneasy at both Liz's reaction and his consequent one.

"Hi, Jerome, how are you?"

"Could be better. Peter's off with a throat thing and I'll be splitting myself four ways."

"Bummer."

"Pretty much. Tell me, when's the PI starting?"

"He started already. Well, when I say started, he's got all the information and he's going to be starting surveillance today. Why?"

"Just wanted to know. Do you think you could get to him to report Liz's movements to us on a daily basis, rather than weekly?"

"Has something happened, Jerome?"

"No. Well, not as such. I'd rather not explain at the moment, Seni. But just see if he can, will you, and get back to me?"

"Sure. No problem. I'll ask him to email it directly to you."

"Okay, I'll see you later, at La Casa, then."

"Sure. See you then."

Seni put down his phone and frowned. Something wasn't right. He picked up his phone again and dialled up Scott.

"What did *he* want?" Jonathan couldn't even say his name.

"He's just busy because of staff problems," Liz answered, running her hand over his bare chest. Jonathan huffed. "Which means he'll be busy over the weekend." Her hand smoothed southward over his tight abs. "Which means he won't care what I'm doing, where I'm doing it and with whom I'm doing it."

Jonathan lazily closed his eyes, relishing her soft, small hands smoothing over him. He wasn't going to be able to hold on to his control for much longer. Suddenly, Liz straddled him and rested her hands on his chest, her hair spilling over her bare shoulders and covering her breasts as she bent down to look at him.

"I'll just take the kids down after lunch on Saturday, so he won't suspect anything, then the rest of the time I can spend most of it here." She bent down and kissed across his chest until she reached the flat disk of his nipple. Jonathan groaned, grabbing her hips. Liz softly bit his nipple and Jonathan jerked. "That's if you like." She smirked against his hot dark skin.

"Oh, I like. I like very much." And in one smooth manoeuvre, Jonathan flipped her on her back and stretched out over her. The air mattress squeaked under them and Liz giggled.

"We really need to get a bed and some other bits and pieces." Liz's eyes flitted around the stark large room with their clothes scattered all over the carpeted floor.

"Just a bed, nothing else." Jonathan held her wrists above her head with his left hand and he guided himself into her with his right. "Because we'll only be fucking in here. From the minute you walk in, to a few minutes before you leave." He thrust hard into her and she moaned loudly.

"Hello, Mr Ferretti."

"Hello, Scott. Just wanted to know if you've started on the job."

"I'm actually on surveillance now."

"You mean you've followed her?" Seni couldn't keep the surprise out of his voice.

"Yes, Mr Ferretti. Mrs Ferretti has been at Prime Model Agency for the last three hours."

"And that's the only place she's been to this morning?"

"No, she took the children to school, then passed by Starbucks and collected some coffees and water and then she came to the agency."

"Oh. Good."

"I'll keep with her until eleven this evening and then I'll switch to the tracker for the night surveillance. I shouldn't imagine she goes out at night, but if she does, the tracker will record her movements."

"Great. Do you think you could do a daily report?"

"No problem. I can email you the report in the morning. Would you like me to email it to you or directly to Mr Jerome Ferretti." Scott was a no nonsense kind of guy. Arsenio had told him exactly the nature of what was going on and he'd grasped the delicacy of the situation.

"Send it directly to Jerome but also send me a copy, separately."

"You'll have a full daily report by ten every morning."

"Thank you. Good bye."

"Good bye, Mr Ferretti."

The lunchtime rush thankfully ran smoothly and Gia sat down heavily at the table with a rather large glass of Barolo and waited for Cosimo and

Arsenio to arrive. It was days like today she realised how much Peter did. They'd coped very well without him, mainly due to Jerome stepping in and Dani sacrificing her morning off. But it was becoming abundantly obvious to Gia that she was getting tired a lot more easily. She loved La Casa but without Jerome or Peter being there, she knew she couldn't manage it alone, not anymore. She stared blankly at her glass and sighed to herself. She wasn't ready to give it up yet. Gia knew it wasn't hers to give up anyway, but La Casa filled a void that the loss of her beloved Alessandro had left. La Casa and her sons were her life now. She knew her sons were on a different path that didn't include her as much, she'd lost them little by little, but La Casa was her constant and being without it was unthinkable to her.

"Mama? Are you alright?" Cosimo's gentle voice pulled her out of her depressing thoughts.

"*Si*. Just a little tired," she huffed to herself. How many times had she used that excuse to cover up what she was really feeling? Lonely, sad, old, depressed and a whole host of other unpleasant feelings, but tired was the word she always used to disguise them.

"You need a holiday, Mama. You work too hard. You never have any fun."

"I have fun. It's fun here at La Casa." She smiled widely at him, hoping it would brush away the concerned look on Cosimo's face.

"It's work, Mama. I mean you need to get out more. When have you booked to go to La Garda?"

"January third. For a month."

"Good. The break will do you good, spending time with the family."

Gia nodded and kept her smile fixed, for the sake of Cosimo.

***

Peter's throat infection kept him off on Saturday too, which meant Jerome stepped in to help out Gia. Cosimo had expressed his concern for her well-being to Jerome at their weekly get together, and Jerome was in total agreement that she needed to work less, but whenever he suggested she take more time off, she just wouldn't hear of it.

Jerome quickly scanned through the monitors in Peter's office before jumping into the shower. He let the steaming hot water wash off his sweat after his work out and tried to relax his tense muscles. He was worried that after promising he would spend more time with Liz the very next day, he was basically neglecting her. It looked like he'd be spending the whole weekend at La Casa. What with Peter ill and his mother showing signs of fatigue, he really had no choice. He rubbed himself down vigorously and dressed, anxious to focus on something other than the negative aspects of his life. Once he was dealing with the smooth running of the restaurant, he'd be able to shelve his disturbing thoughts – at least for the moment.

By the time Jerome entered the restaurant, Dani was already making coffees for the kitchen staff. Her presence had an unexplainable calming effect on him. Dani looked up from the coffee machine, sensing him, and she gave him a radiant smile.

"*Buongiorno*. I seemed to have timed that well."

"*Buongiorno*. Yes you have. Double?"

Jerome nodded, quickly pacing towards the bar, his face softening instantly into a smile.

"I'll take them through for you." He quickly lifted the tray and took them into the kitchen. Within a minute, he was back at the bar where his coffee was waiting and his eyes spotted the open reservation book. "Have you been looking over the bookings?"

"Uh-huh." She nodded, turning around to face him. She took a sip from her cup and placed it on the bar. "It's going to be tight again, but I've managed to juggle the tables, I think." Dani rounded the bar, then proceeded to explain where she had placed the various reservations. Jerome watched her fiddle with a loose piece of hair that wasn't secured in the French pleat she'd styled her hair into. He became totally mesmerized by her and how she was totally focused on what she was saying. "So, unless a few tables linger, there shouldn't be a problem." Dani turned back to look at Jerome.

He cocked his head to one side and nodded. "That's made my job easier today."

Dani beamed back at him. He was about to add something but his phone vibrated, indicating he had an email. He reached into his pocket and pulled out his phone, then opened up the email option. He stiffened slightly and his face hardened a little. Dani frowned at his reaction. For a few minutes she'd seen the charismatic Jerome, but now his face had turned pensive. She was getting used to having him all to herself in the morning and that in itself was unsettling her. She needed to be more careful. Dani moved back behind the bar and busied herself with the tidying up of the coffee machine, leaving Jerome to read whatever it was on his phone.

Jerome perched himself on the bar stool and started scrolling through Scott's report on Liz's movements yesterday. There was nothing untoward. In fact, all she'd done, after dropping the children off at school, was spend three hours at her agents and then went back home. He wasn't sure how he felt about that. He knew he should've been pleased – relieved even – but if he was being honest, he felt a twinge of disappointment. Jerome frowned to himself. *Maybe Liz was making an effort after all. Maybe she was willing to put everything behind them and try harder for him and their family. Wasn't that what this was all about?* He rubbed his forehead, disturbed by his reaction. Jerome closed off the email and pocketed his phone, unsure of what he'd been expecting. He shook his head, deciding again to shelve his feelings and immerse himself in work.

As expected, the Saturday lunchtime trade was steady and constant. Thankfully, by two o'clock, there was a slight lull and Dani felt she could relax somewhat. That was until she saw Liz enter the restaurant along with Kara, Alessandro and Nina. *Crap!* Thought Dani. She prayed that they'd sit at the bottom of the restaurant. She really didn't feel like being snubbed publicly again. Gia fussed over the children while Jerome took Liz's coat. Dani discreetly watched their interaction. Liz had a small fake smile fixed on her face as Jerome scanned the restaurant for a table. They seemed to be skirting around each other. There was no touching or intimacy – they were behaving like strangers, not like a couple at all.

Dani decided she'd better focus on clearing away her table and hope Jerome wouldn't direct them to her section. Gia was about to guide them up to where Dani was now resetting the places, when Jerome suggested another table in Rosa's section that had just been vacated. Dani felt her body relax and breathed a sigh of relief. She wasn't sure why she felt so uncomfortable around Liz. They'd hardly even spoken to each other, so it wasn't entirely fair to judge her on one meeting, but nevertheless, Dani really disliked her. Liz looked stunning in a figure-hugging black dress and knee high boots, and she walked around as if she owned the place. Dani huffed to herself – *well she did, didn't she?*

Gia settled them all in and then went to the front desk as more customers were entering, leaving Rosa and Jerome to deal with the order. Dani's focus was drawn to the front door as it opened and to her surprise in walked Adam and Chloe with their children in tow and Adam's father Ray. Chloe caught her eye and waved to her. Gia smiled widely at Adam, recognising him instantly, then he proceeded to introduce the rest of the family.

"Hey, this is a nice surprise!" grinned Dani as the children chatted animatedly. Chloe settled them down, trying not to disturb the other tables.

"I thought it was time they saw you in action." Adam winked. "And try the amazing food."

"Hey, Ray, how are you?" Dani quickly hugged and kissed Ray, his tall frame engulfing her. Like Adam, he was big and in great shape for a man who was a year shy of sixty, with dark blonde hair greying at his temples. Dani had always liked him. He was the epitome of a gentleman with a wicked sense of humour. Ray was the only grandparent Sophie, Oliver and Rosie had. Adam's mother had left Ray when Adam was only two, and Ray had single-handedly raised him whilst building up his doctor's practice.

"I'm very well. This place is really something." He lifted his eyebrows at Dani and sat down.

"Yes it is. The food's fabulous too."

"And the owner isn't half-bad either." Ray lowered his voice to a stage whisper, making Dani giggle as she handed him his menu. "She called me *Raymondo*. I think I rather like that."

Sophie and Ollie giggled at his comment and Adam shook his head. "She's not the owner, Dad, she's the mother of the owner."

"Well, she's a hottie."

"Otty," repeated Rosie.

"H-h-hottie," corrected Adam and Chloe gawked at him, shocked that he would correct her.

Dani handed out the menus and quickly retrieved a high chair for Rosie, then left them to mull over the choices.

Thankfully, her tables were on dessert or coffee, so Dani was able to spend more time with her family. It made her a little sad to think that her entire family was sat round table twenty-four in La Casa d'Italia, a stark contrast to the Ferrettis and their huge family.

Dani's eyes flitted over to where Jerome was sitting with Liz and their children. The children were talking away and Jerome listened intently to them, only periodically scanning the restaurant ensuring all was running like clockwork. Liz was sitting stiffly picking at a salad but hardly paying any attention to her family. Jerome proceeded to cut up the children's food and wiped their faces. He moved drinks out of their way so that they wouldn't spill anything, while Liz looked vacantly at them and checked her watch.

The next hour moved swiftly on. Dani was distracted by her family and hadn't noticed that Liz had left. Gia was sitting with the children as they finished their meals and Jerome was doing the rounds of the remaining tables. He headed towards Adam's table while Dani continued to serve a new table of guests that had just been seated.

"Hello, Adam." Jerome held out his hand as Adam rose to greet him. "Can't keep away, I see."

Adam chuckled at his comment. "Well I thought I should treat my family, for a change." Adam quickly introduced the table to Jerome, who took time to speak to Chloe and Ray, then deliberately spoke to all three children. Within a few minutes they'd established that the children attended the same school as Kara and Alessandro, though they were in different classes but knew each other. Jerome suggested that Sophie and Ollie go down and join them once they'd finished. Then he excused himself and headed towards the front of the restaurant.

"Well he's so nice." Chloe directed her comment to Dani as she cleared their plates.

"Uh-huh," Dani replied, trying hard to look indifferent.

"And he's *so* good looking," Chloe continued, oblivious of Adam's arched eyebrow. Ray chuckled and Chloe grinned at Adam. "Well, he is," Chloe insisted and Adam conceded with a nod and a grin. "He's quite a sexpot."

Dani gaped at her sister. "Chloe!"

Adam rolled his eyes at his wife and she sniggered.

"Expot," repeated Rosie and before Adam could correct her, Chloe hissed,

"Don't you dare!" causing all of them to giggle.

"Well, I'll be definitely be coming here again. The food is excellent." Ray licked his spoon clean of tiramisu.

Dani cleared her throat. "And the service, Ray. Don't forget the service." She winked at him.

"Of course, the service was second to none," he added, grinning widely. "And the view too. It's worth it just to watch the floor show." Ray jerked his head towards where Gia was stood by the bar talking to Nina.

"Steady on there, *Raymondo*." Adam shook his head, clearly exasperated. "I swear, you and Chloe have to get out more!"

"I think you're right, son." Ray winked at Chloe, then took another spoonful of tiramisu.

21

NOTHING UNUSUAL

K uch flexed his neck from left to right, then rolled his shoulders. "Man, it was crazy tonight. I'm beat."

He'd just finished wiping down the bar. It had been particularly busy and there were a few customers still lingering over coffee. Dani, Kuch, Nicole and Rosa were the only restaurant staff left, and the kitchen had closed nearly an hour ago.

Jerome looked at his watch. It was eleven forty. "You can go, Kuch."

"Thanks, but that's okay, I'm taking Nicole and Rosa home and she's still got two tables."

"I'll take care of them. Mine have just finished dessert so they'll just want coffee. I can manage," Dani offered. She'd had the afternoon hours off today and she was feeling for Rosa and Kuch. It had been their turn to work through.

Jerome turned to look at the four tables left. Rosa's would be leaving any time soon and the two tables in Dani's section would take thirty minutes tops. He sucked on his top teeth. If Kuch left, he'd be alone with Dani. The thought both thrilled and worried him.

"You guys get off, Dani and I can manage these last few tables."

"Are you sure?" Rosa asked as one of her tables asked for the bill.

"See, we'll be out of here in twenty minutes" Jerome jerked his head towards the table. He smiled tightly at Rosa, feeling decidedly unsettled.

Within ten minutes, Kuch, Rosa and Nicole had left, along with one of Dani's tables, leaving Dani and Jerome alone with the two remaining tables of six and four. Both groups were in good spirits and seemed oblivious to the time. Dani cleared the vacated tables and started to reset them ready for tomorrow, while Jerome took the coffee order for Dani and headed back to the bar.

"What do they need?" she asked slipping behind the counter.

"Four cappuccinos and two decaf espressos."

Dani huffed. *Why did they bother with decaf?* she thought. The whole point of coffee *was* the caffeine.

"Pour them some shots of grappa too, on the house."

Dani nodded, quickly putting the drinks on the tray, then Jerome took over the order. She watched as he continued to charm the customers, even though she knew he must be tired and needed to head off to Sky. He assured them they weren't in any hurry and made some joke that they all laughed at. Then the table of four asked for the bill and Dani quickly prepared it and took it over.

"Looks like these will be here for a little longer than twenty minutes." Jerome raised his brows apologetically.

"That's okay, I'll reset the table." Dani smiled up at him. Jerome narrowed his eyes at her and suddenly she blushed at his intensity. She looked away quickly, acutely aware that they were the only staff members left. Determined to keep the conversation on a professional level Dani signalled to the reservations book. "What's it like tomorrow?"

"I'll have a look and maybe we can sort out the lunch and evening reservations while we're stuck here. I'm not entirely sure if Peter's going to be in tomorrow."

Dani let herself look at him and smiled. "Sure. I'll give you a hand."

"Can you manage for a moment?" Jerome signalled to the table and Dani nodded.

Stepping into the cold night air, Jerome felt the damp on his face. He pulled out his cigarettes and lit one, dragging hard. He'd hardly had time to smoke tonight. He looked down at the glowing tip of his cigarette, thinking he really should try and quit. He remembered he only used to smoke four or five a day, socially mainly, but over the past year or so he'd begun to smoke much more and in the last month he was sure he'd smoked over a packet a day. He frowned, then took another drag. What with all the stress, he was surprised he wasn't a chain smoker. He opened the packet and saw he'd only smoked half of them today. He glanced back at the entrance, hearing Dani's laugh. He smiled to himself. She must have gone over to the table again. He leaned over to the ashtray and stubbed out his half-smoked cigarette. *Who was he kidding?* He hadn't really wanted a smoke, the time had literally flown by today and he'd hardly missed his nicotine fix. He'd just needed the distance from Dani.

Dani was standing by the bar looking over the reservations book when Jerome re-entered the restaurant. He took a moment to drink in her profile. The past few days, working closely with her, had been a welcome distraction from the troubles he was facing at home. But he knew he was playing with fire if he let this go further than just harmless flirting. He huffed to himself – harmless was probably not the right word. If Liz was making an effort, then the least he could do was at least try and forgive her. He took in a deep breath and headed in to the bar. "So, have you managed to sort out all the reservations, then?" he joked.

Dani looked up at him and smirked at the playful mocking of his tone, then held up one finger. "Just give me two more minutes," she joked back and Jerome laughed softly at her. He was getting used to her sharp wit. She'd surprised him on a few occasions but now he'd grown comfortably familiar with her unguarded responses. In fact, he looked forward to them. Their conversations seemed to be peppered with some sort of joke or play on words and Dani's quick comebacks kept him on his toes.

He perched on one of the stools and leaned over closer. Dani took in a deep breath, enjoying the familiar fresh scent of his chosen cologne and the hint of smoke.

"You weren't kidding," he scoffed, clearly impressed.

Dani twisted her mouth, stifling a grin, then trained her focus on the book, avoiding looking at him directly. "Well, I've managed the lunches and most of the evening reservations. But this one here, look." Dani pointed to an entry with her pen. "I can't make out if it's three people or eight."

Jerome leaned in closer to get a better look at Peter's bad handwriting, his shoulder brushed against Dani's arm, causing her to step away from him.

"Oh, sorry."

"That's okay," she replied quickly, though she was anything but. Even his accidental brushing had her senses reeling.

"Hmm, if it's an eight we'll need to put them on table fifteen." He swivelled around to view the restaurant. "But if it's a three... table five," he mulled.

"I was thinking table nineteen and if it ends up being eight we can join up table twenty."

Jerome turned back to the bar and pulled at his bottom lip as he thought for a moment, then looked up at Dani, who was waiting for a response. "I think you're right."

Dani's lips curled into a smile, then she wrote the table number next to the reservation. She could feel Jerome still looking at her and instinctively she turned to return his gaze. Her heart raced at his close proximity but she was determined to keep her head. *Keep professional*, she told herself. Dani managed to squeeze out of her throat. "That leaves us five tables free for any more reservations that may come in after nine thirty tomorrow."

"Hmm." Jerome's brow furrowed for a moment. "You've been a great help over the past two days."

Dani shrugged, indicating it was nothing.

"You're making us rely on you," he smirked. "I know Peter does. And Mama."

"I'm happy to help. As I've said before, I really like working here." Dani felt a rush at the idea of being valued by him.

"Good. I know that you're overqualified for this job. We wouldn't want to lose you."

Dani swallowed the lump in her throat, acutely aware that they were a foot apart and his magnificent eyes were fixed on her. "I'm not going anywhere," she answered quietly.

Jerome licked his lips slowly and nodded, he then turned to look at the table of six who were laughing at something one of them had said. "Looks like they're enjoying themselves."

Dani turned to look at the table. "Yes, I should go and ask them if they want more coffee."

"Hmm. I think I'm going to need one too."

"Okay, I'll just check on them and I'll make you one."

"No, it's okay. I'll go."

The table of six ordered a couple more coffees and some more drinks. After Dani prepared them, she pushed an espresso over to Jerome but decided to stay on the inside of the bar, ensuring some distance.

Jerome looked at his watch. It was ten past midnight. "You should go, Dani. It's going to be busy tomorrow. They'll be going soon, I can finish up here. I really don't need you to stay on."

"That's alright. I'll stay." She hated the idea of him sitting here all alone but she couldn't admit to that.

"You've a long drive home." Jerome picked up his coffee and took a sip.

"It's only about twenty minutes at this time. It winds me down after here." She shrugged.

"Yes, I know what you mean. I find it hard to relax after here." He placed his cup down and toyed with the teaspoon. "How's the house hunting going?"

Dani huffed. "Not so good."

"You're not happy at your sister's?"

"I love being there. But I need to be closer to here and I need my independence."

Jerome nodded thoughtfully. There were so many questions he wanted to ask her but he wasn't sure if it was entirely appropriate for him to open up that door with Dani. Not yet anyway. It would change their dynamic, bring them closer together and he knew that could make things complicated for him. His troubled thoughts were interrupted by the urgent ringing of his phone. He pulled it out of his inside pocket and looked at the screen. It was Paul, his head of security at Sky.

"Hi, Paul, what's up?"

"Just checking that you're okay. You're normally in by eleven thirty. Is everything alright?"

Jerome smiled, thankful he had such a good friend, always watching his back. "Yeah, I'm fine. Still at La Casa. How's everything?"

"We're full already. It's going to be a long night," Paul joked.

Jerome frowned, worried he'd neglected Sky on their busiest night. "I'm not sure how long I'll be –"

Paul, sensing Jerome's anxiety, interrupted. "Don't worry boss. Gino and I have everything under control. You've enough on your plate. I'll get Gino to send you the figures for tonight and I'll fill you in on anything else. Take a night off."

"Thanks, Paul. I think I just might."

"I'll see you tomorrow."

"Sure, bye."

Jerome put his phone away and looked up at Dani who was watching him. For some inexplicable reason he felt he needed to explain the phone call to her.

"Head of security at Sky."

"Trouble?"

"No. He was just worried. I'm normally there by now."

"Oh I see. That's nice of him. You're lucky to have such good staff."

Jerome narrowed his eyes at her and a ghost of a smile skirted around his sculptured mouth. "Yes I am," he replied. He paused, allowing his comment to sink in and what it implied, then continued. "He's a friend too. It's important to have people you can trust around you in this industry."

Dani nodded her agreement. "Is that why you employ a lot of your family? Because you trust them?"

Jerome chuckled at her observation. "Yes, one of the reasons."

Dani's eyes widened for a moment. Images of *The Godfather* and the mafia came unbidden into her mind and her face dropped a little. She swallowed, her mouth drying up all of a sudden. Was she working for some Italian mobster family? They had everything they needed: an accountancy firm, a lawyer. She shook her head, trying to dispel her unwelcome thoughts.

Jerome cocked his head to one side. "Mama told you about our family?"

"Er, yes. But to be honest, I couldn't keep up. It was just too much to take in."

Jerome grinned at her. "Yes, we've a very big family. Your family is small, I take it?"

"Just me and Chloe. Our parents died a few years ago. Adam has no brothers or sisters, only his father. So we're pretty small in comparison to yours."

"And yet you chose to live in London, far away from them?" The question was out before he could stop himself. Dani's eyes dropped and Jerome instantly felt bad.

"It was a bad decision on my part," she replied quietly.

Jerome bobbed down to catch her gaze and she jerked her eyes to meet his. "We've all made mistakes, Dani."

Dani took in a deep breath and nodded. "Yeah, just that some are bigger than others." Jerome blinked softly at her, itching to ask more. To find out what had driven her back up to her family, two hundred miles away from her previous job and home. In the few minutes they'd spent together, Jerome felt their relationship had already shifted slightly – exactly what he'd feared. Dani seemed more at ease around him and he in turn felt less guarded and a lot more comfortable. Maybe too comfortable. The last thing he needed was to complicate his life but there was absolutely no doubt in his mind that he liked being around her. He liked it a lot and he knew he had no right to feel that way.

Lost in his troubled thoughts, Jerome had almost forgotten there was a party of six sitting behind him until Dani's attention was drawn to the table. "Time to go."

Jerome furrowed his brow for a moment, confused at Dani's comment.

"They've just asked for the bill," explained Dani.

"Oh." Jerome turned in his seat towards the table, unnerved by how disappointed he felt that their time alone was ending.

Dani quickly prepared the bill and handed it over to them. Jerome pushed to his feet and paced over to wish them a good night and take care of the payment while Dani cleared the table. Jerome locked up the front door behind them as Dani took everything into the kitchen, then she ran downstairs to put on her coat and get her bag.

By the time she was back up, Jerome had switched off all the lights and was waiting for her in the vestibule by the back door. "Here, they left this for you." In his hand was a twenty pound note.

"Oh, thanks." Dani took the note and shoved it in her bag.

"Thanks for tonight." Jerome leaned over and opened the back door. "For staying and helping out with the reservations."

Dani walked out of the door into the cold night air. "No problem. I'll see you in the morning."

"Actually I won't be here. Peter's just texted me saying he'll be back tomorrow." He turned to set the alarm and locked the back door.

"Oh." She couldn't hide her disappointment. "I mean, it's good that he's better," she added quickly. They'd reached her car and Dani fumbled for the fob to unlock it.

"Yes it is." He turned to face her. "But I'll see you tomorrow night at Sky?"

"Yes. Definitely."

"Good. Well good night, Dani. Drive safely." He stepped backwards and headed for his car.

"I will. Good night." Dani slipped into her car and started the engine. Her stomach sank. She'd have to wait twenty-four hours to see him again.

Jerome was sitting in his home office, waiting for his computer to open. After two days of being at La Casa, he had decided to stay home today. He'd already gone for a run and then made breakfast for the kids, allowing Liz a lie in. Nina had Sunday off and would be back around seven, so he was determined to have some quality family time.

He pressed the email icon and waited for his emails to filter through while he sipped his espresso. It was just past ten and he found it hard not to think about what was happening at La Casa. He knew Peter was there and that everything would run like clockwork, but after being there constantly for the last forty-eight hours, he realised how much he missed it and the buzz.

Scott's report flashed up on the screen and Jerome apprehensively clicked to open it. He quickly read it. Liz had been home until eleven and then she had gone shopping at IKEA for an hour. Her appointment with the hairdresser at Level One had meant Nina and the children had met her outside La Casa for lunch, then she'd left alone and headed to the agency. She'd spent two and a half hours there, returning home around six thirty. Jerome noted she'd stayed home all night.

Again, nothing unusual. He tapped his desk, unsure of what he had been expecting. *It was only the second day*, he thought. Then frowned to himself. *Why on earth did he want to find something? Wasn't this what he'd hoped for? Liz to have finished her affair and to be committed to him and their family?* He leaned back on his chair, then clicked to Gino's report from last night. He needed to concentrate on something else, anything other than the unsettling feelings he couldn't quite understand.

Arsenio opened up his laptop, which sat on his kitchen table, and immediately moved his cursor over the email icon and clicked it open. He took a sip from his espresso and tapped his fingertips impatiently on the glass. He'd heard nothing from Jerome and was now eager to see what Scott had to report.

The emails began to filter through and Arsenio quickly opened up Friday's report and read it. He sat back on his chair, unsure of what he'd been expecting, but he was most definitely disappointed. Nothing unusual.

He scrolled down to Saturday's report and opened it up, again reading its contents. He frowned at the screen. Again nothing unusual.

Arsenio drained his coffee and set down his cup on the saucer a little too hard. Damn it. He was sure there'd be something. He was willing to bet his business Liz was still seeing that pumped-up asshole. She was either very clever at hiding it or he was totally wrong. And he was rarely wrong. Over the two days, she'd done nothing other than see her agent, spend time at home and do a little shopping. Granted, he was surprised she'd lowered her standards to shop at IKEA – it was far too functional and wasn't 'designer'. Not Liz's style at all.

Arsenio scraped back his chair and picked up his empty cup and saucer, taking it over to the coffee machine for a refill. Well, it was early days. He just hoped she'd slip up soon, so that Jerome would finally kick her to the curb. He popped another coffee pod into the machine and turned the knob. He rubbed his eyes with his thumb and forefinger. Even if they caught her red handed, straddled over Jonathan, it wasn't enough. Jerome wanted full custody of his children and Arsenio knew that infidelity wasn't going to secure him that. Until he could, Arsenio knew Jerome would sacrifice himself, staying in his lie of a marriage for the sake of Kara and Alessandro. And for the first time, Arsenio couldn't blame him.

As was expected, Sunday at La Casa d'Italia was hectic. Peter took full control again to Gia's relief, easing the pressure off her. Peter disliked being away from La Casa. It was very much part of his life, it was the family he'd never managed to have. Gia sat with him, going over everything that had happened, just before she went to her apartment for a rest after the lunchtime rush.

Dani stayed on in the afternoon with Richard and Augustino but served behind the bar rather than in the restaurant. Peter sat on one of the bar stools sipping his coffee, glad for the break.

"I never had chance to thank you for stepping in, Dani. Gia told me you helped out a lot while I was away."

"It was a pleasure. I'm happy to help out. I didn't do that much." Dani shrugged.

"Gia also told me you've volunteered to teach her how to use a few programs on the computer." He arched his eyebrow at her.

"Yes, I used it all the time when I was in London."

"Well that'd be a great help. We've tended to keep things more..." He twisted his mouth as he tried to find the right word.

"Traditional?" suggested Dani.

Peter chuckled at her delicate choice of words. "Yes... traditional works. Gia's a little intimidated by technology."

"I think most people are. I'll do my best. Start her off slowly. Once she learns a few basics, she'll get into the swing of it."

"She must like you if she's willing to give it a go." He grinned. "I don't have the patience to teach anyone. And to be honest, I only know the basics myself, so I wouldn't be any good at showing someone else."

Their conversation was interrupted by Joseph who had just paid his bill and had headed to where Dani and Peter were talking. He'd come in with Jenny again and his newly recruited team.

"Everything was superb as always, Peter." Joseph's eyes flitted to Dani as he spoke and Peter's lips twitched at his blatant appraisal of her. *He'd have to get in line,* Peter thought to himself. What with Seni drooling after her and Kuch taking her under his wing, he didn't even want to think about Jerome. If the video surveillance over the past two days was anything to go by, Peter was sure their professional relationship had shifted. To what exactly, he wasn't sure, but he was going to need to keep a close eye on them.

"Glad to hear it. How's the hotel coming along?"

"Slowly," he cringed, "but we should be on track for our opening on the sixteenth. I was hoping to see Jerome but Gia told me he wasn't in today."

"He tries to spend Sunday with his family," Peter explained.

"Yes, Gia said. Well, apart from wanting to catch up, one of the reasons I wanted to see Jerome was to give him his invite to the opening." Joseph reached into his inside pocket and pulled out a wad of envelopes. "There's one for Gia and you, Peter" – Joseph leafed through the envelopes, then pulled one out – "and one for you too, Dani." Joseph turned to Dani and held out the envelope.

Dani's eyes widened in shock. "Oh. Er, thank you very much." She flushed slightly as she took the envelope and saw the wry smile Peter gave her.

"It's on a Monday, so you won't be working," Joseph added. He turned to Peter. "I hope you can all make it."

"Thank you. Of course." Peter took the envelopes and placed them on the bar.

"I also wanted to ask Jerome about hiring here."

"La Casa?" Peter asked, clearly puzzled.

"Yes. I was hoping to host my parents' ruby wedding anniversary at the Lodge – that's the hotel – but we just won't be ready in time."

"When were you thinking?" Peter opened up the reservations book.

"Boxing Day."

"Oh, I see. Well, we only open for lunch on Boxing Day."

"It'll be around fifty people. I was hoping to do it early, say six thirty in the evening."

Peter tapped his pen against his lips as he thought. "You should use the private room upstairs. It'll be cosier than down here. We've some function menus you can look at, but basically we can do whatever you like." Peter swivelled round to look at the restaurant. There were a few tables almost finishing and around six new tables in for late lunches. Peter looked up at Dani.

"Can you manage while I show Joseph the room?"

"No problem, Chef."

Jerome started to prepare dinner for Liz and himself while Kara and Alessandro finished up theirs. Determined to carry on the rest of the day together, Jerome suggested for Liz to complete her scheduled workout while he fed and bathed the children so that they could enjoy dinner together before he would need to head off to Sky. They'd spent the whole day just doing the mundane simple things. Eating together, helping the children with their homework, then they'd retrieved the Christmas tree from the loft. Jerome had taken the children to buy some new Christmas tree lights from a local DIY shop, leaving Liz to put up the tree ready for them to decorate it.

It almost felt normal again. Except they were still tip toeing around each other, being overly polite and keeping an obvious distance between themselves.

Liz had been in good spirits and patient with the children, which, granted, had been unusual of late. She seemed happy to stay home, when before, she'd find any excuse to leave the house, probably to ring or see Jonathan. But today, she'd stayed home. All in all, it had been a peculiar kind of day.

Jerome stopped chopping the salad he was preparing and looked at Liz's phone. She'd never left it behind before; she'd always taken it with her. He looked over at his children who were engrossed in a conversation about a TV program they'd been watching, then he picked up Liz's phone. He hesitated for a moment, before sliding the screen to open it up. He tapped onto the "Registered Calls" option, noting that she hadn't made or received any phone calls today at all. He scrolled to the day before. There were only calls to Nina, from himself and a friend of hers. Jerome sighed heavily, then checked her messages – again, nothing unusual. Maybe she really was making an effort, thought Jerome. He knew it was only a couple of days since the investigator had started and it was too early to be absolutely sure, but nevertheless, it did look as though Liz had stuck to her word. Jerome put the phone back down and resumed his chopping, still unable to shake off the continuous doubt that had settled deep into his gut.

"So can you tell me more about these possible jobs Graham's put you forward for? Or are you still worried about jinxing them?" Jerome teased. They were sitting at right angles at the kitchen table. Liz had showered after her workout and was dressed in a thin, silky, light blue robe that accentuated her cool blue eyes.

"I've the dates for the holiday brochure shoot. It's for four days. I leave on the fourteenth."

"Oh, so soon?"

Liz nodded as she chewed slowly on her poached salmon, then swallowed. "Is that alright? I mean, will you manage without me?" She shuffled slightly in her chair, causing her robe to loosen.

Jerome's brow furrowed, slightly thrown off guard by her concern and the fact he could clearly see the curve of her breasts.

"Um, yes. I'm sure Nina and I can." He focused on his plate for a moment, looking down at the rather bland meal he'd prepared. He fleetingly thought that there was no way poached salmon and salad would satisfy him until the early hours of the morning, but he was trying to be supportive to Liz. At least it was a cooked meal of sorts. She'd been living off salad, that disgusting wheat grass drink and protein shakes. Her only indulgence was the odd glass of white wine.

"It's a good contract, Jerome. Thanks for being so supportive." She rested her delicate hand on his forearm and he flinched slightly at the contact. His eyes darted up to her, worried that she may have taken offense to his reaction but she smiled softly at him.

"Well, I just want to see you happy, Liz."

Her smile widened a little, then she removed her hand and reached over to her glass of wine, taking a sip.

"So any more jobs? What's happening with the fashion show?"

Liz licked her lips free of the wine and shifted around so she was almost facing him. "It's still scheduled for January, but they seem to be having problems with the venue. Graham's keeping me in the loop. I'll be having fittings after Christmas." Jerome nodded, looked down at her plate and frowned. She's hardly touched the food. "But the good news is that there's a contract for a protein shake company."

Jerome's attention was diverted to her face. "Oh? A protein shake?"

"Yes, it's a three year contract promoting a new company that specialises in protein shakes, bars – you know, that kind of thing. And they want a face to launch it."

Jerome watched her face light up at the prospect. "Wow. That sounds like quite a job."

"I know. It's not a field I've thought of before, but Graham suggested it. It's going to be promoted worldwide alongside a fitness DVD. The products are supposed to be excellent. Even Holland and Barrett are going to stock them and possibly other large health store chains and chemists."

Jerome put down his fork and grinned at her obvious enthusiasm. "That's incredible, Liz, really."

"I know. I'm pretty excited about it. I'm having my first meeting with them just before I go to Spain. Apparently, they're very particular. They want to make sure that whoever is involved with the product is fit, healthy and glamorous. Its promotional campaign is similar to an exclusive alcoholic drink, rather than the usual beefcake-muscle-man way this kind of product usually gets promoted. It's slick and edgy."

"Well they couldn't have picked anyone better, then." Jerome reached over and squeezed her hand slightly, then released it. Liz instantly shifted her chair closer, which loosened the robe even more, revealing more of her breasts. She crossed her long toned legs so that the robe fell away from them. Jerome's eyes raked over her appreciatively, realising she was naked under the robe.

Liz continued, seemingly oblivious, but Jerome knew her better. She was trying to seduce him and her ambivalence to his reaction was deliberate. She flicked the hair that had fallen over her shoulders back with her hand, then picked up her fork and speared some salmon.

"The best thing is the money," she continued, waving the fork in the air. "Graham's hoping the contract will be five figures with an option to renegotiate after each year."

"That's great, Liz. It's the kind of contract you've always wanted, to be the face of a product." Jerome directed his eyes onto her face as he spoke softly. He didn't want to give her any mixed messages. She was a very attractive woman and he wasn't blind to that, but he wasn't ready for physical intimacy with her yet. It was still too soon and he still wasn't sure if it was over with Jonathan. Jerome kept himself focused on Liz as she enthusiastically continued, trying to banish his constant erratic thoughts.

"I know, right? I know it's not the usual thing I'm into. I'd have preferred cosmetics or a fashion brand, but this has longevity. And it appeals to men and women. It'll cover both markets!"

Jerome grinned widely at her, pleased that she was obviously excited about this. He just hoped it went through for her. He'd seen her being put forward for many contracts and they had never come through. Not because she wasn't good enough – he knew she was. It was just the nature of the business. Too much competition and too many well-known faces that large companies tended to favour. He just hoped this company wanted a new face, for Liz's and his sake. He really couldn't face her depression and moods if she was rejected by them. He'd been there too many times with her over the years.

"So when's the meeting?"

"I'm not sure yet. Graham's going to let me know tomorrow after he's talked to them. That's why I'm spending so much time with him. He's really pushing me forward for this and he thinks it'll lead to other high profile jobs too." Liz fidgeted in her seat nervously.

Jerome's eyes softened at her obvious discomfort. She was worried that her excessive time away from home might be bothering him, especially after they'd promised to spend more time together.

"Hey it's okay. I understand it's for work," he reassured her.

Her eyes darted up to his face. "Do you? I mean, I know we're supposed to be trying, and –"

Jerome lifted his hand and stroked her cheek, "I do. It's going to be hectic for me too this month. Just please let me know what your schedule is so I can at least try and work around it."

Liz placed her hand over his, then shuffled closer. Jerome swallowed hard. He knew what she was doing. She knew exactly how to break him. He only needed to see her a little bit vulnerable, fragile even and he'd let his guard down. Liz knew that, and he wondered whether her concern was genuine or staged. What he did know, though, was that he hated second guessing her motives, watching her reactions and checking up on her. This wasn't what a marriage should be, or what he had envisaged for himself. He really didn't know how long he would be able to carry on like this. Or worse, if he'd ever get over feeling like this at all. Forgiveness he could do, but forget, that was much harder.

He pulled his hand away from her cheek and focused on his plate again. He needed to change the subject. He wasn't quite ready to let her in again and Jerome was worried that an outright rejection might cause another heated argument. After a surprisingly pleasant day at home, Jerome didn't want to ruin that. Luckily for him, Liz provided the change of subject.

"So, what about you? La Casa? Sky?" she turned a little bit so she was farther away from him, then rearranged her robe to cover herself up a little bit more, still leaving a sizeable amount of cleavage exposed. The gesture was deliberate and Jerome wondered if she'd realised that her seductive tactic wasn't working. He took a moment before answering, taking a long drink from his glass of water. Her movements and surprising questions had thrown him off guard again. Liz never asked him about work. She'd made it clear, especially over the last five years, that she had no interest in the business that seemed to consume him.

"Um, fine, they're both doing fine." His answer was weak but he really wasn't sure if she really wanted to know or whether this was all part of her effort to try and be more understanding.

"Are you booked up over the holidays?"

"Yes, pretty much." He cut another piece of salmon and popped it in his mouth and chewed, wishing it had some sauce on it accompanied by a mushroom risotto.

"I take it we'll be spending Christmas Day there."

"Er yes. If that's okay? I can make arrangements not to be there if you'd rather –"

"No, no. The kids love it down there. We go every year and your mother would never forgive us." Liz smiled tightly.

Jerome huffed. He didn't relish the idea of telling his mother that her only two grandchildren wouldn't be down to see her on Christmas Day.

"And Level One?" Liz asked quietly. Jerome's eyes darted to her face, but she seemed overly interested in her salad. He knew it was hard for her to ask and his natural instinct was to make it easy for her, but again, he was caught between what he felt he should do and what needed to be done. He decided rather than make her feel totally uncomfortable, he'd be as economical and matter of fact as he could.

"The new managers have settled in so that seems to be getting back on track. At least they'll be ready for January, you remember how busy it gets?"

Liz turned slightly to look at him and nodded. "Yes, I remember." She reached over for her wine and drained the glass.

Jerome forked up some of his salad and put it in his mouth. Was there nothing they could talk about without one of them feeling uncomfortable, or angry, or utterly wretched?

"What time do you need to go?" she asked, breaking the uncomfortable silence.

"I should start to get ready. I need to be there within an hour."

"You go and get ready, then. I'll clear these up." Liz gestured at the table. Jerome's eyes fell to her half-eaten food.

"You didn't finish it."

"I wasn't that hungry."

"You have to eat something, Liz. You can't live off protein shakes and that wheatgrass." His voice had a hint of exasperation.

"I'm just watching my weight. I can't afford to let myself go, not with these possible contracts coming up."

"You train hard every day, Liz. You look amazing and I worry that you'll make yourself ill."

She grinned at him coyly, "Do I? Look amazing?"

"Trust you to only focus on that part," he huffed, stifling a smile.

Liz stood up and picked up their plates. "A compliment from you is worth ten contracts to me, Jerome. Don't you know that?" She placed the plates in the sink and turned to look at him as she leaned back against the counter.

Jerome scraped back his chair and rose to his feet, his eyes steady on hers. "I thought you knew. You always look amazing to me."

"Well it's nice to hear it sometimes, Jerome." She spoke softly and Jerome could sense her sincerity. "I need to hear it."

Liz lowered her eyes and nervously fiddled with the tie of her robe. For the first time in a while her hard, cool exterior was replaced by vulnerability, like the young girl he'd first met on the photo shoot ten years ago. She still craved his attention after all these years together. Wasn't that what she'd been telling him? Why she'd ended up in someone else's bed? Jerome's heart sank.

"I'll try and remember that," he replied quietly

Liz looked up at him and smiled shyly. "Thank you."

Jerome stepped around the table and edged towards the door, "I need to get ready."

"I know. It's okay. Thank you for today, for spending it with me."

"I'll try harder, Liz, I will, but it's going to be hard this month."

"I know. But at least today was a start."

"Yes, it was."

DESTINY

By the time the staff of La Casa d'Italia arrived at Sky, it was already past midnight. Jerome was sitting in his office with Paul. They were going over the latest information his head of security had managed to gather from his various sources, regarding their continuing problem of drug runners dealing in the club.

"It seems the runners we threw out last week are part of large network, the head being a rather unsavoury but highly elusive character who calls himself Angel."

Jerome huffed, "Angel?"

"Yeah, a charming alias. He probably has some fascination with death or the afterlife... whatever, he seems like a dangerous, delusional fucker. That aside though, his set-up is extremely organised. My friends at the drug squad are finding it hard to track him down. They're not even sure what he looks like or where he operates from." Paul opened up a file he was carrying. "The only pictures I have are of a few chief dealers and some of their runners." He pulled out a wad of around eight photographs. "I've made copies and all the security are on alert for any of these. Of course there may be more. In fact, I imagine there are a hell of a lot more, but this is all I could get. If his lieutenants are clean skins, it's hard to track them."

"Lieutenants? Clean skins?"

"Lieutenants are the next in command. Clean skins are people with no police records or convictions," explained Paul. Jerome nodded, thankful of Paul's continuing ties to law enforcement operatives around the country. He tended to slip into his police-trained terminology when he was discussing security of the club.

Paul continued, "Apparently there's a huge undercover operation trying to track him down, so my friends down in the drug squad were a little evasive."

Jerome looked at each photo carefully and was surprised to see that most of them didn't look like your run-of-the-mill dealer. There were a couple of women too and all of them were well dressed. They looked professional and could easily be accountants, insurance brokers, bankers even.

Jerome scowled and leaned back in his chair. "Understandable, I suppose, but it makes it harder for us. Is this Angel mixed up in any other kind of business?"

Paul knew exactly what Jerome was worried about. He had a family and a restaurant where his mother lived. He knew Ferretti House was safe, but his home and the restaurant could be targeted.

Paul nodded. "The usual businesses that seem to go hand in hand with these kinds of characters."

"Like?"

Paul shifted on his feet. "A bit of arms dealing and illegal gambling."

Jerome let out a deep breath and pulled at his lower lip. He had a feeling Paul was being guarded about the information. He was going to have to up his security. If they rubbed this Angel up the wrong way, he'd come after them, one way or another.

"I'll up the security at La Casa and your house."

Jerome nodded. After working together with Paul for the past four years, he was thankful he didn't need to explain himself.

"I don't want to antagonise anyone Paul, but I won't have drugs in the club. Politely get them out without fuss, and no violence."

"Sure, boss."

Jerome stood up from his chair and picked up the photos, then turned around and attached each one onto his notice board behind his desk.

"Dani, you really have some amazing outfits!" Carmen stood back a little to appraise her. Dani, along with Rosa, Kuch and Nicole, had just joined the rest of the staff at their usual table at Sky.

"Thanks. Eighty percent of my wardrobe is only nightclub appropriate." Dani shrugged and dropped her eyes to her purple silk jumpsuit. She'd paired it with pewter pumps and her hair was put in a messy up-do.

"You're lucky. Mine are all kitchen appropriate!" she snorted.

By one thirty, Dani was ready to cool off on the veranda. She joined Franco, Rico, Augustino and Richard while they smoked by one of the heaters.

"So glad we've got tomorrow off," said Rico, stubbing out his cigarette.

"What do you do on your days off?" asked Dani addressing all of them.

They all answered in unison, "Sleep!"

Dani chuckled. "Isn't that a bit of a waste?"

"That depends on who you're sleeping with," Franco answered, lifting his eyebrows lewdly, causing Rico to laugh loudly.

"You're terrible." Dani shook her head.

Their attention was drawn to the sudden rise in the volume of music, caused by the door opening next to them. Jerome strode through.

"Hey boss!" Rico called him over. Jerome stepped to where they were all standing and shook everyone's hand. Dani watched closely at their interaction. It was clear that they genuinely liked Jerome. Dani noted that all the staff did. He had their total respect but still managed to have a high degree of familiarity with them. Granted, they were related in some way or another, but at La Casa, while everyone worked, they were always professional.

Jerome finally turned towards Dani and smiled softly at her, offering his hand for her to shake. "I hope these lot here aren't leading you astray." His blue eyes narrowed at her.

"Astray?" Dani questioned, confused by his comment and giddy from his firm grip on her hand.

"Smoking?" He cocked his head to the side, his warm hand still holding hers.

Dani reluctantly pulled her hand away and grinned. "I'm not that easily lead."

"No?" Jerome allowed his lips to curl at her comment.

Dani shook her head slightly. "When I set my mind to something, I always follow through."

"So you possess a certain amount of... willpower? Self-control?" His hand circled in the air in front of him as he thought of the correct words, the gesture betraying his ingrained Mediterranean traits.

Dani swallowed all the while he continued to focus on her. *Willpower? Her? Self-control?* She almost snorted out loud. He was lucky he was married and that they were surrounded by people. He looked good enough to eat, standing two feet away from her in a dark blue pinstriped suit, the open-necked shirt he'd paired it with in the same tone, stretched over his broad hard chest. His unruly hair was immaculately tamed and the trimmed stubble he wore so well gave him a rougher edge over his chiselled jaw line.

Dani continued to gape at him, elated that she'd not only seen him but that he had taken time out to talk to her. Jerome pulled out his cigarette packet from the inside pocket of his jacket and flicked open the lid. The rest of the party were talking amongst themselves, oblivious of the sudden highly charged atmosphere between the two of them. Dani felt, once again, their conversation was about something entirely different.

"Yes, I think so," Dani answered, trying hard not to let her voice sound too breathy. Jerome pulled out a cigarette, tapped it twice on the packet and put it to his lips, then after a beat, lit it. He took a deep drag, then blew out a steady stream of smoke. His lips twitched, stifling his smile, and he continued to regard her.

Seeing his amusement, Dani continued, determined to keep their conversation less intense. "However, you have seen me stuffing my face with desserts, so maybe I've just substituted one bad habit with another." She shrugged and looked at him through her lashes. *Shit, what was she doing? She was flirting with him... again. Jeez, she really needed to stop. What did he say about self-control? He was married, for Christ's sake.*

"Ah yes." He nodded and a smile curved smoothly over his sculptured mouth. "You certainly enjoy the sweeter things in life. I'd hate to come between you and those." He arched his eyebrow. "Maybe you need to substitute your *sweet* cravings with something else? Or do you think you're able to assert some level of self-control there too?" His eyes darkened as he continued to look at her.

Dani's eyes widened at his comment, knowing she'd pushed the boundaries and he was following her lead. She straightened, suddenly needing to steer the conversation onto a less volatile path, and answered, "Like I said, I'm quite determined when I need to be."

"That's good to know." His tongue darted over his top lip and he nodded slowly. His eyes narrowed a little from the quick straight answer, grounding him in an instant.

"Well, I'd better get back inside. I think I've cooled down enough." Who was she kidding? She was on fire! Her body temperature had gone through the roof, regardless of the frosty December air. Dani stepped to the side so she could catch Franco's eye and indicated she was going back in.

Jerome furrowed his brow, then turned his attention back to the four men behind him. He'd crossed that line again, that dangerous line that kept him just far enough away but at the same time was intoxicating – addictive, even – pulling him towards it. This time, it had been Dani that had backed off. It worried him that he'd jeopardised the level of familiarity they'd reached last night by his careless flirting.

"So what are you all up to tomorrow?" he asked the four men and was instantly rewarded with the same answer Dani had gotten, followed by laughter.

Dani opened up the door leading into the club and turned around to look at the five of them joking around. Jerome lifted his eyes and his intense gaze caught Dani's, causing her to falter before she stepped into the heat of the club.

Dani fumbled her way through the crowds, back to where everyone was seated. Her head pulsed with erratic thoughts. *What was Jerome doing? Was he interested in her?* She just couldn't work it out. Thank goodness her head was clear of alcohol. There was no way she'd have reined in that highly charged conversation, had she had a couple of drinks. She was going to have to keep her wits about her around him. She slumped into an empty seat and twisted a tendril of hair that had worked itself loose. *Crap*, she thought. She really liked him, *a lot*, and her natural instinct was to flirt back at him. She was really going to have to watch her step.

Dani sat for a while, lost in her thoughts, until the sound of her colleagues greeting someone caused Dani to shift her troubled focus. She leaned to the side so she could see around Kuch's large frame at who had arrived, and was surprised to see Jenny. Dani caught her eye. She beamed back at her and waved. Behind her stood Joseph, along with the two new recruits he'd been dining with earlier.

"Hey, this is a surprise." Jenny had squeezed past Kuch and her slim frame stood in front of Dani.

"Hi. Yes it is. Come and sit down." Dani shuffled to the side making room for her. She liked Jenny – she was warm and always friendly. "Is this your first time here?"

"Yeah. It's really something." She gazed around the club wide-eyed, her cheeks flushed. "We were out having drinks and Joseph suggested we finish off the night here."

"We come here most Sundays."

"Really? Well it's a great club. Your boss certainly has the whole entertainment thing going on," Jenny smirked. She jerked her head towards the direction she'd walked from and Dani looked up.

Jerome was standing by the nearby bar, leaning against it while talking with Joseph. He looked effortlessly handsome, his strong profile silhouetted by the backlight of the bar. Joseph said something to amuse him and he tilted his head back and laughed. Even in the dim light, he looked absolutely breathtaking.

"He's a *really* good looking guy." Jenny's unguarded comment jolted Dani and she shifted to look at Jenny, who had her eyes focused on Jerome, blatantly admiring him.

"Yeah. Married, though." Dani leaned closer so Jenny could hear her over the music.

"The best ones usually are," huffed Jenny.

"I thought that maybe you and Joseph..."

Jenny shook her head. "No, no. We are just good at working together. Joseph's a great guy but I met him when we were working and I was getting over a big break up. He's just a buddy and to be honest, it's not a good idea to mess around with your boss, unless you end up marrying him." She raised her eyebrows and smirked. Dani chuckled and nodded. "I'm not his type, anyway," Jenny added.

"What? Leggy, pretty, blonde who's good with her hands. That's every guys dream, isn't it?"

Jenny gave a throaty laugh. "Yeah, I know, right? No – joking aside, he tends to like curvy brunettes. Anyway he's not *my* type. I like dark broody Mediterranean men, a bit more like your man over there." Her eyes focused back on Jerome.

"Ah, well if he was single you'd probably be *his* type. His wife is leggy and blonde."

Jenny clicked her fingers, indicating she'd missed out. "Too late for me, then," she chuckled. "At least you get to drool over him every day eh?"

Dani shrugged, trying to be as non committal as possible. "He has a very attractive younger brother, though..."

"Really? Do tell." Jenny edged closer.

Dani laughed. "He's a renowned playboy and flirt, though."

"Sounds perfect!" Jenny giggled.

"My staff are seriously impressed with this place. So am I." Joseph took a sip from his drink and then placed it on the bar. He scanned the club, taking in every detail.

"Thanks. It certainly keeps me busy. How's the hotel coming along?

Sorry, I was supposed to get in touch, but I've had rather a lot on my plate."

"Now I've seen this place, I think I can understand. You've certainly tapped into the pleasure market. You've done really well for yourself."

Jerome shrugged at Joseph's remark, unsure of how to respond.

"Well, the hotel's getting there. A few bumps, but we'll be open just on schedule. We had lunch at the restaurant today." Joseph's eyes wandered around the club, clearly searching for someone.

"Oh? I hope everything was okay."

"It was perfect." His roving eyes locked on to the person he'd been trying to locate. Jerome followed his gaze and saw Dani and Jenny sitting on a sofa talking. Joseph turned back to Jerome and continued. "Anyway. I left some invites to the opening. I hope you can make it."

"I'll make sure of it."

"Good. I also reserved the private room for my parents' ruby wedding anniversary. Peter took all the details."

"Oh, wow. Ruby wedding, eh? That's forty years?"

"Yeah. That's something, isn't it?"

Jerome nodded. "Well I'll personally take care of the arrangements."

"Thanks. I appreciate it. So your staff come here a lot, then?" Jerome took in a sharp breath at his observation. He knew Joseph wasn't interested in his staff – he was only interested in one specific member of his staff. Dani.

"Yeah. They come here to let off steam every so often," Jerome answered, purposely omitting the fact they were here practically every Sunday.

"Hmm, that's nice. Well I'll let you get on with whatever you do in this place and I'll go and socialise a bit. It was really good to see you."

"Same here."

Joseph reached over and gave Jerome a hug, then immediately headed straight to where Jenny and Dani were sitting, his obvious eagerness causing Jerome to tense. His discomfort intensified as Jenny vacated her seat and Joseph slipped leisurely into her place.

"Buongiorno, Dani."

"*Buongiorno. Come stai?*"

"*Bene, bene.*" Gia's eyes lit up. "I see Matteo is teaching you well."

Dani laughed softly. "Well, I know roughly twenty words, which is about as many days as I've been working at La Casa. I'm hoping to speed up the process though," Dani chuckled.

"Really?" Gia replied, genuinely interested. She guided Dani through to the lounge area of her spacious apartment and gestured to the sumptuous cream sofa. The fire was glowing and again, Dani marvelled at the stylish decor as her eyes travelled around the room before resting on its equally stylish owner. Even though it was their day off, Gia was dressed impeccably in a dark blue knitted sweater dress and matching knee-high suede boots. The solid colour broken up with a cream, red and blue scarf, tied loosely around her neck.

"Yes. I think I'd like to learn more. A lot more. I really want to visit Italy. Venice, actually – to start with, anyway."

"Venice? You mean for a holiday?"

"*Si*," Dani replied, causing Gia to grin widely. "I think I need to enrol into a class, or get some CDs to learn."

Gia sat down opposite Dani and furrowed her flawless brow. "How about I teach you? If you're going to teach me computers, I can repay you by teaching you Italian."

"You'd do that? I mean, I don't want to put you out."

"Nonsense. It'll be fun." Gia waved her hand dismissively. "Just conversation, though."

"Definitely, I'm not so interested in learning anything less. Well not yet, anyway."

"The best way to learn is just by hearing the language a lot. That's how I taught myself English. When I came over from *Italia* with Alessandro, he used to speak to me in English for a couple of hours every day. I'd watch TV, listen to the radio, that kind of thing. And then after about six months, it just clicked." Gia snapped her fingers, emphasizing the point.

After three espressos and just over an hour, Gia leaned back on her chair, sighing hard. "My brain hurts, Dani."

Dani grinned at Gia. "It wasn't so bad."

"Ha, that's easy for you to say. Right click, left click, double click, drag, copy... ouff, I'm dizzy."

"You did very well, Gia. You just need to practise and don't be scared."

Gia looked at her watch and Dani shifted, feeling that maybe she'd outstayed her welcome. She'd been there almost two hours.

"Well, I'd better go." Dani rose from her chair and gathered up her coffee cup, ready to take it into the kitchen. "I'm sure you've got a lot to do."

Gia nodded. "I do, actually. I'm supposed to decorate the restaurant today. I'm already late. I was supposed to do it last week and to be honest, I really haven't the energy."

"You mean for Christmas?"

Gia pushed to her feet and nodded her reply.

"On your own?"

"*Si*." Gia took the cup Dani was holding.

"Would you like some help? I don't mind."

"Dani, it's your day off. I've already taken up your morning with the computer."

"I haven't got anything else to do today, Gia. Really, if you need some help, I'll stay and give you a hand."

Relief flickered momentarily over Gia's face. "I'd appreciate it." She'd been feeling decidedly tetchy these past few days and her lack of sleep was wearing her down. She was worrying about Jerome. Something wasn't right with him and she knew it was his home life. He had far too much stress with his businesses and now he had the added problems of re-staffing Level One. Gia scowled to herself. He was being pulled in too many directions and Liz was only fuelling his stress. Her demands on him and her modelling career were only going to increase his already overloaded work schedule.

Gia softly squeezed Dani's arm. "*Grazie*, Daniella."

"Are you busy?"

"Um, well, nothing that can't wait. Is there a problem?"

"The reports."

"What about them."

"There's nothing unusual."

"It's only been three days, Jerome." Seni scrubbed his hand over his face, trying hard to keep the exasperation out of his voice. He knew Jerome was impatient but what worried him more was that he was already fighting with his conscience. He was looking for any excuse to call off the investigator.

"She's had plenty of opportunities, Seni." Jerome's tone was cautionary and Arsenio knew he needed to tread carefully.

"Let's give it to the end of the week. It's just another few days and if all's well, we'll stop Scott. At least you'll know for sure by then." The line was quiet and Arsenio held his breath. He knew if he pushed him, Jerome would stop Scott today.

"Fine. Until Friday," Jerome replied sharply.

"Okay." Again the line went quiet. "Look, Jerome, I know this is hard. Really, I understand. But if Liz has broken it off, then it doesn't really matter does it? No harm done. You'll have peace of mind to... well to carry on, right?"

Jerome huffed on the other end of the line. "Peace of mind? I'm snooping on my wife, Seni. You think this gives me peace of mind? I'm the arsehole husband keeping tabs on his wife, invading her privacy. That makes me at worst a total psychotic control freak – at best, pathetic. But hey, I'll have peace of mind, right?" He couldn't have crammed more sarcasm in the last sentence if he tried.

"Jerome..."

"Save it, Seni. Until Friday and then it's over."

Seni looked at his phone as the line went dead. Fuck, Jerome was pissed.

Dani grinned across at Gia as she elegantly bit into her ciabatta sandwich.

"How come I look a total mess, covered in dust? I bet my hair is covered in bits and dishevelled, and you" – Dani shook her head in disbelief – "well, apart from a slight sprinkling of glitter, you look exactly the same." Dani picked at some dried glue she'd spotted on her thumb.

"I'm sure I don't, but it's probably because you practically did all the work." Gia cocked her head to the side and grinned back at her. "You've done a brilliant job, Dani." Gia looked around the restaurant. It had taken them roughly five hours to finish and Gia was thankful that Dani had insisted she'd help.

Over the years, Gia had accumulated a large selection of Christmas decorations and every year she'd either refreshed them by adding a few new ones or on some occasions, bought a complete new set. This Christmas, she just didn't seem to have the drive she had had over the past years, so she'd been quite happy to let Dani take over. They'd pulled out all the decorations from the store room in the basement and then Dani decided which ones would work well together. The result was a spectacular display of multi-coloured jewelled tones against the predominantly cream backdrop of the restaurant.

The lemon tree, in the centre of the restaurant, served as a rather modern slant on a Christmas tree, which was covered in small fairy lights, jewelled coloured baubles and crystals. Kuch's bar was also trans-formed with an array of various decorations hanging down amongst the suspended lighting, seemingly random, yet every one of them strategi-cally placed, continuing the harmonious tones of the tree. Each table had a small arrangement of baubles in a wreath around a candle and the walls had similar large wreaths, which also had fair lights incorporated. The overall effect was a magical array of luxurious vibrant colours, coupled with monochrome lighting, a perfect combination of a modern edge with the warmth of tradition.

They'd sat down to eat some sandwiches Gia had put together while Dani boxed up the unwanted decorations and cleared them away. "I forgot to hang the wreath on the door and we need to hook up the outside lights too." Dani twisted to look towards the front entrance. It was already dark outside.

"Leave the lights. I'll get Peter to sort them out in the morning. You must be exhausted." Gia smiled fondly at Dani. She'd really enjoyed their afternoon together. "You've done more than enough."

"That's okay, Gia. I like doing it. I used to decorate the bar for the different events we did. I loved the process of creating a new look: Christmas, Valentines."

"Well, you certainly have the talent for it. I used to love it too. I just seem to be finding it harder now." Gia shrugged a little. "And to be honest, I can't be climbing up ladders and jumping on and off the bar like I used to either," she chuckled.

"When my parents were alive, Chloe and I used to be in charge of the Christmas decorations in the bed and breakfast we had. I loved this time of year."

Gia furrowed her brow sensing sorrow in Dani's tone. "You don't like this time of year now?"

Dani sighed deeply and wrinkled her nose. "Not so much. It's a time you spend with your family and with my parents gone and Chloe living away, Christmas has always been" – Dani tried to find the right word as she stared blankly at her glass – "empty, I suppose. It's better that I'm with Chloe and Adam this year but..." Dani stopped, finding it hard to express what she wanted to say.

"I think I understand. You're alone. You felt alone even down in London, surrounded by people?"

Dani's eyes darted up to look at Gia and nodded.

"I know what you mean. Since Alessandro died, Christmas has been hard for me too. But I had the boys to focus on. Then, as they've grown and gone their separate ways... well, it's not the same. La Casa helps. It's a good distraction."

"And you have your grandchildren. Christmas is more for children," added Dani.

"Yes, though I don't spend as much time as I'd like with them." Gia smiled tightly and Dani felt that Gia wanted to say more, but had stopped herself.

"I have my nieces and nephew here at least. That will be nice, seeing their faces on Christmas morning."

Gia grinned and nodded. "It really is something seeing your children all excited. That's the magical part."

"Well, I think it'll be a while before I have my own children," Dani huffed. Gia reached over and patted her arm.

"You'll have your own children, Daniella. Don't you believe in... *destino*?"

"*Destino*?" Dani looked puzzled.

Gia twisted her mouth searching for the word and circled her hand in the air, listing the explanations. "Your future... er... things happening for a reason?"

"Oh, um... destiny, fate, that kind of thing?"

"Yes, that's it! Exactly. Leaving London and coming here. It's all part of your destiny."

Dani pursed her lips together. The unwelcome thought of her breaking her heel and finding Julie riding Jez came into her head in a rush. Was that fate? She shook her head sharply in an attempt to rid herself of that unpleasant memory and nodded.

"Maybe," Dani sighed and sat back in her chair, suddenly feeling weary. Today had certainly kept her mind occupied. She's hardly thought about Jez today, until now. This Christmas and New Year's were going to be tough and she was glad she too had La Casa as a distraction. Dani looked up at Gia who was regarding her intently. "*Destino,* eh? My new Italian word for today."

Gia's face broke into a smile, "*Si, il tuo destino*. Your destiny."

23

TRADITIONS

Jerome ran at a steady pace along the riverside leading up to La Casa, his blood pumping fast through his veins, his breath forming rhythmic clouds. He turned into the car park of La Casa, then stopped just outside the back door and bent over, resting his hands on his slightly bent knees to catch his breath. He'd pushed himself today, needing to relieve himself of the pressure he was feeling. Checking up on Liz, organizing Level One and then the possible drug problems at Sky were all playing on his mind. As his breathing began to slow down, Jerome straightened and made his way towards the back door. Continuing to push himself, he ran up the stairs two by two, heading directly to his office.

Within twenty minutes, he was showered and dressed for business. He lowered himself into his chair and brought his computer to life with a flick of his mouse, then clicked onto the email icon and waited. His heart began to beat a little faster as he let the curser hover over Scott's latest report. He opened up the email and started to read.

Again, there was nothing unusual. Liz had done the school run, then after picking up some coffees and health juices, she'd headed to her agent's office, parking as she always did in the underground parking. She stayed there until after lunch, then picked up some dry cleaning, a few groceries and made her way home, staying there all night.

Jerome leaned back in his chair staring at the screen. It was there in black and white. Nothing untoward. So why did he still have an uneasy feeling? Jerome rubbed his face, then closed down the screen. Four more days and he was done.

Dani pushed back through the kitchen doors into the restaurant, having left the staff's coffees, and headed back to the bar to prepare her own and Peter's.

He was sat at the bar with the rota in front of him. "Can you work through today and tomorrow?" Peter asked, his eyes still glued to the rota, tapping his pen against his mouth.

"Sure, but Thursday I have the night off, remember, so I won't be able to."

"Hmm, yes. The rest of the week?"

Dani chuckled. "If no one else can, sure."

"I'm sorry. Am I taking advantage of you?" Peter looked up at her and cringed.

"Totally, but it's okay." She grinned, then started to make their coffees.

"It's just that Augustino is taking a few days off and Pino called in with a stomach bug."

"No worries, Chef, count me in."

"Mama! Wow, you've really outdone yourself this year!" Jerome stood in the main part of the restaurant and looked around, whistling. His gaze moved from one section of the room to the other in total awe.

Gia stood a few feet away from him, her eyes focused on Dani, and she winked at her. Jerome had met Gia in the vestibule as she'd exited the lift and they'd entered the restaurant together. Dani beamed back, thrilled at Jerome's reaction. Feeling her face flame, she quickly turned to the coffee machine and started to prepare Gia's and Jerome's coffees.

"So you like it? Is it better than any of the other years?" Gia coaxed stepping towards the bar.

"Oh yes, Mama. Really. It's most definitely the best." Jerome moved to the bar and greeted Peter and nodded his hello and thanks to Dani as she pushed the coffees towards them.

"Well, I'm very pleased to hear it. But you need to direct your praise to Daniella."

Jerome's eyes darted to Dani and then back to Gia. "Dani?"

Gia perched onto the stool in front of her, next to Peter. "Yes. She came by yesterday. We started my computer lessons." Gia mock-grimaced and Peter chuckled. "She offered to help me out, but as it turns out, it was all her doing. I just held onto the ladder!"

"Really?" Jerome couldn't hide his surprise. And somewhere in the back of his mind, he thought that he'd missed a chance to see her.

"You never said anything to me this morning when I commented on them, Dani." Peter mildly scolded her. Dani shrugged it off and felt her face heat a little more at the sudden attention. "Great job."

Dani scrunched up her face, embarrassed. "Thanks."

Recovering from his surprise, Jerome sat on a bar stool. "Well thank you very much, Dani. You've done an amazing job. No offense, Mama," he added quickly.

"None taken. She deserves all the credit." Gia turned her attention to Peter. "How's the rota?" Peter slid the sheet of paper he'd been scribbling on towards her and began to run through the next two weeks with her.

"You really are full of surprises," Jerome said softly, continuing to stare at Dani.

She shifted on her feet nervously. "I used to decorate the bar for various events," Dani said quietly, by way of explanation.

Jerome nodded slowly. "Well you're good at it. Very good. A girl of many talents." He blinked softly at her. "We need to hang on to you."

The last sentence caught Peter's attention. His eyes shot up in time to catch the undeniable look of admiration on Jerome's face.

"Great job on the decorations." Kuch slipped into his seat next to Dani. Nicole and Rosa agreed with him taking their places around the table.

"Thanks," Dani replied shyly.

"No need to ask what you got up to on your day off, then," Kuch joked.

"No," agreed Dani. "What did you guys get up to?"

"Oh the usual for me: housework and grocery shopping. I live a very exciting life," Rosa huffed.

"Just slept in and chilled really." Nicole shrugged, but Dani noticed that her eyes flitted over to Kuch.

"What about you, Kuch?"

"Same as Nicole," he grinned.

I bet... thought Dani to herself. She wondered to herself how long they'd been seeing each other and if they'd ever be open about it.

Gia, Jerome and Peter entered the room and made their way to their places. It had been a while since they'd all sat down together. She tried hard not to focus on Jerome, who had now occupied the seat opposite her, his perfect frame dressed in a dark chocolate-coloured suit, light blue shirt and dark caramel tie. Dani's mouth pooled with saliva. Thankfully, Peter stood up to make an announcement causing Dani to look away.

"Morning, everyone. I just want to go over our holiday schedule so that we can put our final staffing rota together. As most of you know, we will still be closing, as usual, on Mondays over the Christmas period. Christmas Eve lunch we will also be closed, but our staff Christmas dinner will be held, as always, on Christmas Eve at four thirty. Gia will be sending around the bag with all your names in for you to pick one for the Secret Santa." Gia smiled up at him and passed the bag to Matteo, who was to her left.

"If you pick out your own name, put it back in the bag and pick another. And the gift shouldn't cost more than twenty-five pounds. That's the limit." There was a murmur of excitement as the bag was passed to each member of staff.

"I hope I don't get Gia or Jerome," muttered Silvanna, so only Rosa and Dani heard. "What on earth would I buy them? I'm useless as it is at buying presents."

"And no swapping the names amongst each other," added Peter. "That's part of the fun." There was a mixture of chuckles and groans from everyone at the table. "Of course, we will be open on Christmas Eve night for our gala dinner and then for Christmas Day lunch too. We have two sittings, so we should be wrapped up by five thirty, so you'll be able to spend the evening with your families."

Their attention was drawn to the end of the table where Rico was chuckling. He'd pulled out his own name. He took out another and then put his own named piece of paper back into the bag and shook it.

Peter continued. "Boxing Day lunch is packed out, so I would appreciate everyone working on that day. Even though the main restaurant is closed for the evening, we do have a party booked up here in the private room, so I'm looking for volunteers." His eyes automatically fell on Dani. She smiled at him and nodded.

"New Year's Eve is fully booked, so again I really need everyone here. It will be fancy dress for the staff. As you all remember, last year it was a huge success."

Dani's eyebrows shot up and she looked at Rosa, who beamed at her and nodded. "I'll fill you in on all the traditions we have here at La Casa. It's great fun!"

Peter continued, "And New Year's Day lunch is only one sitting, starting at one, so we can all come in one hour later. I've put all the details on the notice board. If there are any days you cannot work, let me know and I'll do my best to accommodate you."

Dani's attention was drawn to a soft groan coming from Silvanna. She was reading the name she'd pulled out. Dani leaned over to see who she'd pulled. "I knew I'd get Jerome," Silvanna whispered.

Dani's heart dropped. She'd been hoping she would get him. "Don't worry, I'll help you."

Silvanna sighed in relief. "Oh thanks, Dani. I really wouldn't have a clue."

Rosa pulled out her paper and read it and smiled at the name.

"Who did you get?" asked Kuch.

"Ah, ah. It's *Secret* Santa, Kuch," Rosa tutted.

Dani took the bag and mixed up the papers with her hand before pulling one out. She opened it up, indifferent to whoever's name was on there. Silvanna had the one name she'd wanted. The little piece of paper had Jamie's name on it and she smiled. Buying for him would be easy.

"So tell me more about these traditions." Dani turned to face Rosa.

"Well we do Secret Santa every year and exchange the gifts at our Christmas Eve staff dinner. Oh, I just remembered, it's Capo's and Nicole's birthday on Christmas Eve too, so you'll have to make them a cake!"

"Seriously, on the same day?" Dani looked up at Nicole and she smiled apologetically.

Rosa continued. "On New Year's Eve, we all dress up in fancy dress. It's a blast. The customers get a real kick out of it."

"You dress in whatever you want?" asked Dani.

"Pretty much. I think I'm going to be Cleopatra this year." Rosa's eyes widened with excitement.

"Wow, you'd be a great Cleopatra."

"Thanks. Anyway, on New Year's, you're also supposed to wear red underwear for good luck."

"Really?"

"Uh-huh. And after here, we all go down to Sky. It can be quite exhausting but great fun!"

"And everyone dresses up?"

"Yep. Gia, Jerome, Chef, everyone," confirmed Kuch.

"Sounds like a lot of fun."

"It is. You'll have the best time, believe me." Rosa beamed.

Liz checked her watch again as Graham walked up and down his office, talking into his Bluetooth earpiece. If he didn't wrap this meeting up soon, she'd have hardly any time with Jonathan. He'd been waiting impatiently in their apartment for nearly an hour and by the sound of his text, he was getting more and more agitated. She checked her phone again.

The bed's up! Where r u?

Liz quickly texted back that she'd be there soon.

"Sure. Well, send everything and I'll arrange the meeting with Liz... Two weeks tomorrow? Yes, that sounds fine." Graham stared at Liz as he spoke and she nodded, confirming his statement.

He said his goodbyes, then pulled off the earpiece, his wide smile confirming the call had gone well.

"Well they seem keen, Liz. They've checked out your portfolio. They're seeing another two models and one B-class soap actress too, but I don't think they're much competition."

Liz rose from her seat. "So, Wednesday the eleventh, then? In London?"

"That won't be a problem will it?" Graham shifted some papers on his desk as he spoke.

"No. Not at all."

"I would suggest you fly down. I know Jerome would prefer you getting there in comfort," he smirked at her. He'd had a few run-ins with Jerome over the years. He always insisted Liz was treated well. "And you won't need to stay overnight. The meeting will probably take a couple of hours so you can get back by the evening. You're alright going alone? I mean, you're a pro at these kinds of things now, you don't need me to hold your hand anymore and to be honest, I'm stacked out."

"No, I don't need a babysitter, Graham," Liz replied with a hint of sarcasm. "I'll be fine." She was by the door, ready to open it. "Any news on the fashion show?"

"No, not yet." Graham's face hardened.

"What's wrong?"

"Experience tells me that if the details haven't come through by now, there's a problem. But the event organisers are adamant we continue with all the preparations." He sighed loudly. "I just hope this hard work we've all put in isn't wasted on them. I'll let you know as soon as I know." He smiled up at her in an attempt to reassure her, but after working with Graham for over ten years, she could see he was worried. His phone rang and he picked it up. "I have to get this."

"Sure. Email me the details of the meeting. Bye."

Graham mouthed his bye as he answered his call.

Liz had barely passed over the threshold of the apartment when Jonathan almost crushed her up against the closed door. His mouth ravaged hers, clawing at her coat to get as close as he physically could to her. "Jesus, I was going out of my mind." He pulled back, allowing Liz to take a breath. His hands moved restlessly over her as her coat hit the floor. She was wearing her workout clothes. Jonathan's mouth twitched as his gaze raked over her. "You going to the gym?"

"No. But I was hoping we could work out today." She cocked her head to one side. "I brought my iPad for music." She indicated to her bag.

"You came here to work out?" Jonathan stepped back, clearly hurt. He thought this apartment was their fuck pad. Somewhere they could just enjoy each other.

"Just for a bit." She looked at her watch. It was ten thirty. She knew he had to be at his first personal training appointment at one. "I thought we could do some intense training for half an hour then... if you're good..." She looked at him coyly and blinked slowly, making him understand what his reward would be.

Jonathan narrowed his eyes at her. "I thought this place was for you and me to be with each other." He was still wounded and Liz knew she had to win him round again.

"It is, babe, but I have to train hard for these contracts. The Pilates I do isn't enough and I don't want to train with anyone else. You're the best I've ever had. No one compares to you." She slinked over towards him.

He stifled a smile, the double meaning of her compliment not lost on him. "The best, eh?"

"Uh-huh." Liz was inches away from him.

"You look perfect to me."

"You're only saying that because all you want is to fuck my brains out."

Jonathan closed his eyes and groaned. Liz ran her small hands over his chest and he gripped onto her hips and yanked her hard against him so she could feel his arousal.

"And believe me that's what I want too, but *after* you've got me all hot and sweaty."

Jonathan opened his eyes and rested his forehead against hers and sighed softly. "You're worried about these contracts?"

"I just want to be the best I can be." He could sense she was preoccupied. "I'm living off one thousand calories a day and I work out, but I need to get better definition, lose a few more pounds. I have a meeting with them in two weeks."

Jonathan slid his arms around and hugged her tightly. She was so insecure about herself and he just didn't get it. She really was perfect, the most perfect woman he'd ever set eyes on.

"Okay, babe, we'll train. You can't do any more than what you're doing."

Liz furrowed her brow. She had two weeks to get her body fine-tuned and she needed all the help she could get.

"What's wrong?" Jonathan stroked her worried-looking face.

"Do you have any of those slimming tablets? The ones you gave to that girl who wanted to shed some weight before her wedding?"

Jonathan furrowed his brow. "You mean Meridia?"

Liz shrugged. "I don't remember the name. I just know she managed to lose ten pounds in a couple of weeks."

"You really need them? I don't think it's –"

Liz pulled away from him and pouted. "Jonathan, please. I know you can get them." She'd heard him talking on the phone to some relative of his that could get his hands on a number of steroids and stimulants that are usually difficult to acquire, but they seemed to be popular within the realm of fitness and body building.

"You don't need them, babe. Really, you don't," he pleaded.

"It's just until I get these contracts and do the shoot in Spain and then I'll be fine. They'll just help me. I've hit a plateau and they'll just get me past it. Please."

Jonathan hesitated for a moment. "Okay, I'll get some, but just for a short time, until you get the contracts?" Liz nodded, stepping closer to him. "Please don't stress about these jobs. They'll be mad not to take you on." He kissed her forehead and pulled back to look at her. "I'll call Gabe and pass by and get them some time today." He hugged her tightly, then released her.

Liz's eyes shifted to behind him. "So you put up the bed?"

Jonathan turned and looked over his shoulder at his handiwork. "Yeah. It was a bitch to put up," he huffed, then turned his gaze back to Liz. "Right, thirty minutes to get you all nice and sweaty, then the hour after that is *all* mine. We can christen the new bed. Agreed?"

"Agreed."

"Have a good time!" called Dani as she waved to Adam and Chloe. She had Rosie on her hip. Both Ollie and Sophie were on either side of her. Dani closed the door, locking out the cold night air. It was seven thirty and it was the first night off she'd had since she started working at La Casa d'Italia. She couldn't believe it was already Thursday. The last few days had flown by.

"Sooooo, we have the house to ourselves. What shall we do?" Dani ushered the excited children into the sitting room where the remnants of their game of Twister was still all over the floor. "We've an hour tops before bed. What shall we play?" Dani had fed and bathed the children, allowing Chloe to, for once, get dressed up for her first night out with Adam on her birthday.

The day had been filled with various birthday celebrations, including breakfast in bed, made by the children and Dani. Then Adam's father Ray had come around at tea time to have birthday cake and wish Chloe a happy birthday. He bought her a magnificent bouquet of flowers and a spa morning at Level One. Dani had gifted them a night off and had arranged with Peter to pay for their dinner this evening at La Casa. It was the very least she could do for them.

"Let's sing on the karaoke game," suggested Sophie.

Ollie groaned, "I'd rather play Uno."

"Oki!" Rosie wriggled off Dani's hip.

"Okay, we'll sing for half an hour, then play Uno before bed. What do you say?" The three children looked at each other and nodded.

"Good evening, Adam, how lovely to see you." Gia held out her perfectly manicured hand for him to shake.

"Good evening, Gia. You remember my wife Chloe?"

"Of course. How are you? I believe it's your birthday today. Dani told us."

"Yes it is." Chloe held out her hand and Gia shook it.

"Well Happy birthday, Chloe. *Buon compleanno.*"

Chloe blushed a little. "Thank you."

"Shall I show you to your table? Here, let me take your coat."

Within a few minutes, Adam and Chloe were seated in the raised part of the restaurant, sipping a glass of champagne as they looked over the menu.

"It's lovely here. I didn't really take it all in last time we came." Chloe looked around the now almost full restaurant. The last time she'd been there, she'd been preoccupied with the children. "Gia's so..." Chloe furrowed her brow trying to find the right word.

"Charming?" suggested Adam as he peered at her over the menu.

"Yes, and then some. She's gorgeous." Chloe looked over at Gia who was talking to a table. Her flawless figure was sheathed in a figure hugging purple dress with matching sling back heels.

"If I remember correctly, my dad called her a hottie," chuckled Adam. Chloe giggled at him.

"Yes, that's right. What are you going to have?"

"Um, shall we get a few starters to share?"

"You know what, sweetheart? You choose. You know the menu and I eat anything!"

Adam looked up to find Peter by their table. "Good evening, Adam, Chloe. How lovely to see you both."

They exchanged pleasantries and Adam placed their order of carpaccio, deep fried mozzarella with a tomato marmalade and a crab salad, followed by linguine ai frutti di mare and lobster ravioli, accompanied by a bottle of Gavi.

"Holy hell, Adam, no wonder you love this place." Chloe put down her fork after clearing her plate.

"I know, right? And we have desserts too," he teased.

Their conversation was interrupted by Jerome. He'd stopped by La Casa before heading up to Sky. He greeted them both warmly, genuinely pleased to see them both.

"I hope everything's been to your liking."

"Everything's been fabulous. I'm looking forward to dessert. Dani recommended a couple to us," gushed Chloe.

"Ah yes. Dani is quite the expert on our desserts. She's the best public relations we could ever have. Sales in desserts since Dani started working here have almost doubled." Jerome's eyes brightened as he spoke to Chloe about Dani, which did not go unnoticed by Adam.

"She's always raving about all the food, and of course, she loves working here too." A few glasses of wine had made Chloe less guarded. Jerome's smile widened at her comment.

"Well, we're all very fond of her too. She's become an integral part of our family here. She's extremely capable and has learned everything so fast. I know Peter depends on her. We all do." Jerome stopped himself saying any more, sensing he may have been a little too enthusiastic.

"That's lovely to hear," Adam said softly, then he looked at Chloe. "Dessert?"

"Dani recommended the lemon tart."

Jerome stifled a grin. "Yes, one of her personal favourites. And mine." He turned back to Adam.

"The panettone bread and butter pudding for me."

Jerome nodded. "Well, enjoy the rest of your evening."

"Hi, Gabe."

"Hey, J. How are you?" Jonathan grinned at the use of his childhood nickname.

"Not bad. You?"

"All's good. You don't sound so sure, though."

"I'm in between jobs at the moment but things are sorting themselves out." Jonathan didn't want to elaborate on why he'd lost his job.

"You need anything?" Jonathan knew he meant money.

"No, I'm fine."

"I've told you before, I can help you out if you need anything."

Jonathan sighed. He'd been tempted many times to take Gabe up on his offer of a loan but he didn't want to feel indebted to anyone. Gabe had a chain of dry cleaners and had now expanded into contract cleaning. He had become very successful in the ten years since he'd started his business.

"I know, thanks. Really, I'll be fine."

"So what can I do for you?"

"I need some supplies from your guy."

"I see."

"Some Meridia and something for me."

"The usual?"

"Yes."

"Okay. I'll talk to him and call you."

"Great."

"And come round so we can catch up. It's been ages."

"Sure, I'd like that."

Jerome leaned up against the stainless steel work surface, thoughtfully pulling at his lip, watching Carmen put the finishing touches on the limoncello lemon tart. He was feeling out of sorts and he wasn't exactly sure what specifically was bothering him. He sighed deeply.

"What time did Capo leave?"

"About half an hour ago."

"Hmm."

"You look very pensive. You okay?" Carmen looked up at him as she pushed the finish plate into the server's area.

"Uh-huh. You think you could put a piece of that in a takeout box?"

"Sure. For you?"

"No. Actually, put the tart, some amaretto chocolate cake, the cheese-cake, and throw in a few cannolis too. Send it out to table twenty-four. It's for them."

"Sure."

Jerome straightened and went out to the restaurant heading towards where Peter was. "Table twenty-four."

"Adam's table?" confirmed Peter.

"Coffees and liqueurs on the house."

"Actually, Dani's paying for the whole bill. She asked me not to mention it to them until right at the end, otherwise they'd hold back while ordering. She's going to settle up tomorrow."

"Right, er, well in that case, let me sort that out with her when she does."

Peter furrowed his brow at the comment. "Sure."

"She's worked a lot of hours and done the decorations." Jerome looked around the restaurant, gesturing with a swipe of his hand. "I think it's only right we waive the bill," he explained.

"Oh, I see. Well yes. So when she asks tomorrow, you want her to talk to *you*?" Peter clarified.

"Yes." Jerome smiled tightly at him. "Right, I'm off. I'll just go and say bye to a few tables."

"Okay. See you in the morning."

Peter watched Jerome do what he did best. He moved smoothly from one table to the next, checking everything was up to standard, and charmed his way around until he stopped at Adam's table.

"It was nice to see you again, Chloe. I've asked the kitchen to pack up some extra desserts for you to take home."

"Oh wow, that's so kind of you."

"For the children... and Dani."

"Thank you," added Adam. He narrowed his eyes slightly. "Everything has been really lovely, as always."

"Well, good night."

Both Chloe and Adam wished him a good night and then asked for their bill.

They arrived home to find Dani in the sitting room curled up on the sofa watching TV. It was just past ten thirty.

"Hey, did everyone behave?"

"Of course. They were angels." Dani uncurled herself, stretching. "Did you have a good time?"

"Yes we did and what you did was very naughty, but thank you all the same." Chloe bent down and hugged her sister. "We brought desserts." Chloe grinned widely.

"Oh, you shouldn't have."

"We didn't."

Dani gave a puzzled look at Adam's comment. "Jerome sent them for you and the kids." Adam arched an eyebrow. "He had nothing but praise for you, by the way."

Dani squirmed in her seat, thrilled that Jerome had firstly, spoken about her and secondly, sent desserts purposely. She stood up, trying to behave unaffected, but the slight flush that coloured her cheeks betrayed her true feelings. "Really? Oh, that was nice of him."

"Yes it was," Adam said dryly.

"I hope he put in some limoncello lemon tart in."

Adam huffed and walked through to the kitchen with the box of desserts, closely followed by Dani and Chloe.

"I don't think the kids are going to get a look in!" giggled Chloe. Adam shook his head, placing the boxes on the kitchen table, and pulled open the drawer with the cutlery.

"Don't judge me. I don't get out much," whined Chloe. She slumped into a chair and grabbed a spoon from Adam's hand.

Dani chuckled and Adam grinned at Chloe. He turned to Dani and handed her a spoon. "Thanks for tonight. You shouldn't have."

"It's the very least I could do after all you've done for me. It was my pleasure. Now shut up and pass me that tart."

"Spoken like a true Knox. Nothing comes between you and desserts."

24

SECRETS

Arsenio reread Scott's report, trying desperately to find something, anything, that could make Jerome keep him on. The file of photos Scott had taken filtered through by email and Arsenio tapped his fingers impatiently.

Liz had done nothing every day other than take the children to school, stay a few hours at her agent's and then, after a few errands, go home. She was living the life of a nun! His intercom buzzed.

"Yes, Carl?"

"Mr Ferretti's here. He wants a few minutes," his assistant informed him.

Arsenio's heart, dropped realising Jerome hadn't wasted any time in coming around.

"Send him in." It was just ten thirty. Jerome had obviously read the last report, which had come through at ten, then made his way here. He was definitely going to call off Scott.

Jerome stalked into Arsenio's office, his expression unmistakably hard.

"Can I get you some coffee, Mr Ferretti?" Carl asked.

"No. Thank you. I won't be staying long."

Carl nodded and closed the door behind him.

Arsenio knew his brother well. He wasn't going to win an argument with him if he challenged him so he decided to soften him up with a few pleasantries first.

"Morning. How are you? The kids?" He motioned to the chair for Jerome to sit down but his brother ignored it, preferring to stand.

"Morning. The kids are fine." Jerome faltered for a split second, then got straight to the point of his unscheduled visit. "I read Scott's report this morning. He hasn't come up with anything unusual, so just call him off, will you?"

"Of course. Did you see the photos too? The deal was he would send all the photos at the end of the week."

Jerome furrowed his brow.

"Um, no I didn't see any." He paused for a moment, then stepped towards the seat and lowered himself into it. "It doesn't matter anyway. The reports don't have her meeting with anyone other than her agent. She had coffee with a friend of hers on one of the days, nothing unusual at all. What else could the photos show?"

Arsenio had meticulously gone over every report with a fine-toothed comb and had also found nothing unusual. He was glad Jerome was bliss-fully unaware of the fact. It was awkward enough for Jerome that Arsenio knew as much as he did. If he was aware that Arsenio had also been observing Liz's movements, it would only make things more painful for Jerome.

"I'm not sure, but isn't it better to get all the information?" shrugged Arsenio. He watched Jerome battle with his conscience, knowing his brother well. There was no way Jerome would have agreed to a private investigator if he wasn't fairly sure that Liz was still seeing the trainer. The evidence showed otherwise, but Jerome always relied on his gut feeling and instinct. There was a slight chance that the photos would throw up something that the reports did not. He watched Jerome as he processed that exact possibility. Arsenio was also aware that Jerome was uncomfortable with the whole idea of spying on his wife. Which meant it could go either way.

"Just call him off, Seni. Really. I'm done."

Arsenio sighed, "Okay, if you're sure."

Jerome hesitated for a beat. "I'm sure. Get the bill and I'll settle up with you." He stood up abruptly. He needed to get out of there. The whole experience and this past week had made him extremely unsettled. It was time to move on. At least he knew. Now all that he needed to focus on was whether he could get past it. Would he ever be able to forgive Liz?

"Sure. I'll have it by Monday." Arsenio stood up. The worn look on Jerome's face made his blood boil. Liz was putting him through the wringer; it broke his heart to see his brother, who had always been so confident and sure of himself, suddenly begin to doubt his own actions. "I'll see you later, then?"

Jerome looked puzzled for a second, still deep in thought.

"At La Casa? I can't believe its Friday already. Just under a month until Christmas." Arsenio was doing his best to distract him with small talk.

Jerome relaxed a little and forced a smile. "Yes. It's going to be busy from now on." He swallowed hard. "So I'll see you around two?"

Arsenio nodded, then rounded his desk and walked with Jerome to the door. He put his arm around his brother's shoulders affectionately and squeezed.

"Thanks for... well, just thanks."

Arsenio hugged Jerome. "Don't mention it."

As Jerome pulled away, his eyes caught Arsenio's sock covered feet. "I'm sure you have at least twenty pairs of very expensive designer shoes."

Arsenio laughed softly. "It relaxes me. I like to walk around while I work and I prefer to do it without shoes on."

Jerome chuckled and shook his head. Arsenio was pleased this particular idiosyncrasy of his had managed to wipe the pensive, troubled look off Jerome's face, even if it was for just a moment.

By the time he'd seen Jerome out, the photographs had downloaded. Arsenio sat back down at his desk and opened up each one, studying them. There were over three hundred. He sighed deeply. He really should be going through the mounds of files on his desk but he was determined to find something. He loathed Liz and having to sit and look at her cold, hard, albeit very attractive face for the next half an hour only made him edgier. He scrutinized every picture, checking the backgrounds for something. The only thing that riled him, more than looking at her face, was the amount of times she changed her outfits. *Jeez, it was as though she was on a permanent catwalk.* He ran through each of them again. She spoke to no one except assistants in shops. There were a few shots of her on her phone; very few of the pictures showed her smiling. *Miserable bitch,* thought Arsenio. He sat back in his chair and ground his teeth. Nothing.

With a heavy heart, he picked up the phone and dialled Scott's number. He idly clicked through each photo quickly in sequence, so a few of the shots almost gave the effect of a video recording. Then something caught his eye.

Scott's voice on the end of the phone jolted him. "Hello?"

"Oh hi, Scott."

"Arsenio. You've received the pictures?"

"Yes. I'm looking at them now. They took a while to come through."

"I reduced the resolution so that they would come through faster," Scott explained.

"Are these all in sequence?"

"Yes." Scott waited patiently as Arsenio flicked through the photos first forward, then back again. "Is everything alright?"

"I'm just curious as to why, when she leaves her house in the morning, she's in her workout clothes holding a gym bag and then, when she leaves her agent's, she's in her normal clothes. Why does she change?"

"Oh. Yes. That is peculiar. Unless she works out there. Maybe she has photographs taken for fittings and it's easier in gym clothes."

"Perhaps." Arsenio flicked through them again, convinced he was missing something. "Anyway, you've done good work. Jerome was here earlier. He seems to be satisfied that Mrs Ferretti has finished with this trainer..." He was talking mechanically, still checking over each photo. He stopped at one photo that showed Liz's car at the entrance of the underground car park of her agent's office. The quick sequence showed her getting out of her car and talking to a truck driver, which was parked at the entrance. At first Arsenio thought she was arguing with him to move the truck but on closer inspection, he could see that Liz was smiling. The next shot was of her car descending into the car park while the truck opened up the back to unload. There was no follow-on picture but it didn't matter. Arsenio had found that little something he'd been looking for. The yellow truck had IKEA emblazoned on the side.

"Well that's good to hear," Scott answered but Arsenio didn't really register. He banged his fist sharply on his desk. *Yes!* He thought to himself, then focused on his phone call.

"He asked me to stop the surveillance, so I need you to let me know what the fee is up until today."

"Of course, I'll send it out to you."

"Good. I then want you to continue."

"Excuse me?" Scott said, clearly confused. "I'm not sure I follow."

"I think she's using one of the office spaces as some sort of love nest."

Scott took a moment to digest what Arsenio was saying. "That would explain why she changes clothes."

"And why she's spending an extraordinary amount of time at her agent's," Arsenio suggested, his tone tinged with sarcasm.

"It's the perfect cover."

"Yes. It would also explain why she spoke to an IKEA delivery man on Wednesday."

"Furniture? A bed, perhaps. I wish I'd taken more photos." Scott sounded annoyed with himself.

"That's my guess."

"Shouldn't we inform Jerome?"

"No, not yet. Let's just see what else we can uncover. I think we need to put surveillance on the trainer too, and you're going to have to get into the office block and confirm that she's going there, rather than her agent's."

"She must have a second phone too. How else is she communicating with him? Because the trace on the number you gave me doesn't have her contacting him."

Arsenio could almost hear Scott's brain working overtime and he smiled to himself. "Yes, for sure. How can we find that out?"

"Leave it to me... I'm going to need a week or so though, and it'll be pricey."

"I don't care what you need to do, Scott. We need to nail the bitch."

"We will, trust me."

"Good. We've waited this long, what's a few more days?"

"I'll keep you updated."

"Thanks Scott."

Arsenio hung up, then bent down to put on his shoes. He needed to talk to Cosimo. Keeping Scott on was crossing the line, it was out-and-out interfering, but he knew that Liz was still seeing Jonathan and playing his brother.

Within a few minutes, Arsenio was walking through Cosimo's offices and heading towards his suite at the far end. Mary looked up from her desk. "Good day, Mr Ferretti. How are you?"

"I'm well, Mary. You're looking lovely as always. Is he free?"

Mary smiled wryly. She enjoyed Arsenio's playful banter. "Thank you, you're not so bad yourself." Arsenio laughed softly. "He's on the phone... oh, he's just finished, let me buzz him." She readjusted her glasses and pressed the intercom. "Mr Arsenio Ferretti is here... you can go through."

Arsenio winked at Mary and sauntered into Cosimo's office. "Hi, I'm not disturbing you, am I?"

Cosimo stood up and came around from his desk to hug him. "Yes, you are, but it doesn't matter," he joked. Arsenio huffed and sat on the large leather chair and Cosimo leaned against his desk. "So, what's up?"

"It's Jerome."

Cosimo lost his relaxed stance and instantly became focused. "What's happened?"

"The private investigator's reports over this last week showed nothing. It *seems* she's been at home and at her agent's, excluding the school run and few errands."

Cosimo relaxed a little. "You said, *seems*. Does that mean there *is* something?"

"Scott also took pictures which Jerome hasn't seen, because he thinks they'll show nothing, and consequently has called off Scott. But I did look at the pictures and I'm almost ninety-nine percent sure she's renting a space in the office block her agent is in." Arsenio elaborated on the pictures and what he believed was actually happening.

"So, did you tell Jerome?"

Arsenio shook his head. "He's so uncomfortable with the whole idea and I know if he finds out he won't be able to hold it together. You and I know it's a waiting game. In situations like this, you have to think objectively, stay cool and be calculating, and Jerome is most definitely not any of those things."

"And that's where you come in?" Cosimo arched his eyebrow interrupting him.

Arsenio smirked at him. "Yeah, something like that. I've asked Scott to carry on and also check out the trainer."

"You mean extra surveillance?"

"And phone tracking."

Cosimo straightened and paced. "This is crossing the line, Seni. Jerome will flip out, and I wouldn't blame him. You're spying on a member of our family..."

"She's not family, she never has been!" Arsenio jumped out of his seat, his arms moving rapidly. "She doesn't know what the meaning of the word is!"

"Calm down. I know she's not your favourite person but she is Jerome's wife and the mother of his children. For that alone we have to show *some* respect."

"Hah, respect? Like she's shown us? Mama? When was the last time we were invited to their home, eh? Tell me?" Cosimo furrowed his brow. "See, you can't even remember, can you? Because it's over eighteen months ago! When Jerome got his new car and we went round to see it. That's how long ago!" He paced around the office as Cosimo mulled over what he was saying. "I have to find out for sure before I can let him know. He's not handling it all that well. He feels guilty when it's *her* who should be feeling guilty. She's got herself a fuck pad and is making a fool out of our brother!"

"Alright, alright. Just calm down. Have you thought about how you'll handle it when you have the evidence? He's going to be mortified and he'll never forgive you. You're weaving a tangled web, Seni, and even if you're right and you prove it, it means he has to make a decision and maybe he's not ready for that. He doesn't want to lose his kids. That's all that matters to him and he's willing to try and live with her for their sake."

"It's her that's weaving the web, Cosimo, a web of deceit and lies upon lies. She's a self-centred, egotistical... cold-hearted... gah!" he shook his head. He felt frustrated and torn between what he should do and what needed to be done. If he'd been advising a client, he'd feel no guilt or remorse whatsoever over spying. But putting his brother into the mix made it so much harder – firstly, because he'd be hurt that he'd gone behind his back and then secondly, that he'd found out the sordid truth. "She's like a black widow spider, laying the ground work, using him, taking whatever she can and then, pow!" Arsenio punched his fist against his palm.

Cosimo snorted. "Very poetic, Seni." He stifled a grin at his brother's dramatic performance. "We're not in court now."

Arsenio shot Cosimo a frustrated look, then slumped back into the chair. "You think I should stop it, then?" he challenged.

"Is that why you came? To get my approval?"

Arsenio shrugged. He knew it would make him feel better if Cosimo was on his side.

"This is wrong on so many levels, Seni, and I'm not just talking legally. But I know your heart's in the right place. There's nothing harder than seeing someone you love being made a fool of and telling Jerome, when I discovered what was going on, was the single hardest thing I've ever had to do."

"Fucking bitch," muttered Arsenio sullenly.

Cosimo lowered himself back into his chair and sighed heavily.

"Keep Scott on." Arsenio's eyes shot up to Cosimo. "Let's see exactly what's going on and then we can go from there. There may be a possibility that she slips up somewhere. Especially if she thinks she's second guessing Jerome and starts to feel a false sense of security. He may just work it out on his own."

Arsenio shifted forward in his chair and leaned his arms onto his knees. "With the help of a nudge, he will," added Arsenio.

"We have to be careful," Cosimo warned.

Arsenio nodded, then pushed to his feet. "I'll let you get back to whatever you were doing. Any information I get, I'll send to you."

Cosimo gave him a curt nod. "See you at La Casa at two, then?"

"Thanks, Dani," Peter mumbled as Dani pushed his coffee towards him. He was mulling over the reservations book.

"Have you got the bill from last night? I need to settle up."

Peter looked up at her rummaging in her handbag for her purse. "Did they have a good time?"

Dani nodded. "Yeah, they loved everything. Thanks for looking after them."

Peter leaned away from the bar and shook his head, indicating it was nothing.

"So what do I owe you?" she asked expectantly.

"Umm, well actually, Jerome's asked me to let him deal with that." Peter's eyes narrowed a little and Dani's face dropped.

"Oh? Is everything alright? I mean there isn't a problem or anything –"

Peter cut her off with a wave of his hand. She'd mistaken what his comment meant and he didn't want her to worry. The truth was, it was Peter who was worried. For Jerome to insist that he handled this, Peter knew there was an ulterior motive. Jerome didn't waste his time on staff matters; they were Peter's responsibility. "No, no, nothing like that. He just wanted to handle it. So speak to him about the bill. He has a copy of it."

"Oh. Okay." Dani looked at her watch nervously. It was just past ten. She should go up now before they had their lunch. "Well I better go and sort it out, then."

"He just left. He should be back a bit later on. It's Friday, so he's meeting up with his brothers as usual."

Dani nodded and put her purse back into her bag, feeling a little unsettled.

"Jeez, that Dani looks better every time I come in here," Arsenio huffed as soon as Gia was out of earshot. He blatantly stared over at the bar where Dani was putting together a drinks tray for Lucio, who was working the afternoon shift with her and Richard. Jerome stiffened and took a sip from his coffee.

"Seni, drag your eyes away from the poor girl. You'll make her want to leave. You'll make her uncomfortable." Cosimo shook his head. "And by all accounts, she's a very good employee. Very talented," he added wryly, his eyes flitting around the restaurant at the decorations. Jerome swallowed hard and fiddled with his spoon. Gia had been praising Dani constantly throughout their weekly family lunch. Firstly about how Dani helped with the Christmas decorations and then that she'd been taking the time to teach Gia how to use a computer. Jerome's lack of comment or input hadn't gone unnoticed. He was purposely feigning interest.

"Yeah, pack it in, Seni," Peter hissed. He'd joined them for coffee once they'd finished their lunch and the restaurant had calmed down. Peter turned to Jerome and lowered his voice. "Actually, she was asking about the bill. She wanted to settle up but you were out this morning."

Jerome nodded. "Ask her to come to my office around five thirty," he replied tightly, then swiftly got up.

"Sure."

"I'm afraid I've got to go. I've some work I need to get through this afternoon."

Cosimo eyed him, knowing that the week's events were putting a strain on him. He darted his eyes at Arsenio who frowned back at him, then they all rose from the table to say their goodbyes.

Jerome sifted through the pictures Scott had sent him. He may have called Scott off, but his curiosity was still piqued. Even though the reports showed nothing, Arsenio's words had made him edgy. He rationalised his actions. He was paying for the photos so he may as well take a look.

Jerome rested back in his chair and let out a steady breath. The pictures confirmed what the reports had detailed. Liz hadn't been anywhere or seen anyone other than Graham. He felt a sense of relief simply because up until he'd seen them, he'd still been unsure. Arsenio's words had preyed on his mind all morning. Ignoring the photos wasn't an option. He knew his judgment was clouded. He'd be a liar if he admitted otherwise. He didn't want his marriage to end and he wasn't so naive as to think that all marriages ran smoothly, but this was a major blip and he really needed to focus on whether he could move past it.

Liz had been true to her word and had ended the affair. She'd also been home more and he had not. Granted, it was because of his work, but if he was going to make an effort to save his marriage, he was going to have to at least spend more than just Monday night home and Sunday too. They hadn't been away alone for over three years either. He was going to have to make some changes.

Jerome flicked through his calendar. It was jammed packed until mid January. Liz also had her fashion show and Gia would be away until the beginning of February, so there was no chance he could spare a few days off until she was back. He looked at when the children had their half-term break. They had two weeks off starting on the sixth of February. He knew two weeks was impossible, but five days he could manage. Maybe a week tops. He mulled over the idea of taking them away, maybe to La Garda. A Valentine's week holiday. He could take Liz shopping in Milan – he knew she'd love that. There were enough family who adored the children out there, which meant they'd be able to have some time to themselves too. It would be exactly what they needed: time alone to reconnect, away from work and family. The idea made Jerome a little uneasy. That uneasiness alone made him realise that they had a lot to work through, but it would at least be a start, and a step in the right direction.

Dani brushed through her hair and twisted it up into a French plait and pinned it into place. She then slicked on some lip gloss and blotted her face free of shine. *There*, she thought to herself. She looked decidedly better, more appropriate for the evening than a ponytail. Dani put her things away into her locker, grabbed her bag and headed up to the first floor.

"Come in," Jerome's familiar raspy voice beckoned. Dani swallowed hard and stepped into the large office.

The last time she'd been in there was the day of her interview and she'd been so nervous and caught off guard that she hadn't really appreciated its size and decor. It was light and airy, due to the large balcony windows looking out over the river. There was a seating area positioned near the balcony of a large, rich brown leather sofa and two matching chairs. Jerome's desk was dark wood and looked like it must be an antique. The wall behind the desk had an enormous old map, which had a large lake on it, but Dani couldn't make out the place. To the right there were twenty framed certificates arranged in groups of four and a large book cabinet housing a couple of trophies, books and decorative boxes. The office was stylish and traditional but undeniably masculine.

Jerome was seated at his desk wearing just his shirt and tie, his suit jacket flung over the leather sofa. Whatever he was looking at on his computer had him totally engrossed until Dani entered the room. He immediately rose from his large leather chair and smiled. "Dani," he said softly by way of a greeting.

"Hi," she said nervously. Dani suddenly became acutely aware that they were alone.

Jerome rounded his desk and gestured to the armchair in front of his desk. "Please sit down." Dani lowered into the seat and Jerome leisurely rested himself against his desk, crossing his feet at his ankles.

"You have a lovely office." Dani glanced towards the windows and the view over the city.

"Thank you."

Dani looked back at him, then bent down to where her bag was. "I came to pay for the bill from last night. Chef said you were dealing with it."

"Er, yes. But just leave that for the moment. There's something else I want to discuss." He waved his hands in front of him, dismissing the subject.

Dani straightened, dropping her purse on her lap and staring at him a little wide-eyed and confused. "Oh. Um, is there something wrong?"

"No, no, not at all. You've been working for us, what is it? Three weeks?"

"Yes. Though it feels like much longer."

"Oh?" Jerome's brow creased and he leaned back a little, gripping on to his desk.

"What I meant was, and clearly didn't it express well..." Jerome stifled a smile. "Was that I feel very comfortable here, very at home at La Casa."

"I see. Yes, that does sound better. I'm very pleased to hear it." He grinned, his eyes sparkling as he looked down at her. "Well, you've settled in very well here, and Peter has nothing but praise for you." He noted she'd changed her hair from this morning and it distracted him for a second. He forced himself to focus on the reason she was in his office. "I've noticed that last night was the only night you've had off since you started."

"Yes, that's right."

"And you seem to be working a lot of the afternoon shifts too."

Dani nodded, not entirely sure where this was going. "Is that a problem? It's just that I'd rather work as much as possible and –"

Jerome cut her off again, waving his hands in front of himself. *Jeez, did he make her so nervous that every observation he made, she instantly thought he was unhappy with her?* "I was just making sure we weren't over-stretching you. What with helping my mother with the decorations and teaching her how to use computers, you seem to leave little room for... well... yourself."

"Oh." Dani looked down at her tattered heart-shaped purse on her lap and fiddled with the zip. "I'd just rather be busy, that's all." She looked back up at him and he nodded.

"Well don't let us wear you out."

Dani smiled tightly. Little did he know that the last thing she wanted was time to herself. It would mean she'd think more and right now, her defence mechanism was to work so as not to think or dwell on what had happened and where her life was heading. Dani looked out of the window avoiding Jerome's inquisitive gaze. "I can handle it," she murmured.

"I'm sure you can. I know that you're far more qualified for the position and that you're capable of a lot more, but I wouldn't... I mean, we wouldn't want to lose you."

Dani's focus shifted back to Jerome. "I'm happy here. I really don't need the responsibility of a higher position. Not for the moment, anyway." She looked down at her lap and began to open up her purse. *Is this why she'd been summoned? Was he worried she wasn't challenged here and that's why she was working all these long hours?* Well he was almost right. She just needed to be constantly occupied, physically and mentally. *He was worried she might leave.* The thought thrilled her.

"So, what's the amount?" she asked, trying to veer the conversation off the subject.

Jerome straightened and walked back behind his desk. "I don't want any money."

Dani's eyes shot up to where Jerome was absentmindedly shuffling some papers on his desk. "Um, I'm sorry. I don't understand."

"I'm waiving the bill," he answered dismissively, without looking up.

Dani stood up suddenly. "But why? I arranged with Chef that I'd pay Chloe and Adam's bill, as a thank you for having me stay with them."

Jerome rubbed his forehead and looked up at her. "I know; he told me. Are you still looking for a place to live?"

Dani furrowed her brow at his question. He'd just changed the subject and she wasn't done with the bill yet. "Um, yes? But about the bill," she pressed.

"Any luck?" he interrupted.

"Er, no, not yet. The places I like are a little out of my price range." Her head was spinning. They hadn't finished talking about the bill and he was going off on a tangent. "Look, I really want to pay for the bill. I wouldn't feel right..."

Jerome shook his head and then crossed his arms across his chest, "I've told you, I've waived the bill."

"I know, but I still don't understand why." Her tone was a little more forceful.

Jerome took a deep breath and let his arms drop to his sides. "Well you've worked more than you should, you've hardly had any time off, you're in early every morning –"

"Yes, but I get paid for the extra hours I work and the shifts," Dani argued, cutting him off mid-sentence.

He scowled. "But you don't get paid for coming in early or for helping Peter with the reservations..." Dani went to interrupt but he put his finger up indicating he hadn't finished. "For putting up Christmas decorations and for teaching my mother how to use the computer on the day you're supposed to have off."

"I'm happy to help out, Jerome. And besides, Gia said she'd repay me by teaching me Italian conversation." There was no way she wasn't going to pay for the bill.

Jerome snorted. "Did she now?"

"Yes, she did. I help out because I want to. I like helping Gia – well, all of you."

"She very fond of you," he added quietly.

"And I am of her. So please just let me pay for the bill. I wouldn't feel right."

"And I wouldn't feel right taking it."

"But I can't let you pay for –"

"Well I am and I will, so that's it."

Dani glared at him, not entirely sure what to say. She swallowed hard. *Shit, had she just argued with her boss?*

Jerome's face softened. "Dani, I won't take the money, so please just accept it. It's a way of me saying – or should I say *us* saying – thank you." He cocked his head to the side and allowed a soft smile to curl over his lips.

Dani sighed. "I'm not entirely comfortable with it, but thank you. Like I said, I'm happy to help out."

"Okay, understood. So we're good?" Jerome raised a questioning eyebrow at her.

"Good?"

"Well you put up a bit of a fight there, I don't think I've seen anyone so determined not to accept a thank you gift," Jerome chuckled.

Dani's face flushed, mortified that she'd been so ungracious. "I'm sorry, I just don't want to feel indebted, that's all. It was very kind of you. Oh, and I never said thank you for the desserts you sent."

"You're very welcome. Well I know you're battling with a nicotine craving," he joked.

"Hah – you have no idea. If I carry on eating sweets the way I've been eating them this past few weeks, I'll need a bigger uniform. I'm sure I've put on weight," Dani huffed, looking down at herself.

"You look perfectly fine to me," Jerome muttered.

Dani reddened at the comment and bent down to pick up her bag and dropped in her purse. "Well, I better get downstairs."

Jerome looked at his watch. It was almost ten to six. "I'll walk down with you."

"Oh. Okay." She watched him slip on his jacket and then followed him to the door. "Thanks again, and sorry if I was a bit..."

"Forceful? Insistent? Stubborn?" he suggested.

Dani shrugged apologetically and scrunched up her nose in embarrassment.

"Don't be. It was rather entertaining seeing you square up to me. It doesn't happen very often." They walked down the corridor towards the stairwell. "So you can bite? That's good to know," he smirked, turning to look at her.

"Yeah, I bite." She stifled a grin. "But not too hard."

Jerome threw back his head and laughed loudly. She'd thrown back his words at him, from the day of the interview. He shook his head. She really did have a quick wit. "Very good answer."

Dani's heart leapt and she laughed softly, thrilled she'd been the one to make him laugh so unguardedly.

"Nicole, do you mind if I ask you a question?"

Dani and Nicole were getting ready to head up to Sky. Sunday night had come around again so fast. Dani didn't know where the time went. Rosa had been off in the evening, so the female changing room was empty apart from the two of them. The rest of the staff had already left and Dani had offered to drive Nicole up, so that Kuch didn't need to hang on.

Nicole caught Dani's reflection in the mirror as she leaned closer to apply her lipstick. "Sure." She straightened up slightly and watched Dani vigorously brush out her ponytail.

Dani took a deep breath and smiled tightly at her.

"Is anything wrong?" Nicole asked. She turned to face Dani and leaned her hip against the sink.

"No, nothing like that. I... well, I've just wondered why you and Kuch have been keeping your relationship a secret."

Nicole's eyes widened and her pale skin flushed.

"I'm sorry. I didn't mean to make you uncomfortable. It's just he's a great guy and, well, you're so sweet together. I just don't get it."

Nicole sighed. There wasn't any point in denying it. "He is a great guy. The best."

"So why the secrecy? Won't your family approve of him? Is that it?" Dani fixed her hair into a low ponytail and started to pin it into a messy bun.

"Sort of. Well, not exactly. My aunty and cousin don't like relationships developing between staff because when things go wrong it can be... well, there's always an atmosphere. Things get tricky and often problems in your personal life filter into work. I think that's why they employ so much family. Kuch was hired because he's basically brilliant and because his brother also works at Sky."

"So he's not been here that long, then?"

"Nearly two years."

"And how long have you two been seeing each other?"

Nicole pursed her lips together. "Nearly a year."

"What? And no one knows? How is that possible?"

"Well, Kuch had a girlfriend when he came to work here but that finished a few months after he started."

"Probably because of you," interrupted Dani.

Nicole shrugged and smiled coyly, confirming Dani's observation. "He was always a friendly guy and he flirted with everyone. Even when he was with his girlfriend. It's just the way he is. We went out together in a group from here and then working together every day, things just developed quickly. So, as a decoy, when we're together around other people, he carries on as he always has, so as not to alert suspicion."

"Like he does with me?"

Nicole grinned. "Yeah, like he does with you."

"And it doesn't bother you?"

Nicole shook her head. "He doesn't mean it. He's doing it to protect me."

"Protect you? How so?" Dani slicked on some lipstick and started to pack away her things.

"I come from an Italian family. They can be quite... overbearing. To begin with, we just kept it a secret because we didn't want Gia or Jerome to disapprove. Then, as things got more serious, I knew my family would pressure me to get married. Settle down. And I haven't been ready for that."

They'd moved over to the lockers and were putting away their toiletries. "But you might be? With Kuch?"

"I can't see myself with anyone else."

"What about Kuch? How does he feel?"

"He wanted to tell them six months in, but I asked to him not to. So he's doing it for me. Rosa's the only one that knows here. She's our cover most of the time. And Kuch's brother."

"Nearly a year, eh? That's some secret. Well you can count on me too. I won't breathe a word. But I do think that maybe it's time. I'm sure everyone will be alright about it. They really like him."

"They do. And my family love him."

"Your family? I thought you said no one knows." Dani halted abruptly at the door that led to the stairs.

"No, no, they've met him. Whenever they've come here, they've sat by the bar to talk to me and so they got to meet and experience the Kuchiki charm." She smiled widely and her eyes brightened as she spoke about him.

Dani narrowed her eyes at Nicole. "You love him."

Nicole sighed and nodded.

"Of course you do. Come on, poor Chef's waiting to lock up." Dani squeezed her shoulders. "He adores you, anyone can see that. How they haven't realised is beyond me." Dani shook her head. "I suppose people see what they want to see."

"Yeah, they do," Nicole sighed wistfully.

25

MORE SECRETS

Jerome laced up his trainers and looked out of his bedroom window. It was ten to six and still dark outside. Well at least it had stopped raining, he thought. This first week of December had literally flown by for him. December was always busy, but this year he just didn't seem to have enough hours in the day.

La Casa was fully booked over the holidays and Level One was finally in order. The new managers he'd taken on had already eased the pressure off him. In fact the gym and spa were running better than they'd ever done over the last year. The new staff had brought new memberships at a time when they normally tended to dwindle. It had become obvious that Liz had not been running the business to its full potential and for the first time, Jerome realised that his decision to put Liz in charge of it had probably not been one of his best business moves. She'd never been interested in the Level One but he'd wanted her to have something of hers to run. *Hindsight was a wonderful thing*, Jerome thought ironically. If he had never pushed her to run Level One, then she'd have never screwed Jonathan. He shook his head. Well at least she'd been trying to make amends.

There had been fewer problems at Sky too. Paul had only reported one case of a pusher in the club. He knew that they were going to have to be careful. Drugs were big trade and a club like Sky was a perfect dealing ground. And with the holidays coming up, the dealers would be missing out on potentially big business. Jerome pushed himself to his feet, grabbing his sports bag and jacket and headed downstairs.

"Morning. You're up early again."

Jerome found Liz pouring her tea in the kitchen. It was just after six.

Liz usually didn't surface before eight but over the last few days, she'd been up before him. She shrugged, then wrapped her pale hands around her cup and took a sip.

"Is everything okay?" Jerome furrowed his brow as he looked closer at her. She looked tired, drained even. "Are you worried about Wednesday?"

Liz scrunched her nose. "A bit," she lied. She was worried a lot.

Jerome's expression softened. "Hey, don't worry. You're perfect for the job. Graham said so." He paced over to her and rubbed her arm awkwardly. He furrowed his brow. *Why did their time together feel so awkward?*

She gazed up at him. "Thanks. It's a big contract and..." she shrugged again. She'd been feeling edgy since yesterday and she wasn't entirely sure why. Sleep was proving difficult and not seeing Jonathan over the weekend had made her a little agitated. Since they'd acquired the flat, they'd seen each other almost every day.

"Do you want me to come with you?"

"You'd do that?" Liz couldn't hide her surprise.

"Of course I would. I know it's important to you. I said I'd support you, didn't I?" Jerome cocked his head to the side. "Do you want me to?"

Liz took another sip of her tea. Did she want him with her? He began to move smoothly around the kitchen collecting various ingredients. Liz watched him closely. He looked so comfortable and at ease dressed ready for his workout in his black sweat pants and vest that clung to his toned chest. His hair was dishevelled but he still looked stunning. He placed everything on the counter, then started putting various seeds, fruits and protein powder in to the blender. He flicked the switch and the blender jumped to life. Jerome turned off the blender, twisted the jug free from the base and lifted off the lid. "If it's not too much bother, I'd appreciate it."

He turned to face her, resting his hip against the granite work surface. "It's no bother. Did you book your ticket?"

Liz nodded.

"Okay, give me the details and I'll book my ticket as soon as I get to La Casa."

Liz smiled and he could see the relief on her face. "Thanks."

Jerome tilted the jug towards her. "Here's to a successful meeting."

Liz grinned and lifted her tea cup. Jerome clinked the jug against the teacup and winked at her, pleased she looked more relaxed. He really couldn't work her out sometimes. She was so confident and hard most of the time but then she'd show small cracks of vulnerability and all he wanted to do was reassure her. Maybe a day trip to London was what they needed; a small step in the right direction.

He lifted the jug to his lips and chugged down his drink, then quickly rinsed it out and placed it in the dishwasher. "What have you got planned for today?"

"I'll be going to Graham's this morning, then I'll be home. You're going to the restaurant? On a Monday?" She tried to keep her tone even.

"Just going to do some paperwork. Paul's going to be going over the security. Just a check-up." Jerome smiled tightly. "He'll be checking here too in the afternoon, but you don't need to worry about anything, I've told Nina to let him and his team in."

He could've arranged it another day, in fact it would've been easier on any other day but he'd purposely scheduled Paul on Monday, knowing Dani would be at his mother's. He looked at his watch – he was late. "So I'll see you later? And message me your flight details."

"Sure."

Jerome stepped closer to her and leaned down planting a swift kiss on her cheek, then pulled back quickly. "Don't worry about Wednesday. You'll do fine."

Liz stared up at him and nodded weakly. Striding out of the kitchen, Jerome grabbed his jacket and sports bag and headed for the garage. *How on earth was she going to tell Jonathan that Jerome was coming with her?*

"So, do you think you've got the hang of it?"

Gia twisted her mouth and then grimaced. "I'm not sure. It's fine when you're sitting next to me, but I'm not sure I'll remember when I'm on my own."

Dani had been at Gia's for almost two hours, going over what she'd taught her over the last couple of weeks, and was now progressing to more work-related programs. They were sitting in Gia's office rather than her apartment. It was very similar in decor to her home, very feminine with soft pastel colours. Silk curtains framed the large windows, which made the room light. The sumptuous chairs were upholstered in complementary tones. The desk looked like an antique dining table with a matching sideboard, which Gia used as a filing cabinet. The only photos Gia had on her desk were a black and white shot of Kara and Alessandro and a colour family photo with Gia, her late husband, a smiley teenage Cosimo, a moody nine-year-old Jerome and a cheeky seven-year-old

Arsenio. The picture looked to have been taken by an Italian lake. Behind her desk was a sepia framed picture of Sophia Loren in her twenties, posing seductively. The words under the picture read: "Everything you see I owe to spaghetti."

"*Mio Dio!* Is that the time? I can't believe it's already eleven. The time's just flown by. I was supposed to ring the doctor's at ten thirty."

"Ah, that's because we're having fun," joked Dani. "The doctor's? Are you not well?"

"Yes, we are having fun and no, I'm fine. I just need to book in a mammogram."

Dani cringed.

"Yeah I know." Gia shivered at the thought. "We got so engrossed I haven't managed to teach you any Italian today."

"That's okay. I downloaded some course off the Internet and I've been listening to it on my way to and from work. I get at least a full hour coming and going."

"Good idea. That's the best way to learn, listening to it as much as you can. You need a nice Italian boyfriend." Gia winked at her and Dani chuckled. "You still haven't found anywhere to move closer?"

"No. I think I'll just have to put up with it. I'll start looking maybe in the springtime, when my money comes through from my house in London."

"So you've put it up for sale, then?"

"No. My ex-boyfriend is buying out my share. He's promised me the money by mid-January." Dani scrunched up her nose, feeling suddenly embarrassed, her previous good mood suddenly replaced with irritation. Jez had been messaging her sporadically, anything between one message every couple of days to five or six in one day. Most of them made her angry. He could be very bitter when he wasn't getting his way. Some were touching though, which made her heart ache.

"Well at least you're both civil to each other and have come to some arrangement." Gia smiled softly.

"Well, I wouldn't say that. He messages me constantly. Sometimes his messages are nice, or civil at least. Other times, not so much. I choose to ignore them all," Dani huffed, thinking back to the last few rather insulting messages she'd received over the weekend, obviously alcohol driven.

"He took the break up badly?"

Dani rocked her head from left to right and twisted her mouth. "More like he couldn't accept that I'd leave him after he... well, it's complicated. I just want to get my share of the house. Then all my ties with him are done and I can move on."

Gia nodded her head slowly, understanding far more than Dani had admitted to. "And then you'll buy?" Gia's tone brightened as she leaned back on her chair. It was obvious Dani wasn't comfortable talking about her past.

"Yes, I think so."

Gia nodded, "Yes, it's a better idea to invest in property, if you have the cash, that is. And property in London is more expensive, so you'll get more for your money up here."

Dani shrugged. "Well until the money comes through in January, I'll just have to use my commute time to learn my Italian."

Gia chuckled and patted her arm affectionately.

"Alright, then. Let me go make us both another espresso and you see if you can put in those last three reservations," Dani suggested.

Gia's doe-like eyes widened.

"Don't look so frightened. It's only a computer. It won't bite," chuckled Dani.

"Well, not hard, anyway." Jerome's familiar raspy voice made both Gia and Dani jump. He'd been quietly observing them for a minute or so while leaning against the door frame. His eyes glittered, causing Dani's breath to hitch, seeing him so unexpectedly. He winked, acknowledging their private joke, which caused her to blush. He looked stunning in fitted jeans, a light blue V-necked sweater, covered with a leather biker jacket. He wore a light grey woollen flat cap that matched the scarf tied perfectly around his neck. Dani had never seen him in casual clothes before. He was always in suits, which she loved, but this relaxed look on him had her blood pulsing. Jerome straightened and paced over to the desk.

"Jerome, I wasn't expecting you today." Gia beamed up at him. Dani rolled back her chair so Jerome could kiss his mother.

"I'm upgrading the security. So I asked Paul to come today and install it." He stepped away after kissing Gia on each cheek, then turned to Dani. "Hi, how's she doing?"

"Hi. She's a great student." Dani smiled shyly at him. She couldn't believe he was here. Then she cringed inwardly, thinking she must look a mess. In her rush to leave this morning, Dani had pulled her hair into a high ponytail, wearing no makeup apart from a little lip balm. She'd thrown on some old jeans tucked into her biker boots and a thick baggy cream cowl-necked jumper.

"You must have the patience of a saint. No one's ever been able to teach Mama anything technical."

Gia squinted her eyes at him in mock anger and rattled off what sounded like a chastising sentence in Italian that had Jerome laughing. He backed away with his hands in front of him as if he was being held at gunpoint.

"Okay, okay. I didn't mean it." He grinned, causing the wrinkles around his eyes to meet up with the laughter lines around his sculptured mouth.

Dani bit the inside of her cheek to stifle her grin, "I'll go and make that coffee, shall I?"

"*Si*, Daniella. The flat's open. Just go in – you know where everything is."

Dani rose from her chair and slid past Jerome to head out of the office and up to Gia's apartment.

"Joking aside, how's it going?" he asked.

"Surprisingly well. You're right though, she does have a lot of patience. It's really sweet of her to come all this way out on her day off."

Jerome nodded, "It's a long way from Harewood."

"It is. In fact, that's something I wanted to talk to you about. I was thinking we could offer her the apartment."

"You mean my old apartment here?"

Gia nodded. "Temporarily, until she gets her own place. She's going to buy a place at the beginning of the year."

"Yes, I heard." Jerome's brow creased as he mulled over the idea. His stomach turned a little at the thought of Dani being so close. "Have you mentioned anything to her?"

"No, no. I wanted to talk to you first. It's your place, *tesoro*. It's up to you. I know she's only been here a short time and normally we need three month probation before staff are officially accepted. But I think she's an exception, don't you?"

"Yes she is," Jerome muttered. Exceptional, rather than an exception, would have been his choice of words. Jerome lowered himself into Dani's recently vacated seat and sucked on his top teeth as he thought about the prospect of having Dani living in his old flat. She'd be his tenant. The idea did strange things to him.

"You think it's a bad idea?" Gia asked.

Bad idea? thought Jerome. Yes, a very bad idea. She'd be so close to him, day in, day out, almost twenty-four-seven. It was bad enough working alongside her, but knowing she was just up a flight of stairs – the idea both thrilled Jerome and scared the living daylights out of him. "No. I think it's a good idea. But the flat needs to be repainted and a few repairs to be made. Then once they're done, we can suggest it."

"Good. So I'll leave it up to you to sort out, then?"

"Sure. I'll get it organised."

Dani knocked softly on Jerome's door. She could hear he was talking to someone, so she waited for him to call her in.

"Come in." His tone was clearly agitated but once Dani entered, his scowl softened.

"I brought you a coffee." Dani stepped forward and placed the double espresso on his desk.

Paul was sitting in the chair in front of the desk and he eyed her warily. Dani smiled at him, trying hard to place where she'd seen him before.

Jerome stared at her, evidently surprised. "Oh, thank you." Her unexpected visit pleased him.

She shrugged. "I'm sorry I didn't realise you had company."

"Um, yes. Paul, this is Dani. Paul is my head of security."

Paul immediately got up to shake her hand. "Hello, pleased to meet you."

"Hello. I think I've seen you at Sky."

"Yes, that's right."

"Would you like a coffee?" she asked and her eyes darted to Jerome. *Crap, maybe Jerome didn't want him staying*, she thought a second too late. Her worries were quickly dispelled. Jerome had leaned back in his chair and was regarding her with a soft smile.

"No, but thank you."

Dani said her goodbyes and left them to carry on with whatever they were discussing.

"I thought the restaurant was closed today."

"It is. Dani's just here to help my mother out with something."

"Right. Well, like I was saying, I've added more cameras around the back and sensors in the vestibule. All are disarmed with the key pad. The restaurant also has sensors fitted on all windows and doors. I've connected the system to your home computer, office computer and to Peter's, as well as your phone."

"Good. I think that's all we can do, short of having a security guard here permanently."

"We could have someone pass by every hour to keep an eye out."

"I don't think so – well, not yet anyway. What about at the house?"

Paul scratched his head nervously. "Well, again, we'll be putting in cameras to back up the alarm that's already there. But the house is set back, and behind it there are only fields, which is a security nightmare. It's very secluded. We're going to need to put floodlight sensors every-where which will be annoying, since any wildlife that passes will cause the place to light up like Blackpool illuminations," he huffed. "But there's really no way around it. I do think a patrol between midnight and five in the morning would be justified there though."

"Yes, you may be right. You'll be there this afternoon?"

Paul nodded.

"I've let Nina and Liz know. Any other feedback from your friends down town?"

Paul shook his head. "Nothing, but we had an eventless weekend, so I've not been in touch." He got up from the chair. "Right, I'll head off over to yours then."

They said their goodbyes and Paul left Jerome alone in his office.

He took a welcome sip from his coffee and checked his phone. Liz had sent him the details of her flight, so he immediately logged on to the airline website and set about booking his ticket. Once he'd received confirmation, he then checked flights for Milan over the Valentine's weekend. Luckily, there were many flights, so he booked for all four of them to leave on the thirteenth, returning the following Wednesday. As luck would have it, they'd also be in Italy for the annual Carnivale held in Venice. The children would be thrilled. Jerome's eyes rested on the black and white photo of his children on his desk and he smiled to himself, deciding to keep his plans to himself and surprise both them and Liz over Christmas.

Jerome picked up his phone again and searched for Graham's number. He might want to keep the short break a secret from Liz, but he needed to let her agent know she'd be unavailable for those dates. He hit dial and waited for it to connect.

"Jerome, this is a nice surprise."

"Hello, Graham, how are you?"

"Can't complain. What can I do for you?" Graham inwardly cringed. If Jerome was ringing, it normally meant Liz wasn't happy or he wasn't happy. He never called otherwise. Graham prayed it wasn't about the fashion show. He'd confirmation that it had been postponed this morning, but had decided to keep it to himself until after Liz came back from her meeting in London.

"I just booked a few days away with Liz in February and I thought you should know so that if any contracts come up over those days you can reschedule them. Liz doesn't know yet – it's a Christmas present for her, so it needs to be just between us until after Christmas."

"Oh. That's sounds like a lovely surprise. Okay, give me the dates, so I can block them off."

Jerome gave him the information and Graham duly noted them down, pleased, for once he wasn't being chastised by the brooding Jerome Ferretti. Graham often felt intimidated by Jerome's high-handed demands, but Liz had been a good steady income to Graham over the years and now with these recent larger contracts, he didn't want to rock the boat.

"I'll be accompanying Liz on Wednesday. She seemed a little on edge and I think she needs the support."

"Oh? Well of course, whatever you think is best."

Jerome noted the surprise in Graham's voice, which irritated him. "Well, I'm sure you've noticed she's been quite strung out recently. She practically lives at your office," he huffed. "She's edgy and overly obsessed with her weight. I'm concerned and you should be too."

Graham closed his eyes and took a deep breath. *He knew it was too good to be true. And what did Jerome mean, she practically lived at his office? Jesus, how possessive was he?* She popped in twice a week. That was hardly excessive. Wanting to avoid an unnecessary argument, Graham chose not to point this out. "Yes, she's been nervous about this contract. It's not her usual kind of work. I think that's why she's a little apprehensive. It's a big contract with a lot of exposure. But Liz has always been professional in every aspect of her work, as you well know. I have every confidence that she'll impress them at the meeting and with you being there for her, well, I'm sure that means a lot to her."

"Um, yes, well thank you."

Graham sighed, relieved that Jerome seemed to be somewhat pacified.

"Well it was nice talking to you, Graham. I appreciate you looking out for her."

"You're welcome."

Jerome put down the phone and scowled.

"Scott."

"Good afternoon, Seni. I thought I should let you know that the extra surveillance you asked for will start from Wednesday, as well as the phone logging."

Arsenio looked at the clock on his computer. It was after six and he was nowhere near finished. He rubbed his eyes with his thumb and forefinger.

"Good. Not tapping, then?"

"No. That's a lot harder, but to be honest, we just want to prove they're communicating."

"Yes, I suppose so. Any luck on the second phone?"

"No, but it should be easy to find once we get the logs on the trainer's phone – he'll be calling it regularly."

"Yes, of course."

Arsenio stretched his shoulders and stood up. He'd been sitting for too long and his shoulders felt tight. He started pacing around his office, flexing his shoeless toes into the plush carpet.

"There's just one other thing. I noticed today that Jerome had Paul, his head of security, do a full sweep of the house and grounds of his home. He also updated the security, installing cameras and light sensors."

Arsenio stopped by his window and looked out over the lit city. "Really? That sounds a bit extreme."

"Yes, I thought so too. They have a fairly decent security system as it is."

"I'll see what I can find out about that. Thanks." Arsenio looked back at the pile of files on his desk and sighed. He had a heavy week in front of him. "Send me the reports as before but we need to get together, let's say..." Arsenio moved back to his desk and quickly scrolled down his calendar, "... It'll have to be next Monday. Late afternoon."

"That works for me. I'll be in touch if there's anything else more pressing."

"Okay, thanks."

Arsenio pressed the key on his phone and dropped it on his desk. He'd let Cosimo know tomorrow. He didn't have the energy tonight. Arsenio pressed the intercom and Carl answered immediately.

"You're still here?" he asked Carl.

"Yes, I'm just finishing up."

"Do you think you could organise me something to eat? I'll be here for a couple more hours."

"Sure, anything in particular?"

"Anything but Italian," huffed Arsenio. The only Italian he ate was his mother's and at La Casa.

"Sushi?"

"Perfect."

"You need me to stay on?"

"No, that's okay, Carl. I'll leave you it all for the morning."

"No problem. I'll stay until the food arrives."

"Thanks."

Arsenio dropped back into his chair and sighed as he opened up the file on top of the pile.

***

"You're kidding me, right?" Jonathan paced up and down as Liz sat on the bed in their small rented space. "You're going together? Why?"

"Jonathan –"

"Did you ask him to?" he stopped moving and stood in front of her, cutting her off.

"No, he suggested it and I –"

"He suggested it? He's never been to any of your meetings before. Why now? What's changed?"

"Jonathan. listen to me." Liz reached out and took his hand and squeezed it. "He saw I was stressed out, which you know I am, and he suggested that he come with me. I couldn't tell him no. He's got to see I'm trying too. You know this. We've talked about it." She smiled softly, trying to calm him.

"I don't like it." He crouched down in front of her and Liz put her hand on his cheek.

"I know, but all he's doing is coming on a plane with me and sitting in the hotel bar while I have the meeting. It's really nothing."

"He's spending the whole day with you, Liz. Just you and him without any distractions." Jonathan could only just about stomach Liz going back to her home every day, because he knew Jerome worked long hours. And on the days he spent at home there was always the children. This trip would mean they'd be completely alone.

"Yes, but we'll be on a plane and surrounded by people. It's not exactly intimate. And besides, I'm so edgy I doubt I'll be able to string a sentence together."

Jonathan leaned forward and pushed her back on to the bed, crawling over her, pinning her with his powerful arms. "If he tries anything? What if he wants to nail you?"

Liz smiled slowly at him. She loved that he got so jealous. "What, on a plane? Or in the office while I'm having my meeting?" she raised her eyebrows questionably.

"Argh! This is fucking torture. I won't see you on Wednesday. Thursday I'm stacked out with work because of the rescheduling. It'll be Friday until I see you."

"But we'll have five days together. Just you and me." She licked her lips and widened her ice blue eyes at him.

"It's the nights I'm looking forward to." He pressed a rough kiss to her lips.

"Me too, babe."

Jonathan clenched his jaw and sighed. It was just two days. He'd have to suck it up.

"Well, seeing as I won't be seeing you for the next two days." He bent down again and trapped her bottom lip softly between his teeth and pulled it. "We're skipping your training session and I'm going to fuck you hard for the next two hours."

"Fine by me," moaned Liz, arching up to him.

Jerome looked at the time. Just past one. Jeez, she'd been in the meeting for over two hours. They'd set off from Leeds Bradford Airport at eight that morning, arriving at Heathrow just after nine. They'd taken the train into the city, then a cab to the hotel where the protein shake company occupied one of the smaller conference rooms. Jerome was sitting in the hotel bar area and had drunk far too many espressos. He'd been working from his laptop but now his stomach was rumbling and he needed to eat. He was also desperate for a cigarette but he knew he'd have to wait for both food and nicotine until Liz was done. The only consolation was that if the meeting was going on for so long, they must be interested.

Jerome caught the attention of the waiter and ordered another espresso. He pulled out his phone and dialled La Casa, he was bored and needed a distraction.

Gia's familiar accented voice answered the call.

"Mama, it's me. Is everything alright?"

"Jerome, sure everything's fine. How did the meeting go?"

"She's still in," Jerome huffed.

"Well, don't worry about here –"

From his peripheral vision he saw someone entering the bar. He turned to see who it was. "Mama, I have to go, sorry. Liz just finished," he interrupted, then immediately hung up.

Liz practically ran to him, beaming. Jerome was up instantly and she ran straight into his open arms.

"Good meeting?" he chuckled as she flung her arms around his neck and he lifted her up slightly. He squeezed her, Liz's obvious good mood was infectious.

"Oh Jerome, it went *so* well. I mean *really* well. They practically said I had the job, but they've got to see two more before they can officially confirm it."

"That's so great, Liz." He pressed a kiss to her lips, swept away by her happiness. She was so beautiful when she smiled. Jerome placed her back down and Liz slumped into one of the chairs around the table where Jerome had been waiting. "So tell me everything. Do you want a drink? Something to eat?"

Liz shook her head. "They gave me coffee and water and I couldn't eat a thing, I'm so excited."

They sat in the bar for the next half an hour as Liz gave Jerome a full and thorough rundown of the meeting and Jerome gave her his full and undivided attention, revelling in her enthusiasm. It was so good to see her so passionate – it normally took a great deal for her to show so much emotion. The only thing that worried Jerome was that she hadn't eaten anything all day and was agitated. Her eyes were huge and wild as she spoke quickly and she fidgeted in her seat. He'd never seen her so animated before.

"So they said they'd be in touch, probably once I'm back from Spain." She clasped her hands together tightly and clenched her eyes together, showing her excitement.

Jerome laughed softly. "That's so good Liz, really. I'm so proud of you. We need to celebrate. Lunch? Somewhere swanky?"

Liz twisted her mouth. "I'd rather go shopping."

Jerome chortled. "Of course you would. Okay, maybe a dress for tomorrow's charity do?" Jerome suggested.

Liz eyes lit up. "And shoes?"

"And shoes," conceded Jerome, glad to see her so happy.

By the time they got back home, it was just before nine. Nina was emptying the dishwasher as Jerome and Liz walked in from the garage.

"Hi. Did you have a good time?" she directed the question to Jerome, but Liz answered.

"The best."

"That's nice." Nina eyed the large cardboard bag Liz was holding with Stella McCartney emblazoned on the side and she smiled tightly at Jerome. *Jeez, he spent so much of his hard earned money on her and she didn't even appreciate it.* "Well the kids are asleep."

Jerome's face dropped slightly, he'd been hoping he'd catch them before they slept. Liz put down the bag on the kitchen table, ignoring Nina completely, and headed to the wine fridge, pulling out a bottle of Dom Perignon.

"Drink?" she turned to look at Jerome and cocked her head to the side. "To celebrate?"

"Sure."

"You can go now, Nina. Can you arrange to take the children to school in the morning? After we've finished this" – she gestured to the bottle she was holding – "I don't think I'll be in any fit state in the morning." Her comment effectively dismissing Nina. Jerome scowled but before he could say anything, Nina was already by the door.

"Sure. Goodnight." She didn't even look at either one of them as she exited the kitchen.

"Here, you open this while I get the glasses." Liz thrust the bottle towards Jerome for him to take and then she went over to the glass cabinet, retrieving two champagne flutes. "That was the last bottle by the way. You'll need to stock up for Christmas," she said over her shoulder.

"Yes, I will. Let's hope we need to open many more of these in celebration, eh?"

Liz turned around and grinned, nodding. Jerome expertly opened the champagne with a soft pop and poured it into the flutes. He passed one to Liz and lifted his.

"*Salute.* Here's to the new face of I-Gea protein shakes and products."

"Cheers." Liz smiled coyly as they clinked glasses.

"Shall I make you something to eat before I get in the shower?" Jerome coaxed. He was acutely aware that she'd eaten nothing other than a power bar all day.

Liz shook her head, gazing at him through her lashes, taking another sip from her glass. "I'll eat something once you've gone," she lied. Those tablets Jonathan had given her were working wonders. She just wasn't hungry and had dropped four pounds over the last week.

"Okay." Jerome drained his glass and placed it on the counter. "Well, I really need to get myself ready."

"Of course. Thank you so much for today. I don't think I'd have made it through without you."

"I'm glad I was there too." He reached over and gently stroked her arm. Their eyes locked and Jerome took in a sharp breath, then swallowed. She leaned into his touch and Jerome felt that familiar pull. It had been almost seven months since the last time they'd slept together. Jerome wanted nothing more than to be able to be with her again but he didn't know if he could get past her infidelity. He stepped back and focused on the champagne bottle. Lifting it, he poured some more into her glass and then put it back down. "I'd better get ready."

Liz smiled softly and nodded. Jerome stepped around her and headed up the stairs. Liz gulped down the contents of her glass and refilled it. Taking another deep drink, she then took her glass and the bottle and headed to her room. She could hear the shower running from down the corridor as she approached her door. Pushing it open, she quickly put down the glass and bottle, then stripped off her clothes. Slipping on her silk robe, she reached over and drained her glass again, then tiptoed down to Jerome's room.

Jerome rinsed the last of the shampoo out of his hair and turned off the shower. He grabbed a towel and rubbed his hair vigorously, then wrapped another around his waist. With a swipe of his hand he cleared the large mirror of condensation and was met with the reflection of Liz sitting on the lowered toilet seat behind him. He swung around, clearly surprised that she was there. Liz had already risen from the seat and closed the short distance between them. Her robe was loosely tied, exposing her cleavage. There was no doubt why she was here, her posture undeniably sexual, her eyes wild with lust and for a moment, Jerome was stunned at her ardour. She roughly took hold of his face and crushed her lips to his. Jerome hesitated for a second then responded to her urgent mouth.

Liz's hands pulled away the towel around his waist and pressed against him, kissing him fiercely, hardly taking a breath. She knew if she let him think too much, he'd push her away, and she needed this. Today, after everything they'd been through, she needed to know she could break him. Her hand slid down and took hold of him, causing Jerome to jerk at her touch. But before he could protest, she swept down and took him in her mouth, kneeling at his feet.

"Ah, Christ, Liz." She moved over him, licking, sucking, taking him as deep as she could. Jerome gripped onto the vanity unit for support, unable to stop her, not wanting to. He gazed down at her momentarily, and then reality hit him. He took hold of her shoulders and pushed her gently. Her eyes flew up to his and he could see the hurt of his rejection flicker across her face. He clenched his eyes shut. Jerome's gut twisted, knowing his reaction was painful to her. He was going to have to forgive her at some point, he was going to have to try and accept her back.

"Jerome, please let me show you how much I want you. Stop shutting me out, pushing me away. Please," she said, making him feel even worse.

He released her shoulders without a word, his throat constricted by the lump that had lodged itself there. He closed his eyes and leaned back as she pushed her lips over him again. It was totally base, carnal, but he didn't know if it was enough. Jerome's head filled with unwelcome thoughts and a confusing cocktail of emotions he just wasn't able to fathom. He thought that there was no way he'd be able to climax. But he didn't want to hurt her, not after today. He forced himself to relax and empty his mind of disturbing images that had been, until now, haunting him. Liz continued to pleasure him, determined to win him over. Her relentless ministrations were rewarded by a stifled moan and she dared to look up at Jerome.

His head had rolled back, his eyes clenched shut. The strain evident along his neck as his veins stood out, pulsing. Liz, recognising he was close and sucked just that bit harder. Jerome stiffened suddenly, then he climaxed loudly, his hands' vice like grip the only thing keeping him from collapsing on the floor.

Liz rose to her feet, pressing her body against his she curled her arms around his waist and rested her cheek against his shoulder. Jerome's chest heaved as he wrapped his arms around her and kissed the top of her head.

"Thank you for today. And thank you for now," she whispered, then she pulled back from him. "I'll let you get ready." Without another word, she left Jerome standing naked in his bathroom, stunned and confused. Stunned because Liz had for the first time ever, selflessly pleasured him; confused because he knew the only reason he'd climaxed was because he'd been imagining it was Dani that was kneeling on his bathroom floor.

Jerome powered down the bank of the river and turned into La Casa's car park. He slowed down and took a minute to catch his breath, pulled out his earplugs and turned off the music from his phone. He'd needed to listen to music today. Anything to stop him focusing on what had happened last night in his bathroom. The absence of Dani's little white Fiat disturbed him. It was nine thirty – he knew she'd be here any moment with her vibrant smile lighting up her whole face. Jerome shook his head. He needed to get his head straight and while he kept focusing on Dani, he was never going to manage that. *Maybe he should just let Seni date her*, he thought. *Date?* he huffed to himself, *more like screw her!* Then he'd definitely have to get over it. He shuddered. Maybe that wasn't such a good idea.

Graham picked up the phone and dialled Liz's number. He'd put it off for as long as he could.

"Hello, Graham."

"Hi, Liz. I'm not disturbing, am I?"

"No. Not at all."

"Well the guys at I-Gea were very impressed with you. I've just finished talking to them. I can't see how you won't get this contract. Only if you didn't want it."

"Not want it? Are you mad? I'm glad I have the Spain shoot to keep my mind off it. They said they'd know by the end of next week."

"Yes. That's right. Um, anyway, I'm afraid that even though everything's going well there, I have some bad news. The fashion show looks like it's been postponed." Graham cringed, waiting for her reaction.

"What? Why?"

"The venue pulled out, so the events company is trying to find somewhere and as you can imagine, it's short notice."

"I was so looking forward to doing a runway, finally," Liz whined, then proceeded to rant on about how she'd put so much work and time into this show. Graham sat in his office listening, only adding the odd um and ah. Liz eventually hung up, still clearly upset. Whoever thought modelling was glamorous needed to listen in on some of the conversations Graham had with some of his temperamental models.

Liz picked up her spare phone and dialled Jonathan. It rang five times and then she hung up. She knew he was training and couldn't break off but she was hoping to catch him when he was in between his sessions.

She then fished out her other phone and dialled Jerome. It rang twice and then he answered.

Before he could even speak, she was rattling off what had happened. She spoke so fast he had difficulty keeping up. He grasped most of what she said, but what disturbed him the most was how completely out of control she sounded. He swiftly paced out of his office at La Casa and headed to his car.

"I'm coming home, Liz. Just calm down and I'll be there in fifteen minutes." Once Jerome hung up, he dialled Peter, explaining he'd be out this morning. Then he put his foot down and headed home.

Jerome took one look at Liz and knew something was wrong and it wasn't to do with the cancelled fashion show. She was jumpy and her hands were shaking. "Jesus, Liz, what's wrong?"

She burst into tears, burying her face in her hands. He was over to her instantly, sitting beside her on the sofa and pulling her into his arms. As he hugged her tightly, he felt her ribcage and he scowled. She'd lost too much weight. "Hey what is it, come on."

Liz pulled away from him and he passed her a tissue he'd grabbed from the side table, for her to wipe her eyes. "They've cancelled the fashion show."

"I thought you said it was just postponed."

"It's the same thing. It takes months to get venues booked for such a big show. It'll be a long time before it's rescheduled and they may not want me then."

Jerome rubbed her back while her hands fidgeted with the tissue. "I'm sure that won't be the case."

Liz shrugged.

"Do you want me to talk to Graham? See what he thinks?"

She shook her head, "I know he'll do what he can to get me in again, it's just I'm so disappointed."

"I know, darling, but try and on focus on yesterday. I mean, that went so well, it's huge for you. And there's your Spain shoot you're flying out for tomorrow. You've so much going well for you at the moment, don't focus on this one blip. And who's to say it won't happen anyway, eh?"

He bobbed down to catch her gaze and smiled at her. She nodded weakly.

"You're right. I'm just stressed out." She straightened up and blew a sharp breath out of her mouth.

Jerome squeezed her shoulders. His behaviour probably wasn't helping either. He knew she'd been trying to get closer to him. Last night was her way of showing him and he hadn't handled it that well. He was going to have to push himself more for both their sakes.

"You look tired. You should try and get some sleep, now the kids are at school. You're flying out tomorrow and we've the dinner tonight. I don't want you wearing yourself out."

"I just can't sleep at the moment." Liz leaned back against the sofa and rolled her head back, closing her eyes.

"Shall I make something to eat? Some fruit salad maybe or some eggs?"

"Sure, eggs sound good."

Jerome smiled and headed to the kitchen.

By twelve o'clock, Liz had managed to eat some scrambled eggs with smoked salmon and some fruit salad. It wasn't much, but Jerome was pleased she'd eaten something. He'd found some relaxants Liz had once taken when she'd been stressed and he made her take one so she'd sleep. She was so agitated, she was happy to take anything. To Jerome's relief, she fell asleep within an hour on the sofa. He ran upstairs to her room to get her a quilt, so that then she wouldn't get cold.

The room was in a total mess. She'd obviously been trying to pack for her trip tomorrow. There were clothes strewn across the bed where the suitcase was open and her shoes were scattered over the floor. She'd managed to put some items in, but it was clear she was nowhere near done. There was no way he could take the quilt off the bed with every-thing piled on top of it, so he paced over to her walk-in wardrobe to fetch a comforter she had stored in there. Once he'd found it, he headed towards her door. He was distracted by a very faint buzzing sound that went on for a few seconds. It sounded like a phone vibrating on silent. Jerome scanned the room to find what was making the noise. It stopped before he could locate it. His eyes fell on Liz's bag and moved towards it. *The phone was probably in her bag*, he thought. Jerome reached in and pulled out her smart phone. He swiped the screen to open it and looked at it puzzled. There was no missed call or message. *Strange. Oh well, whoever it was would ring back.* He put Liz's phone back in her bag and headed downstairs.

Dani started up her car and turned the heating on full. She really hoped Ollie was feeling better. He'd looked pretty awful this morning and Chloe was wrecked after his restless night. With any luck, she'd have had a nap today so at least she could enjoy her evening out. Dani looked at the time. Four thirty. Jerome hadn't been in at all today and she hadn't seen him yesterday either. She sighed to herself; she was going to have to get over it. Dani turned on her MP3 player and started to listen to the Italian woman's gentle voice spout off today's lesson.

"I'm not going, Jerome. I just don't feel up to it."

"Liz, come on. It's just a dinner. It'll take your mind of everything. Give you a chance to relax a bit." Jerome was pacing in her room while she tried to pack. He was keeping his tone low so that Kara and Alessandro wouldn't hear. "We don't need to stay long, just until ten thirty."

Liz straightened up from bending over her case. She'd managed to sleep for four hours and was feeling decidedly better, but the last thing she wanted was to go to some stuffy Christmas charity dinner. Making small talk with dull people was not something she was good at. That was Jerome's domain.

"Jerome, I need to pack. I'm leaving tomorrow and I really don't need to be going out when I'm already so stressed out. I just want a quiet night."

"We can't let Seni down." Jerome rubbed his forehead. He didn't want to stress her out more but it was hardly a big deal. In fact, a change of scenery would do her good. Keep her mind off whatever was causing her so much anxiety.

"You go on your own. I'll finish packing, then have a soak in the bath and get to bed early."

Jerome furrowed his brow as she stood with her arms crossed in front of her, staring at him. He knew that look – she wasn't going to change her mind.

26

BABYSITTER

D ani dumped her bag on the stairs and shrugged out of her jacket. She could hear Chloe talking quietly in the sitting room, so she popped her head around the door.

Ollie was laid out on the sofa covered in his quilt, looking pale, his eyes sleepy and rimmed with dark circles. *Shit, he looked worse than this morning*, thought Dani. Rosie and Sophie were curled up on the other sofa watching a DVD.

"Hey, how are you feeling?" she asked, coming through the door.

"My throat hurts," he croaked.

Chloe looked worn out. She pursed her lips together and sighed as she put the thermometer in his ear.

"Aww, darling."

"He's really poorly, Dani. Mummy said so. It's in his neck," Sophie explained gravely.

"I know, angel. I just hope you and Rosie don't get it too."

Sophie's eyes widened and she looked over at Ollie, as if the thought of that was terrifying.

"Shall I make you some honey tea?" Dani gently stroked his forehead. It was burning hot.

Ollie nodded weakly.

"Okay, I won't be long." She rubbed Chloe's back reassuringly, then she headed for the kitchen.

Within a couple of minutes Chloe came through and leaned against the kitchen counter. She watched Dani pour honey into a steaming cup of camomile tea.

"How is it?" Dani asked.

"It's thirty-eight point six. The Nurofen must be wearing off. He looks so limp."

"When's his next dose?"

"In an hour."

Dani looked at the clock. It was six fifteen.

"When's he got to take the antibiotics?"

"Eight."

Dani nodded. "What time's Adam getting back?"

"He's on his way." Chloe rubbed her face. "I can't go tonight, not with Ollie so ill."

"I'll be fine with him, Chloe. I'll sleep with him. I won't leave his side."

"I know. I don't doubt that for a minute. But I'll be useless there. I'll be worried and to be honest, I'm so tired too. I didn't sleep last night. I'll be on tenterhooks all night. The last thing I want to do is go to a Christmas charity dinner. Adam will have to go alone."

"Did you tell him?" cringed Dani.

Chloe nodded.

"He knows me, Dani. He knows I'll be worried. I feel bad for him because he'll be on his own, but he has to go. Sorry you wasted your night off."

"Don't be silly. I can help out with the girls. Are you sure? Once he takes the Nurofen and it kicks in, he'll be fine for four hours," coaxed Dani. She knew Chloe had been looking forward to the party. They didn't get chance to go out much and the party was a huge charity event which Adam's law firm organised every Christmas.

"I really wouldn't enjoy it anyway." She shrugged.

"I'll take this through and then I'll bathe the girls for you."

"Thanks, Dani." Chloe smiled weakly.

Dani rubbed Sophie's hair, then started to comb through the curls.

"Let's dry it, angel."

Sophie scooted over to where the hairdryer was and crossed her legs, waiting for Dani to start to dry her damp hair. Rosie was sitting on the floor playing with a box of hair clips and other accessories. Dani gently dried her hair, admiring the curls. They were like loose springs and they bounced beautifully as she straightened them, then let them go. Sophie had Adam's colouring, blue eyes, curly blonde hair and fair skin but she was the image of Chloe. Rosie, on the other hand, had darker hair and brown eyes and didn't resemble either parent. Chloe always said she looked like Dani. Dani glanced over to her as she tried to put a crocodile clip in Rosie's hair. *She was too gorgeous to look like me*, she thought wistfully. Sophie giggled as they watched her continue to put the clips in her light brown hair.

"Do you want me to put in a clip, Rosie?" Dani asked once she'd turned off the hairdryer.

Rosie looked up, her huge eyes like saucers. "Lip!" She held it up for Dani.

"It's clip, Rosie. C-c-c-clip," corrected Sophie.

Chloe walked in as Dani knelt down on the floor with Rosie. "All done?" she asked.

"Yes, we're just putting clips in Rosie's hair," smirked Dani.

"Do you have an evening dress?"

"An evening dress?" Dani furrowed her eyebrows. "Why?"

"I was wondering if you'd like to go with Adam."

"To the party?" answered a confused Dani.

"Uh-huh." Chloe cocked her head seeing her sister mulling over her suggestion.

"I... well, um, what does Adam think?"

"He's pleased not to go alone."

"I don't know, Chloe. I won't know anyone and it's not really my thing, a stuffy dinner full of lawyers." Dani loved going out but her usual venues were bars and clubs, not formal dinners.

"Aw, please, Dani. He's gonna feel like a spare part," whined Chloe.

"And Adam's alright with me going?" Dani twisted her mouth feeling backed into a corner.

"Yes, I'll get him up here to tell you if you don't believe me."

Dani sighed, blowing hard out of her mouth. She glanced at the alarm clock. It was ten past seven. She'd have to be ready in less than an hour.

"Look, think of it as babysitting him instead of the kids!" Chloe laughed.

Dani's mouth opened in shock at Chloe's comment, then laughed. "Not sure I've anything suitable to wear. Does it have to be long?"

Chloe grinned, relieved. "Ideally, yes. Let me check out your clothes." Chloe went over to the wardrobe and opened it.

"I've only got one long dress. I'm not sure if it's appropriate."

Chloe pulled out the long black dress and let out a small gasp. "It's... wow, it's really something."

"I told you. I got it for a nightclub opening." Dani almost looked apologetic as Chloe shook her head and chuckled. The dress was floor length and straight. The material had a slight stretch, which Chloe realised would cling to every curve of Dani's body. It had cutaway shoulders with a thin black-and-gold-edged strap that fastened around the neck. The gold edging continued down the middle of the front, then split in two, curving over to each hip. On the left side, it continued down all the length of the dress. The right side stopped at the hip and curled around to the back. The particular feature that had Chloe wide-eyed was on the left side of the dress, there was a panel of sheer, fine, black gossamer that ran from under the arm down the whole length of the dress, edged by the thin gold trim. On the right, there was also a cut-out, which travelled around the back, also filled in with gossamer.

"It's gorgeous, Dani. Jeez, it's Versace!"

Dani shrugged. "Not really appropriate, though. Well, not for stuffy lawyers."

"Wear it. You'll look amazing. Adam's gonna freak!" Chloe laughed.

"I don't know, Chloe, maybe you should run it by him first."

"Okay. Get in the shower and I'll show him it." Dani shook her head and headed to her bathroom.

"Sophie, go and get Daddy."

Sophie scrambled off the bed and went in search of Adam. Within a few minutes, he came through wearing his bathrobe and remnants of shaving foam on his face.

"Okay, where's the fire?" he ruffled his damp hair.

"Dani has only got this long dress to wear. All my stuff will be too short on her. What do you think?" Chloe lifted it up for Adam to see and his eyes widened before darting to Chloe's face.

"It's a bit sexy," he said tentatively.

"A bit? It's *super* sexy!" chuckled Chloe.

"Exy!" Rosie repeated and beamed up at them.

Sophie giggled. "Those lawyers will have their eyes popping out."

"A few will have coronaries," Adam added.

"I know. She'll look amazing in it though."

Adam nodded. "Tell her to wear it. We'll have a laugh watching everyone gape at her," he chuckled.

Dani had never got herself ready so fast. Adam was sitting downstairs with the girls and Ollie, who, after his dose of Nurofen, had started to come around.

Dani quickly dried her hair and applied her makeup. "I've never been so stressed," she cringed, applying her mascara. She'd styled her hair and left it loose, showing off her layers, her fringe showcasing her large dark eyes. She wore it back every day at work, so it was nice to have it free for a change. Dani slipped on her strappy, black, sky-high sandals and grabbed the gold clutch Chloe had lent her.

" Jeez, Dani, you look gorgeous. I take it you've no underwear on." Chloe lifted her brow.

Dani shook her head and twisted her mouth.

"Look at your boobs!" Chloe shook her head and looked down at her own chest. "Mine used to be perky once. Three kids and breastfeeding – they're like saggy balloons now," she huffed.

Dani walked over to her, towering in her heels over her sister, and hugged her. "I'd rather have the saggy boobs and three kids any day," Dani muttered.

Chloe sighed. "Yeah, me too. Come on. Go and rock the lawyer world of the north," she giggled. "I wish I could see their faces. Actually, it's their snooty wives that'll be pea green with envy who I want to witness."

Within ten minutes, Dani and Adam were pulling up outside Harewood house, a beautiful impressive eighteenth century stately home set in over one hundred acres of gardens. Dani had only been once, when Chloe and Adam first moved up to Leeds. She'd visited the bird garden and they'd been on the lake when Ollie was two. It was a beautiful setting for the dinner and Dani felt a pang of guilt for Chloe – she'd have been in her element here. Not like her. Dani marvelled at the building, beautifully floodlit as it stood in the huge expanse of gardens, and hoped she wouldn't embarrass Adam. She knew this was a big deal for him, now he was a partner.

"I have to say, I feel a little nervous. I didn't realise it was going to be so grand." Dani stared out of her window as they drove up to where the valets were parking the constant stream of cars.

"You'll be fine, Dani. You look amazing. Thanks for coming." He squeezed her hand.

"Thanks, Adam. Shame about Chloe."

"Aw, you're not such a bad understudy," he joked.

Dani snorted, not sure she could ever match up to Chloe.

"Ready?"

Dani nodded.

"Let's knock their socks off."

The dinner was set in an enormous marquee at the rear of the house. Dani had never seen anything quite like it. The floor was carpeted and had a huge dance floor in the centre. The tables were arranged all around the black and white dance floor. There were chandeliers hanging and the ceiling was black, covered in fairy lights. There was no way anyone would have guessed it was a marquee. She looked around the dimly lit area, noting that there were at least thirty tables.

"Oh my god, Adam, it's amazing." Dani looked around in awe.

"Yeah, we really go all out. Well, we charge five hundred pounds a ticket, so it has to be swanky," he muttered.

"Five hundred pounds! Wow, you'll raise loads of money," hissed Dani. "The food had better be good then," she giggled.

Adam laughed and offered her his arm as they walked towards the table plan. "Yeah, we should make over one hundred and fifty thousand. All for a good cause." He beamed.

He stopped to talk to a number of people as they moved around. He proudly introduced Dani to everyone, having to explain why he'd brought her instead of Chloe. Everyone they spoke to openly gawked at her, as well as all the other guests. Dani was glad the lighting was subdued so her flaming face wasn't so obvious. She could handle attention, but in an environment she was familiar with. This event was not something she was comfortable with. She looked around the marquee and realised that the average age of the guests must have been around mid forties, making her achingly aware that she was one of the youngest, as well as one of the most provocatively dressed guests.

Adam collected a couple of champagne glasses for them and they headed to their table. Dani scanned the room, sipping her champagne. There were an awful lot of taffeta and silk dresses. It looked like a show-case for bad bridesmaid's dress of the year, making Dani only more conscious of her super-sexy, slinky number.

Adam pulled out her chair and she sat down. Their table had a total of ten seated at it. There were the other two partners, Philip Cope and Thomas Baxter, along with their wives, and another two couples, who were obviously top clients of theirs. The whole table stared involuntarily at Dani as she took her seat.

Adam went around the table introducing Dani to everyone and yet again explaining why Chloe wasn't able to come. Dani noticed that they all seemed to relax once the explanation was over. Adam took his place next to Dani and patted her hand. "I think they all thought you were my bit on the side," he whispered. Dani flushed and then snorted.

Dani started to relax as the evening wore on. Adam was attentive and included her in the conversation wherever he thought Dani would feel comfortable. She smiled to herself while she listened to him recounting a work-related story. He really was a good man. The big brother she'd never had.

In the twelve years she'd known him, he'd helped her through all her difficult times in her life. When her father died, he helped both Chloe and herself organise the funeral. Their mother had been in no fit state. He'd also been with her when their mother died. Chloe had been in her last week of pregnancy with Sophie when their mother passed away, and had stayed up in Leeds. Adam again had arranged the funeral. When they decided to put the bed and breakfast her parents had up for sale, he'd arranged everything and advised Dani on what to do with her share of the inheritance. He still managed the fund he'd invested it in, sending her monthly reports. And now, he'd helped her to find her a job, sell her car and was in the process of recovering her half of the house she'd bought with Jez.

They were on the dessert course and Adam had done a good job of entertaining their table with another story. The guests at the table all laughed at the amusing anecdote as he finished, and Dani smiled along too, but she hadn't really been listening, lost in her own depressing thoughts of how her life had turned out. The band was playing "You'll Never Find Another Love Like Mine" and the dance floor had a fair amount of couples dancing, but Dani seemed mesmerised by her dessert fork.

"He's not bad is he?" Adam asked Dani.

"Sorry?" The comment jolted Dani out of her daydream.

"The singer. He's no Michael Buble, but he's good."

"Yes, he is." Dani's eyes darted to the band.

"Come on, let's have a dance." He stood up and grabbed her hand. Dani's eyes widened, as she hesitated. He bent down and whispered in her ear. "Come on, let everyone have a good look at you in that dress."

Dani giggled as he practically yanked her out of her seat. Adam was a great dancer. He and Chloe had taken classes before they were married. Both Chloe and Dani had taken ballroom dance classes when they were younger, and Chloe wanted to be able to dance well with Adam at their wedding, so he'd originally only gone to keep her happy. But in the end he'd enjoyed it, so they'd carried on up until Ollie was born.

Adam dramatically swept Dani around the dance floor and exactly as Adam had predicted, everyone's eyes focused on them. She couldn't stop grinning at Adam – his constant joking with her successfully rid her of unhappy thoughts. It really was quite thrilling and Dani felt giddy being twisted around and then back again when the song came to an end. Adam bowed to her and she dipped into a small curtsy. Then he guided her back to their seats, beaming, glad to see her previous melancholy mood had lifted.

"A drink, I think. What will you have?"

"A tequila gold, no ice, if they have it," replied Dani, lowering herself into her seat.

"Sounds good. I think I'll join you. I've a feeling we'll be leaving the car here." He raised his eyebrows in mock horror. And with that, he headed over to the bar.

Dani picked up her dessert fork and broke into her glazed lemon meringue tart with stewed blackberries. She took a mouthful and closed her eyes, savouring the tangy flavour and crunchy texture. She let out a subdued moan. It was delicious. She just loved lemon.

"It must be good, for you to be moaning like that." A vaguely familiar voice interrupted her from behind. Dani pivoted around to see who it was. There, standing in full black tie, looking every bit the wealthy play-boy, was Arsenio Ferretti. His mouth twitched into a grin and his mischievous eyes twinkled.

Dani gasped. *Why on earth was* he *here?* "Oh, hello."

"Hello yourself." He slipped around and sat in Adam's vacated chair. "What a lovely surprise to see you here." His eyes travelled over her, unashamedly appraising her.

The rest of the table watched on and Dani felt herself blush. Arsenio turned to the rest of the table and greeted the two partners. They seemed to know each other. Philip introduced Arsenio to the rest of the table while Dani sat awkwardly fidgeting in her seat, eating her dessert, which wasn't anywhere near big enough.

"I didn't realise you knew our competitors." He smiled wryly at Dani.

"Adam's my brother-in-law," explained Dani.

"Adam Holmes?"

Dani nodded and Arsenio seemed to be pleased with her response.

"So you're here with your company?" Dani asked, feeling like she should make some small talk.

"Yes, we come every year. We've a couple of tables on the other side." He cocked his head to the side, watching Dani take the last forkful of her dessert. "I came to ask you to dance. You looked like you were enjoying the last one."

Dani swallowed her dessert and stared at him. "Adam's a good dancer and he just made me look good," she said quietly. *Crap, she couldn't dance with* him!

"Oh, I don't think you need anyone's help to look good, Dani. You do a very fine job of doing that all on your own." He stood swiftly and held out his hand for her to take it. *Double crap.*

She looked at it warily, then stood up and gently put her hand in his. He gripped it almost as though he was worried she'd change her mind, and led her to the dance floor. The band started up the next song and Dani swallowed.

"Oh, they're playing our song." Arsenio glanced over his shoulder and smirked, winking at her.

Dani furrowed her brow. Our song? Then she recognised "Sway" and her face reddened, remembering their dance in La Casa's kitchen. *Oh crap, now she was even more nervous.*

Arsenio let out a laugh at her obvious embarrassment.

Jerome was sitting with Cosimo at the opposite end of the marquee. They were on one of the tables Arsenio's company had sponsored. He hadn't noticed Dani was there, mainly because there were so many people and he had come in late. He'd been seated immediately as Philip Cope was making his welcome speech, thanking everyone for being generous and raising such a substantial amount of money for their chosen local charity, a safe house for abused women and children. His attention was directed to the speaker and then to his table members once the dinner had started.

Once dessert was served, Jerome had excused himself to go outside for a cigarette, to an area reserved for the smokers. Between Liz's refusal to accompany him to the dinner at the last minute, along with her increasingly erratic moods, his nerves were shot. He knew the postponement of the fashion show had upset her, but she had other contracts. She was just being unreasonable. Jerome hated letting people down. This dinner was important for Arsenio and Liz knew Jerome couldn't cancel at such short notice. He didn't think it was a lot to ask for her to put herself out for him just once, especially considering he'd spent a small fortune yesterday on her outfit for this evening. So much for compromising.

Both Arsenio and Cosimo didn't press him for an explanation. Jerome's expression was enough to make them understand that he wasn't in the mood to elaborate.

Jerome perched himself on a stool at the table reserved for smokers. He glanced into the marquee, through the window at the various couples dancing. He lit his cigarette and dragged hard on it. Reaching over to flick the ash into the ashtray, he spotted Adam and Dani moving smoothly around the dance floor. Dani was grinning at Adam as he spoke to her. He stood up abruptly, riveted. *What was she doing here?* He knew she'd taken the night off – he'd seen it on the rota. He continued to watch, secure in the knowledge that no one could see him. He hadn't seen her in two days, what with his unscheduled trip to London and then Liz's meltdown today. It was only now, once he'd seen her, that he realised how much it had bothered him. He dragged hard again on his cigarette, painfully aware of how pleased he was to see her.

These were feelings he shouldn't be having. If Liz and he stood any chance of piecing together their fragile marriage, he couldn't constantly have his focus directed at Dani. He found himself thinking about her far too often, moving his work schedule around so he could spend time at La Casa. She was occupying an unreasonable amount of time in his thoughts. It wasn't about just physical attraction, though that was a huge factor too. There was undoubtedly chemistry between them but it was far more than that. He relished their time together. Working alongside her was a dream, their verbal sparring and her easy manner made his time at La Casa even more enjoyable. She had a kindness about her that was endearing, yet she wasn't a push over. Their heated discussion over Adam's bill had proved she wasn't scared to stand her ground, and that fire he'd seen in her only made him respect her more.

Jerome let his gaze rest on her laughing face once more and he knew the emotions that ran through him were not only respect and affection. It was unnerving.

He wasn't the kind of man who gave up, and he most definitely wasn't the kind of man who would throw away ten years of loyalty on a passing attraction. Loyalty and trust were everything to him and working through Liz's betrayal was proving to be harder every day, but he felt he at least had to try.

Quickly stubbing out his cigarette, Jerome headed towards the doorway leading back into the marquee. The song was coming to an end and he knew he'd have to go over, justifying his actions as common courtesy, but the thought of it had his stomach in knots. However much he battled inwardly, he wanted to speak to her, see that spark in her eye, feel that undeniable connection they had. The pull was just too strong for him to ignore. He'd missed her.

Jerome pushed open the door impatiently and scanned the room to find where she was sitting. Dani was taking her seat as Adam walked away towards the bar. Jerome took a moment to take her in. She looked stunning. He hadn't seen her with her hair down since the interview. He took a deep breath and leisurely walked in the direction of the table, rationalising his behaviour to himself that it would be rude not to acknowledge her. Before he'd even taken a few steps, he noticed Arsenio walk up behind her seat.

Jerome came to an abrupt stop, witnessing his brother settle himself into the seat next to her. Jerome clenched his jaw. He knew Arsenio was more than a little interested in her. He'd practically salivated when they'd been introduced and was constantly flirting with her whenever he came to the restaurant, even after he'd been repeatedly warned not to interfere with the staff, by himself and their mother. Jerome rubbed his forehead and headed back to his table. He'd have to go over once Arsenio had returned to their table.

As Adam left the bar carrying the two drinks he'd ordered, he spotted Jerome heading back to his table. "Jerome?"

"Hello, Adam, how nice to see you." He immediately put out his hand and his pensive look was replaced with a sincere smile. Jerome liked Adam. He only knew him within the confines of the restaurant but he seemed a genuine person and from what Arsenio had told him, Adam was very well respected in his field.

Adam shook his hand as he juggled the two drinks. "I didn't see you earlier."

"I came in late," Jerome replied and his mind flitted back momentarily to Liz and their argument. His face tightened.

"We're sitting over there." Adam motioned to where their table was and then he frowned when he couldn't see Dani. "I came with Dani, but she seems to have left the table."

"With Dani?"

"Yes, Ollie my son isn't well – laryngitis. Chloe stayed home with him. Dani stepped in at the last minute, so I wouldn't be alone. You should come over and say hi." Adam scanned the room, trying to find her.

"Isn't that her dancing with Seni?" Jerome pointed them out, trying to keep his voice steady.

"So it is." Adam looked at Jerome and raised his eyebrows. "I didn't realise she knew him."

Jerome huffed. "She's met him a few times at the restaurant, but even if he hadn't, it wouldn't have stopped him."

Adam chuckled. Arsenio's reputation was well known. He was relieved that Jerome could joke about it. The idea of Dani and Arsenio didn't sit too well with Adam, and as he looked at Jerome watching them dance, he realised that it didn't sit well with Jerome either. "That could get a little awkward," Adam smirked.

"He's been told he can't date the staff." Jerome shook his head.

"Maybe you should remind him and cut in," Adam laughed.

Jerome cocked his head and thought for a second. "Maybe I will."

Adam's eyes widened in surprise at his comment, then Jerome strolled over to where Dani was being twisted around by Arsenio just as the song drew to the end.

"So are you here with a date, Dani?" asked Arsenio, taking Dani by the waist.

"No. I came with Adam. My sister couldn't come because their son has laryngitis."

"That *is* good news." He grinned cheekily, then his face dropped when he saw Dani's face frown. "About you not being with a date, not about your nephew!" he clarified hastily.

Dani giggled, "Good, I was about to go and sit down."

Arsenio's grip tightened. "Oh no, I'm not about to let you go that easily. You look amazing in this dress. There's not a man in this room who isn't lusting after you, except maybe Cosimo," he smirked as his eyes ran over her body.

"I think maybe that's a slight exaggeration, but thank you for the compliment all the same," muttered Dani. She averted her eyes from his. He was staring at her intensely, making her feel a little uncomfortable. In an attempt to lighten the mood and change the direction of the conversation, Dani asked, "What about you, Arsenio? No date tonight?" she stifled a grin.

"Call me Seni, and no, I don't have a date tonight. I don't mix work and pleasure," he sighed deeply, pulling her a little closer.

"Really? So tonight's strictly work, then?"

"Well, it started out that way. But I must say it's become extremely pleasurable as the evening has worn on." He pulled back slightly so he could look at her.

"Are you flirting with me, Seni?" Dani held his gaze and his face lit up with the huge grin.

"Definitely," he answered and then he twisted her around and pulled her back to him, so her body was flush against his. Dani gasped at the swift, yet perfectly controlled move.

"I think that's enough manhandling of the staff, Seni," said the familiar raspy voice from behind Dani. She instantly drew a sharp intake of breath. Dani swung around and was faced with the excruciatingly handsome face of Jerome. His blue eyes rested on Dani. "You don't mind if I cut in, do you?"

Dani stood stock still, reeling over the fact he was firstly there, and secondly that he was asking her to dance. *Holy mother of God, he was here.* Eventually her brain clicked into gear and she managed to breathe, "No."

His lips twitched into a small smile. "I'll take it from here, Seni." His eyes flitted back to Arsenio, who muttered something in Italian, to which Jerome arched his eyebrow in disapproval.

"Thank you for the dance, Dani." Arsenio took her hand and kissed it, then sent a disgruntled look at Jerome and left the dance floor.

Jerome held out his hand for Dani to take and she hesitated for a second. "I told you I don't bite. Well, not hard, anyway." He stifled a grin at her and she rewarded him with a soft laugh, nervously placing her hand in his.

He looked beyond exquisite in his tuxedo. Dani mused as to which Italian designer had made it; she knew his taste tended towards all things Italian. He looked down at her, his eyes doing that intense staring thing that made her hot and bothered. The band started with the introduction to the next song and Jerome brought her closer. He placed his hand around her waist, his hot palm resting on the sheer gossamer. Dani's heart started pumping and her ears buzzed. She really needed to calm down. The last thing she wanted to do was make a total fool of herself. His neck pulsed, close to her cheek and she wondered what it would taste like if she just could lick it...

"I hope you didn't mind." His comment jolted her.

"Er, no." *Are you kidding me!*

"It's just I know, Seni."

"I'm not sure what you mean."

"He's been warned off you."

What? Dani pulled back and looked at Jerome clearly shocked. "Warned off me?" her voice a little higher, betraying her surprise.

Jerome smiled softly. "Yes. He knows he's not supposed to hit on the staff. It can get very awkward."

"Oh, I see." Dani relaxed a little. "I don't think he meant anything by it. He just asked me to dance and was being friendly."

Jerome took a deep breath and smiled, moving her fluidly around the dance floor as the singer sang "Kissing a Fool". "Maybe." But something in

327

his tone gave away that he thought there was more to Arsenio's seemingly innocent gesture.

"Adam told me you came instead of Chloe."

Dani tried to focus on what he was saying, but she was preoccupied with the feel of his muscles working on his shoulders. He smelled good enough to eat. "Er, yes. You saw Adam?" she managed to squeeze out, past her tightening throat. His hand was hot in hers and she readjusted her grip. He flexed his long lean fingers over her hand, sending a tremor through her now-wired body. The song was slower than the previous one, which meant they didn't move around the dance floor as much.

"He was getting drinks at the bar," Jerome continued. "He lost you for a bit." His mouth lowered to her ear. "But then he spotted you with Seni."

His chest rested against Dani and she took a sharp breath. *Holy shit!* They were getting closer with every second. She really needed to say something, anything. "Are you here with Liz?" Dani asked quietly. *That's it, focus on the fact he's married. Anything to stop focusing on his delicious scent, a perfect mix of his preferred cologne, a faint smell of cigarette smoke and the distinct masculine smell of his skin...*

Jerome cleared his throat nervously. "No, she stayed home."

"Oh." *Good! Not cool, Dani!* she chastised herself. Her hand shifted and she became distracted by the firmness of his shoulders, his amazing hexagonal eyes, his sculptured mouth...

"Did you enjoy the dinner?" he asked.

What? Shit... get a grip! "Er, yes."

Jerome grinned. "When I saw the dessert menu, I thought of you."

Dani pulled back to look at him, her face flushed. "You thought of me?" she said, thrilled that she should even pass through his mind.

"Yeah, you're the only woman I've ever seen openly enjoy her dessert. What did you have?"

Dani chuckled, embarrassed by his accurate observation. "The lemon meringue tart, but it was a hard decision."

Jerome laughed, "I bet it was. I went for the dark chocolate delice. It was very rich."

"Don't tell me you didn't finish it?" Dani stared at him in mock horror.

"I just left a bit." His soft laugh vibrated through his chest. "I'll bring you it over, if it hasn't been cleared away," he teased.

"I hate having to choose just one dessert. I ate half of Adam's rhubarb plate too."

Jerome shook his head and his eyes glowed. *She really was quite beautiful*, he thought.

The song came to an end and Jerome and Dani stood for a moment, still in each other's arms. Then Dani reluctantly released herself from him. "Thank you for the dance."

"It was my pleasure. Let me take you back to Adam. I don't want you being accosted by anyone else tonight." His comment made Dani's heart leap.

Adam was sitting at their table talking to the clients to his left as they approached the table. Jerome pulled out her chair for her to sit down.

"Oh, you're back." Adam turned to see who had escorted her to the table. "So you rescued her?" he smirked at Jerome.

"Yeah, something like that." He glanced down at Dani and showed a small smile. "Well, enjoy the rest of the evening."

"Thanks, you too."

"I'll see you tomorrow." Jerome turned his gaze back to Dani and she tilted her head to look up at him.

"Yes, and thanks again."

Jerome turned and walked away and Dani stared after him, a little dazed.

"Here's your drink." Adam passed it to her and watched her take a large gulp. "Are you okay? You look flushed."

Dani nodded. "Hot... with the dancing," she explained. Adam sucked on his teeth, totally unconvinced that that was the reason and was about to say something, when his attention was distracted by Thomas.

Dani sat looking at her coffee cup, which had replaced her empty dessert plate. Her crush was getting worse. She just hoped no one had realised, especially Jerome. She scooted forward and tried hard not to scan the room for Jerome's table. The man next to her made some comment about the weather and she politely listened and let him carry on talking about their impending holidays. Needing to get out of there, she excused herself and went in search of the restrooms. She felt giddy from the dancing and a combination of champagne, numerous glasses of wine and tequila, mixed with the intoxicating scent of Jerome.

Dani washed her hands idly in the basin and looked at herself in the mirror. She looked flushed and her eyes were sparkling. *Stop crushing on him! He's your boss and he's married!* She scorned herself, shook her head and took in a cleansing breath. It had only been a month and a half since she'd been devastated and walked out on Jez, and here she was wishing for someone who was out of reach and out of her league. It was sobering to realise that her feelings had shifted so far in a relatively short time. Maybe she hadn't been as in love with Jez as she'd thought. Dani checked

329

herself in the mirror one more time, then headed back out to the marquee.

As she exited the restrooms, she saw Cosimo approaching and he smiled warmly at her. He was such a gentleman and was always so courteous. "What a nice surprise to see you Dani." He held out his hand for her to shake.

"Thank you. It's nice to see you too, Cosimo."

"You look ravishing in that dress." His comment was genuine and with no sexual overtones.

"Thank you. I think maybe it's a bit much for this kind of event." Dani wrinkled her nose.

"Nonsense. You've brought some glamour to an otherwise very unglamorous event. Most of the women here haven't got a clue. You've definitely upped the bar," he whispered, checking over his shoulder in a conspiratorial manner, making Dani chuckle.

She really liked him. He was so different from both his brothers. He was calm and gentle, yet not a pushover. He had a quality that made you trust him. Dani smirked to herself, *well he was an accountant after all, you'd have to trust him.*

"Well you most certainly made an impression on my young brother," he added, softly eyeing Dani.

"He was just being polite and asked me to dance," blushed Dani. Cosimo frowned a little. "Seni didn't mean anything by it." Dani felt she needed to defend him. Both Seni's older brothers were obviously displeased with the attention he'd given her.

Cosimo's eyebrows shot up at her comment and he smiled at her wryly. "Ah yes, Seni, um. Well, I better not keep you any longer, otherwise your brother-in-law will be sending out a search party. It was lovely to see you, Dani." He patted her arm gently.

Dani laughed at his comment. "Likewise, Cosimo. See you soon." Then she walked back into the main marquee.

Cosimo smiled to himself, realising that she'd mistaken the comment he'd made about Jerome for Arsenio. He glanced over to his table and caught Jerome watching Dani walk back to her table. *Oh dear*, he thought, *this was going to end up in tears.*

Dani continued to make small talk with the client's dull wife who had squeezed herself into a peach creation that reminded Dani of curtain material. Her thoughts drifted back to Cosimo's comment about the dress sense of the guests, as she continued to listen to the wife drone on about their holiday arrangements, wishing someone would distract her. The wife stopped suddenly and her eyes looked over Dani's head. Dani turned around to see what had made her table companion stop mid-sentence. There, standing behind her, was a waiter holding a large dinner plate. The whole table stopped what they were doing, intrigued.

"I've been asked to bring you a selection of our dessert menu." The waiter placed a large plate down in front of Dani along with a spoon and fork.

Dani's stomach clenched. She knew exactly who'd sent them. She tried hard to stifle the grin that was forcing itself onto her face, and failed miserably. "Oh, thank you." Dani blushed as the whole table looked on.

Adam took one look at Dani, then turned to the waiter. "Who sent them over?"

"The Ferretti table sent them, sir."

Adam nodded and smirked. The waiter left and Dani stared down at the plate. There was a mille-feuille of vanilla shortbread with strawberries and clotted cream, a glazed raspberry and lemon tart served with mascarpone, a caramelised rhubarb crème brûlée served with ginger snaps, a sticky toffee pudding with butterscotch sauce and vanilla ice cream and a dark chocolate delice with hazelnut cream and crystallised nuts. All in mini portions. They looked divine.

"Well, they obviously know you very well," Adam chuckled. "Dani loves desserts. It's the highlight of her meal," he explained to the rest of the table. The guests at the table laughed as Dani shrugged her apology, still embarrassed.

"Well you don't look like you eat so many," added the peach-dressed wife, in good humour. "I'd get stuck in before the ice cream melts, dear."

Dani looked up and offered them to the rest of the table. To her relief, all of them declined. She picked up her spoon and took a spoonful of the dark chocolate delice and placed it in her mouth. It was delicious. Her eyes looked over to the Ferretti table and caught Jerome staring at her. She mouthed thank you and he winked back, then reluctantly dragged his eyes away from her. Dani's stomach fluttered. He'd sent her over these desserts. The very thought made her whole body tingle.

LUCKY

"I'm a very lucky man," Adam mumbled. Chloe wafted the steaming coffee under his nose.

"Yes, you bloody are," she grinned, sitting down on the bed.

He prised open his eyes and watched her put down the coffee cup, then he lunged at her. She squealed as he pinned her down, throwing the quilt off himself, her petite figure no match for his large frame. Growling, he nuzzled her neck as she squirmed under him.

"How's Ollie," he asked in between kisses.

"His temperature is normal and he seems to have got through the worst," she breathed.

He continued to kiss her across her slightly exposed chest. "Where is he?"

"He's sleeping with Rosie in his bed. I brought in the monitor."

Adam stopped and looked at her. "Is that a good idea? Won't she get it too, now?"

"She hasn't left his side since yesterday. She keeps kissing his throat to make it better. We keep telling her not to but she gets upset. So, I think it's a done deal regardless." Chloe shrugged, resigning herself to the fact that Rosie would probably get laryngitis too.

"Wonderful." Adam shook his head.

"Yep. Let's hope Sophie got away with it. She's kept her distance. How was last night? I didn't hear you come in. I was so tired I zonked out at around twelve thirty."

"We got in around two. It was really good, but I missed you." He released her pinned down arms and held her face gently, then kissed her softly.

She smiled up at him, then they sat up and Chloe got under the covers, snuggling into his firm chest. "Did you?"

"Of course I did. Everyone was asking about you." He hugged her tightly as she looked up at him. "They kept giving Dani weird looks."

"Oh?"

"Yeah. I think they thought she was my mistress or something. I spent all night explaining who she was and why you weren't there," he chuckled.

"Poor Dani. She said she had a good time when I saw her this morning, even if she did feel a little uncomfortable. And she looked gorgeous in that slinky dress. I bet everyone was looking at her," giggled Chloe, knowing Dani would have felt a little awkward at such a swanky event. "I hope she really did have a good time. She's had a rough few weeks."

"Oh, I think she did. She was quite the centre of attention." Adam furrowed his brow as an unwelcome thought came into his head.

Chloe caught his expression and shuffled up to get a better look at him. "What?"

Adam pursed his lips. "The Ferrettis had a table last night."

"As in, her boss?"

"Yeah. Jerome's brother – Arsenio, the lawyer – his firm always has a couple of tables and they were all there. Cosimo and Jerome too."

"All of them?"

Adam nodded slowly. "She ended up dancing with him."

"Well he's a renowned playboy, you said. I'm not surprised to hear he was interested in Dani."

"No, I meant Jerome. She was asked to dance by Arsenio, then Jerome cut in and basically sent him packing. He wasn't happy at all."

"Well didn't he ask her to dance again afterwards?" Chloe sat up and crossed her legs, trying to work out why Adam looked so pensive.

"I didn't mean Arsenio wasn't happy, which incidentally he wasn't. I meant Jerome wasn't happy. Apparently they don't like the staff dating the family because it can get awkward."

Chloe raised her eyebrows and nodded. "I suppose that makes sense. It could get messy if they break up, and he does have an appalling reputation."

"Mm," Adam mused. He turned a little and picked up the coffee Chloe had left on the bedside table and took a welcome sip.

Chloe watched him, realising there was something else about last night that he'd omitted. After being together for over thirteen years, nothing much slipped by her where Adam was concerned. "What is it, Adam? Did anything happen?"

Adam put down his cup and paused for a moment. "I think he likes Dani."

"Well, he'll have to sort that out with Jerome –"

Adam interrupted her, grinning at her continuing misinterpretations. "I mean Jerome. I think *Jerome* likes Dani."

Chloe's eyes widened in surprise. "Jerome? Well everyone likes Dani and she's doing well at the restaurant too –"

"No Chloe, I mean he *really* likes her." Adam gave her a "now do you get what I mean" look.

"Oh." Chloe bit her lip and cringed slightly at her misunderstanding. "He's married though."

"Yeah." Adam took a deep breath and pursed his lips. "That could get a bit awkward."

"He's not the first married man to fall for Dani, Adam. She's sensible." It was true, Dani had never been short of admirers, single or attached, even when she'd been living with Jez she was always being hit on.

"That's not what's worrying me. What worries me is that Dani really likes Jerome too."

Chloe's face dropped. She knew that Adam never made assumptions. When he said something, he was as close as he could be to being one hundred percent sure. "Seriously?"

Adam nodded.

"Fuck!"

"Yeah. They'll be doing that too, soon. It's just a matter of time," he muttered.

"Adam!"

"What? It's obvious. They're with each other every day. I thought he seemed a bit too interested in her when she sold her car and then at your birthday dinner, when he sent her those desserts. But last night confirmed it." They sat for a moment in silence. "He sent her desserts again last night too."

"Are you going to say anything to Dani? Shall I say anything to her?"

"No. It may blow over. He's married and I know that might not stop him, but I think it'll stop Dani."

"Yes. I think you're right."

Adam sighed, hoping for Dani's sake that they were right. "Well, let's not get worried about something that hasn't happened." He looked at the clock. It was ten thirty. He'd taken the morning off, knowing he'd be in no fit state to work after last night.

"Has Dani already left for work?"

Chloe nodded.

"And the kids are asleep?"

"Just dropped off about fifteen minutes ago." Chloe grinned.

"Excellent." He grabbed her gently by the arm and pulled her closer to him. "So I have you all to myself for an hour."

Chloe squirmed as he pinned her back down again on the bed and slowly started kissing her neck.

Jerome blew out the smoke from his cigarette and watched it disappear into the cold morning air. The sun was trying hard to filter its watery rays over the city but was failing miserably. Jerome shivered as he stood on the small balcony of his office, taking a final deep drag, then flicking the cigarette into the river. *He really should stop smoking*, he thought. If Seni, Cosimo and his mother had managed it over the last few years he should at least try. Even Liz had stopped. And what kind of example was he giving to his kids? Who was he kidding? With everything he was going through, he was in no frame of mind to quit. He was permanently on edge, constantly over thinking everything. He opened the balcony door and walked back through into the warmth of his office closing out the icy December wind.

Jerome checked his watch. It was just past nine o'clock. He stepped through to his bathroom and turned on the shower. He stripped out of his gym clothes and stepped under the steady stream of warm water. His thoughts drifted back to last night as he rubbed his thick hair and worked up a lather of shampoo.

He felt bad for Liz. He knew she'd had her heart set on the fashion show, but every time things didn't work out for her, he always got the brunt of it. She had known last night was a big event. Jerome rinsed out the shampoo and vigorously soaped the sweat off his body. He knew why he was feeling unsettled. He couldn't be sure if Liz had used the fashion show's cancellation as an excuse to stay home away from him. Or worse, get in touch with or see Jonathan. However much the evidence showed she wasn't seeing him, Jerome just couldn't trust her. She was behaving erratically. Her mood swings and behaviour were decidedly more bizarre. Liz was hiding something, but he wasn't sure what.

Jerome turned off the water and grabbed a towel. Drying himself off, he shook his head. It had come to this: a permanent state of uncertainty. This wasn't him. This wasn't what he wanted, or how he envisaged his life. Whatever happened, he had to sit with Liz and sort it out, for good. He was in a permanent state of limbo; his sense of duty battling with his feelings of hurt and betrayal. He was using work as his crutch and Dani as a distraction, anything to avoid facing his problems at home.

He quickly dressed, exited his office and passed by Peter's door. He hesitated for a moment, then pushed open the door. The office was empty. He glanced over to the monitors and observed Peter sitting at the bar talking on the phone. His eyes wandered over to the parking area where he watched Dani pull up. Bang on time, nine thirty every morning. He smiled to himself as he thought about last night and then scowled.

He'd overstepped the mark again. He knew he was playing with fire. The trouble was he enjoyed being with her, talking and joking around. She was so easy to be with. He sighed. Who was he kidding? He knew it was more than that, a lot more than that. It was bad enough when they were working together, but last night had been extremely difficult. He had been desperate to spend more time with her, but with Adam being there, it would have been awkward, not to mention Cosimo and Arsenio. He'd kept away from her after their dance but his attention was never far away.

Jerome watched as Dani walked into the kitchen, then back to the restaurant, greeting Peter and then starting her morning ritual of making the coffees for the staff. Jerome watched Peter and Dani chat comfortably with each other. *They'd become familiar with each other*, he noted. Some comment made Dani laugh and Peter grinned. Jerome clenched his teeth together as he continued to observe them.

Who was he kidding? He was crazy about her.

Scott was sitting in his car, patiently waiting for Liz as she kissed her children outside the school gates, then waved them off, watching them run into school. He started up the engine of his car and followed her back to her home, where she parked up in the garage and re-entered her house.

Since Arsenio had asked him to increase his present surveillance, Liz hadn't been to her agent's office. She'd been in London with Jerome all day on Wednesday, and yesterday, she'd been home alone or with Jerome again. He looked at his watch. It had just turned nine. It looked like she wasn't going to see her agent today either.

Scott picked up his phone and dialled his employee Gary, who had started his surveillance on Jonathan.

"Hey, where are you?"

"Outside his house," Gary's gruff voice replied.

"He hasn't left yet?"

"Nope, and I don't think he's going training today either. The last two days he was out by eight."

"Okay, well let me know if he's on the move."

"Sure."

Scott put down his phone and picked up his binoculars. He focused them on the house, scanning over each window to see if he could get a glimpse of Liz. He saw nothing. The familiar sound of Jerome's Maserati coming down the road diverted Scott's attention. He sunk down in his seat to avoid being spotted. It was just ten fifteen. Scott quickly scribbled the time in his notebook. This was unusual. Jerome didn't usually come back until late afternoon.

Scott waited for around fifteen minutes, then saw both Liz and Jerome emerge from the front door of the house. Jerome was rolling a suitcase. He popped open the boot of the car and placed it inside. Once they'd both got into the car, he sped off in the direction of Leeds Bradford Airport.

Within ten minutes, Jerome had pulled up to the drop-off area and was retrieving the suitcase, which Scott now realised was only for Liz. Scott watched on as they discussed something by the car. He was distracted by a call coming through from Gary.

"Gary."

"Boss. He's just left the house with his a large leather holdall. He must be going to one of his clients again."

"Just keep on him."

"Sure, boss."

Scott watched Jerome hug Liz, holding on to her for a few seconds, then kissing her softly. She took the handle of her suitcase from him and then made her way into the airport departures building. Jerome stood and watched her until she disappeared through the sliding doors, giving her a quick wave, then he got into his car and drove off. Scott picked up his phone and dialled Arsenio.

"Hi, Scott, everything okay?"

"Fine. Liz has just been dropped off by Jerome at the airport. Did you know she was going away?"

Arsenio's chair creaked as he leaned back in it. "No. But there was talk of a shoot in Spain. Maybe that's where she's going. What about her calls?"

"She probably had emails with all the details. On the odd occasion she *actually* went to her agent, they probably discussed it then. I'm going in to find out where she's flying to."

"Good, let me know."

"Will do."

Scott hung up, quickly parked up his car and headed inside the departures terminal. He dialled Gary as he walked.

"Which direction is he driving in?" he didn't bother with a greeting.

"Northwest."

"I think he's heading towards the airport."

"You think? It's possible. He just stopped off at a dry cleaners."

"Right. Well, I'm just going inside the terminal."

"You're there already?" Gary clearly confused.

"Liz has just gone in alone."

"Ah, I see." Gary now understood Scott's previous assumption of Jonathan's destination.

Scott hung up and stepped through the sliding doors.

Dani played with her fork as Rosa chatted away about her daughter's parents evening she'd attended on her half day off. Dani nodded and smiled but she just wasn't listening. She stared at the empty chair opposite her. It was fast becoming an addictive habit of hers. Where was he this morning? She'd seen his car when she'd pulled up. Her heart always skipped a beat every time she saw it. Dani lifted her fork to her mouth and chewed on the delicious mushroom risotto Matteo had produced for them today. Even his culinary masterpiece couldn't shake off Dani's disappointment this morning. Dani sighed, deeply realising she was just being ridiculous – it was one dance, for goodness sake! She furrowed her brow as she also realised Gia wasn't in too, which was unusual. It was almost eleven fifteen and even if Gia didn't make it on time, she always came in. Come to think of it, she hadn't been there in the morning either – her car had been missing.

Dani quickly got up and helped clear the table, stacking the dirty dishes into the dumbwaiter, then walked over to the window and looked down into the car park. Jerome's car was missing but Gia's car was back. By now, most of the staff had left the dining room and were heading to the restaurant. Dani loaded the last of the items with Silvanna and then they both made their way out of the door.

Gia was just stepping out of the lift as Dani closed the door. After quickly greeting Gia, Silvanna skipped down the stairs to the kitchen.

"*Buongiorno*, Gia."

"*Buongiorno*, Daniella," answered Gia, her smile weaker than normal. Dani noticed she was wearing one of her stylish coats. *Her wardrobe must be huge*, she thought fleetingly.

"Are you leaving?"

"Er, no, I just came back now. I um..." she pushed open the main door that led to the offices as she spoke.

Dani noted a slight crack in her voice, so she followed her. "Gia, are you alright?" they were in the corridor now and Gia's eyes flitted nervously to Jerome's office.

"I just... well um..." Gia's hand shook as she fumbled with the handle of the door that opened to her office.

"Gia, what's wrong?" Dani asked a little more forcefully, genuinely concerned now. She'd never seen Gia so flustered or on edge. Gia pushed open the door and Dani followed her in uninvited.

"I went this morning... for my mammogram." Gia placed her bag and matching gloves on her desk, her back to Dani.

"Oh, I see."

Gia slipped off her coat and dropped it absent-mindedly on a chair. "They found a small lump." Her voice cracked.

Dani stepped quickly to her and instinctively put her arm around her now hunched shoulders. "Oh, Gia."

Gia let out a soft sob and buried her face in her hands.

"Gia don't, please don't worry. Most of the times it's just nothing. Really."

"I know... the doctor said the same..." She spoke through shuddery breaths. "But it was a shock. You know, you go for these routine tests and you think everything's fine and then... I just wasn't expecting it," she huffed. "I suppose no one ever expects it, do they?"

Dani's arm dropped from around her shoulders to allow Gia to find a tissue in her bag. Dani swallowed hard, thinking back to her mother. It was because she hadn't gone for her routine tests that she'd not survived breast cancer. Dani let out a deep sigh in an attempt to calm herself. "So, I suppose you need to have some more tests? What did the doctor say?"

Gia dapped under her eyes. "Yes, I need to go in for a biopsy, to check it out. The lump, that is."

"Uh-huh. Have you booked it in?" Dani asked softly. Her eyes rested on Gia's forlorn face.

Gia nodded. "I booked it for Monday morning." She lowered herself into her chair and took a deep breath.

"Gia really, I'm sure it's nothing." Dani stepped forward desperate to try and comfort the woman she'd become close to over the last few weeks. Her heart broke seeing this normally confident, charming woman look so worried and distraught. "Shall I make you a coffee? Are you hungry?"

Gia shook her head. "No, really." Her eyes looked up at the antique clock behind her desk. It was almost twelve o'clock. "I could do with a brandy actually." Dani's eyes widened at the comment and Gia smirked. "It's not too early, is it?"

"Oh, I think under the circumstances, you're allowed." Dani grinned.

"I've got some in my apartment." Gia pushed to her feet gracefully. "I'm sorry about earlier. I shouldn't have burdened you with it."

"Don't apologise. I'm glad I was here. Are you alright now?"

Gia nodded. "I'm fine."

The phone on Gia's desk rang, causing them both to jump. They both chuckled and Gia reached over to answer it. "Yes, Peter, Dani's with me."

Dani cringed. She was supposed to be downstairs.

Gia's eyes darted to Dani. "I asked her to show me something, on the computer... well, if you could manage for a little bit without her, we're still not finished." Gia winked at Dani. "I'll send her down as soon as we're done."

Gia replaced the receiver and turned to Dani. "Come on, you can go down in half an hour. If I'm going to start drinking before midday, I'm not doing it alone!"

Gia settled into one of her soft couches, nursing a rather large Armagnac as Dani made them both an espresso. Gia had poured one for Dani and left it on the coffee table. Thankfully, Gia was looking decidedly better. She lifted her glass. "*Salute.*"

Dani picked up the heavy crystal brandy glass and clinked Gia's "*Salute.*"

They both took a sip. Dani wanted to gulp it but knew she'd need her wits about her when she returned to work. "So on Monday? What time is your appointment?" asked Dani.

"Nine fifteen. Apparently it will only take about an hour or so and I'll just be a little sore. It's a core needle biopsy, whatever that is." She waved her hand in the air dismissively. "The doctor tried to explain it to me but at that point I'd switched off," huffed Gia.

"Will you be going with anyone?" Gia shook her head. "You can't go alone, Gia."

"I don't want to tell anyone. I don't want them to worry." Dani knew she meant she didn't want her sons to know. "If it's all clear... or not, I can tell them when I know for sure. Why bother them? They've enough on their plates without worrying about me too."

"I'll come with you if you want."

Gia's eyes widened at her suggestion. "I couldn't possibly ask you to do that." Her voice was soft.

"You didn't. I suggested it."

"I... I don't know what to say, Daniella. I mean..." Gia swallowed, unable to speak anymore.

"Say yes. Really. You shouldn't have to go through that on your own."

Gia smiled at Dani, her eyes filling, overcome with emotion again. This young woman had become quite special to her over the last few weeks. She really was so grateful for her. "Okay, if you're sure."

"I'm sure."

"Where's mama?" Jerome scanned the restaurant as he spoke to Peter who was at the front desk. He checked his watch, it was half past twelve on a Friday and it was very unlike Gia not to be down in the thick of things. The restaurant was already beginning to fill up. Jerome trained his focus on the back, which already had a couple of tables, and was surprised not to see Dani there.

"She's upstairs with Dani," Peter answered.

Jerome's head turned sharply back to Peter. "With Dani? Doing what?"

Peter shrugged. "Computer stuff. Not really sure."

"Oh, I see." Jerome hesitated for a moment, then headed to the back of the restaurant, his curiosity getting the better of him. He started to ascend the staircase, taking the steps two by two. When he reached his mother's office, he found it to be empty. Scowling to himself, he turned back around and headed straight for her apartment. He came to an abrupt halt outside the door and leaned closer. There were mumbled voices, but the two inch solid wood door made it hard to hear who was there and what they were talking about. Jerome opened the door and caught sight of Dani embracing his mother gently.

"Oh, Jerome." Gia smiled at him, pulling away from Dani as he came in closer. His expression betrayed his obvious confusion.

"Mama? Are you alright?" His eyes scanned his mother's face, then flitted to the coffee table where the coffee cups and brandy glasses rested. He then narrowed his eyes at Dani.

"Of course. Dani just quickly showed me something I wasn't sure of." Jerome refocused on his mother as she spoke.

"Well, I'd better go," Dani said gently, suddenly feeling very uncomfortable under Jerome's questioning gaze.

"Tell Chef I'll be down in a bit."

"Sure." Dani stepped around Jerome, avoiding his eyes, which seemed to be trained on her.

"What's going on?" He jerked his head towards the coffee table, once Dani had left.

"I just fancied a drink and Dani kept me company." Gia began to tidy up the cups. "Look, she only took a sip." She huffed at the hardly touched glass. "You didn't need to come up and get her, I was about to send her down," Gia called from the kitchen where she was placing the dirty crockery.

Jerome furrowed his brow at her comment, then realised that his mother had presumed he'd come to get Dani, when he'd actually... *come to think of it, why had he come charging up here?* He rubbed his face. He'd instinctively come to find Dani. There was no logical reason for why he'd single-mindedly rushed up, other than... Jerome swallowed hard. He'd just wanted to see her, needed to see her, was compelled to. Just knowing she was somewhere in the building, he had to find her. Especially after last night. It was as simple and as complicated as that.

"Anyway," continued Gia, coming back into the living room, unaware of Jerome's turmoil, wrapped up in her own thoughts and minor deceptions. "If you give me a moment, we can walk down together. I just need to touch up my make up."

"Sure, Mama. I'll wait." Jerome slumped into the sofa as Gia walked in the direction of her bedroom.

He really needed to keep his emotions in check. After last night, he knew his and Dani's relationship had shifted in a direction that was making him feel he had the right to react impulsively. It'd started with him cutting in on Arsenio last night. And now, what was he thinking as he raced up to where she was? Jerome rubbed his face and sighed. He needed to pull back, for his own good and hers.

Scott skulked by the newsagent's stand, watching Liz wait in line to be checked in. He quickly scribbled down the flight number, destination and time, then watched on. Liz pulled out her phone to call someone, when she was disturbed by a middle-aged woman tapping her shoulder. Liz's face dropped when she saw who it was, then recovering from her initial shock, she smiled brightly at the woman. They obviously knew each other. From what Scott could see, they were on the same flight. The middle aged woman was with a man who also knew Liz. She talked with them until it was her turn to check in. Liz passed over her passport and ticket details to the airport employee and then pulled out her phone again. She quickly dialled a number, her previous smiley face replaced with a scowl.

"Jonathan?"

"Hey, babe, I'm on my way."

"Change of plan."

"*What?*"

"I've just bumped into Joan and Ian White. They're on the same flight."

"The members from Level One?"

"Yes," she hissed.

"Fucking hell!" Jonathan punched his steering wheel, furious.

"Get yourself on the next flight out. I'll ask at the desk when it is and text you the details. I'll call you once I'm in the departure lounge."

"I could still come on the flight and sit away from you," he suggested.

"Jonathan, they know us both. Very well. They'll think it strange we don't acknowledge each other and they're bound to tell Jerome they saw me and you on the same flight. It's too big a risk." The woman behind the desk passed back Liz's passport along with her boarding card. "I have to go. Just give me a few minutes and I'll get back to you."

Jonathan looked in his rear-view mirror, then indicated to the right. He swung his car into a side road and did a U-turn, then drove back towards his home, furiously gripping the steering wheel.

Scott watched Liz disappear through passport control, trying to process what he was seeing, when his phone rang.

"He just double backed on himself." Gary's tone betrayed his confusion.

"Yeah, I thought as much. Their plans just got derailed."

"How?"

Scott described what he'd witnessed, filling in the blanks with what he assumed must have happened.

"So, I presume he'll be getting on the next flight out to Malaga," Scott concluded.

"Probably. We didn't get a shot of them together though, and that's what we needed."

"True, but we got the next best thing."

"What?"

"She called him. She called him from her second phone, so we'll have the number now."

"Yes!"

Scott was sure Gary was punching the air and he grinned to himself.

"Keep a tail on him until I can confirm when he'll be flying out and then I'll speak to Seni, see what he wants us to do now."

"Sure, boss. For a minute there I thought we were barking up the wrong tree. They've been lucky up until now, evading us somehow."

"Yeah, well I think their luck just ran out."

"So what do you two want to do today?"

Jerome flipped another pancake to the delight of both Kara and Alessandro.

"The butterfly house," cried out Kara. She was setting the kitchen table for their breakfast.

Alessandro curled his lip, not entirely happy with her suggestion. "Can't we go to Harewood? They have that big climbing frame."

Jerome cocked his head, looking at Kara, hoping she would change her mind without him having to convince her. Jerome had found the butterfly house fascinating the first two times but after his fifteenth visit it was getting a bit tedious.

"Okay, as long as we look at the birds too," conceded Kara. Alessandro let out a sigh of relief and Jerome gave him a silent high five behind Kara's back.

It was almost ten o'clock by the time they were ready to set off. Jerome had decided that he'd spend at least Saturday with his children, giving

Nina the day off. She'd be back for the evening but this way he was able to spend quality time, just the three of them. He was also trying to avoid being at La Casa. He needed to distance himself from Dani and a day totally absorbed with his children was the best way for him to do that.

"I'll just call Mummy first, to see if she's okay."

The phone rang a couple of times and then he heard his wife's familiar voice.

"Hey, how's it going?"

"It's great!"

Jerome smiled as he heard her enthusiasm and the tightness in his stomach eased with relief. He'd been worried that the location may not have been as luxurious as she'd been expecting. By her tone, it was obvious he could now stop worrying.

"The resort is absolutely fabulous! I'll send you the link so you can see it. It's got a spa and a lovely golf course and the view is incredible. They've put me in a really nice villa too. Well, it's off season, so it's not busy. And we've been lucky with the weather. It's forecasted to be sunny and warm for the duration of the shoot." She was talking so fast Jerome found it hard to keep up.

"I'm so pleased, darling. Here, have a quick word with the children."

Jerome handed down the phone and both Kara and Alessandro spoke briefly to her, then they handed the phone back to Jerome.

"Okay, we'll leave you to get on. I'll call you tomorrow."

Jerome hung up the phone and bundled the children into his car and headed off to Harewood.

Arsenio mulled over his phone call with Scott. So Liz was going to spend at least five days in Spain with the trainer, while his unsuspecting brother stayed home, worked like a dog and made her life as easy as possible. The hiccup at the airport, which had thwarted their plans, was just a minor blip. Gary had seen Jonathan take the evening flight to the same destination.

Scott had finally tracked down the second phone number, so they'd have telephone records as evidence. They now needed a photo or video of the two of them together. Arsenio suggested Scott follow them to Spain, which would have secured those, but even though Scott would've welcomed the extra money and an all-expenses-paid trip to Spain, he wasn't about to take advantage. Scott suggested he ask a contact he had out in Spain to take a trip up to the resort and try and get the shots they needed. It was up to Arsenio to find out the location of the resort.

It was already Sunday, and Liz would be back in four days. Arsenio knew he was going to have to pass by Sky after his dinner tonight and make some excuse as to why he was there. Hopefully, he'd be able to get Jerome to tell him where Liz's exact location was. It was a long shot, but he had to at least try.

So much for a lazy Sunday night in, thought Arsenio as he rubbed his stubbly chin and headed off to get himself ready.

"Hey, are you okay?" Kuch scraped his chair closer to Dani. They'd both sat down to eat something in the private dining room, having worked through Sunday afternoon together. The rest of the staff were setting up for the evening shift.

"Sure, I'm fine. Just tired I guess," she lied. She wasn't fine, but there was no way she could confess why she was feeling so unsettled and down.

After seeing Jerome briefly on Friday in Gia's apartment, he hadn't stayed that day or evening. He hadn't come in all day Saturday and it was Sunday late afternoon and he still hadn't appeared. Dani had a distinct feeling he was avoiding her after the charity evening. But she realised she was probably being totally paranoid. Gia had said he was spending time with his children because Liz was away.

"I hope you're not too tired for Sky tonight." He bumped her shoulder.

Dani grinned at him. "No, I'll be there, don't worry."

"Is Nicole coming?" asked Dani. Nicole had tonight off and Dani wondered if she'd be joining them later. It was also a perfect way to steer the conversation away from her and back on to Kuch.

"Um, yes. I think so." Kuch wound his spaghetti around his fork, avoiding any eye contact.

"Stop the pretence, Kuch. I know."

"Know?" he answered warily.

"About you and Nicole. Didn't she tell you?"

Kuch chewed slowly, deliberately prolonging his answer. Dani shook her head and decided to put him out of his misery. "I worked it out that you and Nicole are seeing each other. She filled me in on the details. Don't worry, your secret's safe with me." Dani grinned at his shocked expression.

Kuch swallowed. "She didn't say anything to me," he answered incredulously. "But I'm glad you know," he huffed.

"Yeah, well, you can use me as a decoy anytime. At least I know it's all for show now." Dani bumped his shoulder.

"It's not easy, you know."

"I can well imagine. But I do think the family would be okay with it. They all love you."

"Yeah, as a member of staff or as a friend. The game changes when they know you're sleeping with their cousin! They're very territorial."

Dani fleetingly remembered her past erratic thoughts of the mafia and *The Godfather*. "You mean, 'They'll make you an offer you can't refuse'?" Dani put on her best Marlon Brando voice and chuckled.

Kuch laughed. "Yeah something like that."

"But you're serious, though. It's not just a bit of fun, is it?"

Kuch shook his head and huffed. "As serious as it gets."

Dani turned herself around to stare at him. "Then what are you waiting for, you idiot?"

"I'm waiting until I know she'll say yes," he sighed.

"You think she'd turn you down?" Dani couldn't hide her disbelief. "She's crazy about you!"

"I don't think she's ready. Not for the whole marriage thing. Me, I was ready from the first week we got together. I just knew. But Nicole has her whole family who are pressurising her to settle down and it's an issue for her."

Dani creased her brow. "She's bloody lucky to have you, Kuch, and if she can't see that, then she needs a kick up the backside. What issues? She's a grown woman, for goodness sake. She makes her own choices. Jeez, she's made her own choice simply by being with you."

"In secret though," interrupted Kuch.

"Yes, but she's still with you. She loves you."

"I know she does. That's why I'm happy to wait until I know she's ready. She's not going anywhere."

"No, she's not."

Arsenio rocked back on one of Jerome's office chairs, waiting for him to finish discussing security with Paul. It had been a while since he'd been to Sky. He scanned the office, which he thought was ridiculously small. His eye caught sight of the notice board behind the desk which had eight photos attached to it. Arsenio stood up and leaned forward to get a closer look.

"So what brings you to Sky at eleven thirty on a Sunday night? Shouldn't you be tucked up in some poor, unassuming, young girl's bed by now? Or has the Arsenio charm finally peaked?" Jerome chuckled.

"Ha, ha, very funny, Jerome. Why do you think I'm here? I'm hoping I'll get lucky. I just left a desperately dull business dinner and need some" – he waved his hand in the air – "light entertainment."

Jerome rolled his eyes.

"Who are these?" Arsenio jerked his head to the photos pinned on the notice board.

"Some unsavoury characters that I don't want in my club. They're connected to some big drug dealer."

Arsenio's eyebrows shot up. "Really?" He leaned closer, taking in their faces. "They don't look like drug dealers."

"I know," agreed Jerome.

Arsenio squinted at them, focusing on one of the pictures. "She's quite good looking." He leaned back again and chuckled. "They look more like... lawyers."

"Yeah, well, you both extort money from your customers. They just sell illegal substances at ridiculous prices; lawyers cover them up, get them off, *then* charge exorbitant fees." Jerome stifled a grin as Arsenio's eyes widened in shock.

"Gee, thanks." Arsenio shook his head.

"Just saying how it is, Seni."

Arsenio shrugged, then retook his seat and Jerome lowered in to his. "Joking aside, are there any problems?"

Jerome twisted his mouth. "Not sure yet, but Paul's on it and thankfully his contacts in the drug squad are being as helpful as they can."

"Good. You've enough to deal with. Speaking of which, I hear Liz is on a job."

Jerome pursed his lips together and nodded, bristling at Arsenio's implied comment. "Yeah, she's in Spain, Andalucía. Some five star hotel spa, golf resort thing. Near Estepona. They're shooting a brochure and advertisement."

"Wow. Well good for her." *Jeez, that went a lot easier than I thought it would*, thought Arsenio. "Well, I'm going to go and mingle. I saw Carmen as I came up."

"Sure. I'll see you in there. I've a couple of things to go over."

Arsenio rose from his chair, picked up his drink and walked back into the club leaving a brooding Jerome.

Once out in the club he made his way out to the terrace, which was reserved for smokers, and pulled out his phone. He quickly dialled Scott's number.

"Seni."

"I got the location. Andalucía. It's a five star golf resort and spa, somewhere near Estepona. There can't be that many there?"

"I'll get right on it. I already sent over their pictures. He's waiting in Malaga for my instructions. As soon as I get something I'll let you know."

"Excellent. Bye."

Arsenio shoved his phone back in his pocket and headed back into Sky.

GOOD FRIENDS

I t was past midnight and Sky was already full of clubbers. The music pulsed through the room, vibrations unhindered by the muggy air, hypnotic lights synchronised to the deejay's chosen beats. The atmosphere was a heady combination, teasing all the senses, intoxicating everyone with the highly charged vibe. Jerome took up his favourite hidden spot, leaning his forearms on the chrome railing along the walkway leading from his office, allowing him to oversee the club.

It was good to be back at work after the two days he'd stayed away from the club. He'd cherished his time with his children, but he was itching to get back into the rush of Sky. He loved the buzz; it gave him a thrill and put him on a high. Here, he could forget his personal problems and immerse himself in work. His eyes scanned the far corners of the club, observing his staff charming the customers, tending to their every need, stroking their inflated egos. All part and parcel of the nightclub business. Gino, his manager, did a first-class job of running the club. The staff they'd hired were smooth, efficient, well groomed and skilled. It was one of the reasons Sky was the top club in the city – that and its unique location.

It didn't take long for Jerome to spot the La Casa staff table. Arsenio was already sitting with them, talking to Carmen and Nicole. Jerome searched the club, allowing his eyes to drift from each of the bars on the many levels, down and across the three dance floors. His heart jolted, unprepared for his reaction to seeing Dani dancing with Kuch. The ultra-violet lights that periodically flashed onto the dance floor illuminated them as they moved provocatively against each other. Jerome stood upright, his whole body tensing under his pristine dark blue suit.

Jerome stared on, his eyes riveted as Kuch's hands pressed on Dani's hips and they moved to the throbbing rhythm. They were both clearly enjoying themselves and Jerome realised that maybe Kuch was more than a little interested in her. He'd definitely upped his game. The idea had Jerome tightly clenching his jaw.

After a few more minutes, Kuch made his way back to the table, leaving Dani to head off to one of the bars. Dani was, thankfully, very easy to spot, wearing a white silk jumpsuit in a sea of predominantly darkly dressed clubbers. He watched her take a drink and then head out to the terrace with Jamie, Silvanna and Franco.

Jerome waited for a minute, then headed towards the terrace, convincing himself he needed a cigarette.

"Any chance we can get our Secret Santa shopping done next week?" whispered Silvanna to Dani.

"Sure, how about Tuesday afternoon, between three and five? I'm not working."

Silvanna dragged on her cigarette. "Cool. Any ideas what to get him?"

"Um, yes, actually..."

Silvanna's eyes widened and she shook her head, indicating Dani should stop talking. Dani furrowed her brow, confused at her sudden change of heart until she heard the familiar raspy voice of Jerome greeting Jamie and Franco.

"Hey boss, where have you been hiding?" Franco joked as he shook Jerome's hand.

Jerome gave a soft laugh. "Nice to know you missed me."

Dani had twisted around to see him and he caught her eye. He nodded at both Silvanna and Dani. "Ladies."

"Hey, Jerome." Silvanna grinned at him, then stubbed out her cigarette. "I'm off inside," she said to Dani, shivering, then stepped towards the door, leaving Dani standing awkwardly by the heater.

The men started talking about some football match that had been on that afternoon, so Dani sat down on one of the nearby couches, not wanting to look out of place. She rolled her glass between her hands nervously, thinking she wished it was something a lot stronger than water. Well, at least she'd managed to see Jerome tonight, even if it was somewhat awkward. Dani was just about to get up when Jerome came from around the couch and stood in front of her.

"Hi." Dani looked up at him, unsure of what else to say.

351

"Hi. Mind if I sit?" he waved at the space next to her.

"Sure. It's all yours." Then she stifled a grin, realising her comment had a double meaning.

"Yes, it is, actually," Jerome joked as he lowered himself onto the couch.

Dani chuckled, glad that the tension had been slightly defused.

"Enjoying yourself?" He looked at her sideways, leaning a little forward.

"Yes, very much. It's nice to get out and I love dancing." Dani instantly blushed, thinking back to the charity dinner, three nights ago.

Jerome licked his lips and smirked, obviously remembering it too. Leaning closer, he lowered his voice. "I know."

Dani laughed softly and shifted a little towards him, allowing herself to get a good look at him. The dark blue suit jacket was tight around his muscular arms and his open-necked, matching shirt revealed a light dusting of chest hair. He was always so well dressed, so well put together.

Jerome took a deep breath, turning himself so that he was almost facing her. "You looked like you were really enjoying the last dance." He jerked his head towards the door leading back into the club.

Dani's face dropped, knowing what he was implying. His eyes fixed on her face. "Yes, um, Kuch. He's a good dancer."

"Mmm." Jerome pulled on his bottom lip with his thumb and forefinger thoughtfully.

"He's just a friend," Dani muttered, looking down at her glass, feeling an unavoidable need to explain.

"Do you dance with all your friends like that?" There was a hint of sarcasm in his tone and the minute he'd asked the question, he'd regretted it. He was behaving like a jealous schoolboy, acting on impulse again. *Jeez, he really needed to think before he opened his mouth.*

Dani looked up sharply at him, her expression clearly stunned. *What? What on earth was it to him with whom she danced with and how? What was his problem?* Dani put down her glass on the table and stood up. *Well screw him, how dare he! What was it to him anyway?*

"Only if they're *good* friends and if they actually bothered to ask me." She tried hard to keep her tone measured, but it was obvious she was on the defensive.

Jerome immediately stood up, his expression betraying how mortified he was that he'd offended her. "I didn't mean –"

Dani waved her hand in front of her, interrupting him. "You don't need to worry, Jerome. Kuch and I are just friends. I know you don't like staff being involved. Believe me, it's the last thing on my mind right now. I'm just getting over a very difficult and sticky relationship and I seriously don't need any more grief right now." Dani glared at him as she stood stock still, squaring up to him.

"I'm sorry, that was uncalled for. I apologise." He smiled almost sheepishly.

Dani narrowed her eyes at him, unsure of what to say. Then she sighed and nodded, appeased by his apology.

"Friends?" he coaxed as he held out his hand for her to shake.

"Friends." Dani took his hand and shook it firmly, allowing a smile to curl over her lips. "Just friends, though," Dani added. Jerome cocked his head to one side, confused. "We're not good friends *yet*, so I won't be dancing with *you* like that." She jerked her head towards the door leading back into the club.

Jerome laughed huskily, delighted by her witty comeback. She really was a breath of fresh air. "I deserved that."

Dani grinned back at him, pleased she'd managed to make him laugh. She pulled her hand out of his, realising she was still holding it, and immediately felt the loss of its warmth.

"But you'll dance with me again, then?" his eyes sparkled mischievously.

Dani twisted her mouth, pretending she was contemplating his question. "Maybe I will, if you bother to ask me."

He laughed louder, causing the wrinkles around his eyes to meet up with the ones around his glorious mouth. "I deserved that too. Still biting I see."

Dani pursed her lips together to stifle her grin and nodded. *Jeez, he was just so damn sexy! How could she be mad at him?* "I'm going back in." Dani wrapped her arms around herself, suddenly feeling the cold air and the need to get away from him.

"Of course." Jerome's eyes softened.

"I might see you tomorrow though?" she added as they walked towards the door.

"Tomorrow?"

"At the Lodge opening? Joseph's hotel?"

Jerome had totally forgotten about the opening. What with Liz having her meltdown and her trip to Spain, it had gone clean out of his head.

"You're going?"

Dani nodded. She reached for the door handle, but Jerome got to it first and pulled it open.

"Well then, I probably will see you there." He looked straight into her eyes, invading her space again, knowing damn well he'd make sure to be there if she was.

"Um, sure I'll see you later, then?"

"*Domani.*"

"*Si domani.*" She grinned.

It was almost one o'clock by the time Dani made her way back to the table. She knew she'd need to leave soon if she was going to be any fit state to be supportive of Gia tomorrow.

Dani felt a hand gently touch her waist and she turned around sharply, only to be confronted by a smirking Arsenio.

"Well hello, you. I didn't realise you were here tonight." He leaned up close to speak into her ear, so that she could hear him over the music.

"Hello, Seni." Dani couldn't hide her surprise. "I was dancing and then went to cool off."

"Well, I have to say my evening just got decidedly more interesting." He took hold of her hand and lifted it to his lips, kissing it softly. "Dance with me?"

"I was just about to leave." Dani felt her face flush.

"It's too early to leave and I know you're not working tomorrow. Come on, it's already past midnight, Cinderella, so dance with me. You owe me anyway."

"Owe you?"

"Yep, Jerome cut me short last time and I'm determined to get my full money's worth." He was still holding her hand, making sure there was no escape. He cocked his head to one side and winked at her.

"Okay, just one, but then I really need to go." Dani relented. She knew he wouldn't let her go and to be honest, she didn't mind his harmless flirting.

"We'll see."

Arsenio could dance. Not just the usual rocking to the rhythm kind of dancing, he actually had moves, serious moves. Kuch knew how to dance but it was fun, light and just him having a good time. With Arsenio, it was definitely more intense, and he took total command. Dani had first hand witnessed his dancing skills at the charity dinner, but that was more sedate and graceful. Tonight his movements were fluid, precise and totally seductive. Dani felt like a helpless marionette in his hands. It wasn't quite dirty dancing but it was as close as you could get to flirty dancing without crossing the line.

By the beginning of the third song, Dani was breathless. She was glad that the music was loud, so she didn't need to speak, and that the lights flashed around them, disguising her flushed appearance. There was enough body language emanating loud and clear from Arsenio for Dani to realise she needed to get away. If Jerome had been rattled at how she danced with Kuch, he'd be positively apoplectic at this display. Fleetingly, she wondered why she should even worry about what he thought. It was Arsenio who'd asked her, so if Jerome had a problem with his brother openly flirting with her, he needed to take it up with him.

"I really need to go, Seni." Dani leaned over so Arsenio could hear her, breathing heavily. *God, she really needed to get some exercise.*

"Really? I can't convince you to stay? It's been a while for me to have such a worthy partner," he drawled, his intent unmistakeable.

"Really. Thank you though, for the dance." Dani pulled away from his grasp, Arsenio's hand drifted over her arm, down to her hand, as she furthered the distance.

"Thank *you*." He winked at her playfully and she shook her head.

"You're a terrible flirt, Seni."

He laughed loudly. "Yeah, I am. But you love it."

Dani huffed at his arrogant but truthful remark but decided not to comment. "Bye, Seni."

"Bye *Bella!*"

Dani chuckled and blew him a kiss. Arsenio immediately clutched his chest as if he'd been shot. "You're killing me," he called after her.

Jerome stood by the bar, gripping onto his drink, his brooding jaw set hard as he clenched his teeth. He'd spotted Dani's white jumpsuit when the ultraviolet lights flashed onto the main dance floor as he walked along the walkway. Once he'd realised who she was dancing with, he descended down to the main bar so that he could get a closer look. A few regular customers came over to talk to him, so he couldn't keep his eyes focused on them the whole time, but he'd seen more than enough. *He was going to have to have another word with Arsenio*, he thought, swallowing back a large gulp of his drink. Throughout all his life, Jerome had never been jealous of either one of his brothers – not of Cosimo's extreme intelligence and his perceptive skills, nor of Arsenio's easy-going nature and patience. That was until just now. The sight of Arsenio and Dani bumping and grinding on the dance floor was something he knew he'd never be able to do. Jerome threw back the rest of his drink, excused himself politely and headed towards the entrance.

Dani said her goodbyes and kissed and hugged everyone, then

headed to the foyer where the lifts would take her to the underground car park where her car was parked.

She rummaged in her bag to find her cloakroom ticket for her jacket and stepped through the door, which was instantly opened by security.

"Leaving already?"

Dani turned to find Jerome standing behind her along with two of the security team. He stepped forward and took the cloakroom ticket from her hand and handed it to the girl behind the desk.

It took Dani a second to recover from the shock of seeing him out in the foyer. She'd never seen him out there before. "Um, yes. I've a lot on tomorrow."

The cloakroom girl handed Dani her biker jacket but Jerome took it, opening it out for her to put on. Jerome pursed his lips together and waited for her to come closer. Dani turned slightly so she could slip in her arms, and Jerome helped her shrug into it, resting his hands on her shoulders for a second.

"I didn't realise you were such good friends with Seni," he said breezily, hoping there were no signs of sarcasm in his tone. He saw her shoulders stiffen at his comment.

She waited a beat and fumbled with the zip before turning around to answer him. "Well, I'm not, actually, but it's your fault I had to dance with him," she answered.

"My fault? How so?" Jerome raised his brow, intrigued by her answer.

"Well, you cut short our last dance together, so Seni figured I owed him one."

Jerome chuckled, placing his hand on the small of her back, guiding her to the lifts. "Ah, I see. A very clever argument from a lawyer." Jerome pressed the call button for the lift. "Well, I think the debt has been well and truly paid off now, don't you?"

The lift doors opened and Dani stepped in. "That's not for me to say really, is it? You'll need take it up with Seni." Dani shot him a questioning look and then the lift doors shut, but not before Jerome's jaw dropped.

Recovering from her quick-witted remark, he snorted to himself and shook his head. *She really enjoyed playing with him, didn't she?* thought Jerome, and boy, did he enjoy being played by her.

The waiting room in the doctor's surgery was thankfully quiet. Gia played with her gloves on her lap nervously. Dani picked up a magazine and mindlessly flicked through the pages, not even seeing or registering the images. They'd been waiting for over ten minutes and Dani could see Gia becoming more and more agitated. In an attempt to keep Gia's mind off her appointment, Dani decided to ask her about the rest of her day.

"Are you going to the opening, Gia?"

"Opening?"

"Joseph's Hotel. It's today from twelve o'clock."

"I don't think I'll feel up to it. And I know Jerome was busy at Level One this morning. I'm not even sure he'll be able to make it either. I have the children's nativity play this afternoon too – well, early evening, actually. I should really go, but I doubt I'll even make that."

"Well, I'll be going to it. Well, both."

"Both?"

"Yes. I'll be going to the Lodge and the school play. My niece and nephew," she added as an explanation.

"Oh yes, I forgot, they go to the same school as Kara and Alessandro." Gia smiled. "They do a great production every year and then a small reception afterwards." Dani grinned at her, pleased she'd been distracted for a moment.

"Mrs Ferretti? The doctor's ready for you."

Gia looked up at the nurse who'd come out to find her. "Right. Um, okay." She stood up from her chair and Dani took her bag and gloves from her.

"I'll look after them for you."

"*Grazie*, Daniella."

"I'll see you in a bit. If you need anything, I'm here. You'll be fine Gia, really," Dani said reassuringly.

Gia nodded and smiled weakly at her, then turned away and followed the nurse into the doctor's surgery.

Dani felt helpless as she sat waiting for Gia. She really wanted to know more. She picked up her phone and scrolled down to Adam's father's surgery number. Quickly dialling the number, she waited to be connected. His receptionist answered after two rings. Dani asked if Doctor Holmes was free and after a few moments, Dani heard the familiar deep voice of Ray.

"Hi, Ray, how are you? I'm sorry to disturb you."

"That's okay, you caught me in between appointments. Is everything alright?"

"Yes, yes, I'm fine. I just wanted to know if you could help me. It's for a

357

friend of mine, actually. She's having a biopsy today. A core biopsy I think, for a small lump they found in her breast."

"Oh, I see."

"I know the doctor will probably tell her everything she needs to know, but I just feel a little helpless."

"Well, it's understandable, under the circumstances." Ray was well aware of the heartache both she and Chloe had suffered when their mother died. "Well, they'll send off the biopsy to the lab and they'll probably have the results in three days."

"Three days! That long?"

"I'm afraid so. You know, it's probably just a cyst or a lump caused by the hardening of tissue."

"Yes, I know."

"When your friend gets her results, I'd be happy to explain them to you. I'm sure it's nothing to worry about. How old is your friend?"

"In her fifties."

"I see. Does she smoke?"

"No."

"What about her family history?"

"I'm not sure."

"Well, I'm sure she's in good hands, Dani. They'll have gone through all this with her. Nine times out of ten it's usually benign. Often it doesn't even need to be removed."

"Thanks, Ray. I hope you're right. Sorry to have bothered you."

"Not at all, I'm happy to help. It's normal to be concerned. But all's well with you though?"

"Yes, I'm fine. You know working hard, getting back on track."

"That's good to hear. I'll be seeing you tonight, at the school, right?"

"Yes. You will. Okay, I'd better let you go. See you later."

"Sure. Bye now."

Dani put down her phone feeling slightly more at ease. She picked up the old magazine she'd been looking at earlier and began to flick through the pages again.

After forty-five minutes, Gia came out of the surgery looking a little peaky. Dani stood up instantly and walked over to her. "Well? Is everything alright?"

"We'll know by Thursday morning. That's when I'll get the results."

"Are you in any pain? Did it hurt?" Dani asked, her true concern winning over patient protocol.

"No, I didn't really feel anything but the doctor said that I'll be sore once the anaesthetic wears off. I need to put cold compresses on it to help and he gave me some painkillers too."

"Come on, let's get you home and comfortable."

Dani helped her put her coat on and passed Gia her gloves and bag.

"Thank you for today, Daniella. You've been a great help and a true friend." Gia squeezed her shoulders and gave her a gentle hug.

"It was nothing really, Gia. You shouldn't go through things like this alone."

Dani drove a subdued Gia back to her home. It was obvious she was lost in her own thoughts and Dani didn't press her anymore. Once they'd reach the apartment Gia told her that she really was fine and that if she needed anything she'd call her. It was more mentally stressful than painful and the wait was going to be the hardest of all. After making her a second espresso, Dani reluctantly left a very grateful Gia and set off back home to get herself ready for the opening.

THE LODGE

"What time are we supposed to be there?" Chloe was changing Rosie on the living room floor as she called out to Dani.

"Anytime after twelve. It's an open house kind of thing. So don't stress," replied Dani from the hallway.

"Well it's just gone twelve now. Shall we get going? Then I can feed Rosie her lunch when we get there and she'll be happy to sit in her pushchair."

"Sure. We could even go to Betty's afterwards." Dani stepped through into the living room.

"Oh, Dani, you look lovely. Where have you been?"

"Uverly," repeated Rosie as she sat up.

"L-l-l-lovely," corrected Chloe.

Dani was wearing her cream polo-necked cashmere jumper over a camel-coloured leather pencil skirt and knee-high boots to match. She'd dressed up purposely from the morning, not knowing what time she'd finish with Gia.

"I had a few errands to run. Thanks." Dani looked down at herself. "Well, I don't get to wear these so much." She shrugged. "What with working in uniform and on my day off, I wear jeans. It's nice to wear something a bit smarter for a change." She dropped her cream coat on to the sofa. "Do you need me to do anything?"

"I'll just quickly change into something less casual. Can't let the side down," grinned Chloe. "Just sit with Rosie. I'll be five minutes tops."

Chloe turned in through the huge iron gates of the Lodge and drove up the wide driveway to the parking area. The Lodge was a large grade II listed residence dating back to the seventeenth century, which was nestled next to a large wooded area. Joseph had bought the fifteen-bedroom house and converted it into a boutique hotel and spa. The original building housed the hotel, which had at present, twelve rooms and four suites. It had been extended at the rear of the house where the spa was situated. The hotel was set in extensive, beautifully kept grounds of over twenty acres and was perfectly secluded from any other residence, as well as from the main road.

"Wow this place is really something." Chloe was suitably impressed as she turned off the engine, glad she'd worn something a bit more glamorous than her usual jeans and sweatshirt.

There were already many cars and Dani spotted a large van from the local TV station. "Well Joseph certainly knows how to throw an opening. It's only one o'clock and there's so many people here. Come on, let's feed Rosie, then we can have a snoop around."

Chloe pulled out a small plastic box with Rosie's lunch in and moved to the back of the car to feed her.

Within fifteen minutes Rosie was sitting comfortably in her pushchair and they had headed up to the rather grand entrance. Thankfully, the sun was out and even though it was mid December, it was unseasonably mild.

The reception area was set out with large tables, which held rows of glasses filled with champagne, along with orange juice and peach juice. Dani picked up two and passed one to Chloe.

"Just this one." Chloe winked, glad that Dani had persuaded her to accompany her. "It's very grand isn't it?"

"Yes. It's really elegant. They've managed to make it modern without detracting from the original style. I bet the rooms are lovely. I'll see if we can have a look."

They walked through to the bar area that had the feel of a gentleman's club, with leather sofas and armchairs and a huge marble fireplace. The ambience, however, was not at all stuffy and the lighting, along with the large windows, made the whole room feel fresh. There were already many guests sat down, so Dani and Chloe made their way through to the restaurant.

Dani loved it the moment she walked through. It had been set up for today's event with a buffet table housing various canapés both hot and cold along the far side, and then tables and chairs were scattered around the luxurious room. There was another huge fireplace and timeless chandeliers hung from the ceiling. The room was warm and classic, in hues of cream and sandstone, but what Dani loved was that the chairs were upholstered in an array of different vibrant jewelled colours, giving the restaurant a modern edge.

"It's gorgeous," whispered Chloe, as they stood taking in the room. Dani nodded in agreement.

"We should check out the spa area. Come on, and then we'll come back in and try some of those." Dani signalled to the canapés. Chloe grinned and accompanied Dani in following a sign, which led them to the spa.

A long glass walkway led to the recently constructed spa. Dani and Chloe entered the warmly lit, marbled reception area. There were four light wooden doors that seemed to lead to different treatment rooms, and an archway off the circular room. Dani spotted Jenny talking to a small group of visitors. She caught her eye and Jenny smiled broadly at her.

"That's the manager of the spa, Jenny," explained Dani. She signalled to Jenny that they were going to look around and Jenny nodded, indicating she'd catch up with them.

Luckily there weren't that many people walking around, so Chloe could manoeuvre the pushchair without much problem. They stepped through an archway and walked along a wide slightly curved corridor, which opened up to an indoor pool.

"Oh wow, this is wonderful," Chloe gasped.

The far wall was all glass, showcasing the woodland area at the rear of the hotel. It effectively felt as though the pool was nestled amongst the trees. There were sumptuous loungers placed around the pool, far enough apart to ensure privacy.

"It is. Come on, let's have a look at the other rooms."

They turned back towards the reception and moved from one treatment room to the next. The decor echoed the tones of the wooded area that were prevalent throughout the spa: rich browns, moss greens and warm rust. Each treatment room boasted an array of therapies, ranging from hot stone massages to mud and clay wraps. There was a steam room and a sauna, both with views of the woods. It truly was stunning.

Chloe took in the view. "This place is amazing."

"I'm glad you like it."

Dani and Chloe swung around to see who had spoken and they were greeted with the friendly face of Joseph Mann. He stepped closer to them as his smile widened, his arm extended.

"Hello, Joseph." Dani took his hand and shook it.

"Hello, and welcome. I'm so glad you made it."

"I said I'd come. This is Chloe my sister, and Rosie my niece."

Joseph turned reluctantly away from Dani and shook Chloe's hand. She immediately began to gush at how lovely his hotel was. Her overenthusiastic comments made his smile broaden and after thanking her, he smoothly steered the conversation to pleasantries. "I believe I know your husband, Adam?"

"That's right."

"Yes, he oversaw the sale of this property. His firm have been our family's lawyers for years. He said he was going to try and come today, but seeing as you're with Dani, I presume he won't be making it."

"Oh, he'll be here later on. I came with Dani because she had no one to come with. I think he's coming with one of the other partners."

"Ah, I see." Her comment seemed to please him.

Joseph gave them more details on the progress of the hotel and when he felt it would be fully up and running. At present, the spa was fully operational and half of the rooms were available. Chloe noted he directed all his comments to Dani and sensed he had a lot more to say. Not wanting to make him feel uncomfortable, she excused herself and arranged to meet Dani in the restaurant after she'd strolled around the grounds with Rosie.

It was just past two by the time Chloe made her way out of the entrance and across the beautifully landscaped gardens. Rosie had become very quiet and Chloe knew if she just walked around a little more, she was sure to fall asleep.

"So, did you manage to see all of the hotel?" Joseph asked Dani as they walked slowly back to the spa reception area.

"Very fleetingly. The bar area is beautifully decorated and the restaurant – well, it's stunning, Joseph. You've done an incredible job here. I don't know what state the place was in before but it's certainly lovely now."

"Thank you. It was in an appalling state when I bought it. I actually made up an album of the before and after photos and the work as it progressed."

"What a great idea."

"I'm thinking of framing the best ones and hanging them in the reception. Would you like to see them? They're in my office, just off reception."

"I wouldn't want to pull you away from your guests."

"It won't take long." He stopped walking and turned to look at her.

Dani didn't want to offend him after he'd taken the time to talk to her, so she smiled and nodded.

"Sure, then. I'd love to see them."

Chloe peeked into the pushchair and saw Rosie was sound asleep. She sighed to herself. Well, at least she would be able to sit and wait for Dani in the gardens. The sun was out and it felt bizarrely warm for December. Chloe found a seating area for smokers that had been purposely set up for today's event and settled into a chair. Within a minute, a waiter came around and took her order for a coffee. Chloe picked up the rather luxurious hotel promotional pack that had been left on the table and began to leaf through it.

"Chloe?"

Chloe's eyes shot up, hearing an unfamiliar voice calling her name. She was met by the mesmerizingly blue eyes of Jerome Ferretti. *Whoa... Sexpot!* Chloe gaped a little, then pulled herself together. *Jeez, how did Dani work alongside that all day? He was gorgeous.* "Jerome! Hello." Chloe managed to pull herself together.

"Hello. I thought it was you. I saw you pushing Rosie around over there." He turned and gestured elegantly with his hand towards the area she'd just walked from.

"Yes. I took her for a walk, so she could take a nap."

Jerome stepped around to look into the pushchair and his eyes softened. He crouched down so he was on the same level.

"She's absolutely beautiful." He smiled softly at Chloe and she wrinkled her nose. "Like her mummy," he added, making Chloe blush.

"Oh that's very kind of you, but I think she looks more like her aunty Dani."

Jerome looked back at Rosie as she peacefully slept, blissfully oblivious. He furrowed his brow, then cocked his head in Chloe's direction. "Like I said, absolutely beautiful." Then he swiftly straightened.

Chloe sat dumbfounded for a moment, feeling the weight of what he'd just said. She thought back to Adam's previous observation after the charity dinner, realising he was one hundred percent right. Jerome stepped away from the pushchair and reached into his inside jacket pocket to pull out a cigarette pack, lost in thought.

"She's here. Dani. She's inside, talking to the owner." Chloe eyed him as he stiffened at her comment.

"Oh?" He had known Dani was going to be here at some point after lunch but he was surprised she was here already.

"Yes, we came together."

Jerome had presumed Chloe had come with Adam. He knew Adam's firm were Joseph's lawyers. His eyes looked over to the entrance of the hotel and then in through the French doors behind Chloe, which lead into the bar. "I see. Have you had a look around?"

"Yes. It's really something. I'm hoping Dani can get us to look at one of the rooms too."

"I'm sure Joseph will be only too happy to show you both." He smiled tightly and Chloe sensed he wasn't entirely pleased with the idea. Jerome opened up his packet of cigarettes and offered one to Chloe.

She shook her head, "I don't smoke."

"Good for you," he sighed. "I really should pack it in."

The waiter appeared with Chloe's coffee and placed it on the table, then asked Jerome if he wanted anything.

"I'll have an espresso please." Jerome closed his cigarette pack and put it back in his jacket, deciding he could do without one. "Do you mind if I sit down?"

"No, please. I hope she won't be too long, I'm famished. We're supposed to be going for at late lunch at Betty's later."

"In Harrogate?"

Chloe nodded, noting that he hadn't actually taken a seat.

"You should help yourself to the canapés in there." Jerome motioned with his head. "You go, if you like. I'll keep an eye on Rosie. I have to wait for my coffee anyway."

"Really? Thanks. Shall I get you something?"

Jerome twisted his mouth as he thought. "Sure, why not. Whatever, surprise me."

Chloe pushed to her feet and laughed softly. *Goodness, he was handsome and just so unbelievably nice.* She quickly made her way back to the restaurant.

"Joseph, they're fabulous. This place is going to do so well. You must be very proud."

Joseph smiled modestly. "Thanks, Dani, you're very sweet. We just need to organise suitable staff when the new year starts. As you well know, the success of a place like this is dependent on recruiting the right employees."

Dani nodded. "Well thanks for showing me the photos, I'd better go and find Chloe. I'm sure Rosie is restless." Dani moved towards the half-opened office door.

"Sure. Um, just one thing Dani. Without putting you on the spot, if you ever weren't happy at La Casa, or wanted a step up, I'd really like to have you on my managerial team."

Dani came to an abrupt stop, then slowly turned to face Joseph. He stood, unable to hide the nervous look on his face, and she was sure it was because Jerome was Joseph's friend and he was effectively trying to poach a member of staff. Joseph was crossing a line, offering her a better position. Dani knew she had to tread carefully. If she blew him off, he might take offence, and he was a customer and friend of Jerome's. If she looked as though she was interested, it could backfire if Jerome found out. The truth was, she wasn't ready for more responsibility. It was a relief not having a whole team relying on her. Dani also couldn't think of leaving La Casa. It had become an extremely important part of her life in a very short space of time and even though Joseph's offer was a great opportunity, she knew it couldn't compare to how it felt working at La Casa. She decided to refuse the offer by being as gracious and polite as possible.

"Wow, um, that's very generous of you, Joseph. I'm flattered that you'd even consider me."

Joseph stepped closer to her. "You forget I've seen you at work. Your ability is wasted on just waitressing, Dani. Don't get me wrong, Jerome knows you're good, more than good. But he has an excellent manager. There's nowhere else for you to go at La Casa."

Dani shifted on her feet, caught between being flattered and uncomfortable. She smiled tightly at him.

"Thank you. It's a great offer –"

"You don't know what I'm offering," interrupted Joseph, smiling softly.

"Be that as it may, I'm very happy at La Casa. It suits my needs."

Joseph narrowed his eyes but said nothing. Dani licked her lips nervously and Joseph adjusted his perfectly knotted tie and smoothed down the waistcoat of his dark suit. "Well, if anything should change, at any time, I hope you'll consider the Lodge and being part of our team."

Dani breathed out slowly and she smiled softly. "I will. Thank you again." Joseph nodded slowly, hoping he hadn't blown his chances of recruiting her in the future. His offer had been a little clumsy, but he needed her to know he was interested in having her on his team, this was probably the only opportunity he'd have. Joseph was also interested in her outside of the realms of employment but that was a far more delicate issue and one that he had to strategize more carefully. It was a good thing he was a patient man.

⸻

"Here you are." Chloe placed a small plate with a selection of canapés on the table for Jerome and an equally laden plate for herself.

"Oh thanks. That's quite a selection," Jerome teased. He was still standing.

"Yeah, well I don't get out much," she chuckled. "My birthday at yours was a welcome exception. Thanks to Dani." Chloe lowered herself into her chair.

Jerome pulled out the adjacent chair and sat down. Chloe realised he'd been waiting for her to sit down before he took his seat. "It's hard, I know. You tend to put your life on hold when you have small children."

Chloe nodded as she popped some prawn dim sum in her mouth. Jerome grinned at her as Chloe closed her eyes, showing her appreciation of the tasty morsel. "Unfortunately, I haven't had much of a support system. We only have Adam's father who's a GP and works very long hours, so it's hard for him to drop everything for us. We always needed to plan well in advance. So Dani's been a godsend."

"Yes, I remember your father-in-law. He came to La Casa one lunchtime."

Chloe eyes widened at his observation.

"How's Ollie?"

"My Ollie?" Chloe asked, confused.

"Yes, Adam said he had laryngitis when I saw him at the dinner. That's why you didn't come, right?"

"Oh, yes. He's very well, thanks, back at school today. Adam mentioned you were at the dinner."

"Yes, we go every year. Your husband's company can throw quite a party. It's a shame you missed it."

Chloe shrugged. "At least Dani had a good time."

"Yes, I think she did," he chuckled. Chloe grinned back at him, picking up another canapé, and popped it in her mouth as Jerome continued. "Dani said your parents died a few years ago and she was down in London up until recently."

Chloe swallowed quickly, a little stunned that he was so well informed. "Uh-huh. It's great having her back."

"I'm sure. We're lucky, my mother's always happy to step in – not that she needs to. We've a nanny, so there's less pressure to be organised," he snorted.

"Your wife, does she work, then?"

"She's restarting her modelling career."

Chloe waited for him to elaborate but Jerome just looked at his now empty coffee cup. It was obvious that the subject was a sensitive one. "Oh wow. So, she'll be travelling, I suppose? That must be hard," she said sympathetically.

"Yes. She's actually in Spain at the moment, shooting a commercial."

Chloe raised her eyebrows, indicating she was impressed. She picked up a mini fruit tart and popped it her mouth and moaned.

"You enjoy your food like Dani," chuckled Jerome. "It's very refreshing." He picked up the same tart off his plate and placed it in his mouth, then gestured that she was right, it was delicious.

"Yes, we Knox girls are a sucker for cake. So your wife won't be at the nativity play today?"

"No, I'll be bringing my mother and maybe Cosimo, my older brother."

Chloe smiled softly at him. He looked troubled as he spoke. His eyes had lost their sparkle and the lines on his face hardened. "He's the accountant, right?"

"Yes, he is."

"It must be nice having a big family."

"On the whole, yes," Jerome chuckled. "Though sometimes they can get a bit overbearing."

Dani walked through the reception area where there seemed to be a lot more people than when she was there only thirty minutes ago. She looked over her shoulder and saw Joseph leaving his office, then he stopped to talk to a group of business men. Dani paced quickly over to the bar and scanned the chairs, looking for Chloe. Not finding her, she delved into her bag to pull out her phone. She'd call her. The hotel was far too large to hunt her down. As she looked up, her eye caught the unmistakeable profile of Jerome. Her heart literally stopped. He was sitting outside, listening intently to whoever was accompanying him. She hadn't expected him to be here. Gia had said he was busy at Level One today.

Dani stepped to the side to see who he was sitting with, the wooden frame of the French doors blocking her view. To her surprise, she saw Chloe talking animatedly, seemingly totally at ease. Dani felt her pulse race. For some inexplicable reason, she felt guilty for being here, almost disloyal. She was also unsure of how he'd react to seeing her after their slightly awkward conversations last night at Sky. He was a hard one to work out. He ran hot and cold with her and he behaved like there was something more to their relationship than there actually was, or rather should be. Well she couldn't avoid him here and she wasn't on duty either. Dani took a deep breath and headed towards where Chloe was sitting.

"Hello."

Jerome instantly stood up. "Hello." Dani stared at him for a moment, not sure of what to say and was thankful when Jerome spoke. "Er... Chloe's been keeping me company."

"Well, I think maybe it's the other way around, actually," Chloe huffed.

Dani turned to Chloe and cringed. "I'm sorry, was I too long?"

"No not all. Jerome's been the perfect gentleman and kept me entertained."

"Let me get you a chair." Jerome turned his back to them and went to a nearby table to bring a chair for Dani. Dani pulled a mock horror face to Chloe, indicating she hadn't expected him to be here. Chloe bit her bottom lip in an attempt stifle her laugh and then mouthed, 'sexpot' and blew air up her face and fanned her face.

"Here you are." Jerome brought the seat over and waited for Dani to sit down.

Chloe got up to her feet. "If you'll excuse me a moment. Shall I get you some canapés on my way back?"

"Um, yes, sure. Thanks." Dani knew her sister well – she was tactfully leaving them to talk.

Once Chloe left, Jerome re-took his seat. "It's impressive, isn't it?"

"Yes. It's really lovely. I didn't think you were coming. Gia said you were busy today."

"Well, I was, but I wanted to show my face. He's a friend and you need to support your friends." He blinked softly at her, wondering if she'd picked up on his choice of words. He didn't want to rile her but he enjoyed their mild sparing.

Dani clenched her jaw and smiled knowingly but chose not to rise to the bait. Maybe he wouldn't be so supportive if he'd known what Joseph had offered her not ten minutes earlier. Jerome called over a waiter, ordering coffee for both of them, without asking her, knowing what she liked. She felt beyond thrilled that he knew.

"So did you come alone?" Dani asked. She felt sure that Chef would have been here too.

"Yes." He reached back into his jacket pocket and pulled out his cigarettes. *Jeez, why was he feeling so nervous? Wasn't she the whole reason why he'd driven out almost twenty miles when he had a mountain of things that needed his attention?* He pulled out a cigarette and tapped it on the box before lighting it. His gaze shifted from his lit cigarette back to Dani. "Liz is in Spain for a shoot until Thursday." He wasn't entirely sure why he felt the need to explain.

"Oh, that's nice." Dani smiled tightly. He'd misunderstood her question. Liz was the furthest thing from her mind, but it was obvious that wasn't the case for Jerome. Her previous good mood was replaced instantly with irritation. Now that he'd mentioned her, it would be rude not to acknowledge her, so Dani continued. "It sounds very glamorous. The life of a model, jetting all over," she rambled nervously as he regarded her. "It must be very exciting, seeing new places, wearing expensive clothes, fashion shows..." *Oh God, shut up!* thought Dani.

Jerome sucked on his teeth and then dragged on his cigarette. "Not really. It looks that way but there's a lot of waiting around and rejection. Jobs get cancelled and rescheduled. It's very unstable."

"Oh?"

"Yeah, only last week a fashion show Liz was up for got shelved. The venue fell through. So, until they find another one..." he shrugged.

"Too bad."

Jerome nodded. "She really wasn't happy," he huffed. He took a deep breath. *Jeez, the last thing he wanted to talk about with Dani was Liz.* He flicked some ash into the ashtray and looked out over the grounds.

"Did you get to look around? Chloe said you were with Joseph." Jerome was desperate to get off the subject of his wife.

The waiter appeared with their coffees and Dani was pleased her attention was pulled away from Jerome. She felt her face heat up at the mention of Joseph. She knew she'd done nothing wrong, but the fact that she'd been offered a position here, and only a few minutes ago, made her feel incredibly disloyal. "He showed me what state the place was like before he refurbished it. It was in a really bad way."

Jerome nodded as he blew out a steady stream of smoke. "Yeah, he's done a great job." He stubbed out his half-smoked cigarette in the ashtray and Dani grinned.

"Still haven't managed to quit?"

Jerome licked his lips and smirked. "I'm thinking about it."

Dani raised her eyebrows. "Well that's a start."

"Yes, I suppose. Ever the optimist." His broody expression was replaced by a smile.

"Oh yes, I'm all about positive thinking. I'm always thinking of things I *should* be doing," chuckled Dani. Jerome's face lit up at her humorous reply and he let out a soft laugh. *Wow, how was it possible that he could look even more gorgeous?*

Jerome shuffled forward a little, leaned his elbows on the table and rested his chin on his clenched hands. "Don't you miss it?" His voice was low as he looked directly at her.

Dani took in a sharp breath, caught in the warmth of his gaze. "Sometimes," she admitted. "But when you know it's bad for you, that it's hurting you... it's better to just cut it out of your life once and for all."

"It can't be easy." His voice became softer as his gaze intensified and Dani's eyes stayed locked on his.

He was doing that thing he did. Talking about one thing but meaning something entirely different. He was looking at her so intimately her thoughts jumbled, flying off in all directions and she was finding it hard to concentrate. "It's not," she managed to squeeze out of her tightening throat. "But as every day goes by, it gets a little easier and you begin to realise that you never really needed it after all. That you deserve better."

Jerome narrowed his beautiful hexagonal eyes and inhaled slowly. "So you'd never go back?" he asked quietly.

Staring into his expressive eyes, she saw a myriad of hidden meanings flash over them. Was he really asking about her relationship with Jez? She just couldn't quite work out what he was implying. Maybe he was just asking her about cigarettes and she was letting her overactive imagination run wild again. But whatever was going on between them had her clearly unnerved and totally excited. She couldn't believe someone she hardly knew could have her emotions racing. One thing for sure, though, if she had such a strong reaction to Jerome, whatever she thought she'd felt for Jez paled in comparison. She took in a breath, then shook her head. "No." *No way would she ever go back to Jez.* In that moment she was sure she'd made the right decision.

Jerome exhaled the breath he'd been holding. "You're a very strong young woman, Dani."

Dani shrugged. *You have no idea!*

EVIDENTLY

"I could really get used to this." Jonathan stretched his arms above his head as he admired Liz from the bed.

"What?" she dropped the towel, having just showered.

"Lazing around, waiting for you to finish work so I can fuck your brains out."

Liz's eyes widened slightly. She let her gaze rake over the perfect naked form that was gracing the king-size bed of their luxurious bedroom. Flicking her long blonde hair over her shoulder, she cocked her hip, striking a pose. "You mean be my boy-toy, my kept man?"

"Yeah, I think I could live with that," he grinned.

She slinked over to the foot of the bed, then leaned down, resting her hands at the bottom of the mattress. "If you play your cards right, you may get to fuck my brains out now."

"And what do I have to do to deserve that?" Jonathan levered up on to his elbows, his attention trained on her naked body.

"Keep talking about being my kept man."

"It turns you on? Knowing I'm waiting around for you?"

"Oh yes. Only me, whenever I want, however I want."

Jonathan licked his lips. *Jeez, he was so whipped.* One look from her and he was putty in her hands or rather he was as hard as stone. He couldn't say no to her. He didn't want to. "You want to be in charge?"

She nodded slowly, crawling up the bed until she had him caged, hovering over him on all fours.

"Babe, you're always in charge of me. Don't you know that? One snap of your fingers and I'm panting like a dog."

She stared deep into his eyes and, without losing the contact, Liz lifted her hand and clicked her fingers. Jonathan growled and grabbed her, twisting her underneath him, pinning down her arms above her head.

"Do you want me?" he asked gruffly.

"Yes."

"How?"

"Hard, fast."

"How long have we got?"

"I need to be down by the pool in forty minutes."

"That's just long enough." And before she could answer him, he thrust hard into her, causing her to cry out. "Tell me if I'm too rough," he gasped.

"I want it rough."

Jonathan groaned as he began his punishing assault on her, marvelling at how this ice-cold maiden melted under him. He'd do anything to keep her. Anything to make sure it was him she wanted, only him.

Sam Whitely drove his car through the entrance of the Finca Cortesin Hotel and parked it in front of the impressive entrance. The valet ran out immediately, helping him retrieve his small overnight bag and camera case. Sam looked around the front grounds and entrance of the luxurious hotel and thought it made a welcome change to the usual places he had to hide out in. He was thankful that the woman Scott had asked him to investigate had expensive taste. He shrugged into his dark linen jacket over his T-shirt, smoothed down the wrinkles and headed to the reception.

He'd booked an overnight stay, on the pretence he was looking for a location for a business conference and team-building weekend. Sam handed over his details and was pleasantly surprised to be upgraded to a suite.

"One of our food and beverage managers will take you on a full tour of the resort, then maybe you'd like to use the spa, or play a round of golf."

"Thank you. Possibly. I'd really like to get a feel for the place. From what I can remember, the hotel is quite extensive."

"Yes, twenty-three thousand square metres of grounds and a six thousand square metre golf course," the receptionist replied, pulling together a promotional pack. "These are a little out of date, I'm afraid. But we should have a new pack ready within the month and our website is also being upgraded. We'd be happy to email you the link as soon as it's completed. You said you were looking to book for the end of May."

"Yes, that's right. Well I'll take these and go to my room. What time is my tour?"

"As soon as you're ready, Mr. Whitely. Just call reception and it'll be organised."

"Thank you." Sam smiled widely at the pretty receptionist and followed the bellboy to his suite.

Once he was alone, he set to work assembling his camera, taking just one of his extra lenses, hoping he'd spot either Liz or Jonathan. He just hoped he'd be able to have some time to snoop around without none of the hotel staff shadowing him.

Jonathan kept up a steady speed, running down along the beach and back up towards the hotel grounds. He'd cool off in one of the pools and watch Liz at work. It gave him a thrill, being able to finally watch her pose and play her role. It made her look untouchable, out of reach and he loved knowing that when she was done, he was the one who got to watch her cool exterior dissolve beneath him.

He powered up the steps that lead to the golf course and started pounding around its parameter. *This place was incredible*, he thought. One day they'd come back here, when she was finally his. He just hoped that all these contracts she was working towards would come through. Once she'd start to be independent, she could get her divorce and the hefty settlement she deserved, so they could start a fresh life together.

Jonathan ran up towards the hotel grounds and spotted where Liz was having her shoot today. They were covering the pool area and then the golf course, from what he remembered. He slowed down and paused by a palm tree to catch his breath, keeping out of her field of vision. He didn't want to distract her, though now watching her laid out on the sun lounger, all he wanted to do was screw her until she collapsed under him, just to show all those assholes who were ogling her that she was his.

Sam lifted his camera and took a few shots of the sea shore and then the elevation up to the golf course. Juan, the employee assigned to Sam for the tour, was very attentive, rattling off all the attributes and trivia about the area and the hotel alike. Sam wasn't listening but he nodded and ummed and ahed whenever he thought it was effective. They jumped back into the golf cart and Juan whisked them up towards the hotel. Sam had his camera permanently positioned to the front of the cart, prepared for anything. His diligence was rewarded when he spotted a familiar dark figure leaned up against a palm tree.

"Do you mind if we stop here for a second? The view here is exceptional."

Juan slowed down to a stop, and Sam zoomed in to focus on who he now knew was Jonathan. He clicked away, then lifted his camera to zero in on to where Jonathan's attention was focused. There were a number of people huddled under a large canopy behind a man who was filming. In front of him was a leggy blonde splayed out on a sun lounger, playing out a role with a waiter. Bingo! Sam clicked his camera and then turned it to recorder mode, focusing on Jonathan and moving it to Liz. Well, it wasn't them rolling around in a bed but it was evidence that they were here together.

"Thank you, Juan. I got what I needed."

The golf cart jerked softly into a steady speed, passing Jonathan and heading to the pool area behind where the shoot was taking place.

"The hotel's upgrading their brochure and website and they're doing the new footage over the next few days," explained Juan as they passed the pool.

Sam nodded politely and turned to face the back, lifting his camera up to take a few more shots of Liz with Jonathan lurking in the background.

It took another hour before Sam finished his tour. Juan left him at reception after wishing him a pleasant afternoon and letting him know he'd be happy to show him anything else and he had only to call reception.

Sam closed the door to his suite and paced over to where he had his laptop set up. Copying all the footage and the photos he'd taken, then immediately emailed them to Scott.

***

Arsenio paced around his office while he waited for Scott. It was just five thirty. He checked his watch again. He hoped he didn't keep him waiting. Arsenio's intercom buzzed.

"Yes, Carl."

"There's a Scott –"

"Send him in," Arsenio replied before Carl could finish.

Scott strode into Arsenio's office with a large file under his arm. "Afternoon, Seni."

"Scott. Is that for me?" Arsenio outstretched his hand and Scott pulled out the thick file from under his arm. "Here, let's use this table, it'll give us more room." Arsenio moved to a large glass conference table set to the left. He impatiently opened the file and started sifting through the photos.

"These here are this week's, that I took, and those there..." Scott loosened a bulldog clip that held together a wad of photos. "Those are from Gary and his surveillance on the trainer."

Arsenio leafed through them, careful not to muddle up their sequence. "They're numbered on the back, so don't worry if you mix them up," Scott added, realising Arsenio was being mindful.

The pictures showed Jonathan going to various people's houses where he spent anything from an hour to an hour and a half personally training. On both Wednesday and Thursday, he was home by ten in the evening. On Friday, where they realised he was going to fly with Liz to Spain, he's left later. He'd stopped off at a dry cleaner's, then after double-backing on himself, he then went to the airport for the evening flight. The photos were a perfect representation of Gary's daily report. Arsenio studied them again hoping to find something, but he just didn't see anything unusual.

"They're yours to keep. Look at them again. Something might jump out at you."

Arsenio nodded still scanning the photos. "Any news from Spain?"

"Actually, yes."

Arsenio turned sharply to look at Scott. "What?"

"Sam, my contact, has found them and sent me some shots of them and video footage. It's not exactly what we wanted but it's what we needed."

"I don't follow."

"It places them in the same hotel, but it doesn't show them together, if you get what I mean."

Arsenio furrowed his brow. "It's enough that they're staying in the same hotel and we have the phone records too."

Scott nodded. "Sure. Its damning evidence, she can't dispute it. What's she going to say? It was a coincidence? He stalked her? I've forwarded them to you but they'll take a while to download."

"Good, thanks. When's Sam leaving?"

"In the morning. He's trying to keep expenses down."

Arsenio nodded. "Well, tell him to try and get them at least sitting eating next to each other. A shot of them together will be the icing on the cake."

"Don't worry, he's on it."

"Good. So get in touch with me tomorrow if anything develops and ask Sam to forward his bill."

"Will do."

They quickly shook hands and Scott exited the office, leaving Arsenio leaning over his conference table, studying the dozens of photos that were strewn across it.

"Nothing like the Nativity plays we used to do, is it?" whispered Chloe to Dani as they sat patiently waiting for the performance to start.

Dani giggled and shook her head. "Well, it's a swanky private school, not a small village comprehensive. I mean look at the stage – it could be the bloody West End! We've even got numbered seats, for goodness sake!"

"Shhh," giggled Chloe.

"Hey, sorry I'm late."

Dani looked up and saw the friendly face of Ray as he squeezed his large frame past the other parents on their row.

Adam lifted his eyebrows. "You just made it." Ray shrugged as a way of an apology and lowered himself into the chair next to Dani as the headmaster started a small speech.

Before long, the play was well underway, to the delight of the audience. Christmas songs were sung with dance routines, making the usual sombre traditional nativity play more modern and infinitely more entertaining. All the junior school participated, even if it was just singing. Ollie was one of the wise men, carrying an impressive gold box, and Sophie made a perfect angel. Her soft blonde curly hair was topped with her obligatory tinsel halo. The whole play took just under an hour, and then there were refreshments set up in the great hall for all the audience so they could wait until professional photographs were taken of the children.

Dani walked with Ray towards the table with the wine set out, purposely avoiding the soft drinks or tea and coffee tables. They'd left behind Adam and Chloe to talk to various parents they knew. Ray picked up two glasses of red wine and passed one to Dani. "It wasn't bad, actually. I remember going to see Adam when he was younger. Half the cast cried through it." He rolled his eyes and chuckled.

"Yeah, well this is the first one I've ever been to, so I've no comparison, but it was all very... um... professional. Cheers." Dani clinked his glass and took a sip.

"Private schooling. You get what you pay for." Ray shrugged as a form of explanation and took a gulp. "How's your friend doing?"

"Friend?"

"The biopsy? Did it go well?"

Dani had almost forgotten about this morning, what with the hotel opening, lunch at Betty's, then racing to get the children ready for the play, it seemed like days ago.

"Yes, thankfully. She wasn't in too much pain but mentally it's wiped her out. She gets her results on Thursday."

Ray smiled softly down at Dani and nodded. "Well, if you or she needs anything, let me know."

"I will, thanks."

Ray looked around trying to see if he could spot Adam and Chloe anywhere. "I was hoping to see the children for a few moments before I got off, but I can't seem to spot Adam anywhere and it's getting late." Ray's eyes narrowed behind his designer glasses, focusing on something – or rather, someone.

"Isn't that your boss over there?"

Dani turned in the direction Ray was looking, but she couldn't see anyone through the large number of parents and visitors. Her heart thumped faster at the thought of seeing Jerome again. "I can't see over all these people. But it probably is. His children come here too."

"No, I meant the hottie. Gia, isn't it?"

Dani's eyes widened and made a silent "oh" with her mouth. "I didn't think she'd be up for it after today..." Dani's voice trailed as she stood up on her tip toes, stretching to see over the mass of people. Ray furrowed his brow for a moment at her comment, then discreetly pointed to where he could see Gia with another man. Through a small gap, Dani spotted Gia sheathed in a figure-hugging understated black dress, which only made her look more stunning, talking with Cosimo.

"Ah yes that's Gia and her eldest son Cosimo," confirmed Dani.

"Well, aren't you going to go over and say hello?" urged Ray, straightening himself and smoothing his perfectly knotted tie.

"Sure, come on," Dani grinned.

They weaved themselves through the sea of people until they were just a few feet away, when Gia spotted Dani.

"Oh Daniella! *Che sopresa!*" and to Dani's, Cosimo's and Ray's surprise she pulled her close and gave her a kiss on both cheeks. "I'm so glad to see you, *tesoro*."

"How are you?" Dani smiled, conveying far more to her than her simple words.

"I'm fine. Better," Gia answered in a low voice.

"Good. Um, you remember Adam's father, don't you Gia?"

"Ah, *si Raymondo*, how are you? It's so very nice to see you again." Gia flashed him her most brilliant smile and Ray stood stunned for a second, positively awestruck by the glamorous Gia. She extended her hand for him to shake and he grasped it.

"I'm very well. It's nice to see you too, Gia. You're looking lovely as always." His eyes swept over her, taking in everything, from her glossy dark hair to her black stilettos.

"*Grazie*, and you're looking very... um, dashing," she beamed. Dani bit the inside of her cheek, desperately trying to stifle a grin. The usually confident and self-possessed Ray had transformed into a flustered blushing adolescent before her very eyes. "Let me introduce you to my son Cosimo," continued an oblivious Gia.

Ray reluctantly dragged his eyes away from the warm gaze of Gia and glanced across at an obviously amused Cosimo.

"Cosimo, this *Raymondo*. He's um, well he's one of Daniella's relatives."

Cosimo held out his hand for Ray to shake. "Pleased to meet you."

"Likewise." They shook hands, then Cosimo turned his attention to Dani.

"Dani, how are you?"

"I'm well, thank you. You?" Dani stepped closer to him which effectively gave Gia and Ray some privacy.

"I'm good. Did you enjoy the show?" His eyes sparkled which made Dani smile.

"Yes, it was very entertaining."

Cosimo leaned forward and lowered his voice. "Both of them?"

Dani creased her brow, unsure of what he meant, until he motioned to Ray and Gia behind her, who were oblivious to anyone around them, talking as if they'd known each other for years.

"Ah yes," Dani chuckled. "I think Ray's a little taken with your mother," she whispered.

"I think my mother's rather taken with *Raymondo*!" he replied.

Dani giggled and Cosimo laughed softly. "So, how are you settling in at La Casa? My mother hasn't stopped talking about you."

"Your mother's lovely. She's made me feel very welcome, and she's trying to teach me Italian. Chef is so nice, he's let me get more involved over the weeks. And Matteo, he's just so sweet to me. He's teaching me Italian too."

Cosimo nodded as she spoke and waited for a moment, thinking Dani was going to elaborate more about the staff, specifically his brother. But he noted that she'd purposely omitted to mention Jerome.

"So, you came to see your niece and nephew?" asked Dani.

"Yes, I try and come to most of their school events."

"It's my first time. I've always been too far away to see them."

"Ah, you're a school event virgin, then?"

Dani giggled at his comment and he chuckled at her. "Yeah, and it was far less painful than I expected."

Cosimo laughed, loving her quick response. He liked her quick wit and could see why his mother was so fond of her and Jerome so enamoured with her.

"Here you are?"

Dani tensed at the sound of Jerome's slightly agitated voice.

"Yes, I was keeping Dani company."

Jerome hadn't realised Dani was with him and for a moment was caught off guard at seeing her so soon again. "Hello, again. I didn't realise you were coming tonight."

"Hi. Yes, it's my first time." Dani shot a glance at Cosimo and he winked at her.

"It wasn't half bad," chipped in Cosimo.

"Um. Yes, they did well." There was an awkward pause, only filled with the chatter of the people around them. Dani looked around nervously and realised that Ray and Gia had left them.

"How's Liz doing?" asked Cosimo, his focus on Jerome.

"Fine," he answered tightly.

"She's happy with her present assignment?"

"Yes." Jerome's answer bordered on the dismissive.

Dani looked into her wine glass, sensing there was something unsaid between the two brothers and that maybe she should leave them to it.

"Any news on the charity fashion show? I know she was excited about that," Cosimo pressed.

Jerome rubbed his forehead and sighed. *There was no way Cosimo was going to let up*, he thought, and he knew he was only asking out of concern. "It's been cancelled."

"Oh no. I'm sorry for her," Cosimo said softly. Jerome shrugged.

"The venue backed out," he added, realising he'd sounded a little too brusque earlier. Cosimo was genuinely interested, but the last thing Jerome wanted was to talk about Liz.

"Where's Mama?" Jerome looked around and Cosimo darted his eyes to Dani in a silent plea for help.

"Um, I think she went to get a drink," Dani offered and Cosimo stifled a grin.

"Actually, I wouldn't mind a drink. Shall I go get you one?" Cosimo offered, stepping past Dani before Jerome could answer.

"Sure, the children will be at least another fifteen minutes." Jerome shrugged and Dani shook her head and lifted her half-full glass of wine.

Cosimo ambled his way towards the refreshments tables, leaving an awkward Dani and a tense Jerome behind him.

In a feeble attempt to make small talk Dani asked, "Which venue was it?"

"Sorry?" Jerome looked down at her confused.

"The fashion show? Where was it supposed to be held?"

"At some hotel, I think. Here in Leeds."

"We used to do fashion shows at the bar. Down in London."

"Really?" Jerome's face softened, his previous agitation forgotten.

"Uh-huh. It was great fun and was always very successful. Especially if there were celebrities involved."

Jerome cocked his head to the side. "You sound as if you miss it."

Dani shook her head from left to right and twisted her mouth. "Sometimes. It's a different buzz, the atmosphere in a bar, compared to a restaurant." She was slightly jostled by someone behind her, causing her to step a little closer to Jerome.

"Yes it is. I love La Casa because it feels, well, it feels like my home." Jerome's eyes lit up and he chuckled.

"Well of course it does." Dani grinned back, picking up the play on words.

"But Sky gives me that excitement. It's like I step into a different world, detached from La Casa. I sometimes feel a little guilty when I'm there, having such a good time," he huffed mildly.

"It's almost as though you're cheating on La Casa," Dani snorted, looking down into her glass again and Jerome's face dropped for a split second. "I suppose it's like a parent having to choose which one is their favourite child." She looked back up at him and her heart lurched at the intense way he was staring at her. "Choosing your favourite... um, business, that is."

Jerome nodded slowly and suddenly, Dani's mouth dried up. She swallowed hard but there was no moisture there at all, so she lifted her glass and took a gulp. Jerome licked his lips and stepped forward, closing the already small gap between them, his sudden close proximity causing Dani to heat up. *Shit, what was going on?* They were in a school, surrounded by hundreds of people, and he was looking at her in a way that made her feel like there wasn't a single person in the room. It felt like the air had been sucked from the huge room, all sound and sense had been removed, vanished, and it was just the two of them. *Say something, for goodness sake, anything,* she pleaded with herself. Her cheeks heated as she stood rigid, spellbound by those magnificent hexagonal eyes, unable to look away as his head seemed to inch closer to her. *Or was it because she was leaning?* Drawn to him. Dani took a deep breath. He was close enough so that she could inhale his distinctive and intoxicating scent and the effects of it did the same thing every time. Her pulse raced, her heart beat sped up and the hair on the back of her head prickled. Then from nowhere, her brain seemed to jolt back to life from its halted state, and an idea burst into her head.

"You could do the fashion show at Sky," she blurted out.

Those eight words shook Jerome out of the unexpected intimate moment and he drew a deep breath, straightening, the spell broken, the moment disappearing. "I'm sorry?"

"You could hold the cancelled fashion show at Sky."

"Oh, I see." His brow creased, still reeling at the hasty change of atmosphere, from intimate and warm to decidedly cooler and serious.

"It's certainly big enough and has the right high profile. You could do it on a Monday when it's normally closed. Early." Yes that's it, focus on work, thought Dani. "January. Yes, January's a good time to do it, when trade slackens off, and it would also give you time to organise it."

She rambled on, hardly taking a breath. Jerome regarded her with a mixture of awe and puzzlement. Not a few seconds before, he was seriously contemplating kissing her in the great hall of his children's school. He had an inexplicable compulsion to do so. As though her presence was a powerful magnet, pulling him towards her, drawing him into her magnetic field. And he was totally powerless. He realised she'd felt it, picked up on the shift of chemistry and defused it before it was too late, before they crossed more boundaries.

"It would be excellent publicity for Sky. Not that you need it," Dani continued, on a roll now, her adrenalin pumping through her, after the highly-charged atmosphere only a few moments earlier. She had no idea what had just happened or what Jerome was thinking, but as she allowed herself to glimpse up at him, she noted his eyes had flattened. Part of her was devastated that she'd purposely pushed him away with talk of business. The other part of her wanted nothing more than to let the obvious chemistry explode between them. *Self-preservation*, she reminded herself, mentally patting herself on her back.

"The press would be all over you for doing a charity fashion show. And you could promote Level One too. Use the salon." She finally took a pause.

Jerome took a deep breath and smiled softly down at her beautiful, expectant face. "That's really not a bad idea."

Dani's large brown eyes lit up as she beamed up at him. It took Jerome every ounce of willpower not to bend down and kiss her hard, until she couldn't breathe. Everything about her fascinated him: her wit, her enthusiasm, her kindness. She had the ability to make him forget everything that worried him and see only light – brilliant, vibrant light that seemed to shine from within her.

"Really?"

"Really."

"And it would mean Liz would get to do her fashion show after all," added Dani.

There it was: the slap to the face. The wakeup call. The not-so-subtle reminder from Dani that he was married. Jerome clenched his jaw. *What was he doing? What on earth did he think was going to happen?* He was married and Dani wasn't the kind of girl that went after married men. If she was, Jerome knew he wouldn't be interested in her. He smiled tightly at her.

"Yes, it would..." Before he could thank her, Jerome's eye caught his mother approaching them with, if he wasn't mistaken, Adam's father. His eyebrows rose in surprise, witnessing Gia in full flirt mode and from what Jerome could tell, Ray was blissfully lapping it up.

"Is that Adam's father?" he asked. Dani turned around in the direction in which Jerome was looking.

"Er, yes."

Gia beamed over to Jerome as she saw him. "Ah, there you are."

"Hello, Jerome." Ray put out his hand for Jerome to shake.

"Hello, Dr Holmes."

"Ray, please," corrected Ray. "I was just bringing back your mother." Ray turned to Dani. "Adam and Chloe are waiting by the car. They asked me to come and get you."

"Oh, okay. We'd better go, then." Dani turned back to Jerome to say goodbye. "See you tomorrow."

He smiled warmly at her, "*Domani.*"

"*Domani,*" Dani repeated softly and then reluctantly turned to Gia to hug her. Ray nodded a curt goodbye to Jerome and then turned his full attention to Gia.

"So, I'll be hopefully seeing you soon?"

"*Si,* I'm looking forward to it," she smiled coyly.

"Goodbye, then."

"*Arrivederci, Raymondo.*"

Ray and Dani unwillingly left Gia and Jerome to head back to the car park.

"You seemed to be quite friendly with Gia," Dani commented as they walked through the school's corridors that lead out to the car park.

Ray beamed. "She really is something. I could listen to her talk all day."

"Evidently," Dani said wryly. "So it's the accent, then? Not the fact that she's absolutely gorgeous?" Dani snorted.

"Oh no, that as well," he laughed. "They're all a bloody good looking lot. I can't believe Gia has three sons over thirty."

"Yes, I know. They're all really nice and charming in their own way. But I only really know Jerome, because we work together," added Dani.

Ray slowed down his pace when they reached the door and looked at Dani. Arching his brow, he countered, "Evidently," causing Dani to blush. She stepped through the open door and walked quickly to where she could see Chloe and Adam by their car.

The children were already buckled up in the car and Ray leaned in to congratulate them on their performance. Rosie was almost falling asleep, but perked up once she saw her grandfather. Ray said his goodbyes to Chloe and Adam, then turned to Dani.

"It was nice seeing you, Dani. I'll be in the restaurant on Thursday."

"Oh?"

"Yes, I'll be booking a lunch at La Casa for my senior and junior partners."

"Oh, okay, then. See you then." Dani stretched up and gave Ray a peck on the cheek. "Goodbye, Ray."

"*Arrivederci,* Dani." Ray winked at her and Adam snorted.

"Steady on there, *Raymondo!*" he chuckled and slipped into the driver seat.

Sam Whitely contemplated his next move. Scott had been pleased with the photos and footage, but Sam wanted to get something more conclusive. He'd been in this business for five years now and had always managed to get his clients what they needed. But he never missed an opportunity to get that something extra, go that bit further. He enjoyed the challenge. Sam knew he was at a disadvantage here in this luxurious setting. There weren't enough people to hide himself amongst, so it was important to blend in and not stick out.

Sam sat in the grand dining room of the main hotel and forked around his delicious red snapper. There were roughly twenty guests in the restaurant and no sign of Liz and Jonathan. They were obviously holed up in their room. He took a long drink from his beer. There were really very few options. It was still early, so he hoped he'd get lucky again and spot them in the grounds, but he'd be on foot and the grounds were so extensive without a golf cart and a guide, he wouldn't be able to cover the area. Sam quickly finished his meal and gathered up his camera. Well, if he had to have a guide with him, so be it, he could use him for his cover.

The hotel lobby was quiet and the receptionist at the desk was different from the one in the morning. It didn't seem to matter – she was equally well informed as to who Sam was. He asked if there was any way he could see the grounds again, his excuse being that he wanted to photograph the hotel at nightfall. The receptionist attempted to track a suitable employee who could take Sam around, but because it was the time when the shifts changed, it was proving difficult. Then she came up with an idea.

"We've Segways, if you don't mind going around on your own. I can arrange for the valet to bring you one."

"That would be perfect."

Armed with a map of the hotel, Sam set off around the grounds, his eyes scanning every area as he sped along the various pathways. There was nothing – the whole area was quiet and the few guests staying were either in the restaurant or by the bar. Sam stopped at one of the pools further away from the hotel and looked up at the rooms that seemed occupied. *They could be anywhere*, he thought. He lifted his camera and zoomed in, moving from one room to the next in the hope he'd get lucky again. It was dark now and he knew any window of opportunity he had was diminishing. He lowered his camera, feeling frustrated. Well, he'd tried at least. He slipped his camera over his shoulder and began to set off towards the bar. *He may as well enjoy his evening*, he thought to himself.

Sam looked back at the hotel and noticed a golf cart idling, waiting by the restaurant. He then observed a waiter load up the back of the cart with what looked like one of those special thermal transporters for food. The waiter slipped into the cart and the driver headed down towards where the private villas were situated.

Room service! thought Sam. He turned his Segway and followed in the direction of the golf cart. He came across the golf cart parked outside a small building situated at the entrance of the villa complex. The waiter was obviously inside and Sam wasn't exactly sure what he was doing, until he emerged with a heated trolley and started to load the food onto it. The building was obviously a service station for the villas. Sam waited patiently to see in which direction the waiter wheeled the laden trolley, then moved into an unlit area until he returned. Within a few minutes, the waiter returned and the golf cart sped back to the hotel, allowing Sam to set off in the direction he'd seen the waiter come from.

It wasn't hard to find Liz and Jonathan's villa – it was the only one occupied. The whole villa was well lit, but the private garden and pool were at the rear. Sam parked up the Segway and walked around to the neighbouring empty villa. He was hoping he'd be able to see them from the back.

To the hotel's credit, the villas were as private as they could possibly be, with the gardens not overlooking each other. Unfortunately, this made it difficult for Sam to get a good view. They were separated by a hibiscus hedging and the only way Sam would be able to get a good shot would be to push his camera though the hedge, wedging it into place. After the third attempt, he managed to get the right angle. He could just about see them on the screen. They were eating their dinner inside, by the patio doors that lead out to the private pool. Sam took a few shots of them, hoping the lighting was enough. He then waited and watched to see if they would venture out. It was past eight o'clock already and if he was going to get the damning evidence he wanted, he knew he'd be here for a while. Looking around, Sam grabbed a chair from the patio of the villa he'd come through and positioned it next to the hedging and sat down.

It was almost nine by the time they'd finished dinner. He watched Liz leave from the table and move outside to the patio. She quickly dialled a number on her phone and started to talk to whoever it was. Sam couldn't hear any of the conversation but he caught her laughing and he snapped a few more photos of her. Liz dipped her toe into the pool and gently splashed the water. She was only wearing a short silk robe, tied loosely.

Jonathan then came out to join her, placing two glasses of wine on the table. He sat down on one of the rattan chairs and watched her as she spoke. His knees were bouncing while he sat, indicating he wasn't comfortable listening to the conversation, but it was obvious he wanted to hear it. Sam clicked away, not wanting to miss any possible shot.

Liz ended the call and placed the phone on the table, then picked up her glass and took a sip. Jonathan spoke to her and she answered him with a dismissive flick of her hand, which only seemed to agitate him more. He said something back and Liz cocked her head to one side, as though she was questioning his comment. She picked up the second glass of wine and sidled over to Jonathan, handing it to him. He took it and Liz knelt down in front of him between his legs, resting her elbow on his jumping knee. She was obviously trying to pacify him. Sam continued to take shots hoping that at least he'd get them kissing.

After a minute or so, Liz managed to get Jonathan to smile and she drained her wine, leaving the glass on the table, Jonathan leaned down and slipped his hand around the back of her head and pulled her to him for a fierce kiss. *Bingo!* Sam had his camera on shutter speed, capturing everything, then he switched it to record mode. Jonathan went to get up from the chair as he continued to kiss Liz, but to Jonathan's surprise, she pushed him back down. Liz reached for the button of his shorts and popped it open, then slowly unzipped his trousers.

Holy fuck! thought Sam, *she was going to go down on him out here, on the patio!* Sam tried to concentrate as he watched the scene unfold. It wasn't long before Jonathan was writhing in the chair, and Liz serviced him with obvious enthusiasm. His climax came fast and the look of pure female satisfaction on Liz's face gave no doubt as to what he meant to her. Jonathan wasted no time. He got up from the chair and stripped out of his shorts, lifting Liz onto a waiting sun lounger. He pulled away the tie to her robe, yanked the garment away and proceeded to reciprocate with his own ardent oral ministrations.

Sam sat back from the camera, suddenly feeling uncomfortable and a little dirty. He'd got what he wanted. There was really no need for him to watch or record anymore. The evidence was as damning as he could have wished for. He switched off the camera, slung it over his shoulder and headed back to where his Segway was parked. It was times like this he questioned his occupation choice. He'd got the result he'd wanted, but at some point, this evidence was going to be shown to her husband. Sam was grateful he wouldn't be the one who'd be showing him.

31

UNEXPECTED

G raham looked down at his phone as it vibrated on his desk, and scowled. *Jeez, he really didn't feel like getting another interrogation from Jerome, especially first thing in the morning.* He picked up his phone and pressed the answer key.

"Good morning, Jerome, how are you?"

"I'm well, thank you. You?"

"I'm good. What can I do for you?"

"It's about the fashion show –"

"Look, Jerome, I really can't tell you anymore than I already have –"

"That's not why I'm calling. I was wondering if you were in direct contact with the organisers. I was going to suggest they use Sky for the venue."

"Oh, I see. Er, well... that's actually quite a good idea," Graham stuttered, thrown off guard by the unexpected suggestion.

"Yes, I thought so too. Do you think you could get in touch with them and I can have my team at Sky set up a meeting – if they agree, that is?"

"Sure, I'll see what I can do. Thank you."

"I'm happy to help, Graham, though I have to admit it wasn't my idea. One of my staff members came up with it. I just hope the organisers go for it, for Liz's sake."

"Me too. We've all put a lot of hard work into this fashion show and it really was disappointing for all of us when it got cancelled."

"So, I'll wait to hear from you, then? I haven't mentioned it to Liz, simply because I didn't want to build up her hopes."

"Wise move. I'll keep quiet until we have some solid news."

After saying their goodbyes, Jerome headed into his bathroom to shower off after his workout. Dressing quickly, he exited his office, feeling a lot calmer. He'd noticed that in the last few days his mood had most definitely been more upbeat and at some times, even relaxed. It had been a while for him to feel like that. He'd spent most of the weekend at home with his children and yesterday had been hectic, catching up with work and fitting in the Lodge and the school play. But he hadn't felt under pressure or the usual tension that had been shrouding over him of late. He paused outside his mother's office, seeing the door was slightly ajar, and he popped his head around the door.

Gia was sitting at her desk working on her computer. Jerome's eyebrows rose in surprise. "*Buongiorno,* Mama."

"*Buongiorno.*"

"You're down early. What are you working on?" Jerome stepped closer to her.

"I'm trying out this program for the seating plans and reservations. I think I'm getting the hang of it now."

"That's great."

"Mmm." Gia clicked on to her mouse and moved it around. "It would seem that I obviously needed a better teacher." She arched her brow at Jerome and he grinned. "Speaking of which, have you organised the flat yet?"

Jerome shifted awkwardly and sighed. "No, I haven't. I've just been too busy, what with Liz away and –"

"Fine. I'll do it, then. Give me the numbers of the decorators and the maintenance company." She interrupted him and beckoned with her hand.

"No, I'll do it. In fact I'll go and organise it now."

"Good, because I bet they won't be able to finish before Christmas and it'll be the new year before we can offer Dani the flat." She shooed him out. "Go on." Jerome nodded and paced towards the door. "Oh, and it's Rico's birthday today, so try and make it for lunch," she added, her eyes back to focusing on the computer screen.

"Of course."

Jerome walked back to his office and sat down at his desk. There was no way around it, now that his mother had forged a close relationship with Dani, he couldn't purposely avoid organising the flat anymore. She'd just badger him about it or demand to take over. Well, he'd just have to bite the bullet and get on with it.

"You remember that the limit is twenty-five pounds, don't you?" Silvanna reminded Dani as they stepped in through the doors of Reiss. Dani walked through the smart shop, heading towards the men's department.

"I remembered," Dani answered. They'd headed into Leeds on their afternoon break to buy Jerome's Secret Santa gift as Dani had promised. "Here, look at these." Dani indicated to a display of pocket squares in an array of colours and designs.

"A hanky?"

"No, they're pocket squares. See? Look at the mannequin. Jerome often wears them."

Silvanna looked to where Dani was pointing. "Oh, right," she nodded. "Okay, then, which one do you think?"

"I think this one." Dani pulled out a silk woven pocket square that was predominantly blue with black detail. "It will go with his dark blue suit and the black. He can also pair it with his dark brown one if he wears that dark blue tie, you know the one that's knitted." She smoothed over the fabric with her fingers. "And it's on sale."

Silvanna's eyebrows shot up, clearly surprised at how much thought Dani had put into her choice. "Sure, whatever you say. That was easy. Thanks."

Dani shrugged and led Silvanna to the cash desk.

Jonathan stretched over to Liz's side of the bed and searched for her with his hand. All he could feel were cool sheets. He levered up on his elbows and looked around their room for her. It was empty. A gentle splashing sound alerted him to the patio. He slipped on his underwear and headed over to the French doors, yawning. The sun was just coming up, its watery light illuminating the garden and private pool.

Liz was powerfully swimming around the edge of the pool, oblivious to the fact that she had company. Jonathan furrowed his brow and lowered himself into the rattan chair, waiting for her to slow down and stop. She was behaving erratically. Hardly sleeping and eating very little. *It was time for her to stop those tablets*, Jonathan thought to himself. He kicked himself for getting them in the first place. The problem was, he knew Liz could get hold of them without him. At least this way he was aware of how many she was taking and the quality of them.

It took Liz a good ten minutes to realise Jonathan was watching her. She slowed down and came to the edge.

"Couldn't sleep?" Jonathan tried to hide the concern in his voice.

"I just needed to burn off some energy." Liz pulled herself out of the water and stood a few feet away from him. His eyes travelled over her naked wet body. The shadows under her pale blue eyes and the accentuated protruding of her hip bone were the only things that marred her perfect form. Jonathan reached out his hand to her. "I'm wet."

"That's just how I like you." He winked at her and she smiled, taking his hand. He gently pulled her onto his lap and kissed her fiercely. No one saw this side of her, the vulnerable side. The side that thought she wasn't good enough, pretty enough, sexy enough. She put up an icy barrier and shut people out, but Jonathan knew better. The young, working class girl from Birmingham had made good, but it was never enough for her. She wanted everything her abandoned mother could never provide for her, always struggling to make ends meet, everything she'd dreamed of, and Jerome had provided her with that. But it was still not enough. Liz wanted to be adored, to be put first; she was selfish and self-centred and Jonathan didn't mind one bit. He was happy to fulfil that role because he did adore her and would do anything to keep her happy. He wanted to protect and take care of her, something she craved so badly. She needed to be the centre of someone's world and to Jonathan that was exactly what she was.

"Liz, I think it's time to stop the pills. You're too agitated and you're losing too much weight."

Liz tensed. "I said I'd stop once I got the I-Gea contract."

"I know you did, but you look tired and –"

"I said I'd stop, Jonathan. It's just a few more days."

"Exactly. It won't matter, if it's just a few more days."

Liz pulled away from him and stood up but Jonathan held onto her slim hips. "If I stop, I'll crash hard and I can't do that while I'm working. As soon as we wrap up here, I'll stop."

"Promise?" Jonathan knew she was right, but that didn't mean he was happy about it.

"I promise. Anyway I've some relaxants that I can take to sleep. I don't need to be up for the shoot until twelve, so I've roughly five hours."

Jonathan furrowed his brow. He'd seen too many women become addicted to stimulants and then downers, and the end result meant they headed on a dangerous, downward-spiralling path. He'd dabbled in the odd recreational drug and used steroids, but he was always in control, and he'd never let them take over. Liz's behaviour worried him. He was going to have to wean her off slowly.

"Don't take anything else, Liz. If you need to relax, then you come to me. I'll massage you, make love to you, we can have a drink, but don't take anything else. Trust me, you don't want to get into that cycle."

Liz stepped closer to him, her eyes blinked slowly. "I could do with a massage," she breathed. "All that swimming has made my muscles tense."

Jonathan's lips curled in to smile. "Just a massage, then?"

Liz shook her head slowly and Jonathan's grip on her hips tightened. She ran her hand around the back of Jonathan's head and pulled him closer, his hot breath gusting over her bare lower abdomen, causing goose bumps to appear over her damp skin.

"I need you. I need you to relax me. You're the only one who knows what I need, what I want and how I want it."

Jonathan groaned. In one swift move he was on his feet and lifting her, striding back through the French doors and into the villa. He was going to wear her out until she collapsed. One way or another, she was going to sleep.

"Scott. I hope you've got some good news." Arsenio lowered himself into his chair after shaking Scott's hand. Arsenio had been waiting all day for his visit but his work schedule had meant that the earliest he could see Scott was late on Wednesday.

Scott handed Arsenio a USB stick. "It arrived by courier this morning. When you see what's on it, you'll be pleased that Sam didn't email it to you. You can never be too careful."

"Is it what we needed? The icing on the cake?"

Scott huffed. "It's more like the cherry on top of the icing, with sparklers all around it."

Arsenio's eyebrows rose at the comment.

"I'd rather not be here when you watch it. So if there's nothing else, I'll leave you to it."

"That bad?"

"Let's just say it's more than we ever expected. I know Jerome, even if it is only through past work, and seeing what his wife's up to doesn't sit well with me. Just let me know what to do from now on."

"Right. Well, I think we should keep up the surveillance. We need to have their fuck-pad confirmed. Then, once we have that, I think your work is done."

"Right. They're back tomorrow, so I'll get Gary to carry on from Friday."

"Good. Thanks for this." Arsenio held up the small USB stick.

Scott snorted, "You may not thank me once you've seen it."

Jerome rubbed his eyes with his finger and thumb, slumping in his office chair. He felt exhausted. There were only so many hours in a day and he needed double. Between checking in on Level One, organising work to start on the apartment and the speedy meeting with the event organisers of the fashion show, that by some miracle Graham had managed to arrange, he was wiped out. He had to admit Graham had done good, efficiently setting up the impromptu meeting, as well as playing a major part in convincing the organisers to look at Sky. Jerome knew the minute they saw the place they'd be interested. He looked at the time on his computer. It was almost eight. He hadn't needed to come back to La Casa, but Joseph had called wanting to go over his parents anniversary party. Peter and his mother were more than capable of dealing with it, but after he'd promised to oversee everything, he felt he should at least be there for the first meeting.

It also meant he'd see Dani.

Jerome knew he could have avoided coming in tonight and spent a few hours relaxing at home before his meeting at Sky, but he was behaving like a lovesick adolescent, stealing any few moments to see her. Sighing to himself, he rose from his chair and headed downstairs to the ever-busy restaurant dialling his home on his phone.

"Hey Nina, are they asleep?" He'd managed to cook for and bathe both of his children before coming out, but hadn't been there to put them to bed.

"Kara crashed pretty much after you left. Alessandro is still watching a DVD."

"Put him on, will you?"

There was a slight muffled sound and then Jerome heard his son's voice. "Dad?"

"Hey, you're still awake?"

"Yeah, just watching the end of *Ice Age*," Alessandro yawned.

"Okay. But get to bed after, yeah?"

"Sure, Dad. Will you make pancakes for breakfast tomorrow?"

"You want pancakes?" Jerome smiled to himself. Over the last five days, his children had had his full and undivided attention and Alessandro was making sure he got as much time as he could squeeze in before Liz was back. Jerome tended to take a back seat when Liz was home, but the last few days had made him realise that needed to change.

"Uh-huh," answered a sleepy Alessandro.

"Then pancakes it is. I'll wake you up early so you can help."

"Cool."

"See you in the morning. *Buonanotte.*"

"*Buonanotte,* Dad."

Jerome found La Casa almost full. It would be like this every night, well into the beginning of next year. The holiday season was always busy and Jerome thrived off it. He scanned the restaurant, noting where every member of staff was and which customers he needed to speak to before Joseph's scheduled visit at eight thirty. Adjusting his immaculate tie, he smoothly started his rounds.

Joseph took a sip of his wine, looking around at the restaurant. He'd gone through the menu for his parent's anniversary party, choosing a buffet rather than a set meal, and had selected the wines and drinks. He was sitting with Jerome in the main part of the restaurant in a more private booth, sampling a few dishes that Jerome had suggested.

"I'll also need to decorate the room."

"Of course, whatever you want. Any ideas?" Jerome shuffled the menus and his notes together and placed them in a file. "My mother usually deals with that, it's her department. I'll get her to come over." Jerome caught Gia's attention and she came over to their table.

"Joseph needs some decorating ideas for the party," Jerome explained.

"It's their fortieth, correct?" Gia confirmed.

"Yes, something elegant," Joseph mulled, his eyes wandering around the restaurant again.

Gia slipped into the seat next to Jerome, glad to sit down for a moment.

"You did an incredible job with the Christmas decorations, Gia."

Gia smiled. "Thank you, but it wasn't me who did them. It was Dani."

Joseph's eyes zeroed in on Dani, who was working in her usual position at the rear of the restaurant, then shifted forward in his chair. Gia felt Jerome tense suddenly.

"Really? Well do you think she could be recruited for my party? I'll pay her extra."

"I think we can arrange something. She's very talented. I'll talk to her about it and then maybe we could set up a meeting one morning or in the afternoon. Whatever suits you," suggested Gia. Jerome seemed overly interested in the file he was holding.

"How about tomorrow? Say three thirty?" Joseph answered eagerly as he scrolled quickly through his phone, checking if there was anything he needed to reschedule. There was no way he was going to miss this unexpected opportunity of sitting down for a one-to-one meeting with Dani.

"I won't be able to be here," muttered Jerome, looking up from the file. The prospect of Dani and Joseph working closely together, unchaperoned, made Jerome feel distinctly uneasy. The fact that Joseph had known exactly where Dani was in the restaurant hadn't gone unnoticed by him either.

"That's okay, we've covered everything else. Once Dani's come up with something, then we can talk about the cost." Joseph looked up from his phone expectantly and Jerome nodded, then reached for his espresso and drained it.

Paul eyed Jerome as he stepped back into his office after seeing the event organisers and Graham out to the foyer of Sky. Jerome removed his jacket and hung it on the back of his chair.

"That went well. I didn't think they'd make a decision so fast." It amazed Paul at how smoothly Jerome conducted his business. He'd known Jerome for many years and worked for him for four of them, but he only saw Jerome in the capacity of being his boss, and on the odd occasion as his friend. It was rare times like tonight that he actually saw Jerome Ferretti doing what he did best; negotiating projects, skilful and commanding, taking control of meetings which ultimately led to him closing deals.

"Yes. It's going to be a challenge getting everything ready in a month, but we have no choice. The models, media and participants were already booked for around that date and to reschedule would've been near impossible within the next few months. I think we can get ourselves organised though." Jerome looked expectantly at Gino who was leafing through all the information and criteria that the events team had left him, then lowered himself into his chair.

"We'll manage. We've got a great team and though it's something we've never done before, it's not dissimilar to when we have guest deejays and artists. My only concern is where we can set up the dressing rooms. There are..." Gino's dark eyes scanned one of the open folders on the table in front of him where the various folders were strewn. "Yes, here, there are thirty-two models. Plus, the backstage staff, dressers and stylists, make up, hair dressers and photographers. And do we know roughly how many will be attending? They were very vague."

"From my experience, there'll be around a hundred and fifty VIPs and then anything between two to three hundred non-VIPs."

"We'll need more security." Gino directed his comment to Paul.

Paul nodded. "And not just in the club. Down in the car park and out front."

The three men spent the next hour going over every detail. Their timeframe and the run up to Christmas, along with their already full agenda, meant they'd need to set the wheels in motion, at top speed.

———

Alessandro swung impatiently on the chrome barrier, waiting for a glimpse of his mother. He loved coming out to the airport and Jerome often brought both him and his sister to look at the planes.

"She's taking so long," moaned Kara. Jerome chuckled to himself. They'd just witnessed the plane land and Liz had probably not even disembarked yet.

"Shall we have a drink at the cafe?" he suggested.

"We might miss her."

"She won't be out for at least fifteen minutes," Jerome explained, leading them to a nearby coffee shop.

Scott and Gary shuffled back against the back wall of the airport arrivals lounge, keeping well out of Jerome's field of vision. Scott was glad Jerome was distracted with his children. Had Jerome been alone, he'd have had to let Gary carry out the surveillance alone, as the risk of being spotted was too high. Luckily the airport was busy, so they blended into the background and waited patiently for their subjects to emerge.

"Hi, I'll be out in two minutes. Are you here?"

"Yes, we're waiting outside."

"Okay, see you soon."

Liz hung up her phone and put it in her bag and turned to Jonathan. "He's outside."

Jonathan crushed his mouth to Liz's, kissing her fiercely. After spending six whole days with her, it was killing him to know she was going back to her husband. His patience was waning. It had been bad enough before their trip away, stealing a few hours a day with her before she returned to her other life. But now that he'd been with her constantly, he would be going out of his mind. Jonathan reluctantly released her. "Tomorrow? At nine?" he confirmed.

"Yes, tomorrow. Wait ten minutes and then come out."

"I know. God, I'm going to miss you." His tone was a mix of longing and exasperation.

"Me too, babe."

Liz took her case handle and wheeled it away from him as Jonathan watched her disappear through into the customs area. She stopped and reached into her bag and wiped her mouth with a wet wipe, then quickly applied some fresh lipstick, fluffed her hair and plastered on her best fake smile as she walked through the electric doors into the arrivals lounge.

Jerome eyed Liz from the edge of the bed where he was sitting. The room was in total disarray. Clothes dropped absent-mindedly on the bed where the open suitcase lay. Bags of shoes cluttered the floor and the walk-in closet had drawers open, showcasing Liz's immense collection of clothes. Liz was unpacking her suitcase, hanging the unworn clothes she'd flung on the bed back into her closet. She'd brought back the children a few gimmicky presents and chocolates, which were obviously bought from the airport departure lounge. Little thought had been put into them, but they had served their purpose of occupying the children for most of the evening. Jerome had put them to bed, leaving him and Liz time to discuss her trip. He was itching to tell her about the fashion show but he was biding his time until she'd told him everything. This was her time, and he didn't want to overshadow her successful promotional contract with the news of him securing the show for her. It was his way of showing his commitment to her work and to some extent, their marriage, their partnership.

Her movements were hurried, Jerome noted. She seemed unduly agitated again as she described her stay and how the shoot went. Something was seriously off and Jerome wasn't entirely sure what it was. She looked tired and he was convinced she'd lost more weight. She carried on talking, pulling out various items of clothing. She rattled off a description of the resort and spoke highly of the team she'd worked with. He regarded her intently, not interrupting as she moved quickly around the room, never looking across at him, busying herself with the task in hand.

Liz reached into her suitcase and shook out a thin folded sweater to slip onto a hanger. The sharp movement sent a small plastic bottle, which must have been wrapped within the garment, bouncing on to the hard wood floor, then stopping by the door. Jerome lifted himself off the bed and paced over to retrieve it. He picked it up and looked at the blank label, then turned to Liz. "What are these?" He gently shook the dark brown bottle containing the pills.

Liz's face dropped as her eyes darted to the bottle. "They're... um, they're just some pills. They speed up your metabolism. You know, like fat burners."

Jerome narrowed his eyes at her. Liz's nervous reaction to the bottle was enough for him to put two and two together. "They're slim-ming pills," Jerome ground out. He'd seen enough various pills disguised as a different array of either fat burners or herbal metabolism increasers, over his time in the gym. All of them were a disguise for stimulants that suppressed the appetite but caused insomnia and hyperactivity. Suddenly everything started falling into place; her agitation, lack of sleep, weight loss. *Jeez, he was totally blind, how had he not realised?* He shook his head, annoyed at himself again for not being aware. It was so obvious now and yet he hadn't picked up on any of it. That fact alone had Jerome's thoughts shooting off into different directions. *How had he not seen the obvious signs?* He took a deep breath, knowing exactly why. He was preoccupied and though he was trying to be more present physically now, he obviously wasn't paying enough attention.

"How long have you been taking them?" Jerome asked quietly.

"Not long... um, about two weeks," Liz answered nervously, suddenly very preoccupied with the hanger in her hand.

Jerome's tense shoulders sagged a little, pleased she didn't deny taking them – he couldn't face another fight. "You're not taking any more, Liz." She was about to say something but Jerome glared at her. "No more. You've lost so much weight and you look tired. Are you sure it's only a couple of weeks?"

She nodded.

"Why, Liz? You know how bad these are." Jerome rubbed his forehead with his hand, clearly puzzled and exasperated.

Liz averted her eyes. "I just needed to lose a bit of weight and it just wouldn't shift. Since I've stopped smoking, I just can't seem to keep my weight stable. I was just going to take them until I got the I-Gea contract and then I was going to stop."

"Oh Liz, darling, they're addictive and dangerous to your health. You know they are." Jerome paced over to her. "You really don't need to lose any weight; you're skin and bones."

Liz slumped onto the bed. She felt exhausted and jumpy, all at the same time.

"I bet you've hardly slept in the five days. And I can tell you've hardly eaten." He tried hard not to sound as if he was chastising her, but the truth was he despaired sometimes at her actions. Actions that could cost her far more than what she thought she could gain.

She held her head in her hands and shook her head. "I just want to make a career for myself and there's so much pressure, too much competition. There's always someone younger, prettier or slimmer and I just can't get past these mediocre jobs." She looked up at Jerome who was now in front of her. He crouched down so they were eye to eye. "I want this contract, Jerome. I need it."

He placed the pills on the night stand and took her hands. "You'll get the contract, Liz. They loved you. Graham told you – hell, even they told you. This isn't the way. You'll do more damage than good. Look at you. You can't sit still for a moment. You're not sleeping and your body isn't being nourished. You'll burn out."

Liz nodded.

"Leave the unpacking. Do it tomorrow. Have a hot shower, or better yet, a bath. You need sleep and food. I'll fix you some grilled chicken with my low calorie mustard sauce and salad with a glass of wine. What do you say?" He smiled softly at her and she blinked her cool blue eyes at him, pleased he was taking control for tonight. She was exhausted.

"Sure. I'd like that. I might need those relaxants, though. I'm too edgy."

"Have your bath first and then see." Jerome rose gracefully and dropped a kiss on her forehead. "No more slimming pills." He scooped up the bottle and put it in his pocket, then lifted the open suitcase onto the floor. "Jeez, Liz, you'd lose the contract if they ever found out. They're whole image at I-Gea is all about a healthy diet and organic produce."

Liz looked up at him, knowing he was right. In the interview, the executives of I-Gea had been very clear that their "face" for the product needed to be squeaky clean – no smoking, no drugs. "Come on, I'll start the bath, it's almost nine o'clock."

"Thanks. Aren't you going to the club?" She followed Jerome into her bathroom.

"They can manage without me tonight," he said quietly, his tone betraying his concern. Jerome turned on the water and tested the temperature of the mixer taps, then he poured in Liz's coconut-scented bath oil. Liz leaned against the tiles watching him, her hands fidgeting with the hem of her T-shirt. When he was satisfied, he turned to face her and furrowed his brow. He reached over to stop her twitching hand and pulled her gently towards him.

"Tonight my wife needs me."

32

DATES

Arsenio was sitting at his desk in his home office, with his hands clasped in front of him. Resting his mouth against them, he stared at the frozen image on his laptop screen. After stupidly starting to watch the recording in his office yesterday evening, his curiosity had gotten the better of him tonight. But once the video progressed, he'd immediately stopped it. His stomach tightened and his blood boiled. Over his career he'd seen many stomach-churning and disturbing images and he had always been matter of fact about most of them. He wasn't totally made of stone but he'd become hardened and unemotional over time and generally most things did not affect him. All of his cases, however, were of people he didn't know and had no attachment to. This, though, was a completely different scenario.

It was disturbing enough that he knew the people on the video well. It was devastating that the footage he had in his possession would totally destroy his brother. Arsenio had scanned through the photos Sam had taken again, showing the lead up to where Liz and Jonathan were out by their private pool. He then paused the video purposely, avoiding watching the explicit footage, undecided whether he really needed to see more than the few seconds he'd already seen yesterday evening. He wasn't sure he had the stomach for it. The photos were more than enough evidence. It showed them kissing and that was what he'd wanted. You didn't need to be a genius to know what came next. The thought alone was enough to make him feel queasy.

Arsenio continued to stare at the frozen image of Liz and Jonathan kissing each other. It was no good – he needed someone else's opinion.

He stopped the video, collected the file of photos and the USB drive and headed out of his house.

———————

"Sorry to come around without much notice, but it's important."

"That's okay. You sounded troubled on the phone."

Arsenio snorted. Troubled? He was feeling positively psychotic.

Cosimo led Arsenio through to the kitchen, where it soon became obvious that Cosimo was expecting a guest. The table was set for two and there was wine chilling in an ice bucket. There was a delicious aroma of shellfish coming from a pot on the stove. Arsenio placed the brown file with the photos on the table. "Oh, you're expecting company."

"Yes, um, not until around nine though. So we've time, and you said it was urgent. Do you want a drink?" Cosimo asked, wanting to avoid a cross examination by his brother. He walked over to the fridge and opened it.

"Sure, a glass of wine... anything. It smells good." Arsenio paced over to the stove and peered inside. "Linguine alle vongole? Jerome's recipe?"

"Uh-huh. Here." Cosimo handed him a glass and poured him some white wine he'd retrieved from the fridge. "So what's up?"

"The investigator brought around the latest photos from Spain. Liz's modelling job."

Cosimo nodded and quietly raised his glass and Arsenio reciprocated. Fleetingly, Arsenio thought that maybe it wasn't particularly appropriate to be toasting in the light of what he was about to say, but it was purely an ingrained habit. They both took a sip from their glasses and Arsenio continued.

"The evidence is damning, Cos. They both stayed at the resort, sharing a villa. There are photos of them at the airport and at the resort, and a few shots of them kissing."

"I see. Is that what's in the file?" He looked over to the dining table.

"Yes. The thing is, the investigator also recorded them."

Cosimo's brow furrowed. "At the hotel, you mean?"

Arsenio nodded. "In their villa, while they..." Arsenio raised his eyebrows, hoping he didn't have to spell it out.

Cosimo's face dropped, understanding what Arsenio implied. He took a drink from his glass and placed it on the polished granite surface.

"I haven't seen it," added Arsenio quickly. "I just couldn't bring myself to. It felt, well... oh crap." He took a drink from his glass and put it next to Cosimo's. "It just felt like crossing boundaries." He spoke in a rush, glad he'd been able to unburden the guilt he was feeling. This was his brother's wife they were talking about.

"I think the boundaries have been crossed well before, don't you?" Cosimo said tightly.

"What's that supposed to mean? That I shouldn't have done this? That I should've let that, that *tart* shit all over our brother? Make a fool of him?"

"I'm not pointing fingers, Seni. Calm down, for goodness sake! I'm just stating the facts. We crossed the boundaries the minute we let the investigator continue. I knew once we found out, it would be hard. I caught her, remember? I know what it feels like to know something that will devastate someone you care about."

Cosimo took a deep breath and rubbed his face. Arsenio physically relaxed a little and pinched the bridge of his nose.

"The problem we're faced with now is what do we do with the information?" Cosimo mulled.

"We can't keep it to ourselves, is that even an option? She's fucking some asshole and spending days away with him and we're going to sit on it?" Arsenio's voice rose with frustration.

"I didn't say that. Just calm down, Seni. You need to get your game head on and try not to get emotional. We need to look at the bigger picture." Arsenio went to interrupt him but stopped short when Cosimo lifted his hand, halting him. "Here, take another drink and let's look at this as rationally and as calmly as we can." Arsenio accepted his wine glass for Cosimo and took a gulp.

"So, we know the most important things for Jerome are the kids and his businesses. The businesses are safe. We've been through it legally and she can't get her hands on anything. The kids, though, are another matter. She can bargain them for more maintenance, correct?"

Arsenio nodded.

"To get full custody for Jerome, she needs to be seen as unfit. Screwing around won't cut it. She's not the first or the last. Or, we can try and cut her a deal; a hefty lump sum for her to relinquish custody to Jerome."

"She'll never go for it. She needs an open tap kept running to keep her happy. A lump sum will run out in no time. She might go for it if her career starts up. She'll need to be travelling a lot more. The kids will be in her way."

"That's a bit like praying for a Christmas miracle. Seni," Cosimo replied dryly.

"Then what do we do? Say nothing?" Arsenio shot back.

"For now, yes. Look, it's a week until Christmas. I really don't think we should confront Jerome with this right now. It's the busiest time of the year for him. It'll force him to make a final decision about her, and the kids will be turned upside down, not to mention Mama."

"Christ, talk about bad timing. The cheating bitch is going to get away with it because of a religious holiday. I'm sure there's some irony in there somewhere." Arsenio shook his head, exasperated.

"Seni, we can't hit him with it. It'll destroy him. We need a week, ten days tops. If she hasn't slipped up somehow, we might need to push him into seeing it for himself. We have enough information on her movements; of the trainer's movements. We can set him up to see it for himself. Believe me, Seni, you don't want to be the one to tell him, or be the one to show him the photos and the video."

"I suppose you're right. But it just feels as if we're covering for her."

"It's a waiting game, Seni. If we charge in, we'll not get the result we need, what Jerome needs. That's what you focus on, full custody and her out of his life. Telling him now won't get him that."

They stood in Cosimo's designer kitchen in silence, contemplating what they were doing. Neither of them happy but were equally understanding that it was their only choice. Arsenio knew Cosimo was right, but he just wanted to nail the bitch. This was the first time he'd ever lost his cool and he knew it was purely because Liz was hurting one of his own, his brother, his family.

"I just hope she slips up. I don't want to be the one to show him the video."

"Jeez, it's that bad?"

"I've no clue, I just watched about twenty seconds and stopped it... I didn't need to see *that*. I didn't want those images in my head. I'd seen enough and knew what direction it was going in."

"It stays between us."

"Agreed."

"What about Scott, and the investigator in Spain?"

"There are no copies. They'll say nothing. It's more than their reputation's worth."

"What do the pictures show?"

"Have a look." Arsenio gestured to the dining room table.

Within a few minutes, Arsenio had the photos spread out across the light oak dining table. He'd put them in sequence and included the shots taken previous to Liz's shoot in Spain. Arsenio pointed out the day he presumed furniture had been delivered, the sudden double-backing of Jonathan after Liz had encountered the couple she knew at the airport.

They scrutinised every photo up until the last one taken in Spain of the two of them kissing by their pool. They were so engrossed that they didn't hear the front door open.

"Hello-o-o-o?"

Cosimo stiffened as he heard the familiar voice from the hallway. His eyes flitted to the clock: it was almost nine. *Crap*, he hadn't realised the time and now he was faced with the awkward situation of introducing Arsenio to James.

"In here," Cosimo called out, straightening from looking at the photos. Arsenio did his best not to smirk as he began to gather up everything, tactfully turning away from his obviously embarrassed brother. He was tempted to make him squirm as payback for the constant digs and teasing he'd endured over the years about his inability to have a meaningful relationship. But after what they'd both been through and discussed tonight, he felt he could cut his brother some slack. That didn't mean he wouldn't rib him at some later date though.

"Oh, um, hello. I'm sorry, I didn't mean to interrupt." The owner of the voice halted at the threshold, filling the doorway with his tall broad frame. Arsenio turned around and was faced with a very surprised James.

"Um, yes, an unexpected visit. Er, this is my youngest brother –"

"Oh, you're Arsenio... I'm so very pleased to meet you." Before Cosimo could finish his introductions, James was striding towards them both, beaming at Arsenio and extending his hand. Arsenio took it and shook it, feeling the roughness of James's palms.

"Mr Banks, I presume?" Arsenio said wryly. "Please call me Seni. Believe me, the pleasure is all mine." He flashed James a wide smile.

"Mr Banks? You make me sound like an old man. Is that how you refer to me, Cos? Call me James," James chortled, his sun-worn face creasing into a wide smile at Cosimo.

"No, I don't. Seni was just being, well... Seni. He was about to leave, weren't you?" Cosimo glared at Arsenio.

"Oh, don't leave on my account. It's nice to finally meet one of Cos's relatives, I've heard so much about you all, it's nice to put a face to a name."

Arsenio's grin widened, noting how uncomfortable Cosimo obviously was. He'd spent the best part of his adult life keeping his private and family life separate. And now, they had accidently collided in Cosimo's immaculately decorated dining room.

James was the exact opposite of Cosimo, he was naturally fair but was tanned with an unruly mop of thick strawberry blond hair. His dress sense indicated he was younger than he looked, probably in his mid thirties. His jeans were designer with a few artful tears. The light green shirt he wore matched his eyes and was casually opened at the collar and rolled up at the sleeves, showcasing his tanned, powerful forearms. Arsenio noted that he wore brown, suede Chelsea boots with a Cuban heel which were unique and showed James had a flare for style. The look was casual but perfectly put together and in total contrast to Cosimo's more conventional attire. He was still wearing his conservative, though exquisite, pin striped trousers from his suit, though he'd shed his tie and jacket, leaving him in a crisp white shirt and waistcoat.

"No, I had better go. It's late," Arsenio replied, to Cosimo's relief.

"Well at least stay and finish your wine," insisted James.

"Um." Arsenio's eyes darted to Cosimo, who shrugged in defeat. There was no way he could avoid it, what with James' impeccable manners and obvious curiosity. Cosimo walked over to the kitchen and retrieved another glass and the bottle and took it over to James.

"Oh, is that the Gavi, Cos?"

"Yes," Cosimo replied, pouring James a glass.

"Does that mean that's linguine alle vongole I can smell?"

"That's right."

"One of my favourites. Your brother's a very good cook you know – well, of course you know," James chuckled.

"He is." Arsenio lifted his glass and both James and Cosimo clinked their glasses. "But he's not as good as Jerome – now he's the real chef."

"So Cosimo tells me." James pulled out a chair and signalled Arsenio to sit down, both intrigued and eager to find out more. Then he sat in the chair next to him. "He has that fabulous restaurant by the river doesn't he?"

Arsenio leaned back in his chair, reeling at how genuinely interested James was. He was a breath of fresh air, relaxed and comfortable and so incredibly nice.

"He does. La Casa d'Italia – you should go there," coaxed Arsenio. Cosimo glared at him and stomped back into the kitchen to check on dinner.

"I know. I keep telling Cos that, but he's always too tired to go down to town. He works too hard." James shook his head, then turned in the direction of where Cosimo was. "Seni said we should go down to Jerome's restaurant one evening."

Cosimo muttered to himself in Italian, *that's all he needed, Arsenio encouraging James. He'd bloody kill him.*

"Did you hear that?" James called.

"Yes, I heard," replied Cosimo through gritted teeth.

James gave an exasperated shrug to Arsenio and grinned.

"So, I hear you're a landscaper?"

Dani checked through her work station and saw that she just needed some more sugar sachets. She turned to Pino and told him she was running up to the store room for more, and asked if he needed anything. He quickly checked and shook his head. Dani sprinted up to the first floor and stepped into the store room. She took out a box of sachets from the shelf and then headed back to the restaurant. As she started to walk down the stairs, she heard the lift doors open and Gia stepped out.

"Dani! Great news! The doctor called and everything's all clear!" Gia beamed.

"Oh, Gia that's brilliant news!" Dani hugged her, both pleased and relieved for her.

"I can't tell you how relieved I am."

"I know. That's the best Christmas present."

"It is, *tesoro*, it is. I'm so glad I didn't tell the boys. All that worry." Gia shook her head. "I'll be glad to see this year over. It's been very *sottosopra!*"

Dani furrowed her brow. "Sottosopra?"

Gia chuckled and muttered to herself in Italian. "Um, how do you say? Up and down?" Gia twisted both her hands, left and right in explanation.

"Oh, you mean topsy-turvy?"

"*Si sottosopra!*" Gia laughed, her eyes lighting up, and Dani realised that for the past few days, they'd lost their usual sparkle.

"Ciao, Bella."

Gia's eyes darted up from the reservations book that had her so engrossed. She hadn't noticed Ray Holmes had walked in.

"Raymondo! How lovely to see you again." She smiled widely at Ray, who winked at her. Gia immediately rounded the front desk and reached for his hand, then kissed him on both cheeks, causing the normally unflustered doctor to blush slightly. "I saw your reservation."

"I told you I'd come. Here, let me introduce you to my partner. Elizabeth, this is Gia." Ray turned to look at the woman who was standing just behind him. She was medium height with her grey hair cut into a sharp bob and sparkling blue eyes. She smiled kindly at Gia, whose smile had slipped slightly.

"Pleased to meet you, Gia. Ray hasn't stop talking about how wonderful this place is." She held out her hand for Gia to shake. Gia gracefully shook her hand. "And I'm his partner in his practice. It gets a little confusing when he introduces me that way, out of the surgery," Elizabeth clarified, with a good-humoured huff. Ray's eyes darted to Gia, realising his perceptive partner had picked up on Gia's misunderstanding, and he cringed slightly.

"Oh, he's too kind." Gia gently patted Ray's arm affectionately, her genuine smile returning to its former glory. "The reservation is for six people at eight thirty." Gia blinked up at Ray.

Caught in the warmth of her gaze, Ray took a second or two to answer. "Um, yes, the other junior partners and doctors are coming too."

"We're a little early. Ray was very eager to get here," Elizabeth added, stifling a smile.

"Oh. Well, let me show you to your table." Gia beamed back at Ray.

"By all means, lead the way." Ray signalled with his hand and followed Gia, his eyes transfixed on Gia's curvy form encased in a chic, cream woollen dress as she sashayed towards the back of the restaurant.

Gia made sure they were settled at their table and left them in the capable hands of Dani.

"Oh. My. God. She's gorgeous. And she has three sons over thirty?" Elizabeth whispered to Ray, then she pulled out her compact from her bag and flicked it open. "I look like a hag next to her, she must be my age." She inspected her pale face, then frowned, snapping the compact shut.

"I think she's in her mid-fifties," confirmed Ray. His eyes were still fixed on Gia, watching her gracefully walk to the front desk again.

"Crap, she's older than me. I feel like a frump. Well, she likes you, Ray."

"You think?" he asked eagerly, turning sharply to look at Elizabeth.

"Oh yes. Her face dropped when you said I was your partner."

"Um, yes. I really need to be more specific," he snorted.

Dani came over with the menus and Ray introduced Elizabeth to her. Dani took their drinks order and left them to mull over the menus.

"So what's good here?" asked Elizabeth.

"Everything!" replied Ray with a chuckle.

Jerome opened up the tray and placed it over Liz's legs. She had a long soak in the bath while Jerome had prepared her meal. Then she'd dressed in her sleep shorts and top. Jerome insisted she stay in bed and that he'd bring up her dinner. "There we are. How are you feeling?"

"A bit edgy," admitted Liz. Her legs were twitching as she spoke. Jerome handed her a glass of wine.

"Here, this will calm you down." He sat on the bed and watched her take a sip.

"Aren't you eating?"

"I will in a bit. I just want make sure you're alright first."

He raised his eyebrows and motioned to the plate of food on the tray and gave her an "aren't you going to eat" look. Liz picked up her knife and fork and started to cut through the succulent chicken. She dipped it in the sauce and popped it in her mouth. It was, of course, delicious. Jerome smiled, taking a relieved deep breath, relaxing a little. He picked up his glass of wine from the nightstand and took a sip.

"This is really good, Jerome."

Jerome shrugged. "Well, if you finish it, I'll tell you some good news."

Liz's eyes darted up to his face. "Good news? About what?"

"Ah, ah, ah." He moved his finger from left to right. "Finish your food and I'll tell you," he said smugly.

"That's blackmail," whined Liz, narrowing her eyes at him but enjoying his little game all the same. He was really taking care of her.

"Yep. But it's *really* good news," Jerome teased. She was about to protest when he held up his finger, then pointed to the plate. "Eat and I'll tell you."

Liz grinned at him. She was transported back to when they first got together and Jerome used to create new recipes and make her taste them. They were happy times. Liz cut through some more chicken and forked up some salad, to Jerome's delight. It took Liz around fifteen minutes to work her way through the meal. She kept stopping and asking questions about the good news. "Is it about me?"

"I'm not saying."

"Jerome!"

"Eat it up," he said nonchalantly.

"Gah! You're mean!"

"Yep. Less talking, more eating, please."

Liz chewed on some more chicken and salad while Jerome sipped his wine.

"Is it a holiday?"

"If you don't finish, I'm not saying and if you carry on grilling me, I may not tell you at all!" Jerome mock-glared at her and Liz giggled at his playfulness.

"Okay, okay, I'll finish."

As soon as Liz popped the last piece of salad and chicken in her mouth, she looked up at him expectantly. He refilled her wine glass, passing it to her, and waited for her to take a sip. He was determined to make her feel tired without the use of relaxants. With her stomach full and a few glasses of wine, he was hoping she'd relaxed enough to drift off.

"So?"

Jerome lifted the tray off the bed, deliberately slowly, and placed it on the floor.

"Jerome! Stop teasing me and just tell me!"

"Okay, okay. Calm down." He sat back down again and faced her. "Well the good news is that the fashion show is on again."

"What? How? When did this happen... I don't understand." Liz shifted forward.

"I spoke to Graham about hosting the fashion show at Sky. We had a meeting yesterday with the event organisers and they agreed. So, it's back on."

Liz shrieked with excitement and jumped up from the bed, flinging her arms around his neck, peppering his face with kisses. "That's brilliant news. Why didn't I think of it earlier? You're amazing, thank you, thank you!"

Jerome laughed at her enthusiasm, steadying her in his arms. "So you're pleased, then?" he asked with a hint of mock sarcasm.

"Pleased? I'm ecstatic!" She settled back on her heels, her arms still around his neck and looked at him. "Sky, what a great venue! What a great idea!"

"Well, it wasn't my idea. Someone else suggested it, and as soon as I thought about it, it just made sense. You get to do your runway, Liz. It's your dream come true."

Liz smiled softly at him. "I will. Thanks to you." Liz pressed her lips to Jerome's and kissed him hard. Jerome faltered a moment, then kissed her back, holding her closer, allowing his hands to trail over her back. Liz tightened her grip on him and Jerome knew where this was heading. He moaned softly. It felt good to have her in his arms again. He'd missed the intimacy, of feeling her softness. Jerome gently pushed her back against the bed and he covered her slight frame with his body. Her hands fisted in his thick hair as she kissed him urgently, desperate to break him. Jerome stilled, taking her by the wrists and pulling them away. He didn't want to rush, he wanted to take it slow, ease into it, unsure if he was able to follow through. A rejection would hurt her, but if they started slowly, Jerome hoped the uneasiness he felt when he was close to her would begin to subside.

"Slow down," he mumbled against her neck.

"I want you, Jerome. I need you..." Liz breathed, rubbing herself provocatively against him. "I want to show you how much you mean to me."

She held his anxious face between her hands and pulled him back to her lips. Jerome tried to relax, to clear his mind while her small soft hands roamed over his back. She didn't want him thinking. If he started to think, he'd stop – she knew him too well. He hadn't forgiven her but he was trying to. Tonight had proved that. He'd spent time with her and focused on her needs. Even while she was away he'd thought about her, the fashion show was proof of that.

A cry from the corridor jolted them. "Daddy!"

"It's Kara," muttered Jerome, scrambling off Liz as she eased herself up on her elbows. "I'll go see what's wrong." He headed for the door and Liz flopped back down on the bed, trying hard to hide her exasperation.

Jerome re-entered the room, carrying a weepy Kara. "She's got tummy ache. Probably all the chocolates she ate. I'll give her a mild antacid and put her back to bed."

"Sure." Liz smiled weakly. She knew the moment had passed. There was no way they would pick up where they left off – well, not tonight anyway. She sat up and grinned to herself. The fashion show was on again. This was exactly what she needed: exposure. The only problem was it would be at Sky and Jonathan was not going to be happy.

"So, where shall we go this morning?" Chloe flopped down in the chair next to Dani.

"Well I need to do all my Christmas shopping so, I suppose Leeds."

Chef had insisted Dani take Friday morning off, since she'd volunteered to work every shift over the holidays and work on Boxing Day night for Joseph's parent's anniversary party. She'd also arranged to have

411

the lunchtime shift on New Year's Day off, just working in the evening, as Ray always made an effort and invited Adam and Chloe over for a late lunch, and of course the invitation was extended to Dani too.

"Sure. If you don't manage everything today, you've got Monday too."

"I can't on Monday. I'm spending the morning with Gia. We need to put together some decorations for the anniversary party I told you about. And I need to get a costume for New Year's Eve." Dani cringed. "I haven't a clue what to go as."

"Hmm. Is there a theme?" asked Chloe.

"No, not really, just famous iconic figures. Rosa is going as Cleopatra and Nicole as Grace Kelly, so someone – or should I say some woman – who's iconic."

"Well that's easy: Marilyn Monroe. Who's more iconic than her? Unless you'd rather go as Madonna?"

"Marilyn or Madonna? Well Madonna's Italian, isn't she?" chuckled Dani. "Hmm... but I don't fancy walking around in a coned bustier all night!"

Chloe laughed, "You could pull it off mind you, but you're right, not very practical. I could make you a version of that white halter-necked dress Marilyn wore. I think I have a pattern of something similar that I made for myself. I can alter it a bit," suggested Chloe. "Then all you need is a blonde wig. We could get the material today, it'll give me time to make it for you."

"Would you?"

"Sure, you'll make an excellent Marilyn."

Dani rolled her eyes. Well, she'd have to blonde again, just for one night.

Cosimo slipped his Ferrari into the parking spot next to Gia's Fiat. Cosimo wasn't a showy man by nature. In fact, of all the brothers he was probably the most understated. He enjoyed fine wine and food. His clothes were exquisite and bespoke but not obvious. His home was a modest detached Victorian house situated between Leeds and Ilkley, granting him the distance and privacy he required but being close enough to his family. All the furnishings in his home were original, mixing modern designs with antiques he'd either acquired or inherited.

Amongst these acquisitions was Cosimo's car. Alessandro senior and Cosimo had a shared passion for cars and when Alessandro died, Cosimo was the only son who was old enough to drive, then in his early twenties. Gia knew Cosimo loved her late husband's red Ferrari Testarossa, so she signed it over to him, knowing she would never drive it. Cosimo had kept it in mint condition and its value had escalated to over double what his father had paid for it over twenty-five years ago. Cosimo rarely took it out into the city, using his modest Alfa Romeo for town, but this morning, he'd driven James into Leeds and wanted to give him a bit of a treat.

Cosimo looked at his watch and scanned the car park. It was just after two and the absence of Arsenio's black Lamborghini meant that Cosimo might be able to have a private word with Jerome before they all sat down for their weekly family lunch. Cosimo found Jerome in his office, talking on the phone. Jerome signalled him to come in and sit down.

"Well, I appreciate that very much. I know it's short notice, but the work needs to be finished in time for the painter... Excellent, so I can book the decorator for the twenty-seventh? Thank you again." Jerome set down his phone and looked up at Cosimo. "Hi, just let me make this one phone call."

"Of course," Cosimo smiled, then settled into the chair in front of Jerome's desk, watching Jerome call and quickly confirm the date with the decorator.

"You're having some work done?"

"Sort of. I'm getting the apartment into order. Just a refreshing of the paintwork and a bit of routine maintenance."

"Oh?" Cosimo sat forward.

"Yes, Mama wants to offer the apartment to Dani, temporarily." Jerome's eye shifted to some papers on his desk and he shuffled them into order nervously.

"Really?"

"Yes. Apparently, Dani's thinking of buying her own place next year, but until then, her travelling from Harewood is proving to be tiring and she's helped out Mama a lot, putting in extra hours here too, so..." he shrugged. "It was Mama's idea," Jerome added, seeing Cosimo's eyes narrow.

"I suppose it makes sense. It's just sitting there, and if it's only temporary..." Cosimo smiled tightly, unsure if it was the best idea having Dani living under the Casa d'Italia roof. It brought her into the family, made her closer to them and it was crossing that delicate line of professional and personal. When Chef had been there it had been fine, because he was classed as family anyway – he'd known and worked with the family for over fifteen years. But Dani had only been working at the restaurant six weeks. And of course there was the added problem that Jerome obviously had feelings for her.

"Mama hasn't told her yet. I think she was waiting to see when the work would be completed. She's very keen to offer it to her." Jerome carried on rambling nervously, as if he needed to explain the details or maybe justify them – he wasn't sure which.

"Well, we all know how Mama can be, if she has something in mind," Cosimo said dryly. Jerome relaxed and grinned. "How did Liz's shoot go? She got back yesterday, didn't she?"

"It went well. She was very excited about it."

"Good. I know it's a tricky business. Not stable, I mean."

"Mmm... well, I managed to get the fashion show back on again. We're hosting it at Sky, so she's thrilled at that."

"Oh that's good news."

"Yes, she gets to do a runway."

"So things are getting better, then? I mean, between you? I'm not prying, I'm just concerned."

"We're working on it. It's not easy and I'm as much to blame as she is, but we're trying."

Cosimo's lips thinned at his brother's comment. *So, Jerome felt things were getting worked out, when the fact was that Liz was working him over.* He sighed to himself. The next two weeks were going to prove very difficult for him and Arsenio. They were all going to have to play happy families until they could finally come clean to Jerome.

"So when's the show?"

"Umm... the nineteenth of January."

"Just a month away, then? That's short notice."

"Well, everyone was booked for around that date already, so it's just for us to get the events people in to see what needs setting up. Gino's used to having events there. It shouldn't be much of a problem."

Cosimo nodded and rose from the chair. "Right, well I'll go downstairs and see Mama. See you down there."

"Sure."

Arsenio turned up late, so the Ferretti family lunch was delayed by thirty minutes. Gia played with her spoon nervously; she'd spent the last half an hour checking the time.

"You've not eaten anything. Are you alright?" Cosimo asked.

"Yes, I'm fine. I'm dining out later, so I didn't want to eat anything now. In fact, I need to go. I have a hair appointment." Gia stood up from her chair and all three men stood.

"You're going out on a Friday night?" Arsenio couldn't hide his surprise. "With who?"

"A friend," Gia answered sharply.

"A friend?" repeated Arsenio.

"Yes, I do have them, you know," Gia answered dryly.

"Does this friend have a name?"

Gia blushed, knowing there was no way she could hide her dinner plans. "Of course. It's Doctor Holmes," she answered softly, avoiding eye contact with any of her sons. She felt a little exasperated having to answer to any of them. After all, she was a grown woman and single. It really wasn't any of their business.

"*Raymondo*," Cosimo confirmed dryly.

"Who?" Arsenio furrowed his brow, looking at Cosimo, who was stifling a grin.

"Ray Holmes. He's a customer of ours," Jerome muttered quietly.

"Yes, he is, and he's also a very nice man. I didn't realise I needed your permission to go out on a dinner date," Gia said haughtily.

"You don't, Mama. I'm sure you'll have a lovely time," Jerome said softly.

"Well, um... I'm sure I will. Thank you. Did you managed to get the apartment organised? I meant to ask you earlier and forgot." She turned her full attention to Jerome.

"Yes. It should be ready by the thirtieth."

"Oh that's excellent. I can tell Dani, then. Goodbye then." Gia turned to a still-stunned Arsenio and kissed his cheeks, and then to a very amused Cosimo and kissed him too. "I'll be back by six and then *Raymondo* is picking me up at seven thirty."

Gia kissed Jerome and then flounced out of the restaurant.

"Who the fuck's *Raymondo*?" asked Arsenio as he slumped back into his chair. "And what's going on with the apartment? Jeez, we've been sitting here for over an hour and nobody's said anything!"

"*Raymondo* – Ray – is Adam Holmes's father," explained Jerome, he motioned to Rosa for another espresso.

"Adam Holmes the lawyer?"

"Yes. Does anyone else want another coffee?"

Cosimo nodded and Arsenio declined.

"And how long's this been going on?"

"Oh, they've only recently met. They got chatting at the nativity play on Monday." Cosimo decided that he should shoulder some of the interrogation.

"I see. Well, I think that that's the first date I've ever witnessed Mama going on," Arsenio huffed. "Not sure I'm altogether comfortable with that."

Jerome shrugged and Cosimo raised his eyebrows. It was definitely a new dynamic for all of them.

"Well, he's a nice guy. A gentleman," Cosimo added.

"And the apartment? You're letting it out to Dani?" Arsenio furrowed his brow. "Speaking of which, where is she today?" He looked around the restaurant. Jerome was about to explain when Rosa brought over the coffees. He waited until she was out of earshot before answering.

"She didn't work the lunch shift. She's back for the evening. Mama suggested we offer her the apartment as she travels all the way from Hare- wood every day."

"Temporarily," chipped in Cosimo. His eyes flitted to Jerome.

"Yes, temporarily. Until she buys her own place, that is."

Arsenio widened his eyes. "I see. Isn't that a bit soon? I mean, I rather like the idea of the delectable Dani sleeping in my old bed. I just wish I was in it with her," he chortled.

Jerome's eyes darkened at Arsenio's lewd joke and he took in a sharp breath, making his nostrils flare.

"Seni, honestly. Give it up, will you?" Cosimo shook his head. "You'll scare the poor girl away with your constant flirting. Calm down, will you? It's a temporary solution to a present problem. I'm sure Mama has put a lot of thought into the idea. She's very willing and Mama seems to have a soft spot for her." Cosimo continued in his defence of the idea, allowing the obviously tense Jerome to relax. He glanced at Jerome and gave him a tight smile.

Arsenio huffed, "Yes, well Mama's not the only one who has a soft spot for her."

Jerome stared at his cup, wondering what Arsenio meant. *Surely he wasn't talking about him, was he?*

"Oh?" Cosimo asked, lifting his cup to take a sip.

"I think Kuch is after her too, and a few more of the staff."

"Well, she very likeable and charming. It's bound to happen." Cosimo waved his hand dismissively in the air.

"Talking of charming, how's James?" Arsenio shuffled forward in his chair and looked at Cosimo.

"Who's James?" asked Jerome, pleased they were finally off the subject of Dani and her pack of suitors.

Arsenio turned to Jerome with a huge grin on his face, "Cos's *date* from last night. I met him at Cos's house. He was trying to impress him with your recipe of linguine alle vongole."

Cosimo rolled his eyes and Jerome fixed his attention on to Cosimo, arching a brow.

"I wasn't trying to impress him... he's already impressed," answered Cosimo tartly, which made Arsenio tilt his head back and laugh and Jerome gaped at his older brother.

"Well that told you, Seni. So who is he, and why has Seni met him and I haven't?" Jerome whined, feigning hurt.

"It wasn't intentional. A miscalculation on my part."

"Well, now it's only fair I meet him too."

"He's right, Cos. And you just know James is dying to come to La Casa. You should bring him down. Meet all the family."

"Alright, now, that's quite enough, just pack it in. I'm not sure that would be such a good idea, what with Mama and..."

"Oh, no. Don't make excuses. He said he wanted to come," teased Arsenio enjoying the fact that he could finally get his own back for all the comments and ribbing he'd endured over his sex life.

"Seni. Just stop it," Cosimo shot back, feeling obviously uneasy with the whole idea.

"He's right, Cos. You should introduce us. How long have you been seeing him?" asked Jerome, genuinely interested. He always felt Cosimo's homosexuality had kept him distant from the family and maybe this would be the turning point.

"Umm... about nine months," answered Cosimo quietly.

"Nine months!" Arsenio couldn't keep his surprise out of his voice. "How have you managed to keep him away from us? Doesn't he wonder why? Jeez, I feel sorry for the guy."

"Well, we tend to spend a lot of time at my home and he works most weekends. It just never really became an issue," Cosimo replied quietly, clearly uncomfortable with the interrogation and thankful his mother wasn't here.

"Have you met his family?" Jerome asked.

"No. They, um... well, they're not tolerant of James' sexuality. He has had nothing to do with them, since he came out. He's used to going it alone. So you see, he never pushed to meet any of you."

"That's awful." Arsenio shook his head. "How can people do that? I mean, I get it's hard for you to get your head around, but to cut you off? And he's so nice. I mean really nice."

"You should bring him down, Cos. Really. I'd love to meet him."

"I'm not sure. What about Mama? I don't want her to get upset."

"She won't get upset. She'll be happy if you are, trust me."

Arsenio leaned back in his chair and huffed. "Things are certainly changing around here."

"What do you mean?" Cosimo tilted his head towards Arsenio.

"Well Mama's got a new boyfriend. You're contemplating introducing your new beau to us..."

"You'll be telling us you've finally found some poor woman to settle down with next," Jerome joked.

"Steady on. Don't overdo it!" laughed Arsenio. "The end of this year is closing in and it looks like the new one's going to be decidedly more exciting. That's all I'm saying."

"Well, I think I've had my fill of excitement for this year. I'll be glad to see the back of it. I'm hoping for a much more sedate year, next year." Jerome stood up from his chair and pursed his lips. "I'm afraid I need to get off. The kids will be home and I want to spend a few hours with them before I need to get back here."

Jerome said his goodbyes to his brothers and headed out of the restaurant.

"Did he say anything?" Arsenio asked.

Cosimo shook his head. "Just that they were *both* trying to sort things out and he was as much to blame as she was."

"In other words, he's still clueless."

"Yep. I'm hoping for that Christmas miracle."

"Yeah, me too."

Dani stored all the Christmas presents she'd bought in her wardrobe and flopped onto her bed, glad she'd managed to get all of it done today. She had roughly two hours before she needed to be at work. Dani looked at her phone again and checked her messages. Over the last week, Jez had been sending her several messages. He'd realised that if he wanted her attention, nasty texts were not the way to go. His texts had been more informative, keeping her up to date with what was happening at the bar, and about customers she knew. Some were sweet and some focused on the good memories that they had shared over their five years together. She didn't answer any of them and was secretly impressed at his persistence.

The message she'd received this morning was again sweet, wishing her a good day and that he was thinking of her, with Christmas around the corner, knowing it was hard for her at this time of year. Jez also mentioned that he would have the money for her by the ninth of January. The bank had confirmed it today and he had emailed her the letter of confirmation and the exact amount.

Dani pulled up her laptop and turned it on. Once it had logged on to her email account, she opened up the email with the attached letter. As well as the letter, there was also a link. The email read:

As you know, I'm not so good with words but this song pretty sums up how I feel.

I know you can't forget what's happened but please forgive me. You mean everything to me and I know I've ruined what we had. At least can we be friends? I can settle for that. I hate to think after everything we've been through we can't be friends.

Jez xx

Dani scanned over the letter and forwarded it to Adam, then she moved the cursor over the link and let it hover for a moment, unsure if she wanted to hear, whatever the song was. She'd come a long way in the six weeks that she'd left London, but she still wasn't sure if she was strong enough to deal with Jez. He'd meant everything to her and without him she would never have got through her mother's illness and consequent death. Dani knew she owed him for that, he'd filled a gap in her life and supported her at her lowest. Yes, he'd made mistakes, huge and unforgiveable mistakes, and Dani was sure his motives were less than honourable, even now. But there was no denying it, in the five years they'd been together, he'd been the centre of her world.

Dani looked back at the screen and took a deep breath, then clicked onto the link. Dani's heart clenched as she heard the familiar refrain of "Maps". Her whole body was covered in goose bumps as she read the lyrics that flashed onto the screen to the sound of Adam Levine's distinctive voice, singing about being there for her in her darkest time and where was she when he was on his knees? Why did she run away?

Tears sprung involuntarily into her eyes at the poignant words, and trickled down her face.

33

DILEMMA

Dani slipped the coffee cups under the spout and automatically pressed the button, lost in her thoughts. Since her email from Jez yesterday, she'd felt unsettled and tempted to answer him, but decided she needed to sleep on it and let the cold light of day throw her a new perspective. One thing she knew, though, was that she would have to talk to him eventually – she'd put it off for long enough. *Maybe this afternoon.*

Dani arranged the cups on the tray and took them over to the kitchen. Carmen looked up at her as she entered the kitchen. "Thanks, Dani. I'm going to need plenty of these today. The weekend before Christmas is always crazy."

"What's that you're making?" Dani peered at the large pot Carmen was beating vigorously.

"I'm making lemon profiteroles with a white chocolate sauce. It's one of the new desserts on our Christmas specials."

"Oh God. They sound amazing!"

"I'll get you some to try when they're done."

Dani grinned. "I just love working here." Then she backed out into the restaurant.

Within a few minutes Gia appeared, looking radiant in an emerald green dress with sheer sleeves. "*Buongiorno*, Dani."

"*Buongiorno*, Gia. You look lovely."

"*Grazie.*"

Dani quickly prepared her a coffee and pushed it towards her.

"Did you have a nice time last night?" Dani asked softly.

"I had a wonderful night. It's been a very long time for me to go out with such a gentleman. Actually, it's been a very long time for me to go out with anyone," she huffed.

"Oh, I'm so glad. Ray's such a great guy."

"He is," agreed Gia, blushing at little. "After dinner, he took me to a bar that has a jazz band. Ha! Me in a jazz club! *Incredibile!*" Gia threw her hands in the air and chuckled, as though the very idea was unthinkable.

"Sounds wonderful," Dani sighed. Gia nodded wistfully and the two of them fell silent for a moment, lost in their own thoughts.

"Anyway, enough about that. I've a few things I need to discuss with you before you start work." Gia perched herself on a bar stool, shaking herself and Dani out of their daydreams.

"Oh? Like what." Dani turned her full attention to Gia.

"Firstly, I want to open up a Facebook account."

"Oh. Okay. That's not hard."

"I also want to be more involved with our page for La Casa too. So, that's one of the reasons I want my own, so I can get the hang of it. It also means I can post photos of my holiday."

"You're going on holiday?" Dani asked, surprised.

"*Si*, on the third of January, for a month. I go every year."

Dani scrunched her nose. "We'll miss you."

Gia's expression softened. "Will you?"

"Of course!"

Gia reached over and patted Dani's hand, clearly moved. "I'll miss you too, *tesoro.*"

"Well we can set that all up on Monday, before we leave for the wholesalers."

"Good idea. That's the other thing I wanted to talk to you about. Joseph asked me if we could send him a few ideas via email. He sent me a picture of the cake he's having made, so we can work our designs around that. Do you think you'll be able to spare an hour this afternoon and we can send him some of your ideas?"

Dani looked at her watch. It was just ten. "Do you want to do it now? I've already thought of a few, incorporating some of the Christmas decorations we didn't use."

Gia jumped off her stool and picked up her coffee. "Well, then. *Andiamo!*"

It didn't take long for Dani to download a few images of what she had in mind to send over to Joseph. His response was almost immediate, giving her carte blanche to do whatever she thought would be fitting.

"I'm hoping we can get most of the decorations assembled on Monday, so that we would just need to place them on the day. It's going to be very hectic that day anyway. The fresh flowers we can put together on the twenty-third and they'll be fine until Boxing Day, as long as we can store them somewhere."

"We could leave the decorations here, in my office or the function room. No one will touch them, but the fresh flowers need to be somewhere where there's no heating." Gia's brow wrinkled as she puzzled over where they could keep them. "We could put them in the apartment upstairs. The maintenance will be finished by the twenty-third and the flowers will be out before the painters go in on the twenty-seventh."

Dani nodded. "So you're having work done?"

"Actually, that's the other thing I needed to talk to you about."

Dani turned the office chair around to face Gia. "What's that?"

"The apartment, opposite mine. I was wondering if you'd be interested in staying there, until you find a place of your own."

Dani blinked at Gia, unsure if she'd understood. "You mean move into the apartment upstairs?"

"*Si*. It's sitting empty and you said you needed to be closer to here. Just until you buy your own place."

"I... I don't know what to say. I, um... wow. That's really kind of you but... well, I'm not sure I could pay for such a –"

"Don't be silly. I don't – or should I say *we* don't – want you to pay rent. It's just until you find a place. Take the pressure off the travelling."

"I couldn't, Gia. It's so unbelievably generous. I couldn't live there without paying. I wouldn't feel right. I mean, thank you, really. That's so –"

"Nonsense. You can stay and that's final. You said yourself you wanted to buy somewhere in the spring, so it would be six months tops. I insist. It'll be ready by the thirtieth so you can move in just after the New Year."

"Gia... I don't know what to say. I'm a little overwhelmed, to be honest."

"Say yes and that's it. We'll be neighbours!"

Dani stared at Gia's face as she smiled widely, still stunned at the offer. "Well, if you're sure."

"Do you want to have a look at it?" Gia stood up from behind her desk.

Dani looked at her watch. It was just past ten thirty, "I'm not sure I have time."

Gia picked up the phone and dialled. "Peter, Dani will be a bit late, we're working on something. Make sure you leave our lunch out, we'll be down in twenty minutes." She replaced the receiver and winked at Dani. "There, all sorted. Come on, let's go."

Dani rose from her chair and followed Gia out of her office. "Don't you mean *Andiamo*?" chuckled Dani, causing Gia to laugh softly.

Jerome's attention was drawn to the sound of his mother's laughter in the corridor. He closed the file he was looking over and got up from behind his desk. He was a little curious to find out how her date had gone last night. From the security camera coverage, he'd looked over this morning, he'd seen Ray had behaved like a gentleman – he saw Gia to the door at one in the morning with just a kiss to her cheek. Jerome left his office and headed to the dining room, hoping he'd find her there.

The staff were already sitting down and eating but the chairs his mother and Dani normally occupied were empty. Jerome caught Peter's eye.

"Where's Mama?" he called.

Peter shrugged. "She's with Dani."

Jerome furrowed his brow and left the room, standing for a moment in the hallway. He looked up the stairs and realised they must be in his mother's apartment. He swiftly turned towards the stairs and climbed them two by two.

"Gia, this place is amazing! It's far too big for me." Dani walked over to the balcony window that overlooked the river. She could see the whole city of Leeds. The apartment was spacious and light, thanks to the large windows along the far side. It had a small hall, like Gia's apartment, with black and white chequered flooring that opened up through an archway to the living area. There was a dining area with a large rectangular light oak table that could comfortably seat eight. Above it hung a long chandelier, which Dani knew would make a spectacular focal point when it was turned on. The dining area led to the open plan ultra-modern kitchen, which was predominantly stainless steel, with light oak and frosted glass cupboards, finished off with black shiny granite tops. The whole apartment was furnished in browns, dove grey and cream, its urban, masculine décor evidence of its previous occupants.

The living area had a large, grey, suede U-shaped settee that could also easily fit eight people. It faced a modern fireplace with large grey stones set inside it. Dani presumed the flames would come up through them, creating another dramatic focal point. The coffee table was low and made of frosted glass and in the centre was a large intricately carved box.

Gia took her through to the first bedroom, which had its own en suite bathroom, complete with a wet room and a contemporary bathtub, the kind that filled from a large chrome spout in the wall. The bedroom itself had a walk-in wardrobe and a huge window overlooking the river that the king-sized bed faced. The second bedroom was the mirror image of the first, just slightly smaller and without a bathtub.

Dani walked back into the living area, slightly stunned at its grandiosity. It was a magnificent apartment, fully furnished in designer furnishing, and distinctly out of her league.

"Gia, this place is gorgeous. Are you sure you don't mind me staying here?" Dani ran her hand over the soft sumptuous suede of the settee.

"I wouldn't have asked you if I wasn't sure."

"So you've asked her, then?" Jerome's familiar raspy voice caused Dani to gasp. She sharply retracted her hand from the settee as though it had burned her, and her eyes shot up to where Jerome was leaning casually against the archway, his light grey, large-checked, three-piece suit matching the stylish decor perfectly. He'd paired it with a white shirt, open at the collar, showcasing his Mediterranean colouring, looking so at home in the exquisitely decorated apartment, and positively delicious. There was no doubt that the interior design was a reflection of his particular taste. Everything was well thought out, very masculine, yet with an extreme attention to detail that made the space seem more homely – intimate, even. A smile curved over his sculptured lips as he straightened and stepped forward.

"Oh Jerome, you're here. Yes. Just now." Gia walked over to him and kissed both his cheeks.

"So? Do you like it?" he asked once he'd released his mother. His gaze focused on Dani.

Dani huffed. "Like it? It's amazing... too amazing for me." Her voice drifted off, almost talking to herself.

Jerome tilted his head to one side, puzzled at her comment. "Why do you say that?"

"It's a little out of my league." She looked around the room nervously.

Jerome stepped closer, stopping a few feet from her. "You won't feel comfortable here? Is that what you're saying? Is there something you want to change? Because we can do that, the maintenance team start on..." His spectacular eyes were suddenly marred with concern.

"Oh God! No, I didn't mean it like that. It's perfect – more than perfect, really. I'm just a little overwhelmed and anyway, its only temporary, isn't it?"

Jerome shrugged. Now that Dani was walking around in his apartment, touching its furnishings, looking around his old home with wonder, the idea of her being there only temporarily didn't sit well with him. *He could vividly visualise her making coffee in the kitchen, stretched out on the settee, laid out on his bed...* Jerome cleared his throat and shook his head, ridding himself of his wandering thoughts. "Did Mama tell you that it'll be ready by the thirtieth?"

"Yes, she did. Really, that's fine. I'm still trying to get to grips with the idea of moving in here. The time frame really isn't what's worrying me." Dani turned to look around again not wanting her gaze focused on Jerome for too long. The place looked immaculate and Dani wondered what on earth needed to be done.

"So, that's it? It's settled?" asked Gia expectantly. Dani gave a half-hearted shrug.

"So what is worrying you?" Jerome perched himself on the back of the settee casually.

"I still feel like I should be paying you rent or something."

Jerome immediately stood back up again and Gia shook her head.

"No!" they both answered in unison, causing Dani to laugh.

"You do so much extra work here, it's the least we can do." Gia stepped closer as she spoke, then turned to Jerome, who nodded in agreement. "To make it easier for you."

"But it's temporary, just until I get my own place. I don't want to take advantage," Dani repeated, determined they both understood. She was caught between not wanting to be beholden to the Ferrettis and being totally flattered that they were trying to make her life easier. It was a dilemma she'd found herself in before and no doubt would find herself in again.

Jerome licked his lips and narrowed his eyes, then answered wryly, "I think maybe it's us taking advantage of you. You're making yourself quite indispensable. I think this is my mother's way of keeping you close by, so you don't up and leave us anytime soon."

"I'm not going anywhere," Dani muttered quietly, repeating what she'd told him once before. "Thank you, both of you."

"I'm so pleased." Gia clapped her hands together and laughed softly. "It'll be nice having a female neighbour for a change. Come on, let's go and have our lunch. Peter will be wondering where we are."

Arsenio reread Scott's latest report on Liz's movements since she'd got back from Spain. She'd spent almost four hours at her agent's office on

Friday morning, again arriving in her gym clothes and leaving in one of her designer outfits. Gary's report also confirmed that Jonathan was in the agent's building, but neither he nor Scott had managed to find out which of the offices they were using.

He just knew they were missing something, something important. Arsenio flicked through the photos again, hoping something would jump out at him. They were ingrained into his memory and he knew he was obsessing, but he couldn't face the fact that Liz seemed to be getting away with cheating. He wanted to nail the bitch and make her pay.

Liz stood on the scales again and waited for the screen to settle on the correct weight. *Damn!* She thought. She'd gone up two pounds since she'd come back from Spain. Liz gritted her teeth and stalked naked across the hallway to Jerome's empty bedroom. Her gaze ran around the immaculately kept room, checking every surface for the brown bottle of pills. There was nothing. She paced over to the bathroom and checked in the cupboards and the surfaces. *Nothing!* Her eyes caught the dustbin by the toilet. She flipped open the lid and looked inside. To her relief the bottle was sitting at the bottom of the bin. She reached in and pulled it out and immediately her heart dropped: it was empty. *Shit! He must've flushed them down the toilet!* Liz stalked back to her room. How was she going to get hold of some more? She'd already told Jonathan she'd quit them yesterday, so there was no way he was going to get her any more. If she asked anyone at Level One, it was bound to get back to Jerome. Liz slumped on the bed. The only way was for her to seek out Jonathan's supplier.

Liz looked at the time. It was almost three. Jerome and the children would be home from Alessandro's football match at any moment and then they were going to do some last minute Christmas shopping. She'd have to wait until Monday now. Liz rummaged through her drawers, looking for a packet of cigarettes she kept for the odd occasion that she wanted one. She flipped open the packet, glad to see it was almost full. Hopefully these would suppress her appetite until Monday.

Dani sat in her car, watching the rain splash down on the bonnet. It was four o'clock and she'd an hour or so before she needed to be back at work. She was supposed to have had the afternoon off, but they were busy and she'd stayed on until four. It wasn't worth going back home, seeing as she needed to be back for five. Things would certainly be a lot better for her once she'd moved into the apartment upstairs. Dani peered up at the building. *Or maybe not.* She had a feeling she'd be eating, living and breathing La Casa once she moved in. The thought made her smile. It really was a great place to live. She shook her head, unable to believe her luck.

Dani had come out to her car for some privacy. She was determined to call Jez once she was off her shift and back home, but because she'd stayed on, her car was the only place she could go where she wouldn't be disturbed. She looked down at her phone and swiped the screen to search for Jez's number. He should be getting ready to go down to the bar around about this time. If she didn't ring him now, she'd have to call him late on Monday. She pressed on the "Call" icon and waited for it to connect. Her heart raced at the thought of hearing his familiar smooth voice again.

"Dani?"

"Hi, Jez."

"Oh my God, I don't believe it! It's so good to hear your voice." He sounded as if he'd just woken up, his voice still had a croak in it and Dani felt her stomach clench. Two thoughts sprung into her mind: the first was that she missed being the one who heard his first croaky words when he woke up, and the second was she hoped that there wasn't anyone else who'd heard them since.

"How are you?" Dani cringed. Her question was automatic and she hoped it didn't make him start his usual tirade.

"I'm better. Much better now."

Dani heard a rustle of sheets and she knew he was propping himself up against the pillows. "Thanks for the letter. I passed it on to Adam."

"Oh. Yes. Well, the bank said it would've been earlier but with Christmas and all, it's taken a week or two longer." There was an awkward silence, then Jez continued, with a tentative lilt in his voice. "How are you? I mean, you've a job now, right?"

"Yes. It's a good job. A restaurant."

"A restaurant? That's um... good."

"I'm just a waitress. But the people who own it are really good to me. I didn't want anything more... I couldn't face any more responsibility. I'm happy just turning up and then leaving it behind."

Jez huffed, "Yeah, it can take over your life. Well, you know it can."

Dani sighed. It felt weird talking about work, tiptoeing around each other. It was awkward, there was so much to say, yet they were purposely avoiding any sensitive subjects.

"I'm sorry about what I said, about you having found someone else. I was angry, and I know that's no excuse, but I know you're not like that."

Dani took in a deep breath, unsure of what to say. The last thing she'd expected was an apology.

"And the messages I sent – the bad ones, I mean. I was angry then too. To be honest, I've been angry most of the time these last six weeks," he snorted. "But angry at me, though, and the situation I've found myself in. Losing you."

"I'm not sure what to say. I –"

"You don't have to say anything. I've done a lot of thinking since you left, and a lot of drinking. Not always the best combination," he scoffed.

Dani smiled. It was good he still kept his humour with her.

"The soppy messages I sent you were when I was drunk. They're the ones I really meant. You know I always get soppy when I drink."

"I remember," Dani answered softly.

"I fucked up, Dani, and I know you can't forgive me. Why would you? I can't forgive myself. But I can't face the fact that we can't at least be friends."

"Jez, it's just too soon. I'm –"

"I don't expect us to fall back into being anything like we were, Dani. I hurt you, deeply. But at least we can talk from time to time. We spent five years together. Went through so much, good and bad. I can't just throw that away."

"Jez... I don't know how easy that'll be for me."

"Did you listen to the song?"

"Yes."

"Then you understand. I can't let you go, not yet, Dani. I just can't. So if it means we're just friends that talk on the phone, I can live with that. I'll take that."

"Jez, I don't want you thinking..."

"Right now I'm thinking, 'Thank God you called'. I mean it, Dani. You want to just stay friends, then that's how it'll be."

Dani knew his persistence should have been a big warning bell. It really wasn't right to encourage him, but he sounded so pleased to hear from her. He was allowing her to dictate the terms. If things got difficult, she could cut him off again. She'd done it before.

"I don't want you ringing me all the time. I work long hours. I'm getting settled."

"I understand. I don't want to make things hard for you. Have you found your own place yet?"

"No. Well, not permanently. I'm waiting for the money before I decide."

"And you'll come down? When the money comes through?"

"I'm not sure that's a good idea, Jez."

"But you've your stuff here too. Your books and there are some things in the basement. Some boxes – don't you want them?"

Dani had forgotten that in her hurry to leave, that fated night, she'd only taken her essential possessions. There were many of her parent's things and childhood mementoes she'd boxed in the basement, meaning to sort through them at some later date. He was right; she would need to go down at some point. She didn't really trust him to send them up to her.

"Um, I might come down for those at a later date. I don't think I'm ready to come back down yet..."

"Dani, I want to see you. It's three weeks from now. Please, it's the only thing I've asked from you."

Dani closed her eyes, feeling bad for him but knowing he was doing what he always did. *Manipulating her.*

"The guys at the bar really want to see you too. Earl especially."

Making her feel guilty.

He continued, "Dani, it's just for one day. Can't you do that? It would mean a lot to me."

Persuading her. "I'll see, like you said, it's three weeks away. I need to see about time off at work too. Dani rubbed her face, feeling uneasy at how quickly she'd fallen back into a familiar pattern. He could still do that. Make her do things she wasn't altogether happy about. "Look, I need to go, my shift's about to start."

"So we'll talk later?"

"Yes. I'll call you. Like I said, my hours are irregular. Now I really need to go."

"It was really great talking to you, Dani, hearing your voice again. I miss you."

"Jez, please don't..."

"Okay. I'm sorry."

"Say hi to the guys at the bar for me. Bye, Jez."

"I will. Bye."

Dani dropped her phone on to her lap and buried her face in her hands. Her stomach felt like it had a stone in it and her mouth was bone dry. Thank goodness it was going to be busy tonight. Anything to keep her mind off Jez.

Scott yawned and rubbed his eyes. He lifted his coffee flask to his lips and tilted it back. *Shit, it was empty.* He glanced back at Jerome's house, seeing the security lights switch on at the rear of the house. He checked the time. It was quarter to midnight. Jerome had left at eight that evening. Liz hadn't moved from the house but she was still awake, he'd seen lights come on and off over the past few hours. She normally was in bed by eleven, but tonight she was late.

He furrowed his brow. Why had the security lights come on? The nanny had already left at nine. Maybe she'd come back into the house again or maybe it was a fox that had wandered over. He pulled out his binoculars and focused them on the upper floors where the lights were still on. Within a few minutes, they switched off and the inside of the house was dark, apart from the front porch light that had a timer switch. Scott put down his binoculars, seeing the lights of a car come from behind him and drive on past down the road.

He'd wait until midnight and if there was no more activity, he'd leave. It'd been a quiet day for him today. Liz had played the model mother and wife, spending all her time with Jerome and the children. That was until Jerome left, then her phone log showed she'd rung Jonathan for over an hour. Scott put down his binoculars and sighed. *She really was a piece of work.* He shuddered, thinking about the video he'd seen of her servicing the trainer.

His disturbing thoughts were interrupted by his phone ringing. He looked down at the number and saw it was his friend Paul, head of security for the Ferretti family. Strange that Paul should be ringing him at this time. He swiped open the screen and answered it.

"Hello, Paul, how are you?"

"I'm fine. You?"

"I'm good. What can I do for you?"

"I just wanted to know why you're watching Jerome Ferretti's house."

Scott turned around sharply, looking out of his rear window and down the road where he'd parked. He could only see a few parked cars outside the various houses on the street.

"How did you know I was here?" Scott asked, clearly puzzled.

"One of my men passes by on a routine check. He spotted your car parked up. So, what are you doing there?" Paul sounded irritated.

"I'm on a job, Paul."

"I'm not sure I follow. A job for who, exactly? Did Jerome ask you to keep an eye on the house?" Now he sounded confused as well as irritated.

Scott swallowed hard. How on earth was he going to explain this without offending his associate or betraying Arsenio, his client?

"No, I'm not working for Jerome Ferretti."

"Then who are you working for?"

"Paul, I can't say."

"I see." Paul still sounded irritated, but by Scott's tone, he understood that he couldn't divulge his client. "Does Jerome know?"

"No, he doesn't," Scott sighed, knowing exactly where this was going. Paul was Jerome's head of security, meaning he had to report whatever he saw. So how was he going to explain why a private detective was staking out his house? He'd lose his job if Jerome found out that he didn't tell him.

"Then you're going to have to explain yourself, Scott."

"You're putting me in a difficult position, Paul."

"As are you. You either tell me who you're working for, or I need to let Jerome know."

"I'd rather tell you face to face, Paul. When can we meet?"

"As soon as possible. I don't want to sit on this information for too long. Tomorrow? I'll come round to yours," Paul suggested.

"Call me first. I'll be on the job."

"This same job?"

"Yep."

"I'm not liking what I'm hearing, Scott." There was a warning in his tone.

"You'll like it even less tomorrow."

"Morning! You're down early for a Sunday." Dani grinned at Adam who was making himself a coffee. He looked dishevelled and sleepy, rubbing the back of his neck.

"Yeah, Rosie slept with us last night after a nightmare," he explained. "Coffee?"

"Please."

"So my chance of a lie-in went out the window, along with getting any decent sleep. She's sparked out on my side of the bed with Chloe now." Adam rolled his eyes. He quickly put in a coffee pod for Dani and switched on the machine. "I got the letter. Looks like everything's going to be sorted out next month, which is good news." Adam pulled out the coffee cup and handed it to Dani, who'd sat down at the table.

"Thanks. Yes. I spoke to him yesterday."

Adam lowered his large frame slowly into the seat adjacent to Dani. "You spoke to Jez?"

Dani nodded and took a welcome sip from her coffee.

"And?"

"He was... well, he apologised and he said he wanted us to be friends." Adam snorted, "Wanker."

Dani smirked, "He was actually really nice."

"Dani," Adam chastised softly.

"Oh, I know. You don't need to worry. I've told him we could talk on the phone and stuff but that was it for now."

"And about you going down?"

"I told him I couldn't. It's too soon. But I will need to go and get the rest of my things at some point. Anyway, let's just wait and see. Once the money comes through, I may feel differently."

"Don't let him bully you. You're just getting yourself together. You don't need him screwing that up for you."

Dani grinned, "I won't. Actually, I have some news."

Adam yawned and rested back in the chair. "Oh yes?"

"Yes, Gia offered me the apartment above the restaurant until I get my own place."

Adam's eyes widened suddenly. "Really? I didn't realise there was an apartment over the restaurant."

"There are two. Gia lives in one and the other one was occupied by one of her sons at various times, but it's empty now."

"So, I take it you said 'yes'."

"I did, but I'll move in after the New Year. It's being painted first."

"Can you afford it? I mean, I don't want you struggling. You can stay here as long as you want – you know that, don't you? There's no hurry for you to leave." Adam leaned forward, his concern evident. The last thing he wanted was Dani to leave if she couldn't manage it financially, and he knew Chloe and the children would be upset that she was leaving.

"Actually they don't want me to pay rent. I offered, obviously, but they just want to help me out." Dani looked at her coffee cup, avoiding Adam's questioning look.

"When you say 'they', who do you mean?"

"Gia and Jerome," Dani answered, then took another sip of her coffee.

"I see, that's um, very generous of them." He just managed to disguise his scepticism in his tone.

"Yes. It's because I work extra hours and help out with the decorations, and I'm teaching Gia a few things on the computer." Dani rambled on nervously as Adam continued to furrow his brow. "And it's just temporary. Until I get my own place," she added, but as she explained the terms and reasons for the Ferretti's generosity to him, it still sounded too good to be true.

"Well. You can always come back here if you find that it's too much. Working and living so close together you may get a little... er..." he tilted his head trying to find the right word. "Consuming. You're a good person, Dani, and sometimes people take advantage. I don't want you feeling indebted to them."

"Gia's not like that."

"No, maybe Gia isn't." He paused before adding, "Just be careful." He smiled softly at her, then took a gulp from his coffee cup.

"Talking of Gia, did you know your dad took her out on Friday night?"

Adam choked on his coffee and Dani giggled, then reached over to pat him hard on the back. "My dad?" he spluttered. "Took out 'the hottie'?" Adam coughed some more, then swallowed hard.

Dani nodded. "Yep. Dinner and a jazz club, no less. Don't you dare tell him I told you!"

Adam shook his head, then pretended to zip his lips, which made Dani laugh. "Well, well, well. I didn't think he had it in him. There's life in the old dog yet." He grinned widely. "Way to go, *Raymondo!*"

"So that's about the long and short of it, Paul." Scott shuffled in his car seat uncomfortably. He wasn't happy about having to explain himself to Paul, but he knew he'd been given no choice.

He'd arranged to meet Paul while he was on surveillance outside Jerome's house. It was lunchtime and Jerome hadn't left the house, apart from going out to the newsagents to get some cigarettes and then to a Jewish bakery for some bagels, early that morning. Liz had stayed home with him, playing her rehearsed role of wife and mother. Scott knew the minute Jerome left in the evening she'd be calling Jonathan.

Paul pinched the bridge of his nose. He knew things must be bad between Jerome and Liz from the rumours he'd heard from the staff at Level One. He tended not to partake in gossip, especially when it concerned his boss. But Jonathan's sudden exit from the gym had caused enough of a stir amongst the staff that the ripples had come to his ears. It also didn't make sense that Liz had also stopped working there. Over the years that he'd worked with Jerome, he'd never questioned his actions. He was there solely to make sure that there was never any danger or trouble relating to the businesses and the staff – what else went on was none of his business. When you ran security, discretion was imperative. No questions asked.

"Jesus, Scott, this puts me in a worse position." It started to make a bit more sense now. Paul remembered Jerome asking for a private investigator for a client. Of course he couldn't have asked Paul to do the work. He was too close, and Jerome definitely didn't want his team knowing about Liz's affair or that he was checking up on her.

"I know, but you gave me no choice. I couldn't compromise Seni. You needed to know the facts before you decided to go to Jerome."

"Jerome has no idea. He's just set up a fashion show for her at Sky. He'll be mortified."

"I know."

"So what's the plan? Once you've got all the evidence, you're going to give it to Jerome? Like, 'Hey look, we've been spying on your wife and she's still fucking the trainer'?"

"Not exactly. I'm not entirely sure how Seni's going to tell him. All I know is that he wants every bit of proof he can get, and we've got it. Phone records, photos, even a video."

"A video?"

"Yeah." Scott shuddered.

"Jesus, Seni went all out. What a fucking mess." They sat for a moment in silence. "Look, I'm not entirely sure how I'm going to handle this."

"Your guy, when does he pass by here?"

"Between eleven thirty and midnight, then every hour after that until six in the morning."

"Well that explains why he never saw me until last night. I'm usually gone by eleven. Her car has a tracker, so I know if she leaves in the middle of the night, but she's usually asleep by eleven. I'll make sure I'm not here from now on so your guy won't report my car parked up."

Paul nodded.

"If anything changes, I'll give you a heads up."

Paul took a deep breath, "I'm going to have to speak to Seni."

"Why? I've told you what's going on. If you tell him we've spoken, then I'm royally fucked for divulging the information. He'll go ape shit and I'll lose him as a client."

"I'm being disloyal to Jerome. I need to be able to cover myself too. This puts us both in a difficult dilemma. Why don't you tell him you saw one of my guys driving past Jerome's house and he recognised you. He might come and tell me himself, then."

"He's a lawyer, Paul. He's not going to spill anything he doesn't have to," sighed Scott.

Paul looked out of his window, trying hard to work out how he could cover himself without blowing Scott's cover. "How long do you think you'll be on the job for?"

"Until Christmas. Maybe until just after."

"Okay, I'll say nothing but try and mention about my man to Seni. I'm bound to see him at Sky. He may just say something to me." Paul shook his head. "This is going to come and bite us in the ass. The Ferrettis are good people. I've known them for nearly fifteen years and worked for them for four, but their family comes first and they value loyalty above all else. That bitch is going to mess them all up and us too. Jerome will lose a shit-tonne if he divorces her."

Scott grunted his agreement. From what he'd seen of Liz over the last few weeks, he could see she was just using Jerome.

"He's got a lot on his plate at the moment and I think he's dropped the ball where she's concerned," added Paul. He thought back to the drug runners they were trying to keep at bay and the extra hours Jerome was putting in at Level One. Then there was La Casa, and Christmas was the busiest time of the year for both the restaurant and the club. He was spreading himself too thinly and Liz was taking advantage.

"Do you mind keeping me in the loop? You never know, I might be able to help out."

Scott shrugged. Paul knew the worst of it now, and he didn't see the harm in it. And an extra pair of eyes and experience might spot something he and Seni had missed.

"Sure. I can send you the photos and phone records along with the reports to your email, but believe me, you don't want to see the video."

"No, I don't. Good. I'll expect your call then?"

"Yeah."

"Well, take it easy, then." Paul jerked his head towards the Ferretti house.

"Thanks, you too," smirked Scott.

34

SUGGESTIONS

"I'm *so* ready for my day off tomorrow," huffed Nicole.

"It has been crazy this week," agreed Dani. She was buttoning up her royal blue, slim-fitted trousers, after tucking in a matching halter top. She'd pinned up her hair in a messy up-do, as usual, not having time to restyle it. The rest of the restaurant staff were already at Sky, except for Kuch who was patiently waiting for them upstairs.

"I'll say. The next two weeks will be worse. But it's great fun, especially New Year's Eve."

"You're dressing up as Grace Kelly, right?"

"Yes, I love Grace Kelly."

"Oh, you'd make a great Grace Kelly! And Kuch?"

"Elvis!" giggled Nicole.

"No way! He'd be an excellent Elvis. That's going to be funny. Will you spend tomorrow together?"

Nicole beamed. "Yeah. I love my days off. We just hang out at my place. He cooks for me and we just watch movies all day long. It's perfect."

"You guys should be married. You work together so well and spend all your spare time with each other when you're not. You practically *are* married."

Nicole wrinkled her nose.

"What? Are you telling me if he asked you, you'd say no?" Dani narrowed her eyes at her through the mirror while she applied her lipstick.

Nicole shook her head and blushed. "Of course I'd say yes. But when we first got together, I told him I wasn't interested in getting married. I've had it rammed down my throat since I was a little girl. You know, 'You need to find a nice Italian man and get married.'" Nicole rolled her eyes. "So I think I just became so anti-marriage. A reaction to the pressure. You probably can't understand what it's like living with an overbearing big family."

Dani huffed. What she wouldn't give to have a big family right now. "Yeah, well you and I have different opinions on family life. What about now, though?"

Nicole shook her head. "Not now. Not since Kuch is in the picture."

Dani smiled softly at her. "Can I make a suggestion?"

Nicole shrugged one shoulder. "Sure."

"Why don't you propose?"

Nicole eyes widened. "Me?"

"Yeah, you. You're happy to throw convention out the window regarding the sanctity of marriage, but you're old fashioned enough when it comes to the asking?" Dani raised a questioning brow. "Nicole, you love the guy, he's nuts about you, but he knows you don't – or rather won't – do the marriage thing. How's he supposed to propose if he thinks you'll shoot him down? He doesn't know you've changed your mind. So ask him. Get him a ring and just do it!"

"You're right," Nicole sighed, then she spun around to face Dani. "You know what? I think I will. Maybe on his birthday. It's on the twenty-ninth." She slumped on a chair, a little dazed. Now she was thinking about the prospect of asking him, she wanted to make sure everything was perfect. "My family are coming over from Italy at the end of January. I can tell them then. We'll have to keep it quiet, I suppose, until then. Or maybe I'll wait until I've spoken to them first. I don't want anything to ruin it." Dani heard the excitement in her voice as she cultivated her plan.

Dani sat next to her and squeezed her shoulders. "Well, you've waited this long, a few more weeks won't matter. He's a great guy, Nicole. He deserves the best and he's got it."

"Thanks, Dani. He is the best and he's going to get the best proposal ever. I'm going to blow his mind!"

Paul stood on the walkway, scanning around the club. Over the next two weeks, the place was going to be heaving. All his men were working every shift to ensure they had no more incidents like they'd had last night. Thankfully, they'd managed to see the smug bastard off without too much disturbance. Paul had wanted to wipe the grin off the asshole's face with his fist, but he knew it would only mean more trouble for Jerome and Sky. He'd have to let the dust settle a bit, then in a month or so seek him out. Paul rolled his shoulders, feeling the tension of his pent-up anger. It had taken him a few beatings over the years to realise that if you wanted to be able to control a volatile situation, you needed to keep your head and wait for the right time to strike, when they were least expecting it. He'd learned that the hard way.

Paul's eyes spotted Arsenio walking up towards the stairs leading to Jerome's office. He knew this would probably be the only time he'd catch him without Jerome being around and his only chance to open up a conversation about Scott and his surveillance.

Arsenio was let through the roped-off area that lead to Jerome's office by one of the security men and paced towards where he saw Paul checking over the club from the bird's eye position. He'd come purposely to speak with him after Scott's phone call this morning. Arsenio knew Jerome had asked for more security around his home. According to Scott, one of them had spotted him and he didn't want that information getting back to Jerome. He was here to test the waters with Paul.

"Hey, Seni. How you doing?" The men shook hands warmly. They'd known each other for fifteen years and were familiar enough to feel some sort of camaraderie. It was a friendship built on mutual respect and the connection they had with Jerome.

"It's crazy busy tonight. Don't people have work in the morning?" joked Arsenio.

"Well most places closed on Friday so they're in full Christmas mode." Paul rolled his eyes and rested his forearms on the railings. "It'll be like this almost every night until the first of January."

"That'll be a real headache for you." Arsenio mirrored Paul's posture and leaned on the rail and looked over the club.

"I'll say. We're fully manned up and we still manage to slip up sometimes," huffed Paul.

Arsenio turned to look at Paul. "Trouble?"

"Just trying to keep some unsavoury characters out." Paul pursed his lips together and stood up, crossing his arms in front of him.

Arsenio didn't need much more explanation. He straightened up and turned to face Paul leaning back against the railing. "Yeah, Jerome said you'd had a few incidences. It's a tough time for him at the moment."

"Yep, he's a lot on his plate and when it's silly season, everything just gets that bit worse. He's lucky he has his family around him to watch his back," Paul said dryly.

Arsenio took in a sharp breath, understanding the hidden meaning in his seemingly casual comment. "He's got a good team here too. I'm sure you're all doing whatever you can. These kinds of guys can get personal."

"We're watching the restaurant, keeping a close eye on it. That and his home."

Arsenio nodded as Paul continued.

"Seeing who's around, if anything's unusual. You know, comings and goings. You can't be too careful." Paul kept his eyes pinned on Arsenio.

"No you can't."

Paul pushed a little more. "I'm lucky I have a thorough team. They keep me informed of every detail, any movements. It's amazing what you can pick up."

Arsenio swallowed. "Like?"

"Cars parked up that have no business in being there."

"I see." Arsenio came away from the railing and stepped closer to Paul. "I think we need to talk."

Paul dropped his arms to his sides. "I think we do."

"Come to my office tomorrow."

"I'll be there at ten."

Apart from the unique location and the stylish décor, Sky undoubtedly played the best of the latest music, along with past hits, making it the most popular night club in the city. This was down to the skills of Kuch's brother Max, who was Sky's resident deejay and was known as MK – Maximillian Kuckiki was just too much of a mouthful. The whole club was pulsing with tangible energy, the atmosphere electric, touching everyone. There wasn't any way you could enter Sky and not be drawn into the contagious vibe that exuded off everyone in there and from everyone who worked there. The staff at La Casa had worked long, hard hours over the last week but their tiredness was soon forgotten as they were swept away by the highly charged surroundings.

Dani stood by the bar, near their usual table, talking to Carmen and Silvanna. It was good to spend time with them socially, Dani mainly spent time with Rosa and Nicole during her working day, so it was nice to catch up with the other female members of staff. A clammy hand landed on Dani's bare back, which caused her to jerk and stop mid-conversation.

She twisted around to see who it was that had disturbed her, and to her utter shock was faced with David, the over-familiar client that came into the restaurant.

Shit, thought Dani. Had it been someone she hadn't known she'd have bawled him out, but she knew she couldn't with David. He was a very good customer, so she'd have to be courteous at the very least.

"I thought it was you," he slurred, leaning in to speak in her ear. Carmen and Silvanna gawked at the wiry man.

"Oh, hello, David, um this is a surprise. Let me introduce you to Carmen and Silvanna, they're part of the kitchen team at La Casa. Carmen, Silvanna, David is a regular client of ours." Dani turned away from David, facing her two friends and widened her eyes at them cringing, secure in the knowledge that David couldn't see her. David looked over at them dismissively and mumbled a hello, then turned his full drunkard attention back to Dani. Carmen stood her ground, her blue eyes darkening. There was no way she was leaving Dani. She leaned over to Silvanna, instructing her to go get help. The guy could hardly string a sentence together and he had now put his arm around Dani's waist, almost caging her up against the bar.

"Can I get you a drink?" He swayed, bumping her up against the bar.

"No, that's kind of you, but I've got one. Thank you," Dani replied through clenched teeth. She lifted her glass containing mineral water, so he could see. His grip on her waist slipped and he'd moved it to her hip.

David tried to focus on the glass. "Aw, that's not a drink!" he whined, looking at Dani's glass. "You need a real drink." He stumbled a little and his grip grew tighter on Dani to steady himself.

"Really, I'm fine. Are you with someone, David? Is your wife here?" Dani thought he might sober up if he thought about his wife.

"No, she-sh home. I came with some mates. Let me get you that drink." He waved to the bartender, who came over. The bartender knew Dani and with one look at her stony face, he'd worked out exactly what was going on. "I'll have a whish-ky and whatever this *gorgeousshh* girl wants."

"Really, David, I don't want a drink. Shall we sit down? You look a little worn out." Dani tried to prise his hand off her hip but he dug his fingers in.

"Oh no, you're not getting away from me that easily."

Arsenio met Jerome coming out of his office on the walkway. Paul had moved down a floor and was checking in with each of his staff, leaving the two brothers to look down over the club.

"How come you're here?" asked Jerome.

"I was at a loose end and I don't need to get into the office until late. We're working a skeleton staff over the holidays. Just emergencies."

Jerome nodded, then turned his attention to the club. He was concerned that Arsenio had an ulterior motive. He knew La Casa staff came down on Sunday nights and he was almost sure that he was here for Dani. Jerome searched the area where the restaurant staff usually sat and couldn't spot Dani. He then shifted his focus to the dance floor, scanning it with narrowed eyes, the pulsing lasers making it difficult to see clearly.

"Is that asshole bothering Dani?"

Jerome jerked his head to look at Arsenio, then followed the line of his gaze to the direction he was now glaring at. "Where?"

"There, by the far bar, near the staff table." Arsenio pointed down to where he meant.

Jerome squinted to focus on who seemed to be standing far too close Dani, almost caging her up against the bar.

"Fuck. That's David," he growled and immediately strode across the walkway and ran down the stairs, followed by an equally agitated Arsenio. The pathway to the bar was crowded making it difficult to get past. They had to weave through the bodies, slowing down what should've been a minute's walk. Jerome couldn't see just how familiar David was getting with Dani but he knew what he was like, especially after few drinks. If he had done anything remotely inappropriate, Jerome knew he'd find it hard to rein in his temper. The very thought of anyone manhandling Dani had his blood boiling and made him feel positively violent.

By the time Arsenio and Jerome reached the three steps that raised the seating area where the staff were sitting, Kuch was already by Dani's side, along with Silvanna and Carmen. The girls had strained smiles on their faces, obviously uncomfortable. Kuch had managed to slip his arm around Dani and pull her towards him, planting a kiss at the side of her mouth, playing out his role of boyfriend. "Oh there you are! I was looking for you. Oh, hello, David, how nice to see you. Have you been looking after my girl?" Kuch eased a grateful Dani away from David's grip, then shook David's now-free hand, smiling widely at a confused David.

"Er, yesh. Your girl, eh?"

"Uh-huh, well we're off to dance. See you soon, eh?" Kuch winked at David and whisked Dani away, his arm around her waist, pulling her towards the dance floor.

Dani squeezed Kuch. "Thanks, I was getting worried for a moment. He's absolutely out of his head, he can hardly stand."

"He's an ass," Kuch muttered. His smile dropped as soon as he'd turned from David.

They passed Arsenio and Jerome who'd stopped a few metres away, witnessing the whole scene.

"David's pissed out of his head," hissed Kuch at Jerome.

Jerome nodded. "Are you okay? Did he do anything to you?" His eyes blazed with anger as he spoke to Dani, though his eyes were trained on David.

Dani shook her head. "He just got too close and tried to buy me a drink. He probably won't remember it in the morning." Jerome sighed, then his gaze flitted to Dani's arms, which were holding tightly on to Kuch.

Arsenio huffed, "In that case you should've decked him."

"The guy's an asshole," Kuch said, looking over his shoulder at David who was slumped on a bar stool.

"You did good, Kuch. I'll take care of him." Jerome shot a look at Arsenio and they both went in the direction of the bar.

Dani sat down near one of the heaters out on the veranda. Suddenly she felt very tired. It had been a long week and tomorrow she was going to be busy. It was past one in the morning; maybe she should call it a night. Kuch had brought her out here and then she'd shooed him off, insisting she was fine on her own and just needed some air.

Pushing the door which opened up on to the veranda, Jerome swept his gaze over the area searching for Dani. He spotted her sitting alone on a couch, her head resting on the back with her eyes closed. He immediately paced over to her. "Dani?"

Her eyes shot open and she straightened in her seat.

"Are you okay?"

"Yeah, I'm fine. Just tired." Dani blushed, embarrassed to be caught out almost napping, especially by Jerome.

Jerome stepped around the table and sat down next to her. "David's been sent home. I got security to put him in a taxi."

"He was really drunk."

"He was. I doubt he'll remember a thing."

"I should go too. I've a full day tomorrow." Dani covered her mouth and stifled a yawn.

"Oh?"

"Yeah, I'm sorting out the decorations for Joseph's function with Gia and helping her set up a Facebook page."

"Mama wants a Facebook page?" Jerome confirmed, clearly surprised.

Dani nodded and grinned. "She wants to be more involved with La Casa's page too."

Jerome shook his head and smiled. "It looks like you've opened up a whole can of worms. My mother's really getting the technology bug."

"I hope that's not a bad thing?" Dani asked, worried that Gia's new found interest might be an unwelcome change for Jerome.

"No, no, not all. In fact it'll make things a bit easier."

Dani shuffled around in her seat so she could face him, resting her elbow on the back of the settee and leaning her head on her hand. "I looked over the page when she asked me."

Jerome shifted to face her. "And?"

"Honestly?"

Jerome nodded.

"It needs to be updated."

"I'm listening."

Dani sat up straighter and bent her knee up on to the seat, now fully facing Jerome.

"Well, La Casa's page isn't linked up to the Sky page. I know most people know you own both but they need to associate the two. Their web pages should also be more apparent and the same goes for Level One too. That way, when you have any events at any one of them, the people who've liked the different pages get to know about events at all three. Who manages the Sky page?"

"MK."

Dani nodded. "It shows. He updates it frequently, has interaction with customers and the page's likes are rising steadily. It's a very active page. I know the restaurant isn't the same kind of business but Sky's twenty thousand likes are all potential customers for both La Casa and Level One. You have three markets in the leisure industry, and two of them are the leaders within their own niche, but that doesn't mean that you can't exploit the customer information you hold on each one, to introduce them to the others and so promote them."

"I thought you were tired." Jerome grinned. He'd watched the sudden change in Dani switch within a few seconds, from weary to totally focused and animated. It was obvious she'd given the subject a lot of thought.

Dani chuckled, "Yeah, I was. Sorry, you probably weren't expecting a full analysis of your social media infrastructure at one o'clock in the morning."

Jerome laughed softly, causing the creases around his eyes to meet up with the ones around his mouth, his face totally transforming. However much Dani was stunned by his normally brooding face, when Jerome laughed in unguarded moments like now, he literary blew her away.

"No I wasn't. But it's certainly more interesting than dealing with drunken customers."

Dani shrugged her apology again. She knew she got carried away some times.

"And don't apologise. I love hearing your opinions. In fact, I'm interested in any other suggestions you may have."

"Oh." Dani swallowed, her mouth suddenly becoming dry. He loved her suggestions? Wow.

Jerome reached into his inside pocket, pulled out his packet of cigarettes and pulled one out. "I took up your idea about the fashion show." He slipped the cigarette between his lips and lit it, taking a deep drag, then looked up at her.

"Did you?" Dani couldn't hide her surprise.

Jerome nodded as he blew out the smoke in a steady stream. *Jeez, he looked so sexy. Why was a man smoking so damn sexy? Or was it just Jerome that made it look sexy?* Dani suddenly felt very warm. She needed to curb her inappropriate thoughts and concentrate. *They were talking about work, for goodness sake!*

"Uh-huh. We're hosting it on the nineteenth of next month, thanks to you."

"Wow, that's in less than a month!"

"Yep, I know," Jerome answered dryly. "It's going to be hectic but Gino and his team here are very capable. In the light of what you just pointed out to me, I think I may need to revamp the pages though." He paused for a second, then added, "How did you put it? Ah yes..." He waved the hand that was holding his cigarette in the air, like he often did when he was extenuating a point. "So, in order to ensure the fashion show is a huge success, I need to promote it by exploiting the information I hold for all three markets, as if I didn't have enough to do." He tilted his head to the side and lifted his brow wryly and smirked at her.

Dani cringed and covered her mouth with her hands. "Sorry. I –"

"No, no. Don't apologise. Like I said, I welcome your input. Of course it means you're going to have to help me implement whatever suggestions you made. You're not getting off that easily."

"I suppose that's fair, under the circumstances," conceded Dani, thrilled that he had considered using her suggestions at all and that they'd be working on them together.

Jerome tilted his head back and laughed. "You'd better think next time, before you open your mouth and suggest anything. It'll probably mean more work for you in the long run." He took another drag from his cigarette.

"Yeah, I think maybe I will."

Inside Sky, the lights and lasers pulsed to the rhythm of the music and Arsenio found it difficult to find where Dani may have got to. He wanted to make sure she was alright and maybe coax her to dance with him. He spotted Kuch by the bar talking with Nicole and Carmen and quickly strode over to them.

"Has Dani left already?" Arsenio asked Kuch once he was close enough.

"No. She's out on the veranda."

"Is she okay?"

"Yeah, she's fine."

"I'll go and check on her." Arsenio turned and headed in the direction of the veranda but not before he heard Carmen call out.

"Behave, Seni!"

He looked over his shoulder at her and answered. "Always do, cuz!" and with a wink and a huge grin, he swiftly made his way through the crowd of clubbers and out onto the veranda.

He searched the now-crowded area full of smokers dragging on the cigarettes and caught sight of Dani sitting with her back to him, talking to Jerome. Arsenio started to advance towards them but slowed down when he had a clearer vision of the two of them. He stopped for a second and focused on his brother for a moment, unsure of what to make of his expression. He looked very focused and intense. Whatever they were talking about seemed serious enough for them not be interested in their surroundings. Then someone jostled Arsenio and his attention was drawn to whoever it was. The person apologised and Arsenio brushed off the apology quickly, then headed to where Jerome and Dani were sitting.

"I see you still haven't quit, though." Dani's eyes gazed at the steady stream of smoke Jerome had just exhaled. "So you're selective with which of my suggestions you implement." She threw him a questioning look.

Jerome turned his hand that held the cigarette and looked at it. "I've decided to quit by New Year, actually."

"Ah, delaying the inevitable, and taking full advantage of the satisfaction until then?" Dani stifled her grin, keeping her eyes fixed on his.

"You make it sound even more appealing," he chuckled. "You certainly have a unique way with words, Dani. But yeah, something like that." He leaned a little closer as he spoke. Dani took in a deep breath, drawing in that unique combination of intoxicating scents that always had her pulse racing.

Jerome licked his lips and blinked slowly before adding, "So it would seem I'm not selective at all, and in fact" – he pointed with his two fingers that held the cigarette at her – "I have taken you up on all your suggestions to date."

"Even if you are delaying one of them," Dani said wryly before she could stop herself. He was doing it again, talking to her about one thing but it felt like he meant something entirely different, something more intimate and personal, something that they had no right to be talking about at all. He'd opened that door again and she had stepped through it, without any hesitation, loving every moment.

"The intent is there all the same."

"I'd better be more careful what else I suggest, then," Dani countered softly.

"Oh don't say that! I'm open to all your suggestions. Especially if you think it's a worthy one? It'd be a terrible waste if you didn't, don't you think?"

Dani swallowed, but her mouth was bone dry. "That would depend."

"On what exactly?" Jerome asked quietly, his mesmerising eyes boring into hers.

"The effect it would have on me."

"There you are!" Arsenio's voice jolted both Dani and Jerome from their highly charged conversation. Dani looked up at Arsenio and smiled tightly as he looked down at her. Jerome leaned away and straightened his position, taking another drag on his cigarette. "What are you two talking about so seriously?" Arsenio furrowed his brow and shifted his gaze to Jerome and then back to Dani.

"Smoking," they answered in unison. Dani shook her head and blew air up her face and Jerome stifled a grin.

"Oh?"

"Yeah, I was just telling Dani it's my New Year's resolution to quit." Jerome reached over to the ashtray on the low table and stubbed out his cigarette.

"About time," huffed Arsenio.

"Um, well I'd better be off." Dani stood up.

"So soon? I was hoping to persuade you to join me for a dance." Arsenio made no attempt to hide his disappointment.

Jerome rose gracefully from the settee, "I think she's tired, Seni."

"I am, and I need to be up early. So, goodnight."

Dani looked over to Jerome and he nodded. "Goodnight."

"I'll walk you out," suggested Arsenio.

"You really don't need to –"

"I insist." Arsenio put up his hand to stop her protest, then shot a look at Jerome, who conceded with a nod.

"Okay, thanks."

They passed by the staff table to say goodbye to everyone, then Arsenio led Dani out to the foyer. Dani collected her jacket from the cloakroom girl who batted her eyelids and shamelessly flirted with Arsenio.

"Someone you know?" Dani whispered sarcastically as Arsenio helped her into her jacket.

"Define 'know'," he asked, smirking.

"In the biblical sense," she shot back.

Arsenio laughed, "Why Dani, isn't that a little crude from such a well-brought-up young lady, and so close to Christmas, too? Where's your sense of the appropriate." He mock-tutted.

"Just saying it as it is, Seni. Where's *my* sense of the appropriate? Probably ten steps over yours." Dani shook her head and pressed the call button.

" Jeez, Dani, you don't hold back, do you?"

"Nope, and neither do you. Goodnight, Seni." Dani stepped into the lift.

"Good night, *bella*." He winked and blew her a kiss as the doors closed to the elevator car.

"*Buonanotte*, Seni. *Dorme bene*."

Dani smiled to herself, hearing Arsenio's infectious chuckle through metal doors.

35

UNEXPECTED PLANS

Paul took a sip from his now-cold coffee and placed the cup back on the saucer. He'd arrived at ten sharp, eager to hear Arsenio's full explanation. It had been eating away at him all night. The uncomfortable feeling that he was keeping important information from Jerome was weighing uneasily on his conscience. Having sat and listened to a very detailed assessment, then sifted through the hundreds of photos from Scott and Gary's surveillance, he now wished he'd never pressed Arsenio. When Scott had explained the situation, he'd kept it short and concise. Hearing every sordid detail in Arsenio's uniquely colourful execution made Paul's blood boil. The cold coffee stuck in his stomach and made it churn even more. Paul had never particularly liked Liz. She wasn't a like-able woman and he often wondered what Jerome saw in her, past her good looks. Having said that, he knew Jerome wasn't a superficial person, but Paul couldn't understand how he wasn't able see her for what she really was: a spoilt, self-obsessed, selfish bitch.

Unlike Jerome and the rest of the Ferretti family, Liz looked down on all the staff the family employed and only spoke to them if she needed to. She was the worst kind of snob, coming from a low-class single parent family who now, having married into wealth, thought she was above everyone else. Her mother had been abandoned by her father once she'd become pregnant, meaning her mother had to work in minimum paid jobs just to keep them financially afloat. After remarrying, when Liz was almost ten, Liz's family moved to a better part of Birmingham where Liz's stepfather lived. It was there that Liz started dance classes, her naturally tall, slim frame making her stand out from her fellow classmates. When

Liz was fifteen, the dance school entered her into a national dance competition. It was there that Graham's modelling agency had spotted her and from then on, she had been signed up with them.

"Shall I get you another?" Arsenio looked at the cup Paul had just replaced.

For the last forty minutes Paul hadn't touched his drink, listening intently to the detailed evaluation Arsenio had given him. He'd asked no questions at all. Arsenio gestured to the table and Paul moved over to look at the photos, then he'd sat back down again, to scan over the reports. Arsenio didn't see the point in hiding anything. In fact, he was hoping that now Paul knew everything, he might be able to assist, to see something he'd missed or even suggest a new tactic.

Paul shook his head. "No, I'm fine." He shuffled in his seat, then put down the thick folder on Arsenio's desk.

"What are you going to do now?" he asked gruffly.

"I'm not entirely sure. Cos thinks we should wait until after Christmas to tell Jerome anything, simply because it would disrupt the family and his businesses at the busiest time. Which, incidentally, I agree with."

Paul took a deep breath and nodded.

"I'm not entirely happy with the idea of playing along, but we really have no choice. I'm also not looking forward to telling him. It'll destroy him. Cos is hoping we can steer him into the right direction and let him work it out for himself. But that may take a while. He's pretty blind-sighted when it comes to her and for some reason, she seems to be able to manipulate him." Arsenio shook his head. Paul still said nothing and just sat absorbing the information. Arsenio couldn't tell if his lack of input was because he was angry or stunned.

"Apart from the fact it's emotionally going to disturb Jerome, he also has his businesses to think about. Luckily, she can't touch those." Arsenio saw a hint of relief pass over Paul's face and continued. "But as you know, that's not what's the most important thing to Jerome. He'll want full custody of his children and that is where he's going to have a problem. Judges don't care about affairs and Liz will use the children until she gets what she wants."

"Money," Paul said bluntly.

"Exactly. I don't think a reasonable lump sum will do it. She needs a guaranteed, steady supply. There are a few scenarios that will" – Arsenio waved his hand in the air, searching for the appropriate word – "encourage her to leave the children. The first is if her career takes off and she'll be travelling a lot and earning money, but the chances of that happening are slim. The second is if we can find something on her that shows she's unfit as a mother, so the court will give Jerome full custody. That's why I'm keeping up the surveillance, but after all this time, all she's doing is banging the trainer."

"Is there a third?"

"Yeah, we give her a serious amount of money that makes it impossible for her to refuse. But we'd be talking six figures."

Paul sucked on his teeth. "At least," he confirmed. "That'd cripple Jerome."

"Yes, but he'd do it."

"Unless we dig deeper and find something. We might need more time."

"That's what I want to do but to be honest, every day that goes by I'm finding it harder to pretend I don't know anything."

They sat in silence for a moment while Paul processed everything he'd been told. He leaned forward in his chair and rested his elbows on his knees and his face in his hands. "It's not what I expected to hear." His eyebrows rose. "I've been so preoccupied with preventing the drug problem at Sky. Maybe I should've listened more to the gossip," he huffed.

"Jerome's a private person and he's very guarded about his family, Paul. I had no idea until he told me. I knew she was a piece of work but..." Arsenio trailed off, trying to reassure Paul.

"Who knows?" Paul asked.

"Cos, Scott, Gary and some guy in Spain. That's all."

"And there's a video?"

Arsenio nodded.

"Let me look at those photos again. Now it's all sunk in a bit, I may see something." Paul rose from his chair and paced over to the table. "The trainer isn't working anywhere now, is he?"

"No. Just personal training at homes."

Paul nodded and looked at each photo carefully. Arsenio pointed out different shots that he thought were important and Paul scrutinised them further.

"This photo here, see? And these ones that come after?" Paul picked up a photo of Jonathan getting out of his car and walking into a dry cleaners. They were a succession of photos of him entering, then leaving.

"Yes, what about them?" Arsenio looked closely, seeing nothing unusual.

"He hasn't taken in anything to be cleaned or picked anything up. What date was this?"

Arsenio turned over the photo to show where the date was pencilled on.

"Let's cross reference it with the report."

Arsenio leaned over the table to pick up the file from his desk and opened it up. He scanned the time log. "He was there for forty-five minutes. That's strange." Arsenio furrowed his brow, looking at the report he was holding.

"It's even stranger that it's across town from where he lives and he must pass at least half a dozen dry cleaners on his way there, including some from the same chain."

"You think there maybe something in that?"

"Maybe, but it's definitely worth a closer look."

"I'll get Scott to check it out."

Liz dropped her cigarette butt on the floor and stepped on it. She looked around nervously, then walked through the heavy door into White Lightening Dry Cleaners. She was sure this was the head office. Jonathan had mentioned it was in the Kirkstall area of Leeds. The chemical smell hung heavy in the warm air of the shop front. It was busy with three staff taking different garments and handing over freshly laundered items. The wall behind the counter boasted a two-hour cleaning service at an extra cost, as well as delivery and mending service. Liz could see why the chain was doing so well, with fifteen shops scattered around the region. Liz stepped up to the counter when the previous customer had left.

"I'm here to see Gabe. I'm a friend of his cousin Jonathan, Liz." The young girl, who was dressed in a blue skirt and white shirt with the logo embroidered on the pocket, gave Liz a once over and nodded. Liz watched her go over to a phone at the rear and call someone. Within a few minutes, the girl opened up the security door for Liz to walk through.

"His office is up the stairs right at the end." The girl pointed down a corridor past a number of large double doors. Liz thanked the girl and walked in the direction she'd indicated. There was a rumbling noise, which sounded like several washing machines working simultaneously, and the hissing of iron presses, which only made the atmosphere even warmer. Liz quickly climbed the stairs and found herself on the next floor where two large, casually dressed men were standing by the office door.

"You here for Gabe?" one of them asked her.

Liz nodded suddenly feeling nervous. She'd come to the head office, desperate for her slimming pills, but now she'd finally got there, she felt decidedly uneasy. The upper floor had a distinctly different air about it, but she couldn't quite put her finger on what it was.

Before she could think any more, the second man opened the office door. "Go right through."

Gabe's office was not what Liz had expected. The shop was functional with clean lines and was basic, clinical even, exactly what you'd expect from a dry cleaners. Gabe's office, in contrast, was traditional, remarkably large and tastefully decorated. Apart from the off-white marble flooring, everything else was dark wood, from the antique desk and book shelves that covered one wall, to the mahogany coffee table and rich ox-blood leather sofa and chairs that were arranged away from the desk. Gabe was resting against his desk, talking to three people who were sitting in the seating area. The two men dressed in dark suits and a woman with asymmetrical blonde hair focused their full attention on Gabe, only fleetingly looking over to Liz when she walked in.

Gabe wasn't as dark as Jonathan and his eyes were a lighter brown. He was taller and leaner. Dressed casually in dark jeans and a cream polo-necked jumper, he looked to be in his early thirties. He turned and smiled widely at Liz as she approached, showcasing his perfect white teeth and a small diamond earring that twinkled in his right ear.

"Liz, how nice to meet you." He straightened and stretched out his hand, which Liz took to shake. "How's Jonathan?"

"He's well," Liz answered, puzzled that he seemed to know her.

"And your trip? How was that?"

"Um, it was fine, thank you."

"J told me you were going to Spain," Gabe continued, seeing confusion on Liz's face. "Please, sit down. We're just finishing off." He signalled to a chair by the sofa for her to sit. The three people stood once Liz sat down, smiling tightly at her. Gabe turned his attention back to his employees.

"So I want the sales reports by tomorrow. We need to arrange all distribution channels and make sure supplies are readily available and delivered swiftly. It's going to be a busy couple of weeks. Any problems at" – his eyes shifted to Liz – "points of sale, I need to know."

The three wordlessly nodded and left the office, muttering their goodbyes.

"So, how can I help you?" Gabe lowered himself into the chair opposite Liz, once they were alone.

"Jonathan told me you could get some slimming pills."

"Meridia?" he asked in a soft voice and a gentle smile. His gaze slipped over her.

Liz nodded suddenly uncomfortable with the whole idea.

"I see. You've taken them before?" he slowly rubbed his chin.

"Yes. I stopped a few days ago but I've put weight on and I need to keep in shape for my modelling contracts."

Gabe smiled at her and nodded. "I think I may have some. I carry a little stock, just in case, for emergencies." His smile widened and his eyes twinkled. "How much will you need? A couple of weeks' supply?" Gabe suggested.

"Sure. That should be enough. Like I said, it's just until I get my contracts."

Gabe rose from his chair and headed to the bookshelf, which had drawers at the bottom. He opened one and pulled out a brown pill bottle. He closed it quietly, then opened up a second drawer and took out a small plastic bag, then closed the drawer and paced back to Liz.

"Here you are, there are sixty pills in there which should last twenty days. And give this to J, will you?" He handed her the small plastic bag which contained some white powder.

"What's this?"

"An early Christmas present." He winked at her.

Liz swallowed hard. She didn't need any further explanation. She'd seen enough models who'd been recreational users of many substances over the course of her modelling career. Liz put the pills and the bag of cocaine in her handbag, glad she hadn't mentioned that Jonathan didn't know she was even here. She'd take her pills and leave, and if Gabe said something to Jonathan, she'd find a way to get around him. She always could.

Gabe turned to his desk and plucked a card from a holder. "Here. If you need anything else, call me." He tilted his head to the side and smiled.

Liz took the card and looked at it. The card was a standard business card with the White Lightening Dry Cleaners logo on it, but the number at the bottom was Gabe's private mobile phone number. Liz dropped the card in to her bag, then pulled out her purse.

Gabe shook his head. "I don't want any money for them. If you need anything else, in the future, then..." His voice trailed, implying that then there'd be a charge. He shrugged. Liz was about to protest but he waved his hand, signalling her not to bother. The gesture was slight, but Gabe's stance and slightly hardened expression betrayed decidedly more. He wasn't someone to be argued with. For all his polite and soft spoken manner, he had a distinctly powerful presence. It was well hidden behind his casual dress and his gentle manners, giving an illusion that he was approachable – friendly, even. The interaction with his employees betrayed something entirely different. Liz had only witnessed a few minutes of their meeting but it was clear that Gabe was in full command. Their lack of input and full and undivided attention gave away their undeniable respect for the man, or was it fear? Liz swiftly rose up from the chair, feeling uneasy again. Now that she had what she needed, she just wanted to get out of the place.

Gabe paced over to the door and opened it. "Give J my best." He held out his hand for her to shake and Liz took it.

"I will."

Liz found Jerome pulling out a large tray of lasagne from the oven. The whole kitchen was filled with the evocative aroma of rich tomato sauce, herbs and spices, blended with the distinct smell of strong cheese. Liz's mouth watered. She couldn't remember the last time she'd had lasagne or any pasta, for that matter. She groaned inwardly. She needed to take a pill, otherwise the now three pounds she'd put on would undoubtedly rise to five.

"Hey. How was your morning?" Jerome asked.

"Okay. How come you're home?" Liz asked as she threw her keys on the counter but held onto her bag, deflecting the line of questioning.

"I thought that I'd cook lunch for the kids, seeing as they're on holiday. I don't need to be at Level One today and I'm having a late meeting at Sky about the fashion show," Jerome explained, pulling off the oven gloves.

Liz eyed the lasagne as steam rose from the earthenware tray.

"I made a salad and steamed sea bream for you. Is that okay?"

Liz smiled tightly at him. "Thanks, I'll just go upstairs and dump everything. Where are Nina and the kids?"

"The kids are in their rooms playing and I gave Nina the afternoon off to do her Christmas shopping. I need to see about her time off over Christmas too, but I wanted to discuss it with you first."

Liz scowled. Jerome was always too generous with Nina's time off. Liz often felt he was far too lenient with her. Nina was employed to make *her* life easier, not for them to work around any plans she might have.

"I see. Well, Christmas Eve, you're at the restaurant aren't you?" Liz's tone had an icy tinge to it.

Jerome took a deep breath and leaned against the counter. He was worried that this might escalate into an argument about how much time he spent at both Sky and La Casa over the holidays. If push came to shove, he'd just have to give a little. He couldn't face a tense atmosphere over the busiest time of the year. He was just glad he had competent staff.

"Yes," he answered cautiously.

"And I take it Christmas Day we're still going there for lunch?" Liz arched an eyebrow.

"Only if you'd like to be. If you prefer to stay home and have lunch here, I can organise that." Jerome was determined to make concessions where he could. If he offered Christmas Day, she may be more flexible with New Year's Eve. The staff could manage Christmas Day, but he needed and wanted to be at La Casa and then Sky on the last day of the year.

"Your mother would never forgive us if we didn't go on Christmas Day," chuntered Liz. Gia would be furious if she didn't get to see her only grandchildren on Christmas Day. Liz toyed with the idea of staying home, just to spite her, but the thought of having to cook dinner and clean up after was too much. "We can go to La Casa for Christmas Day and Nina can have the day off. You'll be home for the evening, won't you?"

Jerome nodded. "I'll need to be at Sky by ten, though."

Liz nodded. "And Boxing Day?"

"Well lunch will be busy and then we have a private party in the evening." Jerome swallowed and then added, "But I can work around whatever you want to do." He'd promised Joseph he'd be there, but if Liz was going to be difficult, he'd just have to let him down.

Liz thought for a moment. Jonathan would be frantic that they couldn't spend Christmas together. She was going to have to think of a way to get away on Boxing Day at least, but if she was home alone with the children, she wouldn't be able to leave. If Nina was here, she'd tell Jerome that Liz left, and where could she say she'd gone? Everywhere would be closed.

"Maybe I should go and visit my mum. We never spend Christmas together. At least if I can go down on Boxing Day. She can see the kids too. She hardly ever gets to see them. You'll be busy and Nina can have that day off too. Mum would like that, give her a chance to spoil them."

"Sure. Um, but shouldn't you check first? She may have plans and it's a bit last minute," suggested Jerome.

"She never has plans, Jerome," snorted Liz. It was true, Liz's mother Carol lived a very mundane life. She worked nine to five in an insurance company. Her husband was in corporate banking. They went on holiday twice a year. One holiday would be somewhere in the Mediterranean for two weeks, usually June time, when it wasn't too hot and always an all inclusive. The second was for a week city break either in the UK or Europe, at the end of September, when the prices dropped. They lived a structured and very monotonous life. They ate out every Friday at the same Chinese restaurant and once a month, they went out for Sunday lunch. There was no excitement or spontaneity at all. Their circle of friends were boring and Liz's stepfather's family were dull and tedious. Every time she visited her mother, it brought back memories of the unexciting life she had led and the exact reason for wanting to leave that mind-numbing existence.

"I could leave on Boxing Day morning. I'd be there in two hours, possibly longer if there's traffic. Maybe stay overnight and come back the following evening. Or even the day after. I mean, if I'm going down all that way, I should stay at least a couple of days, and you'll be tied up at work anyway. What do you think?" The more Liz thought about it, the more she liked the idea. She'd be able to leave the children with her mother on some pretext of visiting an old friend, or shopping, and then meet up with Jonathan. Her mother wouldn't even question it or suspect anything, relishing the time with her grandchildren.

"Er, sure," Jerome answered, a little stunned that her unexpected suggestion meant Nina got more than her two days off, his family would be together on Christmas Day and he was able to work at La Casa and Sky at the busiest time. All without an argument or much of a compromise. He'd miss the children but it was the least he could do. Carol only saw them half a dozen times a year because of the distance, so this way she'd get some quality time with them.

"Right. Well I'll go and ring her with the good news and then we can have lunch?"

"Great." Jerome nodded, relieved. He watched a surprisingly happy Liz leave the kitchen and head upstairs. He sighed to himself. She really was trying to make things work. He was going to have to try that much harder to forgive her.

"I need an espresso and I need something to eat!" huffed Gia, lowering herself into one of her sumptuous chairs. She'd spent the first part of the morning setting up her Facebook account and then going over a few basic steps with Dani. They'd then spent the rest of the morning, as well as lunchtime, at the wholesalers, selecting the decorations for the fortieth anniversary.

The Mondays that they'd been spending together had brought the two women closer, creating a unique familiarity between them. Initially, their relationship was fuelled by work but recently, and especially over the last two weeks, their relationship had definitely become more personal. Dani genuinely looked forward to their time together. Gia seemed to fill the gap the death of her mother had left.

The weather had turned just as they unloaded the last of the items into the foyer, and then the heavens had opened.

"I'll make the coffee," suggested Dani. "I didn't think we'd make it in before it started coming down!"

"Me neither. I'll go to the restaurant kitchen and see what I can put us together for a late lunch."

Within an hour, they were in the function room, having quickly eaten some ravioli and salad, and were now organising the decorations. Dani brought down Gia's laptop so they could search a few new ideas while they started assembling everything.

Dani was determined to make the room as chic as possible. There was a tendency to go overboard on a particular colour or element when function decorations were done, and Dani felt they came off a little gaudy and cheap. She'd visualised something that had a touch of red rather than overpowering the whole scheme of the room. Gia fell in with whatever she suggested, glad not to have to make too many decisions, and just enjoying the company of a like-minded, younger woman.

Dani was just finishing off one of the table decorations when Gia's laptop made a pinging sound, indicating she had a message.

"You've got a Facebook message, Gia!"

"Really?"

Gia twisted the laptop around to face her and blushed. "It's from *Raymondo*. We just became friends on Facebook." She couldn't hide her excitement.

"Well, you remember how to answer, don't you?"

"Er, yes. But what shall I say?" Gia darted her eyes to Dani.

"Hello might be a good start," Dani answered dryly.

Gia rolled her eyes. "Very funny. I mean after that."

"Are you seeing him again?"

"Well we didn't make plans as such. He knew I'd be busy over the weekend, with the restaurant, so we left it open ended."

"Do you want to?" Dani asked tentatively.

Gia nodded.

"Then ask him out."

"Me? I don't know, isn't that a little..." Gia tilted her head from left to right.

"Forward?"

"Well yes. I would've said brazen, even," agreed Gia. "Ask a man out?" she squirmed at the thought.

"No! Make it casual. Like... um... 'What are you up to later?' and then he may take the hint."

Gia furrowed her brow and then started to type her message, which seemed much longer than what Dani had suggested. Dani carried on with her task in hand as she heard the messages ping backwards and forwards for the next few minutes.

There were eight table decorations to assemble and she'd managed to complete three. At this rate, she'd be done by eight if she put her head down and got on with it. She looked over at Gia and saw her smiling at the messages Ray was sending her. It didn't look as if Gia was going to be much help either. Dani shook her head and grinned, thinking what an unlikely couple they made, the fiery Italian 'hottie' and the conservative, gentle doctor. Dani thought back to the conversation she'd had with Gia about fate a few weeks ago and wondered whether this would be Gia's destiny, to end up with charismatic Doctor Ray Holmes. The romantic, optimistic side of her really hoped she would.

"He's coming round!" gasped Gia.

"Here?" Dani looked up sharply from the arrangement she was gluing.

Gia looked wide-eyed and stunned at Dani and nodded. "At eight, after he finishes from the surgery. I told him I'd cook," she muttered, clearly shocked at her own forwardness.

"See? Well, that's in four hours."

"I can't believe I just did that." Gia slumped back in her chair.

"It wasn't so hard, was it?"

Gia shook her head. "It's because it wasn't face to face. I'd have never done it if I was face to face with him." She stifled a giggle with her hand.

"The genius of technology," winked Dani. "It makes you brave."

"Or reckless! Now I need to cook and get myself looking presentable!" she huffed. Dani's gaze flitted over Gia who was dressed in a pair of black smart trousers and a cream cashmere jumper with a Versace silk scarf knotted loosely around her neck, and chuckled. She looked lovely as always and she was sure Ray would think so too. "You look fabulous, Gia, you always do."

"What? These boring old things?" Gia swept her hand down her body. "No, no... I'll need to change. Something much more evening." Gia's expression changed as she looked at the array of items scattered around the room.

"Don't worry, Gia, I'll do these," Dani said, realising that Gia had forgotten they had work to do in her excitement. "You go and get yourself together and I'll finish off."

"I'll stay for another hour or so. That'll give me enough time to go make myself look glamorous and steal something from the kitchen downstairs. What's the use in living above a top restaurant if you can't take advantage of it eh?" she winked.

"Totally," chuckled Dani, thinking Ray didn't stand a chance in hell of not succumbing to Gia's undoubtable charms.

Liz lifted her wine glass and then popped a pill in her mouth. She took a large gulp of wine and swallowed. Her mother had been ecstatic to hear that her normally distant daughter had decided to come and spend time with her over the holidays. Carol started planning activities they could do over the couple of days they were over, while Liz was still on the phone.

"We could go to Cadbury World, the children will love it. All that chocolate! It'll be such fun," she gushed excitedly.

"You might have to take them without me to that, Mum. I don't want to be tempted with all that chocolate. Not when I've a few modelling jobs pending." Carol didn't even hear the indifferent tone in which Liz spoke to her and carried on regardless.

"No, of course not, dear. I wouldn't want you to ruin your figure. But you'd be able to come to The National Sea Life Centre, won't you?" Carol asked eagerly. She rarely spent time with Liz and her family. Since marrying Robert, she only spent time with his son and daughter and their families, and though they were good to her, she missed having her own family around her.

"Probably. I may try and catch up with an old friend while I'm down. I'll see. I'm coming down mainly for you to spend time with the kids, Mum. They hardly see you."

"I know, Liz dear. And Robert is so good with children too."

Liz allowed her mother to make plans for the two days and then, after saying their goodbyes, she hung up. It was too risky to ring Jonathan now; she'd wait until Jerome finally left for Sky. Her bag lay next to where she was sitting on the bed. Liz delved inside it and pulled out the small plastic bag, holding it up. She shook it. There was a lot more than she initially thought. So Jonathan liked to get high every so often? The thought both surprised and thrilled her. He was so careful about what he put in his body and kept in fighting shape, it seemed out of character. But then again, she really didn't know much about his past. Deciding she'd hide it rather than flush it down the toilet, Liz went into her bathroom and dropped it into the bottom of her tampon box. She'd leave it there for now.

36

SILLY SEASON

Arsenio stared at his computer screen. He'd read and reread Scott's report from Monday. What was the importance of White Lightening Dry Cleaners? And why had Liz been there too? Scott's report showed Liz had visited the very same dry cleaners, so there was obviously something connecting them to that particular branch, but Arsenio couldn't for the life of him work out what. He looked at the photos Scott had sent him, which showed Liz had neither taken in nor picked anything up. Arsenio reached over to his phone and searched for Paul's number. After two rings, Paul picked up.

"Liz was in White Lightening Dry Cleaners yesterday, the same branch that Jonathan went to," Arsenio said bluntly, not even bothering with the pleasantries.

"I'll do some digging. But it'll be after Christmas now – I'm short staffed as it is and I don't want to put anyone on that I can't fully trust."

"Of course, we need to keep this quiet for now. I'll keep Scott and Gary on it. At least if they're keeping an eye on the place when either one of them goes in. That's something. To be honest, I can't see Liz being away from home over Christmas anyway, unless she's confident that Jerome won't pick up on anything. So for the next few days, things should be quiet," sighed Arsenio. His usual patience was starting to wane. Christmas had now thwarted their plans and it would be the same again over New Year.

"I think you're right. We need to meet up, though. Maybe over the weekend? I'll be stacked out until then."

"I'll keep in touch and send you whatever I get."

"Good."

"Have a good Christmas Paul, and thanks."

"Thanks Seni, you too. I'll be glad when it's over," Paul huffed.

Jerome watched the security camera footage from Monday. Leaning back on his office chair, he grinned to himself, watching both his mother and Dani laughing and running from the car, laden with different boxes of decorations. They'd just made it into the restaurant before the rain started to come down. He scanned through to the function room and watched their comfortable interaction. Gia periodically touched Dani's arm affectionately, as she often did with people she was fond of. They were totally at ease with each other and seemed to be laughing a great deal, constantly joking around and talking non-stop.

It pleased him to see his mother so happy. That wasn't to say she was unhappy normally, but it was good seeing the interaction between the two women. It was even better seeing Gia actually having fun. The computer lessons, along with Dani's continuous company and their collaborating on the decorations, were a new dynamic for Gia. She'd always been surrounded by men and was obviously enjoying the new female companionship she'd now forged with Dani.

Jerome would have been more than happy to sit and watch the whole recording of them both but firstly, he didn't have the time and secondly, he realised it was a little perverse to be spying on them. He moved the recording forward, curious as to what time Dani actually left. The footage showed Dani's little white Fiat leave at a quarter to eight. *She'd really put the hours in*, he thought to himself. Jerome then moved the recording on at a fast speed but stopped it when he saw a dark BMW car pull into the car park. Jerome shuffled forward in his seat. The car looked familiar, but he wasn't sure from where. Then he saw Doctor Ray Holmes step out of the car, holding a large bouquet of flowers and a bottle of wine.

Jerome huffed to himself, unsure of how comfortable he felt about his mother entertaining the doctor at home. He moved the recording forward and watched as Ray was let in by Gia, via the intercom, then he took the lift to the second floor where Gia was waiting for him. She stood in the doorway of her apartment dressed in a figure-hugging blue dress, looking so glamorous, Jerome saw Ray's step falter as he stepped out of the elevator into the foyer. They greeted each other with a kiss to the cheek and then went into the apartment, shutting the door behind them.

Jerome furrowed his brow. His mother had never dated – well, not to his knowledge anyway, though he had a sneaky suspicion that she must have while she'd holidayed back at La Garda. He sighed to himself. She must be lonely and Ray seemed like a good man. He'd just have to get used to it.

His attention was alerted to his phone ringing and he picked it up. He smiled upon seeing the image of Cosimo flash across his screen.

"Hey Cos, how are you?" Jerome paused the security recording, not wanting to miss anything.

"I'm good, thanks. The office is closed, so I'm relaxing. How about you?"

"Not relaxing, that's for sure," Jerome answered dryly. "It's silly season and it's going to be a long couple of weeks." Sometimes Jerome's brothers forgot that when everyone else kicked back at this time of year, he was doing the complete opposite.

"Aw, you love it. Stop complaining," Cosimo chortled. "Look, I know things are crazy for you right now and the last thing you need is any – how shall I put this? Er... drama. But I won't be coming for Christmas lunch this year."

"What? Why ever not?" Cosimo's declaration clearly surprised him.

Cosimo sighed deeply before explaining. "Well, as you know I'm with James now, and he has nowhere to go, no family, so we just thought we'd spend it together. I'll come around and see Mama and you sometime in the morning, but lunch will be just me and James this year."

"Oh, I see."

"I'm just giving you a heads up before I tell Mama. She's not going to like it I know, but –"

"No, she won't." Jerome knew his mother lived for days like these, where she had all her family around her, and this would be the first year that Cosimo wouldn't be spending Christmas with them. To be honest, Jerome didn't want to spend Christmas day without his brother, especially after all the support Cosimo given him over the last few weeks. "Don't say anything to her yet. Let me just smooth the path first."

"You really don't need to do that. I can handle Mama."

"I know... but just let me talk to her first, okay?"

"Okay, if you insist."

"I do. So you and James are serious, then?"

"Well, he puts up with my difficult nature and doesn't give me any pressure at all – I mean, ever. He's the easiest-going guy I've ever met. We've been together nine months now, and that's the longest I've ever been with anyone. He bends over backwards to keep me happy. That's why I can't leave him on Christmas Day and to be honest, I don't want to."

Jerome smiled to himself. Cosimo hadn't answered his question directly, but it was patently obvious from Cosimo's uncharacteristic, candid description of James that he was important to him. So much so, he was prepared to put James above his own family if need be.

"Well in that case, you should spend it with him. I'll call you once I've spoken to her."

They said their goodbyes and then Jerome focused back onto the security video forwarding it to see what time Ray left.

Two twenty-three! The digital clock read at the bottom of the screen. *What were they doing until two twenty-three?* Jerome screwed his eyes shut and shuddered. He knew exactly what they were doing and now he wished he'd never even looked at the God damn tape. He erased the footage and shut down the computer, thankful he'd got to it before Peter had.

"That's delicious!" Chloe ran her finger around the bowl and popped the frosting in her mouth again. "Please tell me you made us one too."

"Of course." Dani smoothed over the chocolate and hazelnut frosting on the hazelnut cake, then picked up the piping bag. She swiftly piped the rosettes around the cake and then placed a chocolate covered hazelnut on each. Capo's favourite flavours were chocolate and hazelnut, so his birthday cake was easy. Nicole had left it up to Dani to choose her cake.

"Oh I haven't had red velvet cake in ages. Is this Mum's recipe?" asked Chloe, watching Dani start to spread the cream cheese frosting over the heart-shaped red sponge.

"Yes, and before you ask, I made one for you too. I put both your cakes in the utility room so the kids wouldn't see them."

Chloe huffed, "The kids are well behaved and won't touch them. It's Adam we need to watch!"

Dani laughed and carried on with her decorating while Chloe started to wash up the few things Dani was done with. "Thanks. I was going to do them once I'd finished."

"It's okay. So what's your programme over the next couple of days?"

"Well, today I'm finishing off the decorations for the anniversary party on Boxing Day. We're having our staff Christmas lunch at four today and then we'll be working tonight."

"And tomorrow? You're working lunch but you'll home about six," confirmed Chloe, trying to remember the schedule Dani had told her. They were purposely delaying Christmas Dinner to the evening so Dani could also be with them. It would be the first Christmas Dinner they'd had together since their mother died.

"Yes, that's right. Then on Boxing Day, I'll be in as usual and working through." Dani picked up another piping bag with red frosting and piped "Happy Birthday Nicole" on the now-white cake. "I'm just glad we can go in later today. It's been so busy and this next couple of days will be even busier." Dani blew air up her face causing her fringe to move to the side.

"Before you shoot off today you'd better try on the dress for your costume. I've altered it for you."

"Really? Oh, thanks. I'll just box these cakes up, then I can try it once I've tidied up."

Jerome tapped on the door of his mother's apartment. He never usually did. The door was always unlocked and he would normally just let himself in. After seeing yesterday's footage though, he thought maybe he should start thinking a little bit more about her privacy. He also didn't want to walk in on something that he'd never be able to forget.

"Jerome! Why did you knock?" said Gia once she'd opened the door.

"Well, I didn't want to just come in." Jerome stepped into the hallway and then followed Gia into the lounge. "You may have been entertaining," he added dryly.

"Oh." Gia furrowed her brow at his comment but didn't deny or confirm that it was a possibility.

"Anyway, I need to talk to you about something."

"Oh, what is it? Is it about work?" She paced through to the kitchen and pointed to the coffee machine, a silent offer of coffee. Jerome nodded and she immediately popped two pods in the machine.

"No, it's about Christmas Day."

"What about it?"

"Cosimo may not make it," he said carefully.

"What do you mean? He never misses Christmas Day. It's our family day." Gia waved her hands dismissively, indicating she thought he must be mistaken.

"I know, but this year, it's different for him."

"How?" She pulled out the cups and placed them onto their saucers.

"Well, he's seeing someone."

"Seeing someone?" Gia repeated, unsure if she'd heard correctly. She pushed Jerome's coffee over towards him. Then her expression changed as she realised what exactly Jerome meant. "You mean he has a..."

"Yes, Mama, he has a boyfriend."

"Oh. I see." She leaned herself against the kitchen counter, absorbing this new information.

"And I know you're not comfortable with the whole idea, but it would seem it's serious," Jerome continued gently, trying to gauge her reaction.

Gia took a sip from her coffee, feeling decidedly uncomfortable with the idea of Cosimo and a boyfriend, let alone one he was serious about.

"So, they'll be spending it together." Jerome watched his mother put down her cup carefully.

"With the boyfriend's family?" Gia narrowed her eyes.

"No, alone. Apparently his family don't want anything to do with James – that's his name. They don't accept his... lifestyle." Jerome couldn't hide the disdain in his voice. *How could anyone reject their own son?* He thought to himself.

Gia hadn't been altogether accepting of Cosimo's sexual orientation but she could never have disowned her own son. Over the years, Cosimo had kept his private life away from his family, mainly because he didn't want to cause a rift between them and Gia respected him for being thoughtful of their feelings, especially when Alessandro senior had been alive. For Cosimo, his family had always come first and Gia knew that for him to decide to spend Christmas with someone other than his family, it meant that this someone was important to him. More important than his own family. Gia sighed deeply; she knew she couldn't hold on to her sons forever. They had their own lives to lead but she also didn't want to push them away by making their lives difficult for them.

She looked up at Jerome who was eyeing her warily, and thought to herself: *she put up with Liz who was cold, distant and self-centred, so why couldn't she put up with Cosimo's gay partner?* The very idea of the family not being together made Gia's heart sink. "Have you met him?"

"James? No I haven't, but Seni has."

Gia nodded.

"He said he was really nice. Very, um, easy going, friendly."

"I don't like the idea of Cosimo not being here, Jerome. Christmas is for family."

"Me neither, Mama. The kids will miss him too, but Cosimo doesn't want to leave him alone –"

"Well of course he doesn't," interrupted Gia sharply. "Cosimo's a gentleman and thoughtful. No one should spend Christmas alone." She finished her coffee and took the empty cup over to the sink.

"Okay, then. I just wanted you to know in good time, so that it wasn't a shock when Cos called you to tell you that he wouldn't be here." Jerome picked up his coffee and drained it as he watched his mother, who was clearly agitated. He sighed inwardly. He was sure she was going to start a shouting match. Her usual tirade, peppered with Italian expletives, expressing all her grievances. Maybe he had to thank the good Doctor Holmes for that. Maybe it was down to him that his mother's fiery temper seemed to have calmed down over the last few days. The thought both disturbed and amused him. Gia turned around to face Jerome and replied.

"Nonsense, I will have *all* of my family here on Christmas day, including James. If the poor man has nowhere to go he's welcome here, at La Casa. Christmas is for family. If he hasn't got one, then he can join us instead."

Jerome gaped at her. An argument he'd expected, an invitation he had not. It would seem that there were Christmas miracles after all.

Capo beamed down at his cake.

"You made this for me?"

"*Si, buon compleanno,* Capo." Dani planted a kiss on his cheek. They were alone in the kitchen; their only company was the familiar voice of Pavarotti singing Puccini. Capo had come in to oversee deliveries and start his preparations. The rest of the kitchen staff would be arriving within an hour to prepare the Gala dinner for tonight.

"*Grazie,* Dani, *grazie mille!* And you made one for Nicole too?" Capo shook his head still smiling widely in disbelief.

Dani nodded shyly.

"Tell me, who makes your birthday cake, Dani?" he asked softly, his voice still betraying his emotions.

"My mum used to, then Chloe. But for the last few years I didn't have one..." Dani's voice trailed and she shrugged. She thought back to her last few birthdays that she'd celebrated. They'd always been at the bar. Jez had made a big show of opening champagne and maybe giving her some flowers, a small gift too, but never a cake. The one and only thing she really cared about, really wanted, was a cake. It could've been a small supermarket bought cake, anything, something that you could put a candle on to blow out and make a wish. But in all her time with Jez, he'd never arranged one, even though he knew it was important to her and that every birthday he had, she'd always made one for him.

Capo frowned. "This year, I make you your cake. Torte al limone? That's your favourite, isn't it?"

Dani smiled softly and nodded. He winked at her.

"Did the flowers arrive?" Gia had ordered the flowers for the anniversary party to be delivered that morning, knowing Capo would be there early.

"*Si,* I told them to put them in the function room."

"Thanks Capo. I'll make you an espresso and then I'll go up."

Dani entered the quiet restaurant. It was still too early for any of the staff to be in and it felt bizarre not seeing Kuch or Nicole behind the bar at this time. It had just turned twelve and the restaurant wasn't opening until seven that evening. The rest of the staff would be arriving at four for their Christmas staff lunch, where they'd exchange their Secret Santa gifts. Dani made Capo his coffee, leaving it on the stainless steel work station and then made her way to the function room, where she immediately set to work on the arrangements.

Dani had chosen ivory scented flowers and various types of greenery for the floral arrangements and added sprays of red berries to tie in with the theme. Using the clear glass vases that she'd found in the basement, Dani inserted ivory raffia with a thin red thread that wound up the inside of the vase. This concealed the flower stalks perfectly.

"Oh Dani, they look absolutely beautiful!" Gia gushed as she walked in through the door. She looked radiant in a red sleek dress and gold stilettos.

"Thank you. I'm nearly done. I've two more to do and then we need to get them upstairs."

Gia sat down next to her and closely inspected the finished arrangements.

"You look lovely, Gia."

"*Grazie, tesoro.* I thought it was the right colour for tonight. Don't you think?"

Dani nodded, then set to work on the last two vases. "I'll put them on a trolley and take them upstairs. That way we can move them all in one go. I'll top up the water tomorrow morning and they should be fine for

Thursday." Gia gracefully rose from the chair, then quickly squeezed Dani's shoulders in silent appreciation. Gia knew there was no way she could have been able to handle these past few days without Dani.

BY FOUR O'CLOCK, the staff had all gathered in the function room, where the table had been laid out. Everyone put the present they'd bought at the place setting of the recipient, ready for them to open. It was Italian tradition to open their presents at midnight, but seeing as the restaurant staff would probably still be working at that time, and the kitchen staff would be on their way home, they had modified the tradition and would open them before their early dinner.

Capo had prepared a traditional Italian Christmas Eve dinner, the Feast of the Seven Fishes, comprising of seven different seafood dishes. It was Dani's first experience of the Italian Christmas traditions that La Casa d'Italia seemed to adhere to. One look at the magnificent table laden with food and presents made Dani realise that working here was like being part of a big family. The Ferrettis didn't need to do this for their staff, but it was obviously clear that they wanted to. They valued everyone that worked for them, from Peter who managed the restaurant like clockwork, and Matteo who ran a smooth, efficient kitchen, to Rico the kitchen porter. No one was excluded.

Everyone took their places and took great pleasure in opening their presents. Jerome settled into his seat opposite Dani and spoke softly to Peter, who was standing to his right and leaning over his shoulder. Dani noticed Jerome tended to allow Peter to take charge of the formalities. It was always Peter who gave out announcements, and went over schedules or any changes that may have arisen. Though Jerome owned the restaurant, he respected Peter's role as manager and very rarely infringed on his authority. Dani tried to avoid blatantly staring at him as he fingered the present set on his plate. He was distracted with whatever Peter was talking to him about and Dani was glad she could steal a look at him. He looked positively delicious in his dark burgundy three-piece suit, paired with a white shirt and thin black tie.

To Jerome's left, Gia gasped, opening a small box that contained a beautifully intricate brooch, which was shaped in the form of a four leaf clover. It was covered in clear coloured stones. Gia looked around the table to see who'd bought her this beautiful gift. Her eyes caught Kuch's and smiled.

"This is gorgeous! And surely over the twenty-five-pound limit!" she softly chastised.

Kuch shook his head. "I found it in a market stall in Ilkley. They're not real precious stones, Gia, but they look real enough." He shrugged. Gia sighed, clearly glad that he hadn't spent too much money, then immediately pinned it to her dress and turned to Matteo for him to admire it.

Dani looked at her gift and smiled. The present was wrapped in red patterned Christmas paper but the wrapping did little to disguise the familiar bottle shape.

"Three guesses what yours is." Rosa bumped Dani's shoulder and giggled.

"Now that's tough." Dani pretended to think hard, tapping her forefinger on her lips. "But at least whoever bought me it knew what I like," she chuckled.

Dani looked down to the bottom of the table where Rico and Enzo were laughing. Jamie had opened his present and was standing having slipped on the apron that Dani had bought for him. It was white with 'Spooning leads to Forking' emblazoned in black across the front. Jamie grinned widely and blew Dani a kiss.

"I love it!" he called down to her. She tilted her head and grinned back, pleased he genuinely liked it.

Silvanna tapped Dani's shoulder, attracting her attention. Dani leaned forward to look around Rosa at her. Silvanna jerked her eyes in the direction of Jerome who had started to open his present. Dani immediately straightened and discreetly watched him as his elegant long fingers tore open the paper to reveal a slim square white box. He carefully prised the lid open to reveal the pocket square Dani had chosen. His brows drew together in surprise and he slightly shook his head, then he gently ran his fingers over the silky fabric. His eyes shot up, searching for who was responsible for his gift. Dani managed to avert her gaze before he looked in her direction, but he saw Silvanna flush. "Did you buy this?" he asked gently.

Silvanna nodded nervously.

"It's really lovely, thank you."

Dani sighed inwardly, feeling her insides clench with excitement. He liked it. He genuinely liked it. That alone was enough of a present for her. Her bottle of tequila was a bonus. Dani focused on her present and ripped off the paper around the neck of the bottle, then stopped. Well there really wasn't any point in totally unwrapping it now. She glanced down the table to see who was responsible for her present, but no one seemed to be looking in her direction.

"You're welcome, but I have to say, I had some help." Silvanna shrugged.

"Oh?" Jerome tilted his head, questioning.

"Uh-huh, Dani helped me choose it. She seemed to know what you might like."

Dani turned her focus to Kuch who was admiring a brown leather belt that someone had bought him, keeping her attention away from Jerome, avoiding catching his gaze, worried that he may read too much into her involvement. Her expression would surely give her feelings away and she was determined to keep their obvious chemistry tightly bottled up. It was a vulnerable time of year for Dani and she didn't want to say or do something she'd only regret later. It was going to be incredibly hard working closely with Jerome over the next week. People tended to loosen up over the holidays, let their guard down. Dani had witnessed it over and over again at the bar. Office parties where everyone drank too much and ended up with someone they shouldn't be with. Not that she thought she'd be so stupid as to act on her attraction to Jerome, but lines kept getting crossed, by both herself and Jerome. And now that she'd agreed to move into the apartment, it meant he was her landlord as well as her employer, their connection to each other becoming closer.

It took roughly twenty minutes for everyone to open and compare their presents, then they settled into the delicious meal Capo and his staff had prepared. Peter made a small light-hearted speech, wishing everyone a good Christmas and thanking Jerome and Gia, along with Matteo and his staff for the meal. Then Jamie and Carmen brought out the two birthday cakes, complete with lit candles, for Matteo and Nicole. Everyone sang "Happy Birthday" while Kuch took plenty of photos with Nicole's camera. Once the cakes had been cut and served, the staff then moved around the room talking freely, thanking each other for their presents. It was a good way to start what was surely going to be a crazy eight days. Some time out for the staff to interact socially before the real pressure started.

Nicole hugged Dani tightly. "Thank you for my cake. It was delicious."

Kuch continued to take photos, predominantly focusing on Nicole until she put her hands in front of her face and demanded her camera back. "That's enough of me."

"But it's your birthday!" Kuch whined, playfully.

"Yes, it is. And when it's yours next Monday, I'll take loads of pictures of you too." Kuch cringed. Nicole held out her hand for her camera and Kuch reluctantly gave it back. "That's better. Now I can take some of everyone else." She lifted the camera and snapped a photo of Kuch.

"Hey, not fair!"

Nicole lowered the camera and winked at him, then proceeded to move around the staff taking various pictures.

Within half an hour, the restaurant staff had cleared the table and all the kitchen staff were in the kitchen, preparing for what was sure to be the start of a very busy few days.

"Santa's been, Santa's been!" Sophie and Ollie burst into Dani's room. Dani groaned. Her room was still dark, meaning it was far too early to be woken up. She prised her eyes open to look at her clock. Five forty-seven. *Oh fuck!* She'd only had just over four hours sleep. She'd left La Casa d'Italia at one o' clock, volunteering to stay until the last of the customers left, along with Peter and Richard. The rest of the staff had managed to get away by midnight. She was going to need a vat of coffee today. Sophie and Ollie were jumping on her bed by now.

"Has he?" yawned Dani.

"Yes. Everyone's downstairs apart from you," Sophie whined.

"Okay, okay. I'm getting up, but I need Christmas kisses and I need them now." Sophie jumped over to her and peppered her face with kisses and then Ollie crawled up to her and paused. "Eskimo kiss?" Dani suggested, seeing his embarrassed reluctance. He beamed and nodded, then stretched over to her and rubbed his nose on hers. "Come on then, there are presents to open and coffee to drink, but can I at least wash my face and brush my teeth?"

It took all of twenty minutes for the children to rip open their presents, leaving the sitting room looking like a small explosion in a toy factory had occurred. Ollie was ecstatic with his new Xbox and Sophie marvelled at her new bike. Rosie seemed perfectly content to roll around in the discarded wrapping paper.

"Sorry about the early morning." Chloe passed Dani a fresh cup of coffee. "But they insisted you came down."

"It's okay, I wouldn't have wanted to miss this. At least I can have an early night tonight and I'm going to need it. Tomorrow's going to be such a bitch," huffed Dani.

"Itch!" repeated Rosie.

"Bitch!" muttered Kuch, so only Nicole and Dani can hear. Nicole stifled a grin while Dani bit her lip at the uncharacteristic outburst from the normally happy-go-lucky barman. Dani stood by the bar, waiting for a drinks order Nicole was quickly putting together.

"I swear she just loves to lord it over us, for no apparent reason. Your cousin has shit taste in women," Kuch snarled at Nicole. Liz had swished her blonde hair over her shoulder, weaved through the tables and stalked over to the bar. She was not best pleased that her bitter lemon was not diet, and she'd told Kuch in no uncertain terms.

"LBB. I told you," Nicole mumbled. Dani creased her brow.

"Don't you mean LBD? Little black dress?" Dani corrected as she stole another look at Liz's perfect slim figure, swathed in a black clingy short dress, showcasing her endless legs.

"No, LBB. Leggy blonde bitch," Nicole clarified, and Dani almost laughed out loud. "That's my nickname for her." Kuch's scowl was instantly replaced with a grin.

There was a slight lull in work between each of the sittings for Christmas lunch and it was at this time that the Ferretti family sat down for theirs. Gia fussed around her grandchildren, as Liz took her place around the table reserved for them. Jerome seemed to be on edge, torn between ensuring his wife was happy and that the customers, who'd honoured La Casa d'Italia with their presence on such an important day, were well taken care of. Jerome looked at his watch; it was just past two. Peter had everything under control; there wasn't a table waiting any longer than necessary and by the time the next sitting came in an hour later, Jerome knew all the tables would be cleared, set up and ready. *He really needed to relax*, he thought to himself. His eyes moved from the restaurant back to his table. Liz smiled at him stiffly. He knew she didn't want to be here but she was putting on a decent show for his sake. He sighed to himself; at least the revelation of his surprise family trip to Italy had made her gaunt face light up this morning.

Cosimo drove his Ferrari into a parking space of La Casa, then killed the engine. He was relieved to see Arsenio's black Lamborghini. At least Seni had already met James.

"So, this is the infamous La Casa d'Italia?" James smirked. "Are you nervous?"

"What do you think?" Cosimo asked dryly. He still couldn't believe he was actually bringing James to the family's Christmas lunch. When Jerome called yesterday, to tell him the news that their mother wanted James to come too, he'd been stunned into silence. James, on the other hand, was giddy with excitement. It meant he would get to finally meet all of Cosimo's family and eat at La Casa d'Italia too.

"It'll be fine. I'm quite charming, you know?" James nudged him playfully.

"I know." Cosimo pursed his lips together and grinned. "But my family is very... Italian. They're very territorial and a little difficult, set in their ways."

"Really? I'd never have guessed that?" James said with mock sarcasm. "Because you're *so* not like that!"

Cosimo chuckled, "Yeah, I suppose if you've put up with me for the last nine months you can certainly manage a couple of hours with the rest of the Ferrettis."

"You bet I can. Come on. I'm starving."

Cosimo lead the way and entered the restaurant holding a large bag of presents for his beloved niece and nephew. James walked up behind him, carrying an arrangement of orchids he'd put together for Gia.

The children were first over to them. Cosimo introduced James as a friend to them both and both children shook his hand and immediately ran off with their presents. Cosimo greeted Peter, wishing him a happy Christmas, again introducing James. The restaurant was still quite full so Cosimo nodded his greetings to the staff as his eyes caught each of them, not wanting to disrupt their work. Jerome immediately rose from the table and strode over, meeting them a few metres from the table.

"*Buon Natale!*" Jerome hugged and kissed Cosimo warmly, then turned to James. "You must be James. Welcome." He held out his hand for James to shake.

"*Buon Natale.* You must be Jerome, I'm so happy to finally meet you. Thank you for inviting me today." James smiled widely, shaking his hand firmly. "This place is amazing!" James looked around the restaurant, clearly impressed.

"Come over and meet the rest of the family." Jerome stood back, allowing James to walk over to where the rest of the Ferrettis were sitting. Cosimo took a deep breath and followed, still uneasy, but pleased to see that James was totally unfazed or daunted at the thought of sitting around a table with his family.

Liz glanced up as they approached. "This is my wife, Liz. Liz, this is James."

James stretched out his hand and she greeted him with a weak smile and a barely audible "Merry Christmas".

"You've met Kara and Alessandro" – Jerome grinned at his two children – "and this is our mother, Gia."

Gia was already standing, having picked up the discarded wrapping paper from the children's presents. She turned to greet James with a bright smile she reserved for business, and stepped closer to where he was standing.

"*Buon Natale,* Mrs Ferretti. Thank you so much for inviting me today. I brought these for you." James held out the large arrangement of orchids.

"Oh, they're beautiful! *Grazie*, you're very welcome, James. I love orchids." Gia took the arrangement and placed it on the table, but not before she smelled their sweet scent. She then extended her hand and James shook it gently.

Cosimo visibly relaxed his tense stance and Jerome patted his back softly in support.

"They're Zygopetalum orchids, one of the fragrant breeds," explained James.

Gia's eyes widened, clearly impressed with his knowledge. She looked at the beautiful dark violet flowers of the orchid. "They smell wonderful. I've never seen this type before. Please, come and sit down." Gia indicated to a chair next to her. James flashed Cosimo a grin, then shook Arsenio's hand, exchanging seasonal greetings and settled into the seat Gia had indicated to. Gia kissed and hugged Cosimo, warmly speaking softly in Italian, then she lowered herself into the seat next to James.

"Your restaurant is beautifully decorated. I love the lemon tree." James directed his comments to Gia.

"Thank you. It's ornamental only. It doesn't flower or fruit, but I rub the leaves and they smell lovely."

"You need to have another tree close by so they can pollinate, though it's quite hard to grow lemons here in England, even indoors – too cold and not enough sunlight."

Gia's listened intently as James explained. "You know a lot about plants."

James shrugged. "It's my job, I'm a landscaper."

"How interesting. Maybe you'd like to see my plants upstairs later."

"I'd love to, Mrs Ferretti." James beamed at her.

"Don't get too excited, she's a few pot plants on the balcony and a couple of herbs growing in the kitchen. They're hardly Kew Gardens," Arsenio muttered, so only James could hear. James chuckled softly.

"Oh, please call me Gia. I hope you're hungry."

"I'm starving and so eager to finally eat here. Everyone I know raves about it," replied James and Gia's face lit up with a genuine wide smile.

"That's lovely to hear. I hope you don't mind, but we've already ordered for everyone."

"Not at all. I eat anything, Gia. In fact, I prefer it. I wouldn't know what to choose." James chuckled and Cosimo shook his head slightly. *James was flirting with his mother and she was lapping it up!*

"Well, drinks first. What are we all drinking?" Jerome asked as everyone settled into their seats. Cosimo took the seat to the right of his mother, sitting between her and Kara, hoping he'd be able to at least monitor what his mother said to James. Taking another deep breath, he looked over to Arsenio who was eyeing both James and Gia with amusement. Jerome poured everyone some Prosecco and passed around the glasses.

Arsenio winked at Cosimo and mouthed, "Are you okay?" Cosimo nodded; his face had lost some of its tightness. The worst was over. He shook his head slightly, listening to James and his mother talk about plants, then lifted his champagne flute to Jerome and Arsenio in silent thanks and took a welcome sip.

By four o'clock, Kara and Alessandro started to become restless, and Liz decided it was better if they left. The restaurant was still full from the second sitting and the Ferrettis were now on coffees, happy to spend the time talking. Reluctantly, Jerome gathered up the children and after they had said their goodbyes, headed with them for the car.

"If you need to stay, Jerome, until it quietens down, I don't mind. I know it's a busy few days for you," Liz suggested, sensing his uneasiness.

"You don't mind?"

"Of course not. The kids will be playing with all their new toys and I need to pack anyway, so..." she shrugged.

Jerome unlocked Liz's car and put the bags of presents in the boot. "I'll have to get a taxi back, or maybe get Peter to drop me off." They'd all driven down in Liz's car as Jerome had been sure they'd be leaving together. Sensing his hesitation, she put her hand out for the keys.

"Really, just go back in. They'll be pleased for the help."

Jerome huffed, then leaned over and gave Liz a swift kiss on the lips. "Thanks, I'll be a couple of hours at the most." He then opened the back door and kissed both Kara and Alessandro as Liz lowered herself into the driver's seat. Once he'd shut the back door, Liz put the car into gear and sped off out of the car park. Jerome took a moment to light a cigarette. He'd only managed to smoke a handful today, but the stress of the lunch had gotten to him and he still had a long night ahead of him. He blew out a steady stream of smoke and watched it disappear into the dusk. *It hadn't been a bad Christmas Day after all*, he thought to himself. Liz had been amiable around his family, though she'd hardly eaten any of the rich food they'd served. She'd forked around her chicken with Marsala, scraping off the sauce, leaving most of it and eating only the green salad and a few bites of sauce-less chicken. Jerome hadn't wanted to draw attention to her, so he'd let it pass. He just hoped it was because the food was too rich and not because she was back on the slimming tablets again.

By the time Jerome went back inside, he'd noticed that Gia and James were missing from the table.

"Where did they go?" he asked Cosimo.

"Mama wanted to show James her plants," he huffed.

"Well, I think they hit it off. He's a great guy, Cos. You must be relieved." Jerome poured himself a glass of sparkling water, wishing it was something stronger.

"Yeah he is and yes I am. I still can't believe she agreed to it."

"Does this mean we'll be seeing more of him now?" coaxed Arsenio.

"Maybe," grinned Cosimo. He glanced up to the bar and saw that James and his mother had returned and were now talking to Dani. He furrowed his brow. "You know Kara asked me if James was my best friend." Cosimo shook his head. "It made me realise that if I start socialising openly with James... well, people will ask questions; judge." Cosimo blew air up his face. "How the hell do I explain to a five-year-old girl that he's my partner?"

"What did you say?" Jerome asked tentatively, a smile curled around his lips at the thought of his inquisitive daughter.

Cosimo leaned back in his chair and answered, "Well, I said yes he was. What else could I say?"

"So James is your BFF? That's a new way of looking at it. Or maybe he's Mama's," Arsenio chuckled, looking over in the direction of the lemon tree, where his mother and James had now moved to.

"Shut up, Seni," said Cosimo and Jerome together.

ANNIVERSARY

S cott put his car in gear and set off, keeping a significant distance behind Liz. He hadn't expected her to be out and about this early on Boxing Day. He huffed to himself. Over the last few weeks, he'd gotten to know a lot about Liz, her tastes, her routine. So much so, he often could predict where she was going just by the clothes she was wearing or what time it was. Today, though, she'd caught him off guard. He'd had to swiftly put his coffee back in the cup holder and leave his half-eaten croissant on the passenger seat, while she reversed her car out of the garage.

It was early for her to be out at just past nine on a public holiday, thought Scott. Well, he knew the nanny was away, so maybe she had no choice this morning. The roads were quiet, making it hard for him not to be detected, so he hung back until they reached the main road leading in to Leeds. Scott had the tracker on, so he wasn't worried about losing her, but he still preferred to have her car in his sight. Liz pulled into a petrol station and started to fill her car, so Scott parked on the opposite side of the street and waited. He glanced discreetly at her car and spotted the children strapped into the back seats. *So she was obviously not going to meet up with the trainer then*, he thought. Liz placed the petrol nozzle back on the pump and headed into the shop to pay. Scott waited patiently, wondering what was taking her so long, then shifted around and squinted. She was on the phone – no doubt calling the trainer. After a few more minutes, she emerged with a bag full of what looked like sweets, drinks and crisps. She handed them over to the children, then set off again.

Scott quickly tapped in Gary's number.

"Morning." Gary's deep voice came over the hands free system.

"Morning. What's Jonathan up to?"

"He's just put a holdall into the boot of his car."

"His training bag?"

"No, the same bag he took to Spain. Why, what's up?" Gary asked, knowing Scott must be on to something.

"She's in the car with the kids and she's just filled up with petrol. She also bought enough snacks for what I think is going to be long journey."

"What about Jerome?"

"He was still at home when she left."

"And the phone logs?"

"A twenty-minute call late last night to the trainer, once Jerome left for Sky. I think she's going somewhere and I'm pretty sure the trainer's going too."

"Did she pack bags?"

"I didn't see because the car was parked up in the garage," explained Scott. "I'll call Seni. He may know."

Scott hung up and then dialled Arsenio's number.

"Scott. Is everything alright?"

"Not sure. Is Liz supposed to be going away today?"

"Away? Not that I know of. Nothing was mentioned yesterday." Arsenio thought back to the Christmas lunch and couldn't remember any mention of another trip. Granted, he'd been more preoccupied with Cosimo and James. Nevertheless, something as important as that he was certain he'd have picked up on. "Why, what's happened?"

Scott quickly gave Arsenio a rundown of what Gary and he had witnessed over the last fifteen minutes and the conclusions they were drawing.

"But she has the kids with her. Surely she's not that stupid." *Even Liz wasn't that brazen*, thought Arsenio.

"Could she be visiting someone? Family, friends?" suggested Scott. He had now followed Liz's Mercedes through the inner ring road and was heading towards the motorway. "She's heading towards the M1."

"Her mother, possibly." Arsenio was clearly surprised. Liz usually avoided visiting her mother, preferring to have her come stay instead. The idea of "slumming" it in a small four bedroomed detached house on an estate on the outskirts of Birmingham was not something Liz relished. "She lives near Birmingham."

"Well, I'm guessing that's where's she's going."

Gia gasped as she walked into the private function room.

"Oh Dani, *bellisimo!* It's so beautiful!"

Dani was securing the last of the hanging arrangements that hung over each of the round tables. She'd left the main restaurant at two thirty and had started to prepare the room for the party, which was due to start at six.

Each table had a dark red slip cloth over the white linen tablecloth. Dani had placed the flower arrangements she'd prepared in the centre of each table, then surrounded them with six small tea light glass holders with candles. The most dramatic features to the whole decoration of the room were the circular wreaths that hung from the ceiling over each table. They were light frames which had been covered in greenery and small, delicate, white silk flowers. At different lengths, clear and red crystals hung down from the wreaths, causing the lighting to sparkle across and around the room. The wreaths themselves were very simple, but the overall effect was magical.

"*Grazie.* I've nearly finished. I just need to put the last of the flower arrangements on the table where the cake will be and then sweep up the floor." Dani stepped down from the ladder and then brushed some debris that had fallen from the wreaths off her skirt. She was going to have to change her uniform – it was covered in specks. "I've taken a few photos too, of the tables and I'll take a few of the whole room now it's finished. You'll be able to post them on the website and Facebook page."

"Oh Dani, you've thought of everything. What a great idea. Joseph is going to be so pleased." Gia looked at her watch. It was almost five. "Shall I ask Jamie to make you something to eat? It'll be late by the time you finish tonight."

"A sandwich will be fine, Gia – really, anything." Gia nodded and headed out of the room, leaving Dani to finish up.

Dani started to reapply her makeup, having managed a quick shower in the changing rooms and restyled her hair from a simple ponytail to a soft French plait. She added a small red jewelled hair slide, to tie in with the decor. Boxing Day lunch had been busier than Christmas Day and Dani needed to freshen up, especially after she'd set up the function room. It would be easier once she moves upstairs, she thought to herself. At least there'd be less planning involved. Dani always made sure she had spares of most things in her locker, from shoes to clothes, as well as hair styling products and toiletries. She furrowed her brow, thinking back to that fateful day in October when she'd broken her heel. *What if she'd had a spare pair of shoes that night?* She shook her head, ridding herself of the question that still preyed on her mind. She'd thought about the events of that night so many times, played out different scenarios in her head, all with different endings. Thankfully, over the last few weeks, she'd come to realise that it was probably for the best. It was like Gia had said: it was her destiny and there was very little she could do to change that now.

Dani sighed, thinking back to her recent Christmas Day text she'd received from Jez. He still wasn't letting up, saying he couldn't believe he'd be alone at Christmas, and that he missed her desperately. *Too little too late*, she thought as she closed up her locker. Dani checked herself once more in the mirror, then headed upstairs.

Jerome put down the phone in his office. He'd spent a few minutes talking to Kara and Alessandro who seemed happy to be spending time with their grandmother, Carol. Liz sounded in a good mood too. At least while she was away he wouldn't feel guilty about all the hours he was putting in at La Casa and Sky. He looked at his watch; it had turned half past five, just enough time for him to freshen up and be down in the function room.

By the time Dani entered the function room, Richard, Pino and Augustino were already upstairs. She'd be working alongside them tonight, which would be fun – they always worked well together. Jamie and Carmen were in charge of the buffet for the evening, giving Matteo the night off. Gia looked sensational in a purple jersey dress, her thick, wavy hair softly styled around her face. She'd changed from this morning, Dani noted. "Gia, you look gorgeous!"

"*Grazie*, Daniella." Gia shifted restlessly. "I'm... er, I've a... date with *Raymondo*," she muttered.

Dani's eyes widened. She remembered Ray saying he was busy on Boxing Day night when he'd been at Chloe and Adam's last night for Christmas Dinner. They'd invited him around for today too, but he'd said he was entertaining. *Ray was turning into a real dark horse*, Dani thought. "Oh, I see. So you're not staying this evening?" Dani asked.

"Well, I'll stay just to welcome everyone but I need to go by seven, seven thirty at the latest. You'll be able to manage without me, won't you?" Gia's eyes twinkled, she was clearly excited. Dani grinned and nodded.

Dani busied herself behind the bar, making sure she had all her supplies. She would be stationed there for the evening. Dani opened the pink Prosecco and started pouring it into the champagne flutes which were set up on a table, ready for the guests to take when they entered.

Jerome strode in through the door and faltered as his gaze swept around the room. Dani allowed herself to take a quick glance at him. He'd changed from this morning into one of Dani's favourite suits: the dark, blue three piece, matching it with an open-necked shirt. In his breast pocket was the pocket square Silvanna had bought him. Dani smiled to herself. It matched perfectly.

Gia paced up to where Jerome was standing and started speaking to him, distracting his attention from the room. Something Gia said caused him to furrow his brow momentarily. She continued on regardless, talking quickly and waving her hands in the air as she always did, and then his eyes searched the room until they zeroed in on Dani. For a split second, Dani froze. The blatant way he looked at her caused her heart to beat in double time. Gia patted his arm, then walked back to where Jamie was now positioning the cake on its designated table.

A soft smile curled over Jerome's lips and he started to step towards the bar, but just as he moved, the doors opened and Joseph walked into the room, his parents just behind him and Jenny bringing up the rear. Dani watched Jerome shift smoothly into his working persona, greeting Joseph, his parents and Jenny, in turn. Gia glided up to the newly arrived guests and, after the introductions, she guided them to where the welcome drinks were. Dani watched on as more guests started to come through the door, all of them gazing around at the decor.

"Dani, you've done an amazing job. It far exceeded my expectations." Joseph smiled broadly at Dani as she arranged the wine bottles on the bar.

"Thank you, but it wasn't all me. Gia and I did it together," replied Dani.

Joseph chuckled, "Well, Gia told me it was all you, so who do I believe?" He winked at her and took a sip from his glass. Dani suddenly felt awkward as he regarded her over the rim of his glass. He was a nice guy, but after he'd asked her to work for him she felt that she needed to tread carefully where he was concerned. Equally though, she didn't want to avoid talking about the Lodge. So, in an attempt to break the awkwardness, she asked about the hotel.

"It's getting there. In hindsight, maybe I should've waited to open after the New Year, but I was desperate to have the spa up and running for over the holiday season and so I had to open at least part of the hotel. A couple more months and we'll be a hundred percent operational."

Dani nodded, pleased he seemed unfazed by her question.

"Well, I better go and mingle. After all, I'm supposed to be the host of this party," he smirked, then drained his glass and headed to where some more guests had just arrived.

It took roughly an hour for all the guests to arrive. They spent some time drinking and mingling and then took their seats ready for the buffet dinner. The deejay had set up and was now playing a selection of easy listening tunes from the seventies, from Stevie Wonder and Abba to Elton John and Fleetwood Mac, they were all obviously from a playlist specific to the Manns' taste.

Joseph made a small speech thanking everyone who'd come to celebrate the anniversary of his parents and then slowly the guests made their way to buffet. Gia checked her watch and then paced over to Joseph and his parents, excusing herself, explaining she had a prior engagement. She then went over to Jerome who was standing by the buffet and quickly kissed him goodbye, then she literally skipped out of the room, but not before catching Dani's eye and waving goodbye.

Once the guests were seated, Pino, and Richard collected the wine bottles and made their way swiftly around the tables, serving them while Dani quickly prepared the few drinks orders for Augustino to serve. As a team they worked well together, and over the next hour, the staff made sure all the guests were given a five-star service. Jerome watched on from the far end of the room, ensuring that all the guests were being attended to, his eyes occasionally falling on Dani. She was preoccupied with the bar which meant he could watch her work safe in the knowledge that she was oblivious. He really needed to thank her for the room; he hadn't had a chance yet, what with Joseph's arrival and his mother's sudden departure.

Jerome moved smoothly around the room, talking to various guests. Some were already customers of La Casa and the few that weren't were surely going to be. Dessert was then served and by nine o'clock it was time for cutting of the cake, along with more pink Prosecco for the toast. Carmen cut up the cake and plated it while Augustino and Richard served it, leaving Dani and Richard to pour the wine. It had been a hectic couple of hours but as Joseph stood to make his final speech and toast, all the guests were relaxed and ready to enjoy the rest of their evening.

His speech was heartfelt and humorous, peppered with family jokes that caused both his parents to well up with emotion. He moved swiftly on to thank Jerome, explaining that they were college friends and that he was pleased to reconnect with him after five years. Joseph then thanked all the staff, giving Dani a special mention for her decorations. After the guests toasted the couple, Joseph instructed the deejay to play his parents' song so they could start the dancing. The introduction to Barry White's "You're the First, My Last, My Everything" started and Mr and Mrs Mann made their way to the dance floor. The area sectioned off for the dance floor soon began to fill up with couples dancing, and the deejay carried on with another slow number.

Dani hummed along to 10cc's "I'm Not in Love" as she prepared the cups and saucers for anyone who wanted coffee. She was thoroughly enjoying listening to the old music. It reminded her of her parents.

"Any chance you could make me an espresso?" Jerome's raspy voice jolted her and Dani swung around. Jerome raised his eyebrows and grinned. "Sorry, I didn't mean to startle you."

Dani shook her head. "I was miles away. It's been ages since I heard this song."

"Yeah, he's played some really good ones tonight, I forgot what a great era for music the seventies were."

Dani pushed his espresso over towards him and he thanked her. "It looks like everyone's having a good time."

"Yeah, they're really happy with everything, especially the decorations." He eyed her over his cup as he took a sip.

"Oh." Dani felt her face flush.

"You did an incredible job, Dani."

"Um, thank you. But Gia helped too."

Jerome cocked his head to the side and regarded her. He knew his mother had helped out, but the majority of the work had been done by Dani. His mother had confirmed this fact too. Apart from being hardworking and accomplished, she was modest too. "Well, Mama says otherwise. You're making yourself quite indispensible again. A few of the guests have asked to hire out the room, based on what you've created here." Jerome swept his hand vaguely in the direction of the room as he spoke.

"Oh. Well, that's good – I mean, good for the restaurant."

"Yes it is. We need to get together." Jerome leaned on the bar, resting his arm on the marble top and shifted his gaze back to the room. He'd purposely avoided coming over to the bar most of the evening, but now once the party was in full swing, he just felt compelled to be closer to Dani.

"I'm sorry?" Dani flushed, unsure if she'd heard him right.

"We need to sort out the websites, the Facebook page, remember?" He turned back to look at her, arching his brow.

"Oh. Yes. Sure. Well, you tell me when it's convenient." She swallowed hard and turned her attention back to re-shuffle some cups nervously.

"Perhaps after New Year. Things will have slowed down a bit and I'll have more time to spend with you..." he paused a moment and Dani looked up sharply at him, waiting for what he was about to say. Jerome took in a deep breath. "So we can get everything updated, I mean," he added.

"Sure," Dani said quietly, then she turned to the back of the bar, avoiding any more conversation. Her heart was racing. *Why was this time of year so emotionally charged? Jesus, he was just so intense,* she thought, and this made it harder for her every moment they were spending together. The thought of working so closely with him filled her with both excitement and fear.

Jerome moved his focus back to the room, aware that he'd crossed the line again. Dani's reaction had confirmed it to him, but for that moment he didn't care. Joseph caught his eye from the far end of the room and headed towards the bar.

Thankfully, Pino came up and gave Dani a coffee order, then left to clear a table, meaning Dani could busy herself, relieving her of Jerome's scrutinising gaze. The music had moved to more lively numbers and the guests were now dancing to Earth, Wind and Fire, and thoroughly enjoying themselves. Dani placed the coffee order on the bar for Pino, who'd come back again to collect it, just as Joseph reached Jerome. "Well, everyone's very impressed, Jerome," said Joseph as he leaned on the bar.

"Thank you. I'm pleased your parents are having such a good time."

"They are." Joseph's eyes flitted to Dani and he smiled at her, then he turned back to Jerome. "You can't drink coffee. This is a party. Come on, what shall we have?"

Jerome huffed, "I'm working, remember?"

"Come on, your staff have everything under control. The meal's been served; it's just drinks now," Joseph coaxed. "Isn't that right, Dani?" He shifted his focus to a now-nervous Dani. She shrugged, not wanting to put Jerome on the spot. "I mean, it's Christmas and we're celebrating forty years of marriage. Surely that's worth a drink?"

Jerome shook his head and stifled a grin. "Okay, just one though."

Joseph grinned and rubbed his hands together. "Great, so what are we drinking?"

"Tequila." Jerome shot a look at Dani and she smirked.

"Excellent. What have you got?" Joseph grinned.

"Give me a second – I've a rather special bottle in my office." Jerome turned and headed towards the door.

Dani shrugged and carried on with another drinks order that Augustino had given her. Within a few minutes, Jerome was back holding a bottle. He placed it on the bar and Joseph immediately picked it up.

"Where did you get this?" Joseph asked, looking at the bottle which had "El Tesoro" written across the top. "It's an Anejo," he said, clearly impressed. "This is one of the few tequilas that's made by hand, you know. This is really good stuff." Joseph looked wide eyed at Jerome.

"I recently became acquainted with it and bought a few bottles. Here, let me open it." Jerome took back the bottle and cracked open the seal with his long fingers. Dani placed two whisky tumblers on the bar on two small white napkins and Jerome poured a generous measure into each glass. "You really know your tequila," Jerome snorted.

"I think you've forgotten I lived in California for the last five years," Joseph replied dryly, picking up his glass. "To old friends and long marriages."

Jerome picked up his glass and clinked it against Joseph's. "Old friends and long marriages." And they both took a sip.

"Whoa, that's smooth." Joseph inspected his glass.

Jerome nodded and snorted, "It is. Worth every penny. I've a feeling I'll be getting a taxi home tonight."

Joseph laughed, "Yeah, we've too much catching up to do."

The party continued in high spirits. The tables had been cleared and all that remained were the glasses that were being used. Jerome had let Jamie and Carmen leave by ten and Pino and Richard left at eleven. Between Augustino and Dani, they'd be able manage the few drinks that were requested.

Jerome and Joseph had now moved to sit at a table and were now on their third large tequila. After a couple of glasses of Prosecco, two glasses of wine with the meal and a brandy, Joseph was beginning to feel the effects of the tequila. Jerome, on the other hand, was decidedly more relaxed and was definitely enjoying Joseph's company, reminiscing about old times, the tequila taking the edge off what had been a stressful few days. Around half of the guests had left but the remaining partygoers were happy to dance away to various songs that were being requested. Jenny made her way over to the bar, now that work had eased up. Dani was pleased to see her again and they made arrangements to meet up sometime after the holidays. Dani liked Jenny's friendly manner and felt for her, being in a foreign country without any family or friends.

Jenny shook her head as she looked over at Joseph and Jerome. "It's good to see him relax. He's been so stressed out with the hotel, but boy, he's going to have a stinker of a hangover tomorrow," she giggled. "Good job I'm driving." Jenny looked at her watch. It was quarter to midnight. "I think I'd better get them all home. Mr and Mrs Mann look worn out." Jenny glanced over to where the anniversary couple were slumped in their chairs.

Jenny said her goodbyes and then went over to Joseph. He staggered out of his chair while Jenny went over to the Manns and gathered up their belongings and presents. Augustino had put them in a couple of boxes and offered to take everything to their car, along with the rest of their cake, which Carmen had already boxed up. Joseph sidled up to the bar, watched under the close scrutiny of Jerome.

"I just wanted to say thank you once again, Dani. You really made my parent's anniversary very special. You're a real gem, sweetheart." His words slurred a little as he spoke. He then took her hand and kissed the back of it. "Goodnight, Dani."

"Goodnight Joseph." Dani flushed at the attention. Jenny waved to her as she ushered out the Manns and once Joseph had hugged his goodbye to Jerome, they left, followed by the remaining guests.

Augustino helped the deejay pack up his equipment while Dani put the last of the dirty glasses into the dumbwaiter, sending it down to the kitchen. She really felt for Rico. He was going to have to face all that in the morning.

It was half past twelve by the time everything was in some sort of order. Augustino helped Dani move the vases onto the bar while he waited for a phone call from his new girlfriend, who was picking him up. Jerome was talking on his phone at the far end of the room when Augustino's phone rang.

"Oh, that's me out of here. See you tomorrow." He waved at Jerome and then all but ran out of the room. Dani continued to move the vases, then started to remove the dirty tablecloths and pushed them into large bin liners ready to be collected by the laundry service.

Jerome shut off his phone and paced over to the bar where Dani had put the now half-full bottle of tequila and his glass, which he still hadn't finished.

"Looks like I'll be here for a while yet. The taxi service we use is stacked out with work." He sighed, then picked up his glass and drained it. "You should try some of this, Dani. You're a tequila lover."

"Um, thanks, but I'm driving," she reminded him.

"Of course, you're right. Why don't you take what's left? Then you can have one when you get home," Jerome suggested.

"Oh, I couldn't. That's kind of you, but really, I –"

"Can you never just say okay and thank you?" he sounded mildly exasperated. "Look, you've worked so hard these past few days. Call it a bonus."

"Okay, thank you." She twisted her mouth in an attempt not to grin. Jerome shook his head and chuckled. "How long will you need to wait for?"

"They said forty minutes." *He could just walk to Sky*, he thought to himself, *but it had started to drizzle and he'd be soaked by the time he got there.*

"Well, I could take you home, if you'd like."

Jerome was about to explain that it was Sky he was going to when he stopped himself, deciding he'd just decline the tempting offer of a lift. The idea of being in the close confines of a car again with Dani disturbed him, even if it was just a ten-minute journey across town. He'd just take the large umbrella they kept in the restaurant and walk. If nothing else, the walk would clear his head. "Oh no, I couldn't ask you to do that, it's out of your way, and –"

"You could just say okay and thank you, you know." Dani arched one eyebrow at him, then pulled the last of the tablecloths off the table and stuffed them into the large black plastic bag.

Jerome laughed, causing his eyes to sparkle. "Touché. Well in that case, okay and thank you. I'll ring up and cancel the taxi."

"I'll just run and get my things from the changing rooms then, and I'll meet you outside."

"Sure."

Once Dani had left the room, Jerome quickly rang the taxi company, cancelling his ride, and then he dialled Paul at Sky.

"What's it like? Is everything okay?" Jerome asked Paul.

"It's hectic, but everything's under control."

"Good. I've just finished off here but I'm heading home. It's been a busy day." Jerome grabbed the tequila bottle, then switched off the lights in the function room and headed down the stairs.

"No problem, Boss. I'll tell Gino and get him to send you the figures."

"Thanks Paul. Good night."

"Night, Boss."

Jerome shut off his phone and slipped it into his pocket. He paused at the door leading to the car park. *What was he doing?* he thought to himself. He knew exactly what he was doing – prolonging his time with

Dani. *Was he really stealing minutes just to be with her?* He'd blown off work at Sky just so that she could drive him the full twenty-minute ride home. Jerome sighed, thinking back to his conversation with Joseph while they'd drank their tequila.

"So is Dani seeing anyone?" Joseph had asked Jerome. The question caused Jerome's scalp to prickle. Images of Kuch dancing with her came to mind, but he rid them just as quickly as they'd appeared.

"I'm not sure. I don't think so," he replied gruffly.

"I was thinking of asking her out. Would that be okay?"

Jerome shrugged in an attempt to feign interest. But his back stiffened and he took a large gulp from his drink. The idea of Dani and Joseph together was seemingly worse than Dani and Kuch.

Jerome switched off the lights in hallway and opened the door. It was only a matter of time before one of her many admirers was going to claim her as theirs. The thought stirred feelings in him that were totally inappropriate. He wasn't thinking straight. Jerome looked at the bottle in his hand. *That'll be the tequila*, he thought, then he tapped in the alarm code, then shut and locked the door. *It was just a ride home, for goodness sake, and he was tired. Yeah, keep trying to convince yourself Jerome*, he reprimanded himself.

Dani was waiting in her car. She'd put the heating on full blast and was twiddling a loose strand of hair that had worked itself out of her French plait. "You need to give me your postcode for the sat nav," she asked expectantly as Jerome buckled up his belt.

"Or I could just direct you," Jerome replied dryly.

"Um, I suppose."

"So, head as if you're going to Harewood, the way home, and then I'll tell you where to get off for Bramhope."

Dani nodded and pulled out of the car park. She was nervous and when she'd suggested the lift, she hadn't thought for a minute he'd accept. She'd hoped though, and here he was, his large frame folded into her passenger seat, looking sexy as hell.

"They're very nifty, these cars. Are you happy with it?"

His comment halted her thoughts. *They were obviously going to partake in small talk*, she thought to herself. *Hmm... well at least they could talk about cars, a safe subject.* Then Dani thought back to their previous conversation about cars – maybe it wasn't so safe after all.

"Yes, it's easy to drive and park, it's fast enough too and economical. What with going back and forth to Harewood," she explained, keeping her answer as simple as possible.

"Well that won't be for long. The apartment will be ready in a week."

"Yes. I have to say I'm looking forward to moving in there." *I can't wait!*

"Oh?"

"I'll feel more independent. I haven't lived alone before, so it'll be a novelty," she mumbled. *And I'll be closer to you.*

"I see. Well, Mama will be next door too, so if you need anything. Actually, talking of Mama, she still wasn't home, was she?"

"Er, I'm not sure. I didn't notice whether her car was there."

"It wasn't." Jerome's lips pursed together. "Oh, um, here, take this next turn off, then just follow the road straight up." Dani took the turning and filtered onto the dual carriageway. Thankfully there weren't many cars on the road. She suddenly felt nervous. He didn't seem best pleased with his mother being out so late. She wondered if he knew who Gia was with.

"It's quarter to one," he muttered. "You know where she is don't you?"

Dani squirmed. *Crap, he did know, then.*

"She's out with Ray Holmes," said Jerome, answering his own question.

"You don't like Ray?" Dani asked tentatively. *He's a great guy and your mother really likes him, can't you see that?*

"I don't know him that well to form an opinion. He seems like a good man."

"He is. I suppose it must be weird, seeing your mum dating someone."

"The dating I can just about handle it's... well... er."

"Oh. I see." Dani bit her lip in an attempt to stop her grin. "She's a very attractive woman." *She's not past it yet, Jerome!*

"Jeez, please don't. I'd really prefer not to think about it. Please change the subject." Jerome shifted in his seat. The idea of his mother and Ray in the throes of passion exploded in his head and he shuddered.

The only sound was the swishing of the wipers as they swiped the persistent drizzle off the windshield.

Silence.

Jerome looked out of the window and Dani carried on driving.

"Crap, now I can't think of anything else!" he grumbled and Dani giggled.

"Put the radio on," suggested Dani

Jerome switched it on and flicked through the channels. Most of the music was slow and romantic. "God, that just makes it worse. We could do with something loud and distracting."

"I'm afraid I haven't got around to putting any songs on to a flash drive yet. I've only my Italian language course."

"At this point, that might be the best option." Jerome shook his head. *So she was serious about learning Italian?* The thought pleased him. "Mama and Ray. Who'd have thought?"

"I think it's sweet."

"Sweet?" snorted Jerome.

"Uh-huh. It's nice to know that it's never too late to find someone."

"They've only been on a few dates, Dani. I hardly think that means that... I thought we were changing the subject," he growled and Dani chuckled.

"Okay." *How could she distract him? Work, talk about work. It's neutral ground. He was a workaholic.* "How's the fashion show coming along?"

"Good, but I'd rather not talk about work." *Christ don't remind me about Liz, not now. Not when it's just you and me. I'd rather think about my mother and Ray!*

"Hmm, you're making things difficult."

"I prefer to use the word 'challenging'."

Dani snorted. *Yeah, you have no idea how challenging this is.* "Okay, can I ask you something?" asked Dani.

"That depends."

"On what?"

"Is it work related or anything to do with my mother?"

"No!"

"Then sure. Go ahead." He grinned at her. *This was fun, she was fun.*

Dani stopped at a red light and turned her head to look at him. "How did you get your scar?"

"You mean this one?" he gently rubbed his middle finger over the one-inch line just under his right eye, which marred his otherwise perfect face.

Dani nodded.

"I tried to stop a fight in a club and the asshole caught me with his ring on his fist."

"Oh."

"It was thirteen years ago, on my twenty-first birthday. I was lucky he didn't hit me an inch higher."

"Nice memento," huffed Dani. She turned back to look at the lights that stayed stubbornly red.

"Can I ask *you* something?"

Dani turned to face him again and furrowed her brows.

"It's only fair." Jerome arched one brow at her.

Oh shit, what was he going to ask? "Okay, but I may not answer."

"Now who's being difficult?"

"Challenging," she shot back.

Jerome tilted his head back and laughed loudly. How he loved the quick-fire banter he only seemed to have with her.

"I'm glad I amuse you." Dani shook her head and Jerome stopped laughing and his brows creased.

Then pulling on his bottom lip he said, "Oh, you do far more than just amuse me, Dani."

What? Dani stared at his face, which was half-bathed in a red glow from the traffic lights. She felt herself suddenly heat up in the small confines of her car. *What did he mean?* Jerome narrowed his eyes a little and released his lip and was about to add something, when a sharp beep came from behind them. Dani jerked her head to look at the rear view mirror and then at the now-green traffic lights.

"Shit!" She pulled away and accelerated.

"Impatient bastard," muttered Jerome. "At the next lights, turn left," he said softly, feeling uneasy at his previous unguarded comment.

Dani flicked on her indicator and turned. "So, what were you going to ask me?"

"Oh, yes. I was wondering..." *why you left London... if you still have feelings for the man you ran from... why did you run from him, what did he do?* "... why you went into the leisure industry?"

"I thought we weren't talking about work," Dani replied dryly.

"So you'd rather I ask you something more personal, then?" Jerome smirked.

Crap, no way. Dani gave a conciliatory sigh. "Well, my parents had a B and B in Brighton, so I've always been surrounded by the business and to be honest, I just love the buzz. People go to restaurants, bars and hotels for fun normally, and to be surrounded in that atmosphere while you work" – Dani shrugged – "it's the best kind of working environment. I like the idea of pleasing people, making their time special."

"Like tonight?"

Dani nodded, "Yeah, like tonight."

"And the baking?"

"I just love to bake," Dani chuckled. "And I really like to eat cakes too, of course."

"Of course." Jerome laughed softly at her remark. "And you're so good at it."

"What, eating cake?" Dani asked with mock horror.

Jerome laughed loudly again at her quick answer, which deftly deflected his compliment. Then he pointed to a large double-gated entrance, which opened up to a sweeping gravel driveway, leading to a very grand house. "It's just here."

Dani's eyes widened as she stopped just outside the gates. *Whoa! His house was huge.*

"Well, thanks for the ride, it was... entertaining." Jerome suddenly felt uneasy. It felt like he should be inviting her in for a drink, as though tonight and the ride home were part of some sort of date. While Dani was driving, their conversation had been fun and on the whole, light-hearted, but now that they were stationary, the atmosphere in the car had shifted. It was more intense. His focus was solely on her and not his surroundings. He could sense she was feeling uncomfortable too. Her driving had distracted her but now she couldn't even look at him. He took a deep breath, in an attempt to rein in the wave of emotions that washed over him. *It's just the tequila, loosening your tongue and letting down your guard,* he chastised himself.

"It's only fair. You've given me a couple of lifts in the past," Dani joked. He smiled at her. She was using humour again to lighten the atmosphere, she was good at that. He'd crossed the line again and Dani was trying to put their complicated, bizarre relationship back on an even keel.

"Ah, so this is payback, then?" Jerome's face softened but his eyes glittered as he spoke.

He really didn't want her to leave.

Dani laughed softly.

"So I can cash in on another lift in the future, then?" he added.

"Sure, anytime." Dani tried to make her comment sound breezy but even she caught the slight waver in her tone. She tried to think of some witty comeback, just to prolong this rare unguarded moment that they were sharing, but her brain seemed to have halted as she gazed into those mesmerizing hexagonal eyes.

She just didn't want him to leave.

"Do you know your way back?"

Dani arched her eyebrows and then tapped the screen on the dashboard.

"Ah yes. The sat nav. Send me a message when you get home. Just so I know you got there, okay?"

"Er, I don't have your number."

Jerome reached into his pocket and retrieved his phone. "Tell me yours and I'll send you a missed call." Dani gave him her number and then, after a few seconds, she heard her phone ring, then stop.

"Well, I'd better let you go. Thanks again." He unbuckled his belt and then reached down into the foot well of the car. "Don't forget to try this." He lifted the half-full bottle of tequila he'd brought with him and set it on the seat, then he opened the door. It was still drizzling. He stepped gracefully out of the car, then stooped down to look at her. "Drive safe."

"Always."

"Goodnight, Dani."

"*Buone notte.*"

Dani watched Jerome walk briskly through the gates and down to his home. He turned to wave at her before he entered the dark house and she waved back, though she was sure he couldn't see her. He'd be tucked up in bed next to his cold, beautiful wife, before she even got home. Leggy blonde bitch. The thought depressed her.

Dani set off towards Harewood with a heavy heart. She really liked him – he was just so perfect. She chuckled at his reaction to Gia and Ray. That was going to take some getting used to on his part. Was he so old fashioned? Maybe it was the Italian in him. And his scar, another indication of his Italian heritage: a fiery temper. Somehow that made him even more alluring.

Once Dani got home, she stepped into the kitchen and took a small tumbler off the draining board. She poured herself a small measure of the tequila and took a sip. The amber liquid slipped down her throat and warmed her body as it moved down. Joseph was right, it was smooth. It was delicious. She pulled out her phone from her bag and opened it with a swift slide of the screen. Dani saved Jerome's number to her contacts and then opened up the message option. *What was she going write?* Something simple.

Arrived home safely

That was short and to the point. Dani touched the send option and sighed. She really needed to get a grip. *He's married.* Dani picked up her glass and drained it. Time for bed. It was the weekend, and it was going to be another crazy few days. Her phone beeped to signal a message had come through. Dani's heart raced as she swiped the screen open.

Good to know. Did you try the tequila?

Dani screwed her face up with glee. *He'd answered. Why wasn't he asleep?* Dani quickly typed out her reply.

I did. It's divine.

Dani kept her eyes on the screen. *Was he going to reply?* Then the phone rewarded her with a ping.

I couldn't have put it better myself
Sleep well

Dani's face split into a huge grin. *He'd sent her a smiley face!* She quickly typed her response.

Dormi bene

Jerome looked down at his phone and grinned. *How on earth was he going to sleep well?*

CHRISTMAS MIRACLE

C osimo stretched out his arms, then rested them behind his head while he admired James as he stooped to pick up his clothes. "Where are you going in such a hurry this morning?" he smirked at James, watching him slip on his previously discarded underwear.

"I thought since you cooked last night, and I don't need to work today, I should take advantage of that fact, and cook you breakfast." James beamed.

"Really?" replied Cosimo dryly.

"What? You think I can't cook? Or are you worried that I might mess up your pristine kitchen?" James arched his brow and put his hands on his hips. Over the last nine months, James had got used to Cosimo's extreme tendencies towards perfection. Cosimo's home was immaculate and organised to military precision. He found it surprisingly comforting, compared to his erratic and disorganised way of life.

"No, not at all." Cosimo furrowed his brow, a little disturbed that James had voiced his exact thoughts.

"Good, so what do you fancy?" James asked haughtily, knowing full well Cosimo was lying so he wouldn't hurt his feelings.

Cosimo raised his eyebrows lewdly and swept his gaze over James, twisting his mouth, his unspoken answer.

"Yeah, yeah. Don't try that move on me, Cos. I'm talking about food," he mock-chastised.

"Spoilsport. Well, in that case, coffee and toast will have to do."

James crossed his arms and scowled. "Seriously? Cos, over the last few months I've spent eighty percent of my time at your house. The most I've

496

ever done here is pour a glass of wine or help myself to a beer, maybe made a coffee. This weekend is the first one I've had off since we've been together and I want to spoil *you* for a change."

Cosimo shuffled up so he was sitting in bed. "You do spoil me, James," he said earnestly.

"I don't mean it like that. We never spend time at my place, so I can't look after you. We're always here and I –"

"Don't you like being here?" Cosimo asked softly.

"I didn't say that. Jeez. Cos, I love it here, you know that," he sighed, unsure of whether he wanted to open up this conversation. "I just can't... ." James took a deep breath and waited a beat. "You know what, just forget it." James shrugged. He didn't want to argue. They'd had such a great few days together, he'd finally met Cosimo's family and he really didn't want to spoil it. "I'll go and put the coffee on." He smiled tightly and headed out of the bedroom, leaving Cosimo staring blankly after him.

Cosimo shut his eyes tightly and fell back against the bed. James was the best thing that had ever happened to him. He put up with Cosimo's long hours, he fell in with his plans and Lord only knew how many times he'd stood him up. He had never demanded anything from him and was the kindest and most thoughtful man he'd ever come across. *The poor guy wanted to make him breakfast – where's the harm in that?* Cosimo chastised himself.

James was right, he practically lived here, and Cosimo couldn't even remember the last time he'd been to James's flat. He thought it was weird that a landscaper didn't have a garden but as James explained, he had a multitude of gardens that he worked on and nurtured every day. Cosimo chuckled to himself, thinking back to when James had first seen his rather sparse garden. Over the last few months, James had transformed it into what could only be described as an enchanting extension of his home. The whole area had been redesigned with vibrant green grass surrounding a square sunken seating area around an outside fireplace. The plants and flowers were fragrant, including an extensive herb garden that softened the otherwise urban design. There was wooden decking and slate paving that connected the different levels of the garden. The only original features left were a magnolia and two apple trees.

Cosimo swung his legs out of bed, quickly washed his face and brushed his teeth, then headed downstairs. If he wanted James to stick around, he was going to have to bend a little.

By the time Cosimo had made it to the kitchen, James had set the table and was checking on some croissants he'd defrosted and was warming up in the oven. "Coffee's ready and these need another five minutes," James beamed.

Cosimo looked around his immaculate kitchen and dining room, noting that James had opened the curtains, emptied the dishwasher and set the table. The radio was playing softly in the background and James was humming along to a Christmas song, totally at home and at ease. "You've been busy," Cosimo said gently.

James shrugged and handed Cosimo his espresso.

"I'm sorry about earlier. I'm just stuck in my ways." Cosimo arched his brow at James who chuckled, knowing he was repeating his own words back to him.

"I know, its fine, really. Just sit down and I'll bring the croissants over, or do you still want toast?" he added dryly.

Cosimo pulled out a chair and sat down, continuing to watch James busy himself collecting jars of jams and the butter dish. He placed them on the table, then went back to place the croissants in a basket. "No, croissants sound better," he conceded, then added, "I want you to feel comfortable here, James."

"I do, Cos, really. Just forget it, okay? You're probably right, I'd make a right mess in here. It's a miracle I haven't trashed anything up until now!" he joked, determined not to ruin their time together. Cosimo hadn't really ever had a long-term relationship before, and after so many years of being alone, it was hard for him to change. James smiled to himself. At least he'd met the family. It was a big step for Cosimo and James knew that.

Cosimo's brow creased and he played with the tie of his dressing gown. The dressing gown James had bought him for Christmas. Joining him, James put down the basket of hot croissants, then his own coffee on the table. He knew James was trying to make light of his previous faux pas, and avoiding a confrontation and self-deprecation was his way of diffusing an awkward situation. But the truth was that Cosimo knew he was at fault. He wanted James here, wanted his company, his care, his easy manner. His day always started better when he woke up next to James and on the occasions when he wasn't around, Cosimo felt like something was missing.

"There we are, I think that's everything," James said brightly.

"Thank you. This is perfect."

They ate for a few minutes, the radio filling in the silence.

"I'm going to have to go to La Casa on New Year's Eve." Cosimo took a sip from his coffee and James nodded. "I'd really like you to come – if you'd like to, that is."

"Of course I'd like to." James shook his head and grinned to himself. Breaking a croissant in half, he buttered it, then added a dollop of apricot jam. "Two family functions in a week. Are you sure, Cos? I mean, I wouldn't want to intrude," he said wryly, stifling a grin.

"James," Cosimo sighed, pausing for a moment. How could he explain that this was still too new for him and he wasn't entirely at ease with this new development in his private life. "I wouldn't ask you if I wasn't sure."

James nodded and reached for another croissant, while Cosimo took another sip from his cup.

"I'll need to go home today; I haven't been since Christmas Eve. What have you got planned?"

"Not much. I was hoping we'd spend it together. Go for a drive somewhere." Cosimo tilted his head to one side.

"Okay. But I still need to swing by my place." James rose from his seat and headed to the kitchen. "Another coffee?"

"Yes, sure. Why do you need to go to your place?"

James started up the coffee machine and slipped the cups under.

"Clothes. I need to put washing in," James muttered. He loved being at Cosimo's, but the logistics made it tiring. He needed to have enough of the right kind of clothes with him for any eventuality.

Cosimo shifted in his chair to look over to where James was leaning absent-mindedly against the kitchen counter. "You can wash your clothes here."

"I still need some stuff though," insisted James.

Cosimo was about to suggest he brought more of his belongings over when he was interrupted by his phone ringing. He still couldn't grasp how James seemed to be happy with very little, living out of a small holdall, with the bare minimum.

Arsenio's name flashed across his screen. "Hey, Seni, how are you?"

"Good – well, not that good actually. Scott followed Liz down to her mother's and the trainer's there too." He didn't see the point in beating around the bush. The situation with Liz was escalating and every day that passed by, Arsenio felt more and more uneasy.

"You mean together?" Cosimo said, clearly shocked, misunderstanding Arsenio.

Arsenio explained to Cosimo that she'd left on Boxing Day with the children, and Jerome had confirmed to him that she would be there until Sunday. Jonathan had also gone down to Birmingham but had checked into a nearby hotel. They'd spent a few hours together on Boxing Day and practically all day on Friday.

"Jeez, she really doesn't care, does she?"

"She's a fucking bitch," snarled Arsenio.

James quietly cleared up the kitchen as Cosimo continued to make arrangements.

"Are you free today? I thought we should meet up at my office with Paul, just so we can see how best to handle this. Scott and Gary have enough information now. I've told them to head back today. The poor guys have followed them all that way and didn't have anything with them," Arsenio huffed.

Cosimo's gaze flitted over to James. He was hoping to spend the whole day with him. Maybe he could meet up with Arsenio while James collected his things.

"What time do you want to meet?"

"Well it's nearly ten now. Can you make it in an hour?"

"Sure. I'll see you there."

By the time Cosimo arrived at Arsenio's office, Paul was already there. He was looking sternly at some photographs on the conference table. Cosimo didn't know Paul outside of the confines of his employment at Ferretti House. He was Jerome's employee and other than the usual pleasantries, he hadn't really had that much interaction with him. He knew he must be good at his job and trustworthy, otherwise he wouldn't have lasted nearly four years working under his very particular brother.

After they'd all greeted each other, Arsenio outlined what they knew were the facts and what they presumed was happening.

"So, the bottom line is she's continuing the affair and Jerome is blissfully unaware. What you speculate, though, is that she's biding her time to either amass some money, secure some modelling contracts or what? Jerome asks her for a divorce?" asked Cosimo.

"Yeah, that way he'll have to pay out a lot more," Arsenio said through gritted teeth.

"So it's down to money, then?"

Arsenio nodded.

"You want to confront him?" Cosimo walked over to the table where all the photos were strewn. "With all this?" he idly swept his hand over the table.

"Basically, yes. We'll wait until after New Year, once business calms down, and then we really need to tell him. It's gone too far."

"I have to agree. I feel disloyal and to be honest if I were Jerome, I'd want to know." Paul shifted in his seat.

"You couldn't find anything more, then? In the photos?" Cosimo directed his comment to Paul. He shook his head, rose from his chair and strode towards the table.

"No. I know we're missing something. The dry cleaner's." He tapped his finger on one of the photos. "Something there doesn't add up. My man starts on Monday checking into it. Hopefully he'll uncover something."

Cosimo picked up the picture of Jonathan going into the dry cleaner's and then dragged the photo that showed Liz entering the business on a different day, so that it was in front of him. Paul peered over his shoulder.

"This woman here. She must be an employee. Look, can you see? It can't be a coincidence the same woman is in two photos on different days." Cosimo pointed to the photograph where Liz was leaving. Through the open door, you could just make out a woman in a business suit standing behind the counter, talking to the cashier. She had a distinctive asymmetrical blonde hairstyle. "And look here. She's coming out of the door as the trainer approaches. She's a little too sharply dressed, don't you think, for a dry cleaner employee?" Paul narrowed his eyes as he focused on the slightly blurred image.

Arsenio paced over to see what they were looking at. He focused on the woman in the photo and his brows furrowed. She looked familiar but he couldn't work out where he'd seen her. Maybe it was because he'd been staring at these photos that incessantly that her image was now ingrained into his head. "She looks familiar, but I can't for the life of me think where I've seen her before," he sighed, voicing his thoughts.

"Yes, she looks familiar to me too," Paul agreed.

"It's probably because we've been staring at these Godforsaken photos continuously for the last few weeks," Arsenio said, clearly irritated. He walked back over to his desk; he'd really had enough of trawling through the photos and not finding anything.

"She looks more like an accountant," huffed Cosimo. "Or a lawyer."

Something in Cosimo's comment made Arsenio remember a similar conversation he'd had with Jerome a few weeks ago. "What did you say?"

"I said, she looks like an accountant," repeated Cosimo.

Arsenio strode back to the table and picked up the photo again. He pointed to the woman and showed it to Paul. "You can't see her face here very well, but on this photo here, see? Where she's standing behind the counter. It's a little out of focus, but isn't she in the photos pinned behind Jerome's desk?"

Paul examined the picture and pursed his lips together. "It could be, I'd need to see them together. Let me quickly go up to Sky and get the photos from my office." Paul looked from one photo to another. "Now that you've pointed it out, I think you're right. I knew she looked familiar." Paul shook his head, annoyed he hadn't made the connection.

"I don't follow. What's this woman got to do with Sky?" Cosimo looked expectantly at both Paul and Arsenio.

"An ex-colleague of mine in the drug squad believes she's working for a big drug dealer up here in the north. She's on our watch list," explained Paul.

"So if the dry cleaners is where she's working from..." Cosimo started to formulate what this implied.

"Then the dry cleaners could be where the drug dealer works from too," Arsenio added.

"And if the trainer and Liz have been frequenting the dry cleaners, for no apparent reason..." continued Cosimo.

"We may have our Christmas miracle after all," sniggered Arsenio, looking pleased with himself.

"I'll go and get the photos," Paul said eagerly. Now that he thought this was a possibility, he wanted to nail the bitch and as soon as possible.

"This makes up for missing Christmas Day with you." Jonathan propped up his head on his hand and looked at Liz who was facing him as they sprawled out on the king size bed.

"All we've done for the past two days is fuck like minxes," she huffed.

Jonathan laughed loudly, "Are you complaining?"

Liz stroked his face. "No."

"What time do you need to get back?" he asked quietly. He knew today was their last day together and she'd be heading back home in the morning.

"I've three hours at least."

"And then back to reality," he mumbled. "How much longer, Liz? How much longer do I have to be second best?"

"You're not second best! I told you, I need to make sure we're financially secure. And then I'll ask him for a divorce. I promise. I just need more time," she pleaded.

"How much time? Weeks, months, years? I crack up whenever you go back to him, back to your other life. I'll be on my own and New Year is in a few days and I'll be alone, *again*, while you're playing happy families with the fucking Ferrettis!" He fell back against the bed covering his eyes with his arm.

"It's hell for me too, Jonathan. I don't want to be there either, but we've got to play it smart." Liz lifted herself up and crawled onto him. "Hey, come on. We have to stick to the plan." She bent down and kissed him softly.

He moved his arm and stared up at her. "Have you fucked him?"

"What?" Liz stiffened at his blunt question. *They'd gone over this a hundred times. Whenever she spent time away he'd ask her the same question.*

"You heard." He clenched his teeth together, dreading her answer. She'd promised that she and Jerome hadn't had that kind of a relationship for over six months. But he needed to hear it, he needed reassurance that she wasn't using him. The longer they spent time together, the harder it was becoming for him to believe that she wasn't sleeping with him. He was her husband, after all.

"I've told you this. How many more times do I have to tell you?" she started to shift off him, irritated at the line of questioning, but Jonathan grabbed her wrists.

"You can't blame me for asking, Liz. You go home to him *every night*."

"In separate rooms."

"Under the same roof," he countered.

"He's not like that," she muttered. Suddenly, the hurt of Jerome's constant rejection stung like salt on an open wound, uncurling an emotion Liz wasn't comfortable identifying.

"He doesn't like sex?" Jonathan snorted.

"Of course he does," Liz huffed. Jonathan arched his brow at her defensive tone. "Just not with me. Not since he found out about us," she added sharply. She really didn't want to talk about Jerome and his unsettling willpower. She'd practically thrown herself at him on several occasions and he'd stopped her, apart from that one time.

"Oh," Jonathan said quietly. He regarded her thoughtfully. *So it was Jerome that wasn't interested – did that mean that she was?* he thought. He could see a trace of hurt in her pale face.

"Yes, so you see, you've nothing to worry about," Liz added haughtily.

She tried to pull her wrists free but he tightened the grip on her. "Where are you going?"

"Just let me go, Jonathan," she sighed.

"I'll never let you go. Ever." He jerked her towards him and encased her slim, pale body against his, then kissed her hard. Liz resisted for a moment but his powerful arms held her steady and she melted against him. Jonathan pulled away from her leaving her panting. "I mean it, Liz, I can't let you go. You're stuck with me." Liz smiled softly at him.

"Good."

Jonathan relaxed his grip on her and she pulled up. "Hey, where are you going?" he pouted.

"Come on, let's do something fun."

"I thought we just did." Jonathan's tone was sulky.

"Actually, I've got something." Liz's eyes brightened with excitement. She hoped this would cheer him up.

"What do you mean?" Jonathan asked, intrigued by her sudden change of subject.

"Wait here, it's in my bag." She jumped off Jonathan and ran to where her bag was sitting on the table at the far end of the hotel room. She rummaged in the small zipped compartment and pulled out the small plastic bag Gabe had given her. She lifted it up and shook it for Jonathan to see.

He immediately sat up. "Is that what I think it is?" he asked cautiously, his dark eyes wide with surprise.

Liz nodded, stifling a grin. She'd been desperate to try some since she'd got it.

"Where did you get that?"

"Someone," she said cryptically.

"Liz." Jonathan's tone mildly chastised her.

"Oh don't be a spoilsport. We'll just do one line and then we can fuck like minxes again. You know they say it makes it feel even better, don't you?" She slinked over to him slowly, and seductively swept the bag against her naked chest and breasts. "Come on. I've always wanted to try it and I don't trust myself with anyone else but you. I know you've done it before."

" Jesus, Liz, you're killing me here," he groaned.

"It turns me on just thinking about it. You all agitated and rough. It'll be the fuck of the century," Liz purred. Jonathan launched himself at her and pinned her under him, unable to contain himself any more. Liz squealed, then laughed up at him.

"You really want to do this?" he asked breathlessly holding down her hands by her head. Liz nodded eagerly, her eyes wide with excitement. He bent his head down and kissed her hard. "Okay, babe, let's do this."

Over the whole weekend La Casa d'Italia had been packed out from the opening doors to when the kitchen closed. The time flew past and before Dani realised, it was Sunday night. Work and limited sleep were finally catching up on her and she was seriously thinking of blowing off going to Sky. Her rational self knew she needed the rest. What with Kuch's birthday tomorrow night, then New Year's Eve mid-week, the next week was going to be just as busy. She also needed to find time to pack her things for when she moved into the apartment on Friday morning. But as Dani wiped down her last table, she knew there was no way she'd miss an opportunity to see Jerome.

Saturday had been hectic and he'd been occupied in the main restaurant, as Peter had taken the lunchtime shift off. On Sunday, Jerome hadn't come in at all, so he could spend all day with his family who'd been away, according to Gia. And with the restaurant being closed on Monday, it would be Tuesday before she'd get to see him again.

Peter locked up the front door and began turning off the main lights, leaving the bar lit while he gathered up his paperwork.

"Are you done?" he asked. There was only Augustino and Dani in the back restaurant finishing off.

"Yeah. I'll just run down and get changed. Is that alright?"

"No problem. I've just got to cash up now, so you're good for fifteen minutes or so."

Nicole and Rosa were already changed ready to meet Kuch who was no doubt pacing up and down in the car park.

"Oh, you both look lovely," Dani gasped.

"Thanks," Rosa and Nicole replied together.

"Come on, we'll wait for you." Nicole waved her hand in an attempt to hurry her along.

"No, don't bother. I'll be up in fifteen minutes tops. You go ahead, Kuch is probably waiting."

"Okay, if you're sure. We'll see you there." Then both of them exited the changing rooms and ran up the stairs.

Dani pulled out her bag from her locker and fished out her makeup bag. Her bag lit up from the inside and she realised it was her phone. Someone was ringing her, though she couldn't hear anything as she'd switched it to silent. Dani grabbed her phone and looked at the screen to see who was ringing her at almost midnight. Jez's face flashed across the screen and her heart lurched just at the sight of him. *Why was he calling her?* He said he wouldn't bother her. All manner of horrible thoughts came to mind and she shook her head in an attempt to rid them. Before she could answer, the phone stopped flashing, indicating that he'd hung up. Dani switched on the ringer and then put the phone back in her bag. She'd call him tomorrow. Whatever he had to say could wait.

Within fifteen minutes, Dani had quickly dressed and retouched her makeup and as she pulled up to the Ferretti House car park, the barrier opened. She drove through, waved on by the car park attendant. *Perks of working for the owner*, Dani thought to herself, descending by two floors until she found a space. She quickly checked herself in the mirror, then as she went to open the door, her phone began to ring again. Pulling it out again, she scowled, faced once more with the smiling image of Jez. Her instinct told her something had to be wrong. Even when she'd first left him, he hadn't rung so persistently. Taking a deep breath, she swiped the screen to answer the call.

"Dani?" Jez croaked.

"Jez? What's wrong? Are you alright?" From his voice, Dani knew something wasn't right.

"I am now. It's good to hear your voice babe." He sounded hoarse.

"You sound funny." Dani felt a sudden wave of uneasiness.

"I've been in an accident."

"An accident! What kind of accident? Are you alright?" Dani gripped her throat in panic. Her first thoughts were: *who was looking after him?*

"Some fucker tail-ended me and I hit my head. Just a few stitches and whiplash. They're keeping me in until tomorrow, to check on my concussion."

"Concussion? Jesus, Jez." Dani moved her hand to her mouth.

"The car's a mess."

"Forget the car! What about you, where are you?"

"In the hospital. I just wanted to hear your voice. I'm restless and the painkillers are playing havoc with my head. I'm going to have a hell of a black eye and I'm sure I've a lump the size of an egg on my head. What time is it?" He sounded disorientated.

Dani pulled the phone from her ear to check. "It's nearly half past twelve."

"So you've just finished your shift?"

"Yes, I was just heading... I was on the way home."

"It's good to hear your voice, Dani."

"Shouldn't you try and sleep?"

"Yeah in a bit. Can you talk to me until you get home? It soothes me."

Dani swallowed hard, trying to dislodge a lump that had stuck there. "Um, yeah, sure. Let me put you on hands free." Dani connected her phone to the hands free and started the engine.

"I miss you, Dani. I'm sorry I called you so late. Sorry I fucked up," he mumbled. Dani reversed her car out of the parking space and ascended up to the ground floor.

"Don't talk about that now. Let's talk about something else." Dani tried to sound chirpy but her heart was breaking, knowing he was laid up in some hospital bed all alone.

" Jeez, my head is banging and these pain killers are starting to make me woozy."

"Well that's good. Once they kick in, you won't be in so much pain. When did they give you them?" Dani pulled out on to the road and headed towards Harewood, her eyes clouding over as tears flooded her eyes involuntarily. For the first time since October, she wished she wasn't two hundred miles away from him.

"Just before I called you. The nurse said they'd start working in twenty minutes."

"When did it happen?" Dani asked trying to keep her voice steady.

"I was on the way to the bar. I think it was six-ish. I hope they managed alright without me tonight."

"I'm sure they did, Jez. Don't worry about that now. Earl's there."

"Yeah, but he's no manager. He's not you." The last three words he spoke were tinged with regret and Dani gasped softly.

"You didn't get a manager, then? Someone to help you?" she asked before she could stop herself.

"No. Who could ever match up to you, Dani?"

"Jez, please don't. You said you wouldn't do this," Dani mumbled.

"Okay. I'm sorry. I'll change the subject."

"Good." In an attempt to lighten the conversation, Dani asked, "Are they looking after you alright? The hospital, I mean."

"I've got a freaking drip attached to me. You know how I hate needles. And they put my head in a neck brace," huffed Jez.

"Oh Jez." Dani tried to contain a sob.

"I'll be fine tomorrow," he yawned. "It's just good hearing you again. Did I tell you that? Did I tell you that I miss you?"

"Yes, yes, you told me, Jez." The tears that Dani had kept at bay finally dripped down her cheeks. He was beginning to sound drowsy, the effect of the painkillers finally kicking in. Jez continued to talk randomly, becoming more disorientated, repeating the same words and phrases over and over as Dani drove home, telling her he missed her and that their home was empty without her. He babbled on and Dani listened to the words that cut through her heart, every syllable a twisting knife in her chest. She'd never wanted to hear his words of apology because she knew what they would do to her, how they'd make her feel. How much of what he said was true and how much of it was drug induced, she didn't know. Regardless, they affected her deeply.

Dani pulled into the driveway of Chloe and Adam's house and cut the engine.

"You must get some sleep, Jez."

"Sleep yes," he slurred.

"Jez? You need to hang up now." *Why was he hanging on?*

"Don't go. I need you.... love you... so sorry."

Dani clenched her eyes shut, the pain of listening to words she didn't want to hear, too much. "Jez? Jez?"

"Dani?"

"I'm here, just hang up. Go to sleep. I'll call you tomorrow, okay?"

"Sleep... tomorrow." Then the line went dead.

Dani disconnected her phone from the car and buried her face in her hands, allowing herself to sob freely after holding back for the entire journey home. The tension of the phone call and her tiredness swept over her like a wave.

Her sobbing was interrupted by her phone vibrating and Dani's heart sank. Looking at the screen, she saw it was a message from Rosa wondering where she was. Dani quickly wiped her eyes and typed back that she was very tired and had come home, but she'd see them all at Kuch's party. Rosa's reply was almost immediate, telling her she'd call her and make arrangements for tomorrow evening. Dani sent back a thumbs up emoticon, then turned off her phone and headed into the house. Exhausted and emotional, she entered her room, praying sleep would numb the torrent of emotions she was feeling. For the first time since she'd started at La Casa, she was glad she had tomorrow off.

Jerome pinched the bridge of his nose, trying to keep calm. He'd just strapped Kara and Alessandro into the back of his car. Liz was acting erratic again, and though she'd promised she wasn't taking the slimming pills, he just knew she was lying. Short of searching through her things, there wasn't any way he could prove it. In an attempt to calm down and to give himself some much-needed space, he decided to take his children out for a few hours, leaving Liz at home to calm down after his inquisition. The last thing he wanted was for his children to hear them arguing. What worried him more was that after three days of peace, he was now edgy and irritated and back to walking on eggshells in an attempt to keep Liz happy. The thought depressed him.

By early evening, once Jerome had returned home, Liz seemed to be less anxious. She blamed the stress of waiting for word from I-Gea as the cause of her mood and being away from home. An hour long Pilates workout and a twenty-minute run on the treadmill had helped.

Jerome wasn't entirely convinced, but he had to admit she looked calmer and her hands and legs weren't twitching. Thankfully, Nina was back, so the children were going to spend their time with her in the playroom.

Jerome looked at his watch. It was almost seven and Liz hadn't made a move to go and change for Kuch's party. He headed to her room and pushed open the door. "We need to leave in half an hour." He found her laid out on her bed watching TV.

"I'm not coming," she said.

"Why not? You never come to these kinds of things." He was trying to sound cool, but he was tired of going to events without her. He'd always supported and accompanied her, whenever she had to go to work-related functions, however dull they were for him.

"I'm tired and I'm really not good company. You know it's not my thing." She sat up and hugged her knees. She hated going to events where she had to mingle with Jerome's staff. She had nothing in common with them.

"Haven't you been sleeping?"

Liz shook her head.

"You hardly ate anything today. I'll make you something."

Liz glared at him, not wanting to start on the same old argument.

"Something light. I've some chicken soup," he suggested.

"Okay. I'll have some soup."

"Some salad? With avocado?"

"Fine."

"Good. I'll bring it up. Are you sure you don't want to come? It'll take your mind off everything," Jerome coaxed.

"No, I really just want to have a bath and try and get some sleep."

Jerome sighed deeply. "You want me to stay?"

Liz narrowed her eyes at him, unsure of what he actually meant.

"I'll stay if you like," he shrugged.

Something in Liz's demeanour and a small spark in her eyes made Jerome realise she'd misunderstood his comment and had read more into it.

"I mean, I'll stay and help out, with the kids. Make sure you get some rest," he clarified. The last thing he wanted was to send her mixed messages.

"Oh. I see." Liz's eyes frosted over at the obvious brush-off. "No, I'll be fine. Nina's here and once I've eaten and had my bath, I'm sure I'll sleep well." She pursed her lips together and looked back at the TV.

"Okay, then." Jerome turned and exited her room, then made his way to the kitchen to quickly prepare her paltry dinner. His stomach was in knots again, the last few days of calm seemingly disappeared, leaving him feeling wretched.

39

KARAOKE

"So what is this place we're going to?" Dani asked as Rosa pulled away from the curb.

Rosa had arranged to pick Dani up so that she could have a drink for once. After her phone call last night from Jez and the hour-long phone call she'd had today from him, Dani really needed to let her hair down. The only consolation was that at least they could talk now, even though Jez tended to get emotional and somehow still made her feel guilty.

"It's a bar that does karaoke," grinned Rosa.

"Karaoke? Seriously?" Dani laughed. *Wasn't that so nineteen nineties?*

"Kuch loves karaoke. Well, he is half-Japanese, so..." Rosa shrugged. "It's great fun. And Kuch can really sing. I think he's a frustrated singer actually," Rosa giggled. "Do you sing?"

"Well I can hold a tune if that's what you mean... ," replied Dani modestly. "But I don't think I'll be doing any singing tonight. I mean, I play with my nieces and nephew on their karaoke game. Sing in the car and stuff – but real karaoke, that's just a bit too scary for me," she huffed.

"Aw, come on, we all do. Once you've loosened up a bit, had a drink. What cake did you make for him?"

"Raspberry and vanilla. Nicole said that's his favourite."

"He'll be thrilled."

The bar was out of town in a rather affluent suburb. Rosa parked up the car and they made their way into the rather smart establishment. Dani walked in, carrying the cake box, and stopped to take in the room. It was nothing like she'd imagined a karaoke bar to be like. She had visions of a dark seedy pub that smelled of stale beer and this was anything but that. It was more like an uptown gentleman's club with leather sofas and soft lighting. The clientele were mainly in their thirties and over, and they all looked professional and smart, though casual.

"Wow, it's a really nice place." Dani couldn't hide her surprise.

"I know. They just do karaoke about twice a month here and we try to come down when we can. It was just lucky it also coincided with Kuch's birthday." Dani followed Rosa idly. Her eyes focused on a man in his late forties singing "Unchain My Heart" in a remarkable gravelly voice.

"He's good." Dani motioned to the man and Rosa smiled and nodded. The bar was pretty much full and the atmosphere was like something Dani had never experienced before. It had the vibe of a live concert but with added intimacy. Dani loved it.

"Here, let's give the cake to the girl over by the bar. We'll tell her when to bring it out."

Dani handed over the box to the girl who seemed to know Rosa. She quickly gave the girl some instructions, explaining she'd tell her when to get it ready, then Rosa led Dani to where the rest of their friends were sitting.

There were roughly twenty of them and they'd taken over a large section of the bar that had six couches with a row of four low tables. The tables were covered in drinks and platters of finger food and dips. Kuch was up instantly, hugging Dani and Rosa.

"Happy birthday, Kuch." Dani kissed his cheek as he squeezed her tightly.

"I thought you weren't going to make it." He looked to Rosa.

"Happy birthday." Rosa hugged and kissed him. "It's my fault, I got lost getting to Dani's," explained Rosa.

"As long as you made it," he grinned, his eyes sparkling.

Rosa squeezed in next to Carmen, who was sitting on one of the couches. Dani looked around at everyone, acknowledging them with a wave as she tried to find somewhere to sit. In all the commotion she hadn't realised that Jerome was sitting behind her. Her eyes widened in surprise. She hadn't thought for a second he'd be here. Her heavy heart that had been weighed down with thoughts of Jez suddenly felt decidedly lighter and began to beat just a little bit faster.

"Well hello, Dani." Dani's attention was drawn to Arsenio who was also sitting next to Jerome.

"Um, hello." She smiled weakly and then looked at Jerome and added, "Hi."

"Hi." A smile skirted around his mouth as he spoke and before he could say any more, Kuch appeared with a chair for her.

"Here, Dani. I'll squeeze you in over here." He gestured to a small gap between two large couches, which placed her next to Jamie and Nicole and directly opposite Jerome. *Oh hell!* thought Dani. That was all she needed.

The singer had just finished. Everyone clapped and a few people whistled as he modestly bowed. The deejay then called up the next name and a couple made their way to the stage. Dani decided she'd keep her eyes on the stage until she could calm herself down. She was beginning to fear this wasn't just a regular crush. Her heart was beating so much faster now, just at the sight of him. The surprise of seeing him in a social setting made it so much more thrilling. The last time she'd been at an event with him was at Adam's charity dinner. Dani smiled to herself thinking back to their dance. She'd only seen a glimpse of him but he looked breathtaking in dark jeans and a cobalt blue deep V-sweater. It didn't help that they seemed to have some obvious chemistry that flared up unexpectedly. What made it infinitely worse was that Dani knew that if he wasn't married, that bubbling chemistry would have most definitely erupted by now.

The couple who had been called up stood nervously while the introduction started, then the audience clapped their encouragement once they'd started their duet of "Don't Go Breaking My Heart". They weren't particularly good but the audience clapped along anyway as the couple loosened up and started to really enjoy themselves. Their performance was infectious and even though their voices were really nowhere near as good as the previous performer, everyone cheered them along anyhow.

"What do you think?" asked Nicole.

"It's really great, isn't it? I thought people would boo them off."

Nicole shook her head. "Most of the singers are good to average that go on, but even if you're not good, the fact that you get up on stage and sing – well, that deserves encouraging. They're all regulars. Everyone knows everyone so it's just a bit of fun."

Kuch perched himself on the couch next to Nicole and handed Dani a drink. "Here: tequila, no ice. So what do you think?"

"I think it's pretty cool. Are you going to sing too?"

"We're up next. You made it just in time," he winked.

"We?" squeaked Dani, her face freezing for a second, hoping he wasn't referring to her.

"Don't panic," Nicole chuckled. "He meant me."

"Really? I can't wait, then," Dani said relieved, grinning at the two of them.

The couple finished and everyone clapped as they laughed and quickly left the stage. The deejay then called up Kuch and he stood up from the couch and waited for Nicole. Then to Dani's surprise, Richard got up too, and Kuch's brother. She hadn't even realised he was here. The atmosphere changed in the bar and everyone cheered as they got up on to the stage.

Jamie leaned over. "They're quite the celebrities here," he grinned. Dani furrowed her brow not understanding what he meant. "Just watch and listen."

The introduction started to "Turn Up the Love" as they took their positions on the stage and then Nicole sang out the first line pitch perfect. Dani stared in awe at her incredible voice. The whole bar was focused on her, but Nicole seemed unfazed as she continued to sing the refrain. Then from behind her, Kuch began to sing the next rap part. Everyone in the bar was clapping along to his performance. Then it was Richard's turn, who equalled Kuch's incredible performance. The atmosphere was electric. Kuch's brother sang his part and then Nicole took over again. If Dani didn't know them, she would have sworn that it was Far East Movement themselves performing.

"Told you." Jamie leaned in so that Dani could hear.

"They're amazing. I can't believe how good they are." Jamie grinned and nodded at her comment.

When they finished, the bar erupted into cheers and everyone was on their feet clapping. Dani allowed herself to sneak a peek at Jerome who was also on his feet cheering. He caught her eye and smirked, then put his finger and thumb in his mouth and whistled loudly. Dani chuckled and turned her attention back to the stage.

The group came off stage back to their seats as the bar calmed down for the next performer.

"You guys were amazing!" Dani gushed. "Wow, I can't believe how good you are."

Nicole smiled widely. "Thanks."

Dani shook her head in disbelief as Kuch came to join Nicole. "It was brilliant."

Kuch beamed back and looked at Nicole. "She's pretty special."

"So are you." Nicole blushed, then remembering herself she reached over for a drink.

"You were all just... I'm blown away. How can anyone follow that?" asked Dani.

The bar calmed down enough for the next singer to take his place on the stage and he started his rendition of Bon Jovi's "You Give Love a Bad Name."

The evening progressed and one by one, a number of the customers got up to sing, either a duet or alone. Granted, it was hard to compete with Nicole and Kuch's performance, but most of the performances were good. Rosa sang an excellent version of Tina Turner's "Private Dancer" to Dani's utter surprise, and Rico sang The Police's "Every Breath You Take". Dani was already on her third double tequila, enjoying the fact she wasn't driving for a change.

The karaoke took a break, mainly for the customers to socialise rather than focus on the stage, and the resident piano player began to softly play a medley of popular songs. Arsenio saw this as an opportune moment to get some one on one time with Dani. She was sitting with Nicole as he sidled towards them. "Hey." Arsenio winked at Nicole. "Shouldn't you be getting the cake or something, cuz?"

Nicole shook her head and raised an eyebrow at him. "You're not very subtle, Seni. Now be nice," Nicole warned as she got up from the couch, allowing Seni to sit down next to Dani.

"So, aren't you going to get up and give us all a show?" Arsenio asked. His face had a mischievous smirk and Dani chuckled at him. He really was a good-looking guy but she couldn't take him seriously and, over the last few weeks, she'd grown immune to his constant flirting and obvious double-entendre.

"I might," she teased. "What about you?"

"Oh, I prefer to give my five-star performances in private." He raised his eyebrows at her.

"Seni, you are incorrigible and you really need to give up. You know I'll never fall for your blatant and outrageous flirting."

"Outrageous, eh? Maybe, but it really is immense fun trying."

Dani shook her head as she stifled her grin, then playfully leaned forward and breathed, "Well, I'd really hate to ruin your... um, pleasure."

Arsenio half-closed his eyes and groaned, "Now you're just teasing me."

Dani laughed, then reached for her drink and knocked it back. *Jeez, she hadn't drunk so much in a very long time and her teasing was definitely a result of that.*

"I may have to get you sacked just so I can actively pursue you," added

Arsenio, signalling over the waiter. "Another straight double tequila for the lady and a Peroni for me."

The waiter nodded and quickly retreated to the bar. Arsenio shuffled closer to her and Dani cocked her head at him. "So, why would I be sacked?"

Arsenio narrowed his eyes slightly, then reached over to tuck a lose strand of hair behind her ear. Dani stiffened at the intimate gesture. Arsenio had always been a playful flirt and he always kept it light hearted, but something had suddenly changed. His demeanour, the way his eyes burned, his body language, suddenly it felt dangerously different and Dani felt herself sober up instantly. She'd been joking around, but one look at Arsenio and she knew there was some truth behind his playfulness. It became acutely apparent that Dani hadn't really seen the true Arsenio playboy at work. He'd hidden it behind his obvious remarks and double-entendres, but that wasn't who was sitting a foot away from her now. She was obviously getting a glimpse of Arsenio's art of seduction and boy was it disarming. It was like watching Clarke Kent change to Superman. He instantly became more serious and smooth. Arsenio licked his lips slowly.

"Oh, I'd never get you sacked. I'd rather you were constantly around, even if it was just for me to look at." His eyes swooped up her body and locked on Dani's. She felt herself take a sharp intake of breath, caught completely off guard by the comment, and he knew it. Arsenio knew she'd gotten the message. "On the other hand." He licked his lips and dropped his gaze to hers. "I'd give anything to be alone with you right now." His voice, a little more than a whisper, had Dani frozen. Her heart raced, totally dumbstruck by the effect his words had on her. After a beat, he leaned back and gave her a full-blown, mega-watt, sexy smile, then shifted back as the waiter arrived with their drinks. And within a millisecond he was playful Arsenio again.

Whoa! What was that?

Jerome had gone out to have a cigarette with Richard and Enzo and had come back in to witness Arsenio tucking Dani's hair behind her ear. He flinched as he watched Dani tense at something Arsenio said. Unable to stop himself, he strode quickly over towards them but his path was halted by Nicole.

"Great, you're back. We're going to do the cake. Can you get everyone together? And here." She handed him her camera. "Take some photos too."

Jerome's eyes flitted to where Dani was. He felt slightly appeased to see Rosa sitting with her now. Arsenio had shifted a little further away from her. He hoped she'd blown him off but he couldn't be sure.

"Yeah sure." He took Nicole's camera as she sped off to the bar to give them her instructions, then went up to the piano player.

Jerome managed to get everyone back to their tables, calling Kuch over last of all, telling him to sit down with the rest of their party. The piano player took his cue from Nicole and started to play as Nicole did an incredible impression of Marilyn Monroe singing "Happy Birthday", replacing "Mr President" with "Mr Kuchiki". The girl behind the bar brought out Dani's cake with one large candle on and put it down in front of Kuch, who had to reluctantly drag his eyes away from Nicole's seductive performance, so that he could have some photos taken while he blew out the solitary candle.

Jerome dutifully snapped away as Kuch posed with his cake, making exaggerated gestures to everyone's delight. Kuch pulled Dani over and kissed her cheek loudly.

"Thanks for the cake."

Dani scrunched up her nose, embarrassed at the attention and backed away so Nicole could give Kuch a peck on the cheek. Dani turned around and walked straight into Arsenio.

"So, I'll need to wait until May the sixth until I can kiss you." He arched one of his brows and his lips curved into a wry smile.

Dani frowned, puzzled at his comment.

"That's when my birthday is. And just so you know, I'm expecting a cake too." He winked and moved back so she could pass.

Oh crap, thought Dani. She was beginning to think that maybe she should steer clear of Arsenio. He'd obviously upped his game. Her attention was distracted by the flash of the camera as Jerome took a few more photos and she focused for a moment on him. Jerome lowered the camera and shot her a penetrating stare.

Oh double crap! He looked angry. She hoped she wasn't going to get in trouble because of Arsenio. She'd really have to watch her step. Then to her surprise, he lifted up the camera and pointed it at her. She stood staring at the lens for a moment paralysed.

"Smile, Dani." Nicole's voice jolted her. Nicole had moved away from Kuch and was about to take the camera back from Jerome when she saw him focus on her.

Dani's eyes jerked to Nicole, then back at the camera lens and she smiled a very small smile. The flash exploded and Dani blinked several times at the force of the fierce light. Then grinned nervously at Nicole and shook her head. Nicole laughed at her and before Dani even realised, Jerome clicked a few more photos of her.

Nicole grabbed the camera and checked out the photos. "They're great, Dani." Dani stood still for a moment, the flash having played havoc with her vision. Nicole stepped towards her to show her. "See? I'll send them to you."

Dani lifted her eyes to look at Jerome, his expression unreadable as he stared at her. Dani swallowed hard, feeling her pulse race, his gaze unfaltering. After what seemed like an age, he tilted his head to the side and allowed his lips to curl into a smile, then he abruptly turned his focus to where Kuch was. *Whoa, what was that all about!*

Silvanna cut up the cake and passed everyone a piece, then the deejay announced the next singer as Nicole. She grinned broadly and grabbed Jerome's hand.

"Come on, cuz."

Jerome sighed and muttered something in Italian under his breath and Nicole laughed.

"Suck it up, Jerome. You know you love it. Come on, it's been a while since we've sang together."

Carmen clapped and bounced in her seat. "Yay. Go on, cuz, show them how it's done."

Jerome reluctantly got up and everyone at their table cheered. It was obvious he wasn't best pleased but he didn't want to ruin the mood, faced with a determined Nicole.

Dani sat down next to Carmen directly in front of the stage. "So Jerome sings too, then?" she asked, hoping she sounded casual.

"Yeah, he can sing," Carmen huffed and Dani instantly knew he must be good. "When we were kids, we used to sing all the time and Jerome has an incredible memory for words – photographic memory or something. Watch: he doesn't even read them off the screen."

"Really?"

Carmen nodded as the introduction started to Eros Ramazzotti's and Anastacia's "I Belong to You". Dani's whole body was covered in goose bumps when she heard Jerome sing out the first line in a hauntingly melodic voice. Her head shot up to see him temporarily close his eyes, continuing to sing in Italian. *Holy mother of God, he looked and sounded sexy as hell.* There wasn't a woman in the bar that wasn't totally mesmerised by him. Nicole then joined him, singing the English part, definitely giving Anastacia a run for her money. Just as Carmen predicted, Jerome didn't look once at the screen. The two of them sang a truly emotional rendition of the love song and Dani, along with the rest of the bar, gaped at the stage. Throughout the song, Jerome either focused on Nicole or closed his eyes until the very end when he allowed his gaze to fall on to the audience – and for a fleeting moment, onto Dani.

Within a second, everyone was on their feet, once again cheering, and Nicole beamed over to Kuch who was on his feet, clapping madly along with the rest of the bar.

"Good, aren't they?" Carmen shouted over the noise to Dani who remained dumbstruck. She nodded, rendered speechless while she clapped. "They used to sing together at school and pretty much at every family occasion."

"You're all such a talented family," gasped Dani.

Carmen shrugged, "I wish Cosimo was here. He does a fantastic version of Volare."

"Now that I'd really like to hear," grinned Dani, sitting back down and taking a gulp of her drink.

"Aren't you going to have a go?"

Dani shook her head. "Not a chance after you lot. I thought I could sing until I heard all of you."

"Well we're staying for a little longer, maybe you might change your mind."

Nicole came over to join them, buzzing from her performance.

"Nicole, you really are amazing. It's like you become a totally different person on stage."

Nicole shrugged shyly, "I just love singing. It helps having Jerome or Kuch with me though – I feel less nervous. What about you?"

Dani shook her head. The next performer was already on stage and Dani made a concerted effort to look only at the stage. She was desperately avoiding any eye contact with Jerome and equally avoiding Arsenio. Fleetingly, she wondered why Liz wasn't there. In an unguarded moment and fuelled by the four double tequilas she'd already had, Dani blurted out. "How come Liz isn't here?"

Nicole pulled a face before she answered, "It's not her kind of thing. She can't sing and between you and me, I think she gets a bit pissy when Jerome gets up. He used to be such fun but over the last five or six years, he just seems... I don't know, less so."

"She should be really proud of him. He sings brilliantly, even if I didn't understand a word of it!" grinned Dani.

"Exactly. And he doesn't care if she can't sing, he just likes the idea that you have a go – you know, loosen up. The mike auto-tunes you if you're really bad anyway. She's just so stiff! LBB!"

Dani stifled a laugh by putting her hand over her mouth and Nicole giggled.

"Aren't you going to sing?"

"Me? No. How can I, after you?" Dani shook her head.

"Oh, come on. Everyone's had a bit to drink. Even if you're not that confident, no one will even notice. Go on." Nicole nudged Dani.

"I really don't feel that comfortable..."

"What if I sing with you?" coaxed Nicole.

"No offense, but that would only solidify how rubbish I am," huffed Dani.

"Look, the bar is half-empty now so there aren't as many people."

Rosa edged in closer. "You know Kuch will be thrilled."

"I'm not sure if they have anything I know," squirmed Dani, feeling pressured.

"Well, what do you know and I'll see if they have it?" suggested Rosa.

Dani thought hard of some song that she hoped they wouldn't have. "Erm... I used to like to sing along to The Corrs, 'Runaway'..."

Before Dani even finished, Nicole was up and almost ran over to the deejay. Dani's eyes followed her and she felt her stomach tighten. *Please, please, please don't have it.* She prayed, watching the deejay enter the title into the computer. Dani's heart sank as she saw Nicole beam and show a thumbs up. *Crap!*

"Looks like you're up," grinned Rosa. Before she could even grasp what was happening, Rosa was pulling her up out of her seat. Dani grabbed her glass and drained it and reluctantly made her way up to the stage where an excited Nicole stood.

"Just focus on the screen and you'll do great."

Dani took the microphone Nicole was holding and turned her attention to the screen.

The distinct violin introduction started and the bar suddenly became quiet. Before Dani could even catch a breath or even compose herself, the words appeared on the screen and in a shaky breathless voice, she started to sing. Her stomach was like a stone, but she focused on the words. By some miracle, she was able to keep up as the familiar words of this much-loved song appeared. She hardly recognised the sound that came out of her throat and ever so slowly, she began to feel a little more at ease as the seconds ticked by. Dani's eyes momentarily flitted up to Nicole, who smiled widely in encouragement. Before Dani even realised it, she'd come to the end of her three-and-a-half-minute performance. Dani blinked rapidly, then looked down into the bar and was rewarded with the sight of everyone clapping, and her party were all standing. Rosa was whooping loudly, with Jamie and Kuch beaming up at her, blowing her a kiss.

Nicole hugged her as she guided a rather dazed Dani off the stage. "You were really great, Dani. You *can* sing, see?"

Dani mumbled something under her breath, indicating it was the tequila. She lifted her gaze from the floor and her eyes locked on Jerome, who hadn't taken his eyes off her during her entire performance. He was at least twenty feet away but for a few seconds, it felt like there was a tunnel between them, blocking everyone and everything out. Jerome slightly tilted his head to one side and there was a glimpse of a smile on his lips. He narrowed his eyes and gently pulled at his bottom lip as though he was trying to work out a puzzle. Then he shook his head and smiled softly at her, his eyes glittering with secret admiration. She'd surprised him. She had a habit of doing that and he was disturbed at how much he enjoyed every new thing he learned about her.

Dani stifled a shy smile back at him, thinking that the nerve-wracking performance was worth every second, just to have Jerome smile at her that way. Suddenly she felt very hot and fanned herself. Spotting a waiter, she asked for water while Rosa and Nicole babbled around her, clearly thrilled at her performance.

It was getting late and a few of the staff had left, meaning that their seating had become decidedly less cramped. Dani focused on Nicole and Kuch trying hard to skirt around each other. She shook her head, grinning to herself. *How had no one worked it out yet?* she thought to herself. The waiter quickly placed the bottle of water on the table in front of her and turned away. Dani scowled at it. No glass. Then from over her shoulder, a glass appeared and she twisted around to see where it had come from. Jerome rounded the couch and lowered himself into the space next to her. "Thanks," she whispered, her heart leaping and thumping against her chest.

He shrugged, indicating it was nothing, and she felt unbelievably thrilled that he'd remembered she couldn't drink out of bottles. He leaned over and opened up the bottle, then poured half the contents into the glass and handed it to her. Taking it, she proceeded to drain it. "Thirsty?" he chuckled.

"Nerves."

Jerome emptied the rest of the bottle into the glass as she held it, scooting even closer and leaning into her so he could hear her over the music. Dani took in a deep breath, breathing in that intoxicating mix of his chosen cologne, a hint of smoke and the distinctive, seductive, scent of Jerome. "You sing beautifully." His eyes were locked on hers as he spoke. "I haven't heard that song for a while."

"Thanks. It's one of my favourites." She felt her throat close up; the intense way he was gazing at her was making her flustered. She took another sip of water, then added, "You have a great voice too, though I didn't understand a word." She huffed, trying to defuse the highly charged atmosphere.

Jerome smiled widely. "So Capo's and my mother's Italian lessons haven't advanced you enough to translate Eros's songs, then?"

Dani laughed. "No. I can barely handle small talk in Italian. I think I need an intensive crash course to get to that standard. Capo teases me all the time. Both he and Gia told me the best way to learn Italian is to have an Italian boyfriend." Grinning, Dani shook her head and placed her glass on the table.

Jerome took in a deep sharp breath and licked his lips. The thought of Dani with anyone disturbed him intensely. "They're right."

Dani's eyes shot up to his. His expression was deadly serious, all humour gone. She swallowed convulsively. *Why did he always make her feel like there was something else going on between them?* He was always so intense with her. She took a deep breath. *Was he talking about himself? No. That was ridiculous. She needed to stop fantasising!* The tequila was playing havoc with her perception, reading far too much into everything. "Well, I'm not sure I'm ready yet," muttered Dani. Jerome slightly tilted his head and narrowed his eyes, then nodded. *Oh crap, had she offended him?*

"Are you sure?" he asked softly.

"Are you ready to go?" Rosa's voice jolted them and they both instinctively pulled back.

"Er, sure," mumbled Dani, then darted her eyes back to Jerome.

Jerome stood up as Dani pushed to her feet. Jerome furrowed his brow, unsure whether her answer was directed at him or Rosa.

Suddenly feeling very tired and extremely confused, Dani felt the need to get away from him. If they'd have continued talking, she really didn't know what she might have done or said. Why was he so damned sexy?

In a hurry to get out from the bar, they quickly said their goodbyes and got into Rosa's car. "I could've got a taxi, Rosa. I'm taking you out of your way."

"Don't be silly. We arranged it and it's only a few extra miles. Did you have fun, then?"

"Yeah, I did. Who'd have thought I'd be singing in a karaoke bar, eh? And all of you! Wow, you can all sing so well." Dani focused on their conversation, trying to rid herself of the riot of emotions she was feeling. *What did he mean by "Are you sure?"* Dani shook her head and concentrated on what Rosa was saying.

"Kuch is great. His Elvis was hysterical! He's a born performer."

Dani smiled and looked out of the window. "He is. And Nicole. Wow, what a voice. And you too. Who would have thought it?"

Rosa grinned, turning onto the dual carriageway. "What did you think of Jerome? I bet that was a surprise."

Dani shifted in her seat. "Yes, that was unexpected. They sang really well together." Dani could hear the nervousness in her voice and hoped Rosa didn't pick up on it.

"He likes you."

Dani furrowed her brow for a second, wondering if she'd heard correctly. "Who?" She turned to look at Rosa's smiling profile.

"Jerome. He's got a soft spot for you," Rosa grinned.

"I don't think so. He's just..." she couldn't find the right word or at least, she couldn't admit the right word... *being nice?* No that wasn't what she was thinking... *intense, sexy, so incredibly yummy...* Dani felt herself heat up as more and more improper superlatives popped into her head.

Rosa, thankfully, interrupted her internal ramblings. "I don't mean it in an inappropriate way. But he definitely likes you."

Dani sat still for a moment, not exactly sure what to say.

Rosa carried on, unaware of Dani's increasing discomfort. "Apart from Silvanna, Vanessa, Richard, Kuch and you, the rest of us are related to him in some way or another. He treats you differently, like you're part of the family. And as for Seni!" Rosa laughed. "He's got the serious hots for you!"

Dani chuckled. "He's just being flirty. He's harmless." Dani looked out of the window again as Rosa babbled on about the evening. She was going to have to keep a distance from Arsenio. He'd unnerved her tonight and she didn't want to send him the wrong signals. She still wasn't sure what to make of Jerome but Rosa's comments had warmed her.

He liked her.

40

NEW YEAR'S EVE

Dani slicked back her hair from her face and put it in a tight low bun at the nape of her neck. She slipped in a couple of grips to secure some loose strands of hair. Carefully, she put on her black top and pulled on her black sweat pants, then she padded over to the bathroom to apply her makeup. She scrutinised the picture of Marilyn Monroe she had printed out and propped it up against the mirror. Then, pulling out her eyeliner, she carefully slicked a line on the top lid of her right eye, and repeated the action to her left. Carefully, she added a beauty spot above the left side of her mouth, outlined her lips in scarlet red and filled them in. Dani straightened up and checked her look according to the photo. *Not bad*, she thought, though she looked too made up for yoga pants. Dani applied a few coats of black mascara, then quickly slipped on her biker boots, collected her garment bag that housed her dress, and her small sports bag that had her blonde wig, stockings and shoes in it. She ran down the stairs. It was four o'clock, her shift started in an hour.

Yesterday had flown by and Dani marvelled at how fast her time at La Casa d'Italia was passing. Thankfully, she wasn't working through the afternoon today, giving her a chance to prepare her fancy dress costume. Chloe had worked her magical sewing skills and made the dress fit perfectly, adding an extra lining so that the dress wasn't see-through.

Chloe gasped when she saw her as Dani walked into the sitting room. "Wow! You look great like that. Your hair looks so good swept back."

Dani wrinkled her nose, "I just slicked it out of the way so I can put on the wig later. I'm getting changed at the restaurant. I didn't fancy travelling down in a flimsy halter dress. I'll freeze."

"Aw, I wanted to see you all Marilyn Monroed up," whined Chloe.

"Don't worry, I'm sure they'll be loads of pictures! Where's Adam? He said he'd take me down. I'm not driving, so I can have a drink."

"I think he's in the kitchen."

"Okay, I'll get him and we'd better get off. It's going to be hectic tonight. I won't be in until very late, or very early, depending how you see it. We're all going to the club after work," Dani grinned.

"You love it. You love the rush," teased Chloe. "How are you feeling?" she added, knowing tonight was hard for Dani. Over the last few years, Dani had spent New Year's Eve with Jez in the bar. She knew Dani would be feeling out of sorts.

"Okay. It'll be mad, so I won't have time to think much. Besides, everyone's in the same boat down there. Most of us are single. I'm glad I don't need to be in until five tomorrow!" Dani shrugged. She was pleased to be working and the whole team was like a big family to her now. Only Matteo, Peter and Jerome were married – the rest were mostly divorced or single. "Okay, I'm off, see you next year!"

"Yeah. See you next year!"

By the time Adam pulled up outside La Casa d'Italia, it was dark. Dani quickly hugged him and got out of the car. She retrieved her costume from the back seat, then waved him off, blowing him a kiss. She felt the usual thrill as she noticed Jerome's Maserati parked up. *He was here early*, she thought. She pushed open the back door and stepped into the restaurant. The familiar music of Verdi floated out of the kitchen and Dani smiled. Matteo would be in his element. The smells were incredible. She quickly ran up to the kitchen door and peeked inside.

"Dani! You look beautiful," Matteo cried as he saw her. He kissed the tips of his gathered fingers loudly. "*Bellisima.*"

Dani blushed. "Thanks, Capo. You want an espresso?"

"*Si.*"

Dani nodded and retreated to the bar. She put down her costume and rounded the bar and set to work on Matteo's and her espressos.

"Can I get one of those?" His smoothly familiar voice sent shivers up Dani's spine. She took a deep breath, then turned to look at the breathtaking face of Jerome. He'd slicked back his hair and was dressed in a nineteen-fifties-styled, pinstriped, three piece mafia suit. His badge pinned on his lapel had *Al Capone* written on it. Damn, he was just so yummy. Dani grinned at him as his eyes widened at her appearance. He inhaled deeply, causing his nostrils to flare.

"Sure, Jerome. You look... er... great."

"So do you. Though I thought you were dressing up as Marilyn Monroe." He slipped onto a bar stool as Dani prepared his coffee.

"I am. My costume's in the bag." Dani motioned with her chin to the garment bag.

"Oh, I see."

Dani placed the coffee on the bar, trying hard not to look at him. Over the last few weeks, she'd started feeling less flustered around him, slowly getting more comfortable in his presence. However, the last few days had proved to be more difficult. She wasn't sure if it was just the time of year or the fact that they'd been working so closely together, but something had definitely changed. They had an unsaid connection that they both seemed to be skirting around, a strong chemistry that he seemed only to share with her. It didn't help that he was always present. Dani knew one of the reasons she loved this job so much was because he was there.

"You look..." He paused a minute, trying to find the right word. Then, realising whatever he said would either be inappropriate or inadequate, he settled with, "It suits you. Your hair back like that. You can see your eyes," he mumbled, frowning briefly.

"Thanks."

He caught her gaze and his eyes bore into hers for a moment, making Dani's heart surge. She looked away and fussed with Matteo's coffee. *Why did he do that?* He always stared at her so intensely. She shook her head and picked up the cup and saucer and headed to the kitchen. "Here, Capo."

"Oh *grazie,* Dani." He winked at her as she shuffled out of the kitchen.

Jerome stayed sat at the bar, deep in thought. He held his chin, propping up his head with his elbow on the bar, looking broody and incredibly sexy. Dani wished she didn't feel what she felt for him. She was trying hard not to imagine what his biceps looked like without the jacket and shirt straining around them when he turned to look at her. She instantly flushed. *Fuck. Why did he always catch her out?* She smiled tightly and came towards him, avoiding eye contact.

"I'd better get changed." Dani lifted her costume from the bar. Jerome drained his coffee and set the empty cup on the bar, then smiled softly at her. "See you in a bit," she added, then scurried off downstairs to the staff room.

Dani smoothed down the skirt of her white dress and checked her reflection in the mirror. Thankfully, no one could see the scarlet red panties she was wearing. She chuckled to herself. She really did look strange. A loud wolf whistle made her start.

"Oh. My. God. Dani you look... well, you look like Marilyn!" Rosa stood behind her and looked at her reflection in the mirror, her Cleopatra eyes sparkling. She was already dressed in her white toga-styled dress and was wearing her jet-black wig. "The platinum blonde on you is weird. You look fantastic, though! Did you wear them?"

Dani grinned, "Yes, I did. Chloe had to line the skirt so you can't see them through the material!" Rosa laughed a loud, throaty laugh. "You look great, Rosa. Are you wearing yours?" Dani turned to appraise her.

"Of course, it's tradition!" Rosa lifted her skirt up just enough to give Dani a flash of her bright red panties.

Dani noted she was wearing flat Grecian sandals. "At least your footwear won't kill you tonight." Dani looked at her white heels and rolled her eyes.

"Kuch is gonna freak when he sees you! Your boobs look amazing in that dress," Rosa giggled.

"Crap, they're not too much, are they?"

"Are you kidding? You look like a fifties sex bomb, which you're supposed be." Rosa squeezed her shoulders.

"Is he here?"

"Yeah. He looks so cool. He keeps gyrating his hips and saying 'uh-huh'. He's so funny."

"Here let me help you with the headdress. I've some grips in my locker."

Before long, the whole team of La Casa was sitting in the function room, being briefed on their positions and the customers they would be serving. It was a set menu tonight, with six choices for each course. Capo had prepared the staff a traditional Italian New Year's Eve dish of sausage, polenta and lentils and they all sat down together to eat before the madness of New Year's Eve began.

The atmosphere was that of excitement. It took a good twenty minutes for everyone to calm down. There were endless pictures being taken. Dani couldn't believe how good everyone looked – they'd gone all out. Eventually, the weird mix of characters sat down to eat. Dani looked around the large table and giggled. They really did all look funny. How often would you see Charlie Chaplin, Clint Eastwood, Pele, James Dean, Julius Caesar, Elvis, Marilyn Monroe, Cleopatra, Grace Kelly, Einstein, John Lennon, Ghandi, Mussolini, Messi and Michael Jackson sitting and eating altogether? Nicole snapped away with her camera and most of the staff also took pictures on their phones. Dani fleetingly thought that Gia would have a few hundred photos to choose from to put up on the restaurant's website and Facebook page.

Peter, who was dressed as Frank Sinatra, also positioned his camera and took pictures as they ate, grinning to himself. He loved New Year's Eve at the restaurant – customers and staff were always on a high. He checked the time. It was quarter to six. In three hours, the restaurant would be packed out.

"Okay. Listen up." He called his staff to attention. They all stopped what they were doing and turned to him. "It's going to be pretty crazy in here tonight. There'll be the regulars in, but there'll also be new customers, so everyone needs to be alert. It will be a fun night but we still need to be professional. I'll be on hand along with Jerome if there are any problems. Finish up and I'll see you all downstairs in fifteen minutes."

Jerome was holed up in his office sitting at his desk. He'd stayed out of everyone's way purposely, to avoid Dani. He looked at his watch. It was seven fifteen. In an hour, the first of the customers would arrive and he'd be able to thankfully lose himself in his work, playing his role and wearing his mask for the sake of appearances. He'd gotten very good at that over the years. He sighed and rubbed his eyes, then with a heavy heart dialled his home number.

"Liz." His voice was soft even though he was anxious.

"Yes, Jerome." Her reply was clipped and Jerome clenched his jaw.

"I was hoping you'd changed your mind."

"Well I haven't. I'm not coming down there. What, to sit on my own while you flit around each table playing the perfect host? It's boring. I'd rather stay in."

"At least come down for the last hour. The kids will be asleep. We can see the New Year in together," he coaxed. He wanted his children to be with him and Gia was desperate to see them too, but he knew Liz would never agree. It would mean she'd have to look after them.

"I'll see," she answered sharply and Jerome inhaled deeply.

"Okay. Bye, then."

"Bye."

He replaced the receiver and sat back closing his eyes. Things were going from bad to worse and he was finding it difficult to stay home at all these days. He'd tried, really tried, but Liz's recent behaviour since coming back from her mother's was trying his already-limited patience. He'd started going home only when he knew his children were there – otherwise, he avoided it. He couldn't face a confrontation, not now anyway, but he knew it was coming.

Jerome heard the familiar footsteps of Gia coming down the corridor and he braced himself for a scolding. She wasn't going to be happy that his family weren't here tonight.

Gia pushed open the door and breezed in. She was dressed in a very conservative blue suit, with a light blue blouse tied with a big bow, and pearls around her neck. Very un-Gia. Her badge had "Margaret Thatcher" on it. Jerome smiled at her.

"Not sure I like that look on you, Mama." He grinned and she rolled her eyes.

"I know. I loved this woman, but her dress sense was too dowdy for me. What time are Liz and the children coming down? I thought they'd be here with us by now." She checked her watch.

"They're not coming down," Jerome answered quietly as he eyed his mother.

"What? Why?" She had edged closer to the desk, clearly agitated.

"Liz might come down later," added Jerome avoiding the question.

Gia huffed and waited for him to elaborate, staring at him, her displeasure apparent.

"Just leave it, Mama. I don't want to get into it. Not now." He rubbed his face.

"Into what exactly? Tonight is about family. Arsenio is coming down and so is Cosimo – he's even bringing James. We should all be altogether." She put her hand on her hip and glared. Jerome sat silently. The last thing he wanted to do was get into a conversation about his crumbling marriage and his unfaithful wife.

"Look, it's difficult with the children, Mama –" Jerome tried to explain but Gia interrupted as he knew she would.

"Difficult? Difficult! Those children are angels. They hardly spend time with us because of *her!*" She mumbled a prayer in Italian under her breath and Jerome clenched his eyes shut momentarily. "I brought up three boys on my own *and* ran a business, and she finds it hard to bring two perfect children to the family restaurant to spend time with their Nonna and uncles! She has a cleaner, a nanny, she wants for nothing. You indulge her in every way. I don't know what's going on, Jerome, but you'd better sort it out. I've a good mind to call her myself." Jerome's eyes darted up to hers and she could tell by his expression that it would only make things worse.

"A fine family we are!" Her voice grew louder. "I have one son who is a renowned playboy and by the looks of it, is never going to settle down."

"Mama please," Jerome said, knowing how this speech was going to go.

Gia ignored him and flung her arms in the air. "Another son who's gay, so I've no chance of any grandchildren from him. And another son whose wife makes our lives a living hell, holding *my* grandchildren to ransom in some sick mind game to punish us all!"

"Mama. Not now." Jerome stood up as his voice rose and he glared at her.

"All I ever wanted was one good daughter-in-law and I get the ice maiden and the wicked witch of the west all rolled into one!" Gia shouted angrily.

Dani had just entered the corridor to collect the party poppers and streamers from the storeroom and stopped, hearing the heated exchange. *Crap, Gia was really angry!* Dani cringed at the descriptive rundown of her family, noting her specific venomous tone when she spoke about Liz.

"Mama, enough!" Jerome shouted back. "I really don't need your lecture now, not tonight!" his voice sounded exasperated and annoyed, he was trying hard to restrain his temper.

"It's never a good time," she continued and then added something in Italian, which Dani couldn't make out apart from "*puttana*", which made Jerome bang his fist on the table.

"Enough, Mama!" he bellowed.

His reaction made Gia stop her tirade in Italian. There was an eerie silence, then Dani heard Jerome apologise for his forcefulness. The room seemed to go quiet and Dani quickly collected the items she'd come up for. She exited the storeroom and bumped straight into a flustered Gia.

"*Scusa,*" she said softly as she looked over Dani. It took her a few seconds to realise who it was. "Oh Dani, it's you. I can't get used to you in that blonde wig. You look fabulous." Her agitation was fading.

"Thank you, Gia. So do you." Dani smiled at her sympathetically.

"*Grazie.* You look so different," she remarked as she reached up and fingered Dani's wig.

"Well they *are* supposed to have more fun." Dani grinned, trying to lighten her mood.

"Yes, they are." Gia chuckled at the thought. "You can tell me at the end of the night if it's true."

Dani laughed, pleased Gia's previous annoyance seemed to have lifted. "I will."

By eight o'clock, the restaurant was ready and all the staff were at their posts. Dani was working in the raised part of the restaurant with

Pino and Richard, who were dressed as Charlie Chaplin and Pele. The curtain had been pulled back for the evening, allowing the guests in the raised area to be part of the whole restaurant. The guests in their section were regulars and all of them were the elite, spending huge amounts of money throughout the year. Dani had got to know them all over the past weeks.

Jerome entered the restaurant looking tense as he walked over to the bar. His mood lightened as he saw Kuch dressed as Elvis and Nicole as Grace Kelly. Kuch instantly poured him a shot of whisky and placed it in front of him. Peter came over to join him, patting his back as he sat down and Kuch poured Peter the same. They clinked glasses and knocked back their drinks. Jerome took a deep breath and turned to survey the restaurant. He smirked, shaking his head taking in his staff dressed up in costumes of Clint Eastwood, Mussolini, Ghandi, Cleopatra, along with the rest of his bizarrely dressed staff working in the restaurant. Peter got up and moved to the front desk where Gia was checking something. Jerome continued to scan the restaurant, his eyes searching for Dani.

He turned towards the private area and his gaze found her placing the party poppers in the centre of the table. He narrowed his eyes at her. She looked so different but she was still incredible and he found himself staring. Dani looked up and her eyes locked onto his. He gave her a puzzled smile, which she returned, as his forehead furrowed. Unable to stop himself, he strode up to where she was working. Dani straightened up upon seeing him approach.

"I nearly didn't recognise you." He looked down at her and Dani inhaled, sharply knocked off balance by the depth of his gaze. She blinked up at him and he shook his head in disbelief. "You look..." *amazing, sexy as hell, gorgeous...* . So many adjectives he wanted to use. Jerome sucked on his top teeth. In the end he settled for: "You look really good."

"Thanks," breathed Dani.

"Crap, David's early," Pino interrupted as he came over to where Jerome and Dani were standing. Jerome dragged his eyes away from Dani and looked over to the front door.

David was kissing his hello to Gia, then entered the bar area with his wife and another couple. They perched themselves at the bar and ordered their drinks.

"I'd better go down," sighed Jerome and he turned to glance back at Dani, raising his eyebrows apologetically, and then he leisurely moved towards them.

"He's such a prick," Pino muttered. "I hate serving him."

"I'll serve him if you like," suggested Dani. She was still slightly disturbed by his behaviour at Sky, but she could handle him.

"Would you?" Pino looked relieved.

"Sure," Dani replied.

The evening progressed smoothly and the clientele were in good spirits, which rubbed off onto all the staff; the fancy dress costumes proved to be a huge hit with the customers and a great talking point. Gia was in her element talking to all the customers, charming the women and men alike. She was a born hostess and had an unbelievable knack for making everyone feel welcome and special. Dani watched Gia work her magic as she brought over the main course to David's table. He made some smutty remark about Dani and Gia mock-scolded him, then she winked at Dani and moved on to the next table where Pino was serving.

Peter watched on from the edge of the bar. David's table of eight had already had a lot to drink and were becoming rowdy. Luckily, no one seemed to mind. It was New Year's Eve and everyone was determined to enjoy themselves.

As Dani poured their wine, Peter noticed David snake his arm around her waist. Dani carried on without flinching. He made some remark to his table which made them all laugh. Dani smiled politely and moved swiftly around the table topping up their glasses. Pino came over to her where she was gathering up an ice bucket and stand, to check she was alright. Peter looked at his watch anxiously. It was ten o'clock. Everyone was on their main course, so the kitchen would be on a breather until the desserts were ready to be served. His eyes restlessly flitted around the restaurant, ensuring all the customers were being attended to and that his staff were managing.

The front door opened and in waltzed Arsenio, Cosimo and to Gia's delight, James. Gia excused herself from a table, her face lighting up as she spotted them and went straight over to greet them. Jerome, who was at the bottom part of the restaurant, beamed when he saw his brothers. They all moved to the bar and Kuch lined up their shots. Dani stepped down to the edge of the bar to collect her order.

"Is David behaving himself?" Peter asked discreetly.

"He's just showing off," Dani shrugged. It wasn't the first time a customer had gotten overfamiliar with her. She could handle it. "He was just telling the table that I had the steadiest hand."

"Nothing else?"

"He made some quip remark, asking me if I was as easy as Marilyn Monroe. It's just talk. You know what he's like."

Peter looked over at David's table and narrowed his eyes. "What are they drinking now?"

"They're starting on the Champagne."

Peter nodded and looked over to where Jerome was standing. Arsenio caught sight of Dani and whistled softly. Jerome stiffened.

"Dani, you look fantastic!" His mischievous eyes twinkled in obvious appreciation. "What you do to that dress..." he raised his eyebrows lewdly.

"Thanks." Dani blushed and shook her head. Collecting her Champagne, she then quickly headed back to her tables.

"Jeez, she's so fucking sexy," Arsenio hissed under his breath and Jerome stared at him.

"Pack it in, Seni."

"I'm just saying..."

"Well don't." Jerome's tone was clipped.

"She. Is. Del-i-c-i-ous. It's like she's made of butter."

"Seni!" Jerome barked.

"What's with you? Lighten up."

Cosimo rested his hand on Arsenio's arm and shook his head in a silent plea for him to stop. Arsenio huffed and turned his attention to Nicole. He was going to have to have a quiet word with Arsenio about Dani, thought Cosimo. His obvious preoccupation with Dani had clouded his usual razor-sharp perception. James furrowed his brow and shot a questioning look at Cosimo as he tried to work out why there was suddenly tension between the brothers. Cosimo darted his eyes in the direction of Dani, then back at Jerome and James made a silent "oh" as everything fell into place.

Jerome looked away and scanned the restaurant trying to avoid looking up to where Dani was.

"Where's Liz?" asked Cosimo.

"She's at home. She might pop down later." His voice was monotone, devoid of emotion.

Cosimo's eyes flitted to Arsenio's and they both cringed. They knew Gia would have been less than pleased that the family weren't together. Their attention was drawn to the private section where Dani had just opened a bottle of Champagne. David's table had cheered as she opened it without any noise and without spilling a drop.

"They seem to be in a good mood," commented Cosimo.

Jerome frowned. "A bit too good. We've another two hours before midnight and if they carry on like this, we'll be carrying them out." Jerome turned to face the rear of the restaurant. He sent a quick look over to Peter and Peter nodded, understanding he needed to monitor the situation. Jerome's eyes then returned to the rear, his eyes darkening as he watched David openly appraising Dani's cleavage as she bent over to pour the Champagne into all the glasses around the table.

Luckily the neighbouring tables were oblivious to the antics of David's table, and so, it seemed, was the main restaurant. Dani cleared the main course plates and headed into the kitchen.

"Dani. How's it going?" asked Carmen as she took the plates from Dani.

"Fine. It should be easier now they're on the dessert." She shrugged and paced back into the restaurant. Pino shot her an apologetic look and Dani winked at him, in a "don't sweat it" gesture.

Peter quickly looked around the restaurant and took a gratifying deep breath. Everyone seemed to be enjoying themselves and his staff had excelled under the stressful circumstances.

Dani swiftly served the desserts, avoiding any unnecessary loitering around the table. As she placed the last tiramisu down, one of the men at David's table goaded David into a bet. He wasn't a client of the restaurant and from what Dani gleaned from the sporadic conversation she'd heard, he was David's brother-in-law.

"I bet Marilyn here can't open another bottle of Champagne without making it pop or spilling it!" His words were a little slurred as he spoke. *Crap!* thought Dani.

"What do you bet?" David's eyes lit up to the challenge.

"I'll pay for this evening if she does," the brother-in-law replied, rather pleased with his proposal.

"And if she doesn't?" asked David.

"You pay."

David looked up at Dani and winked at her. "Deal. Get us another bottle. *Marilyn.*"

Dani clenched her teeth and forced a smile. Pino shook his head, feeling mortified that he'd swapped tables with her. She went down to the bar and placed her order. Peter came over to her immediately.

"What's he ordered now?"

Dani gave him a rundown of the bet and Peter sighed deeply as Kuch placed the bottle on the bar and sent Peter a worried look. Dani took the bottle and headed back to the table. Peter kept his eyes on her as Dani expertly peeled off the foil and eased the cage away from the neck of the bottle.

"Easy does it, Dani. Don't let me down," coaxed David as Dani slowly turned the bottle keeping her hand firmly over the cork. "That's it, my beauty. Luke's gonna have to cough up big tonight." He sniggered, rubbing his hands together in glee. Dani continued to twist the bottle. Her heart pounded as she adjusted her grip. She'd opened countless bottles of Champagne in her time and she'd never spilled a drop, but the added pressure of the bet had made her nervous.

Peter watched on and Jerome straightened up, shifting on his feet. No one in the restaurant was aware of what was happening at Dani's table. They were all blissfully oblivious and enjoying themselves, to the relief of the few whose attention was fixed on Dani. Kuch shuffled up to the end of the bar and stood directly behind Peter, his eyes fixed on David's table.

Dani twisted the bottle a little more, then a few things happened at once. From nowhere, it seemed, Luke had come around behind her, and as she twisted the bottle, Luke reached down and grabbed the skirt of her dress and threw it in the air. It billowed out, revealing Dani's scarlet red Brazilian lace panties and stocking-clad legs. Luke whooped like a baboon at the sight of them, alerting the whole restaurant to Dani's exposed legs and behind. Dani flinched as she uncorked the Champagne without a sound or spilling a drop. David cheered and Luke groaned. Jerome growled a curse and surged forward, starting towards where Dani was, but Cosimo and Arsenio grabbed him back, restraining him.

"Easy, Jerome. Let Peter handle him. We don't want a lawsuit." Cosimo spoke through gritted teeth, feeling Jerome's biceps tense and his jaw strain as he tried to shake off his brothers.

Peter was up in an instant, flanked by Kuch and Pino. Dani placed the bottle into the ice bucket, then turned away from the table. Her face was flaming and her whole body shaking and she politely excused herself. She walked quickly to the rear of the restaurant and out of the back door towards the fire exit. She could hear David and Luke whining their apologies to Peter, saying it was only a joke and that they had meant no harm. Peter's tone was stern as he spoke, but Dani couldn't hear what he was saying. She didn't care, she just needed to get out of there.

Dani pushed open the emergency door leading out to the back of the restaurant, her body shaking violently as the door shut behind her. She pulled off her wig and threw it on the small table that they kept out there for staff to have a smoke. Tears pooled in her eyes and she tried to contain them, but she just couldn't. Her face was burning and her ears buzzed. *She couldn't go back in there again!* She felt so humiliated. It was icy cold outside but she didn't seem to notice. Eyeing the ashtray on the table, she thought she'd give anything for a cigarette right now, then buried her face in her hands and let the tears flow freely down her hot cheeks.

The door opened again, making Dani jump.

"Christ, Dani, there you are." Jerome stepped out through the emergency exit. He jammed it with the table and strode towards her. "He's a fucking asshole! Jeez, wait here. I'll go get some tissues." He speedily turned around and went back into the corridor. Dani wiped her eyes with the back of her hand and tried to compose herself. She hated anyone seeing her cry, seeing her vulnerable. Jerome returned with a wad of serviettes and pulled out a couple, handing them to her. Then he placed the rest next to her discarded wig on the table, released the table from the door and twisted the lock with his key, so they'd be able to open it from the outside. The door re-closed and he turned to look at Dani.

"He's lucky we had a packed-out restaurant, otherwise I'd have decked him. How are you?" He looked concerned as he spoke, his previous anger subsiding. Dani shrugged, wiping under her eyes and nose, avoiding eye contact. "You must be freezing." He shrugged out of his jacket and stepped closer. Reaching around her, he gently placed his jacket over her shoulders.

"Thanks," she mumbled. It felt glorious and warm and it smelled of him, musky. Dani tightened it around her, still avoiding his eyes. She focused on his shirt and tried to control her shuddery breath. He was so close to her she could feel his body heat.

He gently lifted her chin up. "Hey, come on, don't cry." His face had softened and his breath formed clouds from the cold when he spoke. Dani smiled tightly, but tears threatened again as she looked at him. Jerome frowned and instinctively pulled her to his chest and Dani let out a small sob, burying her face into his rock-hard body.

"Shh. Let it all out. I'm so sorry. You shouldn't have to put up with pricks like that. I swear I'll kill that fucker," he muttered almost to himself. He stroked her head until her sobs began to subside.

He felt glorious against her cheek, his heart pumping a steady rhythm, calming her. Dani reluctantly pulled back, feeling even more embarrassed that she'd broken down again in front of him. She was feeling raw tonight. New Year's Eve was always going to be hard, but she really didn't need the added humiliation. Her emotions raged through her in a chaotic torrent.

Jerome smiled softly at her as he lifted her face up again, his fingers holding her chin. "Better?" He asked quietly, his blue eyes glittered, locking on hers. Dani wiped her eyes again and nodded. Unable to speak, for fear of giving anything away, she looked away. *Fuck, he was so damned handsome*, she thought. And the way he was looking at her made her feel unbelievably vulnerable.

He bent down and pressed a kiss to her forehead. Dani tensed. Instinctively, her eyes jerked up to his, her breath catching at the depth of his gaze. Slowly, he licked his lips and Dani's eyes were involuntarily drawn to them, mesmerized. Before she could start to think that all she wanted was those sculptured lips on hers, Jerome sealed her cold lips with his. His hand slid around to cup the back of her head and his other arm circled her waist. His lips felt so soft and warm and he groaned into her ready mouth as she pressed herself up against him. Somewhere in the back of her mind, she registered his jacket falling off her shoulders as she reached up and wrapped her arms around his neck. Jerome kissed her harder and deeper, edging her up against the wall, his hands travelling down the length of her, hitching her closer to him. He kissed her like his life depended on it, as if he had to, as if he couldn't stop himself and Dani revelled in it. She'd wanted nothing else since she'd set eyes on him over eight weeks ago. Dani gripped on to him, desire exploding in her, when suddenly he pulled away, leaving Dani panting and bereft.

"Fuck!" he gasped, pacing backward. He took a deep breath and slowly exhaled, visibly trying to calm down, then stooped to pick up his jacket. For a moment, Dani flinched, thinking it was her he was cursing at, until she heard Peter's voice calling her name. He'd come to find her. Jerome had obviously heard his voice. Dani wrapped her arms around herself feeling suddenly very exposed. *What was that all about? Crap!* Dani looked at the floor nervously, purposely avoiding Jerome's gaze.

"Out here, Peter!" he called, his eyes fixed on Dani as she struggled to calm her breathing. He stepped over to the table and picked up a serviette and roughly wiped the red lipstick off his mouth. Within a few seconds, Peter was opening the door and stepping through the doorway. He looked over at Jerome, then quickly over to Dani.

"You okay?"

Dani looked up at Peter, clenching her teeth, then nodded, closing her eyes momentarily. She was anything but okay. He turned back to Jerome, who was stepping forward towards Dani with his jacket open for her to put on again.

"They left. I think their wives gave them a mouthful. They sloped out thoroughly embarrassed," he huffed. "I told him he'd need to come back and apologize. Fucking asshole. Here." Peter held out four fifty-pound notes. "These are for you. It's your tip."

Jerome snorted as he gently pulled Dani by the elbow away from the wall and draped his jacket around her. She shuffled forward allowing him to secure the jacket, his arm resting a moment on her shoulders.

"I don't want it," she whispered.

"Just take it, Dani. Here." Peter stepped forward and took her hand, squashing the notes into her palm.

"Has it calmed down in there? Is everyone back to normal?" Jerome asked in a clipped tone. He reached into his jacket pocket and Dani stiffened.

What was he doing? she thought, then she saw his hand pull out his cigarettes and a lighter. He pulled one out and lit it as he looked at Peter.

"Yes, the staff did a great job of distracting everyone. Most people are on dessert now. Gia's doing her thing – you know, mingling," Peter smirked.

"Good. Come on, let's get you inside." Jerome guided Dani towards the door but she froze.

"I'd rather not go back in there... I..." she tightened the jacket around herself as she spoke. She really couldn't face anyone. She was monumentally embarrassed and after what had just happened, her wits were shredded. The last thing she wanted was to face a restaurant full of people.

"Of course. We'll get a taxi to get you home." Peter reached into his jacket pocket and pulled out his phone. He quickly arranged their taxi service to come for Dani.

Jerome stood close enough to her that she could feel the heat radiating off his body. She forced herself not to look at him and focused on Peter while he talked to the taxi service, but she could feel Jerome's eyes on her as he took another drag from his cigarette.

The distinct footsteps of Gia approaching alerted them to the door. "Oh Daniella! How are you? That David is such an *idiota*! And his brother-in-law's an ass."

"I'm fine, Gia, really. Just embarrassed," muttered Dani.

"It's okay, I'll look after her. You two go back inside." Gia's eyes darted to both Peter and Jerome.

"I've ordered her a taxi. He'll be here any minute, Gia."

"Of course, she should go home."

Peter moved towards the door and Dani began to remove Jerome's jacket.

"Keep it. You'll freeze." His voice was raspy and he hovered a moment, then stubbed out his cigarette in the ashtray.

"Ask Rosa to bring Daniella's things. She doesn't need to go back through there," added Gia, effectively dismissing them.

"Sure, Mama." And with a brief nod he left. Gia narrowed her eyes after him, noticing black smudged make up on his shirt, then turned her attention back to Dani.

"Everyone was horrified by his behaviour and had nothing but praise for you." She wrapped an arm around her shoulder and squeezed. "How you didn't slap him, I don't know," she snorted. "You're a real lady, Daniella."

Dani sniffed. *Maybe if Gia had been here ten minutes ago, she might not have thought she was such a lady!* Dani clenched her eyes shut as Gia guided her back into the corridor. Gia leant over and picked up Dani's wig, handing it to her.

"So, tell me. Do blondes have more fun?" Gia joked, trying to make Dani come around with humour.

Dani's eyes shot up to Gia's and she smiled. "I'd prefer to be a brunette any day, Gia."

Gia laughed softly. "Me too, Daniella."

Dani slid into the back of the taxi and rested her head on the headrest, closing her eyes. She felt exhausted. At least she wouldn't be in for the lunchtime shift tomorrow. She'd managed to secure one of the half days off, seeing as she hadn't taken any off over the Christmas week.

Thankfully, the taxi was warm; she'd been shivering until it had arrived but that was probably more to do with her emotions rather than the icy temperature. She glanced at the clock. It was eleven twenty. She'd be home in thirty minutes, just in time to see the New Year in, all alone. Dani sniffed, remembering the last five New Year's Eves she'd had. Every one of them had been at the bar and every one of them she had seen in with her kissing Jez at the stroke of midnight. She wondered who he'd be kissing this year. Dani clenched her eyes shut, holding back her tears. It wasn't that she wanted to be the one who he would be kissing tonight, but more the idea of having that special someone. Dani missed having a partner. Though Jez and her relationship hadn't by any means been perfect, his cheating being the biggest red flag, she longed for someone to share her life with. Share moments like tonight's debacle, have someone to support her as much as she supported them. Someone to love, cherish and someone who would be that person for her.

Her mind then shifted to Jerome. Just the thought of him made her heart thump harder. What was she thinking, really? She really didn't know what to make of it all. Sitting up straight, she replayed what had happened. Was he just caught up in the moment, seeing her vulnerable? Or was it more? She knew how she felt about him and there was obviously chemistry between them, but she just thought it was her reading too much into everything. *He was married, for goodness sake!* She shook her head. Whatever it was, she knew she liked it. She liked it a lot and that made it a hundred times worse.

Dani clasped her forehead in an attempt to soothe her mind of all these disturbing thoughts. Well tomorrow was going to be awkward. She just hoped they were busy and she wouldn't be spending so much time in his vicinity. She pulled his jacket around her and slipped her arms into the armholes and nuzzled the collar. *It smelled amazing, it smelled of him.*

Her attention was drawn to her phone that was vibrating in her bag. She quickly pulled it out and stared down at the name that flashed. It was Jerome. *Oh crap! She really couldn't deal with this, not right now anyway.* He was probably worried she'd make things difficult. She silenced it and dropped it in her bag again, scared of what he might say; putting off the inevitable.

In an ideal world, he'd be single. In an ideal world, he would want her as much as she now realised she wanted him, more than anything. He was perfect, perfect in every way. Except for that small detail... he was married. So, maybe not that perfect after all – and her world was actually far from ideal.

Dani realised she had little choice but to quash any growing feelings she had, for her sake, as much as Jerome's. She'd just behave as if nothing had happened, so he'd realise she wasn't going to stir anything up. It wouldn't be easy, but there was far too much at stake. It was more than obvious his marriage was shaky – the argument she'd witnessed with Gia confirmed that. *He was probably feeling vulnerable, as vulnerable as she was. It was this time of the year. New Year's Eve always made people do stupid things, made them reflect on their life, their mistakes. Wasn't that why resolutions were made? Correct the past and move into a new year with new goals.*

The taxi pulled up outside the house pulling Dani away from her introspective thoughts and she clambered out and glanced at her watch. It was ten to midnight. Adam and Chloe would be back soon. She quickly let herself in and flicked on the lights. She headed to the lounge and straight to the bar, poured herself a large brandy tossing it back, glad for the heat it radiated. She felt alone and her emotions were scattered into a million directions. Tired and raw, she headed to her room. She needed to sleep and deal with whatever she had to face tomorrow.

Dani turned on her light in her room, then went over to her bed and flicked on her Snow White bedside lamp, then padded to her bathroom to remove her smudged make-up. *Holy hell, she looked like a car wreck!* Her lipstick was smudged. *Mmm, that'd be the kissing*, she thought wistfully, and her heart stuttered again as she ran her fingers over her lips, remembering how he felt. Her eyes were bloodshot and her eyeliner was bleeding into her top lid and under her eyes. *Panda-eyes would have been a compliment!* She quickly cleansed her face and patted it dry, then stripped off out of her dress, shoes and underwear and slipped on her sleep shorts and vest. As she slid into her cool covers, her phone vibrated. She reached over to it and checked to see who it was. Outside, she could hear people in the nearby houses cheering as the New Year came in.

She had two messages. She opened the first. It was from Jez.

> Happy New Year Dani.
> I miss you. Pls call me x

Why wouldn't he leave her alone? She quickly checked the second. It was from Chloe.

> Happy New Year sis.
> This year is definitely your year!
> Love you xxx

Dani smiled weakly down at her phone. Chloe always knew what to say. Thank God she had Chloe and Adam. Dani switched off her phone and turned out the light, curling into the covers. *What an end to a crappy year*, she thought to herself, snuggling into her pillow. *Talk about out of the frying pan and into the fire!* Dani let out a deep sigh, trying to control her emotions, hoping that her sister was right. Last year hadn't been one of her best and in all honesty, for the last few years she'd been kidding herself that her life was what she wanted. *New year, new beginnings. It was time to forget about the past and look to what the future would bring her.*

Dani touched her lips and shook her head, thinking back to Jerome. She was going to have to be very careful where he was concerned. *She couldn't be messing around with her boss – been there done that and look where it had gotten her: broken hearted, jobless and homeless!* And on top of that, he was married.

Dani clenched her eyes tightly and willed herself to sleep, trying to rid herself of the image of Jerome's face as he'd looked down at her, how his magnificent eyes bore straight into her. Shit, she was in trouble, real trouble. But regardless of how she felt about him, whatever happened tomorrow, she was going to clear the air, say it was a mistake, that she was emotional, no hard feelings. They were adults after all. No one knew anything, so no harm done. The last thing she wanted was to ruin what she'd achieved at La Casa. It felt right, being there, like she truly belonged. It had just started to feel like home and she wasn't going to let a kiss, a stupid, emotionally-fuelled, albeit glorious kiss, ruin everything now. Tomorrow was a new day, a new year, *her* year and whatever she and Jerome had had for those few minutes was just poor judgement. Dani plumped up her pillow and settled her weary head into it, feeling a little more determined, but decidedly more resigned, and for the first time in a long while, slightly more hopeful of what her future might hold.

In the distance Dani could hear the party goers and revellers sing "Auld Lang's Syne" from the nearby houses. She closed her tired eyes and willed herself to sleep, trying hard to eradicate the memory of those hexagonal bright blue eyes that flashed unbidden through her muddled mind and she knew it was wishful thinking.

PLAYLIST

Coldplay – The Scientist
Puccini – Tosca/E Lucevan le Stele
Eros Ramazzotti – Un Angelo Disteso Al Sole
Frank Sinatra – Come Fly With Me
Far East Movement – I Can Change Your Life
Dean Martin – Sway
Lou Rawls – You'll Never Find Another Love Like Mine
Michael Buble – Kissing A Fool
Maroon 5 – Maps
Barry White – You're the First, My Last, My Everything
10cc – I'm Not in Love
Far East Movement – Turn Up the Love
Eros Ramazzotti/Anastacia – I Belong to You
Corrs – Runaway

HEAVENLY FARE

La Casa d'Italia... the key to happiness.
Heavenly Fare
The second book in the La Casa d'Italia Trilogy

A new year begins and Dani Knox moves into the second floor of La Casa d'Italia. Her professional and personal lines begin to blur as she gets swept into a life that revolves around the restaurant and the Ferretti family.

As more deceit, betrayal and unexpected danger unravel within the Ferretti household, can Jerome refrain from crossing every one of his boundaries? Will Dani be able to resist the disarming magnetism and seductive charm of Jerome Ferretti, a man she knows is off limits, or is their fate already sealed?

Here's a little taste of what's to come...

Chapter I
Happy New Year?

Jerome was sitting in his kitchen staring into his coffee cup. He'd hardly slept. By the time he'd arrived home, Liz was asleep, or at least she was in her room. He played over what had happened last night in his head. He knew he'd screwed up. Messing around with your staff was a recipe for disaster. He'd lectured everyone on it and here he was crossing the boundaries he'd vehemently enforced.

The truth was, he didn't feel guilty. He didn't even feel as though he'd betrayed Liz. He felt nothing towards her. What he did feel was an overwhelming need to see how Dani was. David's brother-in-law was lucky the restaurant had been packed and that both Cosimo and Arsenio were there to hold him back. Jerome clenched his teeth, remembering Dani's distraught face.

He picked up his phone and tried her number again. It was still switched off. How on earth was he going to hold it together until five this afternoon when her shift started?

"Morning."

Jerome's thoughts were interrupted by Liz walking into the kitchen. "Morning. Happy New Year." His eyes travelled over her face to see what mood she was in, and to his surprise, she seemed to have calmed down from last night.

"Happy New Year. You're up early." She filled the kettle as she spoke.

"Yes. I have a lot to get through today."

"Shall I bring the children down for lunch? That way your mother will see them."

"Er... yes, sure, she'd love that."

"Make up for last night." She smiled sweetly at him and then busied herself with her tea. "They fell asleep early last night. They'd never have lasted at the restaurant."

"Oh. No. Perhaps not. I called you at midnight to wish you Happy New Year, but you didn't answer. I didn't call the house, just in case I woke the kids." Jerome drained his coffee and stood up.

"I went to bed early and had it on silent. Sorry." She shrugged apologetically.

"Well, I better get into work. It's a busy day. What time will you be down?"

"Two o'clock okay?"

"Sure, and thanks. Mama will be so pleased."

"It's the least I could do. I know she would've been disappointed last night."

A slight understatement, thought Jerome as he smiled tightly.

"Yes she was. Okay then, see you at two. I just need to get my jacket."

Liz nodded and walked through to the conservatory, leaving Jerome, who then promptly headed to the hallway and ran up the stairs two by two, up to his room. He walked past Liz's room and pushed the door ajar. The bed was unmade and her clothes were strewn over the floor. He shook his head and sighed at the mess, then walked to his room. In contrast, his bed was made and the room was immaculate. He pulled his jacket from the hanger, shrugging it on, and walked swiftly down the stairs. He popped his head into the playroom where Kara and Alessandro were watching TV, to say goodbye, then headed to the wine fridge in the kitchen. He pulled out a bottle of Dom Perignon from the rack and furrowed his brow. He was sure he had restocked the shelves with four bottles. Now there were only three.

Jerome slipped into his car and started up the engine, then checked the time. Ten thirty. He put his phone on hands free and called Peter. "*Buongiorno*."

"*Buongiorno*, Peter. Just to let you know I'll be in around twelve and Liz will be down around two with the kids, so hopefully you can squeeze a table in for us to have a late lunch."

"Um, sure Jerome, leave it to me."

"Thanks see you. *Ciao*."

Jerome then pulled out the scrap of paper he had in his pocket and entered the postcode on his sat nav that he'd scribbled down last night. He pulled out of his garage and powered onto the road.

Dani shifted her legs as she turned and felt something obstructing her stretch. She lifted herself up to see what it was and was greeted by a pyjama-clad Sophie sat on the side of her bed holding the Twister box. She beamed at her, her curly blond hair dishevelled from sleep and her bright blue eyes sleep-swollen.

"Good morning, angel. What are you doing here?" Dani rubbed her face trying hard to calm her pounding head.

"Can you play Twister with me? Ollie won't play."

Dani looked at the clock. It was seven thirty. "Can I get up and have a shower first?" Sophie beamed and she nodded. "Then maybe we make some breakfast?"

"Pancakes?" Sophie asked expectantly.

"Sure, pancakes, and then we'll all play Twister." Dani reassured.

"Ollie wants to play on his Xbox." She added sulkily.

"Once we start he'll join in too. You'll see." Sophie clambered up the bed and got into the covers next to Dani. Dani pulled her close to her and snuggled her. "Happy New Year, angel."

"Happy New Year, Dani. Eskimo kiss?" She lifted her face to stare at Dani.

"Definitely." And they rubbed noses and giggled.

Within half an hour ,Dani was showered and dressed. She turned on the coffee machine and started on making the pancake batter. Sophie sat on the kitchen counter swinging her legs, drinking her warmed milk.

"Okay, pass me the eggs. One at a time, though." Sophie set down her milk and handed Dani the first egg. Dani cracked it into the blender. Then Sophie systematically passed the eggs one by one. Once they were all in, Dani placed the lid on the blender and signalled Sophie to press the switch. She grinned as it whizzed loudly. Then, after Dani's instruction, she pressed it off again.

"All ready. Now we need the pan and palette knife and we can start cooking." Sophie jumped down and rummaged in the cutlery drawer, retrieving the palette knife, while Dani pulled out the frying pan.

Before long, they were joined by Ollie, who'd come into the kitchen rubbing his eyes.

"Come to help?" asked Dani.

"Can I flip one?" He asked hopefully.

"Just one, though, and only after you've given me a kiss."

Ollie narrowed his eyes. Dani laughed, knowing he was struggling with the idea. "Okay, Eskimo kiss." Ollie grinned, nodded and stepped closer to Dani. She bent down and they rubbed noses. Dani grabbed him and squeezed him and he giggled. "Happy New Year Ollie."

"Happy New Year."

By the time Adam and Chloe came down, the table was set and the huge stack of pancakes was warming in the oven.

"Wow, you've all been busy." Chloe yawned.

"I'm starving and I need coffee," mumbled Adam, looking a little worse for wear.

"Offee," repeated Rosie.

Chloe grinned at Rosie. "Warm milk for you, baby. Daddy needs coffee because he has a hangover."

"Anover!" repeated Rosie. Chloe stifled a grin as Adam huffed.

"Mummy, we're going to play Twister. Dani, Ollie and me." Sophie placed the syrup and chocolate spread on the table while Chloe put Rosie in the high chair and Adam collected the coffee pot and placed it on the table. He slumped in the chair and held his head. Dani grinned at Chloe who rolled her eyes.

Before long, the pancakes had been devoured and Dani started clearing up the table. Chloe took the children upstairs to get dressed and Adam helped to load the dishwasher.

"How's your head?" Dani smirked.

"Better. Shit, I used to be able to drink loads and be fine the next day. I didn't drink that much." He shook his head in disbelief.

"How was the party?" Dani filled up the coffee machine and switched it on again. She was going to need gallons today. She'd hardly slept. She'd tossed and turned, trying to fathom out how she was feeling. Jez's message had thrown her. She was secretly pleased he'd got in touch, but she knew she couldn't go back there. It was over. After five years of waiting for a commitment, she knew now he was never going to settle down. Not yet, anyway, and not with her. *New year, new beginning. He had his chance and he blew it, big time.*

As for Jerome, that was a lot more complicated. Dani knew how she felt about him and it was wrong, really wrong. He was married and he had kids. She looked over at Adam as he ruffled his curly blond hair and thought how horrible it would be if he left Chloe and the children. Dani's heart twisted. No, however much she felt, she couldn't do that to Jerome's family.

"Good, actually. We don't get out much. Well, not together, anyway, and it was great for the kids too. They'd crashed on the sofas by ten thirty. How was the restaurant?"

"Busy." Adam waited for her to elaborate and when she didn't, he carried on fitting the last of the cups into the top rack of the dishwasher.

There was a thunder of footsteps coming down the hallway into the kitchen and Adam cringed. Ollie and Sophie ran into the kitchen, Sophie clutching the Twister game. "Come on, Dani. Ollie said he'll only play if you play."

"Okay, okay. But Mummy and Rosie can turn the dial for us."

"What's Daddy going to do?" Ollie narrowed his eyes at Adam.

"He'll umpire," suggested Dani, and Adam exhaled audibly, clearly relieved. "Go and set it up in the sitting room. I'll be there in a minute." Dani shooed them out and they ran back down the hallway to the sitting room.

"Thanks, Dani. I swear I don't know where they get their energy from."

By the time Chloe had dressed Rosie, the sitting room had been set up for their game. Chloe settled into an armchair with Rosie on her lap, thrilled that she'd be doing the spinning. Adam sat at the other side of the sitting room with his third coffee in his hand, resting it on his knee.

"Now there'll be no cheating, not if I'm umpiring." Adam put on an exaggerated stern voice and Sophie giggled at him. "Okay, we'll start from the youngest to the oldest, so Sophie's first. Spin the dial, Rosie." He softened his voice as he turned his attention to Rosie. She awkwardly pushed the dial and then clapped her hands, thoroughly pleased with herself.

"That was great, Rosie. Left foot to red, Sophie," instructed Chloe. Sophie placed her foot on a red circle. Rosie spun the dial again after being prompted. "Ollie, right hand to blue." He jumped up and placed his hand in the blue circle.

Within a short space of time, the three players were already beginning to get tangled, to the amusement of Rosie, Chloe and Adam. Dani deliberately stretched into the most awkward position so that they were all precariously balanced. The doorbell rang and Adam looked over at Chloe, puzzled.

"Are you expecting someone?"

"No," she replied, equally puzzled. He put down his mug of coffee and rose from the armchair, stepping over the numerous toys on the floor and heading to the front door. Rosie spun the dial again.

"Left foot on green, Dani." Chloe laughed, knowing Dani would purposely find the hardest position so that Sophie and Ollie would find it funny, and Dani would inevitably fall. Looking through her legs at Chloe, she winked. Her ponytail touched the floor as she bent over double, her bottom in the air and her thin sweater falling down, exposing her middle. Rosie squealed with joy. Ollie sniggered at Sophie, who had her arm extended under Dani's face.

Adam opened the door and was faced with a rather nervous-looking Jerome Ferretti. Adam furrowed his brow, then raised his eyebrows.

"Er, morning Adam. Happy New Year." Jerome shifted on his feet.

"Happy New Year." Adam answered, clearly bewildered as to why Dani's boss was on his front doorstep on New Year's Day, at eleven in the morning.

"Sorry to drop by unannounced. I tried to call Dani's phone but it's switched off and I don't have your home number. Er, here." He thrust out his hand, which was holding a bottle of Dom Perignon. Adam's eyes widened, then he took the bottle.

"Thanks. Um, please come in."

Jerome nodded nervously and stepped through the threshold. "I wanted to see if Dani was alright after last night. She was quite upset."

They were standing in the hallway and Adam turned to look at Jerome as he shut the front door, confused at his comment. "Upset? Why?"

"Well we had an incident in the restaurant last night and she was pretty shaken up. Didn't she tell you?"

Adam shook his head slightly. "No. What happened? What incident?"

"A customer of ours had a bit too much to drink, and as Dani was opening a bottle of Champagne for them, he reached down and lifted up the skirt of her dress. The place was packed out and, well, you can imagine. She was extremely embarrassed."

"He did what! She never said anything. Who was this asshole?" Adam replied, his face hardening.

"He was a guest of one of our regulars. Normally, our customers are well behaved. Don't worry, though, Peter sorted him out. He won't be doing that again. I just wanted to make sure she was alright."

"Sure. She's in the sitting room. Come this way." Adam led an anxious Jerome through the hallway into the sitting room. "She's playing with the kids."

They entered the sitting room to find Ollie spread-eagled under Dani, who had now widened her legs further, her bottom still in the air, bent over. Sophie was bending over Dani's left leg, waiting for her next instruction from Chloe. As Adam and Jerome entered, Rosie squealed.

"Ex pot!"

Dani's blood raced and she bent down further so she could see through her legs, a feeling of dread and excitement rushing through her veins simultaneously. *Holy fucking shit!* There he was, standing in the doorway. All she could see were his unmistakable lean, long legs clad in tailored black trousers and black ankle boots.

"Fuck." She muttered.

"Uck" repeated Rosie.

Heavenly Fare will be published at the beginning of 2018, where Dani and Jerome's story continues at La Casa d'Italia.

ACKNOWLEDGMENTS

La Casa d'Italia is an unattainable dream come true for me. I have always wanted my own restaurant but sadly never managed it. So I did the next best thing and created one in the pages of this book.

La Casa wouldn't be here if it wasn't for Marios, George and Mikey, the three loves in my life. Thank you for putting up with my moods swings and obsession. Your endless teasing made me crazy and laugh in equal measures... sorry I lost my touch!

Thank you to the numerous people who unwittingly inspired this story: the Montani family, especially the dear departed Ida Montani who taught me so much over thirty years ago. I hear your wise words every day. Peter, I owe you a huge thank you for keeping me sane, giving me some of the most valuable advice and unforgettable memories. To David, simply thank you, just for unintentionally inspiring me.

To *mon amie* Jaine, I am so grateful to you for over thirty years of friendship and your constant support, even from twenty thousand miles away, it still astounds me.

A huge, huge thank you to Emma, whose random conversations I cherish. You make me laugh out loud and your words of support have always kept me grounded. A massive thank you to my fun-loving friend Jackie who has been with me from the start. Your continuing encouragement and comments spurred me on every day.

My dear Irina, thank you for being there for me, listening and laughing at my thoughts and just "getting it".

Bella Barbara, my beautiful Italian friend, *mille grazie* for your selfless input.

Mary, you overwhelm me with your animated support and direct questions, always nudging me forward, always positive and with such a huge heart. Xenia you are pure gold, I owe you so much for all the pep talks and Voula, thank you for making me giggle with our long chats and your endless positive energy.

Without a number of dedicated and talented people, *La Casa* wouldn't be here, so thank you Betsy Stainton, James Millington, Roi Ioakeimidou and JC Clarke for bearing with me. You have made *La Casa* everything I dreamed it would be and more.

To my brother Antony, I am truly indebted to you. Your support floors me, and I wouldn't have got this far without your relentless encouragement.

I am forever grateful to my Mum, Helen and my Dad, George. They have taught me that I can do anything I want and have given me the courage to stretch myself and reach for it. I owe everything I am to them.

Finally I'd like to thank you, my readers. Your comments and support mean the world to me. *La Casa d'Italia* took a little longer than I anticipated but you hung in there. I hope it was worth the wait.

ABOUT THE AUTHOR

Anna-Maria Athanasiou is originally from Leeds in the UK but for the last twenty-two years she has lived in the heart of the Mediterranean on the island of Cyprus. Limassol is her adopted town, where she lives with her husband, two sons, golden retriever and two cats. She had her debut novels, *Waiting for Summer Book One* and *Waiting for Summer Book Two* published in 2013 and 2014, having written the series in secret, never expecting to finish them or to be published.

Since then, Anna-Maria has been asked to guest write articles for The Glass House Girls, an online magazine for women, and contributed to two charity anthologies, *They Say I'm Doing Well* and *Break the Cycle*.

Anna-Maria is a member of the Association of Authors and *For Starters* is the first book in the *La Casa d'Italia* trilogy. Her dream was always to have her own restaurant and though she never realised her wish, Anna-Maria managed to create it within the pages of *La Casa d'Italia*, confirming her belief that dreams really do come true.

Loved *For Starters?*

Connect with Anna-Maria:

Facebook: www.facebook.com/annamariaathanasiouauthor

Twitter: @AMAthanasiou

Instagram: annamariaathansiou

23122746R00336

Printed in Poland
by Amazon Fulfillment
Poland Sp. z o.o., Wrocław